He watched her in the gathering darkness, occasionally adding more wood to the fire. The noise caused her to stir slightly but she did not awake.

When an hour had gone by, he rose from the chair where he had been sitting more or less motionless and lay down beside her. She woke then and entwined her arms around him. Her eyes were fully open, dark and round.

"Could you make love to me?"

They came together with the crashing impact of tide on rock. He soared above her and then dived to claim his beloved prey. When the storm subsided they were one. . . .

ALEXA'S VINEYARD

Rosemary Enright

IVY BOOKS • NEW YORK

Prologue

THE HELICOPTER CURLED away over the Jarrah trees, the black and white painted bird greying to a blur. The bird of ill omen some said, and the emblem of Magpie International, although the stock exchange listing always showed the company as MI Trust. The acquisitive, territory-conscious magpie was seen by some people as a harbinger of doom. "Emotions count where confidence is concerned," Richard had said, "why throw down a gauntlet to chance? Hubris infuriates the gods, or so they say."

Alexa mused on the point as she slowly turned away from the verandah rail and walked back through the French windows into the panelled study, wondering if there could be anything in the old saying. Superstitious fool, she muttered to herself furiously. You think of these things to give you an excuse for not working. "Maybe you need a holiday," she murmured aloud, "somewhere well away from the sight of vines or grapes." Pine needles and snow, perhaps. Somewhere cold. Away from the relentless heat of Western Australia or the eye-blinding brightness of Pauillac. Yes, after the *vendange* at d'Ombre, she could spend Christmas at Langstroth Grange and then go to the Haute-Savoie, or even Vail. The idea of skiing in America for a change seemed appealingly novel.

The ceiling fan stirred the air fruitlessly, rhythmically echoing the faint *whup whup* of the helicopter blades, fading in the distance. Alexa waited until her ears were clear of the sound before addressing herself to the papers on the desk. The French *Directoire* writing table was littered with the morning's mail. There were bills from bottle suppliers, fertiliser firms, gratuitous advertising from agricultural machinery distributors and a letter.

1

The letter was hand-written on thick grey paper. The signature was cramped and hedged with secrecy, but it was legible. There was no mistaking the author. It was signed Vincent Lachasse. It was odd, Alexa thought, that she had never known what that man's first name was before. The printed address said he was Monsignor Lachasse, these days. The Church was a career, like any other. She remembered Tilly telling her that. Alexa smiled wryly at the memory. So Lachasse had gained his promotion, just as Tilly said he would.

The narrow drawer slid out easily, oiled by two hundred years of continuous use. Alexa's eyes still rested on the letter whilst her hand contacted the rough texture of the small velvet box and then the smooth cool leather of the other, larger one. She lifted them out and opened them. The pleated rays of sunshine filtering through the closed jalousies splashed onto the jewelled contents. Two magpies, by Cartier. Some forty years separated them, but they had both been made for members of the same family.

And now Lachasse wanted her to give one of them up. There was no reason why not, except for affection, or superstition. Two together was safer than one, alone.

Alexa's mind strayed back into the distances of her own girlhood. Grandad had never liked magpies, or opals. He'd been known to ask ladies to take such gems off in his house and leave them outside in their cars. The big magpie had Australian black opals in its wings. Tante Héloïse had worn it at the christening, all those years ago. It was a remarkable example of the jeweller's art. The gleaming wing feathers of the bird looked as soft and sleek and wicked as the natural thing. Alexa had admired it then. It was unfashionably large, too large to wear. It had looked odd on Héloïse, who was herself such a composition of oddities; and then she had left it to Alexa together with all her other jewels. Who'd have guessed she had so much? Alexa would never wear it. There was no reason why she shouldn't give it to the convent. Héloïse wouldn't have minded, in fact, she'd have been glad. It was difficult to get postulants now, and those they did get, didn't bring dowries like they used to. Expenses were always hard to meet in old-fashioned buildings designed to answer the greater needs of more spacious days. If the order were to survive it would need substantial contributions. Alexa lifted Héloïse's magpie out of its nest of frayed white satin, it would fetch a good sum, if only as a collector's curiosity.

The brooch in the other box was smaller and brighter, its

modern cut stones sparkling with cheerful optimism, the sapphire wings, of varying blues with tiny slivers of emerald, so small you wouldn't know they were there unless you looked closely, was less realistic but friendlier. On an impulse, Alexa removed it from its plush lined case and pinned it to the faded cotton dress. On any other woman, the rich jewel against the shabby background would have looked absurdly out of place. On Alexa, every garment and ornament invariably looked as it should.

Frowning, she bent over the single page of Lachasse's letter and re-read it with displeasure.

Chère Madame,

Whilst it is some years since we met, I am encouraged by your aunt by marriage, Madame La Courbe, to count on your assistance.

Perhaps I should explain that I am now the pastor of a parish in the city of Bordeaux and among the duties I have inherited from my predecessor is that of chaplain to a convent which may be said to have some claim on your consideration.

I understand that somewhat to the surprise of the family, your husband's paternal aunt left a substantial sum to you in her will, together with a collection of jewellery which should, had it not been for the tragedy which later befell, have been presented to your future daughter-in-law.

The convent in which Mademoiselle de Pies Ombre interested herself during her lifetime, and which she had hoped in her youth to enter, is now distressed and in need of funds. I speak of course, of the mother house of the order of La Sainte Vierge in Bordeaux.

It occurs to me, that you would wish to render some financial assistance in view of the well-established family connection. Since you are unable to fulfil the original intention concerning the jewellery, owing to the unfortunate, and indeed deplorable history of your marriage, I presume you would welcome the opportunity to make amends in some degree by liquidating part or all of the jewellery collection in order to make a worthwhile contribution towards the shortfall in the order's annual income. Any sum invested which produced a sum of 1,000,000 francs annually would be regarded as a suitable benefaction.

I am sure you will see the justice of the arrangement I pro-

pose, and be anxious to make this sacrifice in atonement for
what is past and to give effect to what must have been the next
intentions of the testatrix, her original intentions having been
frustrated by the unfortunate turn of events.

Be assured of my most distinguished sentiments.
Vincent Lachasse

The insolence of the letter was breathtaking. Alexa had read
it several times already, disbelievingly. It was typical of Lachasse's unctuous and revolting tone. The calm assumption that
he had any right to comment on her private affairs and the crude,
unjust imputation of guilt rubbed Alexa's nerves raw. But Tilly
had always defended him.

Héloïse's magpie had been Tilly's suggestion. Poor Tilly, she
was trying to buy herself a place in heaven with somebody else's
money. She must be nearly eighty now. Priests had always been
one of Tilly's hobbies. Their undivided attention could be relied
upon. All it took was good dinners and gossip. A little flattery
did no harm, either, and Tilly was an expert at providing them
all. There was no need for a wealthy old woman to forgo the
comfort of male companionship.

Well, they could have it. It was no more than this year's tax
on contentment. There would always be more to pay, until every
last one of them was dead. Until she herself lay in the little green
enclosure beside the vine fields, at the side of her beloved child.

The house telephone rang stridently.

"I've run out of Cash's nametapes." Morag's accent had become a curious mixture of her native Scots overlaid with French
during the past twenty years or so. The sound-filtering action of
the telephone revealed an unmistakable twang of Aussie now.

"Couldn't we get some more in Perth? I don't know if they
have them over here. If not, use marking ink. I'll explain to
Matron."

"Cook would like to know if you'll be having lunch."

"Tell her, no. I'll just have a sandwich on a tray in here. I
have some matters to attend to, and a letter to write."

PART ONE

❦

CHAPTER
1

🙙🙙 THERE IS A keen cutting edge to all big city mornings, a sharp pang of unborn events, struggling free of the womb in London, New York, Tokyo and Katmandu. But at eighteen years old, Paris was as yet Alexa's only city. For her, every new day held a surprise package behind its back as a too-experienced lover will, to tantalise a youthful mistress.

But today, that piquancy was absent because it was the morning of the last day. Nothing more would happen now. It was over. Alexa faced the chore of saying her goodbyes. Making them sound like *au revoirs*, when as everyone knew, they were really *adieux*. After all, good manners require that all parties to a departure should be able to fool themselves that forming the relationship in the first place had not been a waste of time. That was Alexa's instinctive feeling. Or was it a trained response? Sometimes it was very difficult to know what one thought oneself and what one had been brought up to think. At any rate, there was a difference, she had begun to notice that.

Alexa's room-mate, Mia, a cheerful, bustling little Belgian, was leaving for the Gare du Nord.

"Allez, vite!" It was Soeur Clothilde. "Mia's taxi has arrived, time to say goodbye!" She spoke in her clear, rapid French, her pale young face moonlike in the gloom of the convent lobby.

Outside on the pavement, that side of the Rue de Vaugirard remained in shadow, but the other side was already hot and yellow. Water was still running in the gutters. Mia believed in making an early start.

"Au revoir, ma belle capitaliste." Briskly, the Belgian girl subjected her taller friend to the two formal kisses, one on each cheek. Mia was obliged to stand on her toes and grasp Alexa's

7

slender shoulders to achieve this. Alexa leaned down to receive the tribute with the air of bemused tolerance which is worn by the tall when communicating with the short.

They did seem an ill-assorted pair and as such inspired a gentle amusement among the nuns who had surpervised their welfare over the past months. Mia would chivvy Alexa along and mitigate her tendency to be just a little late for everything. The Belgian's loud voice and voluble French contrasted with Alexa's own slow, hesitant speech, uttered quietly but in a range of notes that seemed to command absolute attention.

Mia had a harmless but simple sense of humour. Once she had hidden Alexa's string of pearls and gold bracelet, whilst Alexa was out of their shared bedroom for a moment. Gigglingly, Mia warned the girls in the neighbouring rooms to prepare themselves for the entertaining spectacle of the contained English girl's discomposure.

Alexa, returning along the corridor in the boy's tweed dressing gown she had worn at school, sensed a flurry of interest among the throng of dark-haired girls in flowered *negligées*, standing around in casual conversation.

When she perceived the absence of her jewellery from the dressing table she, unwilling to disappoint Mia, staged a satisfying but synthetic display of alarm.

"Mes bijoux! Où sont mes bijoux? C'est impossible, une voleuse, ici!"

The little thespian talent that she had displayed at school was stretched to its furthest extent. Very quickly, the delighted but unsuspecting audience restored her property with reassurances.

"Did you really think they'd gone?" Mia asked her delightedly.

"Oh yes, for a moment I was terrified." But Mia felt she had been indulged, although within the rules of their private game, she could not say so.

The discreet splendour of Alexa's possessions inspired an awed curiosity among her companions but no hostility. She displayed a certain detachment from material goods and would often give away a cashmere sweater or an ivory bangle saying that she knew these things were an abominable price in France but could readily be replaced for an insignificant sum in England. Nobody quite believed her but Alexa's own apparent conviction seemed to make it all right. She had, in fact, very little appreciation of the value of money but she was sufficiently able to discern which commodities were highly priced in Paris compared to Leeds or Harrogate.

No-one in the convent, with the exception of Mia, credited Alexa with much intelligence. For many months the strain of listening to heated political arguments or cultural discussions in a language which she still understood imperfectly had tended to give her expression a look of anguished confusion, ultimately followed by one of exhausted vacancy. This encouraged the community of French provincials and girls from Italy and Spain to treat Alexa much as a valuable domestic animal is treated.

Sometimes she would endeavour to shake off the torpor of foreignness and enter into the vigorous debates which characterised the students' dinner table: the problems of Belgium; whether or not a film featuring an adulterous relationship should have won the *Prix Catholique*; Britain and the Common Market. She sought information. Normally she would be told to keep quiet with affectionate contempt. One does not require a contribution from a domestic pet, however *recherché*.

"Tais-toi, chérie, tu ne comprends rien."

Later, after each of these discussions, Mia would explain to Alexa, in simple and forceful French, what the main trends of the arguments had been. She would lecture passionately on the problems of her own country, the decadence of the Roman Catholic Church and much else besides, actually shaking Alexa if she looked uncomprehending. Tirelessly, Mia would phrase and rephrase complex propositions until Alexa fully understood them.

Whether it was for love, or because Mia intended to become a teacher and was the daughter of teachers, or from the simple pleasure of talking, Mia's energy and determination succeeded in teaching Alexa French where many others had failed.

The daily effort to understand the things which involved her companions, and Mia's determined pedagoguery gradually delivered the language into her hands. She would catch herself thinking in French. Simple thoughts at first and then thoughts she would have had in her English mind slowly began to unroll themselves, like old carpets transformed by the new colours of the French tongue.

Once Alexa realised that she had laid hold of the language she had the first real sensation of achievement of her life. A barrier in her mind had broken and feelings of potency hitherto unknown to her flooded in. She had got something for herself, a tool that demanded to be used and honed and treasured.

And she *did* use it. She abandoned the turgid grammar classes which she had attended, at first, every morning at the Lyćee Montaigne. The leaden-footed walk across the dusty Luxembourg Gardens followed by three hours sitting in a huge dank classroom with students of many nationalities, cringing from the pouncing questions of the terrifying Mlle. Parmentier, were uncongenial.

Instead, Alexa walked endlessly in the sunlit streets of Paris, learning its ways and observing its life. Very soon she started playing truant from the learned afternoon lectures at the Sorbonne. Another three hours spent sitting on a narrow bench in a windowless amphitheatre while the sun shone outside seemed a wanton waste of life. Talking to shop assistants and artists in Montmartre, haggling with dealers at the Marché aux Puces, ordering food and asking her way, Alexa began to walk in step to the rhythm of the city.

One day, in the gardens of the Tuileries, while she fed the age-crusted carp in the fountain pools with a piece of baguette which had fallen from some office worker's picnic, she attracted the notice of Jean-Claude Jouffre.

. He was hurrying past, briefcase in hand, when he paused to trace the musical sound of Alexa's pure, unaffected laughter. To his ears it was the authentic sound of simple happiness. No Parisienne would have laughed aloud like that. When he perceived the source of the laughter he stepped aside into the shadow of a tree to watch Alexa feeding the fish. They came rushing at her like a pack of friendly, greedy dogs, mouths open and demanding, pushing and shoving each other, almost as if they would climb out of the water if there were further delay.

Jean-Claude observed her covertly and was enchanted. She could not be French, of course. Her clothes alone were a sufficient indication. They were a disaster. Decently dressed she would be ravishing. As it was, the gaucherie of her *ensemble* was almost touching in its *naïveté*. Oh, they fitted well enough, and she was even well-groomed in the casual manner of Englishwomen. Yes. She must be English. He examined her oyster silk two-piece with care. It was absurdly formal for a girl of her age. Not a cheap garment. And the strand of pearls, they were real, very probably. Artifice had nothing to do with the laughing girl standing in the sunlight feeding those ancient carp. Everything about her was genuine. What a rarity!

From time to time she turned her head and Jean-Claude could

see her face in profile. Her nose was almost forbiddingly straight, and even at this distance, he could see the remarkable colour of her eyes, they were ink-blue, lightening to sapphire when the sun cut across the irises. The upper lip was short and the mouth full and generous, passionate and sensuous. Her thick, honey-coloured hair was twisted carelessly into an arrogant knot on top of her head. There was no attempt at a *coiffure*. Jean-Claude liked her more and more.

And then, there was her figure. Jean-Claude would have enjoyed a closer acquaintance with that figure. Oh yes. The tall, slender body with its perfectly articulated limbs was a pattern of uncontrived elegance, it was a pleasure to watch her moving. A pleasure which might be prolonged.

"Pardon, Mademoiselle." Alexa turned to look at Jean-Claude, amazed to be accosted and anxious to know the reason.

"I wonder if you would do me the honour of lunching with me?"

Alexa was momentarily at a loss. It was already two o'clock in the afternoon.

"Monsieur, I . . ."

"You have already eaten? I am desolate. A cognac perhaps?"

"No, I . . ."

"But that is splendid! We shall lunch together. You are alone and I am alone, what could be more convenient? I hate to eat alone, it is a sad business and it is bad for the digestion. Of that I am convinced. You are so young, *Mademoiselle,* it is important you look after the digestion, no?"

Alexa had never attributed the least importance to her digestion. Mention of digestion was confined to nannies and a school domestic-science book which had a chapter on invalid cookery. She looked perplexed. She would *like* some lunch. She should have gone back to the convent, no doubt her absence would cause some comment . . .

"Come, do not disappoint me. You are wondering if I am quite respectable. Well, I am. And to prove it, we shall lunch near here, on a *terrasse,* so the whole world can see what we are doing. And should you become afraid, you need only call out to the passers-by that you are ill-used, and you will be rescued. There, what do you answer now?"

"Monsieur, what can I say but 'yes.' " Alexa laughed again, willing to be won over by the prospect of food and safety. She knew it was not the correct thing to do, not the prudent thing to

do, but in life, she thought, it was necessary to take some calculated risks or nothing ever happened.

They lunched at a discreet, smart restaurant, with a dark-red
awning, its pavement tables protected from the vulgar gaze by
tubs of well-grown box which formed a hedge tall enough to
conceal all but the very tops of the patrons' heads from view.
The green portals of this enclosure were guarded by the sort of
head waiter whose posture conveyed the exclusive nature of the
pleasure which he guarded for those able to pay and appreciate.
Alexa had protested at first.

"Oh, I'm afraid I don't have this kind of money with me,"
she told Jean-Claude in an agonised tone.

"You need money? Please, allow me. How much do you
need?" Alexa was mortified, he had misunderstood her.

"No, oh no. Please understand, I didn't expect to lunch out
today, so I really haven't enough money for this place." Now it
was Jean-Claude's turn to be mortified.

"My dear young lady, you surely did not expect me to allow
you to pay for your own lunch? I am wounded. Do I look incapable of fulfilling the duties of hospitality?"

"Oh, no. I . . ."

"Please relax. You are my guest, of course. What else? Do
young ladies pay for their own lunch in England? What a bar-
barous custom!"

"It's just that . . ."

But a waiter in a long white apron reaching almost to his shoes
ushered them to a table and all Alexa's protests were stifled in
a flapping of napkins and business with water glasses.

Jean-Claude was very good-looking, Alexa thought. Too terrifyingly good-looking to talk to. He seemed the exact reflection
of her own girlish imaginings. He was so handsome that he
might disappear in a plume of faery smoke or a crack of angry
lightning if she profaned his presence with the ordinary, banal
chatter she would have used for the entertainment of less exotic
people. She was suddenly nervous and shy.

"I'm afraid I don't know your name, *Monsieur*."

"Nor I yours, *Mademoiselle*. It is a moment of magic is it
not, when there is mutual attraction, but no corresponding
knowledge? Not even a name. Alas that names should ever intrude on enchantment. Names are such gaolers, carrying with
them the dreariness of family connections, the sentence of occupation . . ."

"But I must know your name," Alexa cut in. She was impatient of this delay in the progress of their new friendship.

"If you must, then it is Jean-Claude Jouffre. And yours?"

"Alexa, Alexa Standeven."

"Alexa? How crisp and triumphantly English that sounds."

Alexa looked down at her hands while the waiter fussed over Jean-Claude with expensively bound menus. From time to time, while Jean-Claude was thus engaged, she looked up at him quickly, her eyes sliding shyly away, unwilling to meet his. She recognised him from an age before her birth. He was the mirror-image of her soul, intended for her and her alone since time began. With a shock she realised the full meaning of the phrase "a marriage made in heaven." It wasn't just a loose phrase, a saying, it described something you could almost touch.

"I have chosen turbot for us. You will like it," Jean-Claude stated firmly. His green eyes flashed in his lean, intelligent face. Alexa watched the long manicured fingers on the wine list. A gold Rolex encircled his wrist where it emerged from an immaculately laundered cuff. His skin was tanned and his rather thin, chiselled mouth was pale in contrast. Alexa was floating, cradled in a warm cloud of roseate unreality, already far distant and protected from the practical world outside the primeval insanity of instantaneous love.

"I'm sure I shall," she murmured vaguely.

"Tell me, shall we drink champagne to celebrate your beauty and my good fortune, or Chablis to honour the turbot? Which?"

"I think champagne would be too busy in this heat, all those bubbles. I would prefer Chablis."

"Aha! A young lady of discernment, I perceive." Jean-Claude made a slight, jocular bow, "Tell me, are you fond of wine?"

"Well yes, my father is interested in it and he keeps quite a large cellar, actually."

"Excellent man. What does he do?"

"For a living? He's a lawyer, actually."

Alexa felt awkward, she heard herself saying "actually" too often. One did, when one was nervous. She was behaving as if it were her turn to sit next to the headmistress. Oh dear, she must think of something more amusing to say.

"And food? You are interested in food?"

"I've never really had the opportunity to be, not before I came to France, at any rate. My mother's interested in food, you know. But she doesn't seem very interested in cooking, though. So it's a bit difficult to form much of an opinion.''

Jean-Claude was delighted. There was an artless candour about this girl that he could scarcely have hoped for. He laughed.

"So what happens? Do you not eat at home? Ah, of course, you dine out a great deal.''

"Well, sometimes, but not all that often.''

"Just when you get hungry?''

"Oh no. She does cook.''

"But what can it be like if the lady does not *like* to cook?''

Alexa bit her lip. She had been drawn into an embarrassing dilemma. Criticising one's own family was not done. But on the other hand she had started this conversation, to slam the door on it would be equally ungracious.

"Well, it's . . . sort of, well, nondescript is probably the best word. Most of the time we've only a fairly sketchy idea of what we're eating.''

Jean-Claude's face was a picture of consternation.

"*Incroyable*. Tell me, what happens.''

Alexa sighed.

"It's quite ordinary really, we eat a lot of frozen meat and boiled potatoes. You see, my parents live in a big house right out in the country. Because it's so far from all the shops, my mother just orders a pig, a lamb and half a cow every so often and gets the butcher to hack them all up into pieces. Then it all goes into this huge trunk-shaped thing, only it's a freezer.''

Jean-Claude shuddered eloquently.

"And then, you see, when she wants to get something out, as she's only five foot high, she leans into the freezer and hooks something up with the handle of a walking stick, or an umbrella. We don't always know what it is till she's cooked it. Even then it's fairly speculative. Quite fun really.'' Alexa made a lame attempt at saving her mother's honour. "And she always does boiled potatoes to go with the meat. She's quite good at boiling things.''

"And other vegetables? Are there any other vegetables?''

"Of course. We are quite civilised,'' she retorted primly. "We have carrots and cabbage and swede . . .''

"And how does the excellent lady prepare *les légumes*?'' Jean-Claude enquired with deepening horror.

"She boils them for about forty minutes.''

"Your father, how does he support it?''

"Oh, he has the wine.''

"He is a philosopher," Jean-Claude's tone was full of genuine respect.

"But now," Alexa concluded, "I am better informed, the nuns' food is always lovely."

Naturally mention of the convent led to a full description of her time in Paris and its purpose. Alexa was doing a short language and literature course, before returning home to go to university in England to read Law. If she was uncertain about this destiny, she did not say so on this occasion.

When Alexa and Jean-Claude had finished eating it was already after four o'clock. She had learned that he was a woollen manufacturer's agent and Alexa had delightedly told him that her grandfather was a manufacturer.

"But I know him! At least my father dealt with him, often."

Jean-Claude found Alexa's amazement exceeded his own by far. She was still young enough to be staggered at each instance of the world's smallness. She did not yet realise that people with something in common, people of means, found each other all over the globe, because such people were actually comparatively few in number. To her, the coincidence seemed like a cosmic seal of approval on her newly formed friendship.

"Well, he's retired now, you know. There's been a manager at the mill for the past five years, and frankly, I think it'll be sold sooner or later."

"That does not matter *ma chère*, it makes a connection between us. It is a sign. We must meet again, no?"

"Oh, yes please. I would like that so much."

Jean-Claude obtained a taxi for her and settled her into it most gallantly. But not before he had made a future rendezvous with the charming English girl. There was, after all, no immediate rush. One did not get girls like this into bed in an afternoon. No, he would enjoy the subtle delights of a slow seduction. Jean-Claude had reached the age when easy conquests had grown uninteresting. It would be challenging to assail this virginal citadel. Her coincidental nearness to his own world added a delicious piquancy. It was dangerous enough to lend flavour to the pursuit, but safe enough in reality. After all, whatever happened, she would never be able to admit it. Jean-Claude promised himself some weeks of leisurely entertainment culminating in a rare pleasure.

The nuns, had they known of Alexa's truancy, would probably have deemed it their duty to inform her parents but Alexa had been away at boarding school and was adept at covering her tracks. Mia too, was careful not to give away her friend's unauthorised activities. Slightly older than Alexa, Mia had wondered if Alexa's unrestrained wanderings in every quarter of Paris were quite safe. Alexa was undoubtedly beautiful and the more worldly Belgian girl feared there might be danger in her conspicuousness.

Her fears were unfounded. Almost ludicrously English in appearance, Alexa had no need to announce her nationality to anyone. She walked with a long athletic stride, a locomotive style reminiscent of busy empire-builders and totally unfeminine. There was no seductive sway to her hips and she was apt to interrupt her swift progress with frequent childish stumbles. She did not look where she was going. Idle youths attempting to attract her attention would be rewarded with a solemn stare of polite attention from the blue eyes. Sometimes she would courteously ask them to repeat what they had said, apologising for her poor French. Ashamed or disarmed, they would say it was of no importance and run away. Alexa was simply unaware that she was attractive.

The eccentricity of her dress was also noticeable against the backdrop of Paris. For so young a woman, to French eyes, her clothes seemed curiously lugubrious and typically English. Nearly all her garments were made of wool, and it was rare that she was dressed naturally for hot weather. The well-cut jersey suits and dark silk shirts were meticulously cared for and correctly adjusted. Regardless of the temperature Alexa would wear beige 30-denier stockings, and most frequently flat, lace-up shoes. Her make-up, which was minimal and added little colour or definition to her features, was approved by her mother as suitable for young girls. Her thick, healthy, honey-coloured hair received scant attention and was normally wound into the casual knot which Jean-Claude Jouffre had admired. Her hair was her mother's greatest despair. All efforts to discipline it, and visits to the most famous hairdressers in the North of England, had come to naught. Alexa herself believed that this glorious asset was an incurable defect. Her usual costume was completed with a handbag rather larger than those that were fashionable in Paris at that date and more suitable for a matron settled into middle life. Her fearless innocence and air of qualified self-confidence were a sufficient protection from harm, her evident nationality which could not always be discerned from her accent, a clear explanation. Alexa corresponded well with the French folk image of a young English lady.

It was the sum total of those parts which had fascinated Jean-Claude Jouffre. There were contradictions about her that charmed, frustrated or amused, but never bored him. At one moment so elegant, the next so clumsy. She was a long-legged filly foal, showing her youth and inexperience but giving intimations of the power and quality she might develop.

She and Mia had become friends because of the chance allocation of a shared room. The convent was run by the nuns as a hostel for female students from abroad and the provinces. It was very *"bourgeois"* and *"convenable,"* which was why Alexa's mother had selected it, despite her profound disapproval of all Catholics. The nuns would take proper charge of her daughter on her first unaccompanied sojourn abroad. A little experience of a foreign city and a foreign language, not to mention foreigners themselves, was a necessary phase of her daughter's education. It was also intended to be an enjoyable treat before the rigours of serious study resumed, a wholesome interlude of something resembling adult freedom.

And so, during the long summer days, Alexa had her first uninterrupted opportunity to consider herself and assess the progress of her short life. At eighteen, she realised that she stood on the very brink of maturity and it was one of those junctures in a human life at which decisions could and perhaps should be made. She tried asking herself grand and sweeping questions like "What is life for?", and found the exercise a failure. The sneaking suspicion grew that such questions were irrelevant and dishonest. Painfully she inched towards more penetrating introspections. What is my life for? *Is* it my life? What am I like?

There were, until the appearance of Jean-Claude, no answers. The purpose of her life was seemingly to please her parents and be the solid academic and professional success they expected, unless she could be mean enough to disappoint them. Her life belonged to them. It had been nurtured and directed by them in every particular until that moment. They expected to resume command of it and continue the careful management of their eldest daughter's existence for several more years. More years, perhaps, than it was possible to contemplate. Could she refuse to re-surrender? It had seemed, for a time, that Jean-Claude was the white knight who would rescue her from uncertainty and redirect her destiny along less shadowed paths. Believing and hoping this, she had shared her perplexities with him.

At first, he had contacted her by telephone, until she begged him not to. It was not pleasant to be called to the Superior's office where the only telephone was. Mother Claire treated telephone calls for the students as being too stimulating for young girls who should be fully immersed in their studies. The only excuse for telephone calls could be a death in the family or serious illness.

"There is a gentleman wishing to speak to you Alexa, a Monsieur Jouffre. I hope you will not monopolise the line too long."

Alexa went into the glass booth, feeling Mother Claire's eyes boring into her back. When she came out, the Superior looked up from her ledger, removing her round, steel-rimmed spectacles.

"I will not insult you, my dear, by supposing that your acquaintance with this man was formed other than respectably. I know that in matters of social intercourse, you will guided by what your parents would wish."

"Yes, *ma mère*. Monsieur Jouffre is known to my family. There is nothing wrong. That is . . ."

"As long as everything is quite *comme il faut*, that is all right. How are your studies progressing, Alexa?"

Alexa made her escape with as few words as possible on the subject of her studies, which were, by now, non-existent in any formal sense.

Jean-Claude had recommended outright defiance of the law books which lay in wait for Alexa. Indeed, he had even suggested that she remain in Paris and continue her studies there or get a job.

"I don't speak French nearly well enough to get a place in a French university for anything except a short language course, like I'm supposed to be doing now."

"Well, what about a job? You speak enough French for that."

"What sort of a job?"

Jean-Claude sighed. No one could accuse Alexa of frivolity. He had found the task of seducing her unexpectedly difficult. In fact, he had achieved nothing yet except a few willing kisses. She did not dream, it seemed, of going further. His exploratory gestures had been brushed aside without a word. A hand on her knee, or her breast, would be so tactfully removed without overt repulse, that at times, it was Jean-Claude who felt himself to be the novice. And all the while Alexa ate. Her appetite and her conversation were seemingly inexhaustible. Still, he did not despair. Between a man and a woman, as he told Alexa, there should first be *confiance*. Alexa merely stared at him as if he had spoken a truth so childishly obvious it might have been taken as read. Of course there should be *confiance*, what else?

"I just want to do ordinary things, you know," she told him. "I wish they could accept that I'm like everybody else. I want to get married and have a house and a family of my own."

"And your mother, she does not understand this?"

"Not at all. She wanted to be a lawyer herself. She puts in quite a lot of time kicking the Aga and snarling 'I am a lawyer, not a drudge.' So I've got to be one instead. A lawyer I mean. It's all so difficult, they just *assume* I'll do it. They don't even ask if I'm clever enough to do it."

Jean-Claude was extremely puzzled.

"I thought you said your mother *wasn't* a lawyer and that that was the whole root of her ambition for you."

"Yes, I know. When she says she's a lawyer, she means she is by inclination and temperament. Perfectly true, she addresses us all as if we were hostile witnesses."

"I see, but *ma chère* Alexa, what is an Aga? And why does she kick it?"

"Oh, it's a solid-fuel stove for cooking and heating water. You fill it up with coal . . ."

"Oh yes, yes, I see. She does not like this equipment because it is the instrument of her culinary torture."

They continued to discuss Alexa's educational prospects.

"You were clever enough to get into Oxford. That is the most difficult part, surely. After that, you know you can do it, because you have survived the competition."

"I suppose so. If only I were a little more stupid they'd be quite keen for me to get married."

This was dangerous ground which Jean-Claude was anxious to vacate as soon as possible.

"Come, I want to show you something."

The something proved to be an *appartement* in the Etoile district. It was empty except for a few sticks of furniture. Jean-Claude had obtained the key from an estate agent.

"Do you like it, *ma belle*? I thought I might buy it. The views are very beautiful, are they not?"

Alexa wandered round the vast *appartement* lost in admiration. The grand, *Belle Epoque* rooms, most with a generous

balcony, were flooded with light. Her eyes shone. Why should
he want to buy it if he did not think of marrying her. That was
what she wanted. Surely it was what they both wanted.

"It's fantastic, Jean-Claude. Just fantastic. It's the most beautiful flat I've ever seen." Not that she had seen many. It suddenly
occurred to her that she had no idea where Jean-Claude lived.
They always met in restaurants and cafés, always in public places.

"Some of the furniture is quite good. It goes with the *appartement*. This bed, for example, is Napoleonic, a campaign
bed. It would be worth having. Let's try it out shall we? I feel
quite tired after drinking all that wine in the sun."

She did lie down on the bed and responded to his embraces
until the point at which a man expects to be satisfied. Then
she drew back. Jean-Claude was angry. Alexa did not understand what she had done wrong and was miserable. Jean-
Claude drove his black Citroën to the Rue de Vaugirard and
dropped Alexa outside the street entrance to the convent. He
was sullen.

"You know I'm leaving at the end of the month, it's only ten
days away. The 31st of July on the evening plane . . ."

"I'll see you before then."

He drove away and Alexa did not see him again. She was hurt
and confused. Her life seemed blighted at the very beginning.
She had met the man of her dreams, dreams she was almost too
shy to recognise herself and certainly could never confide in
another, and now she had lost him already through some mysterious clumsiness of her own. It must be her fault, because
nothing could ever, possibly, be his fault.

So the last few days in Paris were sad. Mia felt her friend's
heaviness of heart but could attribute it to nothing more than
their own coming parting. She seemed more abstracted than was
usual with her and several times Mia was obliged to repeat herself. That was odd. If Alexa had a virtue, it was the charm of
her absolute attention. Perhaps, Mia concluded, in her heart,
she had already gone home.

"Au revoir," lied Alexa kindly, "don't eat too many pastries
before the wedding, or you'll be too fat to get married."

Momentarily Mia regarded her friend with surprise, was this
some misguided attempt at coarse humour? No, it wasn't. Alexa
rarely made jokes. When she did they were always gentle and
very dry.

"No, *chérie*. I'll be careful and whenever I feel I can't hold out against another slice of *tarte aux prunes*, I'll think of your regal self and resist. Anyway, I'll see you in November at the wedding; the day isn't quite fixed yet but as soon as Pierre knows when he can have leave, my mother will send you an invitation."

"Go on then, you'll be late. I'll see you in November." The ghost of a smile illuminated Alexa's features. Mia's train didn't leave the Gare du Nord until noon.

Mia allowed herself to be urged into the taxi and, whilst waving and smiling brightly, understood that her friend was anxious to see her gone. Alexa and Soeur Clothilde waved until the taxi was out of sight and Mia wondered what would happen to Alexa. Could that face bring her good fortune?

Alexa knew that she would never again see the girl who had taught her every word of French she knew. There would be no money to travel to Bruges in November to attend Mia's wedding. She daren't even ask. Her mother would regard any further foreign excursions as wholly inappropriate and quite out of the question during a university term. Other girls went to finishing school and weren't begrudged a year of fun or ever expected to take life seriously at all until their first child was born.

Alexa was wistful about the year that some of her school contemporaries would spend before settling down to a conventional career, the milestones of which would be recorded in the births, marriages and deaths columns of the *Telegraph*. But Alexa's parents had a more sombre outlook on life. Their fervent belief in "careers for women" only involved careers requiring long arduous study followed by yet more, and culminating in "professional qualifications"—a phrase uttered in the same respectful tone as others reserved for large sums of money or heroic deeds. To Elizabeth and Alexander Standeven, "professional qualifications" were indeed equal to large sums of money and acquired only after heroic application of the mind and denial of youthful aspirations. To them it seemed worth the sacrifices. Alexa wondered if anything could ever compensate her for the loss of her young womanhood.

Alexa's parents' love was measured in doses proportional to her successes. Her mother doled out chocolate drops to her miniature dachshunds on just the same basis. Two chocolate drops for instant obedience, one for getting it right eventually and none at all for a failure. The Sorbonne and Paris had been a

treat, a reward for getting a university place, a frivolous interlude before settling down to the law, the traditional occupation
of the clever Standevens.

Inside the convent there was the unmistakable odour which en-
veloped all traditional French households. Alexa never lost her
awareness of it, it never became routine. It was the combined
perfumes of coffee, polish, bread, mothballs and all those things
which add up to modest comfort and habitual thrift.

"I will go upstairs and finish my packing, *ma soeur*."

It had been made evident, delicately but firmly, that the sisters
wished to have their convent to themselves from midday on-
wards. All their students had paid for accommodation until the
hour of noon on July 31st, 1968, precisely. Good and gracious
they might be, but the nuns revealed their utter Frenchness in
their embarrassing exactitude over money matters.

It was perhaps because they were going on holiday, Alexa
reflected as she moved around the barely furnished Second Empire bedroom she had shared with Mia. It was curious how like
a real family they were. The Mother Superior and the older nuns
didn't look at all excited but wore a thin-lipped, harassed expression, like parents who have to arrange about the boarding
kennels and someone to pay the gardener's wages. The young
ones, on the other hand, their check aprons tied round their long
black habits, were beaming and humming as they swept up and
down the stairs, around corners and along corridors. They were
just longing for Brittany, where the order had a house in which
the elderly and infirm sisters lived in retirement.

There was a little private beach belonging to the convent, a
secluded cove where the young sisters swam in the sea. Soeur
Clothilde told Alexa all this when she had been late for breakfast
yesterday. Soeur Clothilde, so normal and human herself, had
circumvented the vinegary little sister who had charge of the
kitchen to procure for Alexa a piece of baguette and some coffee. It was quite extraordinary what ordinary everyday things
these outlandish beings did.

Alexa took a last look around the room which had been home
to her and was now just another place. It had an astonishingly
high ceiling, a wide expanse of polished parquet floor, and an
elaborate black marble chimney piece surmounted with a vast,
age-speckled looking-glass in a heavy gilt frame. The two won-
derfully tall windows which gave on to the neglected courtyard

garden below were a supreme delight to Alexa. They were not hung with curtains and had need of none. The glass casements opened outwards into the garden, but should one want privacy or to escape the glare and heat of the midsummer sun, inner louvered shutters could be closed, permitting the passage of reduced light and any slight breeze there might be. The windows were closed and opened by the marvellous mechanism typical of such windows in France. It was the windows which taught Alexa unconsciously to recognise what was best in the Gallic character: that combination of ingenuity with utility and elegance, which is composed of all those elements but finally is simply itself.

"I shall miss the windows," Alexa murmured to herself. Above, there hung a single unshaded electric light bulb, pale successor to the chandelier that had once undoubtedly depended from the elaborate ceiling rose. Holy poverty had dispensed with some ornament but could not inflict meanness on such a room as this. Two little white beds, a crucifix, two chairs and a cheap wardrobe were the only furniture. Behind a folding screen there was a wash basin and an old-fashioned tin bidet on a wooden stand. Eventually, Alexa had used the bidet quite regularly, unwilling to go through the tiresome ritual of forming up in Mother Claire's office to apply for the key to the bathroom. The key was always sought and found with apparent difficulty and handed over only after a *supplément* to the usual fees had been paid in cash.

Yesterday evening the room had been untidy with clothes, unpacked suitcases, books and records, all the paraphernalia of girlhood on the move. Now it was as calm as a winter lake. Alexa closed the door behind her, the last swan to fly.

Mother Claire sat behind her desk in the dark little office near the front door listening to the indecisive footsteps of Alexa Standeven approaching across the tiled hall. After a lifetime of making little noise of her own, Mother Claire had become accustomed to interpreting the unconscious noise of others. These were undecided footsteps, not certain whether to go fast or slow, unconvinced of their own direction, a clatter of hesitancy. The coolly beautiful English girl in her quiet expensive clothes had the usual gaucherie of Protestants transposed into a solidly Catholic culture. She was not entirely sure what she should say and what she should not say, with the consequence that she said very little and what she did say was quite commonplace, but she herself was not commonplace.

Alexa knocked softly on the half-open door.

"Entrez."

"Bonjour, ma mère, je suis venue . . ."

"To say goodbye," interrupted Mother Claire with the brisk smile she kept for students. "We will converse in English today, a little indulgence for your last day in Paris."

Alexa sighed with relief. These formal exchanges with the Superior were always a strain, and Alexa's French never stood the strain. She always collapsed into feeble incoherence.

"I'm afraid I still find it difficult, *ma mère*."

"I do not really think so," replied Mother Claire. "I hear you and Mia chattering away quite volubly at times. You have improved much."

"Mia is very easy to talk to."

"Particularly as she knows no English and so it is you who are in the position of power. Is that not so?"

"Perhaps, *ma mère*."

"It is so I think. Like all English people you do not like to be caught out in an error. You are too afraid of feeling foolish. It is sad, for you lose many opportunities like that. But you have made a great step forward, I hear."

"Oh, yes, I had a dream in French and I was talking in my sleep. Mia told me about it in the morning. It was about a fairground, but I didn't remember anything about it."

"It is good news. The language has gone deep into you, it is buried in your brain. That is more than grammar books. Your accent, you know, is excellent but your vocabulary is too small and sometimes your idiom is poor. If you pay attention to these things you will speak really well."

"Thank you, *ma mère*."

"What time is your flight?"

"At two o'clock from Le Bourget, *ma mère*."

"That is good, you have plenty of time. It is 11:30 now, I shall telephone for a taxi for you."

"You are very kind, *ma mère*."

Alexa's flight did not in fact leave until six o'clock but she couldn't bring herself to discommode Mother Claire with the knowledge. She really couldn't bear to watch Mother Claire struggle with the idea that unless she offered further shelter and chaperonage until a more convenient hour Alexa would be loosed onto the streets of Paris without suitable occupation or reliable companions. Even worse, there was the possibility that the Superior might suggest extending the hospitality of her convent in exchange for the payment of a *"supplément."* It always pained Alexa to watch others behaving ignobly. In this instance the spectacle would be doubly unpleasant since she had exactly twenty French francs left, just enough for the taxi and the airport tax. Alexa was careless with money. It had never previously mattered whether she actually had any or not. The children of upper-middle-class families are like royalty; they do not need money, since all their needs are provided for by unseen chamberlains, who go before with their chequebooks and make the way smooth. The result is that when first entrusted with a little money these sublimely unworldly youngsters treat the money intended as bed, board and tuition fees as pocket money to be squandered in cafés and shops. Mia had lent the twenty francs. She would never get it back as Alexa was uncomfortably aware because she could never admit to her parents that she had been so irresponsible and ask them to refund the money. The smallness of the sum would not excuse her from the familiar lecture on the "principles involved."

There was nothing to be done except to go obediently to the airport and wait the five hours or so before her flight. She had some magazines in her hand baggage so that she need not seem too obviously at a loose end.

In the taxi she watched Paris slip by with indifference. She had begun to be homesick about a week ago, during a showing of *My Fair Lady* at a cinema. Its French subtitles had seemed such ludicrous translations of what was actually being said that Alexa realised for the first time that a language barrier is not just a question of people using different but interchangeable codes. The words of one language do not mean exactly the same as their nearest equivalent in another language. So people who seem different, because they talk differently and look a little different, actually are different because they are never thinking or feeling quite the same thing as you. It had been wonderful to hear those English voices and see those open, well-bred English faces. They made one think of hot cups of tea, proper pillows and baths. And in any case, Jean-Claude, who had swept so briefly and brilliantly through her life, had quit her orbit for ever. He had left a trail of luminous vapour, an aching realisation of what life could have been like if she had not done whatever it was that she had done that had chased him away. Paris had been wonderful enough before she had known of his existence, but now that innocence was lost, she wished to depart from an Eden so enhanced and yet so blighted by knowledge of him.

Alexa swallowed and firmed her jaw. Jean-Claude was in the past. She would not think of him again.

Jean-Claude ordered another cognac. He savoured it reflectively. The suppressed panic of airport crowds crackled around him. He watched the passers-by, the determined confidence of some, the apparent unease of others. Bewilderment concealed by loud voices and squared shoulders. Jean-Claude had the contempt of all seasoned travellers for mere holidaymakers. Wearing the clothes of revellers, they hoped to disguise the emotions of refugees.

Jean-Claude had been playing a game with himself for the past few days. Which flight should he book for Paulette and the children? She always took Pierre and Louise to their little holiday property in Sardinia for the whole month of August. Unfortunately, it was a busy time in the cloth trade. The *couture* houses and the *prêts-à-porter* were putting the finishing touches to their autumn collections. An agent could not afford to be away. Last-minute orders were not uncommon. It was a question of prestige. A manufacturer would not like to think his agent was absent at a crucial time like this. After all, a small emergency order could lead to a long-term and profitable association between a woollen manufacturer and a world-famous *couture* house. Paulette had always been most understanding about it, fortunately.

Sometimes he wondered if Paulette amused herself on Sardinia in the month of August. He hoped so. Surely a fashionable woman would console herself. Too much flat-footed fidelity on Paulette's part would be bad for his conscience. A certain relaxation of the domestic rules was the purpose of *mois d'août*.

Time and again, during the past week, he had returned to the tantalising question of his family's departure for Sardinia. It was a kind of mental masturbation. He had massaged himself languorously towards a decision, being careful not to touch too early on the climactic date of the 31st of July. The evening flight. Of course, he might not see Alexa. It would give a pleasing uncertainty to the venture. She'd treat him outrageously. A little provincial prude, a prick teaser. Or was she just unbelievably, enticingly innocent. It was his growing conviction of the latter that had led Jean-Claude to see his family off on their annual holiday on the 31st of July. He was naturally drawn to the clean, the unmarked, the pristine. The virgin snow cried out for a footprint. Maybe he would find snow waiting for him at the airport.

Paulette had become impatient. On the evening of the 29th they'd had a row. The moment of decision had come.

"All right then, the day after tomorrow, the 31st. I'll pick up the tickets tomorrow. I can't see that it matters one way or the other which day you go, but if you're so anxious to be away, I'll see to it. I'm very busy at the moment, but I'll see to it. Maybe then I can get some peace."

He saw them off in a fluster of hand baggage and soft toys. Paulette looked meaningly at him, an unspoken apology for the harsh, impatient words which had passed between them. It was all right again. People got tired towards the end of the summer. The *mois d'août* always came just in time. If it were not for that annual respite, how many marriages might not be shattered? Husbands and wives needed a rest from each other. It was understood. Paulette went, harmony was restored and Jean-Claude turned his attention to other matters.

He'd asked the girl at the BEA desk. They hadn't checked the flight in yet, it was too early. But her name was there, on the passenger manifest. It was so endearingly typical. No surprises. Whenever Alexa said she would be somewhere at a particular time, then she was there. It was convenient. In thirty-three years of life, Jean-Claude had discovered that reliability was one of the attributes of victims. Whilst he, a survivor, was protectively unpredictable. He was congratulating himself on the lucidity of his own thoughts when he saw Alexa.

She wore the same oyster silk outfit as she had been wearing when they first met. It looked a little crumpled. Evidently she had been sitting for some time. She was surrounded by her baggage and glanced anxiously up at the departure board as it clacked the minutes slowly by. She had the look of exhausted apprehension which invades the bodies of those who wait alone for an uncertain event. The same aspect was worn by relatives waiting in hospital corridors, and hopeful litigants in the desolate passages of court buildings. It was a posture of extreme vulnerability. Jean-Claude contemplated Alexa with anticipatory pleasure. He had no idea how he would use the moment. It was soft clay to be moulded on a whim.

She sat less than twenty feet from where he leaned against the

little bar. He would not go to her. Only weak men went to women.
He had already put his stamp on her and she should come to him.
It needed only that she should feel the steady pressure of his gaze
and then, she would come to him because, Jean-Claude was certain, the rules of nature would forbid her to do otherwise.

In less than a minute she was aware of him. Her round-
eyed amazement was almost comical. It was succeeded by a
smile of such brilliance that Jean-Claude felt the near physical
warmth of its rays. He had been right to come. Still he did not
move from where he lounged. To his chagrin she did not stir
either but gestured towards her baggage, as if to say she could
not leave it unattended even for a moment. He shrugged.

"I did not expect to see you again," she remarked matter-of-
factly as he sat down beside her.

The sight of Jean-Claude caused a heart-lurching sensation in
Alexa and an uncomfortable fluttering in the stomach, but she
was concerned to appear undisturbed.

"My dear Alexa, I am so sorry. I have been preoccupied
lately. You know there is quite a little flurry of activity in my
business now, I could not get away. But still, I was not anxious,
because I knew that I could always discover your whereabouts
through your family."

Alexa raised her eyebrows.

"It was only a matter of writing to your grandfather, care of
Firth Holroyd Limited, and the slackened cord which bound us
would be made taut again. I was not concerned."

"So why are you here?"

The question was sharp and direct. Alexa, despite her initial
pleasure in seeing him, was wary. His neglect was not so easily
dismissed. He had hurt her with easy, casual cruelty and she
would not be drawn too readily into the trap again. She longed
to excuse him but the sharp pain of his desertion demanded a
better explanation than he had given.

"I came, of course, in the hope of seeing you. Did you not tell
me on what day and at what hour you were leaving? A lover
remembers these things as if they were written in blood. All the
time, in dull meetings and slaving at my desk, I was buoyed up
by the one thought. Perhaps I shall catch Alexa in time to say *au
revoir*. I shall perhaps be able to send my respects to her distinguished grandparent . . . say some of the things I meant to say
before. One never knows how short the time is until it is too late."

Alexa regarded him with a gradual rebirth of hope that was tinged with caution.

"I must check in shortly."

"But not immediately, I think. We have time to say goodbye, to make some tentative plans. Smile, I entreat you. We are not, after all, to be torn asunder without a parting word. You have half an hour at least. You need some refreshment. You look *très fatiguée*. How long have you been here?"

"Quite a while. Some coffee would be nice. Is that possible?"

She was beginning to unbend. He had come all the way to Le Bourget just on the off chance of saying goodbye to her. He cared, after all, it seemed.

"Anything is possible for you, *ma chère* Alexa, anything at all."

"Then I should like to go to the Ladies first. I've been watching over this lot for hours. The BEA people wouldn't look after it and I daren't leave it."

Jean-Claude laughed.

"*Ma pauvre petite*. Why did you come so early?"

"It's a long story to do with nuns and money. I won't be a minute."

He watched her walk away, uncertain what to do next. He was not sure what he wanted to achieve. He needed more time to think. Looking down he examined the rather large quantity of leather suitcases. She would have a fair amount of excess baggage to pay, he wondered if she realised. A small leather grip caught his eye. There was a zippered compartment at the side with documents stuffed into it. The zip was not completely closed. A corner of the unmistakable black and gold passport was just visible. He leaned down. Smoothly he removed the passport and placed it in his own inside pocket. It lay flat against his heart, invisible and secure.

CHAPTER
2

🦋🦋 JEAN-CLAUDE EASED THE Citroën out of the dark cleft of the Rue Monsieur le Prince into the Boulevard Saint Michel. It was nine o'clock. The evening was hot and dusk was falling, pinpointing the coloured lights sparkling in the emerald shadows of the trees. The main artery of the Latin quarter was seething with strollers and traffic.

He had decided, after installing Alexa at the little Hôtel de Picardie, to leave early. It was clear that a reaction had set in and she was tired and withdrawn. Things would look brighter to her on the following day. No doubt losing a passport was something of an ordeal, he reflected. It was not an experience of which he had personal knowledge. He had no idea how badly the telephone conversation with her mother had gone or that it was the chief cause of her introspection.

The business with the British Consul could probably be spun out over a few days, Jean-Claude decided. It shouldn't be difficult to manufacture a few delays. It would give him time to decide whether Alexa would make an amusing August companion or not. If not she should be returned to her parents and no harm done.

The line of traffic ground slowly to a halt. Jean-Claude slipped his hand inside his jacket and withdrew Alexa's passport and examined it. It was new, of course, and it had no story to tell. Like Alexa, it was a blank sheet. Virgin pages waiting for the imprint of experience. He felt a pleasurable stir of excitement. The photograph interested him.

The utilitarian shot was unflattering. Its grey monochrome, removing the honey tones of her hair, the northern translucency of her skin and the ink colour of her eyes, left a stark image of

30

surprisingly strong face. There was a squareness of the jaw which he hadn't previously noticed, and the way her head sat on her slim shoulders gave an absurd suggestion of effort. Almost as if she were supporting the weight of an invisible crown. The neck was stretched up with a kind of agonised pride. She was a dangerous toy. The kind Jean-Claude enjoyed most. He was reassured, she was worth the trouble.

He put the passport away as the traffic lights changed and reached for a cigarette. Thoughts and impressions passed randomly across his mind. Alexa had been seriously distressed by the loss of the passport but she had remained outwardly calm. The visible symptoms of shock had been admirably controlled, her deportment under pressure, exemplary. She had gone a little grey in the face at the check-in desk and her hands had shaken slightly as she searched her bag. But it had all been done with organised deliberation. There had been no frantic scrabbling movements, no exclamations, no tears.

"I am so sorry, *Mademoiselle*, I seem to have mislaid my passport. Perhaps you could attend to these other ladies and gentlemen while I look for it," she had said in perfect French, her voice clearly audible and steady.

Behind her, Jean-Claude had shrugged, throwing the exasperated French girl in the BEA uniform a conspiratorial smile of sympathy. Alexa felt the stares of the others in the queue; she ignored them proudly. They were the stares with which those for whom things have gone well accuse those for whom things have gone awry. You have created disorder by being unfortunate, they seemed to say. She refused to show pain.

"This is a disaster," she told Jean-Claude grimly as she searched her bag again, but without hope.

"Do not exaggerate, *chérie*, it is a little problem, that is all. Tomorrow you can go to the British Consul and arrange for a new passport. It happens all the time. I will help you. The consulate will be quite accustomed to these occurrences. Why else would consulates exist?"

"I'm afraid it's not as simple as that. I do not have a single franc left. Where am I going to sleep, what can I do with all this luggage? I must contact the Consul immediately and I must telephone my parents at once. They will be leaving for the airport; if they get there and find I am not on the plane they will go mad, I know they will."

"I daresay they will be puzzled, *chérie*, and they will feel the

inconvenience of having met a plane which proves to have conveyed nobody of interest to them, but I doubt their hold on sanity
is quite as fragile as you suggest. By all means ring them, there
is a booth over there. Shall I help you get the number?''

"No, it's all right, I know how to do it. Just look after all this
stuff again will you? I expect it will take a bit of time, reversing
the charges, you know.'' She smiled wintrily at him, like a burst
of pale sunshine on a cold and dismal day. Again, Jean-Claude
was entranced, taken unawares.

"Yes, go on. Make your telephone call and then we will make
plans for the evening. You see, there is an advantage hidden in
the most unpromising circumstances.''

But Mr. and Mrs. Standeven had already left for the airport.
Their general manservant answered the extension in his flat.

"Yes, I'll tell them, Miss Alexa.''

"But try and ring the airport, so they're not waiting around.''

"I'll try, Miss Alexa.''

"And say I'll speak to them later, just as soon as I can.''

"All right.'' The Fiddler, as her father called his unsatisfactory factotum, was not reassuring. But it was the best she could
do.

Jean-Claude was obliged to think quickly. He couldn't take
her back to the house, not yet. He had to make the usual arrangements. There could be no sign of domestic involvement.
The Hôtel de Picardie would do nicely for tonight. He and
Georges Caval had done their national service together, Georges
had always been helpful over delicate little extramarital affairs.
Jean-Claude could always come and go as he pleased. It seemed
the natural solution.

Alexa's face was still serious when she emerged from the
telephone booth.

"They've already left.''

"*Pas de problème*, you must ring them from the hotel. The
Hôtel de Picardie is a charming little place and the proprietor is
a friend of mine. Tomorrow we will see what other arrangements we can make . . . should it be necessary,'' he added
hastily seeing Alexa's look of consternation.

"But I told you, I have no money . . .''

"Of course, but that is not a difficulty. My friend will see that
you have everything you require and I shall tell him you are my
guest. Where is the problem? I am a friend of the family, nothing

could be more natural than that I should look after you in this trifling emergency.''

"Oh, Jean-Claude, I'm so embarrassed and I don't know how to thank you. What on earth would I have done if you hadn't been here.''

"Hush, *ma belle*, there is no need for all this. I *was* here, and you are safe with me.''

"My parents will repay you, of course.''

"They will offer, I have absolutely no doubt, and I shall refuse stoutly. The pleasure is entirely mine. Come.''

Alexa had to accede to his suggestion, there was no practical alternative. The Consul could not be contacted at that hour, it was too late to do anything.

"Your passport was probably stolen, you know,'' Jean-Claude told her in the car. "It happens all the time. Do smile.''

Alexa slept very badly. After speaking with her mother she went straight to bed, refusing food and unable to concentrate on anything but her predicament. The stuffy little room had a shower of its own and was quite well furnished but its long shuttered windows looked directly onto the street. At any other time she would have been pleased, but now, the sound of carefree voices simply emphasised her loneliness.

She resented her mother's anger. It was always the same. If anything went wrong, Elizabeth supposed it was Alexa's own fault. Nothing could ever be attributed to mere misfortune. It would be the same for years. She expected a level of performance from her daughter which was inhuman. Alexa cried with anger. Make me proud of you, don't make a mistake, don't be unlucky, don't be inefficient, don't fail, don't disobey. Never compromise my dignity, never let it seem that I have an ordinary daughter like other women, never have opinions which don't coincide with mine . . . Alexa tore at the scabs of her relationship with her parents.

It wasn't that her father was completely innocent of this form of psychological coercion. It was just that somehow, his wife had appropriated the task of speaking for him. She must have done it an early stage of their marriage, because Alexa couldn't remember a time when her father had expressed a wish or a preference regarding herself. But she was always quite clear about his unspoken edicts. Elizabeth never left any doubt in Alexa's mind as to what they were, and Alexander was spared the trouble of expressing them. An impression of omnipotence had been created. There was no step, however dramatic or extreme, that Alexander would not, or could not take to achieve his ends or exercise control over his affairs. And his affairs included his daughter. Over the years the system had generated a subtle miasma of fear in Alexa. In her eyes, Alexander pulsated with silent power.

Elizabeth's words had fallen into Alexa's ears like drops of nitric acid, nor was her ability to disseminate a shower of ice crystals inhibited by a distance of several hundred miles and a poor connection.

"I hope you have enough money to pay the hotel bill, Alexa. I imagine you must be running rather short of funds by now."

Alexa sighed. This was the most embarrassing feature of the whole horrible situation.

"No, I haven't. Enough money, I mean. Monsieur Jouffre is paying the bill here. You can pay him back."

Elizabeth controlled herself. The nightmare of her daughter's failure to arrive at Yeadon airport, the knowledge that she had lost her passport, and that she was, for immediate and practical purposes, destitute in a foreign capital was in no way soothed by the thought of their indebtedness to a strange young man, whatever his alleged credentials. It was not pleasant to have one's daughter dependent for a night's lodging on some individual of whom one knew nothing.

"You had better ring us again tomorrow and tell us what you've managed to achieve. I shall expect your call at about six o'clock in the evening. Daddy will try and make some arrangements with the bank to send you more money and if you don't get anywhere with the consulate by tomorrow evening, we shall contact the Foreign Office."

"Oh don't be so dramatic, Mummy. I'm in Paris not Outer Mongolia."

"You are adrift and vulnerable in a city which is notoriously unkind to young, unaccompanied women. From the point of view of moral safety, I'm bound to say, I should regard Outer Mongolia as entirely preferable. You have no money and are dependent for the moment on someone whom *I* must regard as a stranger. You appear to trust him, but I have nothing on which to base an opinion. I shall indeed telephone your grandfather at once and find out more."

Alexa sighed. It was typical of her mother to blame *her* for whatever mishap befell. Anything that caused her worry was treated as a deliberate act of callousness on Alexa's own part. It was true that the practical emergencies were always taken care of with swift efficiency, whatever the administrative hurdles, but there was never any reassurance. In her parents' eyes, bad luck was never anything more than bad management. Their affection was real enough but it found no kinder expression than the usefulness of connections and cheque books.

"All right, Mummy. I'll ring you tomorrow at six o'clock."

"Be certain that you do. Goodnight, Alexa."

Before she finally slept, Alexa had decided not to go home. Not immediately. She must not be bullied like this. It had to end. Her parents must be made to understand she was a human being and not a possession. Somehow she must find a way of staying in Paris. She was in love with Jean-Claude. When she went home, it would be to introduce her *fiancé*. Then everything would be all right.

It had struck her, that probably nobody received control of their own life, handed, as it were, on a silver salver. You had to fight for it, make a gesture of intent. *Do* something.

Once Jean-Claude had heard of Alexa's determination he was excused the necessity of manufacturing spurious delays. The people at the consulate were calm, but it would take forty-eight hours to arrange for another passport. In the meantime, they hoped Miss Standeven had enough money and somewhere to stay. Everything would be all right, she was not to worry.

Meanwhile, Alexa was intent on finding a job. She had told Jean-Claude this when he came to breakfast with her on the deeply shaded *terrasse* of the little hotel.

"I won't go home, and I wish I didn't even have to talk to them again. I'm so sick of being treated like a criminal. You should try talking to my mother when something has gone wrong, she always behaves as if one had been arrested for indecent assault."

"Do you not think you should go home, eventually?" Jean-Claude enquired tentatively, feeling his way. He was frankly rather bored with the domestic emotions of the Standevens. He did hope that all this would be over soon. However, it would pay to show some interest. It seemed Alexa's parents were positively *driving* her into his bed. Not that they could possibly realise that of course. But it was the lucky effect of Madame Standeven's telephone manner.

"Possibly. I don't know at the moment. I'm too upset. But I can't stay here without money so I just need a temporary job to tide me over. I don't know what though." Alexa was crumbling *brioche*. The action was unconscious, the crumbs fell in untidy profusion over the paper tablecloth. Jean-Claude put out his hand and enclosed hers, arresting the nervous movements of her fingers.

"Be calm, *chérie*, I will attend to everything. You are an adult, there is no reason to fear. Trust me and I will ensure you have a little respite for thought." Alexa looked at him, her eyes warming momentarily to flame-blue. He was so good.

"Now," he continued, "I will call your parents myself, this evening, and explain everything. You have no need to worry."

"You don't understand, that is the very thing which would make them extremely suspicious. Daddy would be on the next plane out here. What could you explain? Alexa isn't coming home because she's . . . well, what?"

"Believe me, *chérie*, I do understand. I am a little older than you, nearer, perhaps, your father's own age than yours. We will have a chat, and then he will understand that if he wishes to keep his daughter's affections he must allow her some adult dignity. You are not a child any longer, I will make him understand that."

"No you won't. My mother will probably answer the telephone, she usually does, and she does all the talking for both of them. It's very rare that my father speaks to anyone at all. He's like a great, wordless god and Mummy is his priestess." Her voice was full of bitter irony.

"Even better. I can talk to women, there are few Frenchmen who cannot."

Alexa shrugged unhappily. Maybe Jean-Claude could make them see. Things could not be worse than they were. She was glad to let him take some of the weight.

Jean-Claude had no intention of telephoning anyone. The utter wrongness of his intended deceit did not occur to him. He had neither conscience nor moral discretion but an absolute inability to connect his present actions with any future consequences. The only son of an elderly father and an eternally self-sacrificing mother, his natural inclinations had never been frustrated since babyhood. The indulgence had been total. Had Jean-Claude ever known what it was to be short of money, he would not have hesitated to steal it. But the wealth of his father spared him that necessity.

In his own way he was as innocent as Alexa herself, only she was accustomed to having her desires frustrated and, until this moment of defiance, had believed that to be the natural order of things.

To Jean-Claude, Alexa was a game. A challenge to his ability. He intended to have her. The complications only sharpened his appetite.

He arranged a little job for her. A small language school which remained open throughout the month of August had a vacancy for a part-time assistant. Her only duties would be to speak in English to a group of down-at-heel businessmen. She would not want to do it for very long, he felt sure of that.

"It's a little shabby perhaps, this school, but it will do for now. Jobs are hard to get at this season. So many businesses closed down for the holidays and student labour so cheap . . ."

"Please, please don't apologise. It's I who should apologise to you for causing you all this trouble. Really, I'm grateful for anything. It's much better than washing up in a restaurant, and really, I thought that was the kind of thing I'd have to do. I don't think my French is really good enough to work in an office, and I can't type. It's just that they don't seem to want me to do very much for my money do they?"

"You see, *chérie*, it is the total immersion method. You mustn't speak in French at all. The idea is that if they hear enough of you, they'll be bound to understand you eventually."

Alexa had been taken on at ten francs an hour for no other reason than that the tired, pasty-faced proprietor of the seedy *Ecole des Langues Etrangères du Commerce Mondial* had seized on her *accent d'Oxford*, as he called it. He could hardly have expected such good fortune. Young English people of good family, if they did this kind of work at all, would naturally find posts at the Berlitz. He was normally obliged to make do with the flotsam and jetsam of long-haired student life which came his way. This well-dressed young lady would lend a certain *cachet* to the establishment, and at no more cost than a cleaning woman.

The school was situated in a run-down building in a small street behind the Boulevard du Montparnasse. She could walk there every day. That was as well, because fares on top of her hotel bill would be impossible to meet. As it was she was anx-

ious that her earnings would be insufficient to support her and
that she would need to find cheaper accommodation. That would
be difficult. All the convents which took students were closed
for the month of August and the cheap warren-like hotels front-
ing directly onto the Left Bank of the Seine frightened her.

A generous supply of money had been wired to the Westminster Bank in the Place Vendôme. It was not intended to last more
than a week at most, however. Alexa went to collect it. The
banking hall had the acoustics of a swimming bath and the bland
solemnity of a mosque. A courtly bank clerk dressed like an
English barrister informed her that he was to make a cheque out
in favour of a Monsieur Jouffre.

"Apparently your father is most insistent on this point. We
have a draft for the purpose. But I'm afraid, *Mademoiselle*, we
need some more details. What are Monsieur Jouffre's initials?
And his address?"

Alexa was not able to help with the latter query. The arrival
of the money prodded her conscience unbearably. Although she
told herself she hated her parents, actually, she could not bear
to cause them disquiet. She wished they would stop worrying
quite so much. It was a form of torture to her, an imprisonment.
Both she and they must be weaned off the mutually destructive
and vicious circle of worrying and being worried about. She had
no idea what Jean-Claude had said to them. When she asked
him what they had said when he telephoned them, he had replied
merely that her mother was a very charming woman and was
being quite reasonable.

"They'll see you when they see you, *chérie*. Just get back in
time for the university term, that's all they're concerned about
really. I told them, you're grown up now and they shouldn't
worry. Did I not say that I would handle your mother? People
always think their parents are not as others are. It is natural, but
it is not so. I have proved it, I think, even to you."

It was so totally out of character. But not believing meant not
believing in Jean-Claude and that was impossible. He was her
love and everything he did must be right, even if it looked odd
at first. After all, why should her parents *not* act out of character.
She had. She had called their bluff and it had worked. It was all
Jean-Claude's doing. It was appropriate that the man she loved
should make her maturity plain to her parents. It had a poetic
symmetry and truth that contented her.

None-the-less, she decided she must write home. She could

not bring herself to speak to her mother again, but she must write. One does not put one's hand into the fire a second time. One uses a spill.

By the time her letter arrived she had left the Hôtel de Picardie. Jean-Claude had decided that the streets of the Latin quarter were perhaps not absolutely safe. There had been some trouble with Algerian students, who, having nowhere worth going in the summer months and no means to go there in any event, were indulging themselves in scuffles with local youths. There were a lot of police around and the white truncheons were seen in their hands more often than was customary. There had been disturbances. She had far better stay in his *appartement*. Jean-Claude exaggerated the dangers of what had been no more than a minor incident.

"It may be reported in the English newspaper, *chérie*, and what would your parents think, if they knew I was allowing you to live in a *quartier* which is unsafe?"

True, his *appartement* was in Neuilly, a long way from the *Ecole des Langues Etrangères du Commerce Mondial*, but she could go there every morning by taxi once her job began. Her protests had been stifled by Jean-Claude's assertion that since she would have no rent to pay, she could easily afford the taxi fare.

Alexander crashed the telephone receiver back into its cradle. The dachshunds on the Isfahan rug looked up gloomily without raising their heads from their paws. Langstroth Grange had lacked its usual ordered harmony during the last forty-eight hours or so. The attention paid to dogs had been perfunctory and restricted to essential services.

Everyone, Alexander steamed, was being most unhelpful. It was Elizabeth's fault. She had acted and spoken hastily. Had she remained somewhat calmer on the telephone when speaking to Alexa they might have had her safely at home by now. She had further compounded the error by taking matters into her own hands the minute Alexa's letter arrived.

He had been over in Manchester acting for a client in a difficult insurance case. It was a long drive over the Pennines and he had left the house early. He had given his wife the number to ring if there should be a call from Paris, or anything to go on. Unfortunately, Elizabeth had gone one better than that and rung Scotland Yard. They had told her that since her daughter had written, there was nothing they could do. The fact she had given no address was a matter of choice or accident. But she was not a missing person within the meaning of their powers. She had stated plainly, had she not, that she had a job and somewhere to live? She was eighteen and had left school. It was no doubt worrying but they would not be justified in mobilising Interpol to find the whereabouts of a person who, evidently, did not wish to be found and was in no immediate danger. They were sorry. No doubt Miss Standeven would be in touch shortly. Young people sometimes did this kind of thing. They almost always turned up quite unharmed.

Alexander was furious.

"You should never have told them about the letter. Her failure to telephone us that evening and the fact that her passport had been lost were sufficient to give rise to concern over the fate of a young British national. Something would have been done. I wish you would do as I tell you. If I'd wanted you to do anything, I would have said so. Really Elizabeth, if only you could sometimes resist the temptation to *do* something. Action is not always the most effective solution. Sometimes, as in this instance, inactivity would have served our purpose better. At least until I had time to think about it. Now we had better trace this Jouffre person. What did your father say about him?"

Alexander had already heard what his father-in-law had said about Jouffre. It was not very enlightening and not entirely re-assuring.

On the day of his granddaughter's expected return home Henry Jagger had been sailing to Copenhagen out of the port of Goole where he had large interests. Henry often went to Copenhagen, no longer to do business, but to see his many Danish friends. His absences there, or in Belgium, rarely lasted more than a few days. After docking he found that there was a message waiting for him in his usual suite at the Europa.

Elizabeth did not tell her father that there was any immediate cause for concern over Alexa. After all, the old man did suffer from angina and his devotion to his eldest grandchild was well known. There was no need, Elizabeth considered, to worry him at this stage. With any luck Alexa would be home before he was. She didn't want any recriminations. Henry had always said she was too hard on the child. "Let her be, for God's sake. You're always on at her. You never stop." He'd said that often in the past.

"Listen, father, did you ever know a man called Jouffre?"
She spelled the name out. The line wasn't particularly good.

"Emil Jouffre? Yes. Why?"

"Alexa says she's met a man in Paris of that name. He says
his father knew you."

"Perfectly true. He used to be a manufacturer's agent before
the war. But then his uncle died and he inherited the family silk
business in Lyons. They were quite a big concern then."

"Were they all right?"

"Of course. Emil was a good friend of mine. Poor fellow
died of a coronary about six years ago. He had a son, Jean-Paul,
or Claude, or some such name. The business went public and
the Jouffres sold out. Young Jouffre went into his father's old
game, agenting. Went to live in Paris and married a nice girl. I
went to the wedding."

"What is he like?"

"Who, young Jouffre? Well, I never thought much of him.
He was nothing like his father. A lightweight. Not much of a
grafter. Had everything handed to 'im on a bloody plate. Seemed
to cause his parents quite a bit of anxiety as a youngster. But
they were very pleased about his marriage. Paulette. Yes, that
was her name. She'd quite a bit of brass of her own, I gathered.
Another big silk family in Lyons. I expect he steadied down.
They had a little boy pretty soon afterwards, that's the last I
heard. Perfectly good family. She won't come to much harm
with them. She'll be home soon anyway, won't she?"

"Yes, father, she will. I just wanted to check what kind of
company she was keeping, that's all. Hope you weren't
alarmed."

"I'm not easily alarmed. That all?"

The news that Jouffre was married was in some degree a
reassurance but if he was, why had he not taken Alexa to his
own home on the day her passport had been lost? There was
something unsatisfactory about the whole thing. Alexa had never
mentioned his wife, let alone his children. Were they dealing
with the same Jouffre?

Alexander knew it would not be difficult to find a textile manufacturer's agent called Jouffre in Paris. Any reasonably competent private-enquiry agent could do that. To find Alexa and
persuade her to come home—that might be altogether a more
delicate operation. He decided to shelve the matter for a few
days, convinced that Alexa's defiance would not last. Dingy

lodgings and inadequate food would soon bring her to heel.
Elizabeth was far from satisfied with this decision but finally
had to be content.

"This is your doing. How would you have spoken to me if
I'd lost my passport?"

"Don't be absurd. You wouldn't have lost an important document."

"It's happened to greater men than me. Even Caesar nods,
you know. Well, perhaps this will teach you a lesson. Your tongue
isn't your most lovable feature, my dear. I'd say learn to curb it,
if it weren't shutting the stable door after the horse had bolted.
I just hope the horse comes back out of habit."

"Don't you think you should go out there and look for her?"

"Why don't you go?"

"You know why not!" Elizabeth was angry with her husband's deliberate obtuseness. "My French isn't as good as yours
and if I find Alexa, I doubt if I could persuade her to come home
with me, now she's taken up this ludicrous attitude towards me."

"What's ludicrous about it?" Alexander's voice was raised in
a rare show of emotion, "She's afraid of us! And you're the one
that's made her afraid."

"You haven't done so damn much about her over the years,
you've always left her to me."

"You've manipulated us both. It occurs to me that I'm hardly
ever left alone with my daughter. When I am, the experience is
nerve-racking for both of us. We don't know what to say to each
other. We just want to escape the embarrassment as soon as we
can. She'll do anything to get away from me. But you're right,
I've hardly ever spoken to her as a father, *or* a friend for that
matter. How have you managed it, Elizabeth?"

Elizabeth slammed the door of the library. She and Alexander
had never before raised their voices to each other in twenty years
of marriage.

Alexa looked reflectively around the stylish but rather impersonal salon of Jean-Claude's *appartement*. It was an essay in
shop-bought good taste. A lot of *Louis Quinze* reproduction
furniture upholstered in dove-grey silk, standing on an expensive pale-grey carpet. The curtains at the tall window were elaborately swagged in silk which matched the chairs, and bordered
with rose pink. The room had no books or flowers but was
immaculately tidy and well-polished. A daily, Alexa though-idly.

She examined the few rather dull signed prints in their cold brushed-steel frames and the small collection of rose-quartz carvings in a reproduction vitrine. The home of a wealthy bachelor.

She had misgivings about living here with him, but what else could she do, she asked herself. Jean-Claude was now her only friend in Paris and she needed him. And also, it didn't much matter what she did now. She had told her parents she was going to stay in Paris until she was ready to come home. It had been an impassioned, ill-judged letter. Despairingly, Alexa faced the fact that she would not easily be forgiven. But it was done now. There was no point in worrying any more. She had acted and now she must face the consequences, whatever they might be.

Jean-Claude came in wiping his hands on a tea towel.

"Is the little bedroom all right, *chérie*? I have thought of everything. No?"

"It's perfect, Jean-Claude. I really feel I'm imposing on you though. Don't you think I should find a place of my own?"

"Later. Wait at least for a few days. When you start the new job, perhaps we will think again, but for the moment, this is best, *chérie*."

"My parents would be terribly shocked if they thought I was living in a man's flat."

"No doubt. But I thought we had agreed, you are to begin to please yourself. And in doing that, you will please me enormously. You will learn, little one, that pleasing other people is important, but it is not a priority."

He cupped her face in his two hands and Alexa responded instantly to his touch. The cool fingers caressed her ears and neck and she nuzzled him, inhaling the astringent perfume of maleness. He kissed her chastely on the forehead.

"Do not worry, *ma belle*, growing up is always painful. But it is most painful for others. To have a beautiful daughter and find she is not really yours, that is always an angry moment for a man. That is nature and nothing can alter it. It is your duty to take possession of yourself. And as for your mother, well, she too is angry because in losing hold of you, she has lost the last shred of her own youth. You can do nothing. She will come to terms with it. Before long, you will find, she will be pestering you for grandchildren. That will be her next object, believe me."

Alexa looked at him. It was the nearest he had come to declaring his own intentions. Her eyes searched his.

"You seem very certain."

"Assuredly, *chérie*. We Frenchmen make a study of women from the cradle to the grave. We know the pattern of their lives, the categories of their thoughts and can map their souls. Our knowledge is the foundation of our fame as lovers."

"I hope you are right."

"Of course I am. Now, let us stop this interminable talk of your respected parents. It is dull. Let us savour your emancipation together. We have a few days before you must report to the language school, so let us enjoy them. Tonight we will go to a *boîte* and dance until we are tired. The music will be loud enough to drown everything but pleasure. You will then sleep like a new-born baby."

"Rhythm to chase away the blues?"

"Exactement, ma petite."

Alexa left him sleeping. She had watched him for a long time, fascinated by the precise contours of his unconscious face. He was as heartbreakingly handsome now as he was when awake. It abashed her. She was sure her face must look slack, with a sort of muscular dishevelment when she slept. But Jean-Claude had a marble perfection of feature which required neither animation or deliberate control. It was unassailable. His face, neck and shoulders lay uncovered on the pillow, lit by the street lamp outside. He was like a marble torso, thrown down in anger but unbroken and impervious to the erosion of time.

His breathing was deep and regular but he made little sound. The eyelids were motionless, their dark fringes curling on his cheek. The pale mouth was curved and calm, satisfied and certain. The sight of him induced a great longing in Alexa to take him up and hold him close and crush him until his substance was forced to blend with hers forever. But of course, that could not be done. An unexpected tear formed and fell with a splash onto his long hand where it lay across his breast. Alexa rose carefully, and left him. Sleep would not come.

She wrapped Jean-Claude's towelling dressing gown about her more closely and leaned over the wrought-iron balustrade of the balcony which opened off the grey and rose-pink *salon* of the third-floor flat. She felt in the pocket of the robe and found a packet of *Disque Bleu*, she lit one and inhaled its pungency, watching with pleasure as the smoke spiralled away down the Rue des Pères in the motionless air of the warm night. A few security lights still illuminated the doors of the smart little houses and the mysterious entrances to grand villas. The trees stood motionless and dark. Occasionally in a neighbouring street there was the sound of a car door slamming. People returning late from parties; the Sixteenth was a fashionable quarter.

Alexa pressed the area between her legs gently through the dressing gown. There was swelling but the soreness was lessening. Jean-Claude had shown her the bright drops of blood on his finger tips. With his eyes fixed on hers he had licked off all the blood and then kissed her and she tasted the metallic flavour on her own tongue. She was not shocked. The shedding of blood and the drinking of it was surely the greatest love-token known to their culture. Jean-Claude could make love with his mind as well as his body.

The slight saltness of his flesh and the sweet odour of his hair came back to Alexa in memory and caused a small, tender convulsion. He had said that he wanted her, not that he loved her. She had had proofs of his need. But there would be love, surely.

In fact, Alexa had ensnared Jean-Claude into the nearest thing to disinterested affection he had ever experienced. There was an absolute simplicity about her which, together with her capacity for wholehearted enjoyment of the moment, made her the most companionable of mistresses. She had a talent for taking delight in small things and she was able to make him feel the value of many things he had never previously noticed or had taken for granted. And then there were her enchanting manners. She was so touchingly careful never to intrude or to impose on him and never, ever to bore him.

In the hot August days that followed, Alexa lived a lifetime of joy. She was lifted above all ordinary sensation. In Jean-Claude's company her face was turned towards him as perpetually as a daisy's to the sun and he shone back on her so that the petals of her sexuality opened ever more widely to greet him. Neither doubt nor anguish intruded on her bliss. With the curiously selfish, two-dimensional vision of all lovers in the grip of sexual obsession she believed that Jean-Claude was the mirror image of herself.

In reality, Jean-Claude did glory in her emerging womanhood. At Le Bourget she had carried herself with an appealing gawkiness. Now she moved with a proud languor. She prowled beside him like a young lioness, mated, sated and triumphant. He wanted people to see her, and to see her with him.

Routine is said to be the enemy of love and yet, the duties of each lover's life, when blended with those of a partner, form a dance of beautiful predictability. Alexa and Jean-Claude's lives pivoted around his daily visits to his office in Neuilly and Alexa's job on the Left Bank. Jean-Claude carried on his business as a manufacturer's agent for the textile trade desultorily in the month of August. His presence there was only marginally necessary. But the time it allowed Alexa was an essential part of his enjoyment of her. And he recognized that her little job and her small earnings were necessary to her self-respect. Shyly she offered him rent or a contribution to the running expenses of the flat.

"But I am using hot water and electricity, eating food and drinking wine, Jean-Claude. Please do not let me be an absolute burden to you."

"I shall begin to think there is something wanting in my hospitality, *chérie*, if you persist in this. One cannot take *rent* from the woman one adores. Please, keep your money. You will need it for something else, I am sure. Women are always so eager to divest themselves of money, but usually it is somebody else's which they wish to spend. You are perverted, *ma petite*. If you yearn for reckless expenditure, buy flowers or clothes or give it to beggars, but I beg you, do not injure my *amour-propre* by these well-meant offers of charity."

"Then I must look for another place to live. Somewhere nearer the school."

And then Jean-Claude had looked at her with sorrow.

"Do not do that, *chérie*, I cannot live without you. What would my life be? I need to have you near me. What is this strange obsession with money? Cannot lovers leave it out of their considerations? We have enough, it is of no consequence where it comes from or by whom it is supplied. Do not be so commercial, Alexa. I shall begin to think you care nothing for me, that I am a mere landlord to you. Perhaps you think I exact sex from you in place of rent. If that is so, then, indeed, we should part."

Naturally, Alexa gave way. Without difficulty, Jean-Claude had put her in the wrong, cast suspicion on the truth of her love for him and imputed vileness to her motives. The manipulation was a complete success and Alexa, afraid to hurt him, or draw down upon herself such dread accusations, said no more about money. In a few more days, with a similar suppleness of argument, clothed in the tenderest words, he had persuaded her to give up her job.

"Think, *chérie*, is it proper that I should allow you to go into a quarter where it is known there are disreputable characters at large, where there are civil disturbances and where your safety cannot be guaranteed? Could your respected parents welcome the man who had exposed their daughter to such an abomination?"

Alexa was almost incredulous.

"But Jean-Claude, I *lived* there for months, I came to no harm then. Why should I now?"

"Then you were protected by the presence of the larger body of respectable students, mostly young French people. Now, having homes to go to, they are gone and what is left is the scum, undesirables. The police in that area take a dim view of all foreigners below a certain age and in the month of August. They are indiscriminate in their arrests. Do you think being English will save you from annoyance? No, I cannot take the risk. Your parents would never forgive me if I were to permit such a mishap through negligence. No, they could not welcome such a man."

This was very dangerous ground. However, Jean-Claude had soon learned that Alexa was too well-bred, and too intrinsically kind to press any advantage. If affairs between men and women could indeed be viewed as a war between the sexes Alexa did not belong to the school of thought that coined the English phrase, "All's fair in love and war." Rather she belonged to that chivalrous company of campaigners who would only fight on open ground, despising the shadowy, murdering dagger held in the hand of a spy. So she said nothing about the future, but acquiesced in his wish. She left the *Ecole des Langues Etrangères du Commerce Mondial*, with the curses of the sweating proprietor ringing in her ears.

Her pupils had scarcely had time to get to know her, but her leaving so soon and so abruptly was a privation. Unlike her predecessor, Jake, she had tried hard to give value for money. She was not allowed to speak a word of French, and she kept to the rule. She had attempted to teach the dim-looking businessmen with their hopeless faces and mock-tartan neckties in the same way that Mia had taught her. She talked, scanning the vague faces before her, until she trapped a fleeting sign of recognition in the glazed unresponsive eyes. Then she would stop, talking over and over the same point in different words, simpler, more complicated, simpler again. She would hold their hands, shake them, and even strike them, playfully but also desperately when she saw attention fade. Her anxiety to teach was partially born of her own loneliness. She wanted to breach the wall of incomprehension and create companionship. But now, Jean-Claude had her all to himself. She did not go again to the Boulevard Montparnasse. She had been there only eight days and had earned four thousand francs.

Each morning Jean-Claude would leave her sleepy and vulnerable.

"A tout à l'heure, ma belle. A midi."

As soon as she heard the outer door close she would rise and shower. She never breakfasted in the *appartement* as she was unable to understand how Jean-Claude's coffee percolator worked. When she was dressed she walked to a hairdresser's in the Avenue Victor Hugo, Ziggy's. Ziggy was a Hungarian and spoke no English. His French was so heavily accented that Alexa couldn't understand anything he said. But Ziggy was a talented hairdresser and enjoyed practising his art on Alexa's good strong hair. He would turn her face this way and that, searching for her best angles. If ever she showed restlessness, Ziggy would give her a gentle slap and wag his finger at her. It was a sincere compliment.

Afterwards, Alexa invariably returned the short distance to the Rue des Pères in a taxi. She felt self-conscious about the contrast between the almost Geisha-like formality of her coiffure and the morning nudity of her face. Once back in the flat she would commence the pleasurable business of dressing for lunch with Jean-Claude and his friends.

He had showered her with gifts of clothing, handbags, shoes and luxurious accessories of every description. At first she protested vigorously against his generosity, embarrassed and guilty. Her mother had taught her that ladies never accepted presents of value from gentlemen unless they were engaged, and never, ever clothing or jewellery. He gave her money, too. The sums seemed enormous to Alexa. He met her objections with insouciant deftness.

"Chérie, never reject the tributes a man lays at your feet. You give pain. All beautiful women receive gifts, it is natural."

"But it is not moral, Jean-Claude. I cannot approve of myself."

"Approval of the self is the contentment of schoolgirls, *chérie.*

That belongs to the past now. You must satisfy yourself with generosity.''

"Generosity?''

"Mais certainement," he placed his hands on either side of her face and forced her to look at him, ''a man in love provides for his mate or he cannot approve of himself. And, you know, when his mate is very beautiful, he is always afraid that his lovemaking will not be sufficient to keep her, so he tries to think of other things that will please her. He makes offerings to his Goddess. Which will you do, my love? Reject my *petits cadeaux* and approve of yourself, or will you accept them and allow me to believe that I am a man in your eyes?''

Alexa, disarmed, allowed herself to be convinced. She began to spend Jean-Claude's money with a taste and discernment which surprised him. She was, of course, a good student and humble before any knowledge superior to her own. She knew how to concentrate and how to ask questions. She brought these qualities to her shopping expeditions in the *grands boulevards*, the Boulevard St. Germain and in the local boutiques. She was a popular customer and the cynical *vendeuses* of Paris became her allies.

In the dusty tedium of August, retailing clothes was normally an uninteresting task. The chic *Parisiennes* were away from the capital on holiday. One occasionally sold a garment to a tourist who cared only for the label and nothing for the art of dress. But the English girl was a delightful diversion. She had money to spend and was so touchingly anxious to learn. For her they would shorten a hemline in the space of an afternoon and send the dress round to the Rue des Pères in time for the evening. After all, she would be back the following day.

At 12:30 Alexa would be ready to leave just as the *femme de ménage*, Madame Dubois, let herself into the flat to clean. Occasionally they chatted briefly over a cup of coffee that Madame Dubois would prepare. On these occasions Alexa tried to find out more about Jean-Claude, but the older woman deflected her questions with the shrugging reply, *"Je ne sais rien, Mademoiselle. Il me paye bien et c'est tout ce que je sais."*

She felt the unspoken reproof acutely. Gossiping with servants, questioning other people's staff, it was unpardonable. Jean-Claude would tell her more about his life when he was ready. In the meantime all she had to do was trust him.

Their daily lunch date in Neuilly always included some of

Jean-Claude's business associates. Alexa basked in their attentiveness. Only French was spoken and frequently under the influence of wine and admiration her careful and correct French
would become a waterfall of quaint grammar and Anglo-Saxon
vowels which charmed her audience. Sometimes the talk was
all of business and she did not say much but devoted herself to
the extravagant food. Often, when she laid down her knife and
fork on a half-finished plate, without a pause in his conversation
or a glance in her direction, Jean-Claude would remove the dish
and hand it to the nearest waiter with a smile and a murmured
"Ça suffit, je pense." Alexa's expression of spaniel-eyed grief
as she watched the remainder of her *entrée* borne away shoulder-
high invariably caused much good-natured hilarity.

"It is for your own good, *chère* Mademoiselle Standeven.
What a tragedy if you were to get fat!"

"You know yourself, *Mademoiselle*, do you not, that if a
starving horse is turned onto a field of clover, he will die of
colic. Is that not so?"

They had all heard the story of the frozen meat and boiled
vegetables which Jean-Claude recounted joyfully at every new
opportunity.

"You know I will give you anything, my darling, but how can
I permit you to injure your figure?"

Many women resent being treated as a domestic pet, but for
Alexa it was a novel experience. She felt for the first time that
she was loved for herself instead of for what she could do. Jean-
Claude had understood her needs so exactly.

They went one day to a race-meeting at Longchamps. Alexa
dressed as a parody of her former self, wearing the outfit of an
English gentlewoman at a county agricultural show, interpreted
with the sly wit and precision of a Frenchwoman. The sparse,
low-key toilette with the severe schoolgirl boater, tipped with
barely discernible coquetry over her eyes, was an instant sensation. Jean-Claude could not keep his eyes off her and his pride
in her was clear to the many acquaintances who asked him to
introduce Alexa to them.

He talked for a long time to an elderly, rubicund gentleman
with a striking air of general benevolence called Monsieur Terry.
Monsieur Terry glanced at her from time to time in a way that
seemed to indicate disquiet. Eventually, Jean-Claude left Alexa
with him while he went to place bets for the next race.

"Tell me, Mademoiselle Standeven, what you are doing in

Paris. *Le mois d'août*, you know, is not an amusing time of the year. Paris is given up to husbands who cannot leave their business, to students who have failed their exams and must re-take them and to tourists who know no better. It is a winter of the spirit in Paris.''

Alexa was taken aback.

"I am here because I decided not to go."

Immediately she regretted the brusque speech. She had been rude. "I think, perhaps, I am trying to grow up a little," she amended.

Monsieur Terry looked sidelong at her, and then down at his small neat feet clad in London-made shoes.

"Come, let us walk a little," he offered her his arm and Alexa, conceding, linked her arm through his, "let me feel a little of what young Jouffre feels when he has you at his side."

If he had hoped that his skilful flattery would lower her defences and encourage her to tell him anything about her relationship with Jean-Claude Jouffre, he was disappointed. She rose a little in his esteem.

"It is very warm, *Monsieur*. Is it always so hot at this time of the year?"

Monsieur Terry chuckled. "When in doubt, the English always talk about the weather," he patted her hand.

"With or without doubt, *Monsieur*, they always talk about the weather."

"Adroit, *Mademoiselle*, adroit. You wrap a rebuff in a pun before you administer it. But, I understand, you do not want an old man's advice."

His gentle insistence unseated Alexa's composure.

"I did not say that, *Monsieur*."

He stopped walking and with both hands turned her to face him. She was a little taller than him and he looked up at her.

"Listen, *ma chère Mademoiselle*. You need say nothing. I have daughters and granddaughters of my own," his eyes dropped and he hesitated, "if anything should . . . if you should need . . ."

Alexa did not hear what he said, perhaps he did not really say anything. He took his hands from her shoulders and gripped her hands for an instant before resuming his place at her side and continued walking.

"Here is my card, I am there most days."

"But *Monsieur*," Alexa exclaimed, "you are a *couturier*!"

"I am a dressmaker, that is so."

"I am very ignorant, I have never heard of you."

"Well, it is a small house. I have a cadre of old established customers and it suits me well. I was perhaps better known in the thirties, along with Captain Molyneux, but now I am content in my obscurity. I cannot bring myself to open boutiques, launch ranges of ties or go into the *prêt-à-porter*. I am an old man. The old ways and the old customers are enough for me. *Après moi, le déluge*."

Two days later Madame Dubois showed Alexa her picture in a gossip magazine. It had been taken at Longchamps and showed her and Monsieur Terry walking together. Alexa was ecstatic.

"Oh *Madame*, may I keep the paper to show Monsieur Jouffre?"

"Certainly, *Mademoiselle*."

She tore out the page and put it in her handbag and raced off to hail a taxi to Neuilly. She was jubilant going up in the lift to Jean-Claude's office. She knew it was silly to be so pleased but she was sure Jean-Claude would share her little triumph.

"Look, we're in the paper," she said putting the page in front of him. Jean-Claude's face puckered with consternation. "I know it's not a very good photograph but you can tell it's me!"

Jean-Claude's face cleared a little but there was no smile. He did not want his photograph with Alexa to appear in any newspaper. If Paulette were to pick it up in Sardinia . . . he did not like to think of the possible repercussions. Extramarital affairs should be conducted with absolute discretion. It was a rule of good breeding. Paulette would mind the breach of correct behaviour very much. And Paulette must be given no grounds for divorce. She had brought a handsome dowry with her. Emil Jouffre had warned his son. "The money, my boy, is not to make you comfortable. They know they can count on me for that. No, it is to ensure your good behaviour. The income from one million francs will be hard to lose. So be careful, *hein*?"

"Don't you think it's fun?"

"Old Terry is a picture of animation, *chérie*. What can you have been talking about? He's not a ladies' man. You have made another conquest it seems."

"You aren't possibly jealous, he's a grandfather!"

"He's a . . . how do you say it in England? A busy bee? It is that, no?"

"I think you mean busybody," Alexa said slowly. She felt deflated. She had liked Monsieur Terry.

"Don't look so sad, *chérie, c'est pas grand-chose*. Smile."

She did smile, a little tremulously. She felt a fool.

"I think I must keep you out of the public eye, *mon ange*. The reputation of a *jeune fille* ought to be guarded. We have been careless."

"I thought I was supposed to be a woman now," she teased bravely, though her eyes reflected hurt. She did not understand why Jean-Claude should not be tickled to see her photograph in the press. No more did she understand his relief that she was not pictured side by side with him.

"You are my woman and a *jeune fille* for everyone else."

With this Jean-Claude kissed her long and hard and Alexa knew that he wished the discussion to end. However, the ambiguity of his last statement, albeit lightly made, introduced a worm of hope into her heart.

Later she lay cradled in his arms, all doubt chased away by the ardour of their lovemaking. Idly, he nuzzled her damp hair and nibbled her ears.

"Jean-Claude?"

"Oui, ma belle."

"Who lives in the rest of this house? The bottom two floors. I saw Madame Dubois coming out of the front door this morning. Should she have been there?"

"Why should she not be there, *chérie*?" He tousled her hair distractingly.

"Well, I just wondered, the house is all shut up."

Jean-Claude sighed. He disliked questions very much.

"The house, my little detective, belongs to a family who are away on holiday in Sardinia. I rent this *appartement* from them on an annual basis. Madame Dubois has worked for them for years, but since she is employed by them only part-time, she also looks after the flat for me. The arrangement suits us all admirably. Of course, I am conversant with many more details of the daily lives of my landlords as I know the family intimately. We each have relatives who are neighbours in the same village near Lyons. May I tell you more?"

Alexa felt her face go hot. There was an acidity in his tone that she had never previously heard. She felt that she had displayed a vulgar curiosity and offended Jean-Claude's fastidiousness.

"I'm so sorry," she was on the verge of weeping. "You see, in England, neighbours look out for each other, it's quite accepted."

Jean-Claude was filled with remorse, Alexa, she was so sensitive. No need to reward her little bout of curiosity so harshly. After all, when the heat of a love affair abated, there must be some domestic conversation to fill the gaps. He sighed deeply.

"No, no *chérie*. I am sorry. The day has not gone well for me. Some mix-up over a consignment of tweed. I get like a cross old husband, *n'est-ce pas*?"

Frank Bottomley was having a pleasant time, and there again, not pleasant. Professionally, things were not proceeding with their customary smoothness. Bottomley and Garside Limited prided themselves on a swift, tidy conclusion to all the investigations entrusted to them. Well, Garside was no longer with the firm, but his name looked good painted in gold on the bubble-glass door of the Cheapside premises.

No, the Standeven case was not proving entirely straightforward. Still, the sun was shining and Gay Paree was living up to expectations. Frank wished he could have brought Edna with him, but it was against his principles to mix work and pleasure. If it weren't for Standeven's voice on the telephone each evening, cold with disappointment and mild with submerged threat, he would be enjoying the change.

Frank had often acted in delicate matters for Standeven, Standeven and Browne. Since retiring from the Police Force, he'd built up a reputation amongst the more distinguished firms of West Riding solicitors. They called him in whenever something needed finding out, quickly, quietly and at a realistic charge. Yorkshire solicitors were prudent when it came to costs. Frank respected that. Only fools threw their money about. Standeven was one of the keenest. But he wasn't averse to putting it about where it could do some good. Remorseless in pursuit, that's what he was, remorseless. And never more so than now. Just thinking about him made the short hairs on the back of Frank's head stand up. Standeven'd have his guts for garters if he didn't come up with something pretty soon.

The thought of Alexander dragged Bottomley's mind back to the matter in hand. He didn't think the sleazy Café de la Rotonde in the sinister little Rue Saint Séverin would have been a likely haunt for a respectable young lady like Miss Standeven. It was patronised by cheap prostitutes and the kind of unlikely-looking characters Frank knew instinctively ought to be behind bars. Still, he showed the photograph he had been given to the patron behind his zinc bar.

The man looked casually at the colour print. It showed a good-looking teenager in a striped cotton frock, sitting in what looked like a large, green garden. The man laughed laconically, and then shook his head decisively. He'd seen her, of course. She'd come often enough in the evenings with that prim-looking Belgian girlfriend of hers, no oil painting, the Belgian. But the Café de la Rotonde wasn't in the business of obliging cops. And *ce type-là*, well, he looked like a cop. The blonde girl, the onlooker, she'd seemed interested in the regular girls. Just curiosity, no accounting for tastes. And the Belgian? She'd have done anything the English piece had wanted her to, you could see that a mile off. They'd been no trouble. Drank a glass of white wine and a coffee or two, paid for it with a good tip thrown in, and then gone off, quiet as you please. Lots of rich girls like slumming. No harm in it.

Frank sighed and turned away, glancing at the photograph himself. Not what you'd call bonny, Miss Standeven. Bit too like her father for that. Handsome, maybe, a proper Standeven. There was a comfortless look about the lass, she'd not be easy.

The trail had gone cold before he'd got to it. At the Hôtel de Picardie he'd drawn a complete blank. It seemed Alexa had never been there. Bottomley didn't like Caval. A hard case, if ever he'd seen one. But nothing could be got out of him. No, he'd never seen the girl in the photograph. No English girl by the name of Alexa Standeven had checked in during the past three or four weeks. Caval showed him the register. It was impossible to check foreigners into a hotel in France without a passport, so whoever the mystery lady was, she had not been in his hotel. Jouffre? Never heard of him.

Bottomley didn't believe him. Not for a moment. He flipped open his wallet casually, ostensibly to replace the photograph, but really to allow Caval a view of the neatly folded, crisp, thousand franc notes. There were a lot of them. Caval shook his head. He and Jouffre had been mates in the army. They'd had some good times together in Algiers. Caval didn't shop mates for a few lousy francs, not over a girl, anyway.

The consulate staff weren't much help either. Yes, they remembered Miss Standeven, of course. They'd issued her with a new passport and they assumed she'd gone home. She'd been accompanied by a Monsieur Jouffre, a friend of the family she'd said. She'd given the address of the Westminster Bank in the Place Vendôme as her contact address in Paris. That was perfectly in order. In fact, they remembered, it was Monsieur Jouffre who had suggested she do so, in case she changed hotels. Quite reasonable.

The bank was no more helpful. They had always supposed Mademoiselle Standeven's address to be that given them when facilities had first been arranged, 147, Rue de Vaugirard. A student hostel, run by nuns. Most respectable. The bank had been notified of no change. They were *desolés*, but they were afraid they could not help. Young people could be a great trial. Poor Mr. Standeven.

The Commercial Attaché's department was obstructive at first. They were not in the missing persons business. Why didn't Bottomley go to the police and so forth. Eventually they agreed to supply a list of all the textile agents in Paris. They did. There was no firm which included the name of Jouffre on the list.

"Perhaps," said the weary young woman diplomat, "Monsieur Jouffre trades under a different name. He may have bought an existing firm, or inherited a partnership from someone with a different surname . . .'

That left the telephone book. There were plenty of Jouffres in Paris. A whole page of them. Three of them had the initials J. C. Bottomley visited each address, one in Passy, one in the Rue Michel-Ange Molitor and one out at the Porte de Vincennes. It was a wasted day. The J. C. Jouffre in Passy had proved to be a double amputee in a wheelchair, the husband of the concierge of a dreary block of modern flats. His wife had spoken a little English. She gave Frank a cup of tea, not bad tea either. It had been the best thing that had happened all day. Tomorrow, he would start going through all the Js. When he'd finished that, he'd visit every textile agency in Paris. Frank Bottomley didn't think of doing it the other way round. He wasn't a lateral thinker. Steady Eddy, that's what they'd called him in the Force. Silly really, his name wasn't Eddy. Frank had never understood it.

That evening, Frank took himself to what he termed a "girlie show" in the Pigalle district. It wasn't much fun, Edna wouldn't have enjoyed it. But he had to do something to get the sound of Alexander's voice out of his ears. He hadn't snapped. He'd just started talking about French enquiry agents. Perhaps a local man might do better. That wouldn't do Frank's reputation much good. It'd soon be round every legal office in the West Riding that he, Frank Bottomley, had come home empty-handed.

He left the show early. He didn't really like the noise and the smell. The girls were uncomfortably close on the little stage. They looked unnaturally large and threatening. You could see the sweat shining on their painted flesh. Hard, leathery-looking skin that was none too fresh either. Their eye make-up was running and their big lips were drawn back in ghastly grimaces of synthetic invitation. He was sickened.

Outside the pavements were wet, a shower of rain had freshened the close atmosphere. Frank sat down in a basket chair on the *terrasse* of a nearby café. He'd have a coffee and maybe a snack. It was too early to go to bed yet. It wasn't crowded, a few groups sat about under the red awning, enjoying the slight cool of the air, the reflection of the neon lights in the road and the pleasant swishing sound of the passing traffic.

The waiter was slow in coming. In the manner of waiters, he was suddenly submerged in the task of clearing tables abandoned by earlier patrons. He had the professional unawareness of the presence of new customers. Frank sighed philosophically. He wasn't in a hurry. Idly, he picked up a newspaper left lying on the chair beside him. It was rather crumpled, a popular rag by the look of it. On the back page there was a photograph of a grand-looking girl wearing a smashing hat. A real corker, it was. She was with a fat elderly man. Disgusting. Frank would like to have put her over his knee. He would too, if she'd been his daughter. It seemed to be on a racecourse. Frank couldn't make out the caption. He threw the paper down disgustedly and concentrated on catching the eye of the waiter.

The next day, before he left for Neuilly, Jean-Claude made Alexa's heart leap with a fearful anticipation.

"Do not meet me for lunch today, *chérie*. Pass the whole day in making yourself look beautiful for me. This evening will be very special, I think you will be happy with the little surprise I have. Yes, *très contente*."

Alexa regarded him in wonderment. "When will you come?"

"At half past eight. Be ready. No?"

Alexa had spent her day in a mist of happiness, preparing for an evening which she was sure would reveal her future to her.

She tried so hard not to think in terms of marriage or a proposal, but it was not possible. She loved Jean-Claude and he loved her. What could stand in their way? She could not control her imagination. It escaped her custody over and over again. She had visions of her mother and father, angry at first almost certainly, but then surprised, and more surprised still at their own pleasure in the notion of Alexa being engaged to be married to a respectable Frenchman. They would lay aside their great plans for her with loving resignation, admitting that her happiness was all they had really ever sought.

They would like Jean-Claude. They could not fail to appreciate his handsomeness and his energetic air. He was already established in business and could support her, there could be no objection on that score. And she would soon meet his family. There would be a long intimate drive in his black Citroën first, to the countryside around Lyons where his mother lived. At least they would know exactly who she was. There would be no suspicion as to *her* family. Thinking about her own parents, Alexa was conscious of a slight frisson of apprehension. But no-one, not even her mother, could deny her the chance of happiness. And if she had Jean-Claude standing beside her, she would be invincible.

All day her mind ran in these grooves. Ziggy noticed her radiant happiness and excelled himself. For some reason Madame Dubois never arrived, but it didn't matter. Alexa relished her solitude because soon it would be a rare commodity. She went out for a walk. But the exercise gave her no relief from the almost exhausting excitement she felt. If on most days people turned in the street to look at her, today everyone did. The exaltation in her face drew every eye.

She tried to eat an omelette and some bread at a pavement café. It was no good, she could not eat a mouthful. The waiter was all flattering concern. She smiled on him but did not see him.

In the afternoon she returned to the *appartement* and tried to rest. It was difficult as she didn't want to disarrange her hair. She dozed a little but her mind was relentlessly busy. At about six in the evening she got up. It was a pity there was no bath to soak in. Realising the absence of that pleasurable prelude to her preparations would leave an excessive amount of time for even the most meticulous toilet, she lay down again on the bed and stared impatiently at the ceiling. At seven she started to dress, proceeding with careful slowness. But these things have a natural pace and the work on her appearance was complete by twenty minutes to eight. It did not matter. She was ready.

Twisting and turning before the cheval mirror, Alexa was pleased with what she saw. She had repeated the success of her experiment at Longchamps, when she had made her clothes express her *naïveté*, and in so doing, hint at a tantalising precocity. The cut of the short white ottoman-silk skirt and its elaborately beaded camisole top was flawless. The rich fabrics contrasted with the almost infantile simplicity of outline. Ziggy had dressed her hair in a severely neat ponytail and adorned it with an enormous black velvet bow. Alexa's slim legs, in pale sparkly hose, descended to fragile inconsequential slippers. It was witty. And it would not have disgraced the front cover of *Vogue*. It was difficult to believe that the glittering sprite reflected in the glass was the same *ingénue* who had so nearly left Paris on Flight BA245 just over three weeks ago. Was that all it was? Alexa shook her head as if trying to clear it.

In the kitchen there was a cold bottle of wine in the fridge. She uncorked it and arranged two glasses on a tray. Back in the *salon* she poured herself a glass. The sting of the first gulp calmed her a little. She put a record on the turntable, the Beatles. Opening the windows of the *salon* wide, she walked out onto the balcony and began to look up and down the street. There were many black Citroëns like Jean-Claude's in Paris but Alexa's heart gave a lurch every time one came into view. The agony of waiting was also a game of solitaire, because she knew that the edge of anxiety she felt would make the eventual relief of his coming and the comfort of his presence a total consummation of her faith.

By half past eight he had not arrived. They would be late, he would have to change. A quarter of an hour later she became impatient. Impatience dissolved into worry. At ten o'clock she tried to telephone his office. There was no reply. By eleven tears pricked threateningly behind her eyes, but she dared not weep, it would spoil her make-up and in Paris, the night was still young. Any minute now he would telephone full of loving apologies and explanations. Something silly had gone wrong. In later years they would often laugh over it.

The sheer tensile strength of her belief and hope upheld her until one o'clock. Only then did despair overrun her defences. Slowly, she undressed and took off her make-up. When Jean-

Claude did arrive, he must not see any evidence of the deep
wound he had inflicted on her. She would be in bed, sleeping.

It was a night of profound misery. She got up several times
and made cups of instant coffee. She played some more music
and smoked cigarettes until she felt sick. At last she allowed her
mind to scream out the pain. Why, oh why had he done this to
her? Had she been so wrong about him and his intentions? Surely
that was impossible? But it was possible. What did she know of
a man like Jean-Claude? Really know. He was at least twelve
years older than she was. She had been an inky schoolgirl when
he had already become a man about town. With those looks he
must have made love to a hundred girls. What had made her
think herself any different? Alexa berated herself with every
reproach her mother could have thought of and more. She wept
with the angry, violent tears of a child. Tears that ravage the
face and alter the texture of the skin. Tears that engorge the eyes
and make a lovely face hideous. The mirror told her that she
was sufficiently punished.

Alexa slept towards dawn. She had sustained a savage emotional pruning. She had felt every cut of the knife and sap had
bled from the stumps. It was an atrocity. But also, it had brought
a despairing calm. Whatever had to be faced, she would con-
front. She would meet each disastrous consequence as it presented itself. But she could not go home, not now.

In the morning she was woken by Madame Dubois who
evinced no surprise at finding her in bed so late. Alexa said she
would get up at once. Madame Dubois always did the bedroom
on Wednesdays. The charwoman nodded approvingly as she
knotted a dressing gown about her and went into the shower
room.

Needles of water impinged on Alexa's tired flesh. She soaped
herself all over, unconsciously trying to wash away her abjec-
tion. What a perfect fool she had been. Jean-Claude would re-
appear or telephone this morning with some reasonable
explanation of their broken date. It was not a great matter. *Pas
grand-chose*, as he would say. She must behave with cheerful
dignity. She was glad Madame Dubois was there. The presence
of another human being made everything seem more normal
somehow.

Returning to the bedroom, Alexa seated herself before the
dressing table. She rather liked being alone with Madame Dubois. The plain Frenchwoman would chat to her in her slow

Sud-Ouest accent about the banal concerns of her farming family, her dog and belief in herbal remedies. She was never inquisitive about her employer's guest, which Alexa thought astoundingly ladylike; she was shamed when she remembered how she had tried to question her about Jean-Claude.

The vacuum cleaner was already in operation and Madame Dubois was absorbed in the carpet. Momentarily their eyes met in the dressing-table mirror and Alexa smiled.

"J'ai une très belle coiffure aujourd'hui, n'est-ce pas, Madame?" Alexa joked indicating the profuse disarray of her hair.

On Madame Dubois' face there was no answering smile. The vacuum cleaner was still droning. Alexa shrugged. The older woman continued to regard Alexa's face reflected in the mirror, running the noisy machine over and over the same piece of carpet.

"Il y a une lettre." The sound of the vacuum cleaner ceased abruptly.

From the pocket of her flowered overall Madame Dubois produced a square white envelope with a typewritten address. Alexa's eyebrows rose questioningly but Madame Dubois volunteered nothing. She took the proffered letter from the other woman's large red hand, searching her expressionless features.

"Je vais préparer du café, Mademoiselle."

Madame Dubois was winding the cable of the vacuum cleaner, her face out of view. Alexa turned the envelope over in her hands, trying to get some clue as to its contents and disliking the flutter of apprehension she felt. It had no stamp.

Chérie,

I have business in Lyons for a few days and cannot see you again, hélas. *My family returns on Monday and life recommences.*

Please leave your key with Madame Dubois, she will need two days to clean the flat. Bonne chance.

J-C

Madame Dubois was taking as much time over making the coffee as she could. The end of August was never agreeable. Monsieur Jouffre never cleaned up after himself. She, Madame Dubois, did the dirty work, all of it. How she despised the bourgeoisie. And how, generally, she despised the grasping insolent tarts with whom her employer usually whiled away the month of August. They had no idea how to speak to a servant. No notion of one's dignity. Still, the extra money was welcome. She patted the five hundred-franc notes in her pocket.

This time, however, had been a little different. Mademoiselle Standeven was young but she had the makings of a *grande dame*. She was polite and tidy in the *appartement*, she did not leave soiled clothing on the bedroom floor or overflowing ashtrays in the *salon*. There was no embarrassing contraceptive equipment left brazenly on view. She was *bien éleveé*, that one.

Madame Dubois would like to have composed a kinder letter, somehow. But writing letters was not her *métier*. Every year she wrote only two, one to her sister in Detroit at Christmas and one to Monsieur Jouffre's summer girlfriend, the latter painstakingly typed with one finger.

"Madame Dubois!"

"Je viens, Mademoiselle."

Madame Dubois braced herself, there was usually some kind of scene. She wiped her hands on her overall and went into the bedroom. "I don't feel terribly well. May I have my coffee in here, *Madame*? I think I will lie down for a little while, if you have finished in here."

"Certainement, Mademoiselle."

"Oh, and will you kindly bring me the 'T' section of the telephone directory."

It was not a question, it was an order. Here was a new and interesting side of Mademoiselle Standeven.

When she brought the coffee to Alexa's bedside, Madame Dubois discreetly palmed the letter which she would later flush down the lavatory.

CHAPTER
3

🐾🐾 *"CHÈRE* MADEMOISELLE STANDEVEN."

Monsieur Terry rose from behind the large walnut partner's desk. *"Quel plaisir."* His rotund figure, flattered by a superbly tailored Huddersfield worsted, rolled smoothly across the faded Savonnerie carpet. Monsieur Terry's cherubic face beamed with sociability above the discreet tie, but the hair on the back of his neck bristled.

Alexa took his outstretched hand, it was dry and warm.

"Come and sit down. Will you take a little something?"

"No, no really, Monsieur Terry." Alexa sat on the edge of the Chippendale carver he positioned for her.

"Come, you cannot refuse. The first time you honour my *salon* with your presence you must accept a little hospitality. You would not refuse an old gentleman, you English are so polite. You will take something, to show we are friends?"

"I didn't want to take up your time . . ."

"A little *marc*? My cousin has a small property where they are able to distill in the old manner." Monsieur Terry raised his hands, palm upwards in the air and shrugged his shoulders, "When he is gone, alas, the licence will die with him. The pruderies of modern government. So, we have a rarity here, *Mademoiselle*. Will you not try it so that I can tell my cousin, as he lies on his deathbed, that his nectar lives on in the memory of the most beautiful woman in Paris?"

"Thank you, you are very kind. Perhaps just a small one."

Monsieur Terry nodded his satisfaction and busied himself amongst a forest of crystal decanters which stood on a massive silver salver. He poured the bright fluid carefully, continuing to talk cheerfully and inconsequentially, sensing the girl's nervousness.

Smilingly, Alexa accepted the tiny cut-glass goblet. The blatant flattery was rendered inoffensive by Monsieur Terry's avuncular manner. If there was a hint of sarcasm in his tone she chose to ignore it.

"Is your cousin dying?" Throughout her life Alexa would cling to the habit of listening intently to whatever she was told even when aware that words had been spoken merely to fill in an awkward interval. It was a habit that many would find disconcerting.

"No, but he is an old man like me and we must consider the possibility that we may go, either one of us, at any time." Monsieur Terry felt he was losing control of the conversation. "*Eh bien*, to business, *Mademoiselle*. Let me guess. You would like a *tailleur* for the autumn. Something in one of your lovely Scottish tweeds transformed by the good fairies in my workroom? Heather colours would be wonderful for you, *Mademoiselle*. Let us drink to the success of our work together."

"Well, actually, Monsieur Terry . . ."

"Ah, it is *une robe du soir. Une grande toilette*." Monsieur Terry chattered on enthusiastically waving his arms around in a sort of frenzy of preliminary creativeness. There seemed to be no stopping him.

Alexa looked out of the window down onto the Place Vendôme. There were drawbacks to a warm reception. She sipped the strong spirit gingerly.

"I'd love a suit or a dress," now Monsieur Terry was listening attentively, "but I need a job."

Monsieur Terry was silent. His head was cocked on one side, questioning and alert. Why did she not simply go back to wherever she came from? A girl like this must have parents, anxious parents. The summer was over and so was her disgraceful little adventure with Jouffre. If she went home now, no-one need ever be any the wiser and no harm would be done. She had no doubt learned several useful lessons and would return to England a sadder and wiser girl. Oh, the English are so careless. What father would let such a child as the lovely Miss Standeven wander alone in Paris like a stray bitch? Despite the affair with Jouffre, it was impossible to see her as other than an innocent. What could have possessed her to enter into an association with such a man? It was unfathomable, unpardonable. Who was to blame?

"Mademoiselle," he said slowly, "what is it that you *really* need?"

"A job," Alexa responded stubbornly.

"Come, come, Mademoiselle Standeven. You cannot impose on me. I told you, did I not, that I am a father and a grandfather. Also," he tapped the side of his nose, "I have a scent of trouble in my nostrils. Go home to your parents, my dear young lady, and forget Jouffre. He is not a good man. I must say," Monsieur Terry added cautiously, "I was surprised to meet someone like you in his company. You are not, if I may say so, his usual style of thing at all. Please take my advice and go home."

Alexa coloured. It was too much to expect that the shrewd little Frenchman would not know all about Jean-Claude and herself, but she had the uncomfortable feeling that he disapproved of her.

"Monsieur, that is exactly what I would do if I could. But I have found that my air ticket is invalid now. I should have gone to have it changed and I didn't. I have no money, I have to earn my fare home."

Alexa thought it better not to weary a potential employer with the tale of the rift with her parents. She suspected it would not improve her chances. She was learning to keep her troubles to herself.

"But surely, *Mademoiselle*, your parents . . ."

"They are already sufficiently angry with me. I will not ask them for help. I can't."

Monsieur Terry looked sorrowfully at the stricken girl. I offered my help, I suppose, he thought. Susceptible old fool.

"Mademoiselle, if that is the only obstacle to your prompt return to the protection of your parents, nothing would give me greater pleasure than to handle your travel arrangements."

Alexa was profoundly touched by the old man's chivalry, but she would have none of it.

"Thank you, *Monsieur*. I can't say how grateful I am to you for your kindness but I cannot accept your offer."

"No?" Monsieur Terry was surprised.

"No. You see, I got myself into this mess and I intend to get myself out of it. You remember, that day at the races, I told you I was trying to grow up?"

"Well, yes *Mademoiselle*, I do. But . . ."

"I don't think I really knew just how much was involved then, but I do now. The experiment was not a total failure. I have learned that being grown up involves taking responsibility for your own actions. And, usually that tends to involve money. I am perfectly serious when I say I want a job."

Alexa hoped desperately that Monsieur Terry would help, but she was afraid to put him, or indeed, herself in an embarrassing position by seeming to importune. Consequently her manner seemed a little stiff and abrupt. Monsieur Terry noticed and realised it was the most reliable indicator of both her inherent decency and vulnerability.

"But, *Mademoiselle*, you wish to train as an *ouvrière* in my *atelier*?"

He was incredulous.

"No, but I could be a model."

"This is a small house, *Mademoiselle*. I employ only two models on the permanent staff. Besides, a model has to be trained, two weeks at least, ideally, four." Monsieur Terry was deeply pained.

Alexa's face registered acute disappointment. She slumped almost imperceptibly but Monsieur Terry could not help but observe it and was stabbed to the heart. She twiddled the empty glass in her fingers and Monsieur Terry felt miserable. A kind heart was a great handicap in business, he mused to himself.

"I am sorry, *Monsieur*," Alexa gathered up her things, "I thought it was worth asking."

"But, of course, *Mademoiselle*. And it has been so pleasant to see you again." There was an embarrassed finality in his tone.

"Could you suggest anywhere else I might try? The collections will begin any time now. Perhaps there is someone who could use an extra, even untrained."

The girl's tenacity of purpose and her well-bred attempt to conceal her dismay and disappointment made his heart ache. But in the *couture* business it is more customers one wants, not more staff.

"One moment, *Mademoiselle*." Monsieur Terry went to his desk and took out a tape measure.

"Take off your jacket please and hold your arms out . . . so."

Alexa put down her handbag and gloves and did as she was told, bewildered but obedient.

"Hmm . . . I want an inch off your waist."

* * *

With the few hundred francs left in her handbag after Jean-Claude's desertion, Alexa was able to secure a hideous little room on the Left Bank. It was situated in the Rue des Feuillantines, a narrow, unattractive street just behind the dome of the Sorbonne. The room was one of many in a barrack-like women's hostel. The administrator was a large, hatchet-faced woman with badly bleached hair and a crudely made-up face. She had no personal interest in the tenants beyond their ability to pay the rent. However, she made no attempt to conceal her curiosity about Alexa who felt her sneering appraisal keenly.

Alexa's passport gave no clues. It said merely that she was a student, a description which covered a wide range of activities or none at all, in Madame Bertin's experience.

"If you will sign here, *Mademoiselle*." Alexa did so.

"Your passport will be returned to you tomorrow evening, the police, you understand."

"Naturally, *Madame*." Alexa knew that this registration of foreigners was routine, but the woman eyed her as if she was on the run.

"Here is your key. Room 203. You will observe the list of regulations which are displayed in the foyer, *Mademoiselle*. There is to be absolutely no cooking in the rooms: all tenants must be in by midnight when the doors are locked and will not be re-opened in any circumstances: clean bed linen will be provided by the management and changed every fourteen days: tenants must sweep their own rooms and brooms are provided for the purpose on every landing; male visitors are not permitted. Tenants may iron clothes in Room 6 between the hours of six and eight in the evening on every night of the week except Sunday. The key to Room 6 is kept in this office and must be signed for in the book. These are the chief conditions of your tenancy, *Mademoiselle*, apart, of course, from the payment of the rent which I receive in the office here every Friday morning at half past seven. I trust you will be comfortable."

Alexa dropped her eyes lest the flare of amusement should be seen. Madame Bertin recited her rules with the settled, sing-song conviction of a country congregation saying the Apostles Creed.

The bleak little cell measured approximately ten feet by eight, Alexa guessed. Its niggardly dimensions and poverty-stricken appointments juxtaposed oddly with Alexa's *soignée* appearance. She sat down on the bed, her eyes almost refusing to convey the images they received to her brain. And yet she felt an odd sense of elation. Since the morning she had got both a job and somewhere to live, and without anyone's assistance. For most girls of her age, she was well aware, that was not a great achievement. But for her, it was a great deal.

An inspection of her new quarters did not take long. The floor was an ugly red composition and quite bare. The modern window had neither curtain nor blind, only a grating metal concertina shutter, a charmless but efficient contrivance. Across the street could be seen similar tenements, some were greyly crumbling examples of Belle Epoque architecture, others were of more recent construction and correspondingly unlovely. There were no trees but the occasional splash of colour from a potted geranium on a balcony proclaimed that the human spirit offered pockets of token resistance even in the desolation of the Rue des Feuillantines.

A corner of the room was curtained off with a scanty piece of cotton to provide a wardrobe. There was a wash basin which boasted a single cold water tap. The water had worn a brownish green stain into the enamel of the basin. The bathing arrangements in the convent seemed sybaritic by comparison. Above the bed, a small bookshelf was screwed to the wall but the only light switch was by the door.

The prohibition against "cooking in the rooms" was an irony. In the first place Alexa had no idea how to go about cooking in a room that boasted no equipment for such an activity and secondly, she planned to spend as little as she could on food. She had four weeks at the most to earn her airfare, in time to get home for the beginning of the Michaelmas term at Oxford. There was no alternative now but to go home, and face whatever had to be faced. She recalled her mother's angry words. She was indeed adrift in a foreign capital. Suddenly, it seemed an unfriendly place. But dignity demanded that she get home by her own efforts. She could not ask for assistance again. The fight for independence must go on, even if the weapons were now changed.

The wages she would receive at Maison Terry would be very low indeed. Monsieur Terry was painfully conscious that the remuneration he could offer was almost impossible to live on, let alone finance a long journey in the near future. He had wished to give more but could not, in justice to Sophie and Marcelle.

"You see, *Mademoiselle*, my two house models are fully trained and experienced. The sum I propose to pay you is only a very little less than I pay them. It would not do, would it, if I were to pay you more? They would feel belittled and insulted. Perhaps they would leave me and go elsewhere." Hastily, Alexa agreed that he could not and should not pay her more.

Sophie lived comfortably at home with her wealthy parents, and Marcelle, well, Marcelle also was taken care of. Monsieur Terry blushingly admitted that Marcelle was a different type of girl. She was older, for one thing, and she lived with a man who was able to provide for her.

Painstakingly, he had explained to Alexa that modelling for a *couture* house was a sought-after occupation amongst Parisian girls *de bonne famille*. The financial rewards were small because competition for these positions was fierce and money was not a great consideration for girls from *bourgeois* homes. "It is true," he had continued, "that occasionally a girl of . . . shall we say . . . a different type works as a model, but I'm afraid, *chère Mademoiselle*, that she always has a protector."

"In other words, *Monsieur*, I have done everything wrong. I have left my parents and I have left my . . . protector, as you put it. Or rather, he has left me." Alexa did not mean to be rude, merely to clarify her own position.

Monsieur winced at his own gaffe. Poor child, her present plight was sufficient punishment for her irresponsibility. How many years was it since he had been so clumsy? But there was something about Mademoiselle Standeven, despite her occasional gruffness. He could not say what it was precisely but she made one relax, put one off one's guard. One found oneself doing a great deal more talking than one ever intended. Absurd. Perhaps it was her astonishing directness of manner and strange way of giving rigid attention to one's lightest word. Unusual in the young, he reflected. She seemed to suck information right out of one's head with those dark sapphire eyes of hers. To make amends for his unwitting cruelty, Monsieur Terry renewed his offer to pay the expenses of Alexa's homeward flight. She refused as he expected. With a sigh he suggested a compromise. Would she consider the cheaper alternative of travelling by train and by ferry boat to Dover? The amount of money involved was so trifling. This offer too, was rejected politely but firmly.

Alexa's work at Maison Terry was absorbing. There was no *Directrice* as in larger houses. Monsieur Terry attended to all the administration of the business himself with the help of his aged secretary, Mademoiselle Babinet. He also trained his own model girls. Like all *couturiers* he had a clear idea of what he wanted from them. At first he schooled Alexa on her own for an hour in the morning and again in the afternoon. He taught her such fundamental tricks of the model girls' trade as how to turn as if on ball bearings, how to trail a rich fur along the catwalk contemptuously while showing a plain grey flannel frock as if it were made of cloth of gold, and how to walk. The walk was the great secret.

"You see, *Mademoiselle*, you place the heel on the ground firmly. Not the toe, you are not a dancer. The heel, the heel, always the heel. And then, when the entire sole of the foot has made contact with the ground, you lift the heel, then the instep and finally the toe. Now the whole foot is off the ground, and you are ready to peel the other one off in the same manner. Behave as though you were walking in glue."

Monsieur Terry demonstrated the technique, which would have been a comical performance to the detached observer. But Alexa was not detached and her seriousness never wavered. She watched Monsieur Terry's antics solemnly and after one or two trials was able to imitate the motion perfectly.

"Bravo, *Mademoiselle*, bravo. You are a good pupil. You feel the tension in the thighs? If you make a habit of walking like this it will save you much tedious exercising, I assure you."

Alexa was enchanted. This simple technique was the key to that enviable swagger.

After a few days of these private drill sessions with Monsieur Terry, he began to think that his philanthropy would be rewarded by the addition to his staff of a competent model, which was more than he had expected. She learned quickly, the English girl. She tried hard, she worked hard and she succeeded well. Monsieur Terry was more than pleased. In three-and-a-half weeks he would present his autumn collection in his usual show. No press ever came and nobody fought over tickets. None-the-less, invitations were sent out to his many customers in France, some in England and a few in Germany and Switzerland. A surprisingly large proportion of these came to the showing, and if the collection was a success, the orders he received on the day of the show got the season off to a good start. Mademoiselle Standeven would supply a *soupçon* of novelty, which could make all the difference. Sophie and Marcelle were good girls. Reliable, skilled, known to the customers and absolutely predictable.

Soon they were rehearsing the show itself, using odd garments from the storeroom to get the necessary pace of the changes. The new garments were not yet complete and the workroom was working overtime to get them ready. The collection was formidable. Between them the girls would show a total of seventy-six *ensembles* ranging from tweed suits to afternoon frocks, cocktail outfits to ball-gowns. The show would culminate in the traditional, single wedding gown. In spirit, it was an old-fashioned collection. Monsieur Terry would not countenance any of the flexible, multi-purpose garments being promoted by his younger competitors.

Tentatively, Alexa questioned him about this.

"I know my customers, Mademoiselle Standeven. They are not mini-skirted starlets, nor are they the wives of property boom millionaires, they are not, in short, *nouveaux riches*. No, the 'mix and match' spirit is not for us. For a race meeting they want a *tailleur*, for a ball they want a ball-gown, not some 'practical' compromise between the two. Let young Courrèges make his satin space-suits, Paco Rabanne his sequinned chainmail; me, I continue to make clothes."

The relationship between Alexa and the two other girls was pleasant but French people do not make intimate friends quickly or casually. Neither did Sophie and Marcelle have much in common themselves. The correctly brought up Sophie had a good, professional working relationship with her colleague, but it was little more. They never mixed socially although they occasionally lunched together.

Marcelle's sleek-looking lover picked her up from work every day and drove her away in a sports car of impossible glamour whilst Sophie returned to her parents' splendid *appartement* in the Avenue Foch by taxi. They viewed Alexa with slight suspicion. Sophie could not understand what Alexa was doing in Paris. She had neither family nor friends, seemingly, and certainly no liaison. Marcelle oscillated between contempt for Alexa's astounding *naïveté* and genuine concern that should her own lover have a prolonged opportunity of inspecting Alexa, her position might be threatened. Consequently, neither girl did much to alleviate Alexa's solitude.

Once they asked Alexa if she would care to join them for lunch. It was clear to Alexa that they invited her only because

her presence in their shared dressing room had made it difficult
not to include her in their plans without crude discourtesy. Naturally, it was Sophie's suggestion. Marcelle had not been brought
up to pretend any care for the feelings of others. Alexa declined
the invitation. She had no money to spare for lunching out.

The lunch-hour was long, it lasted from noon until two o'clock,
and Alexa occupied the time in quietly examining garments in
the process of construction. The workroom continued operations regardless of the sacred two hours of the *déjeuner* and she
helped unobtrusively by passing pins, scissors, holding bolts of
cloth and running errands to button manufacturers and the little
specialist firms that dealt in trimmings. Her enthusiasm gained
the sympathy of the workroom staff who were pleased to initiate
her into the mysteries of handworked buttonholes, raised seams,
the shaping that could be achieved by the application of steam
and a tailor's ham and many other things besides.

Monsieur Terry observed these activities at a distance from
the seclusion of his beautiful panelled office. He never interfered
or gave any sign that he knew. None-the-less, one day he interrupted a conversation with a linen manufacturer's agent to send
for her and the senior hand. They were to go to his office with
a half-completed evening gown which was composed entirely
of fine Irish lawn painstakingly stiffened with continuous narrow
tucks. Monsieur Terry was not satisfied with the drape of the
fabric. It did not conform with the sample he had been shown.
To demonstrate his complaint, the lawn dress was pinned onto
Alexa. The procedure was complex as the dress was elaborately
cut and there were a great many pins. A heated discussion en-
sued during which the workroom hand was dismissed from the
room. Alexa, however, remained, encased in the voluminous
dress, hardly daring to move or breathe. Eventually, after much
argument and counter-argument, accompanied by vivid gesticulations, the two men seemed to resolve their differences and
left the room without a backward glance at Alexa.

They returned one-and-a-half hours later after a convivial
lunch, to find an exhausted Alexa still standing in the dress. She
had been sorely tried by the pins and did not dare move for fear
of injuring the already immensely valuable gown. She knew it
had cost many hours of work. Monsieur Terry laughed.

"Forgive me, *chère* Mademoiselle Standeven. Forgive my
stupidity. You stood there as silent as the tailor's dummy I asked
you to be and you were so convincing in the role, I quite forgot

there was a real young lady in the dress. An estimable young lady. You should be canonised, *Mademoiselle*. A saint of the *couture* trade.''

He lifted the telephone to summon help from the workroom.

"Come and see me here tomorrow morning. I think we should have a talk, you and I.''

"Entrez," Monsieur Terry responded crisply to Alexa's knock.

"Aha, it is you, *Mademoiselle*. I must compliment you on your well-developed sense of responsibility, *chère Mademoiselle*.'' He patted her shoulder awkwardly but affectionately. "There are not many models who would have endured what you endured yesterday and all for the sake of a gown.''

"I thought it was important, it has taken weeks already. Supposing I had spoiled it?''

"It is precisely because you notice these things and care for the work we do here that I regard you so highly, *Mademoiselle*. You are very much interested in this business, I think?''

"Yes, *Monsieur*.''

"Mademoiselle, a model is a model is a model. But you, you are intelligent," Monsieur Terry tapped his broad forehead. "You look, you listen and you learn. Perhaps, you may have a future in *couture*.''

"Thank you, *Monsieur*," Alexa murmured.

"I want to tell you something of the background to my business so that you will be aware of the sort of people to whom I sell my clothes. I believe that if I take you into my confidence you will promote the clothes more successfully. And perhaps, one day, who knows, you may have a larger role to play.''

Alexa's attention was fully engaged.

"My stock in trade is *Le Style Anglais*. There is a section of European society, particularly French society, that adores everything that is English, except perhaps the food," he said meditatively, "and even then, I have known in extreme cases of Anglophilia some bizarre stories . . . *Alors, Mademoiselle*, you understand what it is that I am trying to convey?''

Alexa nodded.

"All the fabrics I use for the day wear collection are manufactured in the British Isles. For the evening wear, I use many silks and brocades from Lyons, it is true, but also some from Macclesfield, and of course, the marvellous velvets from Listers in Bradford.''

Alexa's fascination could be read plainly on her face. Monsieur Terry was most gratified.

"There is for instance, in my opinion, no perfection achieved like that which results from the marriage of a perfect grey worsted from, say, Huddersfield and the handling that it receives here, in my Paris workroom."

For an hour or more, Monsieur Terry expounded his theories and principles, warmed by Alexa's unflagging interest.

"And so, *Mademoiselle*, we come to you and the part you can play. You see, there is an indefinable something about the way a confident, well-bred Englishwoman wears her clothes which is inimitable by a Frenchwoman, however hard she tries. She is *chic*, smart, you would say, but she cares deeply for her *toilette* and it shows. The Englishwoman, once she has left the looking-glass and her maid, has done her best, forgets entirely what she is wearing. She has, in short, an absolute carelessness which is, in my view, the highest manifestation of elegance. You, *Mademoiselle*, young as you are, have that carelessness. Will you use it? Sophie and Marcelle are *sérieuses*. They are French and their care and concentration are not to be despised, but you can add a note of authentic Englishness to our collection."

"Yes, of course, I'll do everything I can, but what exactly?"

"I want you to smile, *Mademoiselle*. Usually a *couture* model shows the clothes with *hauteur*, with disdain. That is the well-established tradition. I want you to break with tradition, to smile, to laugh even. I want you to plunge your hands deep into the pockets of coats, twirl like a little girl showing off a party frock. Be different."

"Smile?"

"Mais oui, Mademoiselle," Monsieur Terry leaned back in his chair, "do you know that your smile is your greatest asset? We see it too rarely. Now I know you do not smile continuously, inanely, like a girl promoting a new brand of cigarettes, but it is a great weapon, your smile. It can illuminate a room. You must learn how to use it to advantage. Today is Friday. All weekend, I want you to practise that smile. Smile first at tobacco kiosks, every single time you see one. Forget that you feel foolish and remember that you look wonderful. When you have mastered the tobacco kiosks, start smiling at all *gendarmes*. They are difficult, *gendarmes*, but they are not as hard as kiosks and they are just as safe."

* * *

Alexa's solitary domestic life was in appalling contrast to the cheerful bustle and luxurious surroundings of her working world.

The greatest vexation was the problem of washing her hair. She could and did wash her entire body, standing up at the basin, in cold water every day. But an attempt to wash her hair in cold water proved as futile as it was disagreeable. She had no option but to invest some of her precious store of money in a miniature primus stove and smuggle it into the building. Using this and a nondescript aluminum vessel purloined from room 6, she managed to boil enough water to shampoo efficiently. The process was lengthy and it took the whole of Friday evening to complete.

Far from making it a cause of resentment, Alexa was glad of the task. She had nowhere to go and no money to spare. In the tenements across the street she could hear the sounds of families preparing their evening meals. The clash of pots and pans, sharp-tongued exchanges and later even the clink of cutlery was audible through the open windows in the fine September weather. Alexa longed to be other than she was. She fantasised about the simple pleasures of belonging to an extended family of working people and knowing the security of closeness. Delicious smells wafted across the street and reminded her that she was hungry.

As far as food was concerned, Alexa adhered to a demanding regime of privation which had more to do with economy than the preservation of her figure. In fact she was becoming very thin. Every second day she bought a *baguette* from the bakery down the road. The day when the *baguette* was fresh bought was a feast day and she ate rather more than half, which left less then half a stale *baguette* to be consumed the following day. The additional items of her diet were Camembert cheese, of which she ate a small section every day, keeping the reeking remainder in its box in a drawer, a few black olives and a glass or two of rough red wine. The wine cheered her a little and helped her to sleep in the noisy street.

The weekends were by far the worst. The endless hours of loneliness trickled so slowly by. On Saturdays she walked in the parks. On Sundays she passed hours in the Louvre, the Jeu de Paume, Les Invalides . . . all tediously familiar to her by now. But on Sundays there was no entrance fee.

Once walking down the Champs Elysées a black Citroën flashed by quite close. It seemed to Alexa that it was Jean-

Claude at the wheel with a dark, hard-looking woman by his side and two children in the back. She couldn't be sure, but the reminder of his presence in the same city winded her momentarily and her breath came short and fast.

During the last weekend before the three consecutive days of the collection Alexa was forced to give way to a gnawing anxiety. Her period had not come. She never kept a diary so she could not be certain whether her worries were well founded or not. But it felt wrong, she hadn't had a period for what seemed a long time now. Every day she had kept watch for signs and every day been increasingly dismayed to find nothing. Sitting down at the plywood table, Alexa searched her memory. She made a series of calendars conditional on certain landmark events having occurred on such and such a day, and so on *ad infinitum*. It didn't matter how you looked at it, Alexa admitted to herself. It was clear that she was at least two weeks late, possibly more.

In a frantic search for refuge from the unthinkable, Alexa's mind flew to the well-worn old wives' tales she had heard. Hot baths and gin were out of her financial reach and there was no wardrobe to jump off. Could she be wrong? At times she was sure she was, at others she had an equal conviction that she was doomed.

She did not walk in the Luxembourg Gardens that Saturday but took her troubles to the nearby Boulevard St. Germain which seemed to offer the most convenient opportunity of both avoiding the crowds in the Boulevard St. Michel and obeying Monsieur Terry's instructions to practise smiling at kiosks. To some extent the absurd exercise took her mind off the frightening possibilities that might lay ahead. Since early girlhood Alexa had always exhibited the healthy discipline of looking her troubles full in the face and then putting them from her until she had an opportunity to take action. And in any case, there could be no question of letting Monsieur Terry down. He had been too kind for that. She began to think of ideas to flesh out his.

On Monday dress rehearsals began in earnest. The collection would be shown on Wednesday, Thursday and Friday of that week. A number of garments still needed final adjustments before Monsieur Terry would be satisfied and what time was not spent in rehearsal was spent in fittings. Monsieur Terry was rising to his biennial crescendo. His normally equable temper was beginning to fray, and at times he was even short with Alexa in spite of his growing fondness for her.

Monsieur Terry had some anxieties of his own. If this collection was not an unparalleled success, he might have to consider closing the doors of Maison Terry. It seemed no one could any longer make a living from the honourable activity of making a quality garment for someone who ordered it, and who paid one a fair price for the materials and the work. Modern mass-marketing techniques were beyond him. He was too old a dog to learn new tricks. He had spent his years at the pinnacle of the garment trade, how could he descend to the gutter of mass-produced ready-mades. They could say what they liked, "limited editions," "exclusive models," and all the other mendacious expressions the marketing people favoured, it was all lies. It was not *couture*.

The girls worked hard. Sophie and Marcelle were familiar with the pre-collection high tension which affected all *couturiers* and Alexa knew enough of business in general to realise that this was Monsieur Terry's only opportunity to show off his wares. Orders were the only test that counted in any business. She was going to do her very best for him.

"Smile, smile, smile, Mademoiselle Standeven. We are kiosks, we are *gendarmes*, light us up, enchant us, but smile."

"Mademoiselle Sophie, tuck in your *derrière*! We are not selling sex here, only clothes!"

Everyone smiled with affection at Monsieur Terry. Nothing except an imminent collection could induce him to abandon the courtly manners which were his trademark. And then, by tradition, Monsieur Terry would bury his face in his hands in mock embarrassment at his lapse which made the models, the workroom hands, Mademoiselle Babinet, and all the carpenters and electricians laugh, as they did every year, twice a year.

At the end of the morning rehearsals on Tuesday, Alexa lingered in Monsieur Terry's office as the others went off to lunch. This was the most beautiful room on the premises of Maison Terry, and as always, it was being transformed into a *salon* for the show. A catwalk was being constructed and lighting equipment erected. The priceless ribbon-backed chairs that Alexa had noticed on her first visit to the office, Waterford chandeliers and the soft English landscapes against the mellow panelling made an ideal backdrop for the showing of clothes to admirers of *Le Style Anglais*.

Alexa was sitting on the edge of the catwalk, her head drooping, when Monsieur Terry caught sight of her. In spite of his preoccupation, something in the girl's attitude moved him to compassion. Perhaps she was very tired. She had hardly had time to develop the stamina of the other girls. But there was something else, beyond fatigue, Monsieur Terry feared.

He had not spent a lifetime in close contact with young women, produced two daughters and several grandchildren of both sexes without knowing a pregnant woman when he saw one. He hoped very much that he was wrong, but the signs were there. It had been the same for several days. For an hour or so after midday, she seemed tired, and then she recovered. The brilliant clarity of her complexion, was, if anything, enhanced, her hair glossier, her bosom fuller. There had been some last minute alterations to Mademoiselle Standeven's garments.

"Come, Mademoiselle Standeven, today you must eat. You will lunch with me and recruit your strength."

Although Alexa had sworn to herself that she would not think about her personal problems until after the shows were over, sudden fatigue had sapped her ability to resist. She allowed herself to be borne away by Monsieur Terry. They lunched splendidly at the Café de la Paix, where Alexa had often eaten a late breakfast in the convent days which now seemed a lifetime away.

Monsieur Terry ordered for both of them. He wanted to give the girl a treat. He couldn't imagine how she had been living. Not comfortably, he was sure.

"I think we will start with a little caviare. It is light and packed with much-needed protein, I think." He smiled quizzically at Alexa. "Have you eaten this delectable roe of the sturgeon before, *Mademoiselle*?"

"Yes, just once. I was fourteen and on a visit to Copenhagen with my grandfather. He has many friends and business acquaintances there, you see. I liked it, the caviare, I mean."

"Good. And then, perhaps, a little dish of *Faisan Normande*." Alexa looked puzzled.

"Pheasant to you, *Mademoiselle*. You are familiar with pheasant?"

"We have plenty of them at home. My mother hangs them for half an hour and then subjects them to fierce heat for approximately two hours."

"This will be quite different, I give you my word."

They snickered conspiratorially together. The curiosities of the English cuisine were among Monsieur Terry's favourite topics of conversation. Good. Her spirits were returning.

"Now, will you take vodka with your caviare?"

Alexa laughed.

"Nothing would surprise me, *Mademoiselle*, you are so much the woman of the world." Alexa bit her lip and again Monsieur Terry had occasion to curse his tongue. But Alexa swept the potentially embarrassing remark away.

"I have an idea, *Monsieur*, a suspicion only, that Sancerre might go very well with caviare." What a very surprising young woman she was.

"Now I know you truly are a woman of the world, my dear!"

"Not at all, *Monsieur*, just the daughter of a man who knows his way about his own wine cellar and likes to have someone to enjoy it with him."

"And you were that someone, *Mademoiselle*? How your father must miss you."

"Well, wine was about our only mutual topic, you know."

But the lightened mood did not last long. Alexa's inner dejection again became visible on the surface and she seemed unable to shake it off. Monsieur Terry watched her carefully, while he talked volubly of his children and their lives, and of his house and garden at Versailles. Something was wrong. It was all too painfully evident. With a sigh he put down his fork.

"Mademoiselle Standeven," Terry's voice was very low. He leaned forward and took her hand. "Forgive my intrusion but I believe you may be in very deep trouble. I pray the good God I may be wrong, but I fear . . ."

Alexa tried manfully to keep her face perfectly straight. Although she managed to guard her features from distortion, neither muscle nor will-power could prevent twin streams of tears from coursing down her face. It was not so much the extremity of her predicament that caused this sudden loss of control, but the misery of knowing that poor Monsieur Terry was powerless to help and that would cause him grief. It was a bad time for him to be burdened with any problems but his own.

"You must wish me a million miles away."

"Indeed not, *Mademoiselle*. Why, you are a natural model, easily the most talented I have met in a long career. I mean that, *Mademoiselle*. I do not say it merely to comfort you."

For a moment they were both silent. Then, tentatively, without looking up from his plate, Monsieur Terry said, "I know little of these things, *Mademoiselle*, but there is something I do not understand. I, you know, have been married to the same

woman all my life. I am old fashioned, and, of course, a Catholic. But nowadays, there are . . . how shall we say? Preventa-
tive measures? Were no arrangements made between yourself
and . . .''

"No. It all happened so suddenly. I would not have known
where to go, or whom to ask. Jean-Claude never did anything
about it. And I . . . Well, it would just have seemed so cold-
blooded.''

If anything, Monsieur Terry liked her even better. Mademoiselle Standeven was such an innocent sinner.

"Well, let us remain calm. You and I, *Mademoiselle*, are
resourceful people, are we not? We shall think of some acceptable procedure.''

The faithful old Rolls inched its way cautiously between the
miles of dry stone walling which lined the lonely and atrociously
narrow road to Langstroth Grange. Why Alexander Standeven
should want to live in this depopulated dale was beyond the
comprehension of his father-in-law.

Henry Jagger glanced out of the car window at the threatening
acres of chalky green and shuddered. He was an urban man.
The hard blue sky, spattered with the golds and bronzes of the
wind-driven leaves, was an alien sky. At home in all the great
cities of the world, and in his native Bradford, Henry would
prefer a day in the First World War trenches to a day in the
countryside. He shrugged himself down into the vicuna overcoat
and lit a cigar.

The back of Sheard's neck, recently barbered, looked enter-
tainingly red and plucked. Henry blew a large cloud of smoke
at it, and then another. It was no good, he wasn't going to rise
to the bait. Why should he? He hadn't risen to any of his employer's teases for twenty years. It was a curious aspect of Henry
Jagger's personality, that for a man of his intellectual gifts and
influence in the world, he had a babyish sense of humour.

"Damn.'' Henry swore under his breath. He had dropped ash
on his stomach. Irritably he brushed it off. His stomach got in
the way of everything. The damn diets were no good. Fifty
Savile Row suits in the wardrobe and not one the same size.
Henry swore again, "Damn and blast.''

Sheard, glancing in the rear-view mirror, studied Henry. It
was a bad business. Miss Alexa gone missing . . . well, as good
as. Not come home at any rate, and not written. Not a dicky

bird for weeks. The gaffer was put about by the whole thing.
You could see that. Roared like a bull he had when Mrs. Stand-
even, Miss Elizabeth that was, had admitted they'd lost her.
Well, the old man would do something. He always did. Miss
Alexa would be home soon, if Henry Jagger wanted it that way.

Henry, had he known the thoughts of his man, would have
been gratified but not in agreement. Once he had got over his
rage at being kept in the dark about Alexa's disappearance, he
had begun to ask the pertinent questions. Had Interpol been
tried? What about a private enquiry agent?

Nothing Elizabeth and Alexander had been able to tell him
had been at all satisfactory. And then he'd had the angina attack.
That was their excuse, of course. They hadn't wanted to tell him
because of his angina. If they'd told him a damned sight earlier,
he might have not have had the attack, and he might have been
able to do something. Elizabeth was his own child, but she'd
always been devious and then on top of that she'd married Standeven. Grand fellow in many ways, but complicated. Never did
anything the straightforward way. They made a nice pair between them, Elizabeth and Alexander. They'd both as many
faces, arms and legs as an Hindu idol. That's something you
couldn't say about Alexa. Straight as a die, that girl. Just like
me, Henry thought.

Langstroth Grange came into view. Standing massive and
foursquare on its gently sloping site, the house was a small
mansion, with an austere Georgian façade of dressed sandstone
and an impressive portico. The gardens were laid out with that
deceptive English informality which is so time-consuming and
expensive to maintain in manicured perfection. It was a good
house, but why here? Henry asked himself for the thousandth
time.

He hurried up the steps at the front of the house, the sound
of bleating sheep in his ears. The Fiddler, wearing a green baize
apron, swung open the door to admit him.

"Good evening, Mr. Jagger. Mr. and Mrs. Standeven are in
the library."

Henry took off his coat and dropped it into the Fiddler's arms
without looking at him. Fellow behaved like a London butler.
Useless at car cleaning and coal carrying, but a genius at smarm.
Henry wouldn't give him house room. Still, it was difficult to
get anyone up here. His real name was Charles, but Alexander

had christened him The Fiddler on the Backstairs for Byzantine reasons of his own and it stuck.

The library was little more than a comfortably furnished snug at the back of the house, converted from the old servants' sitting room. An apple-log fire burned in the grate. The evenings were drawing in now and getting colder.

Alexander Standeven stood with his back to the fire, a whisky and soda in his hand, and Elizabeth sat at the desk with her customary small sherry, her expression grim. Henry shook his head.

"Well, I suppose we'd better get weaving," Henry sighed.

"Drink?" Alexander offered. Elizabeth frowned.

"Should you, Father? You know what the doctor said."

"Gin and It," Henry responded defiantly.

"You shouldn't be drinking cocktails at your age, and definitely not in your state of health," Elizabeth said.

"Aye, lethal," Henry conceded, sinking into the winged armchair by the fire.

"Well, what do we know then?"

Alexander sat down on the old chesterfield opposite Henry. There was a file of papers beside him.

"Precious little. Here's Bottomley's report and the one and only letter we had from Alexa. It was written shortly after Elizabeth spoke to her on the telephone. We must assume she was still at that hotel when she wrote it, although Bottomley cannot say for certain that she was ever at the *Hôtel de Picardie* at all."

"What about the hotel register?"

"Nothing. She just wasn't on it. Bottomley said the owner looked a thoroughly unpleasant type. And I can assure you, everything else that could be done, has been done. The last people to see her . . ."

Alexander noticed that Elizabeth went pale as he spoke. Perhaps his choice of words had been unfortunate. During the past few days Elizabeth had been tormenting herself and him with talk of the "white slave traffic" and fantastic horrors of that nature. Naturally, Alexander had scoffed, saying his wife's imaginings were the result of strain and not of rational deduction. But he was becoming quietly frantic. Bottomley had proved useless and finding a French enquiry agent to act in the matter for him was turning out to be an agonisingly slow business.

Alexander carefully rephrased his information, "The last people, of whom we have personal knowledge, to see Alexa were the people at the Westminster Bank in the Place Vendôme. That's where Alexa had her little account.''

"Well,'' Henry urged, "and is the account empty then?''

Alexander shrugged. "One must assume so.''

"Not necessarily. She must have been living on something. It's possible the account is still live. She may have been back there since. If there's activity on the account that would give us a lead.''

"Highly unlikely.''

"But worth a try, wouldn't you say?''

"*Anything* is worth a try. But I don't imagine for one moment that she's doing anything that isn't paid in cash, of which she will need every penny.''

Alexander's unspoken thought was that things could be a lot worse than he had allowed himself to believe up to now. She could be living with a man, perhaps this Jouffre. She could be . . . well it didn't bear thinking about.

"Assumptions are always dangerous. That's one thing we've got to look into. Now what else have we got?'' Henry asked impatiently.

"Nothing, unless you know the name of Jouffre's firm, if it exists.''

"Well, I don't. But I reckon I can find out pretty damn quick. I'll ring every manufacturer of quality woollen goods for women's wear in the country, starting with Yorkshire. Someone will use him, and someone will know what his firm's called and where his office is. I'll get on to the editor of the *Wool Record* and get an SOS advertisement in. Somebody'll pick it up. We'll find 'im.''

"I suppose Bottomley might have found him by now if I'd left him on the job.''

"Never mind Bottomley. Just get on to the bank first thing in the morning and find out if that account's active. Another thing, you might do better to let the branch manager in Skipton ring up for you. Get more out of the Frogs that way. Bankers don't mind telling tales out of school *to each other*. He sent Alexa's allowance to Paris every month didn't he?''

"Yes, he did, by banker's draft.''

Elizabeth, silent until now, said "We have nine days. The university term starts on the 10th of October. The Warden says if Alexa doesn't present herself at the college on that day without adequate excuse, she loses her place. Those are the rules.''

"That's the least of our problems, Elizabeth," Alexander snapped.

"Aye, we'd all be a sight better off today, if you weren't quite so keen on universities," Henry remarked bitterly.

"Allo Monsieur, you are there? You can hear me? The line is not good. Ah, that is better, less of the crackle now. Yes, I have checked our records. I can tell you that Mademoiselle Standeven makes a small deposit here each week. There was nothing for a while, but then regular sums. This branch is convenient for her."

"Where does she work?"

The Frenchman told the manager of the Skipton branch all he wanted to know before interference on the line made further conversation impossible.

CHAPTER
4

MONSIEUR TERRY COULD not have foreseen the extent of his collection's success. There was nothing beyond the annual subtle adjustments to such matters as hemline, trim detail or some such minor matter to distinguish the clothes from what had been shown in previous years. But the atmosphere in his *salon* after the first show was electric, something like the effect of his autumn collection in 1930 which had first elevated Maison Terry to the ranks of the major *courturiers*. That collection had enabled him to move from the modest fourth floor premises in the Rue de Louvre to his present lavish establishment. It seemed that this collection would keep the business going, at least for the present. And he was glad, for it was Monsieur Terry's wish to die in harness.

It was Alex's doing. Only a true generous man like Monsieur Terry could have admitted to himself that his business had been saved by an ignorant foreign girl, but there it was. Great as Monsieur Terry's optimism regarding her talent as a model had been, he had expected nothing on this scale.

On the first day, the *salon* had been comfortably full with invited customers from all over Europe, but it had not been crowded. Monsieur Terry could barely remember when it had last been crowded. There were no unexpected faces, no strangers sitting in the Chippendale chairs. Alexa's own shy suggestion that Mademoiselle Babinet should not read a commentary on the clothes as usual, but the details should be printed and placed on the chairs, had been adopted. She had further suggested that a small chamber orchestra be engaged to play classical pieces with a strong rhythm. That had proved a stroke of genius. It changed the mood entirely, lending an animation to the move-

ment of all three models and a briskness to the show, which in
no way injured the traditional image of the house but reversed
the air of graceful decline which had begun to creep in. The
audience was delighted.

Alexa herself had shown the clothes allocated to her with a
breathtaking verve and originality. She had insisted on buying
a substantial pair of strong brown lace-up shoes to wear with a
handsome tweed coat and had sent Mademoiselle Babinet out
to scour Paris for a short thick dog lead made of plaited leather
with a choker chain. She had practically stumped onto the catwalk, the lead dangling from the pocket of the unbuttoned coat,
whistling to imaginary dogs, swinging the coat wide, hands in
pockets, head thrown back. She never smiled during this fantastic performance until the very end, when she swept the room
with a beam of light which earned her and the coat a storm of
applause.

She had insisted that Carita dress her hair in a simple pony
tail, allowing the natural movement of her hair free rein. She
wore the black velvet bow that had been Ziggy's idea for her
hair in a dozen different ways. She had wrapped it round the
waist of the fabulous pin-tucked Irish lawn, she wore it round
her neck with a wool afternoon dress, and she sported a small,
pert version round her ankle with a cocktail dress.

Monsieur Terry was dapper as usual and beaming with pleasure. Mademoiselle Babinet was forced to set up an impromptu
enquiries desk as so many ladies wished to make private appointments to view the garments that had particularly interested
them, at their leisure.

By the second day, the bush telegraph of Paris had done its
work. The telephones never stopped ringing. Was there any
chance of getting in at this late stage to see the collection? Would
Monsieur Terry give a short interview to the press?

Ziggy telephoned. Was it really her? His Mademoiselle Alexa? Did she know she had had *un succès fou*? At least that's
what Alexa thought he said. Sophie and Marcelle were generous. After the show they produced a case of champagne. They,
and everyone else, drank to Alexa.

"But, *chérie*, you have a career. A star is born!"

The second show differed from the first in that the *salon* was
tight-packed with people, some of whom were quite unknown
to Monsieur Terry or his staff. There was also a plethora of
camera equipment. The string quartet was squeezed, grum-

bling, into a window embrasure, extra chairs had to be brought from the workroom, the dressing room and anywhere else where so much as a stool could be found. There seemed to be almost as many men present as women. The collection took longer to show because the progression of garments was interrupted by prolonged clapping and in one or two instances, a standing ovation.

Alexa was oblivious to anything but her task. The heat of the makeshift changing room and the breakneck speed at which the changes were effected required the most intense concentration. She did, however, catch a fleeting image of a strange young man sitting on the window side of the catwalk, in the front row. A walking stick leant against his chair. His body seemed long in comparison to his legs, that was all. Beside him a tall woman whose face was obscured by the brim of her hat occasionally spoke to him, touching his wrist with her gloved hand.

When the show was over, Monsieur Terry came into the changing room. He was breathless.

"Well, done, *mes chères demoiselles*. A triumph, once again a triumph. Madame de Pies Ombre would like to see the Irish lawn again, also the navy cashmere coat and several afternoon dresses. We shall take a glass of champagne together in Mademoiselle Babinet's office until everyone else has gone, so relax and then I will send for you, *mes chères*."

Alexa started to sort through the disordered rails, looking for the Irish lawn.

"Ah, *la pauvre petite*. Mademoiselle Standeven has the headache, I think, no? It is no wonder, the heat, the lights . . ."

"No, really . . ." She smiled reassuringly at him, "I'm fine."

She knew he was anxious to spare her further exertion. Although Monsieur Terry was understandably preoccupied with the collection, her pregnancy was never very far from his mind. Frequently, he would signal to her, his eyebrows uplifted enquiring silently if she were feeling all right and able to go on.

"Truly, *Mademoiselle*, there is no need. Sophie and Marcelle can . . ."

"Honestly, *Monsieur*. I'm *enjoying* it. It's exciting isn't it?"

"Your devotion to duty does you credit, *Mademoiselle*, but do not overdo it. Remember, you are not accustomed to all this."

He glanced at her meaningfully, hoping she could understand

his warning. It was not possible to speak openly of her condition before the other two girls.

"*Monsieur le Marquis*, you are not comfortable, allow me to place a footstool, so." Monsieur Terry deposited the low stool before the chair in which the young nobleman sat, clutching his stick between his knees, his right leg dangling awkwardly. Gratefully, the Marquis placed his left leg on the stool and then, clutching his trouser leg, lifted the emaciated limb to rest beside it.

"*Madame*, some more champagne?"

Madame de Pies Ombre held out her empty glass languidly. Terry had always had the manners of a footman. Still, his clothes were superb. This time, they were better than ever. That, of course, was the fundamental difference between Terry and his more successful competitors. He had been getting left behind. Dior, Pierre Balmain, Marc Bohan, they treated one as if they were equals. No doubt the young people like it but it affected their work. The clothes lacked that quality of discreet grandeur which characterised Terry's. He, at least, knew he was making for a class of people whose values were eternal. A good servant knows instinctively what appeals to his betters, whether he understands it or not.

"Well, Terry, shall we go on?" The Marquise lifted her pencil-thin eyebrows.

Monsieur Terry nodded to Mademoiselle Babinet.

"First, I thought, the coat."

Madame la Marquise would not be able to resist the coat. It was just her style of thing. True, she would not pay for it. The accounts would be arrogantly ignored for months on end. Finally when pressure was discreetly applied by the excellent debt-collection agency which Maison Terry employed to handle these delicate matters, Madame would order another garment. That too would not be paid for. The collection agency would begin its routine of gently menacing letters and calls. Eventually, Madame de Pies Ombre's account would be paid by her cousin, the affluent Madame la Courbe. It was exasperating for that poor lady, but the family would naturally wish to avoid the scandal of court action and publicity.

The truth was that *Madame la Marquise* had no business in Monsieur Terry's *salon*. She could not afford *couture*, but she was an addict. Clothes were like a drug to her. If Monsieur Terry did not supply them, some other *courturier* would. To Monsieur Terry it was something of a moral dilemma, but not one which he had ever been able to solve. As Madame de Pies Ombre grew older and her financial resources ever more slender, she became if anything more rapacious. Sadly, Madame la Courbe had indicated that her ability to underwrite her noble cousin's extravagance was not limitless.

"Ah, Mademoiselle Sophie, here you are! Will you come closer please, so that Madame de Pies Ombre can appreciate the quality of this cloth. Yes, *Madame*, feel it, is it not exceptional? *Monsieur*, I implore you to handle this cloth, it is something quite out of the ordinary. The hair of pure-bred Angora goats, but absolutely the finest. It is raised in South Africa and woven in Bradford."

Fabrice de Pies Ombre gave the coat a cursory glance as Sophie spun and turned in front of him. He was not interested. He had known Sophie for years. She was a bore. Half the eligible bachelors in Paris of whatever age had proposed to her. Nobody's fortune had been large enough. Sophie's financial expectations were a joke. Who was she anyway? The daughter of a fashionable physician, that was all. Her looks were fading a little, Fabrice mused, all that holding out for a better price took its toll. He nodded perfunctorily as Sophie was dismissed. His mother was busy discussing the possibility of making the same coat in red cloth. It was not amusing. Why had he come? Because he had nothing better to do. That new girl was interesting, though. She was something quite different, put a breeze through the whole place. Wonder who she is? Might ask Terry for her telephone number. Well, she'd come out for dinner tonight wouldn't she? He'd see her in a minute and he'd tell her then. She wouldn't dream of refusing or making an excuse, not with her employer standing there and his mother's order hanging in the balance. Oh, no. It would fill in the rest of the evening nicely.

Of the garments selected by Madame de Pies Ombre for further inspection, only the Irish lawn had been worn by Alexa. Fabrice waited taut with interest.

When she reappeared at last, Fabrice leaned back in his chair appreciating anew her loveliness, the elusive quality of her charm and singular freshness. As she was about to withdraw, he caught her by the wrist. Alexa, startled, turned to look at him.

"Will you dine with me this evening, *Mademoiselle*? Unless, of course, you have other plans."

Monsieur Terry looked away. He was infuriated by the insolence of the casual invitation to his *protégée*. But there was
nothing he could do. He had been taken completely by surprise.
This was not time for Alexa to become involved with anyone,
it could only lead to further complications. And certainly, the
very last *parti* he would have chosen to publicly escort Alexa
was Fabrice de Pies Ombre. He held his breath. Perhaps instinct
would prompt her to refuse. Frankly, he hoped so.

Alexa's eyes widened in surprise. "It is very kind of you,
Monsieur, but I'm afraid I am a little tired this evening. Perhaps
some other time, when the shows are over."

Madame Terry gave her husband a sharp glance. He was fid-
geting.

The Sanctus washed over Monsieur Terry's consciousness as
it usually did. High Mass on Sunday was his weekly opportunity
to let his mind float free. For the forty years of his marriage to
Bernadette, every week without fail he had accompanied her to
mass, and in his fashion, derived as much benefit as she did.
True, he was barely aware of the stately progress of the liturgy.
He intuited the approximate point the ritual had reached by
means of an entirely subconscious awareness of the state of mental and physical tension exhibited by his neighbours. In general,
his soul was in step, though his mind was elsewhere.

Somewhere in the depths of Monsieur Terry's genetic memory
there was a serene belief, no doubt the legacy of chocolate-
making Quaker ancestors, that any thought that manifested itself
when the thinker is aware of being in the presence of God is
sanctified. Most frequently he found his Garden of Eden amongst
thoughts of the succulent *gigot* that awaited him at home. Tender
and rosy, pierced with slivers of garlic and spears of rosemary,
it was quite his favourite dish. Or there might be an exuberant
feast at the house of one of his children to look forward to, made
merrier by the flower faces of his grandchildren. They were
good, wholesome thoughts, that today eluded him.

Monsieur Terry could find no repose. What course should he
embark upon? He felt altogether at odds with himself. There
were times when he regretted ever having met Mademoiselle
Standeven. Then he dismissed the wicked thought. No sooner
had he consigned it to hell than it came back again. Monsieur
Terry shuffled miserably, his knees uncomfortable on the rush
bottomed prie-dieu. The drifting incense made him sneeze. He

felt in his pocket for a handkerchief. Bernadette's face appeared again from behind her hands, she mouthed a reproof.

Once again, Monsieur Terry combed through the options. She could not marry Jouffre. He was already married. Even, Monsieur Terry reasoned, were a divorce desirable or moral, and it was neither, it would be impossible to achieve. Paulette Jouffre had brought her husband a considerable *dot* on her marriage. Everyone in the textile world knew that. It was common knowledge. So even if Jouffre had loved Alexa, he would always love his wife's money more. It was an attitude that Monsieur Terry understood. After all, he too, was French. Church, family and business. That was what kept marriages together. Mentally he shrugged. *Que faire?*

The best thing, of course, if it could be managed, would be to persuade Mademoiselle Alexa to return to her parents, make a clean breast of things, have the baby and get on with her life. For Monsieur Terry's money, that was the best bet all round. If only she could agree to that. But she insisted that for her, no solution could be productive of more misery for all concerned. Her parents would never understand. This time, Monsieur Terry shrugged physically, which earned him another exasperated glance from Bernadette.

I would not do to appeal to his wife for help in the matter. Bernadette was not particularly open-minded. She was a good woman, but rigid in her views. In spite of the fact that her husband, through his *métier*, rubbed shoulders with the rich and famous every day, Bernadette had insulated herself from what she thought of as the pollution of society by closely guarding the *petit bourgeois* atmosphere of her home. No. A pregnant model girl would receive only a cool welcome in any house over which Bernadette presided.

There was a third possibility, in some ways the most attractive and yet fraught with difficulties. Monsieur Terry had a house, a small holiday house near Arcachon on the Atlantic coast. It was nothing really, just one commodious living room, a tiny kitchen and a couple of bedrooms. But it was pleasantly situated among the pine trees, cool and shaded in the hot summer weather, a welcome retreat after sweltering afternoons on the beach. His children used it in August, just as he and Bernadette had used it when his own family were young. For the rest of the year it was closed up and shuttered. That was the problem of course,

apart from a seldom-used stove in the living room, it was un-
heated and winter was coming.

Leaving aside the practical question of heating, she might be
bored and lonely down there by herself. When it was over, of
course, she could come back to modelling. She was so young
her figure would recover in no time. But could she earn enough
to keep the child? It was doubtful. Should he offer to make her
his *directrice*? Not immediately of course, but train her for the
role. It would justify a larger salary and thanks to her own efforts, it looked as though he might be able to afford it.

Something must be done. Monsieur Terry owed Mademoiselle Standeven a debt of gratitude. She had more than repaid
his original generosity and he was not the man to leave the score
uneven.

Unfortunately, there was yet another factor to be taken into
consideration. That was Alexa's entanglement with Fabrice de
Pies Ombre. Monsieur Terry could not call it other than an
entanglement and he had taken every possible step to sidestep
the acquaintance on Alexa's behalf.

De Pies Ombre had presented himself again at the *salon*, on
the last day of the collection. There had been no seat for him,
but he had stood at the back among a crowd of press photogra-
phers, who had jostled him unmercifully. He could see little of
the show, but he remained throughout, determined to catch Alexa immediately it was over. He was disappointed. Monsieur
Terry hustled Alexa away and down a back staircase after the
show.

"You look pale and drawn, *Mademoiselle*. Go home in a taxi
and rest well this weekend. Eat plenty of good food and come
to me on Monday. It will be time then, to examine the alterna-
tives. No, no, do not protest. I have your best interests at heart,
Mademoiselle. You need quiet. Go now."

Monsieur Terry had returned to the lobby to find the *Marquis*
leaning impatiently on his stick.

"Ah, there you are, Terry. Where is the so beautiful English
model, today?"

The careful idleness of the enquiry did not deceive Monsieur
Terry.

"You wished me to present her to you, *Monsieur*?" Monsieur
Terry said smoothly. He was still smarting from the impudence
of de Pies Ombre's unceremonious treatment of Alexa on the
previous day. He felt the insult not only to his model, but to

himself and his establishment. "*Hélas*, this will not be possible. Mademoiselle Standeven is invited to pass the weekend in the country. She has a long drive ahead of her. Naturally, I encouraged her to leave early." Monsieur Terry spread his hands in a characteristic gesture of dismissal. "I am desolate, *Monsieur*. So unfortunate."

"Then perhaps you will be good enough to give me the young lady's address and telephone number in Paris," de Pies Ombre scowled. The request was framed with an arrogance which increased Monsieur Terry's sense of affront.

"Unhappily, *Monsieur*, that will not be possible," Monsieur Terry's voice was silky. "As I'm sure you understand, I do not feel at liberty to give the addresses or telephone numbers of my models to gentlemen without their own express permission and Mademoiselle Standeven has given me no instructions regarding yourself."

The play of contrasting emotions on de Pies Ombre's face had been interesting to watch. Outrage and anxiety fought over the battlefield of his features, finally resolving themselves into a picture of angry resentment.

But his ruse had proved futile. Somehow or other, de Pies Ombre had made contact with Alexa and their friendship was advancing. In vain, Monsieur Terry had implored her to drop this acquaintance.

"I do not care *chère* Mademoiselle Alexa, if his mother goes elsewhere for her clothes, and in any case, I think it unlikely. The young *Marquis* has really no influence with her at all. What concerns me is you and your life. Please let me impress upon you, Fabrice de Pies Ombre has no money, no profession, and no, how do you say it? Backbone? None, I tell you. He will waste your time. He is not a useful friend for you and he would make a disastrous husband. Come, we have serious matters to arrange. Do not, I beg you, spend time with this man. He can only do you harm."

But she did not listen. She liked him, she said. He was amusing and she felt comfortable with him. It was almost like having a brother.

"Does he know that you are carrying another man's child?" Monsieur Terry had eyed her keenly over the top of the spectacles he always wore for doing his accounts.

"No," Alexa had dropped her eyes, "he does not know that."

"Should he not be told?"

Alexa's eyes were mild and innocent. "I do not think so, *Monsieur*. He is a friend, that is all."

The truth was that Alexa had considered telling Fabrice but had decided that there was nothing about their current, easy-going relationship which justified such a confidence. A few months ago she would have told any man, any friend, everything about herself. But her pregnancy had altered her in more ways than she knew. It was a new protectiveness that was growing out of her incipient motherhood, an impulse to erect fortifications of discretion around herself and the mysterious person that was growing inside her, in secret.

Beside him, Monsieur Terry was aware of Bernadette rising to go to the altar to receive holy communion. He did not join her. He rose himself and sat back in the uncomfortable chair. Looking upwards to the stone-vaulted ceiling, he allowed his mind to curl around the least desirable solution of all. Marriage to de Pies Ombre. It was distasteful, but it was possible. If he became convinced that it was what Mademoiselle Standeven wanted then he, Terry, would get it for her though it should mean burning in hell, as it well might, he thought ruefully.

Fabrice had not been idle over the weekend following the final show of Terry's collection. Nobody, it seemed, had ever heard of this Miss Standeven before she had made her debut at Terry's. Moreover, outside of that establishment she seemed to have no life, and there were no discernible traces. No matter, he would keep watch over the entrance to Terry's premises. After all, she must arrive for work and she must leave. Better still, he would employ some street urchin to follow her. Soon he would know all about her. Terry's obstructive attitude was a trifle. It would not prevent him from knowing the English girl better.

Although the possessor of an ancient name, Fabrice was neither well-known nor well-liked in Paris. A polio victim, he showed none of the graceful and endearing resignation which is so often inclined to make an afflicted human being popular with his fellow men. Fabrice cherished a sullen resentment against his fortune which made those who might have been his friends turn away from him. At thirty, he was unmarried, a situation which the dowager *Marquise* sought, seemingly in vain, to rectify.

The most ambitious of mothers shrank from sacrificing their daughters on the altar of the de Pies Ombres. That altar was, in any case, made of no very solid material. The family properties were in a parlous state. There was only the name. The present *Marquis'* distorted body and unpredictable manners might have been overlooked, but his penury made him altogether unmarriageable.

He was not entirely without charm for his education, undertaken by a series of expensive tutors, had been most thorough. He was a wit, albeit a rather cruel one. But Paris hostesses had learned to avoid inviting him to all but the most essential and large functions. He could be an embarrassing guest at a dinner party. He seemed unable to control his intake of alcohol and then his everyday boorishness descended to viciousness. Nor did he seek sociability. He belonged to no clubs and his acquaintances were restricted to the sons and daughters of his mother's friends.

For a French aristocrat, he was oddly provincial. He did not share his class's traditional attachment to the capital. Each year, he accompanied his mother to Paris where she came to buy clothes and enjoy lunching and dining with her friends, most of them, like her, natives of Algeria who had either married metropolitan Frenchmen, or had been exiled after the catastrophic war of independence and de Gaulle's shocking abandonment of the *colons*. She had long since ceased to expect that many hostesses would be eager to include him in their invitations. Of the six weeks mother and son spent annually in Paris, Fabrice whiled away most of them in heavy drinking at the crumbling Hôtel de Pies Ombre in the Marais. Visitors were rare but his mother gave one reception each year to return the hospitality she had received. Fabrice endured the occasion with a bad grace, bored by the endless, acrimonious conversation of people living perpetually in a colonial past. His behavior gave his mother's friends an annual reminder, that he was, from every point of view, an undesirable suitor.

During the last thirteen years he had escorted most of the socially prominent young girls of his generation who lived in, or who visited, Paris with their families in the autumn. Most of those girls were married now with children of their own. If, as his mother wished, Fabrice were to find a bride, it would have to be from the ranks of those girls still available, in their early twenties. Fabrice did not share his mother's continuing though fading optimism. He knew too well that in a decade where looks, talent and energy were deified to the extent that hairdressers, if sufficiently successful, were constantly photographed rubbing shoulders with princes, he, the indolent, crippled Marquis de Pies Ombre, was likely to remain a bachelor.

He made little secret of his unconcern. In the past, Fabrice might have fancied himself in love from time to time, but such affairs made no lasting impression on him. He was too selfish a man to care deeply for another human being, especially a greedy, clothes-obsessed woman. He supposed that in another nine or ten years, when he was forty, his bachelorhood would be regarded as settled. His mother's anxious, speculative glances would cease. Talk of heirs, duty to the family and continuity would, mercifully, be forgotten.

Such conversations destroyed Fabrice's equanimity. It was useless to explain to the *Marquise* that the de Pies Ombres had little left with which to continue anything. The late *Marquis* had lived in the style of an American millionaire. Every year's income was overspent. Yacht charters, racehorses that never won, ill-advised speculations, suites of hotel rooms taken for weeks at a time in all the capitals of Western Europe had rapidly eaten away the respectable patrimony of the de Pies Ombres. Now lawyers doled out the very small sums that the remaining capital was able to generate.

Talking to the lawyers was something that Fabrice avoided as much as possible. Their slate-eyed faces and eagerness to acquaint him with the most unpleasant facts made their visits to the *Château* loathsome. Their earlier suggestions that he should train for some profession in order to augment his income fell on stormy ground. Fabrice's father and grandfather had never worked. Why should he? Now, fortunately, they had ceased to press this unwelcome idea upon him. It was already too late. Time both flees and drags its feet for those who do nothing. If he felt any guilt or regret at his lack of energy, he suppressed the feeling.

Fabrice clung to the outmoded idea that his position both entitled him to a life of idleness and disqualified him from earning his bread like other men. The truth was that he lacked confidence in his ability to compete on equal terms in any area of endeavour, professional or commercial. His solitary education had denied him an early opportunity of measuring himself against others. The competitive spirit, which is fostered from youth in other boys, had been missing from his own experience. He was paralysed at the thought of having his efforts or achievements compared with those of his contemporaries. He took refuge in a pose of lordly inactivity, an impenetrable shield against failure. The one thing of which he could be certain, the only thing which nobody could take away from him, was his title and his name. He could be the Marquis de Pies Ombre without fear of failure or successful competition.

In vain had the lawyers and the trustees reminded him that he, his mother and aunt could barely live on the annual income available to them, still less would it support a wife and family in addition. Fabrice simply turned away. He refused to grasp it. A wife and family, after all, were liabilities that he might never incur. He would not scramble after cash to buy the right to breed. The prospect of disposing of one moment of his time or one thought of his mind other than at his own exclusive whim was abhorrent to him. Still more so the possibility that goals striven for might not be achieved. The thought of that humiliation was enough to prevent him making any effort. And so he said to his advisors that he found poverty was bearable but the bondage of professional obligations would suit neither his temperament nor his position.

Miss Standeven, however, had had a disturbing effect on these settled convictions. She had stirred desires in him that he could not name. Alexa was quite unlike any other girl he had ever met. She seemed as free as a wind-blown seed. Apparently untrammelled by parents or the expectations of others, she might remain mobile but dormant or there again, at a whim of nature, she might become stationary, lodge herself in some congenial soil and put down roots. Since he had been unable to discover anything about her except the self-evident facts that she was English and worked at Terry's, he imagined her to possess a fascinating arbitrariness which he almost envied. She could not be categorised or compared. Alexa was neither a girl with a commercially minded mother, looking for a husband, nor a keen-eyed adventuress carving out a place for herself in *café* society. She fell entirely outside his experience and occupied his thoughts much.

It was fully five years since Fabrice had been remotely interested in a woman other than the prostitutes he occasionally frequented. He had thought that beyond that infrequent need to discharge a biological function, it was unlikely that any member of the opposite sex would engage his attention. The discovery that his taste for women of a superior type could still be aroused was mildly irritating.

He had employed a messenger to send round his card to Maison Terry. On the reverse he had scribbled an invitation to lunch with him. He would have to wait until after the weekend for her reply. He did not like waiting for anything.

"Get up at once, Fabrice. You are very late."

The *Marquise* entered her son's bedroom without knocking. The morning was already far advanced towards noon. She was dressed with a hard-edged smartness which was thrown into relief by the dust-laden shabbiness of the room and its age-muted colours.

"Late for what. To be late, one must have an engagement. I have no engagement, therefore I am not late. In fact, I embark with conscientious earliness on a day of dullness."

He was taking Miss Standeven to the Bois for a late lunch. His imagination cradled the prospect. He did not care to have his mother know of all his activities. It would be better not to have her picking over the details of a relationship she would perceive as profitless.

Fabrice lay among a pile of white linen pillows in the large gloomy bed. Its tapestries were surmounted by a gilded coronet on which danced two dusty magpies fashioned in painted wood, which were the ancient heraldic emblem of the de Pies Ombre family. There was a large cup of *café au lait* in his hands, and the sheets were bespattered with the crumbs of *brioche*.

"Really you are so slovenly. You will not be able to loll about in this disgusting fashion once you are married."

"Why not?"

"Because you will lose the respect of your wife," the *Marquise* was testy.

"Will it matter?"

"You're a fool. Get up."

"What for?"

"I think you should come with me to Cousin Tilly's for lunch. She won't mind and it will do you good."

The *Marquise* desired her son's company purely as some measure of protection against what she feared might otherwise be an embarrassingly frank tête-à-tête with Madame la Courbe. She *had* been rather extravagant lately and no doubt she had been seen at Terry's collection. Naturally that didn't mean she'd

ordered anything, but then, as Tilly knew, with Suzanne de Pies
Ombre, to see was to buy. It was always Tilly who got her out
of trouble with her debts. But she did it with such a bad grace
these days, so tiresome of her. Anything was better than talking
about money, even Fabrice's company at lunch.

"In what way will lunch in that furniture emporium of an
appartement of hers be of benefit to me?" Fabrice demanded
querulously.

"It will do you good to get out from under your stone, out of
this poisonous room and into the fresh air. I seem to have a
white slug at home, not a son. People must see you."

"The sight of me may well benefit them but I doubt it will
conduce much to my entertainment."

"It will conduce something to our income if you marry."

"My income, you mean."

"Your income is what we live on."

"A pity."

"You must try and marry a girl with some money of her own.
It should not be too difficult. You have charm when you chose
to use it."

"Maman?"

"What?"

"Why don't you get a job?"

"Are you insane?"

"Why not? The lawyers are always suggesting that I get a
job."

"They suggested, Fabrice, that you study for the legal profession. What are you suggesting for me? That I should run a
flower shop?"

"Why not? Duchesses do it all the time in England. The
Duchess of Devonshire, they tell me, has a butcher's shop."

The *Marquise* shuddered eloquently.

"I am not an English Duchess. I am your mother, the Marquise de Pies Ombre, and I do not work. It was not expected or
thought necessary in my day. It is different for you, now everyone is doing it."

"Precisely *Maman*. It is the very point which I have just
drawn to your attention."

The *Marquise* threw her son an angry glance. He could never
resist pointing out her inconsistencies to her. He had a good
mind. It was a pity he did not use it to their mutual advantage
instead of tormenting her with it.

"It is no good, *Maman*. I shan't be hired out like a mule. I am not habituated to the idea of work. I find I have no natural taste for it. I can never understand why the working classes are so keen on it. In their shoes I should regard unemployment with considerable favour. And in any case, it is too late now. What am I trained for?"

"The lawyers will release some more money if you marry."

"There is not much to release. Not enough to keep an influx of new de Pies Ombres in the style to which they ought to be accustomed, indeed in any style at all by all accounts."

"Tante Héloïse will not last much longer and when she goes she will leave all her money to your children if you have any. If you do not have any, she will leave a tidy little fortune to that convent of hers."

"So, it makes no difference, we can always apply to the good sisters for succour. They will see the logic of the thing."

Madame de Pies Ombre picked up the caliper from the day bed at the foot of Fabrice's bed and threw it down beside her son. The incongruity of lecturing him about marrying a girl with money whilst handling this appliance did not occur to her. She had a sublime confidence that if Fabrice would only behave himself and court a suitable girl consistently, the inevitable and satisfactory conclusion would be a prosperous marriage from which she had much to gain. Neither her son's physical defects nor his indigence seemed to her to be any barrier. Anyone would be honoured to marry into the de Pies Ombre family. She had never been informed to the contrary. She tried another tack.

"Fabrice, it is with your happiness and fulfillment in life that I am chiefly concerned. I am not interested in money."

"How deeply relieved I am to hear it, *Maman*. I was beginning to fear you had developed a quite peasant obsession with it."

Fabrice did not, of course, lunch at Tilly's.

"I nearly succeeded in bringing him with me today," Suzanne confided to her cousin.

"Well, I am glad you did not," Mathilde responded while pouring out Scotch whisky into Waterford tumblers. The provision of strong drink was her invariable preliminary to serious discussion.

"He said he had to stay at home to telephone David about the *vendange*. Total nonsense of course, he hasn't a hope of getting

David on the telephone and in any case, when has Fabrice ever cared about the vineyards?''

"Of course, it's nonsense. It is just his marginally polite way of telling us that he does not want to lunch with two elderly ladies and be nagged about his fading prospects. That is why I am so glad he hasn't come, apart from the fact that he never troubles to make himself agreeable. We can discuss those same fading prospects with candour and in comfort.''

The comfort was undeniable. Suzanne looked around her cousin's spacious Etoile *appartement* with an envious sneer. Nothing here was old or worn; even the few examples of black lacquered oriental furniture had been restored to the point where their value was impaired. Tilly didn't know that and if she had she wouldn't have cared. Smartness was what counted. The rest of the furniture was either glass or black leather with chrome frames, most of it Italian. The polished parquet floor was adorned with shaggy white rugs. Huge, wealth-proclaiming bunches of white arum lilies were thrust into chunky vases of Swedish glass. Tilly had married a man with a sugar refinery and the generosity to die of a neat, conclusive heart attack only ten years after their marriage.

"Switch on the logs and pay attention.''

The *Marquise* needed no second bidding. Accustomed to the freezing cold of her two homes, the sulky stoves and unmanageable fuel bills, free heat in the homes of others, from however vulgar a source, was always welcome. She stood up smoothing the elegant cream woollen dress which was still unpaid for.

"I have run out of ideas.''

"Happily, I have an entirely fresh one. I have been talking to Terry.''

"You make friends with the most extraordinary people, Tilly. How can you talk to a dressmaker.''

"Easily, they have mouths like other people and friendship is not an absolute prerequisite of conversation. Terry has a girl.''

Suzanne blinked.

"I am not *au fait* with the family circumstances of my dressmaker.''

"Idiot! The new model. There could be money there. Not perhaps a great deal, but some.''

"How do you know?''

"Guesswork. Hints. It is worth considering?''

"A foreigner? How can one marry someone one does not know?"

"You are not being asked to. Fabrice is."

"It is the same thing."

"The great advantage of the situation is that she does not know him and consequently her objections would be limited to the physical factor."

Tilly looked at her cousin. Underwriting Suzanne's bills had become a bore and an increasing financial strain. Something would have to be done. What had begun as a cousinly gesture during the period of fiscal chaos that befell the de Pies Ombres after Luc's death had become an intolerable burden. It wasn't in Tilly's nature to refuse more help straightforwardly, but she would have to extricate herself somehow.

She had been somewhat surprised when Terry had sounded her out about the progress of Fabrice's search for a suitable wife. He had managed the matter most urbanely, made the questions seem no more than time filling chatter and yet she had discerned some purpose in it all. There was an English girl, it seemed, employed in his establishment, who had taken quite a fancy to Monsieur Fabrice. Apparently the two young people had been seen together once or twice. Ridiculous of course. It was nothing, nothing that need concern the de Pies Ombres. If *Madame la Marquise* was to hear it, it should not cause her the slightest worry. No doubt the *Marquis* was amusing himself. Of course, Mademoiselle Standeven came of quite a solid sort of family. No doubt when she did eventually marry, someone of her own class, naturally, there would be quite a little something to go with her. Such a charming girl and so delighted with Paris. She enjoyed *la vie française* so much.

"Terry intimates that the young lady would welcome a respectable opportunity to remain in France. They can be very romantic about France, the English, you know."

"I am aware of that," the *Marquise* snapped. "It is a respectable connection for my son that I seek, not occasions for philanthropy."

The *Marquise* did not immediately detect the keen edge to her cousin's voice or the lack of warmth in her glance. Tilly rose and went to a drawer in her bureau. She placed a sheaf of papers in Suzanne's lap.

"You see, *ma chère cousine*, I really can no longer afford to dress you," her voice was soft, "and last month Brun came here from the Marais and told me he's received no wages for twelve weeks. Naturally, I told him how busy you were and that it was just some unfortunate oversight on the part of your man of business . . . but . . . ''

"You paid him?''

Brun was the caretaker and general servant employed at the house in the Marais. Were it not for him, the house would probably have become completely derelict.

"But, of course.'' Suzanne's long Norman face was deeply red.

"So, you see, don't you, how necessary it is becoming that some action should be taken to . . . well, let us say, put your affairs on a more comfortable footing. I didn't think that any option, however unlikely, should be overlooked. Do you?''

"Mademoiselle Babinet?''

"Oui, Madame."

"I want to talk to Monsieur Terry.''

"Who shall I say is calling, *Madame*?''

Lately Mademoiselle Babinet had developed more confidence in dealing with customers.

"Madame Mathilde La Courbe.''

Monsieur Terry's voice was jocular. *"Chère Madame.* How good of you to telephone.''

"I think you will find that your benevolent little scheme should prosper now, if only the young lady will do her part.''

"*Eh bien, Madame*, we shall see, we shall see.''

Bon, Monsieur Terry thought. It is another option. It is not the best, but it is a possibility. Something would have to be decided soon.

He had received a curious telephone call only yesterday. The voice had been strange, foreign. The caller spoke in French but with a heavy Belgian accent. He said he was a woollen cloth manufacturer trying to discover the whereabouts of his usual agent in France, he appeared to have moved offices. Did Monsieur Terry know him by any chance? He had tried every dressmaker in Paris that he knew, now he was starting on those with whom he had had no dealings. The caller apologised for the intrusion but said the matter was urgent. Could Monsieur Terry help? Of course he could, but Jean-Claude Jouffre had remained at the same address in Neuilly for some years, perhaps the gentleman had the number wrong. The firm was . . . just a moment, he would get Mademoiselle Babinet to check, yes, Estèphe Guillaume in the Rue de l'Eglise, number 16A. Monsieur Jouffre was now the senior partner. So glad to have been of assistance.

The reminder of Jouffre's existence had in effect panicked Monsieur Terry. Something would have to be done about Mademoiselle Alexa's affairs. Time was passing and nothing was decided. He would investigate the possibilities that might be inherent in her friendship with de Pies Ombre. There was something in the determination with which he had pursued her that had impressed Terry in spite of himself. It could be considered. That did not mean to say that the solution was any more desirable than it had been or that it would be adopted. None-the-less, it would be as well to have the ground prepared.

It was that which had occasioned a series of rather oblique conversations with Madame la Courbe. She was a sensible woman, quick to understand a bargain, even an unspoken one. Her voice on the telephone was syrupy.

"About my account . . ."

"Ah, *Madame*, fifty thousand francs is not an insubstantial sum. But for such a good customer as yourself, a worthwhile discount could be arranged. Of course, should our other affairs proceed to a satisfactory conclusion, I do not see how there could be talk of money between us. *Au revoir, Madame*."

There was a premium to be paid for options, as Monsieur Terry, a businessman, was aware. The full price was not paid until the option had been exercised. He still hoped that they would not be forced on that necessity.

Tilly put the telephone gently back into its cradle. The sugar refinery shares had slipped badly lately. She sighed. If only her other creditors could be bought off with similar favours.

Alexa stabbed the strawberry tart with her fork. She did not want it. The shining cartwheel of crimson displayed on Fouquet's trolley had seduced her eye but she tasted nothing. She realised with a slight shock that for the first time, after many months in France, she was not interested in food. Fabrice had woven a spell. His wit and urbanity combined with a natural ease of manner had made her aware that she had been very tired. Fabrice contrived to be restful to her exhausted nerves, and at the same time a stimulating companion. They had talked about the history of France, its social structure and his own family's place in it. The de Pies Ombres belonged to the pre-revolution *ancient régime* aristocracy and their line stretched back to Saint Louis.

"But what a strange name you have, Fabrice. It sounds like something to do with peas in a shadow, but it can't be."

Fabrice chuckled.

"Being connected with something in a kitchen garden certainly cuts one down to size. I suppose I should be grateful you don't think I'm the descendant of a meat pie. At least you got the pronounciation correct. *Pies* means magpies in French and as you correctly surmise, *Ombre* means shadow. But it didn't really begin as *shadow* at all."

"What was it then?"

"One of my remote ancestors, in the Middle Ages, came from the region of Castile in Spain. He was a nobleman in his own country and his heraldic emblem was a magpie. And, I imagine, because he was a Spaniard he called himself an *hombre*, which just means "man." The other possibility was that he used to greet people by saying *Hombre!*, that means *Man!* Really terribly beatnik and modern if you think about it. And then I suppose people in the district forgot what *hombre* meant originally, dropped the *h* in writing—they would never have pronounced it anyway—lost the accent on the final *e* and the word looked like the French word it actually became with a totally different meaning. So, here I am. The Marquis Fabrice of Magpie Shadow, call me *Peaceombrer,*" he pronounced the words, running them together, with an exaggeratedly English accent, "at your service, *Mademoiselle.*"

"How romantic, Fabrice. What a marvellous story!" The *Marquis*'s eyes glowed, it was pleasant to be appreciated.

During the revolution, many of the de Pies Ombres had perished on the guillotine, a fact which made Alexa shudder with retrospective horror and pity in spite of Fabrice's matter of fact tone when relating this terrible episode in his family's long history. But there had been survivors, all of whom sojourned in England until the terror had passed. As a result, the de Pies Ombres had always cherished an affection for England and the English.

The physical demands of Monsieur Terry's show, the perpetual worries about her pregnancy, the strain of simply keeping going, and apprehension regarding the future had taken their toll. To hear her own language spoken so perfectly was like thrusting her feet into a shabby old pair of sheepskin slippers after a wet, winter walk. Indeed, Fabrice spoke English better than she did. Alexa was astounded to find her tongue stumbling over the words and idioms of her own native language. It seemed incredible that she had spoken English for eighteen years and French for fewer months, yet she was awkward and clumsy with the more familiar words.

"It's awful, I can't speak English any more, and I just don't speak enough French to say all I want to."

"That is unusual, it will take you a day or two to re-establish the English."

"Do you have this problem? You don't seem to."

"Ah no, from an early age I had an English tutor, an Oxford man. So you see, I am genuinely bilingual. There are no dislocating gear changes for me."

"Which language do you think in?"

"It depends on what I'm thinking about. Sometimes both languages at once, mental Franglais. When I am thinking of you, I think in English. Don't try to eat that."

Alexa looked up ruefully.

"I don't know why I took it, it wasn't greed, more absent-mindedness. I was concentrating so hard on what you were saying, it just seemed the quickest way of getting rid of the waiter . . ."

"You don't have to explain to me, Miss Standeven, I am not the nursery governess, you know."

"I'm so used to having to explain."

"You can explain as much as you want to me, when we are married."

Alexa literally gaped. She felt as if her head had been struck, painlessly, from her shoulders. Instead of blood there was a gushing vapour of surprise.

"I should shut your mouth, Miss Standeven. Lovely as it is, it is full of pastry."

Slowly, Alexa brought her jaws together, dropping her eyes.

"What is it, Miss Standeven, is the prospect of becoming the Marquise de Pies Ombre of the Château d'Ombre unamiable?" Fabrice's face was bland. "Or is it my leg? A bit short and spindly, and, of course, quite useless, but not that disgusting. You could have a preview." There was pain in his eyes and his lips twisted in self-mockery.

"Oh, no . . ."

"You consent? Oh good."

"You haven't actually asked me . . . You sort of told me."

"Insufferable arrogance. I apologise."

A glimmer of mischief in her eyes, Alexa said, "I can forgive arrogance. You see, that word cropped up over and over again in my school reports. I used to say that arrogance was the adjective people who felt inferior used to describe people they knew to be their betters. It got me into a lot of trouble."

Loud laughter spurted from Fabrice, startling the sombre clientele of Fouquet's. He laughed uncontrollably till tears began to glisten in his eyes and he choked.

"Monsieur! Monsieur le Marquis. Vite! De l'eau. Vite, vite!"

The waiters scurried around him with glasses of water and napkins. The other lunchers returned their attention to their plates with obvious reluctance. Splutteringly, Fabrice recovered.

"There is your answer, Miss Standeven. It is not, it is true, an answer given directly to me, but to fate, destiny, or what you will. You see, you were born to be a *Marquise*. I have nothing to do with it. I am just the humble instrument of your fulfillment."

Alexa's face was bright with laughter. There was something about Fabrice that reminded her of everything that was likeable about her father. But it was different. He had no power over her and she need not be afraid of him. He was companionable and fun. It was delightful to be with him. Jean-Claude dropped away from her. She looked into her own memory and found that the picture of Jean-Claude was like a yellowing photograph, stored in an attic, debris from the past, empty of meaning. She found she could say nothing about the baby. It was hers, but it had no place in this conversation. She would tell Fabrice all about it later. Yes, later, that would be best.

Fabrice was hardly handsome. His features were too heavy for that: in repose they seemed to glower, but when animated by conversation, they were so informed by intelligence, the eyes so dark and alert, that he appeared enormously attractive. His hands were square with spatulate fingers, they were clean and well groomed but not effeminately tended as Jean-Claude's had been. Fabrice was stockily built. He had massive shoulders and a broad chest but he carried no surplus weight. She searched his face again, trying to read every contour. The jaw was angular, clean cut. Strongly marked black eyebrows brooded over his deep-set eyes, his nose was thin, aquiline. A lock of the thick black hair that was completely straight flopped over his broad forehead. No, he was not handsome, but he was very far from being ugly. He was someone who would make her feel safe. She considered his proposal. Did he mean it?

"I am rather . . ."

"What? Surprised?"

"Well, yes. We haven't known each other more than a few days. It's not long."

"Eleven days to be precise."

"Isn't that a rather short time in which to choose a wife? You still call me Miss Standeven."

"I do that because it amuses me. I like the sound of your name. It suggests solidity, seriousness, reliability . . . in short, all the qualities which I do not possess myself. I think you have much to offer me."

"And what do you have to offer me, *Monsieur*?"

Fabrice looked at her in genuine astonishment.

"My name, my house and my affection. You want more?"

Alexa shrugged, nonplussed. No, why should she want more? Was not respectability, shelter and affection the most any man could offer to a woman. They were enough. She had loved Jean-Claude and he had betrayed her. Affection was a milder, safer thing altogether. There could be no terrible hurts in store.

"No," she said slowly, "I don't think I do want more."

CHAPTER
5

🎕 🎕 JEAN-CLAUDE PUT THE telephone down. The rain lashed the plate-glass windows of his office. Below, the leafy purlieus of Neuilly were troubled by gusts of wind, the wet pavements bespattered by falling leaves. In the distance, the Seine was a ribbon of steel. Autumn had come.

Paulette's voice had sounded brisk and cheerful. She'd just seen little Pierre back off to school for the first time after some trying weeks. He'd recovered well from the whooping cough which had so alarmed them when he was taken ill in Sardinia and had been rushed to the hospital in Cagliari. It had been a nightmarish few days. Paulette distraught, Pierre in the hospital, bewildered and frightened and no-one to take care of three-year-old Louise. Jean-Claude had flown straight out. Madame Dubois had put a few things in a suitcase for him and brought them out to the office in a taxi. And then what had she done? He shuddered to think. Madame Dubois always dealt with these things in her own way. He'd had no time to give any specific instructions.

Poor little Alexa. She had deserved better than that. The diamond ear studs he'd intended to give her were still in his desk drawer. Never mind, he'd give them to Paulette for Christmas. He sighed. Perhaps it was all just as well. Somehow it would have been difficult to explain to Alexa that their *liaison* was just a temporary thing and would have to end. She would never have understood, so moral, so English. Her distress would have torn him apart. He thought with regret of the smooth slender body and the lovely trusting face. Mentally Jean-Claude rapped himself over the knuckles. Never get involved with a woman of family, it only causes complications.

109

Fortunately, things had worked out well, Alexa had made a great success it seemed. Her face in every paper, her name on every lip. But, as yet, as far as one could gather from the popular press, she had no escorts, no evening life. Strange. Perhaps she could not forget him. Jean-Claude studied his reflection in the glass surface of his desk. Was it not he who had shown her the road to independence, fame, even fortune? Had he not introduced her to Terry and had he not given her generous amounts of money to spend on clothes? Yes, he had accomplished a good deal on her behalf and done a good deed that he would never reveal to a living soul. Jean-Claude felt a pleasing and unfamiliar surge of righteous satisfaction.

The intercom on his desk buzzed loudly. Irritated at this interruption to his reverie, he pressed down the switch sharply.

"Oui."

"Il y a deux messieurs pour vous voir."

His secretary's voice was singsong with boredom and routine.

Jean-Claude frowned, flipping through the pages of his diary. It was Tuesday, the fifth of October. He couldn't remember an appointment. Perhaps Giselle had put something in for him. She did that sometimes and forgot to tell him, but no, the page was blank. Well, he was at leisure.

"Qui . . ."

"C'est Monsieur Standeven et Monsieur Jaggair." Giselle pronounced the unfamiliar names awkwardly.

Jean-Claude had a light-headed sensation of unreality.

He rose slowly behind his desk. Henry and Alexander both in turn ignored his outstretched hand. He was shaken by the omission, a fact that was lost on neither of the keen-eyed Yorkshiremen who stood before him.

"What an unexpected . . ."

"Well, Jouffre," Henry Jagger's voice was full of synthetic affability. "I expect you know why we're here. Alexa gave us to understand you were acting as guardian, so to speak. You found her a job, did you? And somewhere to live. Somewhere suitable, like. Well, I imagine she's been living with you and Paulette. That would have been the right thing to do, wouldn't it? Surprising no one kept us in touch, like. It'd have been nice to know how the bairn was going on. Of course, I don't expect you knew Alexa never wrote or telephoned, only the once, at any rate. We've been worried, I don't mind telling you. Still, that wouldn't be your fault, would it?"

It was well known in the international textile business circles which Henry frequented that he had lost his Yorkshire accent more than four decades ago. Any resumption of the vowels and dialect words of his working-class boyhood was a warning signal. Jean-Claude smiled desperately. This was going to be very difficult to handle.

"Well, actually . . ."

"Mind you, I expect she'll be just about packing up to go home now. Just as well. High time she was home. She's got her education to think of, has Alexa. Well, never you mind, lad, we'll call round to your place on the way back to the Crillon. Pass the time of day with young Paulette, like. Now there's a bonny girl. I've not seen her since your wedding day. Aye, time flies.

"You won't have met my son-in-law, will you, Jean-Claude? Alexander Standeven. Young Alexa's father. He's a lawyer, you know. Couldn't persuade him to join us in the wool trade and damn glad I've been at times.

"He's got me out of some pretty scrapes, I can tell you. Nothing like a good company lawyer when your business gets to be any sort of a size, is there? But your father knew all that, of course. I never knew a man as keen to pay for the best advice. He'll have passed the notion on to you, I don't doubt."

"How do you do, sir? *Enchanté.*"

Alexander nodded an acknowledgement of the greeting, his face unsmiling but impassive.

"Can I get you something? Some coffee perhaps?" Jean-Claude looked anxiously into the faces of the two men before him. He wondered how much they knew, how much Alexa had told them. Had they even seen her?

"No lad, you can get us some brandy. I've a feeling we're going to need it." Henry stripped off his pigskin gloves in a gesture that was deliberately threatening.

"Please gentlemen, do be seated. The cognac will be here in just a moment."

A little calm was returning to Jean-Claude's fevered brain. If he managed this carefully and very cleverly he might get away with it. It was not going to be easy. Henry Jagger had a formidable reputation. Jean-Claude's father had warned him never to get on the wrong side of him, he was rumoured to make a most unpleasant enemy. And this tall good-looking man in his forties, he had not spoken yet. Alexander Standeven. Jean-Claude saw what one day Alexa could become. His eyes were like Alexa's, dark blue, but without the warmth.

"We are surprised," Alexander spoke in a neutral tone, "that Alexa has not communicated with us for so many weeks. I have telephoned this number on several occasions and have been told that Alexa was not here. And yet I concluded, perhaps foolishly, that she was working here. Perhaps you could throw some light on the matter. My wife is seriously disquieted."

Alexander picked up his glass and turned it round and round in his hand, bringing it to his nose. His eyes never left Jean-Claude's face.

"Gentlemen, allow me to explain."

"Please do, Monsieur Jouffre."

"Alexa is now working for a *couturier* in the Place Vendôme. Maison Terry. At first, it is true, she worked as an assistant instructor at a language school, a little job I found for her until I was able to arrange this more congenial position. It was a matter of sounding out contacts, you understand. Now, of course, she has had a great success. It is possible, more than possible that she will be offered lucrative photographic assignments in the future. Naturally, she preferred to live independently," Jean-Claude turned down the corners of his mouth in a grimace of sympathy.

"What could I do? You know what young girls are these days. Once they are earning a little money of their own, there is no controlling them. Really she . . . ."

Alexander raised his eyebrows. With detached professionalism he awarded Jouffre marks for the quality of his lie. Always stay as near the truth as you can, it reduces the risk of blundering.

"This is somewhat at variance with my information, Monsieur Jouffre."

Had it not been for the stressful nature of the circumstances, both Henry and Alexander would have enjoyed their brief interview with Alexa's employer. Terry had proved an easy man to deal with. His information had been most helpful. He had not been unaware, he said, that some degree of family tension was responsible for Mademoiselle Standeven's presence in Paris. He had endeavoured on several occasions to persuade her to resolve her differences with her family. He was accustomed to take an interest in the affairs of his model girls, after all, they were invariably so young. Alas, he felt there was a limit to what he could hope to achieve. A girl of eighteen was an adult. It was absurd, was it not?

When pressed, Monsieur Terry had admitted that there did seem to have been some kind of association with Jouffre, and that yes, it was not of a kind that a father could approve. But of course, Monsieur Terry had only encountered Mademoiselle Standeven once during this period. When she had entered his *salon* as a trainee model, the *affaire*, if indeed that is what it had been, was at an end. He suspected that Mademoiselle Standeven had been treated infamously. Not that she had said much about it, Mademoiselle Standeven was so brave, and, he had added, always so dignified.

Alexander appreciated Monsieur Terry's suavity. It was almost the equal of his own. Between them, outraged father and affectionate, protective employer had established the facts of the matter in hand. They had done it without crude accusations or seriously diminishing the dignity of Miss Standeven. It was made clear between them that she may have suffered an injury at the hands of an unscrupulous man, but that she herself, whatever the unsavoury details, was, if not blameless, greatly to be pitied.

Henry had observed this amiable game of pat ball with admiration. On the one hand the Frenchman had succeeded in conveying information he ought to have concealed as a loyal friend of Miss Standeven. On the other he ensured that his *protégée* would be avenged and that the minimum of opprobrium would attach to her. It was all highly satisfactory and the three men were delighted with each other.

However, there were some salient features of Mademoiselle Standeven's situation that Monsieur Terry had thought it better to keep to himself until he had had the opportunity of a conference with Alexa. Things were rather more complex than Monsieur Terry knew how to explain to Mr. Standeven at short notice. The pregnancy and the de Pies Ombre factor were becoming interrelated complications which would require further thought.

Jean-Claude squirmed.

"Of course, *Messieurs*, I do not know what gossip you may have . . ."

Alexander waved his hand in a gesture of impatience.

"Do not trouble yourself, *Monsieur*. I am in possession of sufficient fact to justify my taking preventive measures."

Jean-Claude was now completely out of his depth.

"Preventive measures?"

"But certainly. You yourself mention gossip. As you must realise, your recent, cynical seduction of my daughter, which I imagine you will not now deny, could well give rise to damaging talk. My daughter's innocence is gone. However, reputation, which fortunately is not wholly dependent on innocence, is not yet entirely at a discount. To be more specific, were it a matter of common knowledge that my daughter was a woman of loose morals, it would seriously injure her prospects of attracting the sort of husband I have in mind for her. I propose to take some precautions."

"A marriage has been arranged for Miss Standeven?" Jean-Claude was entirely at sea.

"Certainly not," Alexander snapped. "Nor will it ever be. It is simply a matter of encouraging one sort of suitor and discouraging others of a less desirable kind. We manage these things discreetly in England, as I'm sure you are aware. Moreover, my daughter is far too young to marry. There will be no question of it for a few years."

"Then I am at a loss to see . . ."

"No doubt, but if you will bear with me, *Monsieur*, I am about to put an end to your mystification."

Alexander settled himself more comfortably in his chair, as he warmed to his task.

"Allow me to explain the position. Your wife, I take it, knows nothing of your connection with my daughter. Leaving the question of matrimonial affection aside, I imagine it would be inconvenient to you were Madame Jouffre to have occasion to complain of your behaviour to her. You have at least one child, possibly more. Moreover, a respectable marriage settlement was made in consideration of your marriage. The sum of money involved would be a serious loss, were Madame Jouffre to decide to divorce you."

Jean-Claude was clearly aghast. He had a mental picture of his life crumbling about him. The house in the Rue des Pères would have to be sold, his business would be affected; Paulette had an interest in it. And his children, he could not bear to lose them. Alexander's voice continued inexorably, and for a time Jean-Claude scarcely heard him.

"And so, Monsieur Jouffre, I have worked out a formula designed for your protection and that of my daughter. Be good enough to write me a cheque for the sum of twenty thousand

pounds sterling. You need not be afraid that I shall cash it. I
disapprove of blackmail,'' Alexander added composedly.

Jean-Claude's jaw dropped, not so much in shock at the largeness of the sum as in utter confusion.

"The cheque buys my silence and it ensures yours. If I hear
one word on the subject of my daughter which I might find
offensive, the cheque will be cashed and your wife . . ."

"Put in the picture,'' Henry could not resist interrupting
cheerfully.

Alexander glared at Henry. Retaining the proper tension was
crucial when executing the kill, as any experienced advocate
would agree.

"Precisely. Furthermore, the cheque is to be regarded as a
short term measure only. I shall in fact, require a fixed and
floating charge over all your assets to the value of that sum as a
permanent insurance policy. But all that can be arranged in a
few days' time, when you will be approached by my own firm,
Standeven, Standeven and Browne. Naturally, you can rely on
us to deal with the matter with absolute discretion and striking
efficiency.''

Alexander rarely allowed even the most trying of circumstances to deprive him of a little desiccated fun.

Jean-Claude was almost incoherent as he expressed his gratitude. He scrabbled in his desk drawer and produced a large
company cheque book. He handed the completed cheque to
Alexander who examined it carefully.

"You have assets to cover this amount?''

Jean-Claude nodded.

"Good. Well, we need not intrude upon you further, *Monsieur*.''

Jean-Claude pressed the switch on his intercom down.

"May I have my secretary call a taxi, *Messieurs*?'' The
Frenchman's manner bordered on the obsequious, Alexander
noted.

"We should be grateful,'' Alexander buttoned his British
Warm overcoat thoughtfully.

"You know, Monsieur Jouffre, you are fortunate to have such
a temperate fellow as myself to deal with. In England I should
probably have sued you for 'enticement.' There is no doubt a
similar action available in the French courts. A more energetic
father might have considered it worth his while to pursue his
remedy at law. Still, I always like to avoid unnecessary expense,

not to mention delays. You are enjoying extraordinarily disagreeable weather here at the moment, are you not? One always
thinks of Paris in the sunshine. Goodday to you.''

Fabrice felt good. The specially adapted Jaguar purred along the
Champs Elysées. Marriage to the youthful Miss Standeven was
quite an attractive prospect. She was amusing, undemanding
company. And certainly, her appearance at Fouquet's had caused
a gratifying stir. It was pleasant to be envied.

He glanced sideways at Alexa's unconscious profile, admiring
her insouciant elegance. The beige dress emphasised the faint
rose blush on her rather prominent cheek bone, a simple pearl
earring punctuated the delicate question mark of her ear. Tendrils of blond hair, escaping from the confines of her pony tail,
curled on her temple. It was these touches of unexpected informality, both in her manners and in her grooming, which made
her so different and so desirable.

Alexa's eyes remained fixed on the road ahead. What should
have been a moment of calm contentment, happiness even, was
poisoned by the falsity of her position. The unspoken fact of the
child lay between them. How could she tell him? She must do
so, that was certain.

She did not know Fabrice very well, but his physical presence
beside her in the car irradiated peace. She was loath to wreck
it, both for herself and for him. He was an unusual man, quite
unusual enough to accept another man's child, but he had gone
too fast for her and now the critical timing of this inevitable
revelation had passed beyond her full control.

She was tempted to let it all out in a rush. Just to take her
chance with Fabrice's reaction. Honesty was always best. And
yet, how many times had her father warned her against hasty
speech? The tongue should always follow the mind at a respectful distance. Profligacy with information was something he always advised against. What would he advise now? It was
impossible to imagine because, Alexa knew, the very last thing
her father could conceive of was his own daughter in such an
appalling situation.

"Crippled aristocrat marries mystery model." Fabrice broke
the silence suddenly.

"Is that what the papers will say?"

"Oh, some, I suppose."

"I'll have to telephone my parents this evening and tell them."

"Inevitably, my sweet." Parents-in-law. That was a hazard he'd never thought of.

"What will your mother say?"

"She'll be ecstatic. She'd just about pulled stumps and taken her bat home, resigned to never attaining the status of grandmother.

"She may be a bit . . . well," Alexa was picking her way, "be a bit disappointed. I mean, I'm not an aristocrat."

"I shouldn't worry about that, good solid bourgeois stock. Ideal for renovating the depleted genetic coffers of a family like the de Pies Ombres." No point in telling her that his mother and aunt expected her to restore the financial fortunes of the de Pies Ombres as well. The desirability of Alexa was about the only thing mother and son had agreed about for a long, long time. An odd coincidence.

"Fabrice, I think there's something quite serious we ought to talk about. I mean, something you ought to know . . ."

"My dear little *fiancée*, it is only because you are so young that you think that. Did you not know, that if all the serious things that betrothed parties could know about each other were brought to light at an early stage, no weddings would ever take place. There would be absolutely no takers for the sacrament of marriage. I implore you not to ruin our chances with untimely revelations. Do you have an unsightly mole in a place where only a hallowed husband may proceed? Ah no, it is an ingrowing toenail, or perhaps something more serious still, a conviction that an early indiscretion with a rustic neighbour's son disqualifies you from the privileges of an innocent wife. Be easy on these points, such lapses from grace are very common."

Alexa was silenced. It was impossible to talk to him in this frame of mind. She needed his full and serious attention and she knew she did not have it. A better moment would arise soon.

Fabrice's mood of frenetic gaiety lasted for the rest of the short journey back to the Place Vendôme. He spoke about their future together in a way which Alexa found disturbing. She was uncertain whether to take him seriously or not. How much was mere banter and how much she was intended to regard as a truthful account of his expectations, she could not have said.

"You will not find me an unreasonable husband, but I shall expect you to be faithful for the first six years or so."

"That doesn't seem unduly onerous," was Alexa's light response.

"Perhaps not, but it will be a necessary abstention on your part." A note of seriousness had crept into Fabrice's voice. "You see, my family would like an heir, preferably with a back-up team, and of course, there must be absolutely no doubt as to their pedigree."

"What about you, do you want an heir and a back-up team, as you put it?"

For a moment Alexa's mind grasped at a straw. Perhaps the child she was carrying could simply be born and assumed by all to be the first, and slightly early fruits of her union with Fabrice. She dismissed the thought as unworthy and unsafe. But she dreaded acquainting him with her secret more and more. A family who wanted an heir would object to waiting until the bride's womb was vacated by a previous occupant. Alexa had inherited from her father the habit of brutal confrontation with the facts of any situation.

The more she thought about it the less able she felt to risk losing Fabrice. She wanted him and the safe haven he could offer.

"My own desires have never been a consideration, darling. May I call you that? That charming English endearment. So much better than *Chérie*, don't you think?"

"Yes, yes, I do think so. I always feel like a small round red fruit when somebody calls me that, which is very diminishing somehow. What shall I call you?"

"Darling, I think. Let us be a normal old English couple."

"How lovely. But tell me about your own desires not entering into it."

"Ah well, when one bears one of the greatest names in France, one is under an obligation not to allow it to die out. Like keeping up a rare breed of sheep or horses, you know?"

"Oh yes! I do know! Père David deer and things like that."

"Precisely."

"And you, will you be faithful for six years?"

"Perhaps. Who knows. I am French, remember."

"Is that an excuse?"

"It is a reason, *mon amie*, a reason."

"Ah, *voilà*. The young people return." Monsieur Terry waved away Mademoiselle Babinet. They had been studying the sales figures for the house fragrances, *Lavande du Terry* and *Rose du*

Terry. There had been a sharp upturn in the sales since the collection.

"And where did you lunch?"

Monsieur Terry kept his voice light and inconsequential. There was something in the Marquis de Pies Ombre's manner which filled him with a queer foreboding. Had he stopped to analyse that feeling, he would have recognised the fear that matters had passed altogether out of his control.

"*Monsieur*, in the absence of any male kinsman of Miss Standeven's, you should be the first to know that I have asked her to become my wife and she has accepted." Fabrice's announcement was almost curt.

The smoothness on Monsieur Terry's face remained unruffled. Inwardly he deplored the haste with which this step had been taken. Now he could not consult with Miss Alexa, could not warn her of her father's arrival in Paris, could not discover if the Marquis de Pies Ombre had agreed to accept the child of another man. But then, he deducted rapidly, the matter must have been arranged between them, there could obviously be no engagement to marry otherwise. *Alors*, he thought, so she has done it. Whether it will prove satisfactory and whether the formidable Mr. Standeven will approve it, is an entirely different proposition.

"But this is wonderful! There must be champagne! *Oh magnifique!* I could not be more delighted if it had been one of my own daughters!"

Monsieur Terry was an expert at concealing his own emotions but did not suspect that Alexa's demure expression denoted anything more than a maidenly satisfaction at her betrothal. In reality her downcast eyes concealed the considerable alarm she felt. The difficulty of putting Fabrice in full possession of the facts about her position and leaving him free to withdraw from the engagement increased each moment, with the widening publicity which surrounded them.

Fabrice had no wish to spend any time listening to the effusions of Monsieur Terry.

"I think we will not disrupt your afternoon's work. I should take Alexa to meet my mother before she retires to dress for the Opera."

"Oh no, Monsieur le Marquis, you cannot deny me. One glass, I insist. Mademoiselle Babinet, bring glasses and three bottles of the Bollinger. We must tell everyone. Mademoiselle Standeven is to be married.''

"Mais c'est fantastique," Mademoiselle Babinet's plain face was wreathed in smiles, ''I will go at once, but first there is a message for Miss Standeven. A Mr. Alexander Standeven telephoned from the Crillon,'' she announced with arch satisfaction, ''he said would *Mademoiselle* be good enough to meet him there this evening at eight o'clock. Suite 19.''

Fabrice had gone. He had not made a good impression. The flippancy of his manner had contrasted unfavourably with the gravity of Alexander's.

''So that is your fiancé.'' It was, at least, a statement of fact, not a question. Alexander stood with his back to the room looking out over the lights in the Place de la Concorde. Alexa was sitting on the brocaded sofa.

''Yes.''

''How much do you know about this man, Alexa?''

''Only that he is a French aristocrat and bears one of the greatest names in France.''

Alexa felt protective of Fabrice. Her father did not know him. It was unfair to judge him, as she was certain Alexander would unhesitatingly do, on the basis of a single meeting.

''That is quite correct.''

Alexa glanced at her father in surprise.

''I have been making some enquiries. The de Pies Ombres own a château in the Médoc and an *hôtel particulier* in the Marais. Both properties are heavily mortgaged and in an advanced state of decay. He doesn't seem to be in terribly good shape himself, does he? What's the matter with his leg?''

''Polio.''

It was what Monsieur Terry had told her. It seemed that the *Marquise* had once confided that her son had contracted the disease in early childhood. There was nothing remarkable in that. Before the vaccine became widely available, many children of his generation were unfortunate.

''I see. Do you really want to be married, at your age, to a cripple?''

Alexa made no reply. It was sometimes a good policy when dealing with Alexander to let him answer his own questions. It was a thing he didn't like. In his professional life, he was accustomed to having his questions answered, under duress, if need be. This attack on Fabrice, although predictable, angered Alexa. It was typical of all her dealings with her father. Every pretended discussion was no more than a courtroom interrogation in which her answers to questions would be ridiculed and shown to be either false or dishonest. A familiar panic fought with the determination not to be overwhelmed on this occasion. She had defied her parents once. It was an advantage not to be feebly lost. These considerations completely obliterated thoughts of allowing Fabrice to withdraw from the engagement on the grounds of her pregnancy. She had thought of withdrawing herself without explanation, but now her father *had* thrown down a gauntlet, which the whole history of their relationship demanded she pick up.

"Well?" Alexander demanded after a pause.

"It doesn't seem to me to be the most significant thing about Fabrice."

"You will find it quite significant when you are married. Physically." Alexander uttered the word with loathing. He could hardly bear to contemplate Alexa having anything to do with any man in that way, let alone an incomplete specimen like this Fabrice.

Alexa again failed to respond. Alexander had slipped his knife into a soft and painful area. He counted on her attempting some defence which he could then destroy. But his daughter had grown wise enough to concede ground that was of little value. She knew that Fabrice's desirability was not the real issue.

"He appears to have no profession."

"Aristocrats don't, usually."

"Aristocrats," Alexander spat the word, "usually have some money. On what, pray, does he intend to support you, and, heaven help us, a family."

"We can work it out," Alexa unconsciously repeated the refrain of the Beatles hit tune, "I can work."

Alexander laughed bitterly.

"Alexa, you have lost nothing of your *naïveté*. At what can you work, do you imagine, that will be enough to sufficiently repair the fortunes of a family entirely dependent on the land? The property which supports the de Pies Ombres requires massive infusions of capital. Nothing you can do will be more than a drop in the ocean of their needs. What about Oxford? What about the law?"

"You and Mummy want all that. I don't. I tried to tell you but you just didn't listen."

Alexander was silent. What was behind all this? What possible motive could she have for wanting to marry this sorry individual? What had really happened with Jouffre? He didn't want to know. Elizabeth would go berserk. All their hopes for Alexa down the drain.

"Have you thought what effect this will have on your mother?"

"Yes. I'm sorry, but it's my life," she answered his question coldly. To do otherwise was to risk exposing further weaknesses to her father's probe. It was always Alexander's policy to elicit as much speech as possible from his opponents in argument.

"Not entirely, not yet. Have you realised that I can refuse my consent to this marriage?"

"Yes, Daddy," she was aware of a slight tremor in her voice "but you can't force me to return to England. I can stay in France and I can live with Fabrice, and I have a job."

Alexander smiled grimly, in spite of himself. She wasn't his daughter for nothing. She knew how to think on her feet. She hadn't expected any of this but she was coping magnificently. What a courtroom performance she would have given. Brave, too. Nobody had defied Alexander for years. Odd that it should be the gentle, biddable Alexa to break the pattern. He turned away from the window and faced into the luxurious room.

"Well, since you are determined on this course of utter folly, I had better see what I can do to protect your interests. It won't be much, I'm afraid, but there'd better be some sort of safety net."

The suddenness of his capitulation astounded her. It was as if he had drawn a neat, precise line in his mind that marked the close of their relationship as father and juvenile child.

There was a moment's awkward silence. It was the sort of silence which had so often pushed them apart before. Alexa ended it herself.

"Thank you, Daddy. I'm sure everything will be all right, really."

Alexander crossed the room to embrace her. Alexa was surprised, her father was not a demonstrative man. She could not remember a time when he had even kissed her mother in public. He was surprised himself and oddly relieved. Now Alexa was an adult and he was at last free to be her friend. Gently he disengaged himself.

"Did you know that I have a case of claret in my cellar, Château de Pies Ombre. It's your chap's. Not much good I'm afraid. Still, it's a *Deuxième Cru*, something to work on perhaps?" It was a joke, made to diffuse the intensity of the moment. He was never comfortable in the presence of emotion, and slightly abashed at his own behavior.

"He never mentioned it."

"Not surprising, probably more of a burden than an asset. Classed growths are a rich man's hobby."

"Why's that?" Alexa enquired, her interest awakened.

It was a great relief to talk about anything that didn't have a direct bearing on her personal affairs. With a shock she realised she had obtained her father's consent to a marriage she was not really qualified to enter. There could be no going back now. She would have to deal with the question of her child either by herself or with Fabrice. But her father must never be aware of it.

"Many reasons. One is that only a given amount of wine may be produced from a certain acreage, even if the land would produce more. The quotas are laid down by law. And then of course, only a restricted list of grape stocks may be planted and used in the vinification of claret. Some of these types are tricky and may respond badly in all but ideal weather conditions, with a resulting loss of quality in the end product. What is more, although production quotas are limited, the amount of labour and capital input necessary to keep a classed growth vineyard in prime condition is considerable."

"You said Fabrice's wine was bad. What would account for that?"

"Well, I didn't say that precisely, did I? I said it wasn't much good, which is a little different. It's recognisably claret, the controls take care of that, but it's lifeless and uninteresting. It has the feel of a product that nobody cares about."

"Why doesn't it get demoted, down the ladder? Michelin are always whipping their stars away from restaurants."

"Because, unfortunately, there is no competitive element in this. A classed growth is like a Member of Parliament who's been kicked upstairs to the Lords and never has to fight another election."

"The wine keeps its place no matter what?"

"Correct. It's got its seat in the upper chamber for the rest of its life and doesn't have to do a thing to keep it."

"Oh."

"You see, at the *Exposition Universelle* in Paris in 1855, they identified the classed growths and laid down their relative status. Those classifications just stuck. So an industrious proprietor in 1855 may have created an elevated status for his wine which is still enjoyed today by far less worthy successors."

"So Fabrice's wine is in no danger of ever losing its status?" Alexa pressed the point.

"None at all. Not a lot of good if you can't sell the stuff."

"What would make it saleable?"

"Well, it's always saleable but it's just a case of whether it's good enough to command an economic price."

"What would make it good enough?"

"More care, more knowledge, more money . . . better management generally. Of course, as with any kind of farming, there will always be bad years."

Alexa looked thoughtful. Her father had now wearied of the subject, his mind returning now to more immediate matters.

"Where have you been living?"

"In a women's hostel on the Left Bank."

Alexander wrinkled his nose in distaste.

"What's it like?"

"Pretty awful," Alexa admitted.

"You seem to have been prepared to suffer for your liberty. I suppose that's why I'm giving it to you. You must have been very uncomfortable. I wish it had not been necessary. You'd better go and collect your things and bring them here. You'll need a taxi."

"I haven't got enough cash on me for that."

Alexander sighed. No, she wouldn't have. She'd been living on a knife's edge. Still, it was too late to go into all that now.

"Here you are. Can't have my daughter destitute, nor, I suppose, a future *Marquise*." Alexander tried to smile but his mind was full of misgivings.

Suzanne examined herself carefully in the looking glass. Yes, she was still a handsome woman, she thought. Her large grey eyes had been carefully but discreetly made-up. It was so important not to outrage this little provincial notary's sense of suburban propriety. She must take immense pains to look like the sort of woman a middle-class father could have confidence in. Tilly had explained all this to her in words of one syllable. She was wearing her hair up in an efficient-looking French pleat, it showed streaks of grey at the temples. Paris hairdressers were so expensive and she had been waiting to colour the roots until she got back to Bordeaux, an economy which was more than ever necessary after Tilly's strictures. Well, the grey was just the things for Mr. Standeven. It would make him feel more secure. Grey hairs have a curious reputation for honesty.

She rose, plucking with dislike at the ready-made evening gown she had bought in London five years ago, a response to some sort of sartorial emergency; she couldn't remember what. It must have been dire. The label was that of an English firm specialising in ready-made evening gowns. It was a sheath of aquamarine crêpe with a draped neckline and some sort of beading on a floating panel that depended from the right shoulder. It really was very dowdy but perfect for the occasion, Tilly had informed her heartlessly. It didn't fit, she was conscious of it every time she moved.

"It will be just the kind of dress his wife will wear to upstage the doctor's wife at one of those ghastly middle-class dinner parties. It's perfect, my dear, just perfect." Tilly was the grim impresario of the whole frightful scheme.

Warming her hands at the sulky little fire that flickered intermittently in the marble fireplace, which was the public face of an unswept flue, she gazed at the murky reflection of her bedroom in the spotted mirror. Great grey spaces soared above the dusty canopy of her bed, the seventeenth century panelling, dull from lack of care, was occasionally punctuated by blackened canvases depicting distressing religious subjects, which luckily an age of smoke and dirt had all but obscured from view. There was a network of precious oriental carpets on the boarded floor, their colours dimmed to a dapple of browns and beiges enlivened here and there by more recent traces of spilled cosmetics. The tarnished silver toilet service gleamed dully, catching the odd spiritless reflection from the fire. It was freezing cold and the fire smoked badly, making little impact on the dank atmosphere. Suzanne had lived in rooms like this all the years of her married life. If they had been a little brighter and a good deal cleaner in the early years of her marriage to Luc, she had forgotten.

Recrossing the room, Suzanne went to a tortoiseshell casket and removing its contents, item by item, she studied them. "Nothing flashy," Tilly had said. A superfluous instruction, Suzanne snorted quietly to herself; she had nothing "flashy" left. But something, something to show who we are. It was difficult, the dress wasn't made to wear with jewellery. The people who bought this kind of dress didn't have much in the way of jewellery. The only thing it called for, if anything, was a pair of drop earrings. But Tilly had been quite specific on that point. No dangling earrings, too racy. She inserted some small diamond studded florets into her ears. The diamonds were very small and greyish, outdazzled by the coarse beading on the dress. A narrow bracelet composed of similar stones and an old emerald ring completed the ensemble. Looking again at her reflection she was disgusted by the clumsy outfit. Appalling. Tilly would be delighted.

She could have believed that Mr. Standeven owned a dinner jacket, but that he should have brought it with him, to a city where he could not possibly have any acquaintance, had been disconcerting. Tilly had immediately upgraded the luncheon to a full-blown dinner with a corresponding increase in expenditure that was embarrassing. They would have to put on something of a show. The whole point of the thing, Tilly said, was to reassure Mr. Standeven that his daughter had done rather well for herself and he could leave his previous Alexa in their care without anxiety. And, she had said pointedly, some of his money.

"How do we know if there is any money?"

"Trust me," Tilly had said, "Terry has a nose for these things. Isn't he a businessman?" Grudgingly, Suzanne had agreed. "Anyway, she's said to have beautiful manners and to speak English with *l'accent d'Oxford*. Now, you don't get that without expensive school fees, do you? Be practical, Suzanne, Fabrice isn't likely to do any better at this stage."

"Tilly, do you really think Fabrice will be comfortable with this girl? I don't expect him to be in *love* with her exactly, that's a luxury we can't afford and a folly I imagine him barely capable of . . ." She stopped speaking for a moment, her mind struggling to give expression to unfamiliar feelings. "It's just that he *is* my son, after all, and I shouldn't want him to be tied to someone who would . . . *embarrass* him."

"I have an idea that Miss Standeven will make an admirable *Marquise*, with a little judicious training from you, of course, my dear."

Suzanne brightened instantly at the thought of the forthcoming pleasure of having a daughter-in-law to dominate, as Tilly had anticipated that she would.

"I think she and Fabrice will do very well together," Tilly remarked. "He told me he thought her appealingly vulnerable and not unintelligent. Quite an enthusiastic assessment from Fabrice, I'm sure you agree."

"Intelligence is not the first quality one looks for in a daughter-in-law, is it?"

"Indeed not, but beggars can't be choosers. As I say, this is the best we can do."

Downstairs in the first floor *salon*, Alexa and her father had already arrived. Alexander inspected the room with a mixture of dismay and admiration. It spoke volumes about aristocratic decay and great wealth, long since disappeared. He had seen such rooms, though on a less theatrical scale, in the homes of many of his elderly clients.

Brun, in his threadbare but newly sponged livery, was dispensing champagne with painful slowness. With a forced cheerfulness, Fabrice was endeavouring to instil some normality into the proceedings.

"Let me introduce our cousin, Mathilde La Courbe. Tilly, allow me to present my future father-in-law, Mr. Alexander Standeven. Alexa, Mr. Standeven, Madame La Courbe."

"Ah, Monsieur Standeven, what a pleasure this is. You know, we were almost in despair about Fabrice. He is such a taciturn fellow, no woman seemed able to make a dent in his heart. It was as if he was made of stone."

Tilly prattled on desperately, her speech getting more mannered and artificial. Alexander was indifferent to small talk. His wife despaired of him at social gatherings. He would not talk for the sake of talking or merely to let somebody else feel they were interesting or clever.

Whilst Tilly talked on about Alexa's cleverness in capturing her nephew's intractable affections, Alexander examined her minutely, smiling thinly. A good-looking little woman, he thought, smart but perhaps somewhat overdone. Not quite out of the top drawer, whatever her connections. There is something here, she seems to be interesting herself in this affair to quite an extent.

Tilly gave up the unequal task of engaging Alexander in rewarding conversation. She turned hopefully to Alexa.

"Alexa, *ma chère*, come here, let me look at you. You must call me Tilly, you know, everyone in the family does so!"

Alexa rose obediently and went to sit beside her. As she sat a cloud of dust rose from the sofa. Tilly noted it with exasperation. The very last thing Suzanne would ever do was to roll up her own sleeves.

"I should like that very much, *Madame*, if you are sure it is all right."

"I shall be offended if you don't," she took Alexa's hand and held it firmly. She was a lovely child. Fabrice was much more fortunate than he deserved. Did she guess how she was being manipulated? There was a reserve about her which made it impossible to tell. And her gown, such a success, so entirely suitable. The claret *soie sauvage*, with its neat modest bodice and full skirt echoed by tiny puffed sleeves, had a Victorian flavour, emphasising her youth and Englishness. Around her throat was a choker of seed pearls, three rows, perfectly matched. Edwardian probably, and not bought yesterday. It would be well to handle these Standevens carefully, everything about them spoke of a certain knowingness . . . something, she could not say quite what. She gave up the attempt to analyse the Standevens as Suzanne entered the room.

"*Maman*, you are late. Here are Alexa and Mr. Standeven waiting for you, what can they think of you!"

Suzanne's eyes flicked a startled glance in the direction of her son. He was not given to archness, let alone civility. Clearly, this Miss Standeven had deranged his wits.

"My apologies, I had lost all track of time. Do forgive me Mr. Standeven. So, this is Alexa, the beautiful Alexa. We have heard so much about you, my dear." Suzanne regarded her son's *financée* with a kind of rage. She was beautiful with an air of social relaxation and breeding that was unexpected and not wholly welcome. Alexa felt the cold fingers of the woman's dislike touch her.

With perfect composure, she spread her glowing skirts and executed a graceful little curtsey with a smile of such blinding radiance as to dissolve the older woman's frost in an instant. It was a moment of sheer enchantment. The warmth that had hitherto been lacking entered the room.

Alexander regarded his daughter curiously. Alexa had never done such a thing before. Like him, she was inclined to be a little stiff and remote, not given to effusive demonstrations of any sort. But she had shown great presence of mind and a confident, mature social touch which had surprised him. The curtsey had barely been an obeisance, simply a confiding acknowledgement of seniority. It seemed that, unlike him, his daughter was willing to charm with deliberation. Alexander was fascinated; the subtlety of the Standevens had take on an entirely new mutation.

It was to become typical of Alexa that she would perform best under pressure. She felt herself to be under pressure now. Nothing, but nothing must stand in her way of gaining the acceptance of these people. It was an irony of fate that she would never fully understand how anxious they were to gain an equal acceptance in her father's eyes and thus gain possession of her person. All she knew was that her future mother-in-law, that imposing but scandalously badly dressed female, had begun to dislike her, a danger that was now, temporarily at least, averted.

The presence of Jean-Claude Jouffre's child in her womb had not retired from her mind, but it had begun to take on the status of a near unreality, something that might happen in the distant future. Compared to the emergencies of the last thirty-six hours, the unalterable physical fact had lost its status as a priority.

Fabrice too, was charmed by the surprising curtsey. There was a stylish simplicity to her action that utterly belied her *bourgeois* origins. From some protective impulse he started across the room towards her. He fumbled with his stick and Alexander, on an instinct that was foreign to him, hastened to support him by the elbow. It seemed to everyone that after all, an auspicious start to future family relationships had been made.

As the lengthy and elaborate dinner drew to a close, Alexander, who had drunk with a deliberate abstemiousness, prepared to unnerve his hosts. It was a pity, he reflected sourly, that on the one night of his life when he might have drunk like a duke, he'd been forced to exercise an almost unnatural restraint in the service of Alexa's interests. He hoped, but did not believe, that his sacrifice might be rewarded in the future.

Evidently, there was still wine in these de Pies Ombre cellars that recalled a former grandeur. He had been served the best examples of the best vintages and he had known how to appreciate them, to the surprise and tempered gratification of the de Pies Ombre household. Having given a graceful display of his knowledge, Alexander had asked, "Would you, *Monsieur*, permit me a small indulgence?"

"But of course, whatever is in my power." Fabrice had grown expansive with alcohol. "Name it and it shall be done. Though

I should warn you, that the *droit de seigneur* is no longer an accepted thing,'' he glanced at the pretty hired waitress.

Alexander repressed a shudder. Of all things he detested sexual innuendo, and from a man younger than himself, it struck him as gauche. Alexa was appalled. Fabrice could hardly have damned himself more certainly in her father's eyes. His extreme delicacy in sexual matters was an odd quirk of his character and the few who transgressed in the matter were not soon forgiven.

"If it is not too gross an inconvenience, I should appreciate the opportunity to compare this stunning Château Palmer with a bottle of your own Château de Pies Ombre of the same year. I have, as I remarked, a case of your product in my cellar at home, but unhappily, it is of a recent vintage and a trial proved that your wine requires a sleep of seven years, or so I judge, before it can be fairly assessed. Nineteen fifty-nine was an exceptional year for your region. Do indulge me.'' Alexa heard the thread in his tone which was decipherable to no one else. He intended some sort of reproof. That much was clear. To drink the de Pies Ombre's wine was to drink their blood and he would doubtless find it wanting. There was an inexorable destructiveness about Alexander, a killer instinct that nothing would deny.

After so long and reasonable a speech, there could be no putting him off and Brun was despatched to find and decant a bottle of the '59. He was adept at getting his way, this Standeven. In spite of herself, Tilly warmed to him. He was really very handsome, it was not difficult to see where Alexa got her looks, and there was nothing provincial about his manner or conversation. The barest discernible trace of a northern accent only added to his grave charm. Tilly coquetted and Alexander noticed and gave no sign of it. He was aware of the rapacity of her stare which he regarded with cold satisfaction. That's one off her guard.

"Mmm, did it sell well?'' Alexander indicated his glass.

"I really could not say off-hand . . . the *négociants* and the accountants would know of course but I, unhappily, really cannot keep track of all these things,'' Fabrice floundered.

"You have a professional occupation? Alexa did not tell me. You must indeed have a great deal to attend to. But have you competent agents? Forgive me for asking, but after all, I am, reluctantly, concerned in the matter, as it is so soon to affect Alexa.''

"You say, 'reluctantly,' Mr. Standeven,'' the *Marquise*'s voice was sharp.

"Oh certainly. You know, of course, that my daughter is not of age. I really had never thought of her marrying so young. I feel a natural apprehension in allowing her to commit herself when she is, forgive me, my dear,'' Alexander hesitated, glancing at his daughter, "little more than an adolescent. Come, you would not think me much of a father if I were to consent to the first proposed bridegroom that Alexa presented for my approval. I am not only Alexa's father, her natural and legal guardian, but also her lawyer. I should be in breach of my duties if I did not conduct the most thorough investigation into all those affairs which will affect her security in the future.''

An audible gasp of dismay hung over the table. Fabrice was puzzled. He had been told, although in a somewhat vague manner, that the Standevens would welcome his marriage to their daughter. But that was natural enough. Alexa was somewhat less alarmed. Her father had consented privately to her marrying Fabrice. Whatever game he was playing now, it was played against the de Pies Ombres and not against her. Tilly and Suzanne, however, were taken aback. They had gone to great trouble and expense over this Mr. Standeven's entertainment. Was he about to render their efforts meaningless?

"I am afraid that I must tell you this so-called engagement cannot be regarded as a settled thing until the *Marquis* and I have had a long, and I hope, satisfactory talk. Of course should you care to depute your lawyers, *Monsieur*, that will be acceptable to me.''

Alexander nodded slightly in contentment. He had everyone's undivided attention.

CHAPTER
6

🎵🎵 ALEXA DECLINED THE *Marquise*'s invitation to accompany her and Fabrice down to the Château de Pies Ombre. Suzanne took it that her refusal stemmed from a desire to consider her trousseau at leisure, for she did not really believe that Alexander's threat to put a stop to the wedding would come to anything. Surely he would not deny his daughter the chance of making so advantageous a connection? The more realistic Tilly thought it entirely possible and was determined to do all she could to strengthen the resolve of the bride once she was no longer under the powerful influence of Mr. Standeven's personality.

In fact, Alexa was reluctant to intrude in a house where she felt she had no real right, as she would go there under false pretences. As yet she had found no opportunity of telling Fabrice that he must either accept the child of Jean-Claude Jouffre as his own, or their engagement must be terminated. She was beginning to feel a sort of paralysis creep over her. To break the engagement herself meant facing the cold fury of her father's well-remembered wrath and losing the *fiancé* of whom she became daily more fond. Alexa wrestled with the imprisoning toils of the deception that had grown around her, almost of their own accord. The longer she was silent, the more restricted did her scope for action become. She had tried to tell Fabrice, and Fabrice had refused to listen. Everything was proceeding at nerve-racking speed and there were no brakes that she could apply.

Towards the end of one restless night, she had fallen asleep just before dawn and dreamed of two motor cars, each setting out in the morning, from pleasant suburban houses. One had been green, she recalled later, and the other a white Rover. The Rover was a car her father had once had. In her dream, she knew that the drivers of the cars were set on a collision course. The crash would not happen till the late afternoon, but all day, those cars were fulfilling the choreography of a predestined but unconscious pattern which would lead, inexorably, to death. In one car there was a baby. Alexa was an invisible intelligence. She saw the cars and their drivers, blurred people with no identity, draw closer to their tragedy with terrible slowness. Her screams of warning were soundless, unheard and unheeded. She never saw the end, because she was awoken by her own cry.

Alexander assumed his daughter's unwillingness to accompany him to Bordeaux stemmed from an absolute confidence in his judgement, and a desire to allow him the maximum elbow room in which to manoeuvre. He admired her discretion but deplored her lack of curiosity. He himself would accept the hospitality of the de Pies Ombres for one night after his discussions with Maître Robinson in Bordeaux were completed.

Although the invitation to Alexander had been extended with a superficial grace, it had not been done willingly and had been accepted in the same reluctant spirit. Alexander regarded it as all the more essential to observe the domestic circumstances of the de Pies Ombres since Alexa would not do so for herself. It was a duty he would gladly have shirked, had any other method of testing the quality of Alexa's future life presented itself. He disliked the element of spying involved but it was hardly a mission which he could entrust to the care of a private investigator, who would be unlikely to be able to gather and interpret the kind of information he sought. The memory of Bottomley's blunderings still smarted. Moreover, Alexander dreaded the physical discomforts he anticipated in a draughty, ill-maintained country house no less than the company of the avidly watchful Suzanne. Fabrice he could tolerate. The fellow was quite amusing. He had a bone dry, bitter sense of humour which struck an answering chord in Alexander's own astringent nature.

In spite of his mother's efforts to deflect Alexander's penetrating enquiries, all couched in terms of the most friendly and natural interest, Fabrice had displayed an openness about his affairs that was as engaging as the revelations were shocking. The ingenuousness with which the young nobleman exposed his poverty was almost intriguing. If anything, Fabrice's bald admissions concerning the state of his affairs gave Alexander reason to hope that matters might be capable of improvement. He had always counselled his clients that the extent to which he

could help them was directly proportional to their willingness
to be open with him. There could be no question, he often said,
of losing face with one's doctor or one's lawyer. A full confes-
sion of the squalid facts, or humiliating symptoms, was the only
sound basis for a complete cure. Alexander appreciated Fabrice's candour and he said so.

"You have a great deal to accomplish here. Do you think you
can do it? Do you think you can offer my daughter, and any
children you may have, adequate comfort and security in the
long term?"

"I hope so sir," was all Fabrice answered.

Alexander chose to interpret it as a responsible reply and
preferred it to wild promises.

"Very well, then. I suppose I must give you my permission
to attempt it, if my daughter insists. I give you fair warning,
however: I regard the prospect of a marriage between yourself
and Alexa without enthusiasm, and although I shall not forbid
it, nor do anything to stand in her way or yours, I shall warn her
of what she faces. I shall tell her that she will be poorer than I
ever expected to see her, and I shall advise against it. But no, I
do not forbid it."

Alexa was comfortably ensconced at the Crillon, had daily employment of a more or less respectable nature, and, as Suzanne
had pointed out, the advantage of Tilly's friendly supervision.
Alexander entertained some doubts about the suitability of Madame La Courbe as a chaperone. He was unable to throw off
the impression that she had an interest in Alexa's proposed marriage to her nephew that transcended the understandable curiosity of an elderly aunt. There was an eagerness about Tilly that
disturbed him.

Alexa planned to devote the brief period of her father's absence from Paris to gathering her courage for the terrible scene
which would ensue when she told Fabrice first, and then her
father, that the whole marriage juggernaut must be halted and
why. That would stop the roller coaster of events dead in its
tracks. She must do it, she told herself, but deciding to do it
was something like deciding to commit suicide. It was worse.
While the de Pies Ombres and Monsieur Terry would continue
in their pre-ordained grooves of existence, she would be plunged
into a descending spiral of unknown horror and would be unable
to leave her family behind. They too, would be dragged into the

sucking quicksands of misery. Alexa examined these consequences and the little courage she had recruited melted away.

There remained a single alternative which required only one
victim. Her child could be sacrificed. An abortion might be
possible. However, she had nowhere to turn for help or advice.
Her imagination shrivelled at the thought of approaching Monsieur Terry on such a matter.

One day, after her work at Maison Terry was done, she telephoned Jean-Claude's office. Giselle was clearly confused to
hear Mademoiselle Standeven's voice on the telephone. She responded to Alexa's enquiry as to Jean-Claude's whereabouts
with a mixture of embarrassment and scorn.

"Monsieur Jouffre is not here," she said distantly.

"Then where is he? I must speak to him as soon as possible."

Anxious to protect her boss, knowing that the visit from Mr.
Standeven had in some way disturbed Jean-Claude, and correctly
surmising that he had been no other than Alexa's father, Giselle
insisted that Jean-Claude was out of town and she did not know
where to reach him. That Alexa was quite unaware that her father's
visit to Jean-Claude's office was something of which Giselle did
not know.

"But he will call you, won't he Giselle, to see if there are any
messages? Tell him that I must see him and that I am staying at
the Crillon. Please Giselle, it's terribly important."

The secretary only half agreed to pass on the message to her
employer, and Alexa had to be content with that.

At least, Alexa thought, nobody could have any idea that she
was pregnant. Her figure was still as slender as a willow wand
and the tape measure told her that she was actually thinner than
when she had first gone to work for Monsieur Terry. There was
no thickening at the waist, no distension of the abdomen, but
nor was there any period. It was perhaps two months already.

She hoped to hear from Jean-Claude, he was the only one she
could tell and the only one who could help her. The thought of
an abortion was abhorrent. In spite of her mounting terror of the
consequences of her pregnancy, the presence of the hidden child
had aroused feelings of tenderness in her that she did not know
she possessed. Silently, in her mind, she would talk to it, telling
it that she loved it, no matter how it had come into being, and that
she would think of something. At other times she reproached
herself for the sentimental absurdity of talking to someone who
was not, in any meaningful sense, really there at all.

One lunch time, after a busy and cheerful morning at Monsieur Terry's, she had gone with Sophie to the Boulevard Haussmann. They often had lunch together now, favouring the old-fashioned restaurant on the top floor of *Au Printemps*. On the way, Alexa's eye was caught by a brass plate indicating the consulting rooms of a gynaecologist. She said nothing but tears began to stream from her eyes unbidden. Sophie was surprised and attempted to comfort.

"It is nothing, *chérie*, just pre-wedding nerves. I know how it is, my sister was impossible before her marriage. Now she has three children and she is so happy she has become positively *fat*." Sophie patted her own flat abdomen complacently. "I tell you," she continued, "as soon as the wedding is over, you will laugh at yourself. I should get married as soon as you can."

Tilly was of the same mind.

"You will not think of waiting till after Lent, *ma chère* Alexa."

"What is the significance of Lent?" Alexa was confounded.

"Well, you cannot get married in Lent, can you?"

"Why not?"

Tilly smiled. A little Protestant barbarian. The charming ignorance of the English with their self-invented "Church of England." Who was it, she mused, who had called it "the Conservative Party at prayer"? Poor dear Alexa had a lot to learn. She wondered if it would be possible to get her converted and received into the True Church before the wedding. Perhaps not. Still, it was a pity, a *proper* wedding would be so much more fun to arrange. There was always an element of gloom about these mixed affairs.

"Alexa! It isn't done, *ma chère*. This is a *Catholic* country, remember!"

"Suppose we have a civil wedding."

"Well, you will be obliged to do that anyway, by law, but the heir to the de Pies Ombre name and estates must also be seen to have the 'benefit of clergy,' that is the phrase, is it not? Everyone will expect it. Oh yes, it is essential. The marriage of the Marquis de Pies Ombre is a great occasion. Besides there have been quite a few bishops in the family and there is the position of your son to consider . . ."

"What son?" Alexa spoke sharply, without her usual measured courtesy. She had been thrown momentarily off balance by the unexpected mention of progeny. "I'm sorry, Tilly," she apologised, "I think I'm fairly strung up you know, this has all been so terribly rushed . . ."

"Of course, *ma chère*, you have pre-wedding nerves. What could be more natural. You must be quite on edge, and with Fabrice away it's all so . . . No, I meant, of course, the son and heir we all hope you will give to Fabrice and the house of de Pies Ombre in the not too distant future. That is all."

"What is wrong with a wedding just before Lent?" Alexa had suggested that as a possible date. It would give her time.

"Too drear for words, *ma chère*. And in any case, where is the purpose? What would you do for four or five months? Continue to earn a pittance at Terry's? You could move in with me, of course, and run up handsome telephone bills talking to Fabrice. No, I cannot see any advantage in it. Once one has made up one's mind to marry, waiting around to see if one's mind might change seems a childish exercise to me. All this 'getting to know one another,' however are you to occupy the first year of marriage, before the children arrive to interrupt the tête-à-tête? No, it is much better to leave some topics of conversation untouched, you will need them."

"But that only leaves from now until Christmas."

"Exactly. I saw that when dear Mr. Standeven gets back and has said his piece, you and Fabrice should tie the knot without delay. Poor Fabrice, he has waited so long for this day to come. Why torture him?"

"All right," she responded rather unenthusiastically, Tilly thought, "as long as Daddy has no objection."

"Good. That is settled then. You see how quickly things are decided when women are in charge? I shall give you some more coffee and then call a taxi for you. You need your sleep."

Tilly poured out the coffee from the magnificent Georg Jensen coffee pot wearing an expression familiar on the faces of those who have just completed a difficult phase of a large administrative task. Alexa was not ungrateful for Tilly's interest in her affairs. But she was certain that Tilly would be the wrong person to confide in.

Alexa sipped the coffee in reflective silence whilst Tilly chatted cheerfully about clothes. She was careful to keep her eyes on the older woman's face. It was a trick she had learned from Alexander, though never previously employed. It gave the impression of attention while allowing one leisure for one's own thought. The calm of despair enfolded her. After a while she became aware that Tilly had been talking for rather a long time. Alexa knew she was failing in her duty as a guest. She must make some conversation. Tilly should not be left chattering to herself or entertaining an unresponsive audience. Alexa's early social training reasserted itself.

"Tell me something, Tilly."

"Anything, *ma chère*," she responded lightly, screwing a Black Russian cigarette into her amber holder. What an appetite for information these Standevens have. So thorough.

"What about the vineyards?"

"You mean Fabrice's?"

"Yes, aren't they profitable?"

Tilly sighed. She was tired and a little off her guard. Alexa was a soothing guest, so polite and attentive. She laughed at one's jokes and seemed deeply interested in what one said. In no time at all, one was actually fond of her and treating her as if she were of the same blood. What a curious knack she had. While remaining at a cool and courteous distance, never casual or presumptuous, she actually managed to create intimacy, something that left one longing to reveal more of oneself than was safe.

"No, I'm afraid not. In fact, I think they've made a loss for several years now. Fabrice doesn't take much interest, you know. His father never did either. In fact it would surprise me if Fabrice knew one tenth as much about claret as your father does." They both laughed. "Things have been allowed to slide for twenty years now, since Fabrice's grandfather died. He was the last person to know or care about it."

Alexa's eyes were now alert with unfeigned attention.

"Oh, to be sure, Fabrice does potter a bit. I suppose going to the *chai* every now and again gives him a good excuse to get out of Suzanne's way. Every man should have a job if he does not belong to a club. Now if Fabrice lived in England, he would be sure to go to the House of Lords to doze the day away, just like your English lords one reads about. And when he had woken up, why, then he would go to his club in St. James and doze some more in greater comfort."

Alexa laughed, genuinely amused by Tilly's impression of a day in the life of an English peer.

"But Tilly, quite a lot of our lords, most in fact, spend an awful lot of time in the country. What do you think Fabrice would do there?"

"Examine pigs, one imagines, or whatever frightful animal could be inspected at length and without result."

"Daddy will know that nobody puts much effort into the vineyards, won't he?" Alexa asked seriously. Tilly sighed again.

"I imagine he's bound to, and in any case, the clever man tasted the neglect in the bottle, he won't need to see the weeds, will he?"

"No, he won't," Alexa replied thoughtfully. "Daddy's very interested in wine."

"So we all observed. And not afraid to voice his reactions. Such a confident man."

Consternation spread in Alexa's eyes.

"He wasn't rude, surely, I don't think he meant to be. It's just that he's very interested."

"Oh, *certainly* not rude, but nothing escapes his notice does it?"

"Not much, I'm afraid," Alexa said softly.

"And you too, Alexa. You are an observant child, are you not? For instance, forgive me, but you were aware of some little degree of . . . well, shall we say, hostility for want of a better word—I'm sure it wasn't really as strong as that, but *something* not quite positive in Suzanne's attitude towards you, when we all met at the house in the Marais, for dinner that evening?"

"Suzanne?"

"Yes, *Madame la Marquise*, your future mother-in-law. Soon to be the Dowager Marquise." A note of ill-natured satisfaction was to be detected in Tilly's tone. Her cousin's title had always galled her.

"Yes, I did notice something of the sort," Alexa was guarded, "but what had I done?" The dark blue eyes were fixed invitingly on Tilly's face. If she was in the mood to communicate, knowledge was something Alexa could never have enough of.

"Nothing at all! You were better looking, better dressed and better brought up than she anticipated, you see. Than *any* of us anticipated, frankly. She looked forward to meeting a suburban Miss whom she could easily overawe. What a disappointment! Instead she was confronted by a young woman who was splendidly equipped to take on her role. A supplanter. But you handled it beautifully, *ma chère*, quite beautifully. What an inspiration! That curtsey, so exquisitely done. You would have melted the heart of the Sphinx. But, have a care, I've known Suzanne all my life. She's not very, how do you say it . . . bright? But she is proud, arrogant even, and of course, she is the most tremendous snob. She can be dangerous. Stupid people so frequently are, don't you find?''

Alexa was listening with intense concentration.

''Oh, do not be alarmed, the last thing I want to do is to give you cause for undue anxiety. You will be able to manage her, I have little doubt. Just remember that you have this grumbling little volcano of resentment and snobbery on your hands. She erupts occasionally and the flow of lava, although not impressive, could inflict a nasty burn.''

Tilly's terrifyingly *chic* maid opened the double doors into the *salon*.

''Le taxi de Mademoiselle attend en bas, Madame.''

''There now, time to go and get your beauty sleep, *ma chère*, though heaven knows, you hardly seem to need it. I, unfortunately, do. I must lie down to counteract the merciless drag of gravity. This is obviously the import of the English phrase, 'the weight of years,' you know.''

Alexa laughed. Tilly was a wit. It might not be advisable to trust her unreservedly, but she felt she had made her first friend in Fabrice's orbit. She did not know what the future held, but she was grateful for Tilly's goodwill.

''Goodnight *Tante* Tilly, and thank you, it's been lovely.''

Tilly rose and took both Alexa's hands in her own, looking up into the tall girl's calm and lovely face, the deep velvet eyes so full of intensity. She looked a little pale, perhaps. It would be the strain of waiting, Tilly concluded. But it was the look in the eyes that struck one most forcibly. A thirst, that is it, Tilly thought, a veritable thirst. What is it she yearns for? Perhaps it is everything . . . to do, to be, to know. Ah yes, particularly to know.

''I like you, Miss Alexa Standeven.'' To prevent her from speaking, Tilly increased the pressure on Alexa's hands. She could feel Tilly's rings bite into her own fingers. ''You are better than you know. You have quality. You will make something of Fabrice, of the de Pies Ombres . . . Perhaps because of you, their star will rise again. Take care of yourself, *ma chère*, and *écoutez bien*, if you ever feel the need of a friend, I hope you will come to me, I shall be honoured. Now, kiss me child. All this seriousness is debilitating to the constitution.''

The short taxi ride from the Etoile to the Place de la Concorde scarcely gave Alexa time to ruminate on Tilly's words although she was aware that a good deal of information had been conveyed to her during the course of their evening together.

She was warmed by the worldly old woman's offer of friendship, it seemed sincere. She might need it, but how genuine and how effective it would prove to be when put to the test, Alexa could not have said. It was almost as though Tilly had some presentiment of threat.

Alexa looked out of the rain-splashed windows of the taxi. The lights of Paris seemed at first remote from reality. She ought to regard this city as her own now, the capital city of her country of adoption. What would happen in the end was obscured from her view, like a crucial page missing from a book. But it is impossible to ride through the lights of a great city at night and not feel the heart beat a faint answering tattoo.

By the time she had paid off the taxi, Alexa's spirits had lifted in one of the irrational rising currents which are the privilege of youth. Nothing was better, and yet everything was better, because she was young and could not stay miserable for very long at a time.

She fumbled for her key in her evening bag. Damn, it was not there. She must have left it at the desk. She would have to go all the way down to the ground floor again. She really must adopt one policy for hotel room keys and stick to it, otherwise she could foresee a life-time of trailing up and down in lifts. It was such a tiresome waste of time and energy.

The hall porter on duty had not got it either. There was the empty hook, as he so expressively demonstrated. Suite 19, no key. She searched the small *petit point* bag again. No, it was definitely not there. A comb, an embroidered linen handkerchief, a few francs, a lipstick and a cigarette case. Nothing else. Exasperated, she sorted through the few items on the desk as if trying to make one of them turn into a key. The porter sighed, he disparaged the inefficiency of guests over the matter of keys. The British, he had observed, were outstandingly careless. He lifted a telephone and spoke a few words in the rapid, incomprehensible *argot* of Paris.

"It is all right, *Mademoiselle*. The concierge on your floor has a pass key and she will open the door for you. Perhaps you will find that you left the key inside the room. It happens," he conceded generously. Normally, he would have made more difficulties about the matter. Night duty was inclined to be dull. But the young lady was so elegant. It would be cruel to let her suffer from confusion longer.

"Voilà, Mademoiselle." The crisply uniformed chamber maid returned the pass key on its chain to her pocket. *"Bonne nuit."* Alexa watched her retreat briskly down the thickly carpeted corridor, returning purposefully to whatever were the nocturnal concerns of chamber maids.

.Alexa pushed the door open. Immediately, the rush of air from the darkened room informed her senses that it was occupied. This was not the atmosphere that she had left five hours ago. In a flash of sensory perception, too complex to analyse, her nerve ends picked up the vibrations. There was someone in there. A presence that lay in wait. How stupid. Alexa jeered at herself. If there were such things as ghosts, they did not frequent impersonal hotel rooms. Ridiculous. She squared her shoulders subconsciously, ready to meet the danger which her conscious mind told her could not possibly exist. She groped for the light switch. Her fingers made contact with it after what seemed an age of futile, blind searching. Light flooded the little drawing room and she exhaled breath as a diver does when resurfacing, luxuriating in oxygen and safety regained. For an immeasurable particle of time, her eyes refused to register the male figure seated on the brocaded chair facing the door.

The telephone rang in one of the adjoining bedrooms. Hers, the one Henry had vacated on the day his granddaughter had moved in.

"You'd better answer that. A most persistent caller. Rings every hour on the hour. The *Marquis*, mebbee." Jean-Claude waved a whisky tumbler vaguely in the direction of the bedroom. His speech was slurred.

Mechanically, she crossed the room, throwing a glance at Jean-Claude. His face was flushed, his eyes unfocused. The key was stuffed into his breast pocket. How did he get it? A bribe?

Entering her bedroom, she picked up the bedside telephone while her mind raced with myriad darting thoughts, minnows in a rain-swollen stream. There was nobody there, whoever it was had hung up. The receiver purred emptily, mindlessly in her hand.

She held it for a moment, Jean-Claude was here now. She had wanted to see him, but she was unprepared. She had no idea how to begin this conversation. How did you tell someone you were pregnant with their child and ask them to pay for an abortion?

Her eyes ranged the room as if some clue or inspiration might come leaping forward out of some neglected detail. There was nothing. Her gaze returned to its starting point, to the bedside table. On it there was a bottle of *Arpège*, Parfum de Toilette. An atomiser, with the lid off. She had bought it at Galeries Lafayette only yesterday. Dragging her eyes away, she looked again at the rest of the room. The *Toile de Jouy* curtains were drawn, the toilet articles on the dressing table had been put in order, the counterpane removed and the bed turned down. Her night gown had been laid out on the bed with a respectful carefulness that seemed to mock the inexpensive garment. Everything was, in fact, precisely as usual. Just the one neglected detail.

"*Monsieur Le Marquis*, one assumes. Telephoning to whisper . . . sweet nothings."

Jean-Claude's tall figure blocked light from the drawing room. He kissed his finger tips sarcastically, leaning unsteadily against the door frame.

"Jean-Claude, I am so glad to see you. Thank heaven you came, but you should not have waited. It must have been very inconvenient for you."

"Oh, my dear Alexa, when a *Marquise* calls, one obeys. Particularly," he added, "if she is the daughter of Alexander Standeven." His voice was cold and hostile. He loosened his tie. So he had heard about her engagement. But she did not understand the reference to her father. It seemed of no moment. She must get him to pay attention.

"There is something you ought to know. Shall we go into the other room? I could get you another drink."

"Aha! The *Marquise* waits on the common man! Very laudable, very *grande dame*. No I don't want another drink. I'm drunk, as you can see. Do you know why I'm drunk, Alexa?"

"I think we should go back to the sitting room. It's silly standing here to talk, when it's so much more comfortable in there."

Alexa had never seen him drunk before. Indeed, she had never seen anyone she knew drunk before. She could not distinguish between the ordinary, acceptable cheerfulness induced by wine and the dangerous, mindless violence that some personalities display when distorted by large quantities of alcohol in the bloodstream.

"So much more comfortable in there, is it?" He mimicked her speech cruelly. "Well, you will have plenty of time to be comfortable as the Marquise de Pies Ombre. You are moving so fast into spheres beyond my reach, Alexa. No doubt you were assisted to this high position in the world by the adroit Mr. Standeven. What will he be extorting from the *Marquis* for the pleasure of sleeping with his precious daughter? I hope he can afford it.'' The empty whisky glass dangled from his hand.

"I'm sorry, Jean-Claude, I just don't know what you're talking about. Please can't we go and sit down?''

"Twenty thousand pounds sterling, is what I'm talking about, my dear. And I don't think I've had my money's worth. Do you? So I intend to put that right. We aren't going to sit down, we're going to lie down and I'm going to get a bit of what I came for.''

Alexa's heart sank. This wasn't the way she'd planned things. Jean-Claude was talking nonsense. There was something wrong. It was all going to be more difficult than she had thought.

She walked firmly towards the door, where his figure was silhouetted against the light coming from the room beyond. She tried to push past him. He caught her wrist and held it in a vice-like grip. It was impossible to twist her hand away.

"Let go of my hand, you are hurting me.'' He did not let go.

"Jean-Claude, I do not know what all this extraordinary business is about, but unless you let go of my hand at once, and start behaving reasonably, I shall call for assistance.. I just wanted to talk to you about something, that's all.''

Instantly, he twisted her hand behind her back and wrenched up her arm painfully so that she could not move.

"You may have wanted, a what do you call it? A *chat*, but I do not, I want something entirely different. Something worth money on the streets of Paris if only you knew it. So, Alexa, call for assistance. How will you do it? Be telephoning? By going to the door and shouting? By just shouting?'' He jerked her arm again, painfully. "I think shouting is your best course of action. Of course you will get a broken arm, I shall see to that, but yes, shouting is an excellent idea. Pray begin. Proceed with the shouting, I am ready.''

Alexa gasped with pain, her mind filled with it and unable to encompass any other thought than the need to escape the agonising sensation in her shoulder joint.

"Why *are* you here, Jean-Claude. If you didn't come because I asked you to, what do you want with me? I was under the impression you wanted *nothing* further to do with me, that *was* what your disgusting note meant, I take it?'' She felt his grasp slacken slightly and instantly tried to wrench herself free. It was no good, he tightened his grip again, giving her arm another savage jerk.

"I find, *chérie*, now that I come to re-examine the accounts, as it were, that I have paid rather too dearly for what I had. I have come to claim the balance of what is owing to me. Twenty thousand pounds is rather steep, even for a *Marquise*. I have been overcharged."

"For God's sake, Jean-Claude I still don't know what you're talking about, Jean-Claude, let go!"

"Are you in pain, *ma belle*? I hope so. Who could deserve the experience more? Except perhaps, Mr. Standeven and unfortunately, what I plan for you would not suit him. But you must tell him all about it, won't you? Then perhaps he can think of even larger sums." His lips were withdrawn from his teeth in an animal snarl. Grasping her other arm, he twisted it behind her back so that she had the same searing pain in both shoulders and was held helpless and immobile.

"I have paid, and now you are going to pay. You may enjoy it, I hope you will. But let me tell you, *chérie*, this time, your enjoyment is of little importance to me. This time is entirely for me. For me, do you understand?"

Awkwardly, he manoeuvered her over to the bed, she tried to kick backwards at his legs, to stab his shins with her stiletto-heeled shoe but she only succeeded in stumbling clumsily. He thrust her down onto the bed and held her pinioned by her wrists. At least there was some relief from the appalling pain in her shoulders. A trial told her she could not, even now, escape the grasp.

"Yes, quite a man, Mr. Standeven." She felt the blast of his alcohol-laden breath on her cheek and twisted her face away. "And now, *chérie*, you are going to find out what kind of man I can be. Oh, yes, my breath stinks, no doubt. That is just one of the things you are going to have to put up with." Alexa thought rapidly and decided to make one more attempt to dislodge his hold. She gave a tremendous surge of physical effort, but his weight and the advantage he derived from being on top of her made it impossible. He laughed derisively, beneath his breath.

"No, no Alexa, don't waste your energy. I am going to have you the way I want you and you are going to remember the experience all your life, *ma chère*." He raised his hips and placing one arm across her throat, used his other hand to undo his fly.

I must respond, the thought came to her mind as if from some exterior source. He will relax if I seem to want him. Act. Forget this is rape, try and remember how you used to feel. She raised a hand and tentatively caressed his face. Violently, he knocked her hand aside and wrenched the front panel of her silk jersey dress away, the soft fabric ripping easily in his hands. Alexa, repressing an impulse to vomit, grasped his hand and pressed it to her breast. Simulating a passion she did not feel, she began to move her hips rhythmically, murmuring in a low, languorous tone inarticulate sounds, raising her head, she kissed his face, nibbling his lobes with tiny bites. She felt his body go limp and he too began to moan, his hand searching among her disordered skirts, probing her secret parts.

His face was buried in her breasts and she stroked his hair with her left hand, grinding her pelvis against his. Her right hand stretched out towards the bedside table and closed silently round the perfume atomiser.

"Jean-Claude, look at me, my darling, look at me," she pleaded. There was a moment of absolute stillness before his fists began to flail and his bellow of pain and rage filled the room, the sound reverberating off the walls and seeming to double in volume. With an agile bound, Alexa rolled off the bed gathering the shreds of her clothing about her.

"Shut up. Shut up unless you want to be carted off the premises to the *gendarmerie* as a failed rapist. What a figure you will cut! Get out. Get out of here and shut up."

Jean-Claude was rolling in agony on the bed, his hands to his eyes. Alexa pushed him on to the floor and dragged him to his feet, guiding his stumbling footsteps to the door of the suite.

"You have not had me, you have not had me the way you wanted me, but I *shall* remember the experience all my life. You were right about that. Think yourself lucky if I decide not to call the police."

Pushed by Alexa, he blundered blindly out into the corridor and she slammed the door and secured it. Her mind was clear and alert. The telephone rang in her room. Whoever it is, she thought, I must not sound out of breath. *This has not happened.*

"Alexa?"

She heard her mother's voice, sharp with the anger that anxiety always stimulated in her.

Softly, Alexa replaced the receiver. She couldn't talk to her mother now. She lay down on the bed and sobbed.

CHAPTER
7

🎴🎴 ALEXANDER KEPT HIS promise both to Alexa and Fabrice. He did not, on his return from Bordeaux, withdraw his reluctant permission for the marriage. He perceived the aura of desperation which had surrounded his daughter ever since their reunion in the Hotel Crillon as a fixed determination to marry Fabrice de Pies Ombre at no matter what cost. He felt that Alexa had reached that first moment of true adulthood that enables a child to reject a parent's advice with regret and good manners and proceed to an act of defiance which may separate them for ever. Rather than erect such a barrier as would prevent her from seeking his help in the future, or prevent him from giving it, he chose to make a door. He reasoned that the door would be closed during the period of her marriage for as long as it should prosper, but it could be opened at any time when help was needed.

None-the-less while he was still able, before the day appointed for the wedding, Alexander did all in his power to dissuade his daughter from the catastrophic step she seemed determined to take. He failed, as he knew he would. For the first time in his experience of Alexa, she had distanced herself from all reason. She treated the laws of logic and evidence as if they were the rules of a childish game, useful only in the context of that play, which she had now outgrown. It was not an arena familiar to Alexander and he floundered as any creature will, out of its natural element.

It was in vain that Alexander summarised his long conversation with Maître Robinson, the de Pies Ombres' Bordeaux lawyer. The Frenchman's loyalties had been torn. Like so many Bordelais, he was a Protestant and bore an English name. He warmed instinctively to his English counterpart and sympa-

thised with his anxieties concerning the practicalities of his
daughter's marriage.

"In short, *Monsieur*, I cannot advise it. The de Pies Ombres
are my clients, as they were my father's clients before me, but
my professional loyalty to them does not compel me to pretend
that their affairs are other than in considerable disarray."

Alexander's mouth was compressed into a thin line and his
breath came in meditative puffs. He glanced about the handsomely furnished, dusty room. The breakfront bookcases, filled
with sombre, leather bound tomes, the papers and files, interspersed with silver framed family photographs, strewn in de-
ceptively random patterns on mahogany tables. It recalled the
atmosphere of his own office to him. Maître Robinson was of
his own kind, a decent, scholarly man. A man versed in the
ways of the world, who knew that happiness must be financed
as other enterprises are financed. He shook his head as if to
clear it.

"She seems determined. I cannot begin to comprehend it,
but no amount of argument or warning will dissuade her. And
no, she is *not* a fool. But suddenly she seems impulsive, whereas
before, she was cautious. Sluggish would almost be a better
word. She is, of course, deficient in what my wife calls 'common sense,' she has never been allowed to develop much. She
is not worldly wise . . . how could she be? But I don't believe
her to be a *stupid* girl."

"It is . . ." Maître Robinson hesitated, "forgive me . . . the
title, probably?"

"I have wondered, although I rather doubt it."

"Alternatively, my friend, have you considered, that your
daughter may have . . . er, an emergency of a personal nature?
Perhaps the young people have anticipated . . ."

"That is impossible." Alexander was short. No, he had not
considered it, nor would he.

"Then," said the French lawyer, "we had better make what
arrangements we can."

He pressed a switch down on the desk-top apparatus which
resulted in the appearance of a dapper clerk who was sent away
at once to fetch some papers. He returned some moments later
and helped his employer to clear the top of the partner's desk
and unroll a large map, the curling edges of which were weighted
with random objects, spirit decanters, mineral specimens and a
door stop.

"You see here a plan of the Haut Médoc holdings of the de Pies Ombre family as they exist at the present moment. The relevant areas are all hatched in red. The areas which are cross-hatched in black are mortgaged, and in some instances re-mortgaged, for the most part to the Crédit des Vignerons Bank, here in Bordeaux. These same areas, comprising in total an area of sixty hectares, are under vines, as you would expect. The areas delineated by bold black lines and cross-hatched in green are let to small farmers. They comprise three hectares, no more."

Alexander rose and gave the plan his undivided attention.

"The property is totally encumbered?"

"*Almost* entirely, but you will remark these two isolated lots, here and here," Maître Robinson indicated two small, separate parcels lying away from the main mass of the property surrounding the château itself, "together, they comprise a total of five and a half acres, using your measurements. As you will observe, they are free of encumbrance. They alone remain unmortgaged and unlet."

The lawyers straightened, their eyes met in perfect understanding.

"And what, if anything, is on this land?"

"Nothing. They are virtually derelict. It is unusual in this part of the world, to find land, any land, which is not exploited. However, these two small neglected plots have escaped attention and no attempt to raise capital on them has been made. I suggest we make these the basis of a marriage settlement for your daughter. Land in the Médoc can never be quite worthless. It would be better than nothing. Not immediately useful, perhaps, but . . . who knows?"

"What else is there?"

"Pouf!" Maître Robinson raised both his arms in the air in the classic Gallic gesture of desperation, "Nothing *Monsieur*, nothing. Nothing, that is, except a few family trusts from which the increasingly slender income dwindles ever more rapidly. When the trusts were set up in the time of the present *Marquis*'s grandfather, inflation such as we are experiencing now was unimaginable. No, my friend, take my advice, take the land. Insist upon it."

The Roman Catholic Church used to treat any of its sons or daughters who chose to marry with individuals not of their own faith with a notorious churlishness and imposed a set of oppressive conditions on the non-Catholic party that was apt to provide any such partnership with a set of inauspicious tensions from the outset. Those tensions, for the most part impinged directly on the outraged friends and family of the non-Catholic party and at second hand on the *fiancé* who saw the difficulties merely as stony components of the classic path of true love.

At the time of Alexa's engagement to Fabrice de Pies Ombre, the Second Vatican Council was a comparatively recent event. The radical implications of the resolutions of that historic assembly were not always and everywhere immediately understood, let alone put into practice. Many of the clergy, including Tilly's pet priest, went on as if almost nothing had happened, impervious to the new spirit of oecumenicalism which had found expression at the Council.

Père Lachasse, who regularly dined with Tilly when she entertained her eclectically chosen crowd of slightly *outré* friends, accepted the task of administering pre-marriage instruction and counselling to the Marquis de Pies Ombre and his *fiancée*. Tilly made it clear that if he could achieve a rush conversion of Alexa, she would be grateful. She would rather arrange a *real* wedding, as she put it, than a hole-and-corner affair. Since Tilly had some useful connections amongst senior French churchmen and even a contact or two in Rome, the careerist Lachasse was more than willing to attempt it.

Partly because time was ridiculously short and partly because Lachasse was more comfortable in the company of old ladies than young ones, he set about his task in a manner not calculated to appeal to a proud young woman with a capacity for detached, critical analysis.

Fabrice was bored and embarrassed and Alexa regarded the exasperated priest with the wide-eyed synthetic concentration she had learned from her father. Lachasse, who had never experienced the quality of her genuine attention, decided that in creating Mademoiselle Standeven, the Lord had decided to expend the greater part of his resources on external attractions and practise the strictest economy in the matter of brain and soul.

Alexa might have taken more interest if her heart had been light. As it was, her spirits were crushed on the one side by the disastrous failure of her effort to enlist Jean-Claude's help in terminating her pregnancy, and on the other by the absolute impossibility of now revealing it.

Quite often she found herself on the edge of tears, at one moment speaking soundlessly to the baby, apologising for having intended it any harm, and at another, telling herself there was nothing there which was capable of reproach or emotion, any more than a corn on her foot. And again, for increasingly long periods, she was able to forget all about it as her mind defended itself from stress it was unable to bear.

Despairingly, Lachasse reported his poor progress to Madame la Courbe.

Tilly sighed and gave up any idea of an elaborate wedding. It was a pity. She had been prepared to contribute lavishly to expenses for the pleasure of seeing her nephew and charming young friend launched with style and her own photograph in the glossier society magazines where it had not appeared for a depressingly long time.

In addition to the penal austerities of the permitted ceremony, there was a further obstacle to its smooth performance. Elizabeth Standeven categorically refused to attend any ceremony that took place within the polluted walls of a Roman Catholic church. Accordingly, Tilly decided that it would be most expedient to make the ceremony private. The marriage vows would be exchanged in the *Grand Salon* of the house in the Marais. Alexa was to use Tilly's *appartement* as her bridal headquarters, vacating her room at the Crillon. Alexander would remain there, to be joined by his wife on the wedding eve, when the civil formalities at the Hôtel de Ville would be completed.

The late-October weather was bright, the air just beginning to sharpen, foretelling frost. The special limpidity of Autumn sunlight was frustrated in its attempt to penetrate the *Grand Salon* as all the windows were thickly filmed with dirt, thus diffusing the light and lowering its intensity. The effect was to make the setting for Alexa's wedding and the cast of subsidiary characters who stood waiting for her seem to be one of those hand-tinted sepia photographs in which only a suggestion of colour is overlaid on the general effect of brownness. The result somehow emphasises the gulfs of time and distance between the subject of the photograph and the one who examines it.

It was upon this scene that Alexa broke, dominating it with ease and supplying the brightness to which all eyes were drawn. She herself opened the rosewood doors at the far end of the *salon* and paused for a moment, allowing the full impact of her whiteness to register in contrast with the blackness of the ante-

chamber behind. Leaving the doors for Tilly to close, she walked
alone, the forty feet or so towards where Père Lachasse had set
up his temporary altar on a marble console table, two candles
reflecting dimly in the dingy pier glass behind. She seemed like
a column of white marble being moved into its final position of
honour. There was no smile on her face, nor did she draw any
smiles from those assembled. Momentarily, she turned her head
towards her mother, allowing the navy blue of her eyes to warm
to royal.

In the last few hours before the wedding, Alexa had seemed
to Tilly, who had cosseted the bride since her early awakening,
to be more than usually courteous, gentle, charming and considerate. There was also an atmosphere of other-worldliness
about her which was all most satisfactorily bridal and magical.
For someone whom Lachasse had reported as being totally without any spiritual dimension, on her wedding morning, Alexa
appeared saintly enough to the cynical old socialite.

She had eaten no more than a mouthful or two of *croissant*,
had drunk half a cup of coffee and listened kindly to the garru-
lousness of the hairdresser Carita had sent to attend to her *coiffure*. Mentally, Tilly compared Alexa to Marie Antoinette
immediately before that lady's horrific execution. Her graciousness had that quality about it that made the older woman begin
to tiptoe around the *appartement* as if she were supervising the
last moments of a saint on the threshold of martyrdom, rather
than those of a young girl on the brink of matrimony.

At first, when Tilly had explained that it would be necessary
for her and Fabrice to listen to a series of "little talks" from
Père Lachasse, Alexa had entertained great hopes of the priest.
She would be able to tell him everything and then, he would
somehow help her to put matters right. Very quickly she realised
that there would be no help forthcoming from that quarter. Lachasse gave the impression that he would turn away in disgust
from the sight of a sow farrowing. For Lachasse, the body and
its accidents did not exist. Fabrice had encapsulated the priest's
utter uselessness one day when he had asked Alexa, '"Do you
suppose Lachasse ever has a pee?'' They had both laughed and
agreed he probably found some way to avoid it.

As every possible escape route had closed, Alexa's sensation
of abandonment increased. By the morning of her wedding she
was certain that she had done her best to be honest and that
people and circumstances had closed every door in her face. A

sense of unreality invaded her. She had been left in sole possession of a solitary, important and unstated fact. It was not her
wish and not her fault. She would be blamed for it no doubt,
when it became apparent, but in the meantime she would behave
as well as she could and enjoy her wedding day. Tilly had taken
a good deal of trouble over the affair, and after all, for all she
knew, it might be the last happy day.

When she entered the *Grand Salon*, Alexander perceived that
his daughter had unsheathed a sword of determination from
within the soft scabbard of her yielding exterior, which for so
many years had been the familiar Alexa. In the past few days he
had seen flashes of metal, now he saw the awesome weapon in
its entirety. All along, she had carried something with her, of
which they knew nothing. They had bred her, Elizabeth and
himself; this regal woman was recognisably their own flesh and
blood. The Standevens watched with an ache in their hearts as
the impressive stranger passed them by.

Monsieur Terry was there with his wife at Alexa's insistence.
Her former employer silently saluted Alexa. With a shock he
realised that although he had never intended it to happen, he
had arranged all this. It had been a mere contingency plan, and
rather a long shot at that. He hoped it would all work out well.
Throughout the brief ceremony, Monsieur Terry's thoughts were
occupied with the hair-thin division between taking a Christian
and compassionate interest in the affairs of one's fellow human
beings and dangerous meddling. If he *had* been guilty of the
latter, he hoped God would forgive him. Interference *was* his
strongest temptation after gluttony.

The gown had been Monsieur Terry's wedding gift. He examined it with satisfaction as Alexa passed close by his elbow.
It was probably the best thing he had ever done. It had been
devised to express happiness, solemnity and importance and to
specifically exclude any taint of hilarity, gradeur or self-
importance. The floor-length column of unpressed pleats fell
from a strictly cut shirt-waist bodice, in a fabric of ethereally
fine cream wool used for novices' veiling. It had facings of white
satin which gleamed softly in the reduced light. Tilly had lent a
mantilla of precious antique lace grown creamy with age, and
an elaborate Spanish comb over which to wear it. Around her
neck she wore a narrow velvet band of pale blue from which
depended Fabrice's wedding present, a simple cross of white
baguette diamonds.

As she advanced towards him, Fabrice turned to look at the virtually unknown woman who was his bride. He liked her. He supposed he must love her, that was the view everyone else seemed to take. He shrugged imperceptibly and made a wry face at Alexa who responded with a faint, apologetic smile.

PART TWO

CHAPTER
8

ALEXA'S EYE WAS caught and enraptured by her first sight of the Château d'Ombre. Fabrice called it the "Witches' Hat school of architecture," and although Alexa was amused by this laconic description, she could not endorse the criticism it implied. To her it seemed the embodiment of all nursery imaginings, a random composition of features, whose functions had long been forgotten in the mists of an interesting past. Fabrice was deprecating.

"It's only a pantomime castle, darling. Don't be too impressed."

"I'm impressed just because it *is* a pantomime castle! All our castles are so boringly stolid. It is so absolutely clear from looking at them that life in the Middle Ages was nasty, brutish and *very* cold."

"I'm afraid that the Château d'Ombre didn't exist in the Middle Ages. What you have here is much more ordinary. The core of the house is just a simple, two-storey manor house built sometime in the sixteenth century. Everything else was added at odd times during the last century when there was plenty of money about because of the claret boom. So the riot of towers and turrets is pure Second Empire fantasy."

"It's still wonderful, Fabrice. You can't make me despise it, I've always loved anything remotely 'Gothic' even if it is Victoriana. How many rooms has it got?"

"It depends what you're prepared to call a room. Once, when I was about nine, a young cousin from Algeria came to stay for the summer. I didn't like him much and left him pretty much to himself. He did a lot of what he called 'exploring' on his own. I thought it was a damned cheek. Perhaps I was just jealous that

I couldn't keep up with him. Anyway, he made a very thorough tour of the house and said he counted exactly a hundred rooms. But he would have counted every linen cupboard, pantry and coal cellar in that total, you know.''

"Like small boys do. I should have done just the same.''

"Why? Were you a tomboy?''

"No, not really, but I felt I had to put some sort of an act on to explain the clothes I was wearing. You see unless we were going out or doing something specific, like having visitors, my mother always made my sister and me wear trousers.''

"How very odd.''

"Yes, wasn't it? I suppose the result was that deep down one was much more romantic and imaginative than other children, a sort of resistance to being forcibly desexed. I don't think she *meant* to do that, she was just very careful that nobody should think we were being brought up to be anybody's wives. She was bringing *me* up to be what she wasn't, a lawyer. It was a sort of protective purdah. I suppose if she knew I looked at it like that she'd be terribly shocked. Anyway, I expect it saved a lot of washing too.''

Fabrice laughed. "That's what made you a good model. The exhilaration was real.''

"Oh, absolutely. To be a girl, just a girl, and *paid* for it was like living in a fairytale.''

"And then you married Bluebeard.''

"Very well worth it, to get my hands on Bluebeard's castle.'' Alexa's glance was nervously affectionate.

Their relationship had altered subtly in the few days since the wedding in Paris. The banter continued but covered a growing wariness that was becoming a strain on both. Fabrice waited for Alexa to relax and Alexa, tense with concealed anxiety, waited for an opportunity to unburden herself. Fabrice, half-aware that his wife sought a moment of space in which to make an uncomfortable disclosure and sub-consciously determined to push it away as he pushed all unpleasantness away, covered their mutual discomfort with a relentless levity that drove Alexa into a dark despair. From time to time, her thoughts flirted with suicide and then drew quickly back.

Scorning her own weakness, she reminded herself stoutly that she had committed no crime, and nobody could imprison or hurt her. What she *had* done was commit a social misdemeanour and she was not wholly responsible for that. The confusion would resolve itself and she would walk free into the sunlight again.

A bad conscience and fear of the future are heavy burdens for anyone to bear and, angered that she had done so little to deserve them, Alexa supported herself with silent courage and as much outward *insouciance* as she could muster. A sense of outrage invaded her mind. The punishment for what she had done, and what she should have said and had not, was now enough she felt. But there was no-one to whom she could appeal for a remission.

Unconsciously, she turned away from Fabrice as he provided no respite and encouraged no confidences. He was a continual reminder that she carried around a time bomb which was ticking away in ever-shortening minutes the peace of everyone who surrounded her.

Instead, she fell in love with the unreproachful, inarticulate house. It could not be harmed and it could not judge. It seemed to her, that she and it had entered into a conspiracy. Alexa vowed that if it would only contain and protect her, she would activate the spell that would bring its decaying fabric back to life. It was a lunatic pact, unformed in words and founded on nothing more than a one-sided interior dialogue. But the château's silence was the anvil on which she beat her own flagging spirits into a determination to survive with her marriage and her sanity intact. There would, she was sure, be one single moment, which, if she were only ready for it, would prove the narrow escape hatch into safety.

The cherrywood *armoire* creaked deafeningly. Alexa tiptoed to the door and looked into the dressing room. Fabrice still slept, undisturbed, his breath whistling slightly through his partially open mouth. The coverings of the campaign bed were disordered. Evidently he had had a restless night. The silk robe lay in a confused heap on the floor beside the bed. She would have liked to tidy him up but she repressed the urge. She didn't want him to wake. One day soon, all would be clear and simple between them. But for now, she wanted to explore alone like Fabrice's little Algerian cousin before her.

The consummation of the marriage had gone, as Alexa put it to herself, smoothly. Fabrice had been competent and polite. He had risen after a decent interval, saying he would sleep in the adjoining dressing room so as not to disturb her. Every night since had been the same. Their lovemaking was friendly rather than passionate and always ended in his courteous withdrawal. Sensing Alexa's detachment, Fabrice detached himself. He was mildly disappointed. There was a reserve about her. She was not quite as he had hoped.

In the mornings, he smelt strongly of whisky when he joined her at the table by the bedroom window where she poured out their coffee and made small talk about proposed activities for the day ahead. He was compliant but not apparently enthusiastic about any of her plans and she found herself alone for long periods during the day. Fabrice passed much of the time in a mysterious place called the *chai*, a big barn-like structure behind the house. He had made it clear that he would not welcome her presence there.

"You would be bored. Making wine is a man's business."

Alexa had laughed, privately outraged at the crude rebuff. "You surely don't expect me to believe that do you, darling? What about the champagne widows?"

"Not terribly pleasant types I shouldn't have thought. Anyway, their husbands were dead. I flatter myself I'm still alive. And Bordeaux's a different matter entirely from champagne, a purely masculine product. It would interest you."

Alexa was surprised by his defensiveness but decided to let it go for the moment. They spent the evenings of this brief honeymoon in the château's damp billiard room. Fabrice clicked the balls around the table and Alexa watched him, sitting with her back to an electric fire which stood in the mock baronial fireplace. They were uneasy together. Several times Alexa tried to make an opportunity to say what was on her mind, but the words had always died on her lips.

They were alone in the château, Suzanne having remained in Paris on Tilly's instructions to give her son and his bride a short honeymoon. Suzanne hadn't really liked it, fearing the undiluted impact of Alexa on her territory.

"I don't know that it's really necessary, Tilly. After all, surely the house is big enough for all of us. *I* shouldn't interfere with them. There's nothing as tedious as a honeymoon couple, heaven knows."

"Nor anything quite as indelicate. So I should stay away and let them get the aggressively nuptial stage over at least. You know how it is, eating and drinking in bed, shrieks of laughter in the night and those rather rumpled faces in the morning. No, no, not at all the thing. Far too much for your nerves, dear. What on earth do you want to go down there for in such a hurry? I'm surprised you're not glad of the excuse to stay in Paris for a while.''

Suzanne sighed impatiently. ''I'm afraid she might interfere with things.''

''What things?''

''Oh, I don't know, Tilly. All sorts of things, she might start moving the furniture around, giving orders to Hortense . . . or bothering Héloïse.''

''She might. She might indeed. She'd be within her rights too. You must get used to the idea, my dear cousin, that young Alexa is the rightful *châtelaine* now. It's her house. She is the present *Marquise* and you, cousin, have slipped into the dowager's slot. you can't have it both ways, can you? You've been wanting Fabrice to marry for years now, you must have realised how it would affect your own position.''

''Of course I did. But we never anticipated Fabrice marrying into the English middle classes, did we? The girl is a provincial notary's daughter. She won't have the least idea how to go about things. If I leave it too long, by the time I get back, there'll be chintz covers in the *Salon Jaune* and bacon and eggs for breakfast. Too horrible. Most of all she's bound to have all the hateful energy of her type and feel she has to assert herself over one thing, if not another.''

''Well I have yet to spot anything in the least hateful about the new *Marquise* and as for asserting herself, she does that just by being herself, I rather doubt she'll need the support of chintz. I think she'll do very nicely.''

''I really can't think why Fabrice didn't take her away somewhere. He must have realised how this plan would interfere with my routine.''

''Possibly, he thought you'd be willing to suffer a little inconvenience on the occasion of his marriage. And where would he take her? Winter sports? Laughably inappropriate and too early anyway.''

''Are *all* tradesmen's windows quite as vulgar as you Tilly? What's wrong with the Cayman Islands, or the Seychelles?''

''Money. Simply money. You don't seem to realise that Mr. Standeven has tied everything up very securely. Alexa will be modestly independent but he hasn't provided anything for Fabrice to fritter. If Fabrice pulls himself together and performs, the long-term future might be quite comfortable for both of them but he's made it quite clear, no Standeven money will be invested in the de Pies Ombre affairs until and unless Mr. Standeven feels confident that Fabrice is at least trying to act like a responsible proprietor. He must try to do something for himself, you know. Standeven is a rich man, but he's no fool. Whatever happens Alexa will eat, but there's no guarantee that you will."

"Quite an exercise! We go to all the trouble of marrying Fabrice to this girl and we get nothing, *nothing* out of it."

"Don't be so tiresomely simple-minded, Suzanne. Do you think Alexa's father would contemplate giving *you* a blank cheque, or your son for that matter? If Fabrice can at least try to make a go of the vineyards, I'm sure Alexander will help. He'd like to, I know. But he won't throw good money after bad."

"My God. Is that the way he talks to you? Two shopkeepers together. Does he think the de Pies Ombres are a stock exchange gamble?"

"Something like it. He sees you as a low-priced stock, just possibly under-rated. He's prepared to speculate to a limited extent but he's a careful man."

Talking about money to Suzanne was always a stressful and frustrating business. She had little understanding of it, where it came from, how it was earned and what its value was. Tilly was anxious to terminate the conversation quickly.

"At the end of the day, Suzanne, none of this matters to me. There's a bit more money coming in for Fabrice now. The lawyers are able to let you have some additional funds from the trusts and Alexa may contribute some of her income. She was about fifteen hundred thousand francs a year that she's free to do as she likes with. She may choose to keep every penny. I strongly advise you *not* to irritate the Standevens. Provincial they may be, fools they are not."

"Well, he might have given them a honeymoon, at least," Suzanne countered sulkily.

"Standeven is a gentleman, albeit a provincial, since you harp on the point, but he would not humiliate his son-in-law by offering him the wherewithal to deflower his daughter in a tropical splendour. I doubt he even wants to think about it. My advice to you, Suzanne, is to do everything you can to make Miss Standeven feel at home. If you don't, you can rely on Alexander to take her and her money away. Just give Alexa and Fabrice a little time to settle down. They'll do wonders together if you let them. Frankly, my dear, that young lady is your best hope for the future."

It was thus that Tilly had persuaded Suzanne to leave her son and daughter-in-law in peace for a few days.

Dressing in the freezing bedroom, Alexa realised that five days had elapsed since her wedding and it was Friday. Suzanne was expected to return from Paris on Monday evening. Before then Alexa wanted to take possession of her new home. She must make some plans to welcome her mother-in-law. A warm bedroom would be a good beginning. She glanced at the iron stove in the hearth. It was an odd sight to English eyes. In England such a thing would be used to warm a greenhouse, an artist's studio or a workshop perhaps. She remembered dimly that there had been something similar in the library at school and her grandmother had had one in her beloved conservatory, but they were very old-fashioned, surely.

This one was shaped like a chimney, with a sort of little window, half way up. It was made of iron, probably, and had elaborate, curly legs. It was rusty. The top had a sort of pierced lid which, when you lifted it, revealed another solid lid, very heavy. There was an implement to lift it. She looked inside. It was choked with ash. Behind, a pipe emerged and disappeared up the chimney. The flue recess was lined with blue and white tiles depicting rural scenes. All this could be quite attractive, Alexa mused, if it could be made to work. It must be made to work, she thought, if it gets any colder in here it won't be possible to use this room in winter.

The château's central-heating system was extensive and unused. There was a network of fat brown pipes punctuated by occasional old-fashioned serpentine radiators. All remained icy cold. Fabrice had told her that the system was fired by a solid-fuel boiler in the basement which had been abandoned during the first few months of the war. It took a full-time man to keep it stoked. Obviously it was no good trying to reinstate that. Alexa made a mental note to take stock of all the heating appliances she might find. To get the place warm was the first thing. It will be easier to think when I'm warm, she thought.

Shivering, she left the room dressed in corduroy trousers and a sweater of Fabrice's over her own. There was a tweed jacket downstairs, hanging on a peg in the outer hall. She would put that on as well. On the landing outside her room, Alexa looked down from the stone balustraded gallery into the square hall with its black and white marble floor. The scale was grand, but not palatial. The château had a human feel about it. It had been built to charm rather than impress.

Above, there was another gallery, with a simpler stone balustrade and doors of less lavish design leading off it. The bedroom doors leading off her own gallery were each made of different precious woods, she noted. Some were inlaid, others were carved, a unity having been created by matching marble pilasters and pediments. Far above, at the top of the house, was a ceiling of plaster, painted *trompe l'oeil* to represent fan vaulting, pierced in the centre by a glazed lantern which was fortunately, Alexa thought, not visible from the exterior. The eclectic mixture of style and period achieved an eccentric harmony, showing successive layers of de Pies Ombre occupation, as each generation confronted the handiwork of the last with a triumphant contrast.

Dark portraits of moribund de Pies Ombres confronted each other across the galleries. Their eyes seemed to follow Alexa in speechless disapproval. She looked at each one, staring them out as if they lived. You are only memories, she told them. No, less than memories, flat-painted shadows that once lived in other memories. You can do nothing to me. You are gone and forgotten. For a moment, she hung over the balustrade, defying the images of Fabrice's ancestors and feeling the cold shaft of air at the heart of their house.

Glancing down into the hall, Alexa noticed that there were two yawningly empty fireplaces on either side. They were of mock medieval design. Iron firedogs stood on the hearths which were swept clean. There were no logs or any evidence that the fires had been lit for many years. She felt the chill silence of the château swirling around her and repressed an urge to fill the great void with a shout. The dying spaces all around her cried out to be transfused with sounds, colour and activity. "I'm coming, I'm coming," her lips moved soundlessly as she ran down the shallow stone staircase.

In the basement kitchen, Hortense, the de Pies Ombres' tall, angular cook, was preparing a breakfast tray. It was laid for two. She turned with a look of slight annoyance when she heard the ill-fitting oak door at the bottom of the spiral staircase creak. She did not like interruptions, she was not used to them.

"Bonjour Madame," Hortense splayed the fingers of both
hands on the stomach of her flowered overall as if wiping imaginary dough from them. "You are up early, today." She waited,
unembarrassed by the pause, for the young *Marquise* to explain
this intrusion into her territory.

"Not really, Hortense. It is eight o'clock already. Besides, it
is very cold upstairs, I thought I would eat my breakfast down
here with you."

"As *Madame* wishes." Hortense responded with cold formality. This was not a welcome variation in her routine. She
was accustomed to dealing with her employers at a distance.
Ever since she had come to the region from her village in Nor-
mandy, more than thirty years ago, she had looked on the kitchen
and its subsidiary apartments as her home. It was also her workshop where she executed the orders of the *Marquise*, when she
was at home, in a seclusion that had been absolute since the old
Marquis' death.

"This is the only part of the château which feels inhabited,"
Alexa ventured. Hortense nodded her acknowledgement of the
intended compliment, her lips compressed. "Shall I sit here?"
Alexa seated herself at the table covered with a blue chequered
cloth. On it was a yellow pottery bowl in which some late roses
nodded from exhausted necks. The table was evidently laid for
Hortense's own breakfast. There was a basket of bread, some
apricot jam and a squat *cafétière*. A large handleless bowl such
as the nuns had used for the morning *café au lait* sat waiting.
Silently, Hortense fetched another bowl, her face closed. Alexa
waited patiently, deliberately ignoring the qualified welcome.
Hortense must be won. With an unerring tactical instinct, Alexa
knew that if she missed the opportunity to enlist the support of
the taciturn cook before Suzanne's return, the difficulty of es-
tablishing herself in the house would be greatly increased. She
had identified the strength of Hortense's personality and could
not afford to have it silently undermining the weak foundations
of her position from this basement stronghold.

Alexa had waited in vain for some mention to be made as to
what duties would devolve on her as the new *châtelaine*. Nothing
had been said, from which she concluded that Suzanne intended
to continue at the Château d'Ombre as she had always done.
The struggle, if there was to be one, would have to be immediate
and decisive. Waiting would only make things worse. Alexa
would have been willing to share authority, but if Suzanne would

not share it, then she would have to relinquish it. One way or another I will be mistress here, she had told herself as she lay awake that first night after their arrival. Otherwise nothing will happen, the house will slowly crumble away and I am too young to be buried under the rubble.

In this scheme of things, the child wandered in and out of Alexa's imagination. Sometimes it featured in her plans, sometimes it did not. It was as if its existence was a thing undecided. At times it was as present to her mind as her own face in the looking-glass, at others it was as distant as a mislaid possession which might yet be found, and there again, might not.

Hortense brought the coffee back to the table. She looked at Alexa with faint annoyance.

"*Madame* would prefer tea, perhaps?"

"No, I like the *café au lait*. I have got used to it. Now I don't think I could ever drink tea for breakfast again. Oh, by the way Hortense, thank you for the *cassoulet* last night. It was wonderful, could we have it again soon?"

"*Bien sûr, Madame!* You like my *cassoulet*? It is a rough country dish for those who work hard in the fields, not really for ladies and gentlemen, you understand, but Monsieur Fabrice has always liked my *cassoulet*." Alexa watched as animation touched Hortense's carven features. It was as though they woke slowly, responding to some powerful magic which could breathe life into inert substances. "It is like . . . your Lancashire Hot Pot!"

Alexa smiled devastatingly. "Oh no, Hortense, it is nothing like Lancashire Hot Pot, I do assure you! Lancashire Hot Pot is *horrible*!"

It was done. Almost stupidly simple. Hortense was a cook who liked cooking. She was an artist who needed an audience. She was stony because her art was neglected and unappreciated. She spoke wistfully of Fabrice's boyhood liking for her *cassoulet* and Alexa caught a glimpse of the strong, kind soul that lived behind the wooden countenance.

"Monsieur Fabrice, he is awake? Shall I take his *petit déjeuner*?"

"No, I should leave it awhile, Hortense, I think *Monsieur le Marquis* will sleep a little longer."

Hortense eyed her keenly. Alexa did not miss the sharp look

of enquiry or the shadow of protective sympathy which flitted across the pebble-grey eyes.

"*Monsieur* is happy about the baby?" Hortense glanced away as she spoke. Her voice was elaborately casual. Alexa, stunned, sat motionless. Her mouth was slightly open but no sound came from it.

"I . . ." Alexa was unable to continue. She didn't know what to say anyway. No denial rose to her lips. It was the moment she had been waiting for, the narrow window of time when something could be done. It was just that she had never expected the cook to open the shutters.

"Perhaps," Hortense said quietly, her eyes returning to Alexa's face, "he does not know."

Alexa found her voice at last. "No, no. He doesn't. But how do *you* know?"

Hortense made a noise in her throat that sounded like a dry chuckle.

"My father had a little farm. There were ten of us children and eight of us were girls. I was the youngest. Someone was always pregnant in our house. The dog, the pig, the cat or one of my sisters, like I say, someone was always pregnant. You know, in our village, nobody got married unless they were pregnant, except the chemist's daughter. But then, they thought they were gentry. All swank. You get to know the look, you see. It's easy with dark women, like our Yvette was. She got this brown mask on her face. She's dead now, cancer of the womb. She had six herself. But you, *Madame*, are so fair. Still, I know."

Alexa looked down into the coffee bowl. It was a relief that somebody did know.

"Are you going to tell Monsieur Fabrice?"

Again, Alexa was unable to reply. Words would not occur to her brain.

"Forgive me, *Madame*. I have said too much. It is not my business. I thought perhaps it would help to talk."

"Oh, it does, it does. It's just that I . . ."

Hortense leaned forward across the table suddenly, stretching her bare forearm out across the blue chequered cloth as if she was about to take Alexa's hand. Her face was intent.

"Do not tell him, *Madame*. It will cause . . ." Hortense stopped. It would be presumptuous to say what it would cause, and yet, the girl's eyes regarded her steadily, as if willing her to speak. "It will cause unnecessary distress, and all to no purpose," Hortense concluded, withdrawing her arm.

"What do you mean, Hortense?"

"You will not carry that baby to term. It is written all over you, *Madame*. You do not have the look of a mother. You understand me? Better to forget all about it. There will be another time."

A long, low sigh escaped Alexa. She sat motionless, her arms folded. Eventually, her eyes slid down from Hortense's face and she seemed sunk in thought. She could hardly believe what she had heard. But the old cook seemed so certain, so matter of fact. She spoke about it as if Alexa had been a farm animal and the child she carried a misbegotten puppy.

"How long?" Alexa lifted her face again.

Hortense shrugged. "A week, two weeks? Who knows. Not long anyway."

Two large tears slid from Alexa's eyelids, whether from relief or sorrow she could not tell. Hortense rose and placed her arm around the young *Marquise*'s shoulders.

"Do not grieve, *Madame*. It is better so. Be done with this, and I tell you, there will be another time."

The next day, Alexa again rose early and joined Hortense in the kitchen. She wanted to be near the only person who knew of her trouble, the only person with whom she could lower her guard. Whether or not Hortense realised that the child was not of her master, Alexa did not know. She felt almost guilty in deciding not to confide in the cook but reason told her that it would be poor manners to burden the kind old woman with knowledge that could only implicate her in guilt. Hortense might well suspect, but a suspicion could not compromise her loyalty to Fabrice.

Hortense was welcoming and Alexa was touched to observe that she had already laid two bowls on the table in readiness. They ate together companionably and Alexa exclaimed at the homemade *brioche* that the cook had prepared especially for her.

"Hortense."

"Oui, Madame."

"How do people keep warm in the bedrooms here?"

Hortense shrugged her thin shoulders. *"Madame la Marquise*

has an electric fire. When it is cold she uses two. Monsieur Fabrice, the same.''

"How do you keep warm, Hortense?"

"In winter, I dress in here, by the stove, *Madame.*'' Alexa looked at the iron range. It was a shining black monster with a range of ovens garnished with bright steel handles and hinges. It gave off a powerful heat. Coals glowed cherry-red in a large iron-barred grate.

"Who looks after this? Who cleans it and stokes it?''

"I do, *Madame*. There is nobody else. Oh, *bien sûr*, years ago there was a man, but no longer. There is no one to look after things now except me. I do the cooking; I make the beds; I clean when I have the time. But you see, *Madame*, things are not as they ought to be. One person cannot run a house like this. It is too much.''

"My mother-in-law is very busy I suppose?'' Hortense looked surprised. She had never asked herself how the *Marquise* occupied her time.

"I do not know, *Madame*.'' Hortense stared at Alexa. She was only a young girl, but she was Monsieur Fabrice's wife. Who was she to take her orders from now? Nobody had warned her about any of this. Not even the courtesy of a telephone call.

Alexa turned to walk back along the avenue of slender cypresses. The stone gateposts leaned drunkenly, detached from any wall or fence with might previously have delineated the southern limits of the property. Rusted iron gates yawned meaninglessly on their crumbling hinges. On each gatepost a stone magpie sat with folded wings, its neck encircled by a coronet. They stared sightless over the flat, deserted landscape and the naked bones of the vines. Flakes of pain still clung to the magpies, black and white, with a dulled metallic gold for the coronets. Alexa got a notepad out of the pocket of the tweed jacket and wrote *Magpies = Morale*.

The distance between the gates and the château was, Alexa calculated, a third of a mile. She scuffed her shoes and kicked the loosened asphalt on the rutted drive which ran in a straight line between the cypresses. From this distance the dilapidation of the château was not visible. It appeared tall and white, ribbed at intervals with cylindrical towers, some thin, some fat, all surmounted by a candle-snuffer roof. Delicate iron finials traced their patterns in the sky. She stood for a moment and peered intently at the château, mentally identifying each room that she knew, from its windows. She did not know all of them. An oriel window, looking southeast from a round turret on the right, caught her attention as the filtered sunlight flashed briefly on a pane of glass. There is something interesting there. A special sort of window usually means a special room. Alexa made a note to discover the place. It might have made a charming nursery.

Alexa looked down at her abdomen. So nothing dreadful was going to happen after all. She didn't know why she believed Hortense, but she found that she did. It was something to cling to and something to dread.

Closer to the house, she stopped again and contemplated the ravaged fabric of the château. It was like an aged beauty. From a distance, the magic was intact, come any closer and the grotesque activity of time assaulted the eye to inspire only pity and embarrassment. The stucco was stained with rust from decaying fall pipes and here and there was crumbling away. The green-painted shutters were faded to pale jade, peeling in strips from the silvered wood. Looking up, Alexa saw large sections of guttering were missing, which would explain the ugly black patch on the painted ceiling of her bedroom. Well, she had been warned. Her father had told her that the house was, in his opinion, virtually uninhabitable. It could be repaired but it would take a great deal of money and time was not on their side. She took out the notebook again. *Guttering, stoves, survey.*

The battle of the stoves raged for weeks. At times Alexa almost faltered, but Elizabeth Standeven was as formidable a character as Suzanne de Pies Ombre and it had proved possible to defy *her*. Alexa discovered reserves of will-power in herself that she had not known existed until recent events had forced her to drag them out of storage. Alexa was actually excited by her own temerity and reminded herself constantly that her determination in the matter was justified. In any event, it was a test case. If she could win this round she might survive. Fabrice would not take her part but nor did he take his mother's. He had handed all the household bills over to Alexa, when she urged him to do so. The roll-top desk in a corner of the billiard room was crammed with sheaves of confusing papers, with frightening figures on them and less than courteous demands for payment. *Electricité de France, Postes Télécommunications, Bordeax.* The names leaped out at her.

"When do you pay all these, Fabrice?"

"I don't pay them at all, not unless the threats get too tire-some. My father used to have a secretary to do all that. I'm sure he wouldn't have known the difference between a coal bill and lottery ticket. I'm happy to say I take after him, as much as I can in the altered circumstances, of course."

"You sound as if all this chaos was something to be proud of."

"Well, I suppose it is. Gentlemen don't interest themselves in tradesmen's accounts, that's something for somebody else."

"If there is anybody else."

"There is. You. Darling, you will be my saviour, I'd no idea you could be so practical."

"I'll go through all these and try and understand them and then I can put them in some sort of order."

Alexa was glad of the prospect of work. It would be a dis-traction until such times as something happened to make Hor-tense's prognosis come true. That it would happen was something that she never doubted. She asked Hortense one day if she should see a doctor. But Hortense had looked at her in surprise and said no. Doctors only made a fuss and put one in the hospital. Sometimes they saved the baby, but if nature did not intend a baby to be born, it was a mistake to interfere. Nature knew what she was doing. Hortense hoped it would not be long for the *Marquise*, the waiting was hard.

"Oh yes, I should, if it pleases you," Fabrice continued, stirring the bills around on the desk.

"Then at least we'll know where we are."

"If that will interest you. Myself, I've never had any yearning to know where I am, it's always bound to be somewhere un-pleasant. I'm unable to perceive the advantage of organised debt, which seems to be what you propose. Debt is debt, it is the element which I inhabit, the air I breathe. I doubt I should know what to do without it and in any case, I've never heard of a way to convert it into anything more congenial."

"You must pay for food, at least."

"Oh, I don't know. Hortense deals with all that. I give her some cash whenever she gets too disagreeable. I know her hab-its, you see. Well before there is the least danger of starvation, she begins '*Monsieur*, it will no longer be possible to eat . . .' A week later, we have the second interview which invariably commences with the words, '*Monsieur*, I regret there will be no lunch . . .' There always *is*. I pay up when the *omelette nature* appears, uncharacteristically leathery and served with a glass of mineral water, which is patently absurd since mineral water costs money and wine, at least, is free here.''

"How dreadful! Poor Hortense! Why on earth does she stay?''

"God knows. It may be some sort of feudal devotion to the young master. She was my nursemaid, originally. She was a good sort. We were quite fond of each other, actually.''

"And now?'' Alexa flashed angrily.

"Funny old stick, isn't she? I wouldn't dream of turning her out.''

"It seems to me she'd be a damned sight better off anywhere else.''

Fabrice stared at her. "Alexa, I do hope you're not going to turn out to be a tiring wife.''

"Well you are certainly not a tiring husband . . .'' The minute the ill-considered words were out of her mouth, she realised her mistake. The words hung like the corpse of a suicide, in the motionless air. Fabrice went white. His mouth forming itself into a little round hole of hatred.

"I'm sorry,'' she said quietly. "I think you may have misunderstood what I meant by that.'' Fabrice got to his feet, slamming the top of the desk closed. He leaned heavily on his stick, spinning himself round to face the window. "If it is a frenzy of activity you require, you have plenty to exercise you there. Please consider yourself free to do what you like about it.''

The quarrel was not forgotten but the presence of Suzanne in the house made an armed truce necessary. That evening, Alexa beat Fabrice at backgammon, a game he played well and had begun to teach her in Paris when, isolated from the financial negotiations, they had drawn together in a mutual distaste for the discussions of their elders. Fabrice played the game with skill and determination, bringing all his neglected powers to bear on it.

"This is a little more interesting, Alexa. You are beginning to think. I was afraid you would never develop any aptitude for the game, you appeared to lack the necessary mental aggression. Of course,'' he tapped the ivory chip softly on the marquetry board, "I know you better now.'' His reference to their earlier quarrel was discreet. Suzanne was in the room, seated by the electric fire in the tiny *Salon Jaune*, where the family sat after dinner. She picked desultorily at a piece of *petit point*, which Alexa judged from its grubbiness was a piece of work that had been begun some considerable time ago.

"Did you make anything of those papers I gave you?"

"Yes. But I have not finished yet. I decided to tackle the question of fuel first."

"And what conclusions have you reached?"

"That this house is heated inefficiently and far too expensively. We seem to be entirely dependent on public utilities. It will not do. We should be independent."

Suzanne's eyebrows rose. "You express yourself very forcibly for a *jeune fille*, Alexa."

"*Belle Mère*, I am no longer *une jeune fille*, I am a married woman with responsibilities."

"To what responsibilities do you refer, my dear?" Suzanne's voice was smooth and dangerous. She had been a little bored lately. The opportunity to put her daughter-in-law in her place would be a welcome change of pace.

"The obvious responsibility to see to it that my husband's mineral resources are not expended irrationally. Isn't that what a good wife is supposed to do?" Alexa appealed. Suzanne continued to stare coldly, her needle poised motionless in the air.

"For instance," Alexa continued rashly, "this house is not warm enough. Every room is inadequately heated, if it is heated at all, by electric fires. The bills are catastrophic. It will have to stop. I will see what can be done to repair the old generator in the basement and what it will cost, in the meantime I think we should use the stoves."

"Do you? Do you indeed? You are a most original thinker Alexa. Who do you suppose will carry the coals? Fabrice? I imagine you think Hortense will do it. Of course, a girl of your modest background would not be aware that servants have limits, they cannot do everything and should not be asked to. Thank you for trying so hard to be helpful, I'm sure your intentions are good, but don't you see, a little *bourgeoise* of eighteen can hardly undertake the management of a house like this without a little more," Suzanne hesitated with dramatic effect, "shall we call it, training?"

Alexa rose and walked across the lustreless parquet to where Suzanne sat. She stood squarely before her to the dowager's great discomfort.

"*Belle Mère*, I realise I have little or no experience of running a house of this size, or any house at all for that matter. My parents intended me to do something quite different. But I wanted to do *this*, and I must begin somewhere. There's another thing, my father's house is actually quite large and my parents employ two indoor servants. My mother is very busy with her charities and committees and so forth, but she does supervise the house quite closely. Naturally, she talks about these things, and I would have to have been very rude not to listen to what she said, and very stupid not to have learned anything. So you see, I think I *do* know enough to make a start here.''

Suzanne squirmed, feigning a deep interest in some knotty problem of her embroidery. ''That is very interesting, Alexa. I suppose it is an advantage in some ways, to have a housewife for a mother.''

Alexa kept her temper. She felt the insult to her parentage and background deeply. Suzanne could not be allowed to get away with that.

''I thought a woman took her rank from her husband when she married. You can't have a bourgeoise *Marquise*, can you? That would be a contradiction in terms, wouldn't it?''

Suzanne made a faint gobbling sound which Alexa took to be a reluctant affirmative. The older woman's eyes remained riveted on her embroidery.

''And while we are discussing servants, *Belle Mère*,'' Alexa went on smoothly, ''there is something that has been worrying me. Perhaps you could advise me, because I really don't know what to do about it.''

The dowager *Marquise* looked up almost eagerly. Her opinion had been sought and in a tone of such sweet humility that she was entirely reassured that she had control of the conversation again. Alexa was a little headstrong, but she didn't mean any disrespect, after all.

''But of course, my dear. Anything. You will need a lot of support and I am here to give it.''

''It is just this, *Belle Mère*, Hortense does not seem to have been paid her wages for weeks and weeks now. It's terribly embarrassing. Perhaps we should let her go. My father says it's very wicked not to pay people who work for you what you owe them. It's stealing. If we can't afford to have her, don't you think we should tell her, pay her whatever we can and try and find her another job, preferably a better one, to, well, kind of make up for things? Frankly, I feel disinclined to use my own money, you know. There are so many other things I must spend it on . . . .''

Suzanne flushed. Fabrice's head was bent over the backgammon board.

"Fabrice!" She addressed her son sharply. "Will you please deal with this."

"Oh no, *Maman*. I assure you I couldn't. Alexa is going to deal with everything to do with the house from now on. She seems to have such an appetite for domestic activity. All the hiring and firing and paying and owing and tiresomeness of that kind is entirely her cup of tea. I shouldn't dream of interfering. Really, I daren't.''

As he spoke, Fabrice cringed with comic exaggeration.

"Well, I shall retire now. All this has been most wearing to my nerves. You should have a little more consideration for your elders, Alexa. The evenings are really not the best time to discuss these things, you know.''

"Goodnight, *Belle Mère*," Alexa rose with punctilious courtesy. "I am so sorry to have wearied you. Shall I bring you a glass of hot milk or something like that? I don't feel I can ask Hortense to do it, certainly not until we've sorted something out about her wages.''

Fabrice looked up from the backgammon board, where he had been setting out the pieces again, merely to give his hands occupation and his eyes somewhere to look during the epoch-making exchange between his mother and Alexa. He smiled slightly at Suzanne and shrugged.

"No thank you. I dislike hot milk." Suzanne swept out of the door which Alexa held open for her.

Fabrice tittered. "You were, perhaps, just a trifle harsh. Money isn't discussed on a regular basis in this household, you know. Mainly because it's common, but also because it's so disagreeable.''

"No wonder, you have so little of it, and what you do have you throw away. Oh, I'm sorry, Fabrice, I don't *want* to be horrible, but if I don't say these things, nothing will *ever* be done.''

"Well, as I said, you can do what you like about it and I'll go along with it.''

"Really? What if your mother doesn't like it?''

Fabrice giggled again. "Then that will be most unfortunate for her. She must see there's very little I can do about it when

I'm married to such a headstrong woman with money of her own. I must say, Alexa, you didn't leave us in any doubt about that point, did you? What a bully you are.''

Alexa looked curiously at Fabrice. He seemed to be enjoying the discord which she had sown.

"Fabrice, do you think we're going to be happy?"

Fabrice did not look at her but continued to fiddle with the backgammon counters. Instantly, Alexa regretted the impulse which had made her try to get closer to him.

"I don't know. I don't think I've got a lot of happiness in me. Not brought up to it, you see. Nobody here thinks much about being happy. It's supposed to be enough just to be *here*.''

"Here? Here at the Château d'Ombre, you mean? Or just here on earth?''

"Oh both, I think, but particularly at d'Ombre. That's the great thing, you see, got to stay in the old place. That's a sort of article of faith with the de Pies Ombres. That's our happiness, staying here.''

"I can understand about the house, but it still all seems very sad to me. Isn't there anything else in your life? Me for instance?''

Alexa wanted to shake him suddenly. Or at least, she thought, to shock him out of this emotional torpor. He hardly seemed like a young man at all, and she needed him suddenly, needed him to be young and vigorous at her side.

"Well, of course, you're in my life. That's self-evident. And you're *here*, aren't you? Therefore, I must be happy with you. That's the logic of the thing.''

"That's not happiness, Fabrice. That's mere resignation. And I don't want you to be *resigned* to me.''

"Oh dear, Alexa. This is all becoming very philosophical. Much too difficult for a simple *vigneron* like me to follow. You should ask my Aunt Héloïse about it all. She's a recognised specialist in resignation.''

This was the other side of Fabrice. In Paris his dry wit had been an invigoration. In the country, it had turned to acid, burning everything it touched. He was like a disappointed old man, tasting the bitterness of a wasted life and reporting on the flavour in a series of sour jokes. In the midst of her own troubles, Alexa felt sorry for him. She wished she could reach him, make him smile as she remembered him doing with the sly sweetness of a very intelligent and naughty schoolboy. But what she felt did not always translate naturally into speech.

"I wish you could pull yourself together, Fabrice. We have a lot to do here, and we'd better pull together. It will take both of us you know."

"I remember being told that people from Yorkshire were noted for a singular lack of charm. They talk like blunt instruments, that's what my tutor said. Isn't that right, *darling*?"

Alexa flinched from the sarcastically pronounced endearment. There was a whisky decanter at Fabrice's elbow and he helped himself liberally.

"Yes, I suppose it is. But everyone likes doing business with a Yorkshireman. They do what they say they'll do, they say what they mean and they mean what they say, *and* they pay their debts." Alexa spoke with passionate seriousness, tears of anger and homesickness pricking behind her eyes.

"Well, well, such loyalty to your province. Do you think you could transfer it to the Médoc?"

"I shall have to, won't I?"

There was a smart tap at the door.

"Entrez," Alexa called faintly.

"I am Mademoiselle Héloïse de Pies Ombre," stated the small, upright figure framed in the open doorway. She seemed frail. Her abundant white hair framed delicate, pointed features. Black eyes sparkled with intelligence and good humour lighting a pale, severely lined complexion. "May I come in?" The question was rhetorical. The slight figure advanced towards the bed, supported on an ebony cane with a silver knob for a handle. The worn heather-tweed skirt, which looked as though it had been made for someone much larger than its wearer, did not swing rhythmically, even allowing for its eccentric cut, as it should. Alexa noted that she had a slight limp. Bewildered, she pushed herself up against the pillows, making an uncertain gesture of welcome with her hand.

"Please, *Mademoiselle* . . ."

"Here, let me make you more comfortable." With surprisingly strong and competent hands, Héloïse rearranged Alexa's pillows, deftly plumping them, creating comfort and order without fuss or familiarity.

"I am afraid you have caught me at a disadvantage, *Mademoiselle*, nobody told me that you would be visiting today. Have

you come to see my mother-in-law? Will you be staying the night,
or longer? I must ask Hortense to make you comfortable . . .''

Alexa spoke in a nervous rush. The knock on the door had
woken her from a deep sleep. She was still disoriented.

"Ah, I expect nobody has told you who I am, or that I live
here. No one will have had time, a new bride is not to be bothered with a rehearsal of family skeletons. Naturally, it is *you* I
have come to see.''

Alexa smiled wanly, "Actually, Fabrice did mention you the
other day. But I had no idea that you lived here. It's such a big
house, but I didn't realise it was possible to be in it and not
know everyone else who lived here. He didn't say you were a
skeleton though, surely you are not just yet, *Mademoiselle*?''

The aristocratic old lady smiled politely at the feeble joke.

"If desire for a chair is proof of continuing life, then, I suppose I am not, as you say, a skeleton.'' The black eyes smiled,
giving the lie to the light sarcasm of the words.

"Oh, please, that little embroidered chair by the stove, it's
quite comfortable. But I expect you know that better than me.''

"And why should I? These are the traditional apartments of
the reigning *Marquis* and his wife, so to speak. I have rarely
been in here. Even as a child, formal interviews with my mother
were conducted in her sitting room, next door. Never in her
bedroom. My father would not have liked it. But now, we live
more simply as you already know.''

Alexa was confused. The staccato manner of her visitor was
not exactly unfriendly but it did not seem to be her intention to
soothe.

Alexa was very tired. During the night, in waves of pain and
nausea, the baby had slipped away, like some embarrassed guest
who found he was not expected and not welcome. There was a
lot of blood. Alexa had been woken by the pain. For a time she
lay there, not understanding what was happening. Then the con-
tractions had come on, strong and rhythmic. She sweated and
wanted to vomit. Fabrice was not there. He was sleeping next
door in the dressing room. Alexa was very frightened and called
to him. There had been no response at first. She called and
called until her voice seemed to her to fill the whole château.
He opened the intercommunicating door after what seemed an
age, his face dull with sleep.

"Get Hortense quickly . . .''

"It is all right, *Monsieur*.'' Turning her head, Alexa had seen

to her astonishment and relief that Hortense was already there.
She wore a dark, old-fashioned dressing gown over a white flannel nightgown and her iron-grey hair hung down in two braids.
"Go back to bed, *Monsieur*, it is nothing, just a bad period, I
will see to *Madame*. You need not worry."

She had done everything. In the end, when Alexa lay propped
on the pillows with freshly laundered linen and a clean nightgown, drinking something Hortense called a *tisane*, the old cook
had said, "Now you are safe, *Madame*. You can begin your
life."

So Hortense had known all along. It didn't matter. Nothing
mattered at all now. Alexa had wept quietly most of the night
after Hortense had gone. She felt like a murderer. The child had
gone in the end because she had not wanted it, because she had
made promises to it that could not be kept, because her love for
it was too equivocal. Alexa tormented herself with these thoughts
for many hours, grieving for a soul she had killed with deceit
and indifference. She hoped its suffering was only in her imagination and that if it was not, the suffering would be blotted out
by the comforting largeness of the greater soul it had come from.

She had slept in the end, and awoke to find this strange lady
in her bedroom. Alexa renewed her effort to behave normally.

"I'm sorry," Alexa apologised again, "I'm not terribly well
today, I . . ."

"I know. Hortense told me. That is why I have come to see
you. I thought you would welcome a little conversation. I hope
I am right and that I do not intrude?"

"Of course you are right. I am very grateful for a visitor. It
is kind of you." Héloïse inspected the contents of the china
pitcher which stood on the boulle commode beside Alexa's bed.
"Good. You have drunk all your lemonade. It is important to
keep the fluid intake up. Hortense can take the jug down again
when she comes with our coffee and make some more." She
leaned forward suddenly and felt Alexa's forehead, "Well, you
have no temperature today, but you still look a little grey in the
face. But the day after tomorrow you should be up and busy
again. A dose of flu is nothing to you young people, luckily. It
would have laid me low for a week."

"You say you live here?"

"Yes, in the *Tour du Jardin*, as we call it. It overlooks what
was once the garden, it's all overgrown now of course, no one
has time to look after those old-fashioned knot gardens any more.

Far too labour intensive. When I was a child it was very spruce
but not any longer. I never liked it much anyway, all those rigid
box hedges and dull-looking shrubs. The paths were all gravel
which hurt my feet even through sandals, so knobbly and dry. I
like the wilderness much better.''

''Which is the *Tour du Jardin*?''

''It's the one which faces south-east, you can tell by the oriel
window half way up.''

''Oh, but I did notice that. I thought it looked so intriguing.
It must be a lovely room.''

Alexa remembered sadly that she had seen the place when the
baby was still with her.

''It is. It's my oratory and also my study.'' Alexa was startled.
Glancing at Héloïse she noticed that she wore no jewellery except the plainest of watches and a tiny gold crucifix on a chain
around her neck.

''Now I have embarrassed you, my dear. I'm so sorry. I'd
forgotten how you English shrink at any mention of religion.
It's not done to speak of it in England, however obliquely, is
it?''

''Well, I suppose not, actually. I don't know why really, but
it's the way it is.''

''Religion happens to be my chief interest and indeed my
job.''

''Job?'' echoed Alexa, mystified.

''Yes, I write religious pamphlets. You know, small instruc-
tional works on lives of the saints, you will always see them in
a rack at the back of any Catholic church.''

''I see. Does it, forgive me for asking, make any money?''

''A little only. But it's enough to contribute something to the
expenses of the household. I couldn't sit back and eat my nephew's bread without at least doing something to help. I was never
trained for anything, you see, and this is all I can do. I'm very
fortunate, I have my beautiful tower, enough food to eat and
work I love. I am glad it doesn't make a lot of money, that would
make me feel guilty. One should have just enough and a little
to give to others when they need help. Possessions get in the
way so, don't you find?''

''In the way of what?'' Alexa frowned, dismayed at the turn
the conversation was taking.

Héloïse smiled slightly. ''We can talk about that some other
time.'' Today I wanted to meet you and talk about you and your

life. I have heard a good deal already. You intend to reform us and all our sloppy, inefficient ways, I hear."

"I thought we were spending too much money on the wrong things. I still think so." Alexa wondered if Suzanne had employed Mademoiselle de Pies Ombre as some sort of envoy.

"I entirely agree with you. You face many problems I fear, but you have my poor support for what it is worth. I will do everything I can to help. I am already abiding by your new edict, you know. I carry my bucket of coal up twice a day and I'm getting very slick at cleaning the stove out. You're quite right, you know, and the stove is much cosier than those beastly electric fires."

Alexa looked at the fragile old lady in the embroidered chair. "Believe me, I had no idea that I was imposing this on you. I don't know what to say."

"Say nothing. It is an admirable reform. We were wasting money from idleness and stupidity. You did well to point it out."

Alexa relapsed back onto the pillows. It was all too difficult. Perhaps it no longer mattered very much.

"Of course, you face much more serious problems."

"What do you mean?"

"Have you been into the *chai* yet? No, of course you have not, you have scarcely had time."

"I haven't been in there, it's true," Alexa said slowly, "not so much because I haven't had time, but because Fabrice doesn't seem to want my involvement. He's within his rights. After all, that's his department. He's given me *carte blanche* in the house, the least I can do is stay out of his working world until he invites me into it."

"And do you think he *will* ever invite you into it?"

"That is something I really haven't had time to think about yet. I've been thinking so much about our money problems and how to solve them. We just haven't enough income. I don't know what to do about it. I lie here every night and worry. There must be a solution."

"I'm sure you'll find it, my dear. The house is already cleaner and warmer than it's been for years. That's a great step forward and you'll make bigger strides yet, I'm sure."

Hortense and Mademoiselle de Pies Ombre seemed to be on *her* side. Alexa's mind, tired as it was, snapped at the realisation. The Dowager *Marquise* was not, and her husband was on no side at all, certainly not hers. Alexa shook her head very slightly. They didn't realise, any of them, that she really did not care any more.

Hortense leaned against the kitchen sink, her arms folded, watching the wet sheets crack like a whip in the cold wind which gusted round the courtyard.

Everything had come away cleanly. She had presided over quite a few births and miscarriages in her time. No need for any interfering doctors with their big mouths. The little *Marquise* had suffered enough. What she needed now was work and some company. Monsieur Fabrice hadn't been near her. It was good of Mademoiselle Héloïse to go and see her. She didn't like talking much, as a rule.

"*Voilà, Madame,* your Hortense is a good laundress. Nobody will ever know. *Personne.*"

CHAPTER
9

🙚🙚 "LOT 1-0-1, LADIES and gentlemen, the property of the Marquis de Pies Ombre. Ten bottles of 1776 Château d'Ombre."

Alexa sat rigid on the straight chair feeling the ripple of tension spread across the room. Timothy caught her eye briefly from the rostrum, his forefinger tapped the ivory gavel noiselessly. Coolly, he glanced about the room, assessing the mood, the feel of the auction. He would not let the excitement fade, nor would he flatten it before it had time to build. He was going to milk it for all it was worth. Inside, he felt the excitement of knight errantry. The young Marquise de Pies Ombre had captured his imagination with her beauty, poverty and gaiety.

"Will anyone start me at five thousand pounds?" Timothy's tone was mild and confident. Alexa kept her eyes fixed on the Tremayne Taylor sale catalogue, stifling a gasp. It was twice the figure they'd discussed. It was an insane sum. Five hundred pounds a bottle. No one would bid and then the cost of her trip would have been wasted. I'll kill him, she thought, there must be some rule against it. Alexa's teeth were gritted with rage when she heard Timothy's soothing Etonian voice again.

"Come gentlemen, there must be someone here who can afford ten bottles of history. Here we have it, a sizeable sample of a pre-Phylloxera wine from the world-famous de Pies Ombre property in the Médoc. A wine born into pre-revolutionary France, the very year when George III sat on the throne of England at the time of the American Revolution. A wine that lived to see its descendants accorded the accolade of Second Class growth at the great Paris *Exposition Universelle* of 1855. Just thirty years later the vineyard lay devastated, the vines uprooted. The plague of Phylloxera had conquered. This wine

slept through it all until the renaissance in the 1920s and now
we are privileged to offer it here, just short of two hundred years
since the war of its vintage. Five thousand pounds? Five thousand pounds anywhere? Five thousand pounds I am bid . . .''

It was away, gone away like a fox, the figures climbed and
climbed. The only sound was Timothy's voice rhythmically re-
cording the bids, he settled into his stride, almost chanting the
astonishing figures as if they were the words of a familiar psalm.
His intelligent face was smooth and withdrawn, emotionless and
professional. The enthusiastic ex–public school boy the London
auctioneers had sent out to d'Ombre was gone, metamorphosed
for the moment into a self–contained, precision machine.

''Six thousand, seven thousand, eight thousand . . .'' Alexa
watched his face swing back and forth across the room as if he
were a tennis umpire, ''eight thousand, it's against you, against
you in the room here . . .'' the gavel hovered threateningly over
the desk but the bidding resumed, ''nine thousand, ten thousand, eleven thousand, twelve thousand . . . was that a bid sir?''
Timothy paused, registering irritation that was politely, but not
completely concealed. There was a shuffle, an embarrassed
murmur from somewhere on the front row. The well-barbered
necks were craned almost imperceptibly.

Timothy nodded sympathetically, forgivingly in the direction
of the unfortunate who had caused the check, ''Thirteen thousand, fourteen thousand,'' another pause. ''At fourteen thousand pounds . . . are you all done? At fourteen thousand.'' The
gavel jerked in Timothy's hand, ''Fifteen thousand? Fifteen
thousand I am bid. Fifteen thousand, ladies and gentlemen, for
the last time . . .''

''Sixteen thousand quid,'' a coarse northern voice was heard
from the rear of the room, causing a frisson of distaste to pass
through the polite ranks of those seated. There was a shocked
silence. The silvered heads remained motionless, refusing to
display ill-bred curiosity or discover who had defied convention
by opening his mouth. Timothy accepted the bid.

''Sixteen thousand at the back there. It's against you in the
room, at sixteen thousand pounds, gentlemen, are you all done,
at sixteen thousand pounds . . . seventeen anywhere? Seventeen
. . . No? At sixteen thousand pounds then . . .''

But it was not over, the auction tore away again. Someone,
perhaps the elderly man sitting in front of Alexa, who adjusted
his gold-rimmed spectacles at intervals, would not let the new

bidder get away with it. It was a dog fight. The rhythm of the auction had been shattered. The casually dressed, long-haired man standing at the back insisted on shouting out his bids, throwing them down like an ungainly boy's challenge. He didn't want the wine. Everybody in the room understood that instinctively. He knew it himself. He only wanted to make a demonstration of aggression against a world that would not admit him. It was destined to be a demonstration only. It was soon clear that the determined bidder in gold-rimmed spectacles would meet any new challenge with unassailable calm.

"All done at twenty thousand pounds, twenty thousand pounds . . ."

The gavel came down with a gentle tap of finality. The wine was sold. There was a surge of muffled conversation. Some looked curiously at Alexa. She was the only woman present, despite Timothy's frequent reference to ladies and gentlemen. She had not bid for a single lot. She did not know where to look or what expression to wear. Timothy appeared immersed in papers, consulting with the clerk.

"A message for you, Madam." The porter leaned across to hand her a note.

"I'll ring you this evening—sixish. Okay?" The note was written in a spidery scrawl with a blue biro. Alexa looked up at the rostrum, Timothy's eyes flicked enquiringly in her direction. She nodded slightly and smiled.

"Ladies and gentlemen, lots 1-0-1 to 1-1-0 inclusive have been withdrawn from the sale." The announcement caused a mutter of annoyance. "If we may continue, after that rather epoch making, shall we say, rally," Timothy smiled professionally, "and go on to lot number 1-1-1, two cases of La Mission Haut Brion, 1949. The property of a gentleman. For those of you not familiar with this vintage . . ."

Alexa rose to leave. She was dazed. Her other lots had been withdrawn from sale as she and Timothy had agreed they should be in the unlikely event of any single lot making in excess of eight thousand pounds.

Alexa clambered out of the deep porcelain bath and wrapped one of the Dorchester's huge bath sheets around her. The telephone was ringing in the sitting room.

It was extravagant to stay at the Dorchester, but it was the only London hotel Alexa knew. She always followed her grandfather's advice when it came to travel. When she had rung him from France to say she was coming to London on business, he'd said there was no point in being original about hotels, the obvious place was usually the best place, and the safest. His own idea of economy was to stay at his club, the Devonshire, which, of course, was not open to his granddaughter.

Alexa had made a swift recovery from her miscarriage. It was aided to some extent by the demanding nature of Hortense's invalid cookery. After a few days in bed, obediently consuming a diet of liver, eggs and iron-rich claret, Alexa was forced to her feet, unable to face one more dish of chopped raw liver.

Fabrice had accepted Hortense's explanation of his wife's indisposition. She was run down, and a severe menstruation had coincided with a bout of flu. His own ministrations had consisted of playing backgammon with her in the evenings, on a tray balanced on the bed, and urging yet more strengthening claret on her. It was one of the bottles he brought to her room that alerted Alexa to the potential riches that lay under the château. Its strange shape, the date 1802 moulded into the glass and its undrinkable contents lingered in her memory for days. Eventually she had telephoned Alexander who had arranged for Timothy Bowring to visit the Château d'Ombre just before Christmas.

The new interest helped to blot out both the miscarriage and the mental suffering which had preceded it. It was, as Hortense had predicted, a combination of work and congenial company which had effected the real cure. Alexa and Timothy had worked together on an inventory of the wines stored in the cellars of the Château d'Ombre and then in those of the Paris house. It had not occurred to Fabrice to be jealous of the enthusiastic, youthful Englishman and he saw Timothy and Alexa off to Paris with something like relief. Timothy was no good at backgammon, primly abstemious when it came to drinking whisky and full of tiresomely learned questions about long-forgotten vintages which Fabrice found he could not answer.

Alexa pushed damp hair away from her forehead as she lifted the telephone receiver.

"Yes."

"I have a Mr Bowring on the line for you Madam."

"Yes, I'll speak to him."

"Hello, Alexa?"

"Timothy! I could have killed you! I thought I'd die when I heard you open the bidding at five thousand pounds!"

"Ah, yes. It may have sounded adventurous to you, but a thing is worth what you know someone will pay for it. I heard on the grapevine yesterday that a merchant here acting as agent for an American collector was prepared to stop at virtually nothing to get hold of lot 1-0-1. The year 1776 means a lot to Americans, they take their history seriously."

"Naturally, they haven't got much of it!" Alexa remarked with joyful spite.

"Well, I would hardly say that," Timothy reproved her in his best schoolmasterish tone, "what they lack in chronological antiquity they make up in sheer geographical spread. And don't forget, an American came through for *you* this morning."

Alexa felt faintly impatient of the lecture. Timothy was so deeply courteous himself, he would defend an entire unconscious, and uncaring, nation from an insignificant slight. Living with Fabrice had begun to sharpen her own sense of humour into thoughtless malice. The realisation was a mild shock. Already, she and Fabrice were beginning to grow together. You were supposed to partake of your partner's strengths, though, not his faults.

"Anyway, now he's got something nice to add to his collection of American Revolution memorabilia," Alexa replied hastily. Timothy was so nice, she didn't want to offend him. "And I've got twenty thousand pounds. I think I got the best of the bargain."

"No accounting for tastes, is there? It's all a question of what you want, and having something that someone else wants, of course."

"Well, I can't thank you enough for all you've done. I can hardly take it in."

"You could thank me enough."

"Oh, how?"

"By having dinner with me. There's still a few things we have to discuss, like what to do with your unsold lots."

"Oh yes, of course. Isn't it marvellous, I've still got all the other stuff left over for a rainy day. It would be fun to have dinner, I was just going to have something sent up on a tray. Where shall we go?"

"I think we'd better make it the Terrace Room. We don't want to cause any gossip. After all, it'll be in all the papers tomorrow and the press will have worked out who you are by now. At least, we'd better not take any risks, I don't want to make things difficult for you at home.''

Alexa almost laughed aloud. Compared to what had so nearly happened, nothing could ever be regarded as *difficult* again. She would have to live with the shame and sadness of that secret for the rest of her life. But at least every other problem would seem relatively small. Poor Timothy, he was a dear, but in Alexa's experienced, aged perception, he seemed like an intelligent child. The idea that her husband, the witty, complicated, taciturn Marquis de Pies Ombre, might be jealous of him seemed ludicrous. But she was touched by his consideration and anxious to make him her friend.

''I'll meet you in the foyer here then. About what time?''

''Oh, say half an hour. I only live in Knightsbridge.''

Alexa walked through the foyer, feeling the thickness of the famous medallioned carpet under her thin slippers. She drew admiring glances from both sexes as she rustled by in the short black taffeta. She knew she looked more than presentable and enjoyed the discreet stir she was causing. That was one thing, she realised, that she missed. In the months since she had been married, she had received no compliments, Fabrice seemed to have become indifferent to her appearance. Eventually she realised that her looks were unimportant to him in themselves, only the envious stares of other men. In the country, there was nobody to stare. She hadn't fretted, but had simply forgotten about her looks, she needed to see them mirrored in other people's eyes. Her dressing-table mirror told her nothing. It reflected a face she was familiar with, neither beautiful nor ugly. She enjoyed being mistaken for a beauty, believing always that it *was* a mistake rather than a fact. It was a trick. Something one conjured up with a few sticks and jars of paint, a deft touch, a little self-confidence and a lot of luck. But the masquerade added spice to life and Alexa responded by modelling the dress with a conscious professionalism, which made her seem larger than life.

''I say!'' Timothy touched her arm, ''You look like the front cover of *Vogue*!''

Alexa turned to face him, smiling at the compliment.

''There was a time when I might have been, but I never got

that far. Didn't I tell you about my career as a fashion model? Where did you spring from?''

"I was just sitting here waiting for you, but you sailed past like . . .''

"A ship in full sail," Alexa teased him, smiling. He coloured a little, she had seen into his thoughts.

"Well, a very elegant tea clipper, fast and sleek, or a beautiful schooner, perhaps.''

"I had a friend at school who was crazy about ships. She'd be just the person for you. I'll introduce you one day.''

But I'm crazy about you, Timothy spoke the words in his mind. She really was so enormously attractive. But there was something dark and indecipherable about her character. She was unlike the other girls he knew. With Alexa he always felt that something was held back. At times, at the Château d'Ombre, he had seen her face suddenly in repose, when she had thought herself unobserved for a moment. He read a sorrow there which looked strange on a young girl's face. And then it would be gone, a fleeting shadow engulfed in the light of her smile.

"Shall we go to the Terrace Room for a drink, or stay here?''

"Which would you prefer?''

"Here, definitely. I like to watch the people coming and going, wondering who they are and what they're doing, eavesdropping generally—it's great fun for a provincial nobody like me.''

"Why do you call yourself that? You shouldn't run yourself down, you know.''

"Why not? My dear mother-in-law does it constantly. She is very wise and experienced, and to hear her talk, you'd think I'd just crawled out of a mud hut. Naturally, I pay attention to what she says.''

Timothy looked sideways at her. He was an uncomplicated young man and his simple standards of morality and good manners ruled out sarcasm about relations. He couldn't be sure whether she was being sarcastic or ingenuous. Her face betrayed nothing but a bland matter of factness. He'd thought the older *Marquise* pretty appalling when he'd visited them at the Château d'Ombre, but Alexa had always treated her with perfect, deliberate politeness. The sudden upsurge of repressed bitterness surprised him.

Alexa. How enchanting she had seemed, so full of energy and vitality. Running up and down the tumbledown château in blue jeans and a sweater. Calling him to look at this and that. She was almost like a child on Christmas morning. Zoffany portraits, Sèvres dinner services with more than half their pieces missing, broken-down old carriages in the moribund stables, anything and everything . . . she certainly had an eye for a nice thing. But of course, he'd been sent to assess the wine, and that was where the real treasure lay. In the cellars of the château itself, in the *chai*, stored haphazardly in barns in the Paris house too. An ordinary family could live in comfort on the proceeds for a lifetime. And now here she was in London. Herself, but more so. She exuded confidence and optimism. What did that peculiar husband of hers make of it all? Most of the time he'd seemed strangely passive, as if it were not his possessions that were being considered. He had appeared to regard his wife's activities with a restrained tolerance but little interest.

"What would you like?"

"Oh gin and tonic, please. We don't have it at home. Fabrice drinks whisky all the time and we have so little money, I feel I can't buy imported gin just to indulge myself. But one can't be in London and not drink our national drink."

"Isn't claret your national drink now?"

"Well, of course it is. But I haven't been married a year yet, I'm still suffering from something of an identity crisis, I think."

Timothy ordered two gin and tonics from a passing waiter and then turned to Alexa. "What will you do with the money? I'm sorry, that was rude. Please forget I asked. None of my damn business."

"Not at all! I want as many people to know as possible. I'm going to do some essential repairs to the château, a little redecorating and put in some decent bathrooms. I have *some* money of my own, but it wouldn't be nearly enough and Daddy said I mustn't spend any capital on it. You see I'm going to open a guest-house."

"A guest-house?" Timothy's expression was incredulous. His experience of guest-houses was limited to the exteriors of dingy terrace houses in seaside places, with signs propped in the lace-curtained windows saying "Vacancies."

"Yes, certainly. I considered opening the house on a 'stately home' sort of basis, but then I realised tourists never come to the Médoc, only wine buffs, and there aren't enough of them. In any case, I think you have to have fairgrounds and 'added attractions' to make any money in the 'stately home' racket. I'm sure I couldn't stand it. Anyway, you have to be 'open' for long periods of the year, just on the off-chance that somebody may come and pay you half a crown to nose round the house. No, it isn't a paying proposition, and in any case, Suzanne would never wear it. At least with paying guests you know whether you've got someone coming or not and whether you're free, or on duty. Much better.''

"About the unsold wine, Alexa, what are you going to do?"

"Nothing at all, at the moment," Alexa replied decisively, "it can stay where it is. But when you send in your statement of account, Timothy, include all the lot numbers as if they'd all been sold.''

As she spoke the waiter returned with their drinks on a salver and Alexa addressed herself with guileless enthusiasm to the dishes of pickled gherkins and pearl onions, unconscious of Timothy's open-mouthed stare. When he said nothing, she turned to look at him.

"You can do that, can't you?"

Timothy seemed to find his voice with some difficulty. He took off his spectacles and examined them before replying.

"No, no. I'm afraid I can't. And in any case, what would be the point?"

Alexa looked straight ahead, the colour rising in her cheeks. She hoped it did not show. This first attempt at what she had naïvely conceived to be grown up "wheeling and dealing" had misfired rather badly.

She had worked it all out an hour ago, in the bath. It would be a good thing if the de Pies Ombres believed that the limit of their painlessly realisable assets had been reached. It would discourage frittering. It wasn't that she didn't realize that the manoeuvre would in some degree cloud the real history of the sale, but she was afraid that a full disclosure would encourage her husband and mother-in-law to believe that their resources were, after all, limitless. Suzanne would forget that this new source of capital was only discovered by a combination of fluke and her daughter-in-law's own deductive powers. Fabrice, on the other hand, would view the sums realised as windfalls, enough to keep a few creditors at bay and enable further indebtedness, but not enough to encourage any serious attempt at commercial recovery. But Alexa knew that the money the wine represented was, with self-denial and discipline, just enough to offer the de Pies Ombres a last chance to hold on to their inheritance.

Alexa had suspected that her own plan was flawed, but had hoped that Timothy would see no objection to doing as she asked. After all, she had acted for her husband all along in the matter, her instructions could be taken as his for practical purposes. Now it seemed she would have to think of something else.

"My firm was officially employed by your husband," Timothy broke in on her thoughts, "to dispose of his property. We have to give him an accurate accounting of all transactions entered into on his behalf. Anything else would be a flagrant dereliction of duty and breach of trust. Well, it would be worse, it would be stealing."

Alexa's eyes registered genuine hurt. "But you wouldn't be stealing anything. Surely you don't think I'd ask you to do that!"

"I'm sure you wouldn't mean to. But we should be helping you to steal, which is just as bad, Alexa."

"But *I'm* not stealing anything either. All I want to do is hide the unsold wine for a time. Otherwise it'll just end up in the next sale, and the money will be squandered. If you knew the de Pies Ombres like I do, you'd know they just *throw* money away. If they go on doing it, they'll be totally, totally ruined and there'll be *nothing* anyone can do to save them."

Patiently, Timothy explained Tremayne Taylor's position again.

"And anyway, we can't store the unsold lots, Alexa. We're auctioneers, not wine merchants. Space is at a premium with us."

Alexa's features were spread with perplexity and sadness. "Well, that's the best I could think of. What would *you* do?"

Timothy thought for a moment, his rather large, pink hands clasped between his knees. He studied the pattern on the carpet minutely. After some prolonged moments of thought, he looked sideways at her, without raising his head.

"You know, my father was Bishop of Penzance before he died and my uncle is a big wheel in the Treasury. The Church and the Civil Service, you know, they're much the same, you start at the bottom as a curate, or as some junior assistant, and you work your way up. The administrative skills aren't dissimilar. If you want to get anywhere in this world you mustn't cheat, but it's downright foolish not to play the cards in your hand intelligently.

"When you've got some awkward information to present, it's

a question of presenting it in the right way. Digestibly, indigestibly, garnished appetisingly or wrapped up in a discouraging-looking sauce; it all depends whether you want action, inaction or just delayed action. That's what my father used to say anyway, and he was a dab hand at that sort of thing when he was an up and coming young clergyman,'' Timothy grinned, ''or that's what he told *me* anyway.''

Alexa tapped her slippered foot rhythmically, listening hard.

''Now, if you want that wine to remain unsold, committed to oblivion, so to speak . . .''

''Well, not for ever . . .'' Alexa broke in.

''Just listen,'' Timothy said almost sharply, not liking to have his thread of concentration broken.

''You have to present the relevant information to your superiors, your husband in this case, with the maximum candour and the minimum palatability.''

Timothy sat back in his chair and regarded Alexa patiently, as if waiting for the penny to drop. Her brow was, to his eyes, entrancingly creased.

''Your husband doesn't like reading, does he?'' He prompted gently, ''Not overfond of paper work . . .''

Alexa's eyes snapped as enlightenment momentarily dazzled her.

''Write him a report!''

''That would be the businesslike thing to do, wouldn't it?'' Timothy's chuckle was dry.

''A full, painstaking, accurate report, amplifying the details of your statement of account and all wrapped up in a boring-looking file with tape tied round it!''

''A few graphs never do any harm, and tables, don't forget tables. They're invaluable for explicit dullness. Mind you, you must label the file, and draw your husband's attention to the subject matter. Must give the fellow a sporting chance. Then your duty as a good steward is done.''

''Oh, Timothy. Will it work?''

He shrugged with a faint, amused smile.

''Who knows? But it's a tried and tested technique and a respectable one too. It's stood many an honest career man in good stead. You'd be surprised how many hot potatoes get insulated in thick files and then allowed to cool safely.''

''But it doesn't solve the storage thing.''

''That's a minor matter. We'll move it to a wine merchant's

for you, here in London. You'll have to pay an annual fee but it shouldn't break the bank.''

Timothy chatted through dinner, mainly about his family, his time at Cambridge and his infant career in the world of fine art auctioneering. Alexa only half-listened, her thoughts were preoccupied with the triumph of the twenty thousand pounds and the pleasure of having learned an important diplomatic skill. She savoured the twin components of power, money and knowledge, exploring their possibilities in her mind.

''I'm sorry, I'm boring you.'' Timothy's voice, pointed with hurt, penetrated her consciousness.

''No, I . . .''

Timothy smiled as he watched Alexa's thought-shrouded face above the black taffeta bow slowly unveil as if from deep sleep.

''I suppose a lot's happened today, hasn't it? I shouldn't be prattling on about my dull little concerns. Anyone can see you've got far bigger things on your mind.''

''I'm sorry, Timothy, really. It's unforgivable of me, especially when you've done so much.''

He looked pleased and embarrassed.

''Only my job. Tell me about the guest-house project.''

''Well, I was certain Fabrice would hate the whole idea and probably wouldn't let me do it, but actually, he was marvellous about it. Really, I thought he'd prefer to let the house fall down before he'd have paying guests but he seemed to think it was hilarious and promised to be pleasant to all the guests. He said it was better than having to have lions about the place like an English lord and at least the guests did the paying, instead of him having to buy lions and then pay to feed them.''

In fact, Fabrice had been jocular about his wife's idea because he had found it difficult to imagine that such an unlikely project would ever get off the ground and never seriously expected to be incommoded by the appearance of strangers in his house. But Alexa, seizing on his bare permission, had astonished him by the vigour of her activities to raise funds to repair and redecorate the house. He had stood by bemused while she turned the château and its contents upside down, looking for anything she could turn into money.

Suzanne had found herself at odds with her son, who allowed Alexa's activities to proceed unhindered, remarking only that he hoped they might be allowed to preserve the family portraits. Nor did she find an ally in her sister-in-law, as Héloïse limped around the château, visiting rooms and attics she had not seen for many years, unearthing objects which might be turned into cash including her own grandmother's old dolls' house.

"No! Tante Héloïse," Alexa had protested vigorously, "it's irreplaceable. Not intimate, personal things like *that*."

Héloïse had not understood the distinction. To her all possessions were personal and turning out the château was like her childhood Christmas ritual of ransacking her toy cupboards for things to send to the orphanage, taking especial pleasure and pride in parting with anything that was actually dear to her. The avoidance of pain in these exercises seemed cowardly to her and rendered the activity uninteresting. Since she was not allowed to invest the search for saleable objects with any but a purely practical purpose, Héloïse lost interest in helping Alexa and retired to the *Tour du Jardin* to write a religious tract based on the inadvisability of accumulating material goods. Meanwhile, Suzanne, whose motives were less elevated if less confused, contented herself with semi-audible invective about the money-grubbing *bourgeoisie* and English materialism.

"What does your mother-in-law think about it?"

"Who, Suzanne? Oh well, she's not at all keen, as you might expect, but she lives off Fabrice's income, and since it is insufficient to indulge her taste for both privacy and indolence, she'll have to put up with it, I'm afraid."

"You didn't tell her that, I hope." Timothy grimaced.

"Of course not. She's older than me, and Fabrice's mother. She's entitled to be told unpleasant things as pleasantly as possible. I said we'd find her a sitting room as far away from any possible disturbance as was practicable, but it wasn't very likely we'd be able to arrange for her to have her meals served separately, unless she prepared them herself, of course."

"Oh dear, I don't suppose she'd like that very much. Why doesn't she move out?"

"That would obviously be the best thing. But she can't. She hasn't a bean of her own. All her dowry, marriage settlement, if you like, was in Algerian property. Well, that's all gone without compensation since independence. Her family were diehard *Pieds Noirs* and wouldn't leave until they were forced to. The family had been there since 1840, they just couldn't believe de Gaulle would abandon them till the very last minute. In fact there was some story about the old man, her father, having to be dragged out of the house. He said he'd rather let the FLN shoot him in his own dining room than die like a sewer rat in some miserable little slum in France. So poor Suzanne has nothing at all. It's desperate really. If she'd give me half a chance I'd be truly sorry for her. No wonder she's so bad-tempered.''

''She might try to help you, though.''

''I'm afraid she can't do that either. She doesn't know how. Her only resource is snobbery. She's not terribly well educated, you know. She had a governess and not a very good one at that. All she seems to have learned is *petit point*. Survival skills, like how to do your household accounts and make an omelette, simply weren't on the curriculum.''

Timothy smiled wryly.

''And you, of course, were well instructed in these arts.''

''No, I wasn't. But I was taught that if you can read, you can teach yourself to do anything and you may often have to do so. And I'm not a lawyer's daughter for nothing. I know that no situation is so bad it isn't capable of some improvement. *Something* can always be done. And there again, don't forget, I'm a Yorkshirewoman, born and bred. We work hard to preserve and augment what we've got and we don't let money slip through our fingers.''

For a time, Timothy said nothing at all, pushing the veal cutlet around on his plate. Alexa watched him, her head cocked on one side, puzzled at his lack of response. Eventually, he put the knife and fork down and looked up at her. His intelligent face was defenceless.

''I don't suppose you'd give it all up, leave them to it, and marry me?''

Alexa stared, unable to make her brain absorb fully the sounds that she had heard. She had no idea that she had this effect on Timothy Bowring. Their relationship was friendly, businesslike and comfortable, not like this.

''There's a bit of family money and I'll be a partner one day. . . .''

''Timothy, *don't*. I just can't . . . it's impossible.''

''Yes, yes, I suppose it is. You must be shocked. Me, a bishop's son and all that. I just couldn't help saying it, I can't help wanting it, but I see that I'm not much of a catch compared to . . .''

''Timothy, it isn't that. A proposal from you, or somebody like you, would have been much more popular with my parents, and quite possibly with me, had I ever *had* one from somebody like you. But, you see, don't you, it's too late. And I like my life, really. It's been such a marvellous day, don't let it be spoiled."

"No, no. I'm sorry. Please forget I said anything at all. I thought maybe you weren't happy, that's all, and maybe there was a chance for me."

"*Please*, Timothy, don't say any more. Accidents happen, let's forget it. There's just one thing you should know. Fabrice de Pies Ombre is my husband and the Château d'Ombre is his house and mine. It's also our livelihood. The house, the property and the man go together. It's almost impossible to say where one ends and the other begins. But I *chose* them and I shall stick to them *and* make the best of them.

"And, I'll tell you something else," Alexa noticed with some sense of irony that whilst she had told Timothy to say nothing further on the subject of her marriage or his feelings, she herself was saying rather more on those subjects than she had intended, "nobody in my family wanted me to do it, they were completely against it. So I know, that whatever happens to us, whatever happens to me, or to the Château d'Ombre, I shall never have to look back and wonder if things would have been different or better if I'd had my own way. Because I'm having my own way, right now."

Alexa was embarrassed to hear herself finish on a note of aggression. She smiled apologetically.

"I'm inclined to get on a soap box over things."

She turned her head to allow herself a moment to recover, looking over the bright lights of Park Lane to the emerald-edged trees of the shadowed park, beyond. The strength of her own emotions had taken her by surprise, she found she was breathing hard, as if she had taken strenuous exercise.

"Some dessert?" the waiter interposed smoothly between their respective silences.

"Not for me," Alexa responded to Timothy's murmured enquiry. "I'm tired and I'm catching an early train tomorrow. I'm going to see my family in Yorkshire before I go back to France. They don't say so, but I'm afraid it may be the last time I see my grandfather, so I have to go. Thank you for a lovely evening."

Timothy smiled crookedly at the schoolroom formality that was always Alexa's refuge when she was unsure how to proceed. He rose to pull out her chair.

"How kind you are, Madame de Pies Ombre."

Alexa understood at once what he meant by addressing her by her title. He intended her to know that he was convinced that she was married in her heart to Fabrice and everything he stood for. He saluted her.

She rewarded him with a broad smile like a capsized crescent moon and a light kiss on his cheek.

"Come and see us as often as you like, won't you, Timothy? If you come in the summer, you can see how the guest-house project is doing, and after that, perhaps you can start some favourable rumours!"

Timothy watched her go. He stood motionless with the damask napkin still clutched in his hand. The waiter hovering near attempted to catch his eye with a comradely, tip-winning leer. Timothy, unaware, slumped back into his chair unaccountably drained. A day in the life of Alexa de Pies Ombre was like a year in the life of anyone else. She grew and changed before your eyes, and perhaps, he admitted ruefully to himself, you needed the wings of an eagle to keep up with her.

CHAPTER
10

ELIZABETH LOOKED OUT of the tall window in her daughter's bedroom at Langstroth Grange. The fog prevented her seeing much of the grounds but the sound of tyres crunching on the gravel below heralded the car's arrival. It was a raw dark morning and the Rolls' powerful headlamps picked up a thin sprinkling of snow on the lawns as Sheard swirled the large vehicle into position, as near the flight of stone steps as he could get it. It was eight o'clock. Alexa drank the last of her coffee from the china mug on the tray. The Leeds/Bradford airport at Yeadon was out of commission again.

Her visit had been tinged with unhappiness on all sides. Her grandfather, although protesting that he was fit, had become noticeably more frail since she last saw him. His wasted cheeks and greyish pallor had been a shock. Gently, her parents had warned her that he could not last much longer. He was only sixty-seven, but his was not a long-lived family and the heart condition which had been troubling him for some years was now more severe. He had insisted on making the short journey to Langstroth Grange, to be with his granddaughter during her visit, despite his doctor's remonstrations. It would be safer, the doctor insisted, to stay within easy reach of a major hospital.

Sheard had made his disapproval plain too and eventually Henry had shouted at him that whatever time he had left to him, he was going to live it. He would not waste it hooked up to machinery and subjected to the unwelcome authority of a nurse in a vain effort to extend his allotted span by a few miserable weeks or months.

"What've you to look so down in the mouth about, Sheard? You'll be a free man when I go. Aye, *and* you'll have a tidy little

199

income of your own. I'm going to see my little lass if it's the last thing I do, as it might well be; and *you're* going to drive me there. And I'll thank you not to sulk every mile of the way. I don't want to see a face as long as a yard of pump water every time I clap eyes on you."

On the evening before Alexa's departure, amidst protests about the cold and dark, Henry had invited his granddaughter to take a stroll in the grounds with him. It was a clear, starlit night and bitterly cold. The owls were hooting as their footsteps scrunched on the gravel of the orchard path.

"So, you're going back then?"

"Of course, Grandad. What else can I do?"

"You can do a deal else, if you've a mind to. But if you like this husband of yours and you get on together, you're doing the right thing. Take no notice of them two," he cocked his head in the direction of the lighted window of the library, where Elizabeth and Alexander sat after dinner. "Nobody told me what to do when I was your age and I came to no harm for lack of advice. And I started with a lot less than you and what's 'is name. True, I'd no debts, but I'd nothing at all to start with, not even a roof to my head. I came through all right, so you will too, my darling. Follow your instincts and don't waver. That's the best advice I can give you. Stay firm."

Henry stopped abruptly on the path. His breath was short. After resting for a moment, they returned to the house.

"If I'm able, I'll come and see you off tomorrow morning, but don't count on me. I don't hold with all this rubbish about conserving my strength, my time's almost come." He stopped Alexa's half-hearted objection with a slight shake of her arm. "I just want to keep enough wind in my sails to get back to my own house to die. I'm damned if I'll go marooned amongst all these bloody fields. And I want my own doctor. He's a perfect fool, but I've been telling him what's wrong with me and what to do about it for long enough now, we've just about got used to each other."

Henry paused to adjust the astrakhan collar of his town coat, shivering slightly with the cold. "Think on, now. You do as you think fit. None of us lives very long, not long enough to tell others how to live *their* lives. You do it your own way."

Henry's words to her had been occasioned by Elizabeth's relentless attempts to dissuade her daughter from returning to France. It never occurred to her that it was too late because in the Standeven household, nothing other than death was ever irreversible.

Constantly, Elizabeth had opined that Alexa had been as good as trapped into the marriage and that she need feel no guilt in abandoning a contract she had entered into under what amounted, in Elizabeth's estimation, to duress.

"But, Mummy, he asked me, and I said 'yes.' Where is the coercion in that?"

Elizabeth was stuck for an answer, but her instincts told her that the matter was not as simple as that.

"Suppose he was under pressure from his own family to ask you?"

"Whatever makes you think that likely?"

"Don't be so foolish, Alexa. The de Pies Ombres are desperately short of money and *you*, or rather your family, is not."

"There are far greater heiresses than me, people with *big* money, who really could do something to restore the Château d'Ombre and without all this worry and contrivance. They don't need our sort of money. So I really don't think that can be the reason."

But still, Elizabeth would not let the matter drop.

"There was something rather odd in the way that La Courbe woman," Tilly would always be 'the La Courbe woman' to Elizabeth, "positively incarcerated you on your so-called wedding morning. I never saw such a travesty in my life. It was a flagrant usurpation of a mother's privileges. She must have been afraid that had *I* had the supervision of you that morning, there would have been no wedding. She's shrewd enough, I'll give her that."

The greater part of these exchanges took place without Alexander's knowledge. He had already expressed his disapproval of his wife's attacks on their daughter's marriage when Elizabeth had begun them on the evening of her arrival at Langstroth Grange.

"We had better remember, if we are all to remain friends, and I had rather we did, that Alexa *is* married whether we like it or not," he had said to Elizabeth from his dressing room door as they both prepared for bed. "And until such times as she comes to me and tells me she wants the thing undone, and unravelled, we are bound to pay her the compliment usually due to married women."

"Oh, and what is that?" Elizabeth snapped as she adjusted

what she imagined were the few discreet curlers she had always worn in bed since the earliest flames of conjugal passion in her own marriage had abated.

"We must refrain from abusing her husband and her husband's family. Alexa freely entered into that marriage. It was against my better judgement, but I did give my permission. *I* have no evidence that there was any element of undue pressure put upon her, none whatsoever. And I tell you this, if you don't leave it alone, she may never come home again, and I shall know whom to blame if she does not. You very nearly achieved it before, if you succeed finally because of your damned intemperate tongue, don't expect any congratulations from me."

Alexander had taken a restrained pride in Alexa's enterprise in selling the wine and rejoiced with her at the prices realised. But, he had warned her, it would take a great deal more to put the Château d'Ombre back on its feet. The principal ingredient of recovery, he had remarked, was the determination to succeed.

"And that is really in Fabrice's hands. You must pull together, of course, but it cannot be all your doing. We are expecting some effort from *him*."

Now it was time to go, Alexa could not help but feel relief. She loved her family dearly but that love was always qualified by a fear of the havoc they could wreak in her composure. To be with them, particularly her mother, was to begin to question her own judgement, to doubt her own decisions and to feel helplessly that she would never be allowed to grow up and that, indeed, perhaps that was best.

She had always interpreted her father's silences as tokens of absolute agreement with her mother's spoken objections to anything she might wish to do. And on this occasion, the fact that her father had given his qualified blessing to her marriage and set the seal of his tolerance on it by attending the wedding, was almost overcome to her mind by Elizabeth's perpetual and secretive efforts to undermine it. She was, therefore, all the more grateful to her grandfather for his reassurance. He alone had made her feel that she was entitled to pursue her own affairs and live her own life as she chose.

She had been called at six o'clock and taken to see Henry, who had also woken early, asking to see her, in the large guest room.

"Now, my darling, I can't go with you, and that's a fact. I don't feel so clever this morning and I'd better not risk it. You'll not get away from Yeadon, you know, not in this fog. Better get down to London on the train, Sheard'll take you in the Rolls and then he can come back for me. I shan't be up and dressed till then, so it's no hardship.

"I don't expect we'll meet again, not till we're both twanging harps and wearing nightgowns at any rate, so give me a big kiss. No tears, mind, and remember what I told you."

Alexa leaned over the bed to kiss her grandfather, struggling to control her tears. She could not trust herself to speak but managed a feeble smile. It seemed to her that he was the only one who had loved her unconditionally.

"Most of what I've got goes to your Mummy, you know, that's only right. But you'll find there's something for you to be going on with in the meantime, and eventually, it'll come to you. But you get on making your own fortune. Don't wait for dead men's shoes. Families don't get rich and powerful by waiting to inherit their parents' money. You and what's 'is name get stuck in and work. It's the only way."

Alexa made some incoherent sounds of assent.

"And there's to be no coming to my funeral. Do you hear me? I won't have it. There'll be plenty there, I don't doubt. But you're not to come. It's not healthy and I shan't miss you. Go on now."

Henry dropped her hand and seemed to push her away a little roughly. She looked at him, surprised and hurt, through the mist of tears. He lay back on the pillows, his skin papery. He had talked far too much for his strength. She wanted to kiss him again, but she dare not, so she blew him a kiss from her hand and bade him a whispered goodbye.

Tentatively, Alexa suggested to her mother that perhaps she should not leave as Henry seemed worse.

"No. You know your grandfather. He hates illness, injury, mutilation, misfortune and anything connected with death. He can't avoid the latter for himself of course, but he'd hate it if we let you be involved. I know him. He won't allow himself to die until you're well clear. So, you'd better go on, dear. We'll take care of everything else. You live abroad now. I suppose I must accept it. You'd better get on with your life there if it's what you want. I shan't say another word."

Elizabeth started to strip the bed. She asked herself again, where she had gone wrong that her daughter should marry a penniless cripple in defiance of her wishes. A Catholic into the bargain. Life was very hard. The prospect of grandchildren who were French, a race for whom she had little respect, and *Catholic*, a religion that was abhorrent to her, outraged her sense of fair play. A careful, responsible parent, such as she had been, had a right to expect satisfactory results. The idea that her carefully nurtured Alexa should be subjected to the ignominy of debt, the insecurity and all the discomfort that debt produces, was an insult to her own father's effort to rise above poverty and protect his descendants from it. And yet Henry Jagger had actually encouraged Alexa to persevere in this marriage, if what Alexa said could be believed. No, it was as well that she should go and go quickly before she began to lose her temper not only with her daughter but with her dying father. That would certainly be unbecoming.

"Have you got everything?" she addressed Alexa with as much warmth as she could muster.

"Yes, I think so. Can I take this with me?" Alexa lifted the miniature in question down from its place beside the chimney piece. It was an early nineteenth-century likeness of an ancestor on the Standeven side, a portrait of a rather smug-looking young man in a dark coat and plain neckcloth. Nobody could remember exactly who he was. Elizabeth nodded her puzzled assent.

"I think I ought to have at least one ancestor of my own with me at d'Ombre. My mother-in-law has a tiresome habit of pretending I don't even know who my grandparents were. I wish I had some *prettier* forebears, but this one will do very well for the purpose!"

In Leeds City Square, large, wet flakes of snow fell sparsely on the Black Prince and his incongruous court of naked bronze nymphs.

Sheard had been silent for most of the journey and Alexa was glad. But as he swung the Rolls into the station forecourt he suddenly spoke.

"You do us all proud, Miss Alexa, out there. Think on now."

In common with all Yorkshire servants, he thought nothing of giving instructions to his employer or his employer's family. Their affairs were his affairs, and their honour was his own.

Alexa was touched by this mark of sincere affection from her grandfather's old friend and servant.

"I shall do my very best, Sheard, you may be sure of that."

"Aye. You'll frame all right. I shouldn't be surprised if you didn't turn out to be a proper toff, now, like your grandad."

"Thank you, Sheard," Alexa replied to the carefully qualified compliment. That was another thing about Yorkshire servants, they had a horror of any words that might be interpreted as flattery. Everything must be conditional.

Sheard settled her in the pink and beige Pullman car. He muttered a few words, inaudible to Alexa, in the ear of the steward. He climbed down onto the platform and stood there looking at her. She slid open the window to speak to him.

"I won't wait if you don't mind, Miss Alexa," he touched the peak of his cap. "I've got to get back up that there dratted dale to fetch your grandfather home. It'll take two hours in this fog."

"Yes, of course, Sheard. He's very poorly, isn't he?"

"I don't rightly know, Miss, but I reckon he'll pull round again, this time. He always has before, it's just he seems right depressed at the moment. The country don't agree with him, he'll be better off at home. I'll be off then."

Sheard turned away, straightening his already perfectly adjusted chauffeur's cap as he disappeared into the confusion of the barrier. Alexa watched him until he was out of sight and then sat down and took her gloves off. There was a lump in her throat.

"Would your ladyship care for anything to drink?" The steward bent over her deferentially. Alexa blushed. She wasn't entitled to that form of address. Sheard must have been giving unauthorised instructions to the chief steward while settling about her luggage.

"Beg your pardon, m'lady, but your man said you was a marchioness."

"That's not *quite* true. I am married to a French *Marquis*. It's the same title, but in France, everyone is called *Madame* or *Monsieur*, whoever they are. We're very democratic over there." The steward smiled. "As y'ladyship wishes. We've a very nice dry sherry I can recommend this morning."

The train drew away from Leeds and settled into its familiar, soporific four-beat rhythm. The flat uninteresting landscape of the south of Yorkshire reminded her of d'Ombre, with its impersonal mists and distances. The great difference was the way the wet lay in puddles on the surface of the ground, pools of water could be seen in pastures and ploughlands alike. Here the earth was very dark and looked as rich as chocolate cake. At d'Ombre it was light-coloured thin and stony stuff. There seemed to be no nourishment in it. But that's what the vines liked. They all said that. Poor soil, well drained.

She remembered how one week before Christmas, it had been raining for days. But Alexa's boots had barely been splashed as she walked up and down the lines of amputated vines. The gravel had felt knobbly beneath her feet. The water seemed to drain away instantly, on touching the ground.

She had taken to walking in the vineyards every day, sometimes for hours at a time. Gradually she began to come to terms with the landscape, getting over the uncomfortable feeling of dangerous exposure that all hill-bred people experience on plains. The sheep-dotted dales of her home and similarly populated fells of her school days had imprinted on unconscious conviction on her mind that the sky never formed more than one third of any landscape. To live in a place where the pattern of the world was turned upside down was, in itself, a fundamental disturbance to her equilibrium, or so she had told herself. In fact there had been more than a trace of agoraphobia in her reaction to the outdoor world of the Château d'Ombre.

The indescribable mental pressure of her concealed pregnancy, and the associated fears, had found their expression in this one neurotic symptom. She was unaware of its cause, and hardly aware that it really existed. And yet she had found herself pausing at the doors of the château, asking herself if there was any reason why she should go out. Eventually, recognising something that was akin to fear, she had fought it down and forced her unwilling feet to carry her out into the open air. And, over a period of days, the mild winds blew sadness and guilt away. That was all done with now and she must make good her pledge to serve the house, property and family with all her strength. They had saved her somehow, and though they would never know it, they should be repaid.

Contrary to expectation, human beings do not always form the strongest bonds with places where they have been happy. Alexa, like many others, forged cords of attachment to the place where she had live most intensely. Although it had been an intensity of suffering, it was the most vivid experience of her life. Long after it had been submerged in more immediate troubles and happier events, it would be the unnamed, unacknowledged child she had lost during her first few months of residence in her husband's home that formed the longest and strongest root which she put down in the soil of Château d'Ombre. And, like the vines, unbeknown to herself, she would draw up sustenance and stability from the depths she had penetrated.

As she walked, Alexa had looked down at her feet, scudding occasional pebbles with her rubber-clad toes. The long distances which lay exposed in every direction were veiled with a thick mist rising off the river to the east and the more distant Atlantic to the west. The ordered ranks of the harshly pruned vine stumps were shadowy, their tormented outlines disappearing quickly in the mist.

The gnarled vine stumps gave no clue to the extent and spread of the roots beneath. She felt an instant comradeship with them in that they, like her, were shorn of all fruit, flower and leaf. But Alexa already knew enough to realise that their power lay in what was invisible and that they would come and come again, year after year, despite rain and pestilence. If the wine was not good one year, it would be another and she took some courage from the lesson of their endurance. All we have to do, she told herself, is stay near them. As long as we have them, they will pull us through in the end.

While she drank a cup of coffee she had ordered, Alexa thought of Fabrice. Up to now, their sex life had not been a success. She blamed herself entirely for that. Or at least, she tried to. He had done what he no doubt considered his dynastic duties, but the necessary qualification in her self-giving had put a barrier between them. Every night he went through the routine of increasingly mechanical foreplay, penetrated her gruntingly, as often as not with the aid of a gynaecological preparation which, he said laconically, was an admirable substitute for passion, and quickly reached a climax from which he subsided onto the bed beside her. He would lie there for a little while, staring at the ceiling as if he were asking himself what had gone wrong.

Alexa was always left with a feeling she could not have put into words. It was a feeling of having been cheated of something at the last moment, when the prize was almost hers. It made desolate tears come into her eyes. She would lie still in the dark beside him, her finger tips wiping away the wet on her cheeks. She did not know what, in precise terms, had gone wrong, she was only sure it must be her fault, something to do with having cheated him.

Every morning he continued to go early to the *chais*, the long low buildings behind the château where the wine was made. But what he did there remained a mystery. He never talked about his work and brushed aside Alexa's tentative enquiries brusquely. Once she had asked him how his day had gone and he had said, "Oh, don't be so middle-class Alexa. Is that what your mother says to your father when he gets back from his office or wherever it is he works?" She had not replied. It was exactly what her mother said to her father when he came home in the evenings. Conversation about the day's business was routine in her parents' home and to know nothing of the way in which her husband earned their living was alien to Alexa.

And yet there was some warmth in his odd, off-hand acceptance of her in his home. Unlike Suzanne he never made her feel that her position was equivocal or that of an interloper. The day Alexa had said she would move an elaborately painted screen from an unused bedroom to her own, partly to protect it from damp and partly because she admired it, Suzanne's automatic protests had been quelled by Fabrice instantly.

"Naturally my wife will exercise her discretion in these household matters," he had said, masticating *rognons de boeuf* with rhythmic steadiness. Alexa was so grateful to him she came very close to thanking him for his intervention. But she could not afford to admit that there was any tension between herself and Suzanne or that any arbitration between herself and her mother-in-law was necessary.

"Perhaps, *Belle Mère*, you would like the screen, yourself," she had said, "it's so pretty. It doesn't matter where it is as long as it isn't damaged."

"You'd better take it if you want it, though I hope there will soon be an end to all this continual upheaval. I cannot see what you hope to achieve. It is busyness for the sake of busyness. Very vulgar. Excessive activity is a symptom of common blood."

"Whereas," Fabrice had countered cheerfully, "sustained inactivity is generally thought to be more symptomatic of death than good breeding."

Suzanne had looked sharply at her son and daughter-in-law as she saw the slight smile pass between them. Their most natural moments together often came as a result of teasing the dowager *Marquise*. As far as his mother was concerned, it was the worst feature of Fabrice's marriage, that he now had the whetstone of Alexa's appreciation to sharpen the edge of his tongue.

Alexa drank the last of her coffee reflectively, smiling at the recollection of that scene. There were times, like that one, when she felt a piercing happiness in her husband's company. It was made all the more poignant by his unexplained, lightning withdrawals into himself. If only she could find the key to his heart and keep it instead of forever mislaying it as she seemed to do. He was always correct, sometimes affectionate in his remote way, but never passionate. Her hand tightened unconsciously on the handle of the coffee cup. She would have to try harder to win him. It was another challenge. She would do him so much good, she would make him love her.

At King's Cross, once settled in the taxi, Alexa felt around in her coat pockets and looked in her handbag. She shrugged charmingly and spread her hands in the way Monsieur Terry so often did.

"I'm so sorry, I don't appear to have any change," she told the porter with a beaming smile. He smiled himself, torn between anger at her parsimony and euphoria at the benediction of her smile. The cabbie grimaced into the rear-view mirror. He didn't like picking up women. Particularly these monied, la-di-da types. Never did have a penny on them when it counted.

"I 'opes you've got the fare, lady."

Alexa allowed her eyes to widen in synthetic outrage.

"Why shouldn't I have? Heathrow please, terminal two."

She shuddered slightly at her own meanness. But from now on it was going to be imperative to look after every centime. You couldn't go wasting money on people you were never going to see again. Everything could be learned, including economy. She must remember to tell that to Fabrice.

At Heathrow, the check-in girl on the Air France desk looked curiously at the titled second-class passenger.

"There are some telegrams waiting for you, Madam. I have them here."

Surprised, but with no sense of foreboding, Alexa slit the first one open and smiled at the message of congratulation on her success and the warm welcome home to France. It came from Tilly. It was just like her, to do the unexpected, slightly crazy thing. Still smiling, Alexa turned to the other, running her thumb under the flap of the yellow envelope, expecting something in the same vein as the first telegram. Her eyes glued horribly on the ugly, type-written word.

Grandad died at noon. Quite peaceful. Last message to you was "Good Luck." Very insistent you do not come to funeral. Telephone when you get home. Mummy.

Poor Sheard, he never did take Grandad home. His master died among the sheep-ridden fields, after all. Alexa couldn't help smiling as she thought of the strong will of the man who had caused a telegram to be sent to someone at Heathrow on the morning of his own death. That took character, and if it was all that he had bequeathed her, it was the best inheritance.

CHAPTER
11

❧ ❧ FABRICE CAME TO meet her at Mérignac. Although practically speaking, there was nothing else he could have done, Alexa was surprised at her own delight in recognising his lopsided silhouette in the small crowd waiting in the arrivals concourse. When he turned slowly on his stick, using it as a pivot in his characteristic manner, his eyes caught hers and he smiled. She had not seen that special smile of his, mocking and bittersweet, since the day when he had taken her out to lunch at Fouquet's and proposed to her. Something of the dull ache of the news of Henry's death lessened as she contemplated his wisdom in sending her back to her husband.

"Hello, *ma belle*, I've missed you."

"I've missed you too," Alexa said almost too dutifully. Even her brief absence had been long enough to make her a little shy of him. His greeting was so open and warm she hardly knew how to respond. It was unlike their usual habit of sardonic banter. There was a momentary pause while each regarded the other with hopeful affection but slight unease. Fabrice made the first attempt to overcome the awkwardness. He'd forgotten how lovely she was.

"Here, let me take that for you." He leaned down effortlessly to take her small dressing case.

"I can manage it," Alexa replied with an unconscious lack of grace.

"I'm well aware of that, but I shan't be able to manage your suitcase when it appears, so I'm doing what I can to help."

"Sorry, I'm not very tactful, am I?"

"It's one of the things I've missed. Your honest to God clumsiness, dressed overall with perfect schoolgirl good manners.

211

Your amusing little bouts of downright savagery are quite diverting too. *Maman* has had an easy time of it lately." In his disappointment Fabrice spoke with more sadness than ferocity. It was so rare that there was any deep harmony between them. For a moment he had hoped that they might both overcome their innate diffidence with each other. They'd had so little time to get to know each other. Alexa always seemed so busy planning or achieving something or other and now she was back, no doubt full of her first real triumph.

Alexa too, understood that an opportunity she had not known how to seize had passed. She fell back on the usual companionable banter.

"Oh, Fabrice. What an awful thing to say! How is she, anyway?"

"Impatient to see you and your twenty thousand pounds sterling, of course."

Alexa turned to him sharply. "Fabrice, no! You promised I could spent it on my project." She looked fiercely at him. "I *can* spend it on the project, can't I?"

"But of course," he mocked gently, "isn't that why we endured a week of that buffoon Bowring's company? The way he looked at you I thought I should die of laughter long before he died of unrequited love. Hardly old enough to have given up pawing boys of his own age in the English fashion. What an effect you had, darling. I think *Maman* was somewhat discontented. She would have considered it polite if young Bowring had at least attempted to moon over *her* a little. Any nicely brought up young Frenchman would have understood what was required. Anyway, she was a little cross about it."

"She's always cross about something or other. I'm just concerned that she understands that this has all been for a *serious* reason, not to extend her wardrobe."

"What did you get for the rest of the wine, by the way?" Fabrice changed the subject smoothly, anxious to get away from the contentious matter of his mother and her curiously large appetite for top-quality clothing.

"Oh, I'm afraid it didn't sell. I've written you a comprehensive report about everything. The file's in my luggage. You can go through it in the *chai* tomorrow morning."

Alexa winced inwardly as she heard her own voice give the small but vital twist to the truth. Fabrice wouldn't be interested in reading about anything that had been found to have no marketable value anyway. Still, the file was there with all the facts, she hadn't really concealed anything. A slip of the tongue.

Fabrice grunted. He was grateful to his young wife for taking some of the domestic paperwork off his hands, but news that she was now beginning to generate business paperwork of her own was not so welcome.

"You know my grandfather died."

Fabrice registered instant shock and sympathy, but dependent on one hand for the support of his stick and finding the other occupied with holding Alexa's dressing case, he stumbled slightly in an attempt to move closer to her. Alexa put her arm out to steady him and found herself embracing him at the very moment in which she would have liked to feel the weight and warmth of his arm encircling her own body. There were already so many times she could recall, when it was *she* who had made the warm and sympathetic gesture whilst in need of it herself.

"I'm sorry," he said. "I didn't know him, did I? I mean, he didn't come to the wedding, did he? Is that yours there?" Fabrice pointed to a pigskin suitcase with her grandfather's initials stamped on it. Henry had lent it to her when she first came to Paris more than a year since.

"Yes." Alexa was struck by the macabre coincidence but said nothing. "No, you didn't. Know him, I mean. It's all right, I loved him, but he was ready to go. He sent us a last message. It was a telegram I got at Heathrow. 'Good Luck,' it said." For an instant her features were convulsed. "I'll get the suitcase. I hope the car's not too far away, it's terribly heavy, that thing."

Fabrice turned the old Jaguar east from the airport to Bordeaux.

"Aren't we going home?"

"Not immediately. I've got to see the *négociant* in Bordeaux, first. He rang me this morning and said he wanted to see me about something. You'll like Chirac, he's an agreeable type. He'll probably give us lunch too. That's if you feel up to it."

Fabrice glanced at her sideways. She seemed perfectly calm now. Her sudden storm of grief beside the car in the airport carpark had been violent but mercifully short-lived. He'd been helpless, unable to do anything. He had felt inadequate and embarrassed, patting her with his free hand.

"They keep a very good table at their premises. Directors' dining room, proper chef, antique silver—it's all pretty much like a London merchant banking outfit. I used to go sometimes with *my* grandfather when I was a small boy. Anyway, Chirac Frères deal with the marketing side of the wine business. Château d'Ombre isn't the only property they handle, of course, but it's one of their more important ones. So I expect they'll make a fuss of us, especially as I've got you with me. They've probably laid something fairly spectacular on for the new *Marquise*. I said you'd be with me.''

Alexa was quiet, watching the ugly suburban sprawl speed by. Exhausted and relieved by her recent paroxysm of sorrow, she listened to the pleasing sound of her husband's voice. She liked the way he spoke. His voice was light, the French musical, crisp and correct. Better still, Fabrice spoke as though he was almost proud of her.

Without answering him, she examined her face in the mirror concealed behind the sun visor. Her face had recovered quickly from the bout of weeping. She decided not to add any face powder. It was usually a mistake after tears. It only made it more obvious.

The leaf-green coat and sable pill-box were smart enough. The coat had been a gift from Monsieur Terry. A cancelled order that fitted her perfectly. Clothes were becoming a problem. The idea that model girls get *couture* clothes free or nearly so had of course, proved to be a myth. Her mother had given her a generous cheque for a trousseau and she still had some clothes left over from the period spent with Jean-Claude. She daren't thrown them away, but at the same time she was loath to wear them. She had spent her mother's cheque on repairs to the guttering at the château. She had her allowance of course, but her instinct was to save every penny that she could.

"What are you thinking about, darling?"

"Clothes."

"Oh. When a wife says that she really means money."

"I don't. At least, I mean how not to need any clothes and therefore how not to need any money."

"How refreshing you are. My poor dear mother views the problem of howsoever she shall be clothed from the entirely opposite angle. With her it is a question of how to need clothes and therefore how to need money. It is a problem for her as she does nothing that justifies her being clothed. She is a true lily of the field.''

"Then she had better try trusting to providence like it says in the Bible!'' was Alexa's tart rejoinder. Fabrice sighed. It was his own fault. He should have kept off the subject.

"Now, look. This is old Bordeaux. We Bordelais find it far finer than Paris.''

Alexa was captivated. They were passing through cobbled streets so narrow that it seemed incredible that the Jaguar could squeeze by without injury. The grey houses were tall and gaunt so that the streets seemed deep fissures in the earth's crust. The shadow in them was complete. No ray of sun could hit the cramped thoroughfares directly. The pearly quality of the Atlantic light was dimmed over by a miasma of ancient gloom. Here and there an elaborately carved stone doorway announced a former grandeur, the crispness of the stonemason's work long since blunted by time and the relentless massage of centuries of salt-laden winds.

Untidy men with dark oily curls and sallow complexions shambled in the streets. Their clothes were a peculiar assemblage of limp and matted garments. Many wore leather slippers with medieval-looking curled toes. There were garishly dressed girls, their faces enamelled with unnatural vividness, and black-clad old women carrying laden shopping bags, one in each hand. They seemed compressed with the weight of years and misfortune.

Glancing upward she could see shutters half opened onto filigree balconies, decorated with scarlet geraniums. Long lace curtains veiled the unimaginable lives lived within.

The dusty, untidy shop windows displayed tin cooking pots of strange design and piles of the oriental-seeming footwear. Spools of greyish meat spun on vertical spindles, making the air savoury.

"This is the Arab quarter. A lot of seamen from North Africa have traditionally made this their headquarters.''

"What are all these women with the peroxide hair? They're not Arabs, surely.''

Fabrice grinned. "They are not the sort of women one discusses with one's wife, but they're mostly good sorts and keep these chaps from molesting decent French girls. Every port has a certain population of them.''

Occasionally there were glimpses of the broad Gironde, the watery artery which brought the world's trade into the heart of Aquitaine. There was something familiar in the atmosphere, if not in the visual aspect of the place.

"It feels a little like Liverpool. I went there once to meet my grandfather off a boat. There's the same feeling of actual international relationships happening on the dockside. It's different from the theoretical feeling of cosmopolitan intercourse you get in capital cities. The goings and the comings are right there in front of you. The buying and the selling, the bills of lading, the customs houses and seamen's missions, they're the same, whether it's Liverpool, beaútiful Bordeaux, or just boring little Goole."

"I must take your word for that. I have never visited either worthy borough."

"You should. That's one of the problems with you French, you're apt to think that the world begins at Calais and ends at Marseilles."

"My father didn't."

"I bet he never set eyes on an English commercial port apart from London. The so-called international set are woefully ignorant of the way in which the real world works."

Fabrice did not answer at once. His face was set. Eventually he said, "It would be more becoming, darling, if you refrained from pontificating about matters of which you can know little. It is not graceful and it is not well-bred."

Alexa was stung. Angrily, she turned her face away and looked out of the window to her right, affecting to have paid no attention to him. The atmosphere in the car was strained. Fabrice made a clumsy bid to rectify matters.

"I don't know that I approve all that much of talk about breeding, well-bred, ill-bred, that sort of thing. But sometimes it seems to be necessary. After all, I wouldn't want anyone to get the wrong idea about my wife, simply for want of a word in season from her prematurely crusty husband. Come on, don't sulk, Alexa, it's not like you."

But she would not respond to the thinly disguised apology. What made matters worse was a painful awareness that he was right. She *was* apt to be too free with facile opinions, she usually did it when she felt nervous. It didn't make her any less nervous to have the fault pointed out. And nervousness made her aggressive.

"I suppose," she snapped, as the car drew to a halt beside a discreetly grand eighteenth-century building on the waterfront, "you would prefer a wife without any opinions, an animated doll making the expected noises at the expected times. I must try to behave like a superior model."

"Ah, the beautiful bride. At last we meet her."

Georges Chirac spoke in English and without any trace of accent but betrayed his Frenchness by the formality of his phrases. He was tall and dressed in impeccable pepper and salt tweeds garnished with the sort of tie that Alexa had seen on the Rue de Rivoli. They were an elegant and witty interpretation of prestigious class badges worn by Englishmen proud of their school, their university or their regiment. His face looked as though it had been conceived by the Royal Mint to look good in profile on a coin of the realm. A Gascon face.

"And you have had a great success, we hear, quite a triumph. You have a true helpmeet here, Fabrice. I congratulate you."

Chirac looked with interest at Alexa. Since her marriage, little had been heard of her despite the speculation. A common adventuress some said, a vastly wealthy heiress, said others, whose father had bought her a title. A nobody, anyway.

"I hope you can spare him, my dear *Marquise*," Chirac indulged her with the title, "for a few minutes only, I promise. Fabrice and I have some little business to settle and then we shall have luncheon. You must be hungry after your journey. I am so sorry to be the cause of imposing this tedious detour on you. I hope you can forgive me."

"Very readily, *Monsieur*, if I may look at all these wonderful things while you are talking." The room was lined with glazed cabinets, each displaying wine labels, many in series with each other showing a different label for each vintage of a single château. Other vitrines showed small silver dishes—*tastevins*, corkscrews and other memorabilia of wine drinking.

"I doubt if they are wonderful, *chère Madame*, except, of course, to people like us. Wine is our obsession, our hobby, our livelihood, but I do not pretend that a young lady would find its charms quite as limitless as I do myself. But if you will indeed be so kind as to cast an eye over our little collection, I shall bring your husband back to you before your boredom becomes terminal."

In the event, Monsieur Chirac and Fabrice were shut in an inner office for more than half an hour. When they returned, Monsieur Chirac was all courtliness, dispensing professional charm with a liberal hand. By contrast, Fabrice seemed moody and withdrawn. Alexa noted it without particular alarm, attributing it to the sharp exchange of words which had taken place between them immediately prior to their arrival. She had rather it had not been so, but now she felt it was her responsibility to maintain dignity and proceeded to ignore Fabrice's unsociable behaviour. Marital squabbles should never be allowed to inconvenience other people.

Monsieur Chirac took Alexa by the arm and led her into an adjoining apartment. Three great windows, reaching from ceiling to floor, uncurtained and unshuttered, invited the Gironde and its rippling, flickering light into the room. The glass and silver on the long marble-topped table glinted and flashed in the moving light and the Irish chandeliers which hung above added their subdued twinkle to the symphony of cool illumination. Opposite the great windows was a curvili near chimney-piece, carved from the same grey-veined marble as the table, and surmounted by an expanse of gilt-framed mirror glass, which meant that the diners must always be surrounded on both sides by the river. On the floor, herringbone parquet, faded almost to silver by the incessant, unstopped light, shone with wax polish. The result was a room without colour but consumed by light.

"It is a wonderful room, *Monsieur*."

Monsieur Chirac nodded his satisfaction. "Don't you think it needs cheering up? A little colour perhaps, just a splash?"

"Garnet, maybe, to give it definition, dark red . . ." Alexa caught the smile in Georges Chirac's eyes.

"You did it for the wine, didn't you? The garnet comes from the wine in the glasses, it's all the colour you need."

"Or want, *Madame*. Bravo. Your husband must count himself a lucky man, he has found a wife with both beauty and brains." Fabrice made a *moue*. Was it the cliché he disliked or the compliment paid to her?

Fabrice felt an obscure anger. Alexa, to his mind, had an indecent knack of attracting attention to herself. It gave him a feeling of insecurity, a sensation of being out of control of the one thing he most desperately wanted to control. He knew that his feeling was unreasonable and he avoided confronting it objectively in case the sensation of outrage should dissipate in the light of judgement, and leave him feeling empty.

A relatively simple luncheon was served. A little parade of *hors d'oeuvre* appeared, each starkly perfect in itself, unconfused with garnish or any sauce but mayonnaise or olive oil. The *entrée* was lampreys at which Alex balked, having a fear of anything tubular, the more so if it came out of water.

"I beg you to do me the honour of trying, *Madame*." Alexa's gorge rose as the manservant, discreet to the point of invisibility, stood beside her chair, silently proffering the salver on which the loathsome fish reposed. "It is but an eel." Hardly a comforting statement. "Your Henry II was very appreciative of lamprey. It was a Plantagenet taste, of course, originating here in France, where the Plantagenets had their roots. Please indulge me, I planned the lamprey myself, in compliment to the cousinship of our two people. Here in Bordeaux, we like to honour the English connection."

Overcome by his obvious sincerity, Alexa served herself from the dish, feeling herself to be in the same position as one who is confronted with a sheep's eye at an Arab feast. In fact it was delicious, rich and delicate.

During lunch, Alexa and Georges Chirac talked with increasing mutual liking. Fabrice remained preoccupied, answering most questions with little more than a murmur or a grunt. Eventually, he was excluded from the conversation altogether, as Monsieur Chirac firmly refrained from addressing any further remarks to him as if he were a sulky child. Alexa, embarrassed but helpless, followed his lead.

"How does one become a *négociant à Bordeaux*?"

"It is usually a family thing, *Madame*, as it is in our case. Chirac Frères is not an old house, however. It was started by my grandfather in the early years of this century."

"How did he begin?"

"Very simply. He owned a small property, a few hectares, no more, which his father had obtained cheaply during the barren years of the Phylloxera plague. My great grandfather was a peasant, he could barely read and write, but he foresaw that there might again come a time when land in the Médoc could become productive and valuable. He left the land to my grandfather who planted it with vines grafted on American rootstocks. It was the law, by that time, you understand."

"Why the American rootstocks?"

"Oh quite simply because the American native vine had proved resistant to the Phylloxera."

"Forgive me, I am interrupting."

"No, no, you do right to ask. These facts are so well known to me, so much the bedrock of my heritage, that I forget they are not obvious. But, as I say, Grandfather planted his vineyard and by the end of the First World War, his first full harvest was gathered by my grandmother who tended the vineyard whilst her husband was in the army. Grandfather was a good *vigneron*. He marketed his product personally, visiting local cafés and restaurants and taking samples with him in a pony and cart. Eventually, the *patrons* of these establishments asked if he could supply them with other wines, white wines, for instance, so that they would not have to bother with other individual suppliers. Being by nature an entrepreneur, Grandfather said yes, and began to travel to more distant parts of the region in search of wines that might please his customers. Sometimes he bought these wines outright and at other times he merely negotiated a price on behalf of the vineyard proprietor, taking a commission for his trouble. By 1928, this work was the mainstay of his livelihood and his brother, my great uncle, joined him in the business. You see both their portraits in the anteroom where you were examining our collection."

Alexa's attention was rapt and not merely polite. Fascinated by this story of humble beginnings and surrounded by the results of great achievement, she recognised a history not very dissimilar to her own grandfather's. There was nothing, it seemed, that could not be done or reached with steady, plodding determination. Fabrice paid no attention, he had heard it all before, nor did he consider it to have any relevance to his own position. If Chirac chose to entertain Alexa with the well-worn history of Chirac Frerès' rise to prominence, there was, unfortunately, nothing he could do about it. When one was first married, he mused, there was bound to be a fair amount of this sort of tedium until the lore and legend of generations was transmitted to the bride who would, in her turn, become weary of it. Sighing, he shut out the sound of Alexa's eager questions and Chirac's delighted responses.

"And the original vineyard, did you carry on with that?"

"Oh no, it was too small and formed such an insignificant part of my grandfather's income, that we gave up producing wine of our own altogether when my grandmother died. She had some affection for those few vines and kept them in production while she lived. But seriously, by that time it was only a hobby."

"How very sad! Those few vines are your roots, the beginnings of your success. An ancestor's farsighted legacy. It gave you everything you have!"

"I had not perceived it in quite that way before, *Madame*, but no doubt you are right."

"Oh, I'm sorry, I'm boring you," Alexa said hastily, feeling she had rather overstepped the boundaries of politeness. Chirac regarded her speculatively, he had rarely encountered so charming a young woman. Her looks and vitality were amplified by the intense quality of her concentration. There was nothing so calculated to beguile as this obsessive, dissecting interest she displayed in everything that was said. And she was unpredictable. At one moment she seemed retiring, at another she was vivid with enthusiasm, and always there was the formidable, blue-eyed attention.

Her personality seemed to be undergoing one of those maturing metamorphoses that happen in the post-adolescent period. It could give a jerky effect, like a youth's voice breaking. Her schoolroom polish which betokened a careful education was at times disrupted by an unexpected forthrightness which Chirac suspected originated with more fundamental qualities, bred in the bone. He hoped young de Pies Ombre was up to the demanding task of being this girl's husband. If she could only communicate some of her burgeoning interest in the wine trade to *him*, it might be a very good thing for them. If she could do it in time. As he entertained these random thoughts, he glanced at the glowering Fabrice.

"No talk of vines is ever boring here, *Madame*, I do assure you. Your interest is most flattering. May I make a suggestion? Why do you not undertake the restoration of my grandfather's old vineyard yourself? When you have succeeded, no doubt we could come to some equitable arrangement about the profits."

"But *Monsieur*!" Alexa was aghast at the turn the conversation had taken and uncomfortably aware that it was far from pleasing to Fabrice. "I know absolutely nothing about vines!"

"I hardly think we need regard that as a totally disabling factor. If I may say so, *Madame*, for a person of your commanding temperament, there can be no better way of learning anything than active involvement. And how appropriate the lessons would be. Soon you will be assisting your husband in the management of his property. Is that not so Fabrice?"

Fabrice's mumbled reply was dismissive. Tactfully, Chirac offered Alexa an escape route, "Of course, I appreciate you will be very busy just now," and to his regret, she took it, explaining in some detail her plans for the guest-house project.

"Think about it anyway. The vineyard will wait upon your convenience."

He was not going to take no for an answer, Alexa thought, and so smiled her pretended agreement. Why a kind, intelligent man should insist so on an absurd joke was puzzling in the extreme.

Monsieur Chirac understood that his suggestion had been waved smoothly aside and he regretted it. He was a rich man and in a position to give an informal wedding gift to this charming bride. It would be a diversion for her, one that she might well need. Marriage to Fabrice de Pies Ombre would not be an easy row to hoe. The little scheme might even have provided a modest income for them in due course. In the light of his recent conversation with the *Marquis*, it could well be needed. Monsieur Chirac detected reserves of strength in this young girl which might be the salvation of her husband. A pity she hadn't seen the opportunity and grasped it. It was the only thing he could do to help. Chirac Frères was not a charity though, heaven knows, where some proprietors were concerned it seemed much as if it were. Still, one was obliged to draw the line somewhere.

When the salad had been served, Alexa had eaten enough.

"But you will have a little of this cheese, to please me, *Madame*, surely. And another glass of wine. Jaime, bring Madame de Pies Ombre another glass." Turning towards her, he said, "There is a wine I want you to try, I should value your opinion."

"I am sure my opinion could be of no value to you, *Monsieur*."

"On the contrary, if we can assume your palate is untutored, as you seem to be claiming, it is ideal for my purpose." The manservant filled Alexa's glass until it was a third full. "Now, take a good mouthful. No, no, not a ladylike sip, a good womanly mouthful, that's right. Now what do you think of it?" Alexa was nonplussed, uncertain where to begin. "Take another mouthful and I will ask you specific questions. No, don't swallow it, swish it round your mouth like mouthwash, chew it, let every part of your mouth feel the wine." Alexa did as she was told, her eyes holding Georges Chirac's. "Now, you may swallow. By now, you must have in your mouth, a memory. If I ask you quickly, you will be able to answer my questions."

"I will try, certainly."

"Good. Is the taste still in your mouth?"

"Yes."

"So that tells me it has what we call *length*. Does your mouth feel dry, your tongue, furry?"

"Yes, it does."

"That is the tannin. It comes principally from the *Cabernet Sauvignon* grape. It gives the wine its ability to endure, to develop any other qualities it may possess, usually after a number of years. It is, if you like, the skeleton on which the flesh and muscle of wine is draped. Do you find the feeling of astringency unpleasant?"

"No, not exactly. Of course, I have experienced it before, my father buys and drinks quite a lot of claret."

"Does he indeed? He sounds like my sort of Englishman. So if the tannin is not exactly unpleasant, what would you call it?"

"Strong, perhaps, or metallic. And there is something else, too . . . it's almost like vanilla essence. Does that sound mad?"

"No, but it's a decided bonus. That vanilla savour, it comes from aging in new oak casks. The newer the casks, the stronger the flavour. We haven't used many such casks for this, it's an expensive treatment. Would you say that was about all, as regards flavour, I mean?"

"As distinct from *feel* or sensation, yes."

"Hmm, and tell me, was there anything about the wine that seemed to be different from that hard, metallic quality, a texture perhaps, subordinate to the main impression?"

"Yes, I *think* so. A sort of slithery feeling, a little like a drift of silk chiffon passing across the tongue, perhaps almost slimy, but not disagreeable, maybe you could say . . . *soft*?"

"You certainly could say soft. That is the *Merlot* content, a different sort of grape which is often but not always included in Bordeaux reds, claret as you call it. Have some of this cheese, just a thin slice, it will help to rest your palate, the effort of concentration must be quite great for you."

"I will, thank you. But isn't it Edam?"

"But of course, the only cheese to eat with Bordeaux."

"Isn't that very odd, when you have so many marvellous cheeses of your own in France?"

"Bordeaux is not France. We still feel very independent here you know, even after all this time. The three hundred happy years we spent under English rule, and indeed, our habits as international traders before that era, have never entirely been bred out of our blood or our corporate memory. We tend to look outwards, rather than inwards as the great majority of French-

men do.'' Alexa could not resist throwing Fabrice a triumphant
glance, to which he seemed oblivious. ''The cheese was brought
to us by the Dutch merchantmen who used to sail up the river.
It was received with enthusiasm here and adopted as the ideal
accompaniment to our native product. Mild, creamy but firm,
always flavoursome but never competitive, it is a great working
partner for claret.''

''It was always my favourite when I was little.''

''An early instance of your sound taste, *Madame*, and perhaps
a foreshadowing of your future home?''

Alexa laughed at the absurd speculation. ''I don't think so,
it's just very nice cheese!''

''Now, try again for me, *Madame*. This time we will consider
the bouquet, as we should have done first. The nose.''

''The nose?''

''Yes, the smell, we hope the perfume. Swirl the wine around
in the glass, that is correct. How elegantly you do that, *Madame*,
almost as if you had been born to it, hold the foot of the glass,
if you want to be really *'comme il faut,'* wonderful. Now tell
me, what is your impression?''

''Really, I don't honestly *have* a very strong impression. I
suppose I am showing my appalling ignorance.''

''Not at all, *Madame*. You are showing your absolute honesty.
The wine has little to commend it in this direction. Undistin-
guished. Taste it again, this time I want you to look for something different. Fruit. Not necessarily grape, but any instant
reaction you may have, just say what it reminds you of. Straight
away, don't think about it.''

''Blackcurrant?''

''Bravo. My own reaction, precisely. Fairly usual, in Bordeaux, and very acceptable, even desirable.''

''Is this wine something special?''

''No, *Madame*, it is not. Well, that is to say, we hope it will
be something special in its category. What we are doing is
making a blend of various wines we have bought in. The wine
is to sell abroad, as genuine *Appellation Contrôlée* Bordeaux,
respectable in every way. Not the product of any one château
but a number of different properties, all conforming of course
to the statutory requirements for Bordeaux.''

''And what is the reason for doing this?'' Alexa asked the
question almost as if it were her preordained part in a play,

knowing it was the expected enquiry and willing to know the answer.

"It helps us to market the wine of numerous unimportant growers, who make a respectable wine and do not have the financial resources to age their product themselves. You realise, of course, that wine in the barrel is not money in the bank. To many producers, that is an important consideration. You need capital to produce wine that is mature. We have that capital, and by mixing the wines of various properties, some good, some perhaps a little less wonderful, we can produce a reasonably priced claret that the man in the street can afford to drink at any time."

This theme struck a chord in Alexa and she was anxious to ask questions about it, but glancing at her watch decided to deny herself.

Fabrice did not seem disposed to take the initiative about leaving and eventually Alexa, interested as she had been by all that Georges Chirac had told her, felt that they must go if only to allow Monsieur Chirac to continue with his afternoon's work. It was after three o'clock when she said firmly that she and Fabrice must take their leave. She had been taught that if one was invited out to luncheon, it was unmannerly to remain until one's hosts felt obliged to offer one tea. Elizabeth Standeven had been very clear on that point.

"It has been a great pleasure to meet you *Madame*, I hope your next visit to Bordeaux will not be too long delayed. And remember, I meant what I said, if you should ever feel you have sufficient time on your hands, I would welcome your interest in the matter of my grandfather's vineyard."

"Well, Alexa, you made quite a little impression on Georges Chirac, didn't you? Though I doubt it will be enough to save our livelihood."

"I didn't *try* to make an impression on him," said Alexa, stung by the implication that she had been showing off. "Someone had to make some conversation. He laid on that magnificent luncheon for us and you hardly said a word. I was embarrassed. And worried."

"What are you worried about?"

"You, of course, weren't you well?"

"As well as a man can be when he's just been told that his wine isn't good enough to sell."

"What?" Alexa said, largely to gain time. Her mind raced.
So that was it. Everything her father had suspected about the
vineyards at d'Ombre had been true. Tilly had said they weren't
profitable, but she hadn't taken that too seriously. She had supposed that she meant they didn't provide a rich living in their
present condition. "What do you mean, not good enough to
sell?"

"What I say. He says he can't move Château de Pies Ombre
at the price set last autumn. Chirac told me I'd have to find
someone else to handle it. Or market it myself directly, which
is frankly impossible. I just don't have those sort of resources."

"What will we do?"

Fabrice ignored her use of the mutual pronoun. "He's given
me a year to make other arrangements. Oh of course, he says
he's very sorry and all that. It's tragic to see a classed growth so
debased, *et cetera*. He's sorry for my grandfather's sake who,
of course, gave his grandfather his first opportunity to handle a
really important wine, but he's got himself to think of . . . All
the stuff you'd expect. And that, incidentally, is the reason he
made that lunatic suggestion that you should take on his old
vineyard. A sort of sop to me. Quite pointless, of course, you'd
need some money to put that on its feet and if it ever did make
a success, it would be years before we saw any return. We could
be dead of starvation before that."

"But I don't understand, he offered it to *me*."

"Certainly, to spare me the humiliation of being offered a
manager's job on a small, inferior property." Alexa somehow
did not think this was an absolutely accurate reflection of Monsieur Chirac's motives.

"But Fabrice, this is really terrible. *Why* is our operation in
such a bad state?"

"No capital. I need to spend a great deal of money at
d'Ombre, and you know very well, there's hardly any money at
all."

"There is now, I could let you have half of what I got for the
wine and just do what I planned to the house more slowly as the
profits from the paying guests built up. I'd just have to do it on
a smaller scale, that's all."

"Alexa, you don't begin to understand, I need to spend about
a thousand pounds an acre at d'Ombre, and we have sixty hectares, that's £150,000. You'd better go all out to get some money

out of those Americans, it may be the only hope we have of eating.''

Alexa was silent for a moment. ''Is there nothing I can do to help?''

''Yes, do what you planned to do and leave me to manage my own business without interference. Georges Chirac's flirting with you doesn't make you into an instant *régisseur* or *maître de chais*. Even if you knew everything there is to know about claret, it's money I need, not advice.''

''Fabrice, what happened to all the money?''

''My father was a bastard. He spent every penny. My grand-father, and his father before him, had made a great deal out of the vineyards, and other interests too, of course, but my father just threw everything away. He left me with nothing. He never liked me. It was a deliberate gesture, he didn't want me to have anything.''

''But Fabrice, darling why? You must be wrong, no father could feel like that.''

''Mine did, he didn't want a cripple for a son. He wanted to punish me for not being like him. I hated him. Sometimes I wake in the night, sobbing. Actually crying real tears. Do you know what it is? I can't get over the fact that the bloody bastard died before I could get even with him. You see, I promised myself that one day I'd kill him.''

''Fabrice! Stop it! It's unhealthy. You must put it out of your mind. We have a problem, we must deal with it. Blaming some-one who died a long time ago, even if it was his fault, just isn't going to help us solve it.''

''It's my problem, and I may solve it, or I may not. It'll still be my problem.''

''Alonzo! Alonzo McIntyre! What kind of creatures can they be?'' Suzanne lounged on the threadbare chaise-longue in the *Salon Jaune*.

''Mr. and Mrs. Alonzo McIntyre are Texans. No doubt they will seem strange to us, but they will be our *guests*, and that is how we must treat them. They're paying very dearly for our hospitality, we must give it ungrudgingly. Two hundred thou-sand francs is an enormous sum of money. They have a right to expect everything they want, and warmth, *Belle Mère*, warmth.''

Suzanne looked genuinely puzzled for a moment.

"Are we talking about carrying coals again? I really don't think I can manage much more . . ."

"No we are not, *Belle Mère*. We are talking about a genuine and generous welcome."

Explaining what was expected of her to Suzanne, who had finally expressed a grudging willingness to be involved in the entertainment of her daughter-in-law's first guests, was an uphill task.

"One can't just switch it on like a light," Suzanne objected, although to all outward appearances considering this matter of the quality of the welcome with heartening seriousness. But Alexa was too exasperated to be patient.

"Can't one? I've done it, you *must* do it, or we'll be finished before we begin."

"*Bien sûr*, a professional *mannequin*—a near tart, no doubt *you* can turn it on for anyone." Alexa compressed her lips. Some day, please God, she would be rid of this woman. It wasn't her viciousness so much as her total absence of brain that tried Alexa's patience.

"I'll ignore that, Suzanne. Why don't we look at it another way? Tarts and *grandes dames* can make anyone feel wanted. It's a trick of the trade, common to both vocations."

"*Touché, Maman*, I think," Fabrice awarded Alexa the point in the manner of one umpiring a Sunday afternoon cricket match, relaxed but fair. Alexa rounded on him angrily.

"Life is one long spectator sport to you, Fabrice. It's time you started participating. You could begin by reacting like any normal man whose wife has just been called a *tart*!"

"Oh no, I couldn't darling. I'm not a normal man. I'm a cripple, I have to be forgiven a lot of things. But I *am* looking forward to these Texans of yours, they will be a great diversion. I intend to be most amusing."

"I want you to be kind to them Fabrice, nothing more."

Alexa sat as she did every afternoon, at her desk in the turret room of the *Tour du Jardin*. She was adding up the tradesmen's accounts for redecoration and plumbing work. The early spring sunshine shouldered its way through the lancet-shaped lights of the oriel window. It was warm enough to leave the stove unlit. She thought with a pang of conscience of poor Héloïse, lugging scuttles of coal up the winding staircase throughout the damp winter months. It was almost as though she had succeeded in forcing the older woman to give up her study through sustained torture. But Tante Héloïse would not listen to such fears, simply insisting that Alexa needed the room more than she did herself.

Alexa would love to have known Tante Héloïse better. But Héloïse held her, as she held the rest of the world, at arm's length. It was an austerity which Alexa could, with a great leap of the imagination, understand.

Fabrice had confided that in her youth Héloïse had longed to become a nun but no community would accept her. She would have had a magnificent dowry to bring and her name, although officially buried forever, would in fact had shed lustre on any aristocratic convent. But no superior felt able to accept a disabled novice. The physical rigours of conventual life were deemed too great to be endured by any except the fully fit. Héloïse's burning enthusiasm, they said, was no substitute for health. And as there was no practical possibility of success, there could be no genuine vocation. It was an injustice, no doubt, and a humiliation certainly, but one which Héloïse had learned to live with. She tried instead to live by a modified monastic rule of her own. It involved strictly rationed conversation and an avoidance of day to day gossipy involvement with other human beings. Héloïse was a species of anchorite.

"It's something to do with a Third Order, sort of being a plain-clothes nun, if you like. But anyway, either Tante Héloïse keeps more rules than she need or they've given her a whole load of extra ones to keep her appetite for holiness satisfied."

Alexa learned these things from Fabrice, one evening after dinner. Suzanne had retired early, as she had taken to doing ever since she had been informed that an invasion of American visitors was imminent. She had decided that a regimen of early nights and hot possets of mulled wine prepared by Hortense was her best defence against future exhaustion. It left Fabrice and Alexa alone, to share each other's company, more often than since their short, dull honeymoon.

During these periods, Fabrice became more inclined to talk under the influence of whisky and told Alexa details of family history, hitherto unknown to her. Héloïse's story interested Alexa greatly, the more so because of the way in which Fabrice told it. Alexa had never seen him so frank, nor so communicative. His usual sarcasm was absent, and his eyes in the lamplight reflected a stark pity for his aunt's lonely struggle to achieve sainthood without the official recognition of her church. It would have been possible not to understand what was being said. But Fabrice's description of the practice of self-immolation was both graphic and profound. Alexa looked at him and listened to his voice with wonder. There was a fluency and power she had never seen before. His capacity to be involved intellectually and emotionally with the obscure problems of his aunt was a side of him which Alexa never suspected.

She also recognised dimly that he was not talking to her at all but to himself. This whisky-generated fluency was a means of communicating thoughts to whatever sounding-board happened to be present. At any rate it was a great deal better than the edgily sociable evenings over which Suzanne usually presided, alternating inane observations with stabs at her *petit point*.

Lying uncomfortably awake that night, because Fabrice lay across her arm, snoring slightly, after a more prolonged and satisfying sexual encounter between them than was usual, Alexa concluded that she was now in possession of the turret room solely because Héloïse had taken a genuine if perverted pleasure in giving it up, and not as she had always suspected, because of the tiresomeness of carrying coal buckets up there. There was something undeniably creepy about living in the same house as a religious maniac and that was what, by all normal standards, Héloïse must be. And yet, it was Héloïse who was the one member of the family to whom Alexa felt most inclined to turn in any practical difficulty.

She recalled the afternoon when she had first visited Tante Héloïse in the tower, her study. It was the first time Alexa had ever been there. She'd ventured up the winding stairs to ask Héloïse's advice. Alexa had begun to have misgivings about the heavy cost of advertising for paying guests in the *New York Herald Tribune*. It was so terribly expensive and they hadn't had a single bite yet, as she explained to Héloïse.

"Maybe it's the advertisement itself that's wrong. Could you look at it for me?" Héloïse had adjusted her spectacles and taken the folded newspaper that Alexa held out to her. The shameless advertisement ran:

> "Le Marquis et la Marquise de Pies Ombre
> cordially invite you to pass a few nights at
> their world-famous property
> Le Château d'Ombre

Board and Lodging 100,000 ffs per night. Conversation Free. Brochure on Request. A unique opportunity to experience the company of genuine European nobility. (The present Marquis's ancestor Estèphe de Cordoba was created Chevalier des Oiseaux Pies in 1076, nearly a thousand years ago.

Live as one of the family and find out what it's like to be an aristocrat.''

Fortunately, Fabrice and Suzanne had not seen Alexa's little effort at copywriting as she had deemed it wise to conceal it from them.

She had kept them both busy with preparations. Unpacking old footmen's uniforms from trunks in the attic and finding willing volunteers to wear them for a small hourly rate of pay, had been Suzanne's especial care. Fabrice had been told to gather as much wine and brandy together as he could find, which guests could drink without destroying the archival succession of vintages in the cellars, or drinking anything that might fetch a sum in excess of ten per cent of the cost of a night's entertainment at the château.

"This is really very good, my dear," had been Héloïse's surprising verdict on the startling advertisement. "I'm not too sure about anyone actually being *created* a *chevalier.* Mind you, I'm not up on heraldry, it's not one of my things. But it does seem to me that if the gentleman arrived from Spain, which is what we all suppose, already bearing arms, it would have been natural to assume he *was* a *chevalier*, or gentleman of the horse-riding class, already. Anyway, I don't suppose most Americans will care about these details. What does Tilly think of it? I'm sure you would have asked her." Héloïse was sly.

"I did ask her, of course, I suppose I thought you might be upset by it. It might make us sound ridiculous."

"What ever does that matter?"

Alexa shrugged. There was no point in trying to get involved in Héloïse's upside-down reasoning. "Tilly said it was 'barbaric but brilliant,' but the fact is, I haven't had a single response."

"Keep your nerve. There is nothing wrong with the advertisement. It is simple, honest and enticing. I should know, I write for a living. You can't expect a rush of bookings all at first, it's a lot of money you're asking. But something will happen soon to break the ice. The business will come, never fear. In the meantime, I think we should arrange a little headquarters for you. An office. This one." Alexa's face registered her surprise although she was momentarily speechless.

"But you *can't*. It's yours Tante Héloïse. I can't take it from you."

"It is not in your power to take it. I am giving it to you. It would be an act of meanness to refuse my little gift, I'm sure you agree."

"With arguments like those, you could make anyone do anything." Alexa smiled.

"You must accept. You have a great task ahead of you and precious few tools with which to perform it. I can give you the one simple basic necessity that every worker needs."

Alexa's brows lifted.

"A place to work is essential," Héloïse continued. "The lowliest tradesman has at least a shed in which to keep his materials and practise his craft and you are the *châtelaine* of a great house, and now the manager of a business. So, it is agreed then. Yours is the larger responsibility, and you must have the best premises. These, my dear, are they."

"But Tante Héloïse, what will you do?"

"Me? Find another shed, of course, one more suited to my station as a minor breadwinner. I feel confident that *you* are going to be our support from now on."

Alexa felt overwhelmed by the prediction and not a little flattered. But she was glad that Fabrice had not overheard the conversation.

"There are no words sufficient to thank you, Tante Héloïse."

"I don't want your thanks, I only want your success." Her voice was gruff.

"I shall go now. You will want to plan revisions to my decorating scheme. I shall return only by invitation. These invitations will not be too frequent. We both have work to do."

Alexa had looked round her domain. Héloïse's little gift was in reality a considerable one. The battered desk, uncluttered now, the mounds of typescript and the ancient typewriter having been removed; the pale mark on the wall where the large, gaunt crucifix had hung, beneath it a prie-dieu which Héloïse, for some reason, had not seen fit to take. All spoke of a lifetime of honest thought and hard work, but they would have to go. In this room Tante Héloïse had won wisdom, overcome disappointment and forged a mighty personality. It will have to serve me in the same way, thought Alexa, but I shall need a different backdrop for my efforts. The anchorite's cell will become the eagle's nest, the she-wolf's lair, even the miser's counting house. She's right, it's all I may have for years and years. But she had felt pure exhilaration.

She looked down at Fabrice's sleeping face. It had a peace and purity about it that stirred her emotions. We shall have a race, you and I, my darling husband, and see who can make the most of you and your name. Shall it be wine or Americans that make our fortunes?

The McIntyres came and filled the house with joyous if unmusical sounds.

Sadie McIntyre was a well-exercised, well-corseted woman in her late fifties, whose features cheerfully bore the honourable scars of early hardships. Her hair was a highly improbable blue-black which contrasted smartly with her accurately lipsticked mouth.

Her voice was very loud as if she expected it to convey information over vast distances and its stringy, sinewy vibrations crackled with warmth and interest. Alexa liked her immediately.

Her husband Alonzo was the quieter of the two. He was short and balding which did not prevent his barber from cropping what remained of his hair to a fascinating tactile fuzz. Alonzo's eyes were pale but attentive, flicking swiftly from face to face and object to object. Alexa felt her welcome to him become both stilted and gushing as she stumbled over the suddenly unfamiliar English words. Alonzo was not the man to help her with the difficulty. His large dry hand pumped hers rhythmically whilst his eyes studied her face with unsmiling concentration. His wife compensated for the flat, cool greeting with an enthusiasm which threatened to burst her small frame asunder.

It became clear that their visit to the Château d'Ombre was a grace note, added at the last moment to their tour of Europe at Sadie's insistence. Clearly her husband could deny her nothing. His marble eyes only warmed when they fell on her. He exuded the air of one who was indulging the whim of a dearly loved child, but had scant hope of enjoyment himself.

Alexa followed the McIntyres and the pretty village girl that Hortense had recruited and rudimentarily trained as a *femme de chambre*. She was keen to gauge her guests' reaction to the decor of their room.

The lofty chamber had elaborate *boiseries* and plaster mouldings. The painted ceiling, similar to the one in her own room, showed a composition of pink, classical nymphs, sporting in blue sky furnished with cumulus clouds and wisps of diaphanous drapery, intertwined with flowers. The work of restoration had been very costly, but the effects, Alexa believed, quite glorious. There was a faded woven carpet on the floor which appeared to echo the design of the ceiling exactly, and the colours, though pale and faded, were the same. Alexa had found it rolled up in the attic. Unrolling it, with difficulty, she had recognised its relationship to the ceiling in the bedroom. It was very dirty and ugly stains disfigured it. The carpet had some rents in it too. It clearly could not be used in that condition. More money had to be spent on professional cleaning and specialist repairs. But it was worth it.

Even Suzanne had given her grudging approval to what Alexa had achieved in the English Room. It was so named by common consent, purely for the traditional English chintz that Alexa had chosen to complement the pale, faded blue of the *boiseries*. The room had been repainted but deliberately rubbed in places, a little dark paint being added to the blue, here and there, to give an impression of wear and the fading effect of centuries. Light, spindly satinwood and kingwood furniture, encrusted with ormolu, surrounded like courtiers the great bed that Alexa had contrived, using a plain iron frame knocked up in the *chais*. The effect was achieved solely by the sheer quantity of the chintz drapery and its extraordinary complexity. Alexa had worked in the kitchen with Hortense for many evenings stitching this masterpiece. Hortense had called it a *robe de bal* for a bed, which her young mistress had agreed was a good description.

Curtains of the same chintz cascaded lavishly from the giltwood pelmets, with panels of cheap machine-made Nottingham lace, looped back from the panes, softening the stark view of the still-wintry vineyards outside. The newly painted magpies on the gateposts were visible in the middle distance.

A concealed doorway led into a modern bathroom that had been created in the old dressing room. It had everything. A cheerful fire burned brightly in an open fireplace to turn the chill of the evening, reflecting its light softly in the glaze of the blue and white Dutch tiles that Alexa had found in a junk shop in Bordeaux.

Bowls of early daffodils rested on every available surface in the bedroom and a bottle of vintage champagne was set in readiness in a porcelain ice pail. Alexa was proud of her handiwork. It was a beautiful room, full of precious things, welded into a composition of airy elegance.

Marie busied herself patting imaginary creased out of the satin counterpane, tweaking daffodils and straightening towels. The McIntyres said nothing at all and Alexa found she was holding her breath.

"Will this do?" The question was meaningless. It was the only room ready for occupation.

"It's marvellous honey, just marvellous. You see Alonzo! Have you ever seen anything like it in your whole life before? In hotels you just don't get any idea . . . Oh! *Louis Quinze* isn't it?" Sadie's fingers touched the tiny *bonheur-du-jour* with something like reverence. "The real thing? What do you call this wood? It's kind of stripey."

"Kingwood," rejoined Alexa happily. She could have kissed Sadie McIntyre, at least she knew what it was all about. Alonzo's approval was more contained and expressed in terms of a solitary nod. He was a man who had become accustomed to confirming his acceptance of hotel bedrooms and seemed unaware that the enjoyment of his visit depended to a large extent on his willingness to connive at the fiction of a private, social guest-and-host relationship with the de Pies Ombres.

"If you would like Marie to unpack for you, you have only to ask. We shan't be dining until nine o'clock, and if there is anything you would like to eat in the meantime, just ring this bell and someone will come."

There had been a fair amount of discussion about the business of guests' unpacking. Suzanne had stated that no guest could be allowed to unpack their own cases, even if unaccompanied by a personal valet or maid. These were points of etiquette outside the range of Alexa's own knowledge. However, she had recognised a flavour of authenticity in Suzanne's shrill insistence and had decided to check the point both with her mother and with Tilly in Paris. Both had confirmed that strictly speaking guests should not be required to unpack for themselves, but both had said it was very old-fashioned when, really, nobody had the staff to keep up with that kind of thing. And so a compromise had been reached. The service would be offered but not forced on people who, no doubt, had not stowed their intimate belongings with a view to having them exposed to the censorious examination of a stranger.

"Sure honey. You just relax, we'll be fine," replied Sadie who was skilled at the art of creating ambiguous pauses in which she could study the form before making any decision as to how to proceed in the social arena.

While dressing for dinner herself that night, Alexa remarked that the McIntyres seemed an ill-assorted couple. Sadie was so bright and appreciative and Alonzo seemed to find any kind of response a tremendous effort. "I expect they think we're a bit odd ourselves. Creatures from outer space if that man's stare is anything to go by," she commented.

"It doesn't matter much what they think, does it, as long as they enjoy themselves and think they've had what you call *value for money*?" Fabrice was tying a white bow tie. The effect under his dark, sardonic features was to make him look almost like a hero of romantic fiction, as Alexa told him.

"You disappoint me, I was going to do my best to looking thrillingly sinister. You, however, do look like a romantic heroine."

Alexa was wearing the red gown she had worn first when she and her father had dined at the *hôtel* in the Marais. She put her head on one side and regarded her reflection in the glass with moderate satisfaction. She started to clasp the seed pearl choker about her throat when Fabrice unexpectedly appeared behind her and closed the fastening for her.

"Tu es très belle, chérie." She was startled. He rarely, if ever, addressed her in French when they were alone. His voice had entirely shed its light, sardonic tone and sounded thick and husky. *"Un moment, je reviens."* He went into his dressing room and emerged a few moments later carrying a flat leather case, square and rather battered.

"This is all there is left, virtually. Most of the things I should have been able to give my wife were sold a long time ago to settle some of my father's debts. Some weren't considered important enough to sell, this is one of them. I think it will go with your dress. Let us try it."

Alexa was both touched and excited by his mood of simplicity and gentleness. He placed the case on her dressing table and she opened it. Lying in a nest of worn cream plush there was a diadem of Bohemian garnets, a small tiara.

"Oh, Fabrice, how charming. But I can't wear it."

"Why not? It's the same colour as your dress and it would look wonderful against your hair." He removed the little tiara from its case and held it against the dark gold glints of her hair. They both regarded the effect in the looking glass.

"But honestly, don't you think it's rather ridiculous. It might embarrass the McIntyres. It's going too far, surely."

"Don't you think it's all rather ridiculous anyway, a bankrupt farmer and his wife making a sideshow of themselves and their family in the forlorn hope of keeping a roof over their heads and continuing to eat? Wear it for God's sake. The McIntyres have come to see a spectacle. By all means, let's make a spectacle of ourselves."

She'd hurt him, without meaning to, but the sharpness in his voice concealed his wounded feelings. Alexa agreed to wear his offering in a spirit of conciliation, extremely anxious to avoid discord on this crucial evening. "Of course I'll wear it, Fabrice. It's a lovely thing. Suzanne will laugh, but I don't care. Help me put it on."

Alonzo McIntyre owned a firm supplying drilling equipment to the oil industry. It was a *multigh million dollar concern now*, as he informed a startled Fabrice. He had started it from nothing when still a boy. "My folks was sharecroppers and it was a mighty hard life. Me'n Sadie got wedded when she was fifteen. Her pa was lookin' to keep her home for a few years to help her ma, but she and I just upped and left. Judge in the next county married us and we haven't regretted it a single day. No sir. Not once."

The de Pies Ombres were interested but embarrassed. It was difficult to know what would be a suitable reply to this intense statement of their guest's commercial and romantic career.

Having given so free an account of himself and his affairs, Alonzo felt entitled to reciprocal frankness. Fabrice bulked at the penetrating enquiries into his income and the manner in which he acquired it.

"My husband's vineyards are going through a tough time at the moment," Alexa interposed anxiously. "There have been some disastrous harvests in recent years. We thought we'd better supplement our income and diversify, I think that's what you call it, and earn some money in the hotel trade. You are our first customers."

"Well, it sure is nice to be here, honey," Sadie McIntyre said soothingly. Alexa somehow gained the impression that she had spent a lifetime soothing Alonzo and now did it automatically, whether it was required or not. "Honey, would you get one of

those cute flunkeys to get me a glass of water? I can't drink wine
you know, it goes straight to my head, doesn't it Alonzo?''

It turned out that neither of the McIntyres cared for wine,
indeed they had never drunk it. This devastating revelation so
bemused Fabrice that, to Alexa's relief, he was unable to evince
any reaction that would be noticeable to a stranger's eye. Suzanne responded by drinking a little too much herself as if to
demonstrate the wholesomeness of the family product. Fortunately, the results of her indulgence were rather more comic
than shaming and she undertook to favour Sadie McIntyre with
the address of a local dressmaker who executed commissions
for persons of moderate income with an emphasis on fitting
awkward figures. ''I never use her myself, of course,'' Suzanne
finished brightly, ''but she does wonders for the middle class.''

Alexa caught Sadie's astonished eye and engaged her sympathy by choking messily, whereafter both dissolved into a fit of
immature giggling. Suzanne looked on, secure in the knowledge
that she had been gracious and helpful. She was sublimely unaware that Mrs. McIntyre could have afforded to employ the
Dowager Marquise de Pies Ombre as a private secretary, had
the notion entered her head, and had Suzanne possessed the
ghost of a skill which might justify such a charitable exercise.

Fabrice looked at Alexa through the forest of silver gilt can-
delabra and *épergnés* on the endlessly long table. His face betrayed a total lack of comprehension. Whatever was happening
at his dinner table that night, he had given up any effort to make
sense of the proceedings. He joined Alonzo McIntyre in a glass
or two of Laphroig, a substitute for the requested Bourbon, and
which the American grudgingly admitted to be a drink of passable quality.

Apart from a disappointing inability to appreciate the product
of their hosts' property, the McIntyres were good guests. They
exhibited a wholesome lack of awe and were prepared to be
impressed but not to be intimidated. They had paid for an experience and they planned to enjoy it in their own way. Like
adults who had paid a steep entry fee to an exhibition, they dealt
out praise and criticism with an even hand. Their questions,
uttered in the main by Sadie, were both intelligent and searching.

Sadie had remarked on the dilapidated condition of some exterior shutters on the ground floor of the château. To her it
seemed no more than a repair job to be brought to the attention

of the man of the house at an early opportunity. Her surprise that Fabrice had not already "fixed" the shutters left Alexa at a loss for an answer that Sadie could possibly have understood, nor was she aware of the general handiness of all American husbands at whatever level of society. But she understood that the notion of some tasks being suitable for gentlemen in their own estimation, and some not, would be an alien concept to Sadie. And so it ought to be, she thought with some annoyance.

As a result of knowing Sadie McIntyre, Alexa learned a respect for the many Texan women she subsequently entertained, the lifelong companions of larger-than-life, self-made millionaires. Their education as young girls had often been entirely neglected and they had frequently known hardships which Alexa's imagination could barely encompass. But when money and leisure came, they set about amending the deficiencies in their own information and experience with commendable zeal. Their willingness to learn from a girl less than half their age impressed and humbled Alexa. If she could have given her Texan women guests a motto, it would have been "It's never too late, it's never too difficult and we're never too proud." But it took an English-woman to appreciate the Texans.

Throughout most of the McIntyres' two-day stay, Fabrice had laughed. Laughed with the unseemly gusto which often follows the unexpected announcement of a death. Fortunately it hadn't mattered. The McIntyres too were sufficiently polarised by the culture gap to assume that their host's continual hilarity was occasioned by geniality rather than by hysteria.

As she closed the great door after waving their hired car out of sight beyond the magpie gates, Alexa turned to her husband and remarked hopefully.

"We shan't need to go to Disneyland now, shall we, darling?"

Fabrice was not amused and stared at her starkly and uncomprehendingly. A depression settled on him after the departure of the McIntyres and Alexa strove to reassure him, whilst being herself conscious of failure. Fruitlessly she argued with him that not all Americans could be like that. The United States of America was a vast country in which many and varied people lived. The McIntyres were not typical Americans. They were just typical of a *type*.

"Do you really think this is going to work, Alexa? I mean, I had the impression I spoke English but whenever I said anything they looked at me as though I was out of my mind."

"Perhaps they did. That's their privilege. It doesn't matter what they think of us, as you said yourself. I just hope we're outlandish enough to encourage them to send their friends here."

"It's so tiring talking to people who don't understand a word you say."

"Never mind, they liked the sound of our voices."

Reassuring Hortense was more difficult still. The amount of food which had been returned to her kitchen, virtually untouched but pushed to the side of the plate, wounded her as no other insult could have done. Hortense was determined to wallow in feelings of rejection and was grim-faced for days. Alexa's attempts to make her see that the food had not been despised, but merely been too rich for palates accustomed to plainer fare, was met with the granite unresponsiveness of which Hortense was master.

"In the future I think I should write in advance and ask them what their preferences are. You mustn't blame yourself for this, Hortense, we shall learn as we go on."

Almost disastrous as the McIntyre experience had been, Alexa learned several useful lessons from it. She would never again assume anything about her guests' tastes for food and drink.

Suzanne, so far from being a liability, was a positive asset. Her capricious appearances and absences at meals lent a certain thrill of uncertainty to the daily format. Her studied elegance and innocent rudeness to the McIntyres had captivated them entirely. They had come to see what they termed "old-style aristocrats," with the emphasis on the second syllable, and Suzanne fulfilled their highest expectations. The delicate punishment she meted out to Alonzo McIntyre was received with admirable calm. Alexa had acted as guide around Suzanne's manner and manners and thus she had been accepted as a monument to the bad days that would never come again.

Suzanne had appeared both evenings *en grande toilette* as Alexa and Fabrice had also dressed. The McIntyres were unresponsive to this, which may have triggered Suzanne's kindly condescension in the matter of a dressmaker. Sadie merely changed her slacks and put on a clean shirt. The dress of the resident household was regarded as theatrical costume and nothing to do with real life.

Suzanne's reactions to the McIntyre episode were surprisingly positive. She said she felt like a station at which a brief halt had been made and where the refreshments had been found more or less passable, and the staff good humoured, if ill-trained and overdressed. She hoped the McIntyres had profited from their visit, by which she intended to convey that a ringside view of the domestic manners of Suzanne de Pies Ombre could only enhance those of the observer.

There was a worrying interval of some weeks before Alexa received any further bookings. During that period, the spring weather established itself and the vines came into leaf.

CHAPTER
12

ஐஐ *"ENTREZ."*ALEXA THREW down her pen on the accounts book. It was laborious work. Figures had never come easily to her, but she improved with the daily discipline of calculating the receipts and outgoings of the guest-house business. And then there was the excitement of watching the profits grow, at first little by little as capital expenditure was recovered, but lately the books had shown the business to be in real profit.

Monsieur David stood in the doorway, his alleged seventy years of age at odds with his black hair and upright posture. The brown eyes were sombre and wary. His blue denim dungarees were worn and patched but clean and well pressed. Instead of the expected collarless shirt, he wore a good-looking pinstriped shirt, the knot of the red silk tie supported with an old-fashioned gold collar pin. His sleeves were rolled up with a military precision. The conker-brown shoes bore a superficial film of dust over the polish which seemed regularly and lovingly applied. A proud and fastidious man, Pierre David neither cringed before, nor fawned on any man.

"Ah, it is Monsieur David, isn't it? Please come and sit down. I am sorry to take you away from your work, but in all the circumstances, I am sure you will forgive me. I think we should talk."

"Madame," David bowed with stiff correctness, indicating his total disagreement. Alexa was momentarily puzzled by the old man's imposing manners. But then, she reflected, he had spent his whole life on this property in daily contact with the male members of the de Pies Ombre family, as had his father before him.

"Monsieur, I fully understand your instinctive reticence and

242

appreciate the loyalty which it betokens, but I am bound to say, I am powerless to help my husband if I know nothing of what led to this terrible business."

"It is over. It should be forgotten, buried."

"I doubt that I could forget it. A wife does not forget that her husband is so unhappy he wished himself dead. Nor will forgetting it prevent a further attempt. An attempt which will probably succeed. He was prevented this time only by a fortunate coincidence. Won't you please tell me whatever you know that may shed some light on my husband's state of mind? And frankly, I should like to know the circumstances in which you found him. Believe me, *Monsieur*, I am as interested in rendering service to your master as you can be." Alexa inclined her head towards a vacant chair.

Slowly, rigidly, with a reluctant flexing of his joints, David lowered himself into a battered wing chair. The young woman expressed her thoughts with great facility. There was something almost shockingly forward in her fluency, not quite decent, David thought. At all events, he did not intend to be rushed. He examined his shoes carefully.

When he raised his head, he looked out of the window of the turret room, staring into the horizon. He turned his head and regarded Alexa unsmilingly. She returned the gaze steadily, her expression bland but watchful. To hurry him would be fatal. He would resent it.

David was wondering about the propriety of revealing anything to Monsieur Fabrice's wife. She was his wife, yes, but an outsider after all, and a foreigner. There'd always been a certain solidarity between the male de Pies Ombres and their upper servants. It wasn't friendship exactly, it couldn't be that, but it was loyalty. Mutual dependence. David cleared his throat at length before speaking.

"I heard a noise. A sob. I was working later than usual in my office in the *chai*. *Madame* has never been there."

"No, I haven't," Alexa replied quietly.

"My office is adjacent to *Monsieur's*, that of the *maître de chai* is on the other side. Of course there is no *maître de chai* nowadays. It is a role which *Monsieur* fulfils himself."

"You are the *régisseur*, *Monsieur*, are you not?"

"That is correct, *Madame*." David nodded gravely. "I am responsible for the vines themselves, their cultivation. I deliver the harvest to the *cuvier*. After that, the making of the wine is the responsibility of the *maître de chai*, in our case, Monsieur Fabrice, himself.''

"Please go on. I am sorry to interrupt you, but you know I know nothing of these things. I want to get it clear."

"As I said, I heard a noise, not a natural noise, coming from *Monsieur's* office. I was . . . concerned. Naturally," the old man shrugged, "I went to investigate. What I saw . . ." He broke off and stared through the lancets of the oriel window once more. The silence was prolonged and Alexa feared he would not resume his narrative without some coaxing. She leaned forward from her desk and softly stroked his work-worn hand. It was risking a rebuff, she knew, but she must recapture his attention and draw him back to her, from the horror of recent memory. "Please. I need your help." The simple appeal seemed to reach him and he turned again to face her.

"Monsieur Fabrice was standing, with his back to me. At first I could not see . . . he was a little bent over, leaning his back against the desk, facing the window. I thought he was ill. I went towards him and then I realised. He was bending over so that he could get the muzzle of the shotgun in his mouth. He was trying to depress the trigger with the end of his stick." David dropped his eyes from Alexa's and passed his hand over them momentarily. Then he seemed to recover from his obvious distress.

"Somehow, I pulled the gun away from him, out of his mouth. I knocked him back. It's difficult to say exactly. It happened very fast, you understand. Now I know I should have knocked the stick out of the way, simpler and much safer. But . . ."

"I understand. You saved him anyway."

"*Grâce à Dieu*, yes, I did. The gun went off but nobody was hurt. There is a hole in the ceiling now."

"Better than in the roof of his mouth and the top of his head, isn't it?''

"*Madame* is not afraid to call things how they are. You should have been in the resistance, *Madame*." Alexa, guessing at the type of man she had to deal with, understood the statement to be a backhanded compliment. On the one hand he disapproved of her unfeminine, unflinching imagination, on the other he applauded her courage in facing the ugly facts.

"Thank you," she responded gravely. "But you know words are cheap. I doubt I should have acted as promptly as you did. There are, of course, no adequate expressions with which to thank you. Perhaps you could tell me why my husband wanted to take his own life. That is really what is important here, is it not?''

Again he shrugged. "It is the château, what else?'' Seeing Alexa's obvious confusion he hastened to explain, "No not the house, *Madame*, you do not understand. Here in the Médoc, château does not mean any particular kind or size of house. It means the property, the vineyards. That is all. Many châteaux have no house to speak of. Maybe a simple farmhouse, but that is all. Here at d'Ombre, we have a château in both senses but in many cases the only buildings of any size are the *chais*.''

David did not add that, in his own opinion, Monsieur Fabrice was oppressed by his marriage. Oh, he had said nothing, nothing at all. Very probably he hadn't realised it himself. But all the same, he, David, had known *Monsieur le Marquis* since babyhood. He had an instinct. *Monsieur* was experiencing the very thing he had never previously known in his life, competition, and that competition was coming from his wife. There was constant talk of what *Madame* was doing, what *Madame* was achieving up at the house. The men in the *chais* all had wives or mothers who talked to Hortense in the village and some of them even had casual cleaning jobs up at the château. There was no doubt that the young Madame de Pies Ombre's enterprise was prospering and that *she* was the author of success. And then, there was real trouble in the vineyards, an unfortunate contrast. From time to time people joked that *Madame's* touch was needed. They even said it to Monsieur Fabrice himself. But to him, it was not a pleasantry, but a taunt. It was an additional pressure just when everything else was going wrong. But looking at her, David absolved this Englishwoman from knowingly hurting his young master. Her genuine anxiety was written plainly on her pretty face.

"Also, *Madame*, are you not aware of the significance of the hail-storm we had on that night? Once the *véraison* has occurred, bad weather can end all hopes of a satisfactory harvest. As usual of recent years, the quality of the *vendange* will be below the desirable standard, and now the quantity is likely to be limited too. We operate on a knife-edge here, there is no cushion to allow for natural disasters, no insurance against the weather. We have no second wine here, as many châteaux do. We will simply have to make Château de Pies Ombre with fruit that is both substandard and very scant. Poor *Monsieur*, he has had as much as any man can take.''

Somehow, looking into those searching blue eyes, so honest and clear, David found he couldn't bring himself to explain about *Monsieur's* fragile self-regard, and her own part in diminishing it. It wouldn't make sense to her. She was too like a man herself, a good man. There was no artifice, no pretence and no weakness. She wouldn't understand.

''What do you mean by the *véraison*?'' Alexa asked, her attention caught by the technical expression.

''That is when the fruit has begun to turn colour. It is less resistant to damage then.''

''And what is wrong exactly with the château?'' Alexa knew what was wrong, she had heard it from Fabrice's own lips, but there was no harm in hearing it again, she thought prudently, from an independent source.

''Everything, *Madame*. We need money. There is no money for fertiliser for the land, no money to replace old stock, no money for new casks, no money for enough labour or machinery to weed and cultivate the land. No money to buy the chemical sprays we need to guard against pests, we are a prey to every plague Fate sees fit to send us. There are many things we need for the *cuvier*. A new wine press, labour to operate the old ones is hard to get these days, and too expensive if we could get it. So, much of the harvest is out of condition before we can even press the grapes. *Madame*, there is nothing we do not need.''

''My husband, does he really know anything about making wine?'' Alexa was prepared to have her enquiry rejected with contempt. Questioning a servant about his own master's competence was to invite a snub. But she had to know what was going on in the *chais*. If Fabrice would not tell her himself, she would be driven to these methods.

''*Bien sûr, Madame*. He knows more than his father ever did. When he was a little boy, Monsieur Fabrice used to follow me about the place, watching everything that was done. And when his grandfather was still alive, the old *Marquis* used to bring him to the *chais* every day. He would say to him, 'We make red gold from these grapes, *mon petit-fils*, and we are the alchemists. You must learn the secrets, so that after I am gone, there will be someone to carry on the work.' ''

''I confess, *Monsieur*, that I am somewhat confused. I had gained the impression from my mother-in-law, that my husband knew little of viniculture and cared even less. Are you telling me that this is not the case?''

A barely discernible expression of contemptuous dismissal crossed the old man's features. Alexa noted it with interest. It was clear that Monsieur David had not the smallest regard for the opinion of Suzanne de Pies Ombre.

''Certainly, *Madame. Monsieur*, your husband, does not wear his heart on his sleeve. That is not his way. If *Monsieur* cares about anything, it is about the vineyards because his grandfather, who was the only one to act as a father to him, also cared about the vineyards. But what can you do? When you see someone you love dying, or *something* you love falling into decay, then you try to prepare, do you not? Prepare to live without them. You teach yourself indifference. It is a kind of courage. Me, I could never do it.''

''But what about his father?''

''Ouf! What indeed? He was always abroad somewhere with his wife. They spent very little time at the château. No, they left the boy here in the care of Hortense. She was his nurse, you realise, *Madame*. There was his grandfather, too, of course, until he died, poor gentleman, and then the tutors. All Englishmen.'' Monsieur David looked disdainful. ''Fabrice was very much indulged as a boy. He was lonely and a cripple. *Que faire?* We all tried to make things up to him. Sometimes, his parents would visit for a little while. They brought presents. Such presents! Electric trains, a car, yes, an electrified car he could drive about the grounds, and once there was a pony. But the pony had to be sold. Monsieur Fabrice was afraid of it. The tutor he had then, it would be . . . Greville, yes, Mr. Greville, did not go about things in the right way. He shouted at the boy. It made things worse. Naturally, his balance was not good. This man Greville did not understand that it would take our young master longer to gain confidence than other boys. It was not good. Monsieur Fabrice lost his temper and hit the pony. Mr. Greville hit Fabrice. The old *Marquis* dismissed him and the pony was sold. That is the story of your husband's life. Attempt, failure, destruction.''

''I am not the only one unafraid of calling things by their proper names.''

The old man bridled, his weather-beaten features darkening.

''If it is pretty phrases *Madame* is looking for, she must look elsewhere. I am a plain man with no liking for aristocrats. I pity

the man and would help him if I could. I respect his suffering
but not his position.''

David spoke with a kind of embarrassed brusqueness. He had
gone too far, said too much. He had no desire to become involved with the family concerns of *Monsieur* and *Madame*. Their
personal relationship was no business of his. He had allowed
himself to be lulled into foolish reminiscences, memories of the
old days. It would all come to an end soon and each would have
to pursue his own destiny. He, Pierre David, would manage. He
had saved a good deal over the years. What poor Monsieur Fabrice would do was another matter. Perhaps he would be forced
to swallow his pride and depend on the wits of this clever young
woman. She had wheedled more out of him than he would have
believed possible.

''I see,'' Alexa answered thoughtfully, directing a steady and
enquiring gaze at him. ''May I ask why you work for a family
like this if these are your sentiments? I need hardly remind you,
I am a foreigner, there are so many things that I shall never
understand unless they are explained to me.''

She had perceived his weakness instantly. Monsieur Pierre
David could resist the attractions of the opposite sex because,
in his experience, they were always allied to frivolity, vanity and
idle curiosity. These things repelled him, which is why he had
remained, as Hortense had told her, a bachelor. It might be a
different matter if he were to encounter good sense and modesty
in the very quarter where he least expected to find them.

''My family has always worked for the de Pies Ombre family,'' David found himself replying. ''It is true, if I were as good
a communist as I am a *vigneron*, I would have moved to the
city, worked in a modern industry and joined a trade union. But
I love vines. I cannot help it. It is in my blood. I should die
away from them. They are the rootstock onto which my life is
grafted. Without them, what should I be? It is a tragedy to see
them neglected like this. I am glad the old *Marquis* did not live
to see the decline of this property. But his son, he spent all the
money. He did not care.''

Alexa studied the man in the armchair. Her heart went out to
him. His impotence in the face of the ruination of his old master's work was the greater tragedy. His loyalty to d'Ombre was
organic. Something he could not help even if, as he seemed to
indicate, he would like to.

''*Monsieur*, I am grateful to you for your frankness. As you will know, I am young enough to be your granddaughter, and I would not presume to teach you your business. But would *you* consent to teach it to me? I think I could begin to help with the finance side of things, but I would need to have some understanding of what is required and why. I do not ask more, I know you cannot transmit the experience of a lifetime and the inherited wisdom of generations. But if I could know just a little of what you know, I think we may still see the vines flourish again. Do not let us despair, not just yet. Will you help me to help the Château d'Ombre?''

"Certainly, *Madame*," David spoke in the tone of one who is anything but certain; "but . . ."

"My husband will have to be persuaded that you and he cannot carry this burden alone any longer. I realise that in your eyes I must be disqualified from helping on three counts. I am female; I am young; and I am, of course, English." Alexa's smile dizzied him.

"I assure you, *Madame* . . ."

"Perhaps you could introduce my husband to the idea of my participation gently." She rose to signify the end of the interview. David got up and extended his hand. The handshake was to seal a bargain. His eyes met hers with a mixture of hope and admiration. As he closed the thick wooden door, he tapped his own forehead contemptuously. Old fool. Mesmerised by a girl. She listened well, and that unexpected smile, well, it was unfair on a fellow. But what could she do? What could anyone do?''

"What do you want? Two minutes' silence?''

Alexa was torn between exasperation and commiseration. Whenever they were alone Fabrice relapsed into an almost catatonic state. For the past few days he had gone through the motions in the *chais*, been punctual at meals and had entertained Alexa's paying guests conscientiously enough, but with a stiffness and hauteur that was beginning to provoke adverse comment. She had heard the stifled conversations on corridors and landings. It was worrying commercially, and most of all, Alexa could not live with the sense of failure that his unhappiness imposed on her.

Fabrice sat on the edge of the bed with his head in his hands, silent at first, in the face of her angry question. He had torn off his dinner jacket and his bow tie hung loose about the open collar of his shirt.

"I wanted rather more than that. An eternity of silence. That's what I wanted. But no. Somebody had to interfere. The old, old story again. Anything for Monsieur Fabrice, as long as it is not what he wants. When I was a child, a boy, I wanted love and instead, I got things. Now I want things, I cannot have them. I thought at least I could have death, a long sleep, freedom, instead . . . I am getting what I suppose you call love."

"And you never acquired the knack of making use of love?"

Alexa spoke with a coldness which she knew was unfair and unkind. But the evening had not been a success. Her guests had not enjoyed themselves and had retired early to bed with excuses about their long journey on the following day.

Fabrice shook his head, wearily, "No."

"Didn't your grandfather love you?"

"With him it was mainly pity. He was a fair-minded man. He knew it wasn't my fault I was a cripple, but he wanted a strong, handsome grandson, who would grow into a man he could be proud of. He kept making it very clear that his son had disappointed him wilfully and I had disappointed him innocently. He used to say, 'Poor boy, poor boy. You will do your best, I know.' "

Fabrice mimicked the sound of an old man's reedy voice with what Alexa guessed to be chilling accuracy. He must have done it many times as a lonely, resentful little boy.

"Stupid, vile old man," Alexa struggled with the back zip of her gown.

"No," Fabrice sighed deeply, "he wasn't stupid, he simply wasn't the man to pretend that things were as he would have liked them."

Alexa sat down beside her husband, and tentatively put her arm around his bowed shoulders. He did not shrug her away, but leaned his head against her shoulder. She clasped him strongly for an instant and then moved away.

It was obvious that he was very tired, but he must be braced.

"It was brave of you to come into dinner, that night. Really, I'd no idea. To have a shotgun in your mouth one minute and *filet de porc* the next seems pretty stylish to me."

It was days after the event that she had discovered that her husband had been seconds away from death and that only a matter of hours later he had helped her to entertain their guests. It was Hortense who had alerted her to Fabrice's real state of mind, a hint no more, but with gentle persistence, Alexa had got the whole story out of her. Pierre David had come up to the house for his customary glass of wine with his old friend, Hortense, and described what had occurred in the *chai*.

Incredibly, Fabrice grinned at her. "What is that phrase? Calling a spade a spade? Your manner of describing things would be uncomfortably graphic for most people, Alexa. Isn't it lucky I have a strong stomach?"

Alexa brushed this red herring aside impatiently.

"Fabrice, didn't you think for one moment that I might want you to stay alive?"

His eyes widened. "What benefit would you derive from my continued existence? I don't even support you. In fact, you seem to be supporting all of us. You even told me I wasn't an adequate lover. Why should *you* miss me?"

"You misunderstood what I said then," Alexa replied briskly. "It was clumsily phrased. In any case, there was an occasion on which you were more than adequate. At least a part of me must have thought so, because rather a large part of me is getting larger."

There was a long silence. Fabrice continued to look down at the floor, his elbows supported by his knees. Alexa felt sure he could not have understood. Perhaps it was all wrong to tell him now. But it was a question of finding a reason, giving him a reason to want to live. Would it be enough? He was unpredictable, his performance as a human being, patchy. She sat down at the dressing table and examined her face. Some pins were falling out of her hair. She moved them and began to brush it with long vigorous strokes, enjoying the stimulating touch of the bristles on her scalp.

"Now you have everything, Alexa, don't you? You are not only mistress here in my house, but you are the master too. You wield the power, pay the bills and carry the heir in your belly, the ultimate weapon."

"The heir to *what*, Fabrice. Heir to a guest-house?" She swung round on the dressing stool to face him. "It's not the *heir* in here," Alexa clapped her hand to her stomach. "It's a child, *our* child, Fabrice. Do you want it to grow up unloved and lonely, like you? Or do you want to protect it from that? I want to bring it into a happy house where both parents struggle against their difficulties together and try to build something to secure its future. We have an absolute duty to pull together. Somebody else is depending on us and I can't do it on my own. You have to co-operate or I might as well arrange to have an accident right away.''

Alexa had no idea why she had said that. It emerged from her mouth without any permission from her brain. It was a form of mindless violence occasioned by the infuriating, self-pitying weakness of her husband. She didn't care what he thought or even what he did, if only he could be roused from the shifting, sinking sands of his self-indulgence. She was beginning to feel a sensation like panic. How could he leave her to fend for herself when she wanted and needed him so much? He didn't really have to do anything except be there, be there for *her*, a shoulder to cry on, a body to lean on. She could do the rest herself.

He looked up, his face white and the mouth formed into the round hole of shock which she had first seen on the day she had seemed to taunt him with sexual inadequacy. She had learned to interpret it as a sign that he was dangerously angry. ''Don't you *ever* say anything like that again, do you understand? Never. I don't know where you get these filthy ideas, but don't bring them here.''

His unexpected anger was exhilarating. Alexa experienced a strong sensation of arousal excited by the knowledge that there was still vivid life in Fabrice and that he could care so much about anything. And it was *her* child he cared about. Her relief was so great, she wanted him to shout and rave, so she could immerse herself in the sounds of his positive determined life.

''Aha,'' she challenged triumphantly, ''so you *do* want the child!'' He got up from the bed and came towards her swiftly, leaning only lightly on his stick. For a moment she half feared he meant to hit her and she dodged slightly, but only as she might have dodged a storm-tossed branch. She could forgive him anything now, anything as long as he would be alive.

''Of course I want the child. It'll be the first thing I've ever wanted and actually got, if I do get it, that is. Something will go wrong, you watch. Something will happen to take my child away from me, because that's what always happens.'' To Alexa's intense delight he was shouting, and smiling all at once. She placed her own finger to his lips and taking his free hand placed it on her abdomen. ''Maybe you can't feel anything yet, but I assure you, it's there. It will be born at Christmas, I think. So the Christmas house party idea I had is off for this year. It will be well after the *vendange*, at any rate, so it won't interfere with that.''

"If there is one."

"There'll be one. You can be certain of that. It's not a good time for you, I realise that, but we'll manage."

"I don't see much point in even picking the grapes this year. I may as well uproot the vines and use them for firewood for all the use the harvest will be." He didn't even notice her attempt to reassure.

"Now it is you who is talking filth. Those vineyards have served generations of your family well, and I assure you Fabrice, with a little manoeuvring, they will serve the next generation just as well. I've already made quite a bit of money this summer, and it isn't over yet. Soon I'll be able to contribute to the expenses of the vineyard. We'll pull it round because we've *got* to. There is nowhere else to go. If you give in now, we lose everything, the mortgages will be foreclosed, the loans called in. We will have nowhere to live and no income of any sort to live on. And the next Marquis de Pies Ombre will have to live on charity. You will have to let me help, Fabrice, for the sake of the future." Again Alexa touched her abdomen.

"I suppose the mother of my son can have anything and do anything she wants. Anything else would be a serious risk to her health, especially in your own case, my darling. Oh, Alexa, if only things could be the way you see them."

In his sudden euphoria he had given way and Alexa's path into the *chais* was now clear. She would begin to learn what she needed to know on the following day.

"They *will* be exactly as I see them. All you have to do is believe it. The rest will follow naturally."

Georges Chirac leaned back in his chair and regarded Alexa with amazement. How quickly she grasped things. Something to do with her extreme youth, a flexibility of mind that went with the pliability of youthful muscles. But then, he had noticed that extraordinary quality of attention of hers before. It must charm some and embarrass others, he reflected. His lips twitched. Yes, to have this slip of a girl noticing that the sounds one was making did not actually mean very much must be very disconcerting.

She had matured considerably in the months since he had last seen her. Her slight air of hesitance was gone together with the soft, hazy quality of her beauty. In their place was a surefootedness, a briskness and a brilliance of eye and complexion. She was impressive.

"And so, Monsieur Chirac, there is absolutely no reason why our château should produce a vintage this year. Is that correct?" Alexa crossed her long legs neatly at the ankles as she spoke. Georges Chirac kept his eyes firmly on her face.

"Perfectly, *Madame*. You can do as you suggest. Harvest the grapes, press them, and I will buy the must from you. As soon as the malolactic fermentation is over, it can be removed to my *chais* here, and I will act as *enleveur*, handle the wine as I think fit and then use it for a blended claret. Once those grapes are gathered, apart from the very first stage of vinification, they need not be any further trouble or expense to you. I am afraid we shall not have much of a harvest this year anyway. The recent storms will have made serious inroads into the quantities we might have hoped for. Still, if the months of ripening are good and we suffer no further climatic disturbances, there might still be some quality wine made."

"But not by the Château d'Ombre."

"*Hélas*, no, *Madame*, not this year. But I applaud your strategy. You have devised an excellent programme for recovery. First, avoid damaging the reputation of your property further by producing a poor wine and selling it as Château de Pies Ombre. Second, concentrate on getting the land back into good heart. Third, re-examine the style of your wine in the light of current market conditions. When you have done that, we can think about what your re-stocking policy should be. I think you are right about the *hardness* as you call it. It was all right when people were prepared to buy claret in large quantities and wait a minimum of seven years before broaching the first case. But, as you say, the pace of life is different now. It is a good thought, that. To be frank, I hadn't thought of it myself. And your point about smaller, modern houses without cellars . . . No, *Madame*, it is not ridiculous. It is something we should consider. You are right. Our market is changing and we should move with the times.

"There is a wine, Château Pétrus, it has enjoyed an enormous success lately. It was not one of the great classic wines of Bordeaux, not even particularly highly regarded in its bracket, but the qualities you mention are precisely those exhibited by Pétrus. We could all take a lesson from it. The *encépagement* there is almost a hundred per cent *Merlot*. That would be a departure in the Haut Médoc, of course. It seems *Madame*, that you are ahead of the times. But I give you fair warning, that vine flowers early, it's a frost risk . . .''

Monsieur Chirac was now as oblivious to the beauty of his visitor's legs as to the time. He would talk contentedly for hours about his favourite subject and, ordinarily, Alexa would have been as delighted to listen to him as he was to talk, because vines were fast becoming her own preferred topic of conversation. Unfortunately, she must risk seeming a little rude. She had already waited for a natural pause in the *négociant*'s discourse, but none had come.

She rose to take her leave with an apologetic smile. "Oh, surely you are not going, you will stay and lunch with me."

"I wish that I could, *Monsieur*, but unfortunately, I have another appointment."

"That saddens me, *Madame*. I had hoped to keep you here a little longer. It is not often I get to talk to somebody whose enthusiasm for wine is just developing. I wanted to indulge myself, I confess."

"You are very good and patient to act as instructor. I know it is not your job to do it, and believe me, *Monsieur*, I am grateful."

"*Madame*, it is my very real pleasure. You will succeed in your task, I know. You have a feel for the land, for living things, for tradition and yet you have the spirit of adventure which will enable you to develop and build on tradition. It is a combination of qualities that will marry as well as the classic grapes of the Médoc. The result, *Madame*, will be a memorable and lasting wine." He raised her hand to his lips.

Alexa turned the battered blue Renault down the narrow Rue Gilbert. Her appointment was at noon, which should allow her time to get back to the Château d'Ombre in time for luncheon.

She had three resident guests at the moment, the Scheitingers from Houston and their New York banker, Richard Lockwood. An oddly attractive though rather forbidding man, Mr. Lockwood was apparently their guest. Alexa was faintly irritated to find herself so much aware of a man who made so little social effort. Most of the day Lionel Scheitinger and he were busy in the library where they seemed to be discussing business matters intensively. In the meantime Ariel Scheitinger was rather at a loose end and Alexa had given her as much companionship as she could. None-the-less, whatever the business negotiations were, they were always broken off for meals and Alexa was punctilious about being present herself, even if Fabrice could not manage it during the middle of his own working day. As she constantly reminded herself and Fabrice, they were not running a hotel, but offering hospitality of a kind that few people ever experienced and could never normally buy.

Fabrice had seemed more settled during the past week. Alexa visited the *chais* at intervals during the day. She understood the work that was going on there in only the most rudimentary fashion. Her unpredictable and unannounced visits were designed to break up Fabrice's day and act as a counter-irritant to his depression. Despite his capitulation on the night he learned of his own imminent fatherhood, his attitude at first had been one of surprise, but as she established the habit he became welcoming, and at times almost tender. As she walked around the semi-subterranean galleries with him, looking with awe on the serried ranks of casks, the men involved in tasks such as racking and turning the barrels glanced warmly at her. Her presence was an encouragement. Where Madame de Pies Ombre was, there employment and prosperity would soon follow. Had he told them she was *enceinte*, Alexa wondered, at a loss to account for her welcome? Surely not, it wasn't officially confirmed yet. Not that there was any doubt.

Doctor Gaultier confirmed the pregnancy smilingly.

"And you are well in yourself, *Madame*? Is there any early-morning nausea as yet? No, it must be long past, if there was any. You have not rushed to find yourself pregnant. Most ladies would have been here after the first missed period. I compliment you on your healthily relaxed attitude. There is really no advice I can give you, you know. Just do whatever you do normally, whatever seems natural to you. There is no occasion to make any sort of fuss about pregnancy, it is not an illness, after all. Pray do present my compliments to Madame de Pies Ombre, and to Mademoiselle Héloïse, of course. How delighted everyone must be. And your husband, his happiness must be beyond . . ."

"I am concerned about my husband, actually," Alexa broke into the empty felicitations quietly. She had no wish to be rude, but a doctor is supposed to listen and this one clearly had a marked preference for the sound of his own voice. Concisely, and without revealing that Fabrice had attempted to take his own life, Alexa described Fabrice's depression.

"Things will be better now, *Madame*. I assure you that the period when a man's first child is coming is a proud and happy time. A man feels himself fulfilled and justified, he flexes his muscles in preparation for the moment when he must begin in earnest the business of being both protector and provider. The years before the children come, that is just a rehearsal."

"Well, in our own case, the rehearsal has been rather short."

"And all the better for that, *Madame*. It is the business of a young wife in your position to provide babies, is it not? Particularly boy babies. That is a little old-fashioned now, perhaps, but all the same, a great property like yours must be served by the generation of heirs. I am sure you agree with me. And in any case, a woman needs babies. Children complete her life. I am confident, *Madame*, that you will be the triumphant mother of many healthy children."

Doctor Gaultier would have continued with more of these anodyne reflections had Alexa not signalled her desire to speak with some slight asperity. Doctor Gaultier ceased speaking himself with slightly raised eyebrows, pointedly joining the tips of his fingers. He smiled faintly, surprised that his helpful remarks had not been heard patiently to the end.

"I wanted to know what to do about my own diet, and things like that."

Gaultier threw back his head and laughed in a way that Alexa found disagreeably patronising. She was not aware of having said anything amusing.

"Your diet? Why *Madame*, would I have any advice to give you about your diet? You surely do not contemplate a slimming regime just at present? Eat what you want, as much as you want. Your body will tell you what to do. Trust it, *Madame*. That is the best dietary advice for a pregnant woman. Indeed it is the best advice in all connections. The same goes for exercise. Do as much as you want, as much as you can. When the time comes that you can no longer do a thing, then do not do it. It is as simple as that."

He spun himself round in his swivel chair and looked out of the window, his fingers still steepled. "Of course, it is essential to keep the bowels open and for that I will give you some suppositories. The bowels are the key to everything, never underestimate the bowels, *Madame*."

Alexa solemnly assured him that she would not neglect this important matter and left his consulting rooms somewhat deflated. She would have found it pleasant to be told to take care of herself, to rest, in fact. That rest would be out of the question in no way lessened her irritation. It seemed that she would have to take her own advice in bringing this baby, this doubly precious baby, safely to term.

When Alexa got home to d'Ombre it was already nearly two o'clock, so she was surprised to find that everyone was still in the *Grand Salon*. Opening the double doors, her ears were immediately assailed by the sound of champagne corks being indecorously popped by Jean and Pierre.

"Surprise!" shrieked Ariel. "This is a pregnancy party!"

"Oh," said Alexa, a trifle flatly, noting Richard Lockwood's absence from the room with a mixture of relief and disappointment. It was strange how these Americans could somehow take your life straight out of your hands and give the confiscation all the appearance of the utmost good-nature and generosity. And what an odd, ill-omened idea. Suppose the pregnancy didn't go well, or there was a still birth or something wrong with the baby . . . Well, they meant to be kind.

Fabrice came towards her, with a look of shy enquiry on his face. He handed her a champagne flute saying quietly, "It's all right, isn't it? Gaultier confirmed it?"

"Of course he did. I really don't know why one has to have these doctors to tell one what one already knows. They make a fat fee out of stating the obvious. I'm sure people didn't go to doctors in the old days when they were pregnant. They were just pregnant."

"And a lot of babies died, *and* a lot of ladies died too."

"Tilly!" Now it was Alexa's turn to shriek, or almost. "How did you get here? Oh it's so marvellous to see you!" It *was* marvellous to see her. The only member of Fabrice's family who seemed entirely normal. Héloïse was normal but only within the geometry of her own self-imposed oddness.

"Tilly, how awful of me, I never thanked you for your telegram."

"Which telegram?"

"The one I got at the airport after I'd sold the wine in London!"

"Think nothing of it *ma chère*, I send telegrams to everyone all the time, I enjoy the drama. It gives me the illusion of still being in the mainstream of life."

"But how did you get here? Why did you come? Not that is isn't marvellous to see you. I'm afraid I have no time for family entertaining, or money either," Alexa added.

"I flew down this morning. Fabrice picked me up at Mérignac. He told me the news at seven o'clock! Can you *imagine*. When the phone rang I thought there must be a revolution or something going on! I don't know anyone who's ever *experienced* life at seven in the morning. Really, I feel quite the pioneer." Oh it was good to see her and hear her light, mocking voice again. And it was wonderful to know that it was Fabrice who had told her the news. The thought that he had been eager to tell someone about the expected child was surely proof that he was throwing off his depression.

"Alexa, my dear, dear Alexa. Bless you, my dear child. Kiss your disreputable old Tilly. It's marvellous to see you looking so well. And it's more than wonderful to see what you have achieved here. I told you, didn't I? You'd put your mark on poor old Château d'Ombre. What a transformation! I may even take to coming here on a regular basis if you can find a cut-price room for an indigent old relative."

Ariel Scheitinger had joined them briefly, hoping to draw Alexa away to her group on the other side of the room. Richard Lockwood was there too now. Alexa saw him wave away a glass of champagne with an impatient, restless gesture.

"Oh, Tilly. You can come here any time you want to, you know that surely. Don't take any notice of her, Ariel, Tilly's rich."

"A lot richer since *you* started supporting the de Pies Ombres, I can assure you of *that*," Tilly said in a low aside to Alexa. "Look who's here, it's that crazy old woman. However do you get on with Héloïse? She's a bit of a spectre at the feast isn't she?"

"No, Tilly. You're very naughty. Héloïse is a darling. I don't know what I should do without her."

"Does she usually come into lunch, and looking like that? *Tiens*, she will frighten all your custom away!"

"No, she doesn't. In fact, she's never joined us at all before now. I should welcome her if she did. Héloïse is the most marvellous conversationalist I've ever come across, apart from my father."

Lately, Héloïse had consented to surprisingly frequent conversations with Alexa who was rapidly becoming a favourite with her. They talked mainly about vineyards and what parcels of land had been acquired by what local proprietors and at what price. Héloïse conveyed these interesting nuggets of information to her young friend in an austere but anecdotal style. Alexa had been so amused by some of the stories that she wondered if Héloïse's alleged dislike of gossip were not an established tactic for avoiding vapid exchanges with Suzanne. After all, her brother's marriage to Suzanne must have taken place within a few years of her rejection by the convent. Facing a lifetime in the same house as her sister-in-law, Héloïse may have given herself an unassailable excuse for unsociability which would have the added advantage of an aura of sacrifice. Alexa dismissed these unworthy deductions as they did not conform to Fabrice's version of Héloïse's chosen style of life. However, from time to time, Héloïse allowed Alexa to see an unholy twinkle in her eye.

"Ah, yes, Mr. Standeven. Does he know yet?" Tilly was clearly more interested in hearing news of Alexander than ruminating on Héloïse's capacity for civilised conversation.

Héloïse advanced across the faded Aubusson carpet. She wore an alarming *ensemble* in cyclamen pink, a departure from her usual vague colour schemes. Alexa understood that the startling hue was intended to express a spirit of congratulation and celebration.

"Alexa, dear child, it is welcome news. Tidings of a forthcoming child are always good to hear. I hope we are not being too previous in celebrating in this way. But poor Fabrice could not contain himself this morning and once he had let the cat out of the bag . . ." she shrugged, "there was all this."

"Oh, it doesn't matter. And anyway, Doctor Gaultier seemed to take my pregnancy rather less seriously than a pimple. So I'm quite glad *you're* all making a fuss of me. I suppose I must regard myself a public property from now on. I *do* like your suit, Tante Héloïse. What a stimulating colour it is." Alexa could not help noticing the astounding jewel she wore on the lapel of the aggressively tailored jacket. It was in the form of a magpie in flight, the white parts of the bird formed from blindingly white *pavé* set diamonds, the black from slivers of black opal, which gave the petrol-like sheen of the dark feathers.

"Yes, I bought it for my brother Luc's marriage to Suzanne. It would be 1934. So it has been very serviceable."

Tilly repressed a shudder.

"Really, I must talk to you about clothes soon," Alexa said

to Tilly. "They're becoming a problem. Monsieur Terry is really so kind to me but he does not have endless cancelled orders. I wonder if I could make arrangements with any other of the *couturiers* in Paris to pick up showroom models. Do let's go and talk to the others, they must think us very rude."

The Scheitingers came to look on Alexa's lately discovered pregnancy as a stroke of good fortune with untold promotional benefits. It seemed the purpose of their visit to the Château d'Ombre was to discuss with Richard Lockwood the financing and launch of their latest business venture. Lionel Scheitinger had purchased two brownstone houses on Riverview in the Sutton Place area of New York with a view to turning them into the most exclusive maternity clinic in the world. The long-range plan was to franchise the exercise so that within ten years there would be a Scheitinger Clinic in every state in America. Already vast sums had been spent on the very latest equipment for the care of expectant mothers of the upper income brackets and a staff that had been lured away from teaching hospitals and universities around the globe with the offer of princely salaries. Alexa was both awed and intrigued by the sheer scale of the plan and the sums of money she had heard discussed.

The audacious business philosophy behind the move was that no family with money could resist the very best care for its pregnant women. Other pleasures and luxuries might be forgone to ensure a privileged start in life for the infant heirs of some of the wealthiest families in the Untied States and beyond. It was cynical, perhaps even a little distasteful, but Alexa could see, without the need of any persuasion, that the venture could not really fail.

"I've a helluva lot of dough down, and when Lionel Scheitinger has dough down, that's because a helluva lot more is gonna jump right back. I got every goddamn thing there is. I got scanners; I got heart monitors; I got machines I don't even know the name of. I got a whole bunch of medical boys with degrees from here to New Mexico and I got a great gang of nurses, real easy on the eye. What I need now is a dame, real pregnant and real classy, all on the right day."

Lockwood leaned back in his chair, toying with a piece of bread. He was not a talkative man. During the three days that he and the Scheitingers had been at d'Ombre, Alexa had hardly known what to make of him. His accent was devoid of class or

national characteristics. It had if anything a slight American bias
but there were other ingredients in it which she could not identify. His clothes were correct but appeared designed to disguise
any personal taste or glimmer of individuality. In later years she
would identify the determined, well-bred blandness of the
Brooks Brothers style, but at that moment it was inscrutable to
her.

About himself he had said virtually nothing. The bare fact of
his occupation as a banker was all that was known to Alexa and
he volunteered nothing further. He had no particular likes or
dislikes and took no more part in mealtime conversation than
was consistent with the barest politeness. He listened to the
others talking as if they were voices on a radio and could be
switched off at will. It seemed that he tolerated the noise as a
background to his own thoughts. Between him and Fabrice there
was a slight tension. Although of a similar age, the two men
avoided conversation. From time to time, Alexa noticed Lockwood observing Fabrice through narrowed eyes. There was a
look of cool appraisal on his face.

She herself often felt Lockwood's eyes on her as she went
about the château. At first she was untroubled by it. Alexa was
accustomed to being observed. So accustomed that she was
largely unconscious of the continual interest of other people in
her appearance and her doings.

But the touch of Lockwood's eyes was unmistakable. She felt
it as certainly as she would have felt a warm, dry hand resting
on the nape of her neck. It felt surprising, shocking even, but
not actually unpleasant.

Once or twice Alexa had found herself looking round. She
began to feel the absence of his regard as a chill, the sudden
withdrawal of a warm garment. She noticed with wonder and
some irritation at herself that all actions had less flavour if he
were not there to observe them. Dull things, daily things, the
filling of coal scuttles and log baskets, the arranging of flowers
and laying of tables, were all vitalised by his silent interest. She
knew it was not the tasks themselves that caught his attention,
but the manner in which she either fulfilled them herself or
supervised the work.

Two days after his arrival with the Scheitingers, she had encountered him in the main gallery. He was leaving his room and
she held a pile of clean linen in her arms. No smile of formal

recognition altered his features. He merely said, "One day, *Madame*, you must come to New York."

"But why should I do that," she had countered more or less playfully, "when everything I want is here?" Lockwood stood unflickering in the muted light of the gallery.

"You have no idea what you want at your age. You cannot know all there is to be had. Your choices are uneducated."

The linen was heavy in Alexa's arms. Suddenly she was annoyed. She did not care to be on the receiving end of portentous lectures from a near stranger in her own house.

"No-one knows all that life has to offer, Mr. Lockwood. One makes choices from the limited range of options available to one. That's all."

"That is true perhaps, for most people. But you are not most people, are you? It is too early for Alexa de Pies Ombre to think of accepting limitations surely?"

For a moment it seemed as if he were about to lift the linen out of her arms and Alexa, uncertain of his motives and a little afraid of him, took a step backwards. But he did not come any closer. He stood silent for a moment, searching her face, and then turned and walked away as if she were no more than a chamber maid with whom he had indifferently exchanged the time of day.

And now she heard his voice say, "Perhaps our hostess would consider having a check-up at the clinic. That should put the right seal of approval on it for you, Lionel!"

"Oh, Alexa, do! Wouldn't that be just perfect, Lionel? Alexa needs a trip, she works so hard, honey, you've no idea *how* hard. It's just so perfect, I can't believe it. Richard's a genius. Here we've been for days and days trying to find the best way to stage the launch. Do you know, we've been through every pregnant actress in Hollywood? I tell you Alexa, either they're not classy or they're not pregnant. And all the time we've had a pregnant *Marquise* right here! You'll do it won't you, hon? Say you will. Lionel's been like a grisly bear with a sore head trying to figure this one out."

"I say, Ma'am, would you do it?" Lionel's face was bright with the dawn of solution.

"Well . . .''

"Free trip, won't cost you a dime. Best of everything when you get there. Ariel's fixed up those old brownstones like you wouldn't believe. A goddam palace. That's what they are. You should see what's she's got in there. Antique furniture, real good paintings, sterling cutlery for the suites, best damn linens you can buy. There ain't a millionairess alive who won't feel right at home there. And you can have all the tests. Anything you 'n' Fabrice, here . . .''

"A regular funfair, in fact,'' Fabrice interposed, his sarcasm vaporising harmlessly.

"Aw, come on now, fella. It's a regular, high-class operation, like you got here, just a different kind of customer. Everything the best. I tell you, the days a' coming when it's going to be a real social advantage to have been born in the Scheitinger Clinic, New York. Yessir, Scheitinger, Andover and Harvard, the classic life-plan for the world's best babies.''

"Will they all be American then, the world's best babies?'' Fabrice enquired with dangerous ingenuousness. Alexa interrupted him swiftly.

"When do you plan your official opening, Mr. Scheitinger?''

"As soon as I find the right dame.''

"I think a change of scene would do me good.'' Alexa allowed her empty champagne flute to chink decisively on the marble chimney-piece. Lockwood's eyes trapped the blue flash of challenge in her eyes. He could not have said at whose feet the gauntlet had been thrown, but he held her glance just a split-second longer than he knew was polite.

CHAPTER
13

🎗 🎗 THE OPPOSITION TO her going had been fierce. Tilly said it was too late for her to travel safely, Suzanne said she couldn't and wouldn't manage the household and guests on her own and Fabrice agreed with Suzanne. Héloïse expressed her own misgivings. "These people," she said, "are no doubt all very well in their way, but Alexa, *ma chère*, you realise their standards of morality are clearly rather different from our own."

It turned out that Héloïse felt there was something sinister in making blatant class and financial distinctions between infants still in the womb. Alexa scotched these arguments by saying the distinctions already existed and what Mr. Scheitinger was doing was accepting the reality and proposing, in his own colourful phrase, to make "an honest buck" or two out of an established fact.

"All he is doing," she expostulated in despair at the end of a long argument with Héloïse, "is being open and honest about it."

"No, he is being cruelly blatant about it and I really don't think we should lend our name to it, Alexa, I really don't."

"Oh, so the de Pies Ombres are socialists, are they? I wish somebody had told me before now. It's useful to know the political flavour of one's own family, however unexpected it may be."

Héloïse sighed. Alexa was being deliberately, logically, infuriating. It was a tactic she made use of sometimes, to get her own way.

"Well, I shall ask our Lord what he thinks about it when I go to Holy Communion tomorrow," Héloïse stated with resignation.

"Oh," was Alexa's hasty riposte, "is that His time for giving rulings on matters of moral perplexity?"

Héloïse wore an expression of wounded wisdom which made Alexa realise she had behaved very badly indeed. But not knowing how to retract such a cruel and clumsy gibe, she was forced to let it die and draw the discussion to a close.

"And in any case," she continued to argue, "don't you see? The publicity advantage to the Scheitinger Clinic in having Madame la Marquise de Pies Ombre as one of their first patients cuts both ways. I'll get a chance to tell everyone in America what *I* do for a living and give the Château d'Ombre a publicity boost. It's thousands of dollars' worth of advertising which we couldn't possibly afford any other way, a chance not to be missed."

"It's publicity purchased at rather a high price, Alexa, and it strikes me as being in doubtful taste."

Impatiently, Alexa pointed out the obvious. "Publicity and good taste are naturally mutually exclusive, Tante Héloïse. You didn't mind me advertising our hospitality and aristocratic company, *that* was in terrible taste."

"It was mitigated by the fact that nobody's feelings could be injured by it but our own." Héloïse was quite as deft, and almost as remorseless in debate as Alexa herself.

"All right, we must agree to differ. I accept this performance may be vulgar, but, believe me, it is necessary. Firstly, I need to get away. Secondly, it's an opportunity to bring the Château d'Ombre to the attention of thousands of the right kind of Americans, and others too, and all without expending a single *centime* of our own money. There's no-one I'd rather please than you, Tante Héloïse, but evidently, it can't be done. You must let me be the judge of what is expedient."

Héloïse raised her hands and dropped them heavily in her lap, acknowledging defeat.

"And there's another thing," Alexa rammed home her victory, "Suzanne's precious Doctor Gaultier had nothing better to offer me in the way of medical advice than to do whatever I feel like doing. He clearly doesn't expect to see any more of me until I either lose the baby or it's halfway into the world. Frankly, I don't think that's good enough and I have a chance to get some better advice now, and I shall take it."

Her determination undented by any argument the family could offer, Alexa was momentarily disturbed by David's misgivings.

He worried that, without his wife's vigilance, his master might make a further attempt on his own life. But this plea also was eventually rejected, after some hesitation.

"The immediate danger is over and in any case, I cannot be his gaoler for life. My husband has everything to live for now. If he is not persuaded of that, then no power on earth can keep him alive. I shall be away about a week, no more. I rely on you, Monsieur David, to keep him busy, excessively so. I strongly suspect that very tired people don't kill themselves, you would need some energy for that."

David looked at her in admiration. Right or wrong, the young lady knew what she wanted. And what was more, she was intent upon getting it without the wheedling wiles he had so much despised in other women.

"*Madame*, for you, I shall do all that is in one man's power to keep another alive. Go, enjoy your holiday. I, David, will watch over what is yours until you return." And with that stout declaration he spun on his heel and stumped down the staircase from the turret room with an unaccustomed grin on his face.

Alexa looked at the door which had closed behind the departing David. I have done nothing to deserve this, she thought, but as soon as I can, I will show David that I know how to reward loyalty that has been given in advance of payment.

Manhattan staggered Alexa. Adjectives disintegrated in her mind before she could apply them. She had seen the unreal pictures, heard the terrifying stories of crime and violence but their impact had been similar to that made by the gruesome fairy stories of her childhood. There was a hugeness about the place that the mind could not encompass. She could not remember a time when she had felt so dwarfed by the things that other men and women had made. Wearily she concluded that there must be a massiveness about the American character that a mere European could not hope to comprehend.

The crags of concrete and the seething crowds intimidated. The streets were dark with the shadows of buildings of seemingly limitless height. The heat steamed like a kitchen at the crescendo of creation. But there was no window to open, no breath of air to be had. The only way to escape the August heat was to go indoors. The coolness there was not the gently civilised cool created by louvred shutters as in France, but a dismal chill generated by air conditioning. When she was out of doors she longed to be away from the exhausting humidity, when she was indoors, she rubbed the goose pimples on her arms frantically. The New Yorkers complained of the discomforts of their own city good-humouredly.

But amidst it all, Riverview Terrace was an oasis of urban charm. The brownstone houses had been tactfully melded into one, their Victorian splendour undiminished but rounded out to a wry maturity which could not fail to gain the appreciation of the most critical European eye. A green and flowery margin separated the houses from too intimate a contact with the highway and the East River. From the houses, the river was a pleasing view of commercial activity, but not permitted to soil the hem of Riverview Terrace with its plebeian touch.

Ariel had indeed done wonders with the interiors. She led Alexa from room to room, on a tour of exploration. Every room or suite had a theme, a period or exotic motif, all made some allusion to the motherhoods of history, myth or allegory. Alexa was lost in admiration, understanding the talent, effort and expense which had gone into this triumph. There was not a room amongst the dozens she saw that she would not have liked herself.

Ariel's characteristic touch was light and idiosyncratic, interpreting antique models and themes with an affectionate disparagement. Her fidelity to her theme was never too academic or exact. The Tudor Room, in spite of its massive oaken bed, imported in sections from England with the crudely carved cradle, was wittily hung with printed fabrics rather than the heavy, predictable embroideries. "I tried it, but sent the embroideries back to the dealer, the whole effect was just so oppressive, I couldn't stand it myself, so I'm sure it would have made me suicidal if I'd been pregnant," Ariel explained. It was the same in the Chinese Suite, which she had decorated with a hue of cherry, rather than the angry red of authentic Chinese rejoicing.

"So what do you think of my efforts?"

"Oh, Ariel, it's all marvellous! What a wonderful place to have a baby, in any time or place the imagination can conjure. I just can't praise it enough. You're a genius. Do you know you could make a great deal of money doing this sort of thing for other people? Tell me, where do you get all these fabrics printed, they look something a bit special to me, not the sort of thing you can just order in a shop."

"Ah, those. Well you're dead right, there's this amazing little

factory I've found right here in New York, really old and small.
It's in a place called Flushing. A family of Quakers who've been
there since I don't know when, since the *Mayflower* I guess, and
are still running it. They use these fantastic old wooden printing
blocks and the stuff they do is just fascinating. You must come
with me and have a look before you go. There is maybe something for your château.''

"I'd love that.''

"Now," Ariel suddenly became less of the enthusiastic young
hostess and more of the professional clinic proprietor, "be sure
to get plenty of rest, honey, the press conference's tomorrow
morning at a half after eight, so you'll need to be fresh.''

Alexa groaned. "How early you Americans seem to do
things.''

"Home of the working breakfast, hon. No loafing in the Big
Apple!''

Ariel closed the door of the delightful Antoinette Suite after
her. Alexa looked at it thoughtfully. She really did like Ariel.
She seemed overshadowed by Lionel, the forceful tycoon. But
Ariel had talent and personality of her own. They could become
friends if only the frenetic pace of her life and Alexa's own
commitments in France would allow it. A friend of her own age
seemed an unattainable luxury at the moment. Friendships took
time, and that's one of the many things I don't have, Alexa
sighed without bitterness.

She had snapped open the locks of her grandfather's pigskin
suitcase, an undisputed possession she supposed, since his death,
when a uniformed nurse in dazzling white linen, cap and shoes
appeared noiselessly.

"I'll do that, Ma'am. I'll just get out a robe and a night gown
and you can slip into bed right away. Or perhaps you'd like a
shower first while I finish up in here?''

"Couldn't I sit out on the balcony for a bit?''

"Don't recommend it, Ma'am. Too darn hot for that.''

"Yes, I think you're right," Alexa said obediently. "A shower
and bed, that sounds good to me.''

Alexa didn't have a shower, but sat for a while in the sunken
marble bath with its gilded-swan faucets. The huge bathroom
was like a small ballroom with chandeliers and flower arrangements reflected in looking glasses. There was a glass-fronted
cabinet containing a selection of luxurious toilet articles from
what seemed like every famous French *parfumier*, all in the

most extravagant packs. She made a note to use some of these ideas for her own guest accommodation at home and was very glad she was not paying Lionel Scheitinger for the luxurious results of his wife's limitless imagination.

"What's your name?" Alexa asked the nurse as she turned down the bedclothes for her.

"Louella Parkin, Ma'am. I'll be looking after you."

"Where do you live, Louella?"

"Why right here, when I'm on duty, but my home's in Queens."

"Louella, tell me something. Will they *let* pregnant women travel on aeroplanes to have babies here? I mean, won't it be a bit late for air travel, at that stage?"

"Well, Ma'am, I reckon anybody with a private jet will just about bust a gut to get here to have their baby, once we're open. This ain't no ordinary clinic. And remember, the staff here will be giving our patients all their prenatal care as well. It's as easy to get from Washington to here in a plane, if you've got one, as it is to go down the street. The standard of obstetrics here just isn't available anywhere else. It's the staff you see, some of the best people in the world."

"And you're one of them," Alexa heard herself say as she drifted off to sleep, grateful for the American nurse's soothing, unobtrusive pampering.

"I guess so, Ma'am," Louella said with quiet confidence as she closed the door softly.

When Louella opened the curtains in the morning it was half-past six. The sky was murky with a yellow haze that betokened great heat and humidity to come. Sitting up in bed, Alexa could just about see the East River through the windows. Barges and little cargo boats were busy with unknown tasks.

"Couldn't we open those windows, Louella?"

"Don't even think about it, Ma'am. It's getting real hot out there already, and it's noisy too. I'd stay with the air conditioning if I were you. You gotta be fresh as a daisy for the photographic session this morning. The hairdresser's coming right after you eat your breakfast."

Prodded by this gentle reminder that she was enjoying the Scheitinger Clinic's delights in exchange for her part of the agreement, Alexa embarked on the epic breakfast which Louella set before her on a silver tray. There were strawberries, Chinese gooseberries, paw-paw and hot-house grapes, together with what looked like real French croissants. Parma ham reposed on a gold-rimmed plate, its rosiness emphasised by a ripe, quartered fig.

"You eat your bran now, Ma'am, we don't want no constipation, do we?"

Alexa wrinkled her nose. She did not like bran nor the reminder of Doctor Gaultier's single piece of medical wisdom.

The press conference was held in the Venetian Room, as the Clinic's magnificent reception area was called. Alexa enjoyed it. The journalists were a thrusting group of New Yorkers, their questions were fired fast and furiously. They appreciated a witticism and their cameramen were delighted with her photogenic face and willingness to help them get good pictures. Very soon a camaraderie was established and Alexa's replies to their questions drew shouts of appreciative laughter.

But it became clear that the pack had just been settling into their stride as a more searching line of questioning began.

"Don't you think this is all a helluva rip off? Thousands of dollars just to have a baby?"

"No," Alexa replied thoughtfully, "I don't. Having a baby, especially a first baby, is a transforming experience in any woman's life. It's like being born yourself, everything is new and nothing will ever be the same again. There's no going back and nobody can change what has happened to your body, or to your life. Too many hospitals belittle the event, and in doing so, belittle the woman. Now that can't be a good preparation for motherhood.

"What the Scheitinger Clinic is doing, apart from providing a most distinguished prenatal and obstetrical service, is ensuring that no expectant mother who comes here risks being treated as a number in a surgical gown. Here she will be treated like a princess about to perform magic. It puts the focus on *her*, not on the doctors, not on her mother-in-law, not on hospital routine but squarely on *her*. And that's absolutely right, you know. It's the mother who will have to live with the consequences of the birth for the rest of her life. Isn't she entitled to some respect? Here she's absolutely in charge. She has her own room, bathroom, sitting room if she wants one, and can entertain her family and friends just as she would at home, in surroundings which are designed to make her feel like a queen. Mothers need to feel powerful, they're in for a tremendous task."

The suave young people from Lionel's public relations agency smiled approvingly. They couldn't have put it better themselves, not on the spur of the moment. They'd briefed Alexa of course, but basically, it was in her hands, and it seemed as if the *Marquise* had come through with the goods.

"What about all the millions of mothers and their families who can't afford this set-up?"

"In the Middle Ages, nobody except royalty could afford glass in their windows, but we all have it now. And what about electric light? Only a few millionaires had that in their houses, not so long ago. Now we can't imagine what it would be like to depend on oil lamps and gaslight. You have to begin somewhere, usually at the top."

There were scattered grunts of approval for the way in which the hostile questions had been answered. The pressmen went on trying for half an hour to break her steady, reasonable replies to their challenges. But Alexa had been brought up in Alexander Standeven's house and she had learned the techniques of counsel for the defence over the family breakfast table.

"What about taking all these medical guys with their fancy degrees out of circulation just to dance attendance on a few rich dames? Wouldn't they do more good in the Third World, or just looking after ordinary people in big teaching hospitals where their skills would benefit a higher number of mothers?"

"Possibly. But the opportunity of working together with other specialists who are first in their respective fields will give them all the chance to broaden their experience and enhance their knowledge. The admittedly large salaries they earn here will enable many to return to the teaching role or engage in independent research to the benefit of all."

"Will you come back here to have your baby, Ma'am?"

"No, I'm one of those who can't afford it. I'm still happy that such a place exists, it will set standards of care that will be copied everywhere."

"They say you run the most expensive boarding-house in the world, back in France, Ma'am. Is that true?"

"I certainly hope so. If you hear of anywhere more expensive, let me know, I'll put my prices up! Seriously, gentlemen, the Château d'Ombre gives value for money, a unique experience. You must all come and visit me some time, I can always make special concessions on price for the press! I mean it, you know, you'll have something worth writing about if you come."

The public relations executives forbade any more questions, using Alexa's own pregnancy as an excuse to draw the taxing interview to a close. They began to hand round generous glasses of Buck's Fizz and canapés designed to look like breakfast dishes in miniature. Gratefully, Alexa sank into a chair on the temporary dais. Lionel and Ariel thanked her effusively.

"You're a real pro, hon. Those bastards were putty in your hands. You think like a Philadelphia lawyer," Lionel beamed.

"Not bad, *Madame*, not bad at all."

The voice in the crowd had something familiar about it though she could not immediately have said whose it was. After a moment's searching, her eyes found their mark on Richard Lockwood's face. It had not occurred to her that he would be there, but of course, it had been inevitable. All this was as important to him as it was to the Scheitingers.

"Thank you, Mr. Lockwood." There was no need to respond to this grudging compliment with more than the barest civility. Alexa found herself nettled by the minimal praise. After all, it had been his idea that she should come to New York and now he behaved as if her performance had been no more than adequate. She really had done quite well, and she wasn't exacting a fee for this appearance.

He studied her for a time, his glance taking in every detail. He looked at her as if inspecting something he owned with a secret, if qualified, satisfaction. Alexa felt herself grow restive under his wordless examination. The several feet of distance between where he stood and the small podium on which she sat felt as if it were joined by a thick cord of invisible membrane. Conscious of an impassable barrier, none of the milling journalists walked between them.

"I'll call you." The words were emphatic, a flat statement of intent. He turned to go without acknowledging the Scheitingers. "Maybe we'll take in a show," he threw the words over his shoulder as he stepped over some camera equipment left lying on the floor.

Ariel broke in on the capsule of silence that surrounded Alexa as she watched his retreat with open-mouthed astonishment. "Come on honey, there's so many people just dying to meet you. You've made a fantastic impression and there's plenty of people here who could be really useful to you. Let's go."

"Does he speak to everyone like that, or just women?"

"Who? Oh, Richard. To tell you the truth, honey, he doesn't

talk to anyone, not even guys, if he can help it. It's business only with Richard. Terribly British, isn't he? Looks bored out of his skull most of the time. I guess he could be shy. Really brilliant men like him often are. He thinks you're just marvellous. Says he's never seen a woman work like you before. Something he said about method and leadership. Lionel was amazed. He said he'd never heard that guy say two words together that weren't about business.''

"British?''

"Sure. Didn't you know? He's a New Yorker now, of course, but he wasn't born here. No, some place in the North of England. Never says much about it.''

Alexa's heart skipped a beat. She was angry with herself. Why should that boor have any effect on her?

"How do you know he thinks I'm 'marvellous'?'' She hesitated over the word. "The way he looks at me, I think he thinks I could do with a wash!'' Ariel looked astounded.

"Oh no, you mustn't think that! He just can't take his eyes off you. Well, who could? Just look at you! And he said he'd call you, didn't he? If you ask me, the Marquis de Pies Ombre had better watch his back.''

"Yes. He said he'd call me. I suppose that means he'll whistle me up like a sheep dog, or does it mean he'll telephone? And about what, anyway? Brevity can be the soul of downright bloody rudeness.''

"You just don't know him, that's all.''

"Do you?''

Ariel sighed, she was becoming impatient with her guest's unwillingness to let the subject of Richard Lockwood drop.

"All I can tell you, honey, is that Richard Lockwood is a great guy. You ask Lionel some time. And he's paid a lot more attention to you than he's ever paid to *me*. I tell you, there are quite a few women in New York who'd cheerfully tear you limb from limb, if they knew.''

Somewhat to Alexa's surprise, the rest of the day was taken up with a photographic session for American *Vogue*. They were doing a feature on Bloomingdales' new Manhattan Mother department. Alexa was to model a selection of designer maternity garments. It seemed she was not entirely unknown, as some of the *Vogue* staff had seen the shows Alexa had done for Maison Terry. The hyperactive young photographer in black jeans and shirt, with his dark hair worn long but drawn back into an eighteenth-century *queue*, looked appreciatively at his model. Her abdomen swelled slightly beneath the elegant tunic of dark linen. Her long slender arms were bare and he could see that the clean line of her shoulders had not been blurred by a prenatal accumulation of fat. Her face too was lean, showing the fine bones to perfection. And her hair and complexion shone with health. Coming close to her, and holding her chin, he turned her face this way and that, looking for her best side. He must do something with those blue eyes, he thought, they are wonderful.

The vast antique mirrors and their infinite inter-reflections would make marvellous, mysterious photographs, full of atmosphere, like some dark Renaissance painting, with colours emerging as individual statements, struck by isolated rays of light.

The Venetian Room was another monument to Ariel's exceptional skills as an interior decorator. A place of glints and shadows, intriguing depths and looking-glass dreams. Alexa responded sympathetically to the mood of the interior and to the photographer's conception. Once he had told her what he wanted to achieve, her face assumed an aspect of ghostly remoteness, as if she were looking out into the future, from a distance of centuries.

"You should go back to modelling," the photographer commented whilst a mini-skirted girl from *Vogue* helped Alexa to change into a velvet dinner gown. "There'd be lots of work for you, right here in New York. I'd like to work with you again."

"No, I have my vineyards to run. It's a full-time job, like having a baby," she smiled, "you have to be there all the time."

"Oh, I thought it was a hotel you had."

"We do, but the vineyards are the real business, the guest-house side of things just helps my husband with expenses. We're doing a lot of re-stocking and that comes expensive." Alexa was quick to correct the impression that the vineyards were her own. She was learning to be careful of what she said in front of people who worked in the media.

"Well, it's a real shame. These pictures are going to be all-time classics."

There were clinical tests too, of course. Alexa was less interested in this side of Lionel Scheitinger's business, although the benefits were one of the reasons she had advanced for coming to New York.

The shining consulting rooms and adjacent examination rooms with banks of glittering machinery and equipment were less friendly and less interesting than the beautiful accommodation. She could take little interest in this side of the clinic's investment, as she had no knowledge with which to judge what she saw.

She was passed between a variety of obstetric specialists, but she grasped almost nothing of their individual areas of expertise, despite Lionel's painstaking and wordy introductions. All the doctors were charming. Most were Americans, but there was a sprinkling of Swiss and Germans, a tiny Japanese lady and a solemn Swede with bifocal spectacles. It was, as Lionel repeatedly said, a truly international "portfolio" of talent. Alexa had interviews with all of them. One, Doctor Heinz, asked her what hereditary diseases her own or her husband's family suffered from. Alexa laughed.

"Please excuse me, if it seem to you an impertinent question. But we are going to do a variety of tests, which amongst other things will tell us if your infant is suffering from any genetic disorders which may be conveyed through the blood lines from one generation to the next. I am a geneticist, *Madame*, not an obstetrician."

"Well, I appreciate your concern, but I can assure you that there is nothing of that kind." Dr. Heinz nodded.

"None-the-less, *Madame*, if you would kindly oblige me, I would like you to think really hard. You know there may be something, something to which you yourself are so entirely accustomed, look upon as so natural, that you have not realised that it is an inherited gene."

"I don't see what you are getting at, Doctor. My eyes are blue, as are those of all my own family, but blue eyes are not a disorder, surely."·

"Indeed, they are not. But how about your husband's family? You can think of nothing there?"

"Absolutely nothing."

The morning after the photographic session, Alexa and Ariel were breakfasting together seated at a small table overlooking the river in the Antoinette Suite's *Louis Quinze* sitting room.

Louella came in with a fresh pot of coffee in one hand and a letter on a silver salver which she offered to Alexa.

"Brought round by messenger, Ma'am, just this minute."

"Open it, honey, it looks exciting. You've hardly been in New York forty-eight hours and already you have correspondence. That's what comes of being a *Marqueeze*." Ariel never made any concessions to French pronunciation.

Puzzled, Alexa slit open the thick white envelope; it contained a cheque drawn on a famous American bank, of which even Alexa had heard, its name redolent of world power and financial sophistication, undreamed-of in provincial France. Attached to it was a printed piece of paper which said: *With the compliments of Condé Nast Publications*. The stupefying sum typed on the face of the cheque was two thousand dollars.

"I suppose this is for the Bloomingdales photographic session?"

"Let me see, honey. Yes, that's your fee. It's okay, isn't it?"

"I thought I was doing it for you."

"Well, you were, but you weren't doing it for Bloomingdales, or for *Vogue*, were you? We thought it was a great idea of Richard's. Lionel said it was a pity Claver and Spell couldn't come up with these ideas, then he wouldn't mind paying their huge monthly retainer fee."

"Claver and Spell?"

"Sure, honey. You know, the public relations people. I've got a feeling Richard has a slice of their action too. Of course he hasn't said so."

Alexa poured herself another cup of coffee. At the time, she'd been startled by the assumption that she would model clothes for *Vogue*. Rapidly she had searched her memory to see if it had been mentioned as part of the agreement. She couldn't remember. But Lionel and Ariel weren't the sort of people it was easy to deflate. Their hospitality had been so generous and the warmth of their welcome so overwhelmingly genuine, that it hadn't occurred to her to call a halt. She hadn't minded doing it, in fact she had enjoyed herself, but now, the feeling that strings were being pulled in the background by the taciturn Mr. Lockwood made her feel uncomfortable, and curiously angry. Mr. Lockwood, it seemed, had been determined to squeeze the maximum return on the cost of her visit.

"Well," she conceded, "the cheque's nice anyway. That'll buy a few casks."

"Oh, you and your vineyards. Why don't you buy yourself something pretty while you're here? You'll probably get a fat discount at Bloomingdales once they've seen the proofs of those photographs. You're going to need some more maternity clothes aren't you?"

"Not nearly as much as I need casks. Do you know, to make good claret, you need to keep stocking up with new oak casks? The older they get, the less flavour comes out of them. It's terribly important. They cost about two hundred francs each."

"No, honey, I didn't know. I've never met such an unnatural woman as you. Here you are, a top model again overnight, young and lovely and in New York and all you can think about is *barrels*. When are you ever going to have any *fun*?"

"When I can afford it, Ariel."

The Dunhill razor in Richard's hand interrupted its steady course across the flat plane of his right cheek bone. He felt his chin with his left hand. Peering into the magnifying mirror, he noted the length of his nails. Perhaps he should have gone to Pete's for a manicure and a haircut too. Bloody fool, he castigated himself. Behaving like a pre-adolescent American boy before his first date. Taking another man's wife out for a night on the town, *pregnant* wife he reminded himself, is nothing to get your truss in a knot about. Another man's wife? Well yes, we'll see.

In Richard's experience, nothing was as fixed as it looked. Fortunes were made and lost overnight, but in fact, nothing was *lost*, the fortune just changed hands, that was all. It might well be the same with other things a man could desire. His thin, mobile mouth twisted. It was the nearest it ever got to a smile. He'd been too busy amassing a fortune over the last nineteen years to concentrate much on being agreeable. The cultivation of charm was a luxury rich men's sons enjoyed but not him.

Richard had moved to New York soon after the end of the war, in 1947. He was the son of a mining engineer who'd gone bankrupt a few years before. The family home in the flat, fertile countryside near Selby in East Yorkshire had been sold. Richard had been forced to leave Drax Grammar School at the age of sixteen, and was put to work in the very bank which had foreclosed on his father's debts. An intelligent lad, destined for university, perhaps even Cambridge if he could have got a County Major award, the blow had been harsh. He had been popular at school and was captain of the school's first cricket eleven. But after his father's catastrophe, he withdrew into himself and became bitter. Bitter against his father's naïve business methods and bitter against the rapacity of the bank which had turned them all out onto the street and curtailed his education.

Silently, Richard began to work. Fuelled by anger, his energy was unflagging. He pored over the ledgers and dealt out the pound and ten shilling notes to the bank's customers with conscientious courtesy. It was a small branch and its customers were small people. For two years he slogged diligently, quietly returning in the evenings to the sad little terrace house in the village of Cawood that his parents now occupied at a peppercorn rent from some relatives. There he read books on economics, stock exchange reports and everything he could lay his hands on, until the small hours of the morning. His father's health had declined rapidly after the failure of his business and his depression spread to Richard's mother who lived resolutely in the past. She would not stir herself to learn how to live comfortably on the narrow income that Richard's modest wages supplied.

After two years at the Selby branch of the Yorkshire Trust Bank, he was offered a transfer to the big commercial branch in Leeds. The manager told him, "This is your chance, lad. Make sure you grasp it and hold tight. You could go anywhere you want to, you know. I'm right sorry to lose you, but it wouldn't be fair holding you back. I've been happy being manager of this branch, respected citizen and all that. But it wouldn't do for you, and you can't wait, I know that. So go on, see what you can do." Richard had turned to leave his office, grimly delighted with his promotion. But he was called back, "Oh, and look, lad, I'm sorry about your father. But you know how it is. You know all about it now. I'm not a free agent here, I can't do as I like, not above and beyond a certain sum. It was a sorry mess. Happen you can put it all right now," the manager concluded hopefully. For Richard, the half-hearted, embarrassed apology had come too late. And in any case, there was nothing to apologise for. His father had overreached himself and that was all. He had to live with the consequences.

He found lodgings with a Jewish widow in the growing suburb of Alwoodley. She didn't need the money that Richard paid her each week for his pleasant room overlooking the leafy garden, but she needed the company. Through her he met many of her family. The Goldsteins were a large and vigorous tribe dedicated to the pursuit of success. They took young Richard warmly to their hearts and watched his progress and steady promotion with interest.

"Jewish or not," they muttered to each other, he was a good lad, an exemplary son and a hard worker. He had been kind to old Miriam too. Didn't he buy a bouquet of flowers for her every Thursday evening on his way home from Park Row? He said they were his contribution to *Shabbat*. He, of course, would not be there. He went home every Friday evening, like a good son should. Yes, when opportunity arose, something should be done for young Richard.

The Goldsteins' charitable feelings towards the young gentile in their midst were motivated by honest admiration for his hard work and obvious talent. With a number of family members in the banking and accountancy business, they knew the grammar of money themselves, and they knew that Richard was rapidly making himself the master of that language. There was, however, a more practical motive for wishing to promote the career of Richard Lockwood. It was a pity he wasn't Jewish, but he wasn't and nothing could alter that. It would be a good thing, they reasoned over the Sabbath meal, if Richard could be got out of the way. Young Rachael, Gideon's girl, was in a fair way to making a fool of herself over him. Now, it was true that Richard had never seemed to notice her, kept his eyes to himself, as it were, but there was no knowing what a healthy, good-looking Jewess could do if they should chance to be left alone even for a moment. "But she's only *fifteen*, Uncle," the younger Goldsteins remonstrated. "And how old was Ruth, or Hagar?" the old man demanded. Further argument was useless. His own Lithuanian mother had married at fifteen and he himself had been born little more than a year later. "Where is the difference? Tell me, where is the difference?" And the older members of the family had shaken their heads in mournful agreement that Gideon's girl was at risk.

There were a number of these conferences. Strangely, at no time did the Goldsteins think of the simple expedient of telling Richard that it was no longer convenient for him to continue to lodge with old Miriam. He had become part of the family and Miriam loved him like a son. The Goldsteins did not desert their friends, even if they *were* goys. But they did not marry gentiles and Uncle Joe, the patriarch of the family, was determined to take no risks.

They settled on Michael Goldstein. He had a nice little banking business in New York, whither he had taken himself after the disgraceful business of that goy school-mistress he had insisted on marrying. He had no son of his own because the school-mistress had left him after a year and Michael, although devastated, had refused to return to the fold and had never married again. None of them had seen him for years. So a carefully worded letter was sent to Michael Goldstein in New York. His reply stated that he would be glad to offer a post to a promising young man and was all the more inclined to offer it because the party in question was a gentile. The Goldsteins, in their relief, swallowed the intended insult almost gratefully.

So at the age of nineteen and a half, Richard set sail for America. He went third class on the *Queen Mary*. The Goldsteins had wanted to pay his passage, first class, but Richard stubbornly refused. "A job is one thing, charity is another."

The Goldsteins were torn between hurt feelings and admiration. "My boy," said Uncle, who was Miriam's elderly brother-in-law, "would it hurt you so much to travel first class and make an old man happy?"

"Yes, Uncle, it would. The day I travel first class, it will be because, I, Richard Lockwood, can afford it."

Uncle sighed. The terrible pride of these gentiles. He tried again. "Miriam will worry. She will worry about the food and the beds and the sort of people you will meet. You have been a son to her. If you won't do it to please me, do it to stop an old lady worrying." But Richard was obdurate. There was help that he could legitimately accept, but mere luxuries he would earn for himself or never have.

Over the years, Richard worked with Michael Goldstein in the merchant banking house he had founded and which bore his name. "I hoped to have a boy of my own, but I never did. You are the nearest thing I shall ever have to a son. When I die, I shall leave control of the bank to you. The family don't need it and they shan't have it. I don't forget how they treated Margaret when she married me. That's why she left me. She thought she had isolated me from my tribe and she had been cruel in marrying me. But I never went back and I never shall. You are the son I never had. You get the bank."

Working side by side with Michael, first as his private secretary and finally as chief executive, Richard learned the intimate secrets of the international banking world. The rudiments he had learned in Park Row in Leeds, but the creative, imaginative

flights of the merchant banker's art he learnt at Michael Goldstein's side. When the old man died at seventy after a series of
heart attacks, Richard felt raw grief. Michael had been his only
companion for all the years he had been in America. Apart from
a brief, disastrous affair with the beautiful daughter of a client
in the early years, Richard had lived and dreamed only money
and the business of banking. His only intimate companion had
been Michael. He had become a rich man, but deprived of his
teacher and surrogate father, his enthusiasm had dwindled. The
intricate adventures they had hatched and successfully concluded together were tasteless without old Michael. The years
were flat. The firm of Michael Goldstein continued to expand,
but the joy of raiding, capturing and king-making was gone.
Richard was thirty-nine and he had never been married.

He looked in the cheval-glass. The room reflected behind him
was immaculate, expensive and impersonal. Richard had bought
the apartment on the Upper West Side on the day of Michael's
funeral. Before, they'd lived together in Michael's palatial penthouse in Sutton Place. "Not Jewish territory, my boy, but I
enjoy lowering the tone. You see this hat?" It was an exaggerated black homburg of the sort seen in the diamond district of
47th Street where the Jewish merchants carried on their precious
commerce in the streets, "I would never be seen dead in a hat
like this on Wall Street, or in London, but I cannot resist wearing
it here. Oh, you should see the faces of all those Daughters of
the American Revolution types who live in this building. It is
poetry my boy, it is a psalm. I wish the whole Jewish race could
see those faces. The pogroms, Belsen, Dachau? Who would
remember them? My hat, it is the revenge of the chosen people."

Their old home in Sutton Place held too many painful memories. The new apartment, with its view over the Central Park
tree tops and its large private terrace, was just a place to sleep.
There were no reminders of the only human being Richard had
ever truly respected apart from himself.

The white tuxedo looked good. His stocky 5'8" frame appeared even broader in the white dinner jacket. Michael had told
him during his first year in New York, "You're not a big man.
It hardly matters. Actually size has little to do with measure-
ment, that's all psychology. Some of the smallest men in this
town are frequently described as tall. It's a question of domi-
nance. But people must think you are tall. That's important. It's

a primitive instinct to fear size and I don't want to think there's anyone out there in that jungle who isn't afraid of you. Work on it.'' And Richard had.

There had been other lessons too. Michael told him that the less he spoke the more certain people were to listen to him when he did. The advice was superfluous in Richard's case, the convivial nature of his early boyhood had been submerged in taciturnity when his father's affairs had collapsed. Michael had also told him never to smile as a matter of course or mere courtesy. ''There are those who achieve something in that way, no doubt, in the world of WASPs and old school ties, but we do not belong to those worlds, we are outsiders. We must never give the impression we are anxious to be seen to be anything else. That would only weaken us. We are apart.'' And that too, fitted exactly with Richard's increasing tendency to smile only when he was genuinely pleased or amused. And outside the penthouse in Sutton Place, that was rarely.

But turning to observe his features closely once again in the shaving mirror, Richard saw in his own light-blue eyes a neediness that shocked him. He wanted Alexa de Pies Ombre to like him.

The Plaza was the venue Richard chose for Alexa's last night in New York. Its Edwardian splendour was the equal of anything Europe had to offer. He'd considered a small restaurant in the Village, but decided against it. It might appeal to her, but he would be uncomfortable in the informal surroundings. He caught himself wanting to impress her and he despised himself for it. He was uneasily aware that impressing a woman was not the same as charming one. But he was at a loss to isolate the difference.

It wasn't that he didn't like women, but since that early and unhappy adventure, he had had almost nothing to do with them. They took up too much time, they were not interested in the things which interested him and fundamentally, they were dull. But Alexa, Madame de Pies Ombre, was not so dull. He had investigated her background and knew far more about her than he would ever allow her to suspect. Lockwood was in the risk-taking business, but only fairly assessed risks were worth taking.

Her people were rather top drawer, of course, in the quiet understated way he admired. There was a modest fortune, a fine house, but only one, and generations of education and cultivation on the Standeven side. And yet young Alexa had done the unusual thing. She had jacked it all in for a far less secure way of life. And then there was that rare capacity for work, steady, ordered, unhurried and always purposeful. With it, he perceived a readiness for risk and adventure. They had something in common.

Their conversation over dinner had been stilted. Richard strove manfully to entertain his guest, but he had never developed the skill of general small talk and found himself floundering in awkward silences, from which Alexa, although she responded politely to all his remarks, showed no inclination to rescue him. From time to time, Richard found himself on the edge of asking her what Heinz had said to her but he felt the question would be unwelcome. He would ask her, but not yet. He would wait until her guard was down. At the moment, he sensed, it was very much in position.

"Was the cheque satisfactory?"

Alexa frowned slightly.

"*Vogue's*? Yes, I didn't expect anything."

"Why not? You did the session, didn't you?"

"I did, Mr. Lockwood, and very surprised I was to be doing it at all. Nobody asked me about it. I gather it was your idea."

"It was, and a good idea too, I thought. I didn't ask you, because I thought there was a small risk you might refuse. An instinct I had about that family, the de Pies Ombres."

"*My* family. Yes, they may have objected. But isn't what *I* feel important?"

Richard was taken aback. She'd confronted him with a question to which there was no graceful answer.

"You've got me there. I'm afraid I didn't think about it. You seemed happy enough to come over and do the press conference, I didn't see much difference frankly. Anyway, I thought I'd reduce the chance element to a minimum. *Vogue's* got a big circulation among the kind of women we want to reach. Those pictures of the Venetian Room should do a power of good. Can't harm you either and I wanted you to have that cheque. I negotiated the best rate I could. I doubt you'd have done any better on your own."

Alexa blushed faintly. "Mr. Lockwood, I know you are used to managing other people's affairs but you will forgive me if I point out that they commission you to do so. You received no such commission from me and I don't like being manipulated.

I was carried along on a tide of events, as you knew I would be, and you also knew I wouldn't dream of upsetting Lionel and Ariel, particularly Ariel, who has been a wonderful hostess. I'm sure they thought I knew all about it.''

"I'm sorry," he answered stiffly, "I thought you'd be glad of the fee.''

"Don't misunderstand me. I *am* glad of the fee, I just wish it hadn't been placed in my hand like a tip.''

Richard pushed his plate away in exasperation. "Oh, come on now. Aren't you overstating the case somewhat? I've had my knuckles rapped and I'll remember my place in the future. Can't we just leave it alone now?''

But Alexa worried the point like a terrier with a bone on which there still remains a little meat, dissecting the question of whether or not it had been right to lead her into earning some money without consulting her as to the manner in which it was to be earned, if earned at all.

"Christ! I didn't think you'd give it a thought.'' Richard was at a loss. He never expected her to react so touchily. Stupid of him. Why wouldn't she object? He'd cut up pretty rough himself all those years ago, when old Uncle Joe Goldstein had offered to pay his fare, first class across the Atlantic. He hadn't liked being patronised, neither did she. She ran the show at Château d'Ombre, that was obvious. People like her didn't take kindly to other people running their lives for them. *They* liked to do all the running. It was natural. He wondered what Michael would have made of her.

"There are only two sorts of people in the world," Michael had once remarked, "the sort who do and the sort who are done to. See to it that you remain in the former and more desirable category, my dear young friend." Clearly, Madame de Pies Ombre, young as she was, was painfully alive to the difference.

"Look, I said I'm sorry. I mean it too. Couldn't you just let it go now. I didn't mean any harm. We could have got another model, they do exist you know, but I just wanted you to have that money.''

Tired by the arguement now, Alexa let it drop. She didn't really like the man, she decided, but he'd made a mistake and apologised for it. Nobody could do more. And she had got the money.

If only he wasn't so stiff. It was impossible to relax in his company. He was constantly alert and watchful and he listened

with such exhausting attentiveness to one's lightest word that it
made one chary of saying more than the minimum. He had a
way of making one feel foolish and that was intolerable. Alexa
did not realise that she had often had a similar effect on people
herself.

"And what will you do with the cheque?"

Alexa glanced briefly at him. Not content with hiring her out
without her consent, he was now prying into her financial concerns.

"I shall buy some equipment for the château. Wine-making
equipment. We need new casks, we could do with an *égrappoir*,
that's a de-stalking machine . . ."

"Don't. Give it to me."

Alexa's eyebrows shot up in amazement.

"No, you don't understand. Give it to me so that I can make
it work for you."

Alexa began to protest.

"Listen, you'll have that de-stalker and the barrels and a lot
of other things too, if you take my advise. Trust me, I know
what I'm doing. I promise you, if you let me manage those two
thousand dollars for you, this time next year they will have turned
into twenty thousand dollars, at least."

"How?"

"The first thing I'd do, if you'd let me, is invest in the Scheitinger Clinics. You know we're franchising the operation and
we're going to the market before the end of the next twelve
months, at least on present scheduling, and I don't foresee any
amendments to the timetable. Lionel will let you buy in. For
that amount you're no threat to him, but when the company goes
public, you'll be worth a lot more. You could cash in your shares
then, but I'd advise you to hang on to them. The Scheitinger
Clinics are going to be big and there'll be a lot of mileage in
them. You can trust me, a lot of people do, remember. If anything looks like going wrong, I'll get you out in time."

"All right. I suppose I can afford to take a chance. It's money
I never expected to have. I don't know why I'm doing this, you
know. It could have something to do with you being a Yorkshireman," she smiled forgivingly, "sheer sentiment."

"Not at all, it's good judgement. You'll congratulate yourself
before you're much older. Come to think of it, how old are
you?"

"Nearly twenty." The reply almost made Richard smile. But

he kept his amusement to himself. He had a feeling she didn't like being laughed at. Alexa had not liked to be asked her age but there was no point in trying to deal with Richard Lockwood. He thought he could treat her casually because she was half his age. He was a rough diamond at best, beneath a layer of superficial polish, and too old to be taught any manners. It was better to overlook his rough corners if he was going to look after her money, and try and establish a working relationship with him.

"I was about your age when I set out to America to make my fortune. But then, you didn't have to do any such thing, did you?" He was trying to get her to talk about her marriage and her life at d'Ombre, to describe what had brought her there. But he had no luck.

"My grandfather was a self-made man, Mr. Lockwood, and it never inhibited him from being a gentleman."

"Shall we stop trying to get a rise out of each other and just enjoy the evening?"

Alexa's smile struck him as suddenly as a bolt of summer lightning, flashing and blinding. "Deal, Mr. Lockwood."

"It's Richard. May I call you Alexa?"

"You may."

"Alexa, can I ask you a personal question?"

She laughed, "Haven't you asked me quite enough personal questions? How old I am and what I'm going to do with my money . . . but yes, if you must. But I shan't know if I mind or not until I've heard the question, and then it will be too late, won't it?"

"No. You needn't answer if you don't want to, so you've still got control and that's very important to you, isn't it?"

"In my own limited experience of life, things go better if I've got control, so yes, I prefer it."

"That's what I thought." He studied her carefully. Just what did make her tick? "Tell me, what motivates you?"

"Psychology now! Well, I don't know, I just do what there is to be done."

"No," Richard said slowly, "it's not quite that. Nobody told you to turn that château of yours into a goddam guest-house instead of knocking it down or selling it. You went for the harder option and look at it. It's a success in every way. The whole idea was stylish, original and well executed. You have a feel for making money. There were so many reasons for it to fail but it didn't. Actually, you could sell off those vineyards to someone with the capital to manage them properly and live on the income from the house, quite comfortably. But not you. Oh no. I've been watching you. Sooner or later, you're going to take over the wine business, aren't you?''

What is this man *after*, Alexa wondered. "Actually, if we sold off the vineyards, we could live in comfort without having to manage the house as a business at all. Land in our part of the world fetches a high price and we have a lot of it. But, we do intend to hang onto it. Every last hectare, and buy more if it's possible. Money has a way of disappearing, land is always solid value. And yes, since you ask, I think my husband will find my involvement in the wine business encouraging.''

"Don't become the prim schoolgirl with me, Miss. You just think you'll manage things better than him, don't you?'' He tapped the side of his wine glass with a fork, which made it ring, a light cheerful sound, as if to denote a correct answer on a television quiz show. "That's it, isn't it?''

"You are rather impolite.'' Alexa was genuinely shocked by this accurate reflection of her own private thoughts. It was totally out of order for a stranger to give voice to them.

"Maybe, but I'm right aren't I? You'll find being right is more important in life than being polite. I must warn you, Alexa, you'll very often be right and just as often unpopular.''

Intrigued, in spite of herself, Alexa asked him how he knew.

"Because I'm usually right myself and very unloved. I recognise the type you see. We're two of a kind, you and me. You'd better get used to it, nobody likes a success, not really, and I reckon that's just what you'll be if you stick at it.''

"I don't think anyone dislikes me particularly.''

"Oh no? Your mother-in-law's not crazy about you, you've bested *her* too many times. And your husband, you've given him a pretty unflattering yardstick to measure himself by, haven't you? I should watch out if I were you.''

"Please remember,'' Alexa said through gritted teeth, "I'm carrying my husband's child. And I do *not* think he dislikes me,'' she added with emphasis.

"Sorry!'' He held his hands up in mock surrender. He was wary of her now. "I stepped out of line again. What is it then, what makes you start and keep going?''

Alexa bit her lip angrily. He was going too far again. In spite of herself, she answered him. "I need to be safe. And to feel safe, I have to be in charge.''

"That's it, is it? It's a very masculine motivation, that."

"Well, masculine or not, it's mine."

Their talk turned to less inflammatory topics. After the confrontation and verbal sword crossing, conversation came more easily to them but Richard's mind was busy, sorting and categorising the things he had learned about Alexa. She had recognised and resented his manipulation, although he had acted from the most sincere motives of goodwill. At d'Ombre, his experienced banker's eye had noted how the land lay. God knows why this girl had married Fabrice de Pies Ombre, but in doing so she had found a stage on which to act out her capacities, an anvil on which to beat the hammer of her will. And, too likely, the scene for a bloody messy ending.

Alexa Standeven, that was, was a doer and a getter, one of his own stamp. And yet there was something different about her, something not entirely materialistic. Was it a creative impulse perhaps? Something which he lacked himself and envied in others. The trouble with creativity was it never flourished where there was no love, no vulnerability. It was her greater danger. And yet, she had that hill-bred, West Riding hardness. She was one of those to whom reality was a face to be looked upon, and as often spat upon. The survivor's instincts were bred in her bones.

The next morning, Richard arrived early at the Scheitinger Clinic, in time to countermand Lionel's order for a limousine to take Alexa to Kennedy. He did not find it too difficult to persuade him to delegate the duty of escorting Alexa to the airport.

As Richard's Lincoln cut through the New York traffic, they chatted desultorily. The conversation was jerky, stopping and starting as the demands of the traffic took Richard's attention away from time to time. After a loud verbal altercation at some traffic lights in which the drive of a yellow taxi screamed incomprehensible insults, he asked casually, "What did the medical boys say to you?"

"Which one, there were a lot of them."

"No particular one. I don't know all their names. We had a specialist recruitment firm do the head hunting. I just meant, did it all go all right. What did they do?"

"Nothing much, just took some blood samples and things. I'm sure they were just going through the motions with me. And really, should you be asking what her doctors have said to a pregnant lady?'' The query was without sting.

Richard had to be satisfied with that.

"Listen, about that money. I'm sorry I acted up so, but I'm really not sure about investing in the clinic. I'm sure Lionel's a good businessman, and all that, and Ariel's a darling of course, but I really could . . .''

He interrupted her swiftly, ''You leave the money with me, the Scheitinger Clinic's all right.''

''I'm sure it is commercially but . . .''

''Look, *Madame*,'' he pronounced the French title with sarcastic emphasis. ''I don't back ventures that stink. I can afford not to. The clinic's okay. You found some pretty good things to say about it yourself, didn't you? Things I'll tell the ad agency to put in the brochure. I'm seeing the proofs today, and they can damn well alter the copy. Really, trust me. And leave the cash with me. I'll take care of it. Two thousand dollars you can live without. Just be a good girl and leave it right here, and before you know it, I'll have turned it into some grown-up money.''

''I'm sorry, it's Tante Héloïse, she got me worked up about the whole thing before I left. She thinks it's a racket, preying on the vulnerability of a lot of women because they happen to be rich.''

''Oh, that old bird.''

''That old bird, as you call her, happens to be very intelligent, and she doesn't talk for the sake of talking.''

''Already she's gone up in my estimation. That's Mademoiselle de Pies Ombre, isn't it?''

''Yes, that's right, my dead father-in-law's sister, Tante Héloïse. You met her. She's a writer, religious pamphlets actually. So naturally, when she smells a moral rat, she's inclined to hunt it down.''

''Why is she lame?'' Alexa looked at Richard. He was looking straight ahead as he drove over Queensborough Bridge, but listening intently for her reply.

''I don't know. Arthritis, I imagine. I never thought to ask. A lot of elderly ladies aren't totally secure on their pins. Why should I be particularly curious about Tante Héloïse?''

''Hmm. What's he got?''

''*He?*'' Alexa's voice sounded a warning note which was ignored by Richard as he persisted, ''Yes, him. What's wrong with his leg?''

"Polio, actually," she replied with an icicle glance.

"He told you that?"

"No. Actually, I was told by a mutual acquaintance. The man who introduced us, my former employer."

"He'd know, of course."

"I presume so, though I'm at a loss to know what concern it is of yours."

"Agreed. It's not my business."

"Quite."

At the barrier, Richard took some envelopes from his inside pocket.

"You may want to look at these on the plane. They're the reports from all the medical guys who gave you the once over. Ariel said to give them to you."

"Thank you." Alexa was curt.

"I don't suppose you'd let a guy give you a respectful goodbye kiss —on the cheek of course."

"I think that might be arranged, Mr. Lockwood." Alexa turned a cameo cheek and received the kiss with all the *hauteur* of a pope receiving a kiss of veneration on the toe. She rejected the pressure of Richard's hand on her upper arm with a barely perceptible, but angry, little shrug. He presumed too much.

She watched him go, wishing somehow that she had been a little less churlish. She rubbed the place where he had laid his hand.

"Your Perrier water, *Madame*."

She was alone in the first class cabin on the Air France jet. Desultorily, Alexa began to open the white envelopes, each with its SC monogram. The reports all told her that she was in splendid health but the dietician suggested she was a little underweight.

"In spite of current obstetrical fashion," it read, "in my own view, the theory that a pregnant woman should carry no weight in excess of her normal weight other than that which can be accounted for by the weight of the foetus, with some allowance for the amniotic fluid, is grave error. This belief can lead to serious malnutrition of the foetus culminating in the birth of an infant which is dangerously underweight."

Diet sheets were appended to the report together with dire warnings about the dangers of alcohol and tobacco.

The last report bore the type-written legend, "The Report of

Dr. Rudolph Heinz.'' There was a long string of letters after his
name and ''University of Cologne.'' That was the barmy geneticist. Ålexa remembered the conversation about blue eyes.
With pursed lips, Alexa slid her forefinger under the flap of the
envelope, swearing softly as it cut her finger. The preamble
thanked her for her tolerance in answering his questions and
went on to make some generalised comments on the science of
genetics. It was the third paragraph which Alexa read and re-
read as if it were not possible she could have gathered its meaning in a single glance.

> *''Whilst no precise detection methods have yet been evolved,
> in view of the history of your husband's family, so far as it is
> known and has been described to me by Mr. Richard Lock-
> wood,''* Alexa's eyes fastened on the name with shocked dis-
> belief, *''it must be acknowledged that an element of risk
> attaches to your current pregnancy.''*

The calm rational words leaped off the page as if they had
been alive, poisonous, evil creatures. With half-averted eyes,
Alexa forced herself to read the rest of what lay in her hands.

> *''There is no certainty that the child you are carrying is pos-
> itively affected. However, previous generations have suffered
> at birth from the uncommon condition known to medical sci-
> ence as* Osteogenesis Imperfecta. *This genetically transmitted
> disorder rarely arises in the human species but is familiar in
> canines. The symptoms are extreme brittleness of the infantile
> bones and fracturing, arising from even the most cautious
> handling of the affected infant, is almost inevitable.*
>
> *''Currently, the only known treatment is careful bone set-
> ting and the administration of a course of cod liver oil. This
> admittedly crude remedy does rapidly clear the condition,
> which does not recur. However, the bones broken and set in
> infancy rarely knit satisfactorily and result in a permanent
> deformation of the affected limb or limbs, or other bones,
> throughout the life of the patient.*
>
> *''Having regard to the probabilities in this case, and the
> incomplete nature of the treatment available, I would urge
> you to return in not less than twenty-eight days for further
> tests. Whilst the presence of* Osteogenesis Imperfecta *itself is
> undetectable, a sample of amniotic fluid may, on analysis,*

show us a genetic irregularity which would strongly suggest the presence of the condition. In that case, a termination should be considered at an early date, to minimise the distress this will inevitably cause your family and the dangers to your own person.''

She crumpled the letter fiercely and ordered a copious lunch, guided by the suggestions of the diet sheet. When she had eaten, she smoothed the letter carefully and put it in her handbag.

CHAPTER
14

&8 &8 THE HOE TORE through the light limy soil, viciously extinguishing the lives of infant groundsel and shepherd's purse. Weeds in the rose beds were the only victims Elizabeth could find on which to revenge herself. Vengeance was all that would ever bring her peace or release again, she was sure of that. But nothing, nothing she could suggest in the way of retribution, had been acceptable to Alexa. She had allowed herself to be shamefully used and she was going to take no action whatever. She actually proposed to carry that filthy creature to term. God knows how it would turn out.

Alexa kept saying, "It may not be affected, it may not be affected," like a tedious, nerve-wearing litany. It was as clear as day that the geneticist thought the risk high. And I am going to be the grandmother of a deformed child. And if it seems all right, it will still carry the gene forward with it and I shall be the ancestress of an interminable race of degenerates, because these appalling people will do the same thing again to some other foolish girl. For all she knew, they had probably done it to plenty of women in the past, each new generation sucking in an innocent, with some tale of polio or a riding accident followed by the birth of a defective child. The mother, of course, by that time, a conspirator herself.

These dark thoughts went round and round in Elizabeth's head as she struggled to come to terms with what had happened.

And this time, the victim was her own daughter, who would in turn become a liar and a deceiver in defence of the creature to which she had given birth. She stopped herself abruptly. It would, after all, be the child of *Alexa*, if the thing really was born. Surely Alexa wouldn't palm it off on some unsuspecting

girl and her family as a *polio* victim. But you couldn't tell, could
you, what a mother would do? Elizabeth was only too aware of
the fierce, amoral nature of a mother's love for her child. God
knows, blithering idiot though Alexa is, I'd kill for her.

Abruptly, Elizabeth threw the hoe down and turned to sit on
the stone seat. Staring ahead she noted the Fiddler attempting
in his incompetent way to mend some collapsed fencing in the
orchard. Alexander must have told him to get it done today.
Waste of time, it would only have to be done again when Wilfred
came on Saturday. Yes, Wilfred. The municipal roadman with
the stutter who worked part time at Langstroth Grange. *He* was
a case in point. Able-bodied but the worst speech impediment
she'd ever encountered. God, how I hate the disabled and dis-
advantaged. I know it's wicked of me. You just can't say these
things out loud. She'd said them to Alexa, though. It *must* be a
healthy reaction. No bitch will feed a deformed pup. She *knows*
it's a mistake, something which *she* as part of nature must put
right. What in the name of Heaven is the *matter* with Alexa?
She's *my* daughter. And she's obsessed with that crumbling old
house and a business that'll go belly up inside a year. It's like
an evil spell. If only I'd known, I'd have locked her in a dungeon
before I'd let her go to France. Oh my *God*. What an unholy,
God-awful *mess*.

Alexa had left the day before on the nine o'clock plane from
Yeadon. Elizabeth had taken her in the Wolseley. It had seemed
pointless to ask Alexander to go with them. For the first two
days after Alexa's announcement he hadn't spoken and now he
had retired into silence again. He was as appalled as she was at
the thought of this monster growing inside his beautiful daughter's body. They'd both racked their brains for some way to
persuade her, all to no avail. Poor old Rory Fullerton had been
dragged out of retirement to add his pleas to theirs. He had been
Henry's physician, of many years' standing, until his retirement,
and one of his oldest friends. He had delivered Alexa himself at
Henry's Heaton mansion, one rainy night in June. His broad
face beaming with pleasure and satisfaction as he wiped his
hands on a towel.

"She's a bonny bairn, Bess," his strong Ulster brogue boomed
round the large bedroom, "and steady as a rock. Good little
nervous system. Well up to it."

"Up to what, Rory?" Dr. Fullerton was well known for his
cryptic style of conversation.

"Life," he had answered, triumphant with the pleasure his night's work had given him.

Elizabeth remembered the conversation so vividly, the inevitable odour of methylated spirits which Doctor Fullerton used as disinfectant, and which accompanied him everywhere, filled her nostrils once again. Tears pricked in her eyes. There would be nobody to say such a thing to Alexa about her first born. Poor kid. Poor, poor, silly Alexa. A termination could so easily have been arranged. The network of doctors and lawyers would have drawn together to make it possible, even at this late stage. *"We shall doer summut,"* as her father would say in any family emergency. She wished he was here now. He had been close to Alexa and maybe he could have talked some sense into her. He'd always hated the abnormal himself. It was a family sensibility that seemed to have missed Alexa entirely. And it could all have been managed so easily. There was *nothing* that couldn't be solved with a lot of professional expertise and a little cash. But how can you rescue someone who's determined to suffer?

Elizabeth drew an elegant white square of linen from her gardening-coat pocket and blew her nose. She examined the handkerchief and its exquisite white embroidered monogram. There were half a dozen of these. Alexa had given them to her for her last birthday present. Good taste. That was Alexa all over. Good taste, good manners and no bloody sense. Well, she was three generations away from the gutters of a West Riding mill town on her mother's side and two hundred years away from them on her father's. No wonder she lacked the survival instinct. It had been bred clean out of her. This is what we work for. To bring up our children as ladies and gentlemen and then we find we've disabled them in the process. A disaster.

Her telephone conversation with Suzanne de Pies Ombre had been vitriolic. Suzanne had been evasive to begin with. She opened with the absurd claim that she didn't know what Elizabeth was talking about.

"Heredity? *Osteo* . . . whatever it was you said. I know nothing about it, I think you must have taken leave of your senses, *Madame*."

"We'll see how far from my senses I am when Alexa's marriage is found null and void and you and your bloody son are faced with a bill for substantial damages."

"Is this blackmail, *Madame*?" Suzanne had said with freezing dignity.

"No, it's a downright threat and not, I assure you, an idle one."

Eventually, Suzanne crumbled under Elizabeth's astute and aggressive cross-questioning. Elizabeth didn't have much to go on, just suspicion and an almost superstitious belief in medical opinion.

"Well, *Madame*, what did you expect me to do? Tell the world my son was unmarriageable?"

"Of course. What other honourable course was open to you?"

Elizabeth continued to harry her prey for a full fifteen minutes, during which she reduced Suzanne to hysterical tears.

"And you, *Madame*, what would you have done if it had been your child, and you saw a chance of happiness for her?"

"I should have at least warned the wretched suitor and his parents, if any, of the risks involved in marriage to my daughter. I should have done it, moreover, before the young people were too deeply committed to draw back. Any alternative procedure would have been both dishonest and cruel, as yours has been, *Madame*."

"I congratulate you on your self-confidence, *Madame*," Suzanne's voice was now more controlled. "Few mothers would claim to retain such an admirable control of their children's feelings." To Elizabeth's acute ear, the Frenchwoman was attempting to negotiate an honourable peace.

Unappeased and uninterested in further dealings with Suzanne de Pies Ombre, Elizabeth slammed the telephone down, delighted to tread on her enemy's neck now that she was well and truly down.

But it was all fruitless. Alexa, normally so reasonable, had resolutely refused to even discuss an abortion, nor would she countenance a divorce. Her mother was at a loss to understand how she contemplated spending one more night under the roof of people who had so ruthlessly and heartlessly deceived her.

Nothing was to be done which might jeopardise her *position*, as she called it.

"What *position*?" Elizabeth had angrily demanded.

"The position I have." It was the only stubborn reply she could get out of Alexa.

"Why did you tell me all this, Alexa? You won't let us help you, so why, *why* have you put it all on *us*? We'll do anything, anything at all. But how do you expect your father and me just to sit idly by, accepting the news that we're to be the grandparents of a seriously damaged child, fathered on you by that deceiving bastard and his conniving coven of witches? It's very, *very* cruel of you.''

Alexa raised her eyebrows in polite amazement at her mother's immoderate language. Inside she was warmly grateful that Elizabeth was willing to tear the kid gloves of civilisation off without a second thought, to fight her battles. Elizabeth was proving of more use to her than she knew. In expressing the rage that Alexa herself felt, she was removing that tiring and unproductive emotion from her own shoulders. Elizabeth could rave, relieving her daughter of the need, and leaving her free to plan.

''Mother,'' for the first time, Alexa abandoned the childish form of address, ''I needed to tell someone. Someone of my own blood, don't you see? Nobody else could be angry enough for me. Let's face it, anybody else would just be embarrassed and that's no good to me. I'm sorry you and Daddy have been so upset. Of course, I knew you would be, but I didn't realise just how badly it would hit you. If I had, perhaps I wouldn't have said anything. You may have found out later, maybe not. *I* seem to have used *you*. I didn't mean to and I'm sorry. But please understand, it's enough now. I have to get on with things, whatever happens.''

After this final and carthartic exchange, Elizabeth embraced her daughter with more warmth than she had ever done. ''I shall never understand, I suppose, but you will do as you like and I cannot help it, so I must endure it. What will you do with your Grandad's legacy? Not spend it on those vineyards, I hope.'' For once, Alexa was able to satisfy her.

''No, I shall spend it on the sort of nursery that will be a happy place for my child to grow up and one which will attract the very best kind of nanny, which you, Mother, are going to help me recruit. I have to go home now to help pick the grapes.''

The first two weeks of September were fine. The warm sunshine encouraged David to delay the *vendange*.

''The crop has sustained a good deal of damage, *Madame*, but what there is will be better if we can leave it on the vine to gain strength in the sun. We will get a bigger price from Chirac Frères, if the must has some vigour.''

''What does *Monsieur* say?''

''He says he will leave the decision to me and to you, *Madame*.''

"Then I will be guided by you, Monsieur David. Your instincts are all we have to rely on. The weather does look settled."

"But at any moment, the first nip of frost could come, and then we are done for."

"I have confidence in *you*, Monsieur David. We will do as you say. You are the *régisseur* and you have faced this decision every year of your life since you were a young man."

The old man nodded, "As *Madame* wishes."

He left the turret room well satisfied. It was good to work for one who knew how to take the advice she paid for. At least this year we will sell the wine, all of it. And if we do not prosper, we shall not starve.

During Alexa's absence abroad, Fabrice had found himself besieged by constant visits from David, who seemed to come to his office for consultations on the most trivial matter. Bewildered at first by these continual interruptions to his own musings, Fabrice had at last tumbled to the reason. "I see that after all, my wife has left nothing to chance, David. These extra supervisory duties must be taxing for you, my dear fellow. Allow me to lighten your load. My enthusiasm for eternity has dwindled somewhat of late. You know I am a man of varied interests and lately I have become intrigued by the idea of fatherhood." Fabrice was not deceived by David's awkward denials. "Come, come, we both know *Madame*'s thoroughness when it comes to her own concerns, I am only too delighted to find myself one of them. But I confess, I should not object to the occasional period of, shall we say five minutes, in which I might consider myself at leisure." After that, David had been obliged to adopt less transparent methods of surveillance.

Alexa had already undertaken the payment of all the regular staff of the château and vineyards. Their wages had been raised and were now regularly paid. Inevitably, there was a subtle shift of attitude amongst the workers in the *chais* and the vineyards. It was something in the atmosphere, foreshadowed by their easy acceptance of her when she had first made her appearance in the *chais*. Her reputation for halting decay and promoting new life had preceded her from the house. Her status with the men was further enhanced by the unspoken but evident support of the *régisseur*. If old Pierre David, misogynist as he was well known to be, approved of *Madame*, then she must be very special indeed.

Hearing his wife's name on every side, Fabrice was at first unresentful and even a little amused. He carried out his own tasks desultorily as before but found that his few orders were no longer received as law. "Perhaps we should wait until *Madame* comes back, and hear her views," David had said to him during the few days of Alexa's absence abroad, when his master had made some remark concerning a supplier's bill. Fabrice had frowned but said nothing. David would resign on the spot if it came to words between them, and that he could not afford.

Fabrice felt the change in his environment rather than noted it. There was an indifferent look on the faces of his workmen, their morning greetings were perfunctory and casual, the sort of salutation reserved for an uninteresting colleague, not even that with which an unpopular superior is placated. David, however, sensed the way the wind was blowing through the *chais* as it had through the château and he was sorry for it, but could do nothing. He was a Gascon himself and you cannot tell an independent-minded Gascon how to arrange his face or modulate his voice. The Revolution had come and gone long since.

As David negotiated his way down the spiral staircase of the *Tour du Jardin*, he shook his head in wonder. Less than a year, and look what she has done. It was a great pity that Monsieur Fabrice's interest appeared to be lessening just as his wife had brought hope to them all. Hope of once again taking pride in the name of Château d'Ombre.

Alexa spent more and more time in the turret room. She and Suzanne exchanged only the most necessary words. Deep down Alexa had never truly believed that her strained relationship with her mother-in-law was capable of development into anything more relaxed than an armed truce, but the knowledge that she had deliberately concealed the genetic fault in her family withered any desire Alexa may have had to enrich the unpromising soil in which it was planted. Fabrice claimed he hadn't known, he had always been told he'd had polio as a very young child. He had practised no deception. He could not be held responsible. Héloïse too, was vague. She had supposed Alexa knew. She had never thought about it. Surely it was not a great matter. And in any case, regardless of what Alexa conceived to be her wrongs, surely a child was a child and welcome no matter what affliction God should choose to visit upon it. Héloïse said she would pray for Alexa. Alexa was outraged at the impudence. There was a coolness between them which saddened them both.

The infant inside her was moving, its early flutterings a strange and delightful sensation laden with emotion. This child was a second chance and nothing, but nothing, should hinder its coming. Her anger with the de Pies Ombres never spread to the child in her womb.

Alexa felt a growing calm descend on her. Perhaps Richard and his prying researches had led him and Doctor Heinz to exaggerate conclusions. There was no certainty that the child would be affected and she began to look forward to its coming. She would have someone of her own blood. A companion whom nature had programmed to sympathise with her every breath. A human understanding that could not be surpassed by any other. She would have a completeness that the childless never knew.

At times she wondered at the curiosity of the man which had led to the discovery that had all but torn her fragile domestic happiness to shreds. His instinct, she realised, had been supported by what she saw around her and what he himself had observed when a guest at Ombre. The family portraits might have served her as a clue, but they had not. It had been left to Richard Lockwood to make the vital connection between the living members of the de Pies Ombre family and their painted ancestors.

Alexa was not a stranger to ancestral homes. A school-friend's, Laquair Castle, was full of family portraits. In that Scottish house, for every charming lady in antique dress, there was a soldier, an officer in the uniform of his regiment, usually painted full length, or a young squire mounted and surrounded by his dogs. There had also been a number of groups of children painted in the Victorian era. They were sentimental and pretty and they showed the children playing with their spaniels and ponies.

In the Château d'Ombre there were no full-length portraits. Nearly all the male ancestors of the de Pies Ombres were depicted from the waist up. Their oddly regimented appearance had struck her within the first few days of her coming to her new home, but she had never interpreted it as more than an oddity of taste.

Since she returned from Yorkshire, Fabrice had come to her bed repeatedly. On those occasions, despite his earlier denials concerning his own condition, Alexa was unable to respond warmly or to stimulate any feeling whatsoever. She wondered, too, why he now displayed an enthusiasm for love-making which he had previously lacked. The thought that he harboured a submerged fear of losing her did not occur to her. Nor did Fabrice consciously know of his own apprehension, but her power to transform all around her was interpreted by some hidden corner of his mind as the power to destroy him. His need to dominate her sexually became acute. Alexa could not submit to that need, nor understand the reasons for it. Whether it was because she was mistrustful of his declared innocence, or because of an innate fear that her pregnancy was too far advanced to make intercourse wise, she did not know.

Unbidden by any message from her conscious brain, her hands one night pushed his away and her face turned on the pillow to avoid his urgent, demanding kisses. "I'm sorry, I can't help it, I'm afraid for the baby." Fabrice tore his body away from hers, shining with sweat, his hands finding his stick on the carpet beside the bed.

"You deep-frozen bitch," he flung at her and slammed the door of his dressing room. Alexa lay for a long time, uncovered, as Fabrice had left her. She willed her legs to move, to go after him and reassure him, but they would not obey her. She had apologised once too often for things that were not her fault, or not a fault at all. She drew the sheets back over her shivering body and slept.

In the morning they had avoided each other's eyes. Suzanne breakfasted in her room as did all the guests. Alone with the decision to end or mend their quarrel, and with no unconscious bystander's conversation to protect them from the sharpness of the dilemma, the silence took the imprint of their thoughts. Neither one was willing to speak first, but Alexa, making bread pellets between nervous fingers, eventually forced sound from her throat. She must give in, because she was the only one who was able to do so. "Look Fabrice . . ." she had begun slowly, "last night, I don't think we should take it too seriously, these things happen . . ."

"Nothing happened, as usual. There is nothing therefore to discuss." Fabrice left the room, his back rigid and unapproachable. Alexa stared after him, hearing in the dying vibrations of his voice the sound of a door slamming.

Alexa rose from the table and walked over to the tall looking-glass which surmounted the chimney piece. The *Salle à Manger* reflected behind her was dim in the old glass, only her face seemed in focus. Leaning forward she silently enquired of her own image, why she was always left alone?

At last David announced the start of the *vendange*. Pickers who had been working on neighbouring properties in previous weeks were recruited and accommodated in bunk beds in one of the old, disused *chais* which had long been used for the purpose. Alexa and Hortense were busy, sweeping and cleaning, preparing the braziers which would warm the workers in the chill of the evening and planning how to feed fifty people after a hard day's labour on the vineyards. Most of them would be students from the University of Bordeaux, and many of those from the Department of Oenology. Their knowledge of wine, David had hinted, would far exceed her own. Alexa was determined to work alongside them and pick up what she could.

"*Madame* is mad," said Hortense to David. "Already the child must weigh on her. Oh, she gives no sign, she *runs* up and down these kitchen stairs and there is no telling her. She heeds no warnings. Can you not do anything?"

David raised his shoulders with a grimace. "What does one say, to the Marquise de Pies Ombre?" His smile betrayed his contempt for the rank.

"You could tell her she would be a hindrance to you, that she'd get in the way of serious work. You know how she would feel about *that*."

"I could tell any other woman to go indoors and mind her pots and pans, but not *her*. What she has achieved here entitles her to some privileges. Don't we owe her anything? Isn't she entitled to get in the way of her own pickers?"

Hortense put her hand in front of her mouth, her steely eyes wide with surprise. She knew, of course, that her mistress paid her from the profits of the guest-house, but had not guessed how heavily burdened with commitments those profits were. *"La pauvre petite,"* she murmured, "does she carry everything on her back?"

"She will pay them this year, and every year from now on, if you ask me. That's if she manages to save the château."

"If that is her intention, then she will. I have had experience of that young lady's determination. It is an uncomfortable thing. But Pierre," Hortense appealed as she poured the frothing eggs into an iron pan, "she is risking the child's life and her own. Someone must stop her. I try to tell her but all she says is that she has no time to take things easy. It is not right, I tell you. She will kill that baby. I wonder sometimes if that is what she has in mind.''

"*Tais-toi*, woman," David glanced around almost furtively. "What if she does, who could blame her. It is not our affair. Madame de Pies Ombre is a good mistress. She has had much to suffer here." Nodding her agreement, Hortense flipped the omelette expertly from the copper pan onto the plate which she set before David.

They both knew of the flaw in the blood of the de Pies Ombres, it was a matter of local lore, one of a set of facts handed down from father to son and mother to daughter. It was like all the stories of the locality, however fantastic, they were true, because every generation had solemnly assured the next that these were matters of history and not of legend. But the recurrent trouble of the de Pies Ombres was not discussed, even though, of all the local legends, it was the one most self-evidently true and which renewed itself in virtually every generation. Every time it happened some euphemism was settled upon and somehow or other, the servants and the village people, without need of words or direct orders, were made aware of it. In Monsieur Fabrice's great-grandfather's time, it had been "a badly set bone after a fall from a carriage" and nobody had dared say anything to the contrary. Both Monsieur Fabrice's father and grandfather had escaped, but Mademoiselle Héloïse was afflicted. With her it had been "infantile arthritis," and now, of course, it was just "arthritis." The village people of Ombre had ceased to ask themselves how women could be found to risk carrying such tragedy in their wombs. It was no good trying to fathom the minds of the rich, they reached as deep as vine roots, maybe that was why their breeding lines lasted so long.

Picking grapes for many hours of the day was hard labour and fraught with constant alarms. The vines were abundantly populated with a variety of snail which inspired Alexa with an absurd and nearly uncontrollable fear. More than once she had found her finger adhering to one of the soft, slimy little bodies as she parted the leaves to cut the bloom-dusted, purple grapes from their stalks. Prudently Alexa soon gave it up. The house guests took up a fair proportion of her time and then there were the pickers to feed. She insisted on assisting Hortense to serve the pickers' meal and joining them for a glass of wine before going back to the house to change for dinner with her American guests. It was a gruelling programme.

Alexa looked at the vivid young faces sitting round the scrubbed table in the courtyard outside the old *chai* and marvelled that in many cases, these youngsters were exactly the same age as herself. She felt herself separated from them by a gulf of experience, by events that possessed the texture of time that had passed and carried her forward, beyond the world of those who shared her chronological age. They were young in a way that she was no longer young and she observed them with an eye that was distanced by a precocious knowledge of life's realities. Their faces were happy, unmarked by fear or anxiety, but she could not envy them. I have all this, she said to herself, and all I have to do is to hold onto it until it sticks to my hand of its own accord.

The students taught her new things about the life of the vine and the special nature of her own soil, its unbelievable complexity and variety. And of course, there were those who, less discreet and observant than their fellows, told her a great number of things she already knew. Kindly, Alexa never gave a sign of impatience. They were eager and proud to impart their knowledge to the pretty English *Marquise*, so charmingly and obviously pregnant.

"The vine, you see *Madame*, must suffer to prosper. A rich soil is no good, the roots must dig very deep for their sustenance. They drive deep into the subsoil and from there bring treasures up into the fruit."

"You are very poetic, *Monsieur*," Alexa responded seriously to the fine-looking boy with the dark, sculptured curls. He was always so anxious to capture her attention.

"Bah, do not listen to him," interjected a bespectacled youth, "he is no scientist. His father owns a property in the Beaujolais, they are all the same there. Understanding vines is a matter of painstaking analysis, not flowery generalisations."

"Well, we have a task, here in the Médoc, do we not, friend? Every step on this land and the neighbouring properties is different. For all we know, each individual wine produces a must of a different character. No one has ever had the time or the courage to test it."

"What do you mean?" Alexa turned eagerly towards the source of new information. This lad was a second-year student.

He blushed as Alexa fastened her unblinking, cornflower-blue gaze on him, demanding an explanation.

"Well, *Madame*, the soil variations in Pauillac alone are enough to keep a team of analysts going for a lifetime. All we can be sure of is that the gentle slopes you have here and the surface gravel drain the land superbly. That appears to be the quality factor. The better the land drains, the better the wine. The roots of the vine are obliged to dig many metres deep and in that way ensure a supply of nourishment which is not subject to fluctuations. But each root may well touch subsoil of a different composition from that touched by its neighbour."

"But they cannot dry out, nor can they be flooded, result consistent quality?"

"Bravo, *Madame*, you begin to understand the basics!" There was a generally laudatory murmur and Alexa smiled thinly to herself. These charming young people had no conception of how much she already knew of their subject. But their affectionate patronage and evident admiration were as warm and consoling as the repeatedly presented paw of an uncritical and adoring spaniel. She left their company each evening somewhat strengthened for the strained encounter with her husband and the difficult duty of entertaining her American guests without giving a hint of their own domestic coolness.

One subject of conversation with the students gave her food for thought. The gravel on the de Pies Ombre property remained unweeded. The weeds shaded and prevented the larger stones from absorbing the heat of the sun and reflecting it back onto the lower bunches of grapes, which would hasten the ripening of the less advantageously placed fruit. Once again, it was a question of money, and while she smiled and talked through the evenings, she thought of the price of weedkiller.

But if the student pickers did not think much of the way the property was run, they appreciated her hospitality and told her dire tales of greasy stew and gristle followed by damp blankets at other châteaux. "The pay is better, *Madame*, but the comfort is non-existent." Hortense provided great *daubes*, *cassoulets*, and sauces, to be eaten with chunks of fresh bread. Then there were always generous bowls of salad glistening with olive oil and cheeses with the early apples and plums of the region. On the final day of the *vendange*, a dish of roast partridges appeared. David had shot them among the stripped vines as each hectare yielded up its harvest.

"This is one good reason for not going to the city, *Madame*," David announced on the last day of the *vendange*, holding a brace of birds aloft. "How many workers in the town get the chance to enjoy *la chasse*? I confess it is my weakness."

"It might be a good idea to get people to come here in the autumn specially to shoot the partridge," Alexa said thoughtfully. David pounced on the remark with enthusiasm.

"*Mais oui, Madame*. I have said the same thing to *Monsieur* on many occasions, but he has no interest. He says he cannot afford to build butts for proper shooting parties, but *Madame*, if it were possible . . ."

"It *is* possible. You give me an estimate of what it will cost to erect the butts, how many we need and where they should be placed and I will see about arranging shooting parties for next autumn." David's eyes shone.

"After all, why not, once the grapes are inside the *cuverie*, your task is done, is it not?"

"Oh, not entirely, *Madame*. I begin to prune, you know. We use, or should use, the prunings for fuel. I should be taking cuttings and grafting them for new stock and putting the pressed grapeskins on the land to manure. There is always plenty to do. *Beaucoup à faire*." He sighed.

"Do you *do* all these things, Monsieur David?" Alexa had caught the tinge of defeat in the old man's voice.

"I do some of them, *Madame*, some each year. I'm afraid there is not the labour to do all that should be done. I am only one man and we have a large property here, sixty hectares is a lot of land to cover by myself with the little help Monsieur Fabrice can afford to give me."

Alexa noticed that David was always correct. Whatever he knew of the real situation, he never gave her the impression that he knew or cared that his master was not ultimately in control of Château d'Ombre. She tried always to respond in kind, referring to herself as her husband's deputy or lieutenant. If she was ever tempted to say "I" instead of "we," David soon reminded her wordlessly that it would not do.

"We should be able to afford more next year, and if not that, at least some new machinery. At any rate, you can count on your annual treat. You'll supervise our shooting parties for four weeks after the *vendange*. We go back to worrying about the wine after that. How much have we got, by the way?"

David raised his eyes to heaven, rolling his eyeballs in the manner of one who calculates roughly and from experience.

"Approximately a hundred *tonneaux*. It is half of what this château usually produces, but thanks to the late sunshine, the quality will be adequate for blending. I think you will get a fair price for it."

"It will be good to get any price at all. I don't think much of last year's vintage was sold. And another thing, Pierre," Alexa addressed him informally, by his Christian name, without thinking, "what about the snails?"

"Snails, *Madame*?" Sometimes, David had difficulty keeping up with the mercurial flow of her thoughts. She would suddenly ask a question unrelated to any previous discussion, as if she expected instant comprehension.

"Yes, certainly, the snails. Actually, if you want to know, that's the real reason I gave up helping the pickers, I'm terrified of the things. But couldn't we *do* something with them?"

David scratched his head in perplexity. "Well," he said slowly, "sometimes we eat them . . ."

"Precisely. And in England they are regarded as a great and sophisticated luxury. If we could just find some way of preserving them, we could export them. Another crop and all for free."

"But, *Madame*, gathering them . . ."

"Let me worry about that." First one looks at the potential in a situation, and then one considers the problems to be overcome. It was a principle she had unconsciously absorbed from Henry Jagger. He didn't allow difficulties to get in his way if there was a profit to be made. "Are snails *ever* preserved in France, frozen, bottled . . . ?"

"Not to my knowledge, *Madame*. But there is a cannery in Pauillac. You might ask them if it is possible."

"Thank you Pierre!"

Alexa saw the grapes de-stalked by hand with pain. It took too long and absorbed every hand on the place. Machinery, it must be her priority even before the land. The grapes were crushed and tipped into the oaken vats. The must would lie with the skins taking colour and tannin from them for twelve days according to Fabrice.

"It is too long. The wine will be stewed." Alexa stood watching Fabrice as he walked from *cuvée* to *cuvée*, feeling each of the wooden tanks with his hand, testing and assessing the temperature.

He turned to her, outraged at this intrusion on his especial territory. Catching sight of her in the gloom of the *cuverie*, his heart clenched with a painful emotion that was separate and distinct from his anger. Her advancing pregnancy had done nothing to mar her beauty, but it had changed it. The increasing bulk she carried before her made the delicacy of her bones seem more pronounced and emphasised a new confidence and precision in her movements. There was a majesty about her now, a pride and authority in her carriage which he wanted to possess himself. She was *his*, but she withheld herself and it heated him with an indefinable desire. He was jealous of her own thoughts, envious of the emerald-green silk that clothed her body, enraged by the pearls that encircled her neck. They were none of his giving. She adorned herself out of her own sufficiency.

He did not answer her, but began, painfully and dangerously, to climb the wooden staircase that led to the companion-way that enabled him to look down into the huge wooden *cuvées*. In his mind, his hands tore at her clothes, he wanted everything that was not his discarded and dishonoured. He wanted her naked and needy, dependent on him. He could see her below. She stood with her arms folded, looking up at him.

"Did you hear me, darling?" The sound of her voice echoed slightly in the dark cavern of the *cuverie*. They were alone, the men had gone home for their noonday meal. "Don't you think you should come down? You don't look safe, I'll go up and look for you." He stopped half way up the staircase.

"Too *much*?" Fabrice asked quietly. "Stewed? What do you know of the matter? You are *maître de chais*, now are you? We all know that you are accountant and paymaster. Judging by appearances, you plan to be *régisseur* as well, do you really think you can combine all these roles? You are not usually quite so immodest. Do I take you seriously, or do I dismiss your megalomania as an unfortunate symptom of your condition?" Fabrice turned himself on the narrow step and began to descend.

Alexa walked towards him, her arms already extended to meet him, "Listen, Fabrice, darling. I don't want to tread on your toes and of *course* I don't know anything like as much as you do about it, but aren't we forgetting something?" Fabrice regarded her, plainly puzzled, but for the moment, placated.

"We're not making Château de Pies Ombre this year. The

whole of the must is going to Chirac Frères for blending. They don't need it too 'hard.' We've got ninety per cent *Cabernet* in the *encépagement* here, you told me that yourself. If you steep that stuff any longer, nobody'll be able to drink it for at least seven years. If it's like that, Monsieur Chirac won't be able to use much of it. They're making a 'high street' wine. The man in the street wants a bottle of wine he can buy and take home to his wife for supper. And he wants to do it often, so the price has got to be right. If the wine needs too much aging, then we're right up the creek, the sums don't work out.''

Fabrice grasped the handrail at the bottom of the staircase and hooked his stick over it. He steadied himself before replying. ''That is your opinion, and it is worth *that*.'' He made a vulgar gesture that was unfamiliar to Alexa but there was no mistaking its import.

Alexa's eyes narrowed. Fighting down an instinct to step backwards, she moved towards him. Nothing ever worked with Fabrice except words she would rather not say. She braced herself for the coming confrontation, relieved, like a soldier, that diplomacy had failed and her waiting period was over. It was better to be out in the open.

''Next year, Fabrice, we're going to do things my way. Oh yes, I know, I have a lot to learn, but the thing is, Fabrice, that I *do* learn and go on learning. I don't imagine that what has to be learned is finite, like you. I listen to anybody who will talk to me. Sometimes I find things out, sometimes I don't, but my knowledge goes on growing. It may not be as great as yours yet, but it will be, some time *soon*, and it will overtake yours very quickly. Because what you know about your own business is set in concrete. Why don't you just get out there and *talk* to somebody, Fabrice?''

''I don't remember calling for your advice and I don't want it. Just get out of my way. Amuse yourself with the house, and David if you like, but keep out of things you don't understand.'' Fabrice was shouting, his face white. Alexa looked over her shoulder, afraid that anyone should hear them.

''Then your business will go under. All the purse strings are mine and I shan't open them for something over which I have no control or influence.'' Fabrice grasped his stick and, descending from the lowest step of the staircase, stepped closer to Alexa. She shifted her balance immediately, responding to an instinct for flight, but she forced herself to hold her ground.

Never show fear, her mother had taught her that during her endless lectures on managing dogs.

"Just how much have you made this summer, Alexa? How much have you made out of my name and out of my home? Because that money is *mine*, not yours."

"That's arguable. I have done everything and you have done precious little except put on a dinner jacket every night and talk in your damned condescending way to people. What do you want me to do? Pay you *rent* on the house? Who pays Hortense's wages and how? Who pays David's? Don't be a fool, Fabrice. There's no future for you or the Château d'Ombre without me."

"And don't I know it! I'm a nobody on my own property and it is you who have dispossessed me. You're a thief, Alexa. You've taken everything from me including my self-respect."

"There wasn't much to take, Fabrice."

It was one of those moments when time becomes slimed and viscous. Action in the thickened minutes oozed slowly through the changed texture of awareness, visible in every forensic detail. She had known it was dangerous as she uttered the words. But she was like a gambler treating herself to a flutter in the near certain excitement of loss. She saw his face, already pale, change to a papery mauve, his mouth form a crater of rage. Its dark hole sucked breath in hungrily and his pupils dilated till his eyes were entirely filled with black. He raised his free hand to strike her. It described an arc in the air, almost fascinating in its precision. Alexa's eyes followed it, riveted. She was too late to step out of the way and Fabrice's hand made contact with the right side of her face. He had struck her with considerable force. Her hand flew automatically to her face and, staggering, she stumbled and fell.

For a moment she waited. Waited calmly for the head-spinning dizziness to stop. There was silence. Her mind examined every inch of her body. Searching for sensations that might give a clue to serious damage. The side of her head hurt, and her face—there would be a bruise. People would see it. As long as the baby was safe. Her fingertips made contact with dirt and grit on the floor of the *cuverie*. It was the most unpleasant thing. Coldly, Alexa made a mental note. The floor of the *cuverie* should be swept and disinfected tomorrow morning.

"Alexa, I'm sorry. I should not have done that." Fabrice looked down at her, a frightened look in his eyes.

"No, you shouldn't, should you? Help me up." She held up

her hand to him. It was a gesture that combined command with pardon. Instantly antagonised by his wife's unconscious but complete control of the moment, Fabrice turned away furiously. He could knock her down, but he could not subdue her.

"I can't. You'll have to manage. I'm going to change." The great door with its automatic closing device let in a slice of daylight to cut the gloom, and then wiped it out as it swung home on its hinges.

For a few moments more, Alexa lay there on the dirty floor, her eyes fixed on the ancient wooden rafters far above. The child stirred inside her. I shall never forgive your father for this. No-one will ever know of it, but I shall not forget, you may be certain. He will *never* be safe from me.

Ariel's hired Mercedes drew up in front of the château.

"My, you've made some improvements here, honey. Didn't recognise the drive, my teeth still seem to be in place." She touched her fingers to her jaw in mock investigation.

Alexa laughed delightedly, it was good to see her again.

"Come in, Ariel. It's wonderful of you to come like this. One of the pleasures of being rich, I suppose. I couldn't go anywhere without prolonged planning or a major confrontation."

"Aw, honey, don't be bitter. You'll make it. I know you will. Anyway, I'm a businesswoman in my own right now, it's all tax allowable. You could always pull something like that if you could get away to come and see me."

"No point in anything being tax allowable if you're so poor you don't make profits to be taxed on," Alexa grimaced, never willing to admit to success prematurely. "Well, anyway, come up to my special place. I'll tell you all about your commission."

"Yep, sounds great. What about the bags?"

"Leave them, the problem may disappear."

The two girls climbed the narrow spiral staircase talking excitedly to each other. Ariel's arrival was like a holiday to Alexa and she was longing to show her the new things she had done in the château. In the turret room, some changes had taken place.

"Well, you *have* made yourself comfortable in here, honey. It's a delight. An Ideal Home for the Lady of Shalott." Ariel looked round appreciatively at the little room. The roughly plastered walls had fresh white distemper on them and were decorated with tiny canvases collected from various unused parts of the château. Some were richly framed and mounted and others remained unframed, in the same state that they must have lain against the walls of the artists' studios, long ago. Plain, painted wooden shelves held a collection of books, chosen as much as anything for their decorative bindings, interspersed with obviously practical manuals on accounting and tax.

The stove was burnished with black lead and looked almost silver in the fractured light from the oriel window. The floor was spread with faded oriental rugs and an old china hand-basin stood on the battered *torchère* near the door. It contained an effusion of wild grasses, flowers, reddening vine leaves and late-flowering herbs. There was only one chair apart from the gilded *fauteuil* at the desk, a sagging armchair in a faded, ill-fitting chintz which Alexa had found in a junk shop in Pauillac. It was the sort of familiar furniture that was completely absent from the château.

"Yes, it's coming together. There's no rush for this place, of course. I just pick things up as I see them, live with them for a while and decide whether I like them and then rearrange a few things to give the latest object a more advantageous home. It's like that. But there's something that *is* urgent. That's why I asked you to come. You see, partly because I've been so busy and partly because of a sort of superstition, I've done *nothing* about the nursery."

"How long is it, now, honey?"

"Six weeks, I suppose."

"Then we'll have to work fast."

"Faster than you think, the project I have in mind is really equivalent to fixing up a small house. The attics here are extensive. They used to sleep about twenty indoor servants, it's like a small town up there. I want to use a large part of it to make a really splendid nursery for my child and the nanny."

"But, honey, is it practical? All those stairs . . . and isn't it a fire risk? Nanny and baby would have the least chance of getting out if anything were to happen. These old houses can go up like a hay rick."

"I know, I've thought of all that. I'm going to put in a modern lift which will communicate directly between the kitchen quarters and the nursery and there will also be a Davis escape apparatus."

"Jesus! What's that?"

"Oh, we had them at school and had to use them every fire practice. In the army they call it abseiling. You climb out of a window and strap yourself into this harness thing and then you lean out at right angles to the wall and sort of walk yourself down it."

"It sounds crazy to me. What if Nanny's not a gymnast?"

"She *will* be, or she won't work here."

"And what about the baby? How can she walk down a wall with a baby in her arms?" Ariel was plainly aghast at the thought.

"I'm having a special sling designed. Don't worry, it'll all work perfectly. Your job, if you'll kindly undertake it, is to make the most beautiful, comfortable, stimulating nursery in the world for a child who *may* be disabled and for the top-flight nanny I shall find for him. Make a place that no one in their right mind would ever want to leave. A magical world that will make the people who live there feel on top of the world, like eagles in a very safe eyrie."

"Alexa, honey, I'm so sorry, I didn't know there was anything wrong with the baby, I really didn't." Ariel was appalled. Medical information at the clinic was privileged. Even the directors knew nothing of what passed between patient and consultant.

"Nor do we yet, it's just a chance. Didn't your Mr. Lockwood tell you about it?"

Ariel looked dumbfounded. "Richard? No. It's not his line of country. How could he know, unless you told him yourself?"

"It wasn't quite like that," Alexa said drily, "more a question of him telling me." Quickly she turned the conversation back to the nursery. At least she had established one interesting fact. Richard Lockwood wasn't a gossip, whatever else he might be.

"What about you, honey? You make it sound as though this magical world isn't going to have very much to do with *you*. Aren't you going to be a feature of fairyland?"

"Oh yes, for one thing, I'm creating it, with your help. For another I'll be visiting the eagle's nest with nice fat worms, baby rats and digestible titbits of that sort on a regular basis."

Ariel smiled broadly, "It does sound as though this baby is going to be brought up to be a regular carnivore!"

"Oh it is, my dear, it is. Haven't you noticed how herbivores only prosper in herds of great numbers? Once my little one has flown the nest, he'll have to survive on his own." There was an icy chill to Alexa's words and this time it was Ariel who was glad to escape the subject of the baby.

"It's a great commission. A fantastic first job for a would-be interior decorator. I've got to thank you for giving me the chance.''

"But it's not your first job, you did the clinic and utterly stunning it is too.''

"Ah, but you know what I mean. I did that job as Lionel's wife. It's not the same as earning money for it. You know how it is when you work for your husband? Somehow you're always a cheaper alternative to somebody better, no matter how good you are. I guess it's just a fundamental rule of matrimony. Nothing you can do about it, isn't that so, hon? How much can I spend?''

"You can spend around eight thousand pounds in English money. That's to include your fee, mind. It should be enough. You can buy a decent little house in a respectable area for that amount of money in England. Am I being unrealistic? My grandfather died and left me a bit of money, that's why I can afford to do it.''

That explained a lot. Ariel had been frankly amazed at the generosity of the budget, Alexa was usually so careful with money. But even so, it was a lot to spend on a nursery for anyone. There were things in Alexa, shadows and ghosts that never walked out into the clear light of day. You couldn't get to know her easily.

"No, I don't think so, honey,'' Ariel answered the question. "Can we go up and look at the site? Oh, I'm sorry, perhaps it's too much for you. Just give me directions and I'll find my own way. You *do* look tired, Alexa. Why don't you take better care of yourself?''

"Don't you start, Ariel. I'm *fine*. I'm not one of your rich Scheitinger Clinic mothers, you know, I have to work, pregnant or not. And I'm much luckier than most. I live where I work, I have enough to eat, a warm, clean place to sleep. There are thousands of wretched women all over the world who can't say as much.''

But Ariel heard the huge omissions. She said nothing of love or of adequate medical support. Alexa looked strained and though her natural elegance was intact, her bloom was dimmed. The assertions she made about being all right sounded a false note. Uneasily, she followed Alexa up the steep, dusty staircases which led to the attics. She wanted to ask about Fabrice, it would be natural, but there was an indefinable something in Alexa's manner that forbade even the formal enquiry. She had a way of

making you aware of which questions would be welcome and
which would not. There was a faint mark on her cheek, like a
smear of charcoal, it might be that. They used it on the stoves
as well as vine cuttings.

There were no more visitors that year. The bookings had tailed
off and Alexa had told the remaining enquirers that the season
was now closed although it would be extended next year for
shooting and a Christmas house party was projected. She was
too weary now to do any more and was anxious to be relieved
of her burden. The few dresses she had were tired and she was
becoming short of breath and impatient. If someone did not hear
what she said the first time she snapped at them. The effort of
repeating herself had become great.

Every day she climbed up to the turret room. There she sat
in the old sagging chintz-covered chair with her feet up on a
footstool. Ariel had found the footstool in the attic room she
was engaged in turning into the nanny's bathroom.

"Why do you struggle up here, honey? It's too much for
you."

"Ariel, this room is my private place, more home than anywhere else in the château. And it's my counting house," she
added with a smile. But Ariel's American practicality was unsatisfied.

"What are we going to do if the baby starts to come? We may
not hear you, and if we do, how are we going to get you down?"

"Don't you think I can control when the baby comes?"

"No, honey, I don't. You can control most things, but not
that. You're getting a little crazy, you know." Alexa took her
friend's hand and squeezed it.

"I know. I'll be better soon. I promise you."

Héloïse tapped on the door of the turret room one day and
entered bringing a tray of tea. Alexa struggled up from the chair
to help her. It was the first time Héloïse had sought her out since
the time of their acrimonious conversation about the baby. Indeed, Héloïse had never come to her before, preferring to be
visited if at all in her new study on the ground floor.

"Lapsang Souchong," she announced triumphantly. "Just
the thing for discriminating English ladies, or so Hortense tells
me. Oh, I'm so very sorry, *Madame*," Héloïse caught sight of
Ariel. "I only brought two cups." Héloïse fixed the young
American woman with a gimlet eye. Ariel understood that she

was dismissed and, preparing to leave hurriedly, cannonaded into both Alexa and Héloïse at the door, where they were trying to negotiate both the tray and Héloïse's stick into the room.

Alexa took the tray from Héloïse who sank into the little *fauteuil* gratefully.

"We are both helpless, aren't we? Can't even get a tea tray into a room without a major fuss," Alexa began cautiously.

"You are never hopeless, *ma chère*, but the rest of us would be without you. I'm here to apologise. You've been so much on my conscience. I hope you can forgive me."

"Tante Héloïse, whatever is there to forgive?"

"Well, let us not pretend that I was not insensitive and stupid. I am a childless old woman, what do I know of a mother's concerns? I have been lame all my life, it is like having brown eyes instead of blue, to me."

"But once, Tante Héloïse," Alexa said softly, "it prevented you from doing what you wanted to do, didn't it?"

"It did, *ma chère*, and I deserve to be reminded. But you must believe me when I say that I had no idea that you were unaware of the position. You see, being a useless old maid, I never thought of it at all. And then, I must confess, I was infected by self-pity. You see, it hurts to think of myself as a baby and realise that you would not have wanted *me*. I suppose I wondered about my own mother, so silly really. All that is in the past. It is the new generation we have to think of and pray for."

"Please, don't say any more. I'm sorry too, I never wanted to quarrel with you, none of it is your fault. There's nothing more to be said."

Héloïse had, with the best of motives, played most effectively on her feelings. And not, Alexa realised, without some deliberation. There was no doubt of Tante Héloïse's genuine goodness, but she was also prepared to exercise an aristocratic wiliness in any cause that was near to her heart. Alexa knew there was more to this than met the eye and she was tense with the unwelcome expectation of a lecture on some other matter.

"Oh but there is, *ma chère*, there is. We have all bitten the hand that feeds us from time to time. No, no," Héloïse waved down Alexa's attempted protest, although she noted shrewdly that Alexa had instantly recognised the feeding hand as her own. "Perhaps because it is a stranger's hand. Without you we should all have had to leave this place and live . . . who knows how?

The château would have crumbled away to dust and maybe some rich proprietor would have bought the vineyards and paid off the debts, but there would have been nothing left. What would an old fool who lives on a few francs from writing religious pamphlets that nobody reads have lived on? What would poor Suzanne have done? And Fabrice?''

"What about Fabrice, Héloïse?'' Alexa feared that they were now approaching the nub of the matter.

"You must try to forgive him. I don't know what has passed between you, but he has no other resource but you. You make him feel he is of no account . . .''

"Well, he isn't, is he?'' Alexa cursed Héloïse in her mind with a mixture of affection and amusement. She was well and truly cornered and her sharp reply had been verbal play, an attempt to wriggle out of what was coming.

Héloïse looked down. It was hard to live with the naked logic of this girl's mind. Her merciless adherence to the facts.

"If you cannot love him, and you cannot forgive him, perhaps you could pity him.''

"Tante Héloïse, do you know what a holy terror you are? An absolute scoundrel. I will do the best I can with myself and Fabrice, but at the moment, as you can see, I need most of my energy for myself.''

CHAPTER
15

🎜🎜 THE UGLY LITTLE church was stuffy, filled with almost the entire population of the village of Ombre. The Christmas Eve mass attracted even the most atheistical among the population. It was a family affair. Tired children were grizzling and it was obvious that despite the traditional fast, the young men had been carousing uproariously in the two *cafés* which the village of Ombre offered for the recreation of its residents. Madame Charbonnier, as became the proprietor of the superior establishment, was to be seen amongst the congregation, resplendent in an aged ocelot wrap she had got, rumour had it, from a lover long dead and gone who had left her the capital to purchase La Perdrix d'Or. The *patron* of the less salubrious Café de Pauillac cared more for his Christmas Eve takings than for a seasonal show of respectability, for he and his numerous family were absent, no doubt cashing up, as Héloïse remarked with a kind of holy cattiness, as the party from the château surveyed the gathering of their rustic neighbours.

Alexa turned to Fabrice, "Why are Catholic churches always so awfully vulgar?"

"Religion has nothing to do with good taste," he muttered, "that's an error made by you English. Good taste varies from place to place and from generation to generation, but vulgarity is universal, something you can rely on. It's a question of enduring values." Héloïse, catching the drift of this whispered conversation, nodded in agreement as she leafed through the pages of her missal and changed her spectacles, in readiness for a major confrontation with the mysteries of faith.

And yet, even to Alexa's jaundiced eye, the church had a coarse charm. The electrified halo of the Virgin shone with bra-

zen happiness and the vacuous, painted faces of the lesser saints
seemed to have a touching vulnerability on this night of nights,
when emotions are stirred and ordinary judgements suspended.

Fortunately, thought Alexa, the cruel bas-relief stations of the
cross were not polychrome, but in some form of alabaster. Their
pallor allowed the beastliness of their message to fade out of
mind, if not out of sight. And everywhere there was the strange
sense-stirring odour of incense, its blue clouds drifting above
the heads of the congregation, hanging beneficently beneath the
stone-vaulted ceiling of the old church.

She wondered why she had insisted on coming. The baby was
already a week late. Doctor Gaultier had been vaguely reassuring. It was often the way with first babies, he said. There was
not the slightest occasion for concern at this stage. But still, she
was heavy and could not really stand for prolonged periods. She
was sitting now, the corner of her eye level with the middle
button on Fabrice's dinner jacket. She felt a little sick. The sound
of the Credo came as if from a distance. Through the forest of
standing figures, she could discern the choir of village boys,
their red *soutanes* cheerful and vivid against the lace-trimmed
cottes, snow-white and lovingly starched by proud mothers. She
felt sick. Why had she come? To assert herself. It had been taken
too much for granted that she would not come, an assumption
which, to Alexa's strain-tattered nerves, was intolerable.

The table for the *réveillon* had been set in the *Salon Jaune*. It
was warm and cosy in there and there would only be the four of
them. Hortense had arranged matters so that they could serve
themselves from the heated trolley. She had invited Pierre David
and his widowed sister to join her in the kitchen for the first
festive meal of Christmas. Once Alexa had learned of this convivial arrangement, she had insisted that their celebration was
not to be disrupted by calls for service from the *Salon Jaune*.
"It is Christmas for everyone, *Belle Mère*, Hortense must have
her little party. We can manage very well on our own."

She felt sick. She looked down at the voluminous blond folds
of the enveloping mink Suzanne had loaned her when once she
had realised that Alexa could not be prevailed upon to absent
herself from the mass. It was an unfashionable coat, made in
the era of Dior's New Look, just after the war. Ideal for a heavily
pregnant woman, it fell opulently to the ankle. It was too hot.
She could smell faded perfume and face-powder lingering on
the collar of the fur. There was a pain, not unlike a period pain,

gathering in her abdomen. It would go off if she ignored it. She began to sweat.

Fabrice spun round at the touch on his hand.

"I'll have to leave." He looked down into her grey face. It was beaded with moisture.

"Can you hold on?"

Alexa smiled up at him. The world of joy which shone in his face wiped out everything that had gone before, for this single moment of greatest intensity. She was broken up with pity and remorse for all they had done to each other. That single schoolboy enquiry, "Can you hold on?", as if she were about to wet herself instead of have a baby, was full of simple affection.

"I think so," she was panting slightly. Carefully, he edged himself out of the pew, leading Alexa by the hand. The manoeuvre involved pushing past Suzanne, who wore a look of triumphant satisfaction, overlaid with a paper-thin look of concern. She had been right to advise Alexa against coming. Alexa had seen the same expression on her mother's face many times before. Héloïse laid down her missal with a look of enquiry. Fabrice nodded. Quickly she put away her spectacles in the *petit point* case and, genuflecting stiffly, prepared to follow Fabrice and Alexa up the central aisle of the church.

They seemed to make their retreat slowly and painfully, and as they did so, a muted ripple of concern and congratulations accompanied them. *"Bonne chance,"* *"Bonne chance, Madame,"* "Bravo." Hands reached out to touch them gently as they passed. Among the haze of faces, some came into sharper focus than others. Alexa recognised men from the *chais* and part-time maids from the château. They all wished her well. It was as if she and Fabrice were themselves the holy couple, almost as if they had stolen the night from its rightful owners. But the people of Ombre shared no such fanciful thoughts. The whispered advice and encouragement, "Relax *Madame.*" "You will have a son before the night is out, *Monsieur.*" "I have had six, it is like shelling peas." "Nothing to it *Madame*, but breathe deeply," became louder until, after an age of walking when they reached the door, the groundswell of good will had become an audible, unified sound, like waves crashing in a muted roar on a distant beach.

Alexa stopped on the churchyard path for a moment to catch her breath. She looked back at the lighted church, its one and only stained-glass window spilling colour onto the asphalt.

"Alexa?"

"Mmm."

"Come on, darling. We've got to get you to bed."

At that moment a flood of water burst from her and drenched her thin evening gown and stockings. Alexa burst into tears. "Come on, it's all right, darling. I'm sure it's normal. Come *on*."

They had taken the baby away. The birth had been rapid and painful, taking place before the doctor could get to her. Gaultier arrived two hours after the four-hour labour was over, expressing amazement that a first infant could have arrived so quickly. He stood beside Alexa's bed, rocking judiciously from toe to heel. "Truly, *Madame*, I thought I had time to finish my brandy, and," he added with synthetic roguishness, "to be frank with you, I thought I had time for another. What an impatient young lady you are to be sure. Never happy until a job is done, if all I hear is true. You will not catch me napping again, *Madame*!" Alexa turned away from the sound of his voice in disgust.

She had no clear recollection of the events of that night after leaving the church. It was a black hole in her memory. An impression of pain, mess and panic remained but there was no record of action or result. The only thing she knew was that the child had been born alive but he must have something wrong with him. He was in Paris, at the paediatric orthopaedic unit in the American Hospital at Neuilly.

Suzanne and Fabrice had left the same night, Fabrice accompanied the baby in the private ambulance and Suzanne followed in the Jaguar. Alexa was left behind in the care of Hortense and Héloïse, to recover as best she may. It was almost like a still birth, she thought, lying in the great bed alone. The months of growing larger, of becoming aware of an active, benign parasite, the crisis of parturition had all culminated in an absence that was tangible. There ought to have been something there, but there was not. It was an odd feeling.

Alexa was relieved to be excused the suddenness of the confrontation that bearing a child involves. To have an infirmity that takes human form in an unpredictable instant, and to be required to welcome it like a long-lost friend seemed unreasonable to her. And instinct and experience told her that she would have been pestered and reproached for standing back from the baby. But she would stand back. You have to get to know people. It's not like a puppy or a kitten whose attractions are immediately obvious. Charles and I will get to know and like each other when we know where we stand. What's wrong with him and whether it can be put right or not. We have to know the facts. We'll work it out together over the years. But we won't be rushed. No. I will begin to love him when I know what it is I have to love. Not before.

Alexa indulged these rebellious reflections for hours at a time. It was protection, a pre-arming against demands she anticipated with dread. Deep in her heart she loved the baby passionately already, no matter what he was like, but she feared that her love would be supervised and made to correspond to someone else's idea of what that love should be.

Nobody rang her from Paris for two days. Eventually she telephoned the house in the Marais herself.

"Hello?"

"Oh, Suzanne, it's me. I wondered . . ." her voice trailed off. She wondered *what* she wondered. She wanted the baby to be all right, but she knew it could not be. She wanted to hold it in her arms but dreaded that moment of final truth, knowing that from that instant in time, she would never be free again, her heart would be tied by steel cables to the child, to his ancestral soil and the home his forebears had built to nurture and protect their posterity.

"I am rather busy at the moment, Alexa. I imagine you want to know how your son is?" Suzanne's voice rang tinnily with the self-importance of a woman who is temporarily busy after a lifetime of indolence.

Not really, Alexa thought suddenly. I want to know . . . what has become of *me*. I'm beginning to feel rather thrown away, a husk. Actually, I feel angry. Nobody will want to hear that. In the confusion of her thoughts she felt an urgent desire to see and hold her child. If it did not come soon, it would not be hers. But she answered Suzanne with guarded composure.

"Yes, I suppose so."

"Charles is perfectly all right. A healthy little boy. There is nothing wrong with him at all."

"I see." The shock of relief swept over her.

"Yes. You and that *extraordinary* mother of yours have made fools of yourselves, and ruined our Christmas into the bargain. I suppose we shall have to forgive you, pregnant women are notoriously unstable. Fabrice insists that we put it all behind us.

Charles is a new beginning. Let us remember that.'' Alexa's
hand ached with the tightness of the grip she exerted on the
telephone as she fought for self-command. Suzanne's new pose
as law-giving matriarch was as dangerous as it was ludicrous.
Why, oh why, had she allowed them to spirit the baby away from
her like this?

"If there's nothing wrong with the baby, bring it back here,
at once.'' She put the telephone down abruptly.

Suzanne intended to regain the ground she had lost by dominating the nursery. The smug, possessive tone of her voice
struck ugly notes on the ear of Alexa's embryonic motherhood.
It was as if being the mother of a man who had sired a child
was a kind of promotion. As if Suzanne had acquired something
by merit. She *must* be kept away.

Elizabeth pushed the eggshell-thin cup and saucer towards
Morag Anderson's large, outstretched hand.

"Please, Miss Anderson, do make the tea. Everyone says I
have absolutely no idea how to. Shall I lift the kettle for you?''
The silver kettle sat high on its spirit lamp, the figure-head of
the magnificent Georgian tea equipage spread on the folding tea-
table between the two women. A fire blazed fiercely in the marble hearth, flicking its lights on the gilded picture frames and
intensifying the rose tints of the Standevens' tastefully appointed
drawing room. One did not interview potential nannies in the
kitchen. It was important to be able to assess how they would
perform under a little social pressure.

"Oh, Mrs. Standeven, this china is quite beautiful. I do like
nice things.''

"It's Crown Derby. Derby Posy. I'm fond of it myself. Now
tell me about your last appointment, Miss Anderson. The agency
has sent your references on and they seem very satisfactory. I'd
like you to just fill the picture in a little. For example, why are
you planning to leave Mrs. Balfour's employ? She has nothing
but praise for you and her children are still very young, I gather.
She must be upset at the prospect of losing you.''

Elizabeth observed the young woman closely. She handled
the precious tea-things deftly in spite of her size. There was a
tendency for big people to be clumsy. Not to know their own
strength. This girl was enormous. Six foot, Miss White had
said, and rather sensitive about it. Can't think why. She's a fine
enough specimen. Good teeth. Not pretty, of course, but her

features were agreeable and there was a youthful comeliness
about her. Her soft Highland accent was acceptable too. Didn't
grate. The white Viyella blouse and neat tartan skirt were good
quality and suitable. Evidently she has some judgement.

"Well, you see, Mrs. Standeven, I do want to travel. When I
saw the advertisement in *The Lady*, I just had to apply. Mrs.
Balfour *is* a little upset, but she understands. I *have* been with
her three years and that's longer than most nannies stay these
days. It's not like the old days. You live so much on top of the
family that they get a bit, well," she hesitated.

"Shall we say, over-accustomed to you?" Elizabeth interrupted helpfully.

Morag Anderson smiled gratefully. "Yes, and to tell you the
truth, Mrs. Standeven, that's not one-sided either."

"I'm sure it's not. But of course, we are offering totally independent accommodation which should remove that kind of
stress, and some domestic help. You needn't be afraid of being
expected to double up as a housemaid. My daughter is very keen
that whoever is appointed should feel herself to be an important
and respected member of her household."

"That's what attracted me, Mrs. Standeven. It's a chance to
practise my profession properly in the kind of conditions that
don't often crop up these days."

"Hmm." Elizabeth watched the careful way Morag put the
kettle back on its stand. "Turn that little screw, the flames go
down. That's right. Just keep it low and the water will stay hot
for us. Tell me, Miss Anderson, what your reaction would be,
if I were to tell you that this appointment depends on the applicant's willingness to consider the position as being long-term.
We hope to avoid many changes for my grandson. The family
has a history of what might be termed delicate health, and my
daughter is fully occupied with business affairs. Some stability
is what is required. Do you, for instance, have any plans to get
married?" Not very likely at six foot, Elizabeth thought complacently. Still, you never know, nature seems to throw up partners for the most unlikely people.

"No, Mrs. Standeven. I have no plans to get married. But I
should like to one day."

"Of course, that is only natural. But can you see yourself
staying with my grandson until he is, let us say, ten?"

Morag put the exquisite cup down carefully.

"I'm afraid I couldn't be as definite as that. Ten years is a long time and someone like me doesn't find someone to marry very easily. I'll have to grasp my chance with both hands. I'm sorry if I've wasted your time."

"I wouldn't say that you have done that. There's a lot to be said for realism. Have a scone, I made them myself."

"Thank you, they look delicious." As Morag took one of the large misshapen scones between her finger and thumb, her little finger stuck out. No doubt she called it her pinkie. A good old-fashioned upbringing in a lower-middle-class family in Scotland. It was ideal. She'd do. Elizabeth watched calmly as the girl's jaws worked systematically on the scone and her expression remained politely bland. Elizabeth had never seen anything wrong with her scones. Their sensible size and sandy texture were a byword amongst her friends and family, but she herself remained blissfully unaware of it. Scones were dull by their very nature. It was the way they were. Filling.

"Miss Anderson, I understand that you cannot give us any undertaking regarding the length of your stay with us, with my daughter rather, and I must thank you for being so frank about it. I think you might suit us."

Morag's face flushed faintly with pleasure.

"Oh, that's wonderful, Mrs. Standeven."

"Hmm. Pour us another cup, would you? I like mine really strong. Now tell me, my dear, how old are you?"

"Twenty-four next week."

"And what are your hobbies? Do you have any kind of sporting activity?"

"I've done a bit of rock climbing, I can swim and I lift weights to keep fit. I like dressmaking and I can knit quite well. I always helped my parents in the garden, and I'd like to think I'll have one of my own some day. I really enjoy gardening, Mrs. Standeven. Does Madame de Pies Ombre have a garden?"

Elizabeth ignored the question, noting only the Scots girl's mispronunciation of Alexa's name.

"You pronounce the name 'Pies' as in garden *peas* and 'Ombre' almost like Umber, that brown colour in your paint box if you have one. Tell me, do you speak any French, Miss Anderson?"

"Well, I did do it at school, but I didn't pass any exams in it. I can manage a few words, but not much more." Excellent. Elizabeth's mind was busy with the various perfections of this applicant's qualifications. A rock-climbing monoglot was pre-

cisely adapted to the management of a Davis escape apparatus
and the upbringing of a little boy surrounded by the pernicious
influence of a French-speaking family. Charles was her only
grandchild so far, he must speak his grandmother's language or
he would be of limited interest.

"I don't think that matters. My daughter is English of course,
and the family all speak English fluently, so you will have no
difficulty communicating. The cook, Hortense, and the maid,
Marie, speak only French, I understand. But you'll soon pick
up enough. The family are Catholics, of course," Elizabeth
picked her way with the delicacy of a cat, "and I suppose
that . . ."

"I'm Presbyterian, but I'm not bigoted . . ." the girl spoke
anxiously.

"Splendid, splendid. That all sounds most satisfactory. Now,
you'll stay the night, won't you? You've brought your things, I
see. I would hate to think of you travelling back to Edinburgh
on a night like this. Quite impractical."

As Elizabeth ushered her recruit out of the drawing room and
up the main staircase, she turned to her and said lightly, "I want
you to feel that I am *always* available. If you feel the least puzzled about anything in France, you aren't to hesitate to get in
touch with me. You'll have a full list of contact numbers, my
address here of course, and you can write to me or telephone at
any time of day or night. Now you do understand that, don't
you?"

"Oh, yes, Mrs. Standeven. That's very reassuring."

"I would never forgive myself if I thought I'd marooned you
in a strange foreign household without any back-up. And mere
distance shouldn't prevent me from being a fully supportive
grandmother, should it? Now, here we are."

Elizabeth opened the door of the blue room. A coke fire
glowed in the Edwardian cast-iron grate and the velvet curtains
were drawn against the chill of the night. The white muslin
hangings on the half-tester bed looked feminine and fresh. It
was a standard of luxury to which Morag Anderson was almost
certainly not accustomed.

"I think you'll have everything you need here. There's a bathroom next door and you've got it to yourself. You'll find towels
in there. Do have a rest and perhaps a nice bath. There's plenty
of hot water. We eat dinner quite early when we're on our own.
Half-past seven. You've plenty of time, so just relax. And you

will remember what I said, won't you? When you get to France, you can call on me at any time, for anything."

"Yes, I won't forget. And thank you. For everything." Morag gestured round the room. "This is like a film."

Elizabeth smiled to herself as she made her way down the stairs. That would do perfectly. A nice girl, an honest girl and just sufficiently intelligent. She would telephone Alexa immediately.

Tilly clasped her jewelled hands together in admiration, looking round the spacious, slant-ceilinged day-nursery.

"It's divine, Alexa!" Her Frenchwoman's eye calculated the cost of the room's decoration and every carefully chosen item. The March light shouldered its way in at the dormer windows and slid a knife of brightness through the tiny lancet slit in the pepper-pot turret in the corner, illuminating the flower-strewn meadow of carpet. It had been specially woven by a small Brussels firm. The walls and recesses were cunningly lined with glass-fronted cupboards to hold games, toys and books. Already there were building-blocks and soft toys, marshalled for the amusement of Charles Philippe Alexandre de Pies Ombre. Tilly's hand rested for a moment on the shining leather saddle of the dapple-grey rocking horse. It oscillated silently, the light glinting in its long silky mane. Where had Alexa got the money? The Standevens probably, they'd be sure to look after their own grandchild. The slopes and planes of the ceiling had been transformed into a glorious canopy of blue sky, populated with fluffy, pink-tinged summer clouds which dipped down, here and there, onto the walls and cupboards. There were no curtains, only painted shutters; innocently white when open, but closed, they revealed paintings of wild animals, foxes, rabbits, birds and badgers, sleeping in their lairs, nests and sets, in peace and innocence.

"For once," said Tilly, "Suzanne is perfectly correct. You must trust me in this. Remember, I have always been on your side. The advice I give is sound. *Chère* Alexa, this is something about which you know nothing."

"But Tilly, I don't like him." Alexa slumped crossly into the spindle-backed American rocker which Ariel had seized upon in a Greenwich Village antique shop. Her hands gripped its age-polished arms irritably.

"Don't sit down, Alexa, you'll crease your dress," Tilly said automatically, absently. "Liking has nothing to do with the choice of godparents. When you select a grape variety for your vineyard, you don't choose them because you like the *taste* of them, do you? Still less the look of them. Dear me, no. All that counts is the probable flavour and quality of the future wine—and its value, of course.''

Sighing, Alexa rose obediently, glancing behind at her skirt. She wandered towards the place where the de Pies Ombres' christening gown had been laid out in readiness on the table. She fingered the elaborate confection of antique lace and satin. It was gossamer-thin with age and repeated launderings. She frowned slightly. Why, of all the men in the world, did they have to pick Père Lachasse as godfather? Of course it was Fabrice's privilege to select a godfather for their child, but why Lachasse? They both despised the oily, bullying little bigot in his silly old-fashioned biretta. So *why*?

Tilly was almost exasperated with her. Alexa was so clever, so energetic and resourceful, but she did have this tiresome blind spot. She was quite clever enough to know she was on ground that was mined with other people's emotions but she persisted in wilfully stamping as if she wanted an explosion to occur.

"Look, Alexa, a powerful friend in the Church is always useful. At one time we always tried to have a Bishop in the family. Unfortunately, younger sons are not so biddable as they were when it comes to a choice of career. Let me see now,'' she did some calculations on her fingers. "The last one must have died in 1910. And he got Marguerite de Pies Ombre out of a perfectly frightful marriage. So you see, one cannot always quite foresee the reason, but let me assure you, it is an area of influence not to be neglected."

Tilly had not long since forgotten that she was Suzanne's cousin and not a de Pies Ombre by birth *or* marriage. She had adopted not only the noble family for the sake of the social cachet she believed it gave her, but its whole history too.

"Lachasse is powerful?"

"No, not at the moment, perhaps. But by the time his godson is grown up, he almost certainly will be. His promotion is virtually guaranteed. The Church, you know, is a career like any other. Not every priest is a selfless saint, in fact, very few are. Lachasse is ambitious. He comes from a large family, many of whom are priests and nuns. You could say it is the family occupation of the Lachasse tribe. They keep a few on one side for breeding purposes, but the rest, and probably the best, go into the Church. He has an uncle who is a cardinal in the *Curia* and two cousins in the *Rota*. Friends in Rome, Alexa. It could be *useful*.''

"How?'' Alexa sat down again defiantly. She was impatient with the discussion and hadn't really been listening for once.

"Well, for instance—getting a divorce.'' Tilly stroked the brim of her velours hat. Its lemon colour was glorious in itself but unbecoming to the elegant old woman's battle-hardened features. She was surveying the room with the desperation of one who seeks a looking-glass and is frustrated.

"I thought it wasn't allowed.''

"It isn't, unless it's called something else. An annulment is allowed. It depends on knowing the right people, quite frankly. Knowing intelligent, influential people who can think flexibly. It's the only way a Catholic can put an end to an unhappy marriage, marry again and stay inside the Church. I told you about Marguerite, didn't I? Her cousin, the Bishop, got her out of the marriage and then some competent lawyer got her money out of the clutches of her husband's family. That's just one example.''

Alexa shrugged. "Frankly, I'd rather have had the lawyer for a cousin.''

"Ah well, *ma chère*, you are biased, and understandably,'' said Tilly, patiently, determined to keep her temper. "I think your father would understand our reasoning though, given the circumstances. Dear Mr. Standeven, such a *subtle* man. It is such a pleasure to see him again. And I'm sure you must be glad to see your parents here at last, whatever the occasion. Do cheer up, Alexa. And think of poor Héloïse. It's a great occasion for *her*. A little nephew being received into the Church. You couldn't spoil it for her by sulking, now could you? I wonder what she'll wear? I shall die of embarrassment if she wears that appalling pink suit again. What a scarecrow she makes of herself. Whatever will Mr. Standeven think?''

"Nothing at all, I imagine. He hardly ever looks at women.'' Tilly bridled, offended. "A daughter is hardly the best judge of such matters.''

"Well I think it's a pity Fabrice couldn't come up with someone a bit more normal. Of all the people he ought to know, I think it's absurd. And it's hard on me expecting me to be civil to that revolting creature. He was barely civil to me you know at the end of our wedding. He actually treated me as if I were a leper. Always talking about *mixed marriages*, as if I were some undesirable *parti* who'd bought or blackmailed her way into a respectable family.''

Tilly decided to let it pass. Alexa was rarely moody and she had some sympathy for her resentment. But there were some things she would have to live with, even if she could never understand them.

"Talking of Fabrice, how is he?'' Tilly was peering into a tiny handbag mirror, twisting her head this way and that, her lips pursed, in what she had been told in her youth was a seductive pout. "He doesn't seem very cheerful to me. I can't think why, he's got everything he could want now.''

"Who knows what he wants. He's Fabrice. Up and down, drunk and sober. Difficult to say anything about him. What's true one minute is untrue the next. He is like the weather. A variable factor that affects one, but a factor one is powerless to affect. I've learned to live with the idea that he doesn't love me, or only sporadically.''

Alexa rose from the chair again and paced up and down the room restlessly. Since the baby's birth, to her hurt and surprise, she and Fabrice had drifted still further apart. To please Héloïse, Alexa had made every effort to fill in the cracks in their relationship and to soften, or disguise, her increasing influence in the *chais*. It wasn't easy, the men came naturally to her now with problems and queries. Suppliers and their representatives from fertiliser companies, machinery distributors and others asked for her by name. With a discretion she had learned the hard way, Alexa would direct all these people to Fabrice's office and as often as not, they would come back, saying *Monsieur* would prefer *Madame* to deal with the matter.

It was embarrassing, and eventually, after a bentonite salesman had fled from Fabrice's office, leaving the building without speaking to anyone, Alexa gave up the pretence. She had found Fabrice sprawled in the chair behind his desk, his features slack and his eyes flat. He was clearly very, very drunk. A tumbler was lying on its side near his elbow, and liquid was dripping into his lap. Even Alexa had known it was pointless to speak. She sent for David, and together, they had got him back to the house and in through the kitchen courtyard. Fabrice had cursed incoherently but Alexa and David had said nothing to each other.

"Come, come. I shall be thinking you're suffering from a classic case of post-natal depression. Of course he loves you.

He married you, didn't he?'' Tilly's voice broke through the memory of that awful afternoon. She was still busy with the mirror. She had given up the pout, and stretching her lips over her teeth in a wide grimace applied a red lipstick with slick precision, accentuating the bow of her upper lip.

"I sometimes have the feeling he was more or less *instructed* to marry me, you know." Alexa looked at Tilly, who flushed slightly and turned quickly as she heard a door open.

Morag Anderson came in from the adjoining night nursery, neat and efficient in her Norland Nurse's pale-brown uniform. The baby in her arms was alert, round brown eyes taking in his surroundings with the unwinking stare of a newly woken infant. Morag stroked the soft down on his delicate skull gently as he began to struggle and whimper.

"Ah, Nanny. My great-nephew. And how is he?"

"A wee bit fashed, Madam. I had to hurry his bottle, but he'll soon settle if I can get his wind up."

"Here, let me, Nanny. Come to your Tante Tilly, little precious . . .'' Tilly stretched out her arms, the yellow barathea of her sleeves rode up to reveal great cruel-looking gold bracelets, studded with gems. Alexa caught Morag's horrified glance.

"I wouldn't, Tilly," Alexa warned drily, seeing the uncertain look on Morag's face. "He's perfectly capable of spewing up all over your beautiful dress, the smell is incredible.''

"Oh, well, I expect you're right. Another time, precious, when we're not all *en tenue*.'' The jewelled hands were dropped hurriedly.

Charles Philippe Alexandre de Pies Ombre mewled bad-temperedly in Morag's strong arms. He clearly was not going to act like a model baptismal candidate. Alexa silently thanked God she would not have to hold the squirming infant during what promised to be an alarmingly long ceremony. The young Comtesse de Bouverie de Rivière would have that doubtful pleasure. She had been roped in by Suzanne as Alexa had no Catholic acquaintance of her own generation.

Alexa wished heartily that they would leave her out of the whole thing. She had no interest in these arcane rites and no influence on their performance. For once, the de Pies Ombres held all the cards and were acting in concert to her exclusion. It didn't matter. A christening was no very great matter. It would be over soon and then she would resume command.

* * *

It was a relief to get away from the reception in the *Grand Salon*. The baptismal ceremony had been long and gloomy. Anyone would think that they had just witnessed an exorcism instead of a christening. As if poor little Charles was a time-bomb packed with sin and vice. That was what Elizabeth had said to her daughter and Alexa agreed wholeheartedly with her mother.

"Well, it's their day. It can't harm Charles and the worst it can do is annoy us. Normally, the boot is on the other foot. Have some more champagne, Mummy, and forget about it. They've had their baptism and we've got the baby."

"Ssh. Alexa! You're a very naughty girl. You must have had too much to drink. No, I won't have any more, darling, and I don't think you should. You've had two glasses already."

"And I'll have another two if I want. I'm grown-up now." It was essential to keep the mood light. Elizabeth and Alexander were not to be worried. She had made them suffer enough. They must be shielded from the consequences of her actions. She felt tenderly towards her parents, now that she too had a child. They had wanted to protect her and now she would protect them.

"Yes, you are grown-up, aren't you. Quite different." Elizabeth looked appraisingly at her daughter. She seemed very much in command of things here. Morag Anderson's reports were breathless with admiration.

"Who is that man over there, Alexa?" Elizabeth would never do anything so rude as to point a finger, or as common as to jerk her head in the direction of the object of her curiosity, but Alexa knew at once to whom her mother referred.

She glanced towards the other side of the room where Richard Lockwood stood talking to Madame Terry. It was kind of him to be attentive to the *couturier*'s wife. Poor Madame Terry was out of her element, shy and oddly dowdy in her fashionable hat and military-style coat. It was hard to believe that her husband had made those clothes. In all probability he had not, he had never been able to persuade his wife to take fashion seriously. She was the living proof that opposites attract. While Monsieur Terry slipped beamingly about the room, joining group after group, but always returning at intervals to her, Madame Terry was grateful for the protection of this handsome man's incomprehensible discourse on the Paris *Bourse*. She looked up at him, hardly hearing the words he spoke but charmed by the strange emphasis he gave to the French language. Richard concentrated on her fiercely, anxious that she should not fear that his attention was focused elsewhere. Alexa was glad to have her most vulnerable guest so kindly taken care of, but she responded to her mother's question coolly.

"Oh, his name's Lockwood. He's a banker. I met him when he came to stay here last summer with some clients of his. I didn't actually invite him. He came with that girl there, Ariel. Her husband had a smart clinic in New York."

"Is he the one who brought the two kittens?"

"Yes. Extraordinarily beautiful. But what an odd christening present, don't you think?"

"Shows some imagination. A lot more use than silver cups and sugar-coated almonds. Animals are good for children." Mrs. Standeven selected a caviare canapé from the salver which rested nearest to her.

"He's all right, a bit pushy."

"Very good-looking."

"Mummy! I didn't think you thought about these things!"

"All normal women think about these things from time to time. I think your Mr. Lockwood looks a splendid fellow."

"Well, he's very old."

"Don't be silly, Alexa. He's thirty-eightish, forty at the most."

"Twenty years older than me is old if we're talking about looks."

Alexa glanced back at him. He had moved away from Madame Terry who had been rejoined by her husband, who had taken her arm and was leading her reluctant steps towards a chattering group. Richard had fallen into conversation with Tim Bowring. He felt her eyes touch him, and glanced in her direction with a quick smile.

His coming had been a surprise. She had invited him, but only in an oblique way, saying to Ariel that if Richard cared to come, she might bring him if it suited her. As it happened, it had suited her very well as business kept Lionel in New York and Ariel would prefer to have a face she knew with her at the de Pies Ombre christening. Alexa would obviously be very much occupied with family guests.

The kittens were enchanting. She had been a little unnerved to see the figure of Richard Lockwood descend from the same car as Ariel, but when she saw the contents of the basket he carried, her self-consciousness melted in the excitement of their beauty.

"Oh how exquisite! Are they something special?"

"Well yes, they're called British Blues and they're my christening present to the baby. They slept most of the way over but they had a meal on the hop from Paris, so they'll be fine for a few hours."

Alexa had looked at him with surprise. It was clear that he liked animals. It was the last thing she would have thought about him. The knowledge spread ripples in her mind. The pansy faces of the smoke-blue kittens looked up at her, their yellow eyes confident and unblinking.

"How clever of you, Richard. I'm sure my son will love them and enjoy them for years to come. I know I shall. We'll take very great care of them. Look, Morag. Look at these wonderful baby creatures. They're for the nursery."

Morag Anderson exclaimed over the kittens and asked Richard all sorts of questions about their diet and care which he answered naturally and with good humour. Alexa watched him. He seemed a different man. In fact Richard was relieved at the warmth of the reception of his gift. Never sure-footed when it came to the art of pleasing, he had begun to be afraid, halfway across the Atlantic, that his originality might prove a nuisance to Alexa and do nothing to increase his popularity with her.

As Morag bore the kittens away to establish them in their new home, Alexa spoke again to Richard.

"I really didn't expect you to come all this way for a christening."

"I wanted to see you were all right."

"Of course, I'm all right."

"And I saw those chaps and I just wanted to bring them to you and the baby." There were so many things he wanted to bring her, and so many things he wanted to say, but it was safer to stick to proven ground.

"I must tell Hortense that we have another house guest. You see, I really didn't think you'd come. I thought you'd be far too busy."

"Well the busyness of bankers is a bit of a myth. Meetings can always be rescheduled. But there's no need to put me up. I've a meeting in London tomorrow. This trip just fitted in nicely."

"Oh, I see." Alexa felt oddly deflated.

Elizabeth's voice recalled her to the present moment.

"Your father is sick to death of that La Courbe woman. Go and rescue him. I think he'd like to look round the sharp end of operations here. Can't you show him some wine or vines or something?''

Alexa smiled at her mother and walked across the room to where Tilly was flirting abortively with Alexander. His face wore an expression of mild martyrdom, his navy eyes narrowed to let in the minimum visual impression of the gabbling woman. He was not listening but nodded gravely from time to time, allowing the corners of his mouth to curve both upwards and downwards at irregular intervals. It was a technique he had perfected over the years. He could appear to be participating in conversations of which he had actually heard not one word. He had acquired a wholly undeserved reputation for being a good listener and a man of considerable charm. He saw Alexa approach from the corner of his eye.

It was almost a shock to see how much she had changed. When she had last been in Yorkshire several months ago, the impact had been similar. But then her subdued anger and advancing pregnancy had dimmed the stunning effect of her dawning maturity. She walked like a queen. But it was not just her appearance. There was an aura of certainty about her, a quality of absoluteness that belonged to all leaders.

"Madame La Courbe has been telling me so many things . . . ."

Alexa knew perfectly well he would have no idea what things Tilly had been telling him and so she responded to the cue.

"Oh Tilly, how sweet of you to look after Daddy. Shall I take him over now, I haven't seen him for ages and we have so much to talk about.'' She trotted out the conventional phrases, amusement dancing in her blue eyes.

Tilly looked suspiciously from father to daughter. Alexa never gushed and Alexander was not the sort of man to be mothered by his daughter. You could never get the better of these Standevens. Tilly sighed resignedly. Perhaps the new lemon hat was not her colour.

But Alexander professed himself to be too tired for a tour of the *chais*, preferring to see them the following day when the men would be back at work.

"I had rather hoped you might show them to me.'' Richard Lockwood spoke. Alexa spun round. He had been standing directly behind her. She was trapped, she could hardly refuse without embarrassing everyone, and yet she felt a little spurt of apprehension at the thought of being alone with this man.

"But of course, if you would like it. I'm afraid you may be

bored, it's all rather technical.'' Richard's expression was serious.

"I will do my best to follow. Understanding other people's business is *my* business, you know. You can't put your money into something you don't know about. Wouldn't you agree, sir?'' He addressed Alexander who observed him dispassionately.

"I wouldn't have said so, no. Alexa, I don't believe . . .''

"Oh Daddy, this is Mr. Lockwood from New York. He came here a few months ago with some clients of his.''

"I see,'' replied Alexander easily. "Well why don't you show Mr. Lockwood what he wants to see, Alexa, since he is so eager to be informed.''

They walked out of the front door of the château. The vines were all pruned now, a single pair of arms or *guyots* apiece, tied into the trellises. Soon the buds would burst and the whole cycle of life begin again. The orderly rows of miniature crucifixions, like the logical slaughter of some crazed despot of classic times, stretched away from the house on every side.

"Who was that woman in yellow talking to your father just now?''

"Oh that was my mother-in-law's cousin, Madame La Courbe. Aunt Tilly we call her. She's nice but terribly wrapped up in clothes and funny little power games of her own.''

"She talks too much. Your father looked as though he was about to pass out.'' Alexa smiled.

"I don't think he'd be too pleased to hear you say that! He believed he looked riveted. And really, I'm sure most people would have thought he was fascinated, so you must be exceptionally observant.''

"Well, I think Madame La Courbe thought she had his full attention, so that's all right. She could have knifed you when you came up and interrupted them.''

"I don't think so. Tilly and I have always been good friends.''

Richard eyed her covertly. There are some things she did not notice, perhaps wilfully. Or was it that she was too young to imagine that anyone her father's age could be attractive to women?

She shivered slightly in the chill of the March afternoon. The skirt of her fine woollen dress whipped around her legs in the stiff breeze. The old mac which she had slung round her shoulders in the hall before they left the house fell to the ground. Richard stooped to replace it for her.

"Things seem to be going well around here, now," he ventured.

"What makes you think they weren't before?"

Ah yes, be careful. Presume nothing and lay claim to no information she has not authorised you to have. He began again, more circumspectly.

"Everyone I have spoken to tells me what vast improvements you have made here. Your agent—Chirac, isn't it?—and quite a few other people." Mollified, she put her head on one side thoughtfully.

"Well," she replied slowly, "the house itself is coming together gradually. There's more to be done on the redecoration front, of course, but the most urgent repairs have been done. The surveyor says the structure's sound, thank God."

"That fellow Chirac says you're going to pull the vineyards round." Richard looked speculatively at her. She laughed.

"I think that's more of a bet than a prognosis. I've got a plan. Whether or not it'll work, and whether there's time for it to work, that's a different matter."

"Hmm. He seems to have confidence in you, based on what, of course, I don't know."

"Based on the fact that he's a middle-aged Frenchman and I'm a passably good-looking young woman. And a Frenchman will go soft on a well-groomed tram smash, just as long as it's a female tram smash, you know."

"You do yourself an injustice. He says your grasp of the wine business is remarkable considering how brief a time it is since you knew nothing at all about it. I think it's very commendable."

"I'm glad you approve."

"And I'm glad that you're glad." His voice was low and thick. Alexa did not know what to say in reply and pretended not to hear. Something in his tone had pinged at her nerve ends. He disturbed her. And now he was becoming unpredictable. If he was flirting with her, he was doing so in the most depressing way. If he was making an out and out sexual play for her then he ought to have his face slapped and hard. But she could not assume that. She shook her head slightly to clear it of the confusing and unwelcome thoughts.

Alexa was holding the key to the small building which housed the offices and communicated with the *cuverie*. As she turned the key in the lock, a clattering and chattering in the air caused them both to look up. "Those are our magpies. The first bit of our family name comes from them and it's Fabrice's crest. A magpie with a golden coronet around its neck."

"So I noticed." Richard watched the handsome pair of black and white birds dashing about overhead, busying themselves with domestic matters in the group of ancient Spanish chestnut trees which stood to the rear of the house and shaded the court-yard when in leaf.

"Two for sorrow," he murmured under his breath, "isn't that what they say?"

Inside, the comfortless office was cold. The stove had gone out and not been relit. There would be no work done in the *chais* that day. The day on which the heir was baptised was a holiday and accepted as such, even in modern republican France.

Richard looked about him with interest tempered by distaste. He sat down on Fabrice's chair after examining it closely, touching his finger tips to the seat. He detested dirt and disorder. Its squalor was deepened by Alexa's own exquisite neatness. He watched her move around the room, the pale cream of her wool voile skirt moving easily and naturally with her lithe movements and her blonde hair gathered into a smooth chignon by a black velvet ribbon. He watched her small, pink-tipped hands handle some papers, and he winced with displeasure as he felt the dry film of dust irritate the nerve ends of his own fingers.

"You ought to get someone to clean this place up for you, Alexa, the dust can't be good for you."

"This is my husband's office."

"Ah," he said softly. The single statement that the apartment they now sat in belonged to Fabrice de Pies Ombre told him a good deal. Firstly that the *Marquis* was a slob, secondly that his wife was too impatient or resentful to clean up after him and thirdly, that, as yet, there was not enough money to pay some-body else to do it.

"Would you like to see the *chais* and the *cuverie*?"

"Yes, I would, very much. And, Alexa," he put his hand on her elbow, "I do appreciate this." She looked at him, puzzled. He was making a great deal of nothing.

"It's nothing, Richard. I'm happy to show you."

They walked out into the corridor and through the door which communicated directly with the *cuverie*. It was a little warmer than the office despite its far greater size.

"There's no wine in those vats now, just a cleaning solution.

It's where the grapes are put to ferment at first when they've been crushed. The skins are still in with them, of course. They're open at the top—you can't see from here, but a sort of double valve system keeps mixing in the skins with the juice, otherwise they'd just float on top.'' Alexa looked at her companion. His face remained impassive. He wanted her to continue with her presentation.

''If the *chapeau*, as they call it, stays on top it can lose contact with the must itself, so it doesn't take enough colour. You get a layer of carbon dioxide which is all right as long as you don't trap air and bacteria as well. That can spoil the wine. If we had stainless steel, sealed tanks, there would be no risk.''

''Hmm, and then what happens?'' He watched the glow of animation and intelligence suffuse her features. She had almost forgotten him. It was as if she spoke to herself with a concentration that was total. Her eyes seemed suddenly larger and darker as the pupils dilated in the gloom. A single dark lash had fallen onto the curve of her cheek. Richard could not take his eyes off it, he itched to remove it, to touch her.

''Well, when the wine has got enough red from the skins— whether fermentation has finished or not—it's pumped out of those vats and into the press here. The wine that runs free is the best—comes out easily, of its own accord—and it goes into one or two of these concrete, sealed tanks to finish fermenting if need be, or to wait until the second fermentation starts. Then the same with the rest, the wine we have to press the skins harder to get, the *vin de presse* as they call it, that's kept separate, it has more tannin in it. It can be used for topping up the rest, according to taste, so to speak. Unfortunately, we don't have a second wine here, so it's a case of either wasting some of the *vin de presse*, or shovelling it all into the main brew, whether or not it's a good idea. Not so hot, for an allegedly up-market wine, is it?''

She turned to face him. She was only a little shorter than him. His eyes rested on her shoulders, he could feel their delicate bones under the pressure of his palms, but his hands remained by his sides. He could imagine the feel of her skin if his thumbs were to rest at the base of her neck, the spring in the escaped tendrils of hair that curled around her ear lobes. He remained quite still.

''I see.''

''What I'm telling you is in confidence, of course. Naturally, other proprietors always know something about what goes on on rival properties, and then there's the whole world of wine writers and so forth. But I don't want to disseminate any negative reports myself, do I?''

"I'm used to keeping my mouth shut. I think you can rely on me.''

"Good." She nodded seriously and Richard kept a straight face with difficulty. It wasn't that she was absurd, far from it. But her solemnity induced a wave of tenderness in him. It was the same sensation that came over him when watching very young animals go purposefully about their work of survival.

"When the wine ferments a second time, usually of its own accord, it's called the malo-lactic fermentation." Richard's mouth quirked imperceptibly. It was difficult to know whether she was powerful or vulnerable in her new-found knowledge. She was so charmingly didactic. Never could so lovely a child have so resolutely put play aside. But she was not a child and he must guard against thinking of her as such. She was a wife and mother, a businesswoman with fast developing acumen and, of course, a titled lady of France. He had the feeling, that although she was modest about it, it was something she would not like to give up.

"Malic acid converts to lactic acid," she continued. "Apparently it's a good thing because it makes the prolonged bottle aging process possible. Essential for claret. Mind you, I'm a bit cynical about all this aging mystique. I wonder if we wouldn't do better to find a formula for making a wine that grows up a bit faster, so we can sell more of it, more often. Wouldn't that be better, don't you think?'' She paused, her head on one side, apparently awaiting some comment from him, but he made none.

"Anyway, our last lot finished the second fermentation last week, and I'm nervous of it standing around on the lees too long. Monsieur Chirac says it'll be all right for another few days and then he'll come and fetch it away in tankers.''

"Ah, yes, that's right. You're not declaring a vintage this year. Your idea, I'm told.''

"Yes.''

"Very sound. If you can't make a top product don't palm it off on the buyers as if you could. The day you say Château de Pies Ombre is back in business, the more likely they are to believe you.''

"That's what I thought. Well guessed.''

"Quite." His mind had strayed again from her words. Her nearness was half intoxication and half torment. Her essence swirled around him like a disorientating fog, misting his vision, distancing the clear bell of her voice and disturbing his balance so that he felt drunk. He strove to regain command of himself, if he could only speak, hear the sound of his own normal voice, the world would stop spinning.

"What do you think of these wooden vats, then?" Richard tilted his head back, to look up to the top of the vast structures. He clung to the banality of dutiful questioning, like a schoolboy who is anxious to show that he has been paying attention.

"Well, they're very traditional, of course, but they're hard to control. If the initial fermentation starts too fast at too high a temperature, the wine gets a *stewed* taste, like tea that's been standing around too long."

"I doubt if I'd know the difference quite honestly. I just rely on the price of a product to tell me it it's any good or not. If it costs a bomb, chances are it's okay, if not, it's probably not up to much."

"Richard, how *common*!" He grinned cheerfully, relieved to have recovered his equilibrium, "Well, I don't think I've got what you'd call an educated palate. Anyway, what's the cure for stewed wine?"

She began to tell him about possible treatments and more about the disadvantages of wood, the cleaning difficulties, the cooling problems, the loss by leakage and other things. He listened, enchanted by the seriousness of her discourse, the fullness of her knowledge and the clear music of her voice. He was awed by the sheer power of her mind and energy, it was a furnace enclosed inside a skull of supreme elegance, showing its blue-flame power in her eyes. "So you see," Alexa concluded her lecture, "wooden vats leave a lot to be desired."

"What would you replace them with?"

"Oh, stainless steel, every time. But that's a long way off, I'm afraid."

They walked away into the cold caverns where wine was stored in barrels, Alexa shivered at the abrupt change in temperature. Without a word, Richard took off his jacket and offered it to her. Alexa took it with casual gratitude and he was glad that something of his would embrace the body he so longed to crush with his arms.

* * *

Alexa sat with her father in the turret room. He had admired her sanctum sincerely. The garden below attracted his notice, however, and about that he had not been so pleased.

"That lets the whole property down, you must do something about it."

"I've no spare hands for gardening; when I have, I *will* do something about it. In the meantime, every penny we have has to be spent on the land and equipment, as well as the house of course."

"Well," Alexander thrust his hands deep into his trouser pockets and leaned back on his heels as he sometimes did when he was about to make an announcement. His mouth was fighting to be allowed to smile, but he kept it under control. "I think I should like to give my grandson the stainless-steel vats as a christening present. Say three."

"Oh, Daddy, they're very expensive . . ."

"I'll worry about that. You just keep learning all you can and putting it into practice as soon as you can. Have you any wine aging in the cask at the moment?"

Alexa made a face. "Stacks, for all the good it'll do."

"Why do you say that?"

"Well, I bet the wine was stewed in the first place, or the harvest was too early or too late, or it got a bacterial taint, or something. Even if it was perfect, there are no new oak barrels, so the flavour is going to miss something, isn't it? I'm saving up for new oak barrels at the moment. I have a special fund for it."

"Hmm, well, a birthday present perhaps, we'll see. Let's get through this next year first and see how things go."

"Don't do too much here, Daddy. I couldn't let you spend all this money without telling you how dicey things are. It really is hand to mouth. You know the vineyard isn't paying its way. Fabrice couldn't even pay the wages now if I didn't subsidise them from the house."

"I'm aware of all that, Alexa. I can assure you, I've no intention of *investing* in any serious sense for a long while yet, if ever. No, I have to keep my powder dry. I'm bound to say, dear, whilst I don't decry your efforts here, it could well be too little and too late. I'm holding myself in readiness for the day you and my grandson turn up on the doorstep at Langstroth Grange seeking the support of your aged parents. And very welcome you will be, of course." Alexa bit her lip. He was a master of the small compliment, buried beneath the avalanche of politely phrased insults. He would never change. Caution was always allowed to obscure his generosity.

"I liked that Lockwood fellow, incidentally. Sound, very sound."

Alexa shrugged. "He's all right. He's looking after a bit of money for me."

Alexander arched his eyebrows. "That's very wise of you, darling. I shouldn't be in a hurry to take it away from him, if I were you. I think that young fellow knows what he's about. He seems to have taken rather a shine to you." Alexander regarded his daughter quizzically, his left eyebrow lifted.

"Oh, I don't think so. And I'd hardly call him *young*, he's a lot nearer your age than mine. Our paths just happened to cross, that's all. He may be a bit lonely. He really is rather dull."

"I bet all his bills are paid. You might find that a more attractive quality in a man as you grow older."

"All *our* bills will be paid eventually. And then perhaps Fabrice will cheer up a bit and be as marvellous as he can be."

"Ah, how *is* your husband? I don't seem to have spoken to him much."

"He seems very happy about the baby."

"Don't you *know* how he feels? When you were born, I could hardly bear to have your mother out of my sight."

Alexa knew better than to falter. A thousand skirmishes with her father had taught her that he would pounce on any hesitation as proof that her next statement was contrived, if not falsehood. Now she had lost any reason or desire to hide anything from her parents, she found she must. They had a right to some peace now and she could not burden them with the facts of her relationship with the husband they had begged her not to marry. Her reticence was also born of the knowledge that a child's cry sits ill in the mouth of one who has declared herself adult and encouraged others to rely on the truth of it. Her father could not help.

"Fabrice is a very complex personality, Daddy." She heard the tell-tale defensive note in her own voice. "Full of surprises. One just doesn't get to know him all at once."

"Doesn't one? I might have hoped your understanding of him had increased somewhat. My own interest is limited to how well he is treating you, and if he is supporting you. I gather, however, that it is *you* who are supporting *him*. Everyone I speak to here seems to regard this as a notable triumph. It strikes me differently, I must confess. It strikes me as most unsatisfactory. In fact, I think it's shameful." Alexander looked at her challengingly, his jaw jutting pugnaciously. Alexa had seen it all before. His routine for eliciting information that he felt certain was being wilfully withheld rarely varied.

"Fabrice is a good husband in many ways, Daddy. But he's no businessman. But he's very good with my American guests, you know. He always turns up on time and talks to them . . ."

"Your loyalty does you credit. But if the skills of a geisha girl are a significant advantage in a husband, then I must concede he appears to possess them in some degree. But I would have thought that the first duty of a husband is to support his wife, by the labour of his own hands, if need be."

"Not every marriage is the same, Daddy."

"Well, they ought to be the same in certain bare essentials, otherwise how do we define a marriage?"

"Daddy, please don't let's argue."

"We're not arguing, Alexa. I never argue." The fact that Alexander spent his whole life arguing, devising arguments and projecting them, subtracted nothing from his oft-pronounced belief that he never argued. Alexa concealed a smile. The most infuriating characteristics of a parent become endearing foibles when they are no longer a daily irritant.

Awkwardly, Alexander put his arm around his daughter. "It's you I'm worried about, and now there's the baby. Everything seems to be on your shoulders and I wish I could lift it off. But this is what you chose, darling. Believe me, I wish you every success. I just hope you're strong enough."

"Of course, I am, Daddy. I'll be fine. And so will Fabrice."

"The baby came through all right, then?"

"Seems so."

"Quite."

"Wouldn't Grandad have been pleased? His great-grandson, a future *Marquis*, that *would* have been something to trail his coat about at the Club. It doesn't mean much to you, though, does it?"

"Not a thing. As long as he's healthy, that's the main thing. Of course, I shan't really be easy in my mind until I know he's as clever and brave as his mother." With that unaccustomed and illogical compliment, Alexander signalled the end of the discussion.

Outside, the magpies flapped around the roofs of the château, engrossed in some problem of nest renovation. Alexander had fallen silent. He watched them outside the oriel window.

"Have they any fledglings yet?"

"No, I don't think so. Not yet. Why do you ask?"

"What do they say? One for sorrow, two for a boy and three for joy. I've probably got it all the wrong way round. Anyway, let's hope it adds up to joy in the end."

PART THREE

CHAPTER
16

⅏ ⅏ "LOOK MUMMY! WE'RE on top of the clouds! It's like a huge, lumpy white eiderdown, going on and on. I'd like to bounce on it, but I'd go through, wouldn't I?" Charles stood excitedly in the space between the seat in front and Morag's knees. "I expect so, yes, darling," Alexa replied without looking up from her papers.

"Mummy's busy, sweetheart."

Charles turned complainingly to Morag Anderson. She had the answer to everything, well almost. "Mummy's always busy. Other people speak to her when she's busy. Why can't I?" Like all intelligent children, he saw the possibilities in playing one adult off against another but with rare exceptions, when the lines of communication between his mother and his nanny had temporarily become confused, he never succeeded.

"Let's play dominoes, shall we?" Morag reached into the soft leather bag at her feet. It was old. The same one that Alexa had had with her at Orly airport, the day she had decided not to go back to England. Morag rooted amongst its contents unaware. Alexa's eyes slid towards it. It's the little things that never change. An old travelling bag. Something you never think about, and yet it's there, when friends, and hopes and dreams are gone, for ever. She shuddered at herself a little. Her life was what she had made it. There was no room for ephemeral dreams and hope was confined to the vintage. Château d'Ombre, the house, and Château de Pies Ombre, the wine. That was all that mattered, and Charles, of course.

"And other people always say *'Ssh Mummy's busy,'* but *Mummy* always says *'Ssh Mummy's thinking!'* " Charles' brown eyes sparkled with mischief. "Doesn't her brain ever hurt?"

"There's no difference, Charles. Thinking is busy and busy is thinking. And yes, sometimes my brain does *kind* of hurt, but not in the way you think. You'll understand what I mean when you're older." Alexa was crisp. She never talked down to her son. It wasn't a matter of high-minded nursery policy, she didn't know how to talk down to another human being. Sometimes Charles would gaze at her with a child's unconcealable hurt, when she crawled about the nursery floor with the blue cats. With Quink and Waterman she would abandon herself to a sea of silly endearments and passionately expressed affection. It shocked Morag to the core. "Mummy's little flower faces," she crooned to them. "Aren't I your flower face, Mummy?" "No, you are a little boy," she had replied once with totally unconscious brutality. Charles' face had crumpled tragically. "Don't cry, darling," Alexa was bewildered. The cats *did* have flower faces, they were like two blue dahlias. Did Charles want to look like a flower? Really, children were so heart-rendingly unreasonable. "Anyway, they're *my* cats, Richard Lockwood gave them to me," Charles had bravely gone on the offensive. And now she was going to see Richard again, after six years. Would he help?

She returned her attention to the cash flow projection she had been poring over. *Cash flow projection*, Alexa turned the phrase over in her mind. Wasn't it just another way of saying "If wishes were horses, beggars might ride?" What banker would want to lend on a wish? On the fringes of her mind she heard Charles begin to object to yet another game of dominoes. He was being difficult.

"It's all right, Morag. I'll have finished in just a moment and then we can talk."

She put the papers away in her briefcase. It might work, it might not. If not she'd just have to consider using her own money. It was a lot to risk. Not a lot of money really, but all she had of her own. Ombre was back on its feet again and making a wine to be proud of. It was gaining an increasing reputation and fetching higher and higher prices. Every year there had been new investment. The achievements, modest at first, had been steadily built on year by year until Château d'Ombre could almost, tremulously at least, hold up its head as one of the world's great wines.

Its essential underlying character was unchanged. Alexa had moderated her early enthusiasm for an *encépagement* in which the *Merlot* grape featured more strongly than any other. That was something she would reserve for her own wine, when it happened, if it ever did. No, the staying power of the *Cabernet Sauvignon* was one of the things that lovers of high-quality claret were prepared to pay for. That had to be borne in mind.

Without any sense of conscious preciousness, Alexa began to think about the wine that now obsessed her mind. The words used by others to describe it had at first seemed pretentious, an absurd posturing, and she had felt embarrassed to speak of the product of Château d'Ombre in such terms. Eventually, she realised that if she did not, then she would remain dumb. The affected expressions and descriptions were no more than the everyday working vocabulary of the wine trade. Without that vocabulary, her wine could not be promoted to the people who counted, and so, getting over her embarrassment at the flowery phrases, she had begun to use them herself.

The well-remembered flavour of Château de Pies Ombre slipped over the mental tastebuds she had developed. The classic profile of fresh blackcurrants, cigar box and a very elusive hint of sweetness flirting with the dryness, these were the things that its admirers loved about Château de Pies Ombre. They were prepared to wait for them and to pay handsomely for them. And more, the high *Cabernet* content ensured that a buyer had a steadily improving wine, an appreciating asset. There were still enough buyers of that stamp around to make a wholesale change inappropriate. It was frustrating, but it was hard commercial fact. As she herself had remarked to Chirac, ''It seems I have been wrong, for the time being at least. We cannot make expensive changes for the sake of change while the product continues to please.''

For two years now, the vintage was sold almost before the malo-lactic fermentation was completed, so eager were the buyers. The château was prospering, but how long would it last? A bad harvest or two, the growing threat of competition from Spain to deflate prices, anything. A wine grower, as she had stressed over and over again to herself, is only a farmer. And farmers must expect bad times as well as good. The great thing was to be prepared. As soon as the wine business was stabilised, she had formed it into a *Société Anonyme*.

''We must limit our liabilities, Fabrice. If one thing goes wrong, it need not be the end of the world. As things are at the moment, that vineyard can pull us all down with it. We simply aren't secure yet, perhaps we never will be. It's a high-risk business.''

The conversation had taken place early one autumn evening in the billiard room. The newly arrived guests were resting and bathing before dinner and Alexa was checking the spirits in the silver tantalus that always stood ready for gentlemen guests who wished to use the room after dinner. The old blue damask curtains had been cleaned a year after Charles' birth, but the ancient silk had disintegrated in the process. A Lyons weaver had copied the fabric from a scrap that was salvaged and later, the conker-brown and gold Spanish-leather wall covering had been expensively restored.

The room now wore an aspect of solid luxury. The singing gentian colour of the curtains reflected the blush of light shed by apricot-shaded lamps, their colours reflected secondarily in the heavy, painstakingly waxed mahogany furniture. The gruesome, moth-eaten heads of animals killed in the chase long ago had been removed and in their place hung English oil paintings of dogs and horses and sporting prints of anglers and shooting parties. Every one had been picked up at a junk shop price and money had been spent on cleaning and reframing. They gave the room a look of cheerful masculinity and energy recalled in tranquillity without evoking the charnel-house gloom of many country-house billiard rooms.

Everywhere, at this season of the year, there were vases and bowls of rich brown and orange chrysanthemums, their earthy, autumny scent complementing the aromas of cigar smoke and the resinous perfume of the logs burning on the firedogs. At first Fabrice had scoffed at the flowers. "You don't put flowers in a room to be used by men," he said. But Alexa ignored him. In her experience, men liked flowers as much as women, they just didn't say so.

"Down where?" Fabrice grasped maddeningly at the metaphor in Alexa's warning about their liabilities. He had developed the tiresome habit of asking the same sort of literal-minded questions that a child asks. It was partly an attempt to draw her attention away from the subject on her mind and, at least partly, a deliberate ploy guaranteed to infuriate Alexa by disturbing her concentration on the matter in hand. Fabrice had found that the sport of baiting his mother worked just as well on his wife. It was just a case of choosing different lures. But once she understood it, Alexa developed the counter-tactic of patient, cruelly frank replies to the simple-minded questions. Invariably, Fabrice found himself worsted in the encounter.

"Into the gutter. Where would we all go if this house had to be sold to pay the debts of the wine business?"

"Yes, what about the house?"

"That's to become a *Société Anonyme* too."

Fabrice looked at her incredulously, "My *home*, a limited company?"

"Yes, why not? The guest business has been supporting the wine business ever since I married you. I thought it was time to put it on a more formal footing. In the future, when money is taken from the proceeds of entertaining guests here to bolster the château there will be a full record of it and it will be in the form of a *loan*, Fabrice. Eventually, it should be paid back to the house, or rather to *A & F de Pies Ombre et Fils. Société Anonyme*."

"*Loan?* You mean I have to pay back my own money? To myself?"

"Yes. And I am the Managing Director of A & F de Pies Ombre, so you will have me to answer to if you are late with repayments."

"I see. Does this mean you are going to confine your activities to the house from now on?"

"No, of course it doesn't. It just means that there is going to be tighter control of the toing and froing of money between wine business and guest business. After all, Fabrice, there's really quite a lot of money now, we had better know exactly what we're doing with it and where it all goes."

Fabrice had been about to reply when the door was pushed open by a Mr. Turcot from Connecticut. Instantly, Fabrice and Alexa had smoothed their faces and become the delightful, welcoming couple the world had begun to expect them to be. Mr. Turcot was down early. Was he well rested? Could they do anything for him? Dinner was not served until nine. Would he care for an aperitif with them, here by the fire? The *Grand Salon* needed more people in it to be comfortable. They had some rye, even some ice-cold beer. It was absolutely no trouble, they would be delighted. But Mr. Turcot just wondered if he'd left his reading glasses in there. He was going outside for a breath of fresh air until he guessed it was time to zip up Maisie's gown. That was Mrs. Turcot. The door had closed behind the pleasant-mannered American and the expressions of conflict had resumed their places on the features of Madame and Monsieur de Pies Ombre.

"It's *my* money, Alexa. Don't forget that." Fabrice pushed a log further into the fire with his toe. Alexa's face darkened. He didn't get any easier to live with or to reason with.

"Without me, Fabrice, as you know damn well, you wouldn't *have* any money at all. And probably no house or visible means of support of any kind."

"I wasn't aware that marrying the granddaughter of a tradesman was going to put my birthright in jeopardy."

Alexa's mouth tightened with hurt and irritation. "He wasn't a *tradesman*, Fabrice. How many times do I have to point out the difference? My grandfather was a manufacturer. Where I come from that's a proud title. He was Master of Oakfold Mills and on his own patch, as big a man as any bloody duke. Bigger. He was as far away from being a *tradesman* as you are." The continual jibes about her family were the one thing against which she could present no wall of indifference. Every time she rose to the bait. And every time she cursed herself for a fool. Seeing her stung into hot defence gave Fabrice a petty satisfaction that made her ashamed both of him and of herself.

"Thank you for clarifying the position, darling. I'm sure your grandpapa was all very well in his way, but I'm at a loss to see how that affects *my* position. As far as I am able to determine, this house is still mine, and the vineyards are still mine. Whatever you do here, you do with my permission, or not at all."

Alexa had grown accustomed to these postures. They meant nothing. In the end, Fabrice always gave in. She had learned, slowly because she was unwilling to be disgusted, that as long as Fabrice was allowed to imagine that he had shamed her, made her feel awkward and at least momentarily unsure, he would allow her to carry her plans forward. He never had anything to put in their place. There were times, however, when she could not bring herself to take the easy way out. Instead of contriving to falter and adopt a submissive but persuasive manner, she sometimes risked his prolonged displeasure by allowing her ire to show. It delayed matters by a few days, very rarely more.

"You very nearly lost it all, and without my enterprise and bloody hard work you would have done!"

Fabrice took a cue from the rack and began to click the coloured balls about the table idly. "Well, that may be so, but it doesn't alter the fact that you will need my co-operation to chop my belongings up into little companies. I shan't stand in your way, of course, but there has to be a benefit in it for me. I've

learned that much from you, Alexa. Fair exchange is no robbery.
Isn't that what they say? So my price for signing everything you
and Maître Robinson want signing is full access to all the funds
available at all times.''

Alexa ignored the naïve, bullying bravado. She could trust
Maître Robinson to paint a picture of sufficient gloom about
liabilities and collateral and all the doom-ridden rabbits that
lawyers and accountants were so good at pulling out of their hats
when necessary. Fabrice would give in. He no more wanted to
lose Château d'Ombre than she did.

"To spend on whisky? Try making your own, Fabrice. You're
sure to make at least as good a job of it as you did of making
claret!''

But he had frightened her. She went to Maître Robinson. There
must be some way of understanding Fabrice's attitude. Some way
of controlling his irresponsibility and ingratitude. Surely all her
work gave her some rights.

"I confess to you, *Madame*, that your father and I were always
very concerned about your future with that family. I am glad
you have come to me, but truly, unless it is a divorce you are
seeking, I do not think that I can be very helpful. Not directly.
Unless it comes to an open rift between you, it will be difficult
to establish exactly what your rights are.''

"Listen, I realise that on the face of it, everything at d'Ombre
is Fabrice's. But you know, in the early days I put my own money
into repairs. I actually spent my trousseau money on new guttering! And what am I to make of these veiled threats. I do not
want to see my work destroyed. I do not want to be treated like
a manager who is paid a salary. For one thing, *Monsieur*, I am
not paid a salary. All these years, I have clothed myself with my
own small allowance and help from friends in the *couture* business in Paris. It has not been easy. I need clothes to give the
right impression at d'Ombre. People pay to see an old-world
grandee and his wife. Not a struggling young couple with a
mortgage and a disabled child.''

"Ah yes, the child. How is he?'' Alexa shrugged. Her slender
shoulders as expressive now as any Frenchwoman's. "Both legs
were broken when he was a toddler, as you no doubt heard. The
bones knitted and after a regime of cod liver oil there were,
thank God, no further occurrences. But as is typical with the
condition, the bone grafts were imperfect. There is distortion to
both legs, they're not quite the same length and he walks with

an ugly, limping gait.'' Maître Robinson stared at her. This frigid recitation of the facts was formidable. Few mothers could have looked reality so firmly in the face and give so unwavering an account of it. ''My poor son has worn long trousers ever since he was three years old.''

''Everything you have achieved for the property will benefit him some day.''

''I hope so. If his father doesn't ruin it first. But there is more to it than that. I want rewards of my own. I am not content to work for a lifetime and have nothing to show for it.''

''Aren't a successful *Premier Cru* claret and a beautiful house, both of which will pass to your son, 'something to show for it,' as you put it?''

''I really don't know how I can put this any more plainly, *Monsieur*. I mean I want something of my *own*. Money to spend. Power to exercise. The right to say 'I sell,' 'I buy,' 'I liquidate,' 'I destroy' . . . *that* is what I mean by something of my own. Do you understand what I mean now?''

''Yes.'' Maître Robinson was silent for a moment. ''The only way you can be sure of acquiring the authority you seek is to start a new enterprise.''

''With what?''

''With your own land and capital.''

''It is not enough,'' Alexa said flatly.

''Enough for what, *Madame*? Have you thought what you might do with it?''

''To be frank, no I haven't. Until this moment I have been busy trying to save d'Ombre for my husband and son. Now that there is some occasion for cautious optimism about the future, I am reminded in no uncertain fashion that neither house nor vineyards are mine, nor ever will be. It makes me afraid for my own future *and* ambitious too. I know what I can do when I have to. I should like to do it all again, this time for myself. Those little plots of land will never make me enough money to be independent.''

''I would not be too sure of that, *Madame*. For one thing, little plots of land can be added to, can they not?'' He selected a pipe from the rack on the chimney-piece in his office and, gesturing for her permission with easy politeness, lit it. He sucked meditatively, glancing sideways at his client.

For the first time, Maître Robinson began to regret his readiness to act for Madame de Pies Ombre. Of course, it had seemed natural. She was the wife of an established client, and Fabrice de Pies Ombre was only the last in a long line of de Pies Ombres that had been served by his firm. But he now had the uncomfortable sensation that the interests of Alexa de Pies Ombre were beginning to diverge from those of her husband to such an extent that she might be better advised by somebody else. But it was difficult to say so. Her lovely face was redolent of all the trust she placed in him. Had he not told her father, the excellent Standeven, that she must look on him as she would her own father when it came to matters of personal business? But nobody could have foreseen how great her business would become. And then, if he were to listen to his own instincts and recommend her to some other lawyer, it would feel as if he were tipping her over the brink into the loneliness and insecurity of divorce. There was the child to think of. No, no, he must try to serve the *family* as a whole, however difficult.

Alexa gave the proposal that she should buy more land some moments of consideration. "With land prices the way they are now? It will be difficult and will involve borrowing. I'm not very keen on borrowing. It never did the de Pies Ombres much good."

"With respect, *Madame*, they did not manage affairs with your competence. I would be the first to agree that borrowing money is not an enterprise for the incautious or unwary. But you, *Madame*, do not fall into this category."

"No, I suppose not."

"And why are we talking about wine?" Maître Robinson caused an expansive puff of smoke to cloud the air above his head. It hung there like a misty-blue halo denoting sudden enlightenment. "It is not the only thing in life."

Alexa eyed the elderly lawyer with surprise. "Isn't it?"

He smiled. She really was very lovely. "Ah, *Madame*, it has not taken very long to turn you into a true *vigneronne*! What, then, shall we do? You could sell your land, the oil refinery in Pauillac is always hungry for new sites, administrative offices . . . that kind of thing."

"No." Alexa's voice was sharp. It was against her instincts to sell anything. It could always come in useful and if it didn't, it was still there to sell if things became desperate, if you were actually hungry. "I'm sure it's a mistake to sell anything unless you have to. And land, it can only get more valuable. Oh, yes, I know what you are thinking, 'What is it worth if the country is invaded? What is it worth if it is confiscated by an occupier,' but these things do not seem likely at the moment.''

Maître Robinson's pipe emitted several small, quick puffs of astonishment. Indeed he was *not* thinking of invasion or occupation! Young Madame de Pies Ombre was either very farsighted or deeply pessimistic. Perhaps it was the same thing. ''In that case, *Madame*, unless you can think of anything else, it must be wine. You will need capital, you know. It is a risk.''

''What I have in mind isn't nearly so much of a risk as producing château-bottled claret. But you're right, I will need capital and I will need it long term.''

''Will the doctors in America be able to straighten out my legs, Mummy?''

Alexa kissed him and drew the eiderdown up around his shoulders. They were staying overnight with Ariel in her penthouse at the top of the Riverview Terrace clinic. Lionel was away on business in Chicago and Ariel was delighted to have their company.

''I don't know, darling. We can only ask them. I'm sure they'll help if they can.'' Alexa looked at him. It was impossible not to love him. ''Look, Morag's just in the next room here, she's having her supper on a tray because Mrs. Scheitinger and I are going out this evening. We'll shut the door so the television doesn't disturb you.''

''Oh, Mummy,'' Charles began to wheedle, ''can't *I* watch television too? I'm not tired, really. I had a long rest.''

''No, you certainly can't watch television. It's nearly nine o'clock already, way beyond your bedtime. And what about poor Morag? She hasn't had a rest and she must be very, very tired. And we've all got to be up tomorrow in time for your appointment. Go to sleep now, Charles.''

Alexa walked firmly to the door. She wasn't very good at disciplining her son, though she knew it was necessary. She hoped he would be good. Morag's first transatlantic trip hadn't agreed with her. She was suffering from jetlag and was clearly unable to cope. Charles on the other hand seemed indifferent to time zones and had kept her busy most of the afternoon, despite his much-vaunted ''nap.''

Alexa looked back at the handsome little face with the curly black hair on the pillow, so different from Fabrice's own severely straight locks. The face contrasted tragically with the misshapen limbs. He looked almost like a miniature jockey or a case of infantile rickets. He was so bright and confident. Could he ever go away to school like normal boys? The risks to his self-confidence in sending him away seemed too great to take, but as Alexa argued herself, the risks of him never knowing what it was to have to adjust to his peer group or stand up for himself seemed even greater. Suzanne disagreed profoundly and lost no opportunity to say so.

"Goodnight, Morag," she addressed the grey-faced Scots girl slumped on the sofa. "I think he'll fall asleep almost immediately. I don't think he knows how tired he is. Will you be all right? Your supper will come soon and it will be *sumptuous*. Try and eat something and then get an early night. We shan't be late. If you need anything, just ring."

"I'll be fine. You enjoy your evening." Dear Morag, she was so dependable. Nothing would have been possible without her. Alexa went to her own room to collect her bag, her thoughts still running on Suzanne. In her memory, she could hear her good forceful French, and feel the peculiar sensation of rage that came when you realised that the beautiful vowels and crisply articulated words added up to arrant nonsense. Quite a number of people only heard the impressive resonance and never got round to noticing the false coin of her words.

"You English, you are always so eager to be rid of your children. And a crippled child . . . how cruel." Patiently, Alexa explained again and again the psychological damage that could be done to Charles by isolating him from others of his own age and background. "He will grow up eccentric. He will imagine he is of the first importance in everyone's opinion because, at home, that had always been his experience. It will make things very hard for him when he is grown up. Look at Fabrice. He has great difficulty relating to men of his own age and class."

But Suzanne was not convinced. She had kept Fabrice at home, or rather left him behind, and was not willing to admit that any other procedure might have been more successful. Infinitely worse, she would hint to her grandson that unless he was careful, his mother might send him away. Always there was the unspoken implication that Alexa was a cleverly disguised witch, if not a wicked step-mother.

Alexa discovered this one night when she went from her own room up to the nursery in the late afternoon before changing for dinner. She went every evening after her work in the *chais* or the turret room was finished for the day. For an hour she would sit with Morag and Charles on the squashy sofa before the nursery stove. It was a precious time. They read the classic nursery tales of Andersen and Grimm, of A.A. Milne and Beatrix Potter. The warmth and closeness in the charming nursery quarters made Grimm's worst efforts at horror only enhance the safety and comfort of that delightful suite of rooms.

In the winter months, Morag made toast and brewed tea for the three of them. Elizabeth sent pots of the honey from Alexander's hives, sometimes they had Hortense's special, tart, damson jam. It was the hour of the day when Alexa felt closest to Charles and through him, to her own blood and ancestry. There was nothing French about those nursery gatherings. All was ordered with a kindly discipline which was designed to give a framework of security and peaceful predictability.

On one such afternoon when Charles was five, he leaned against Alexa, cradled in her right arm while she supported the story book in her left. The warmth of his confiding little body was soothing. Quink was lying on his back, blue-grey stomach exposed, before the glowing stove. He wore that curving smile of feline triumph which betokens a cat's total satisfaction with life. Morag had taken the tea-things into the nursery kitchen and could be heard moving around softly, not wishing to clatter and disturb Alexa's reading of the *Snow Queen*. It was a sad story and when Alexa felt Charles' body convulse she dropped the book and put both arms around him, enfolding the little bundle of distress closely.

"Darling, I *told* you it was a horrid story! But you made me read it. It's only a silly fairy tale, don't think about it. I never liked it when I was little. Let's read a bit of *Pooh* to cheer ourselves up. Come on, sweetheart. Cheer up." She held him tightly, rocking him slightly, but the sobs increased. "What is it, Charles, tell me. You mustn't take these things seriously. I knew it was too grown up for you!" Alexa would have done anything to stop him crying. She felt him pull away from her violently.

"I'm going to be like those children," he sobbed, "all on my own. You're going to send me away. I'll be all cold and lost. And there'll be other children there, horrible children who'll laugh at my legs and make me cry." Alexa was genuinely puzzled. "What? What do you mean, I'm going to send you away?"

"Yes, you are. *Grand-mère* told me. You're going to send me away to a cold place in England where I'll be all by myself, and people will be cruel to me." The sobs quieted. He'd said it, the terrible thing that had preyed on him for days and made him restless at nights. Morag had said he seemed peaky.

"Oh, darling, darling. My little Charles. I think *Grand-mère* hasn't explained it properly. First of all, there are lots of different places in England for little boys that you might *want* to go to when you're older, but not for *ages* and *ages*. And I *promise*, you shan't go to any of them, ever, unless you want to. And we shall look at lots and lots and you can help choose. We might even look at some in America where Auntie Ariel could keep an eye on you. But you don't have to go, if you don't want to. And another thing, Charles. Everyone in the world has something about them that makes them different from other people. Those things can be good or bad or not one thing or the other. What matters most is the good things. If those things are good enough, things like cleverness, kindness, good temper and braveness, nobody will laugh at you about your legs. If they do, you have my permission to hit them. But you probably won't want to. You see, you'll feel so sorry for them, that they feel so uncertain about themselves that they have to draw attention to your legs to take everybody's mind off what's wrong with them. No, I don't think you'll feel like hitting poor people like that." Gradually she quieted him.

"Morag, tell Hortense to stall dinner for half an hour, I'll give Charles his bath this evening."

"Yes, *Madame*." Morag gave her halting message over the house telephone which had been installed soon after Charles' birth. In the five years she had served the de Pies Ombres, her French had improved very little. She did not mind her isolation, Charles was enough to her. She was mistress in the large and beautiful nursery, it was her home.

Alexa picked Charles up with difficulty, he was a heavy child. She carried him into the nursery bathroom. It had been decorated by Ariel to represent the inside of a yellow submarine. Painted cartouches around the walls showed marine views of underwater life. While she undressed him, Alexa questioned Charles casually.

"When did *Grand-mère* tell you this silly thing?"

"I don't know." No. Five-year-olds did not have calendars inside their heads. It couldn't have been that long ago.

"Well, was it in the morning, or at lunch-time?"

"In the morning." Charles looked away from his mother, he didn't like being questioned. He began to reach for his model boats. Alexa kept her hand on his arm, anxious that his attention should not wander just yet.

"Where does she talk to you, Charles? She doesn't come up here, does she?" Alexa hoped not. The thought of Suzanne invading this most carefully guarded territory outraged her.

"No. She talks to me in her room, I was playing in the gallery and she called me. She often does. She shows me things."

"Really darling, what things?"

"Things." Alexa soaped Charles thoroughly all over with the Johnson's baby soap that reminded her of her own nursery days. The faint odour was the smell of safety and security. She made a foamy lather so that Charles looked more like a fluffy lamb than a little boy. Charles loved that. She dotted a knob of foam onto his nose, to recapture his attention.

"Yes, darling, but what sort of things?"

"Pictures mostly."

"How interesting." Keep it light, she warned herself. You know how he can clam up and he mustn't be frightened. Above all he must not be frightened.

"Ladies and gentlemen in funny clothes. Quite a lot of them have walking sticks. She says they're my family and the walking sticks are the curse of the de Pies Ombres."

"Ludicrous!" Alexa muttered the word under her breath. "Does she, darling? Anything else?"

"There's a big white house with lines of island bushes around it. She says its called *La Roseraie*, and it's in 'Geria." Island bushes was Charles' name for palm trees, since he first recognised them in illustrations of pirate stories and saw the usual token palm tree on the small round desert isles of childish legend.

"Ah, it's where *Grand-mère* used to live, when she was a little girl, but not any more."

"I know, some robbers stole it before I was born. When I'm grown up, I'm going to fight to get it back for her. *Grand-mère* said the robbers stole a lot of people's houses and we can get them back if we fight and are very brave. She says it's the sort of fighting you don't need strong legs for. I'm going to help do the fighting but first I have to drink a lot of milk and eat lots and lots of food to get strong enough. Can I have some bread and jam?"

"No, sweetheart, you'll get too fat if you keep eating starchy snacks. Get out now, Charles."

"Oh Mummy, can't I stay in and play? Morag lets me." His attention had wandered away, distracted by his flotilla of boats bucking in the tidal wave created by his mother's soap-chasing hands.

"I know, sweetheart, but Mummy has to go down to dinner. Look, I'm not even changed yet and I want to tuck you up and kiss you goodnight." Grumblingly, Charles clambered out of the yellow bath and consented to be wrapped in the huge fluffy towel that Alexa held out to enfold his small body. She hugged him strongly. The poisonous old woman was filling his head with her hysterical, dangerous ideas. In an elderly woman they were merely silly and a bit sad. But if she communicated those ideas to an imaginative, impressionable child, who might well develop a burning need to prove himself, God only knew what the end could be.

Alexa had been dimly aware of the existence of a small party of displaced Algerian colonials who nursed an unquenchable thirst for de Gaulle's blood. But she had never imagined for one moment that their unrealistic hopes of returning to their North African home was shared by Suzanne, frequent as her bitter references to the glories of her colonial youth had been. Torn between hilarity and anger, an icicle of fear entered her mind.

Alexa very nearly laughed aloud at the notion of Suzanne in the role of ex-colonial dissident and would-be urban guerrilla, or whatever it was she had in mind. But trying to turn Charles into a future terrorist? That was not a matter for amusement. It must be dealt with quickly and decisively. These, she told herself, were the real dangers of stupidity. It would be of no use to reason with Suzanne. Something guaranteed to give a definite and permanent result was called for.

"Come on now, put your slippers on. Bed now." They went into the night nursery where Morag sat in the armchair mending a pullover with her exquisite darning stitches. Of all the nursery apartments, this was the most ordinary. There was nothing in it to fire a restless imagination with ghostly, night-time terrors. Everything was made pretty but commonplace and there were no pictures. Even the wardrobe doors had been purposefully designed to slide on runners so that no cupboard door that swung open or was left ajar through inadvertence could cast a frightening shadow.

"I wonder if you're a big enough boy to understand this?" Alexa sat down on the edge of Charles' little four-poster bed. Morag, sensing a confidential chat about to begin between mother and son, got up to go away, but her mistress motioned her to stay where she was. When it came to Charles' welfare, Alexa had no secrets from Morag Anderson. She would explain the details to her later.

"Understand what?" Charles began to marshal his teddy bears and soft toys in the strict order of precedence which they were made to observe for "sleeping." It left very little room for Charles himself, but he would not rest until the ritual positions had been established and he had carefully disposed his own body in the narrow space left.

"Well, it's a secret. A grown-up secret, I think you're still too little," Alexa sighed elaborately. It worked. Charles was like his mother. The threat of missing out on information riveted his concentration.

"I'm quite big now, *Grand-mère* says so."

"Well, you *might* just be big enough to be trusted. It's very serious and grown up. Keeping a secret like this is a big responsibility for a little boy, darling." Charles' face was as anxious as that of a puppy, afraid that its dish is going to remain empty. His entire being was focused on extracting further speech from his mother. His brown eyes sucked with the same power as his mother's blue ones.

"All right. Remember what I'm going to tell you is what we call 'in confidence.' That's a very grown-up thing. It means you must never tell anybody else about it. It's an important secret just between the two of us." The eyes sucked brownly while Alexa arranged the lace-edged pillows more comfortably behind his head. "When people are as old as *Grand-mère*, they sometimes get a bit, well, silly, you know. Start telling things that aren't exactly fibs, but aren't quite true either. They can't help it, they don't mean to do it. You see, their brains get tired and so they get things muddled up. They mix up true things with untrue things until the true things are turned into untrue things. Do you understand? So although they aren't liars, which would be awful and *very* naughty, you mustn't believe what they say, because they'll have muddled things up so badly."

"So there isn't a white house?" Charles' face fell.

"Oh yes, darling. There *was*, and there may still be if the Algerians haven't knocked it down. That's a true bit. But, you see, it'll be all broken down now and nobody would want to live there any more. And robbers didn't take it. There was a war. Algeria is a country that used to belong to France, but eventually, France decided to give it back to the people who lived there. It's all quite, what we call, *legal*. The people who own the house now if anybody does, it might be the government, really do own it. If anyone tried to take it away from them, *they* would be the robbers. You'll understand all about it when you grow up and do history at school. Poor *Grand-mère* has forgotten the proper story. Her brain's tired.''

''And you aren't going to send me away?'' Charles had plucked a small clump of plush hair from the body of his favourite teddy bear and was tickling his nose with it rhythmically. He often did that when he was sleepy.

''Of course not, darling. That was terribly naughty of *Grand-mère*.'' Alexa noticed her own slip immediately and it was seized upon instantly by Charles with his child's stunning logic.

''It's not naughty if she can't help it. Wasn't her brain being tired again, Mummy?''

''Yes, darling. Her brain was tired when she told you that. You might go away if you want to, later. That was the true bit. But I shall never *send* you away and I wouldn't let you go to a cold or nasty place even if you did want to. Those were the untrue bits. She can't help it. It happens to a lot of people when they get old.''

''How old is *Grand-mère*?''

''Oh, about fifty-six.''

''Gosh! Will I live to be that old?''

''Oh yes, a lot older I should think.''

''Won't my brain go funny?'' You can never be too careful or too honest when talking to children, Alexa cursed herself.

''Well, that's the interesting thing, Charles. The more you work with your brain, and the more careful you are *always* to tell the truth, even just to yourself, the more likely your brain is to stay strong and young all your life. I tell you what, if you were to do a few sums, or even make up a poem—that's even harder but more fun—in bed every night before you fell asleep, just after your story and before your prayers, I should think we needn't have any worries about your brain.''

''Dividing?'' Charles was one of those rare children who actively enjoyed arithmetic.

''Particularly good.''

"Does Tante Héloïse do dividing?"

"I suppose she must, darling, I've never asked her."

"She must do lots. She's much older than *Grand-mère* and *she* hasn't got a tired brain, has she?"

Suzanne's campaign to subvert Charles' affection foundered on the velvet-covered rock of Alexa's diplomacy. Charles was only five but he enjoyed the pleasurable secret of *Grand-mère*'s tired brain and making his nightly reports of fresh instances of its decay more than the vague promise of participation in a dangerous fight in the far distant future. Alexa was not Elizabeth's daughter for nothing. Surveillance was the key to control. And it was for everybody's good.

Morag wrote her regular monthly letter to Elizabeth. Her naïve but accurate description of the latest domestic power struggle went unread by her mistress. In the early days, Morag had confessed to Alexa that she kept up a correspondence with Mrs. Standeven and that although she felt some unease in doing so, since it might be interpreted as disloyal, she was powerless to end the communications without Alexa's own interference. Mrs. Standeven had written first, and her letters demanded a reply, which in politeness, she did not know how to avoid.

Alexa had set the nanny's mind at rest.

"My mother likes to know everything that is going on, you know. I always found her a relentless correspondent when I was at school. Twice a week, Wednesdays and Saturdays, there would be a letter from her, mainly asking questions to which I either did not know the answer, or would rather not have replied. She quite destroyed my taste for letter writing.

"If I were you, Morag, I should keep on writing, if it doesn't bore you too much. Just don't give her a lot to worry about, that's all. It will be a real service to me. Send her my love when you do."

In that way, Alexa kept her mother supplied with sufficient material to content her appetite for private intelligence and ensured the loyalty of Morag Anderson. The inclusion of a formal message of affection from her daughter each month was an endorsement that warned Elizabeth that Morag was, at best, a double agent but a useful conduit of two-way information. Elizabeth preferred her relationships to be complicated. It was dull in the Yorkshire Dales.

If, when reading Morag's latest letter at the kitchen table of Langstroth Grange, Mrs. Standeven had twinges of conscience about her rival being unchivalrously disqualified on grounds of senility, she smothered them. Alexa had to use the weapons of defence which came to hand. Not that Morag actually mentioned "senility" as such, of course, but she had a rare talent for reported speech. A good plain Scottish education. Very workmanlike.

*

CHAPTER
17

IN NEW YORK the cold bit ferociously. Sharp winds fun-
nelled down the endlessly tall streets and avenues, lurking with
unsheathed blades to cut the flesh of unwary pedestrians. Accustomed now to the kinder winters of the Médoc, Alexa was
as startled by the bitterness of the cold as she had been years
before by the steaming humidity of the summer heat.

"There's snow coming, honey, I can smell it," Ariel was
pouring maple syrup on a pancake for Charles who was enchanted by the classic American breakfast.

"Smell it?"

"Sure. Alaska, Siberia, that's where it comes from and there's
always a smell first. I suppose it's like a very dry white wine but
with an earthy taste, a clear coldness in the head, and what you'd
call the *goût de terroir.*"

"Would I?" The other girl laughed. "I must be an awful
bore."

"No, just wrapped up in what you do. It's rather charming,
actually. The baby tycoon."

"Well it sounds as if your snow is going to taste nice when it
comes. I just hope it doesn't stop me getting home again for *too*
long."

Ariel's new apartment was on the Upper East Side. It was
smaller than the Riverview Terrace penthouse had been and
crowded with Ariel's accumulated possessions. She and Lionel
had separated. Ariel's own career had given her little time to act
the part of a big-time American businessman's wife and she
wanted no children of her own. "It wasn't fair to either of us,
to carry on," Ariel had remarked philosophically. "We just
found we wanted different things and those things just couldn't

be made to knit together. Lionel needed me to act out the part of the adoring, grateful wife and brilliant hostess. I didn't want to do it. He wanted an all-American princess with the regulation two or three kids and the look of a future First Lady. I said 'no deal' and he packed his bags. Naturally, I didn't let him get very far with that. After all, why should he have gone? It was his place anyway. So I got out myself. The best thing, every which way you look at it.''

Alexa had admired the hygienic simplicity with which Lionel and Ariel had arranged their affairs. For them it was so uncomplicated. No strings, no regrets. They both had skills they could exercise anywhere and no millstone of history, obligation and custom to impede their flight from an unsatisfactory situation. They could both make something out of nothing, and then move on to the next thing. She couldn't help comparing their situation with her own and Fabrice's. Neither she nor her husband were anything without Château d'Ombre. They were tied to the soil which made them what they were. Madame and Monsieur de Pies Ombre were nobody, together or individually, without the few acres of land which gave them their name, their reason for being, and which supplied their income. The need to feed on that earth kept her and Fabrice together as inexorably as if they had been tied at birth by a cord of indivisible flesh.

"Mummy, if it snows, can we go tobogganing in Central Park?"

"Yes, darling, yes. Of course we can. If there *is* snow and enough of it, Morag shall take you to Macy's and buy you the best sledge in the store. That's a promise.''

"Can I get down, now?"

"No, poppet, you may not," Morag interposed. "Ask properly, and we'll see.'' Charles sighed. He was a well-trained child but sometimes he tried for a burst of independence.

"Please may I leave the table?''

"Yes, Charles, you may, if Mummy and Mrs. Scheitinger have no objections.''

"That's quite all right, Charles,'' Alexa addressed her son. "Run along with Morag now and do your tables. I want to hear your eight times this evening, quite perfect. You can do it if you just *concentrate*.''

"Aren't you pushing him a bit hard, honey?'' Ariel looked at her friend anxiously. It must be tough to have such a severely damaged child, but wasn't she over-compensating?

"Certainly not. I went to school when I was four and I could read fluently at that age. I don't know why you Americans wait so long. The sooner a child can read, the sooner it can amuse itself, and, what is more, educate itself. And that's the best kind of education, you know. The things you find out for yourself are so much more valuable than things other people tell you because they think you ought to know them."

"But, Alexa, we weren't talking about reading. We were talking about math."

"I know. I've always had problems with figures myself. I can see Charles going the same way if it isn't tackled early. With any luck, Charles may have a lot of money one day. He's got to know how to look after it. It begins with simple addition and knowing your multiplication tables, not to mention subtraction."

She didn't tell Ariel that she knew she pushed Charles and had every intention of continuing with the programme she had instituted for her son's early education. He had such a serious disadvantage, one that might never be removed, it was important that he should also have very serious *ad*vantages to compensate. Next year he would begin to play a musical instrument. The year after that she planned to have a pony. If Charles could ride, he would have a sport in which he could compete on equal terms with other boys. She would teach him herself and succeed where his father's tutor, Mr. Greville, had failed.

"Well . . . Doesn't he ever just *play*? He's only seven for Chrissakes!"

"Of course, he's a small boy. He plays at adapting Hans Andersen for the stage. Morag seems to spend a lot of her time dressed up as a witch and he's even roped Hortense in before now. And he plays at dressing vines. He's always got some bush or other in the nursery that he's subjecting to new mutilations in the name of experimental viticulture. It's all good, serious, creative stuff. I'm pleased with him, intellectually."

"And, physically . . ." Ariel probed. Alexa's face lost its customary bright hardihood and registered the nearest thing to despair that her friend had ever read there.

"He's reached his full potential, considering his age and disability. In a year or two I'm going to start him riding. I suppose I ought to be doing something about swimming too. But frankly, I dread exposing him to the curiosity of other people. I know it's got to happen some time, otherwise I'd be scheming to build a private pool. It's just a matter of taking the plunge, for him *and* me. Literally and figuratively.''

"Couldn't the doctors in France come up with *anything*, honey?''

"There's no medical cure, I know that. I thought something might be achieved by surgery but nobody in France or England seems to agree. I just hope the attitude here is more enterprising. We've got an appointment tomorrow to see Doctor Heinz's friend, Doctor Kilpatrick, at the Kennedy Institute. I'm counting on him having some ideas. America seems to be the place for innovative medicine these days.''

Ariel placed her hand impulsively over Alexa's, "I'm sure he'll think of something, honey. Charles's just so darling, he *must* do something.''

Doctor Kilpatrick was Boston Irish. He was smooth and professionally affable. The horn-rimmed spectacles flashed enthusiastically on his well-fleshed face. His shoulders were so broad, they seemed to stretch out in a firmly graphic expression of East and West. The geniality spilled from him like loss-leader cans of baked beans in a supermarket. Alexa found him overpowering and not altogether agreeable. He, on the other hand, approved of the beautiful young aristocrat who sat before him. She had real style. European style. He looked forward to a long and profitable relationship.

"If you just run along now, sonny, into the next room, Nurse will be able to find some cookies.''

"Cookies, sir?'' Charles was perplexed.

"Yes, son, cookies. You like cookies don't you?'' He tousled the small boy's hair familiarly. Charles pulled away disgustedly from the unwelcome caress. Alexa watched thoughtfully. Children and animals. They always know. She was a little shocked at her own reaction. *Run along, sonny*, was not the way to address her son. With surprise she noted her own resentment of the scant respect shown to him, Monsieur Charles de Pies Ombre. It was the first time she'd ever thought of him in that way. It had taken a stranger to make her aware of her own child's dignity. Alexa's hackles rose.

"My son does not eat biscuits or sweets, Doctor.'' She shot Charles a warning look.

"Aw, come on, Mom. You don't expect an old hand like me to believe that, do you?'' Alexa froze. No-one had spoken to her like that for a very long time.

"Charles, darling, go into the next room as the doctor asks. Perhaps Nurse can find you something to read." Charles executed a sketchy bow in his mother's direction. She suppressed the smile that rose to her lips.

"I repeat, Doctor, my son does not eat biscuits or sweets. I would have thought you should have approved. Oh, and by the way, perhaps your nurse didn't tell you, his name is Charles."

Richard put the telephone down crisply. Excellent. She was within his grasp at long last. Somehow, he'd known it was only a question of waiting. One day, she'd be back. And now she was. For seven years now, he'd watched and waited, certain that some inevitable action of cosmic organisation would bring her within his orbit again. He had begun the process himself by taking a little of her money into his care. This time he would attach silken threads to her and she would never be lost to him again. There were always strings in business. Strings that were resented and chafed at, but the gossamer filaments with which he would bind her would thicken into cords so strong she could never break them and never wish to.

He'd seen her a few times during the past five or six years, but she had never seen him. The little Landais woodman's cottage outside the slumbrous village of Villandraut in the Sauternes district had been ideal. He'd bought it for a song the summer after Charles had been born. Little by little, with help from local labour and doing a good deal himself during his annual summer vacation there, *La Garenne* had become a luxurious retreat inside a rustic shell.

No-one knew him in the sleepy village of Villandraut. He was just a rich American *célibataire* who came every summer to enjoy the pleasures of poor men. He chopped wood for winter fuel he would never use, he replaced the old terracotta tiles on the roof, Lafon the carpenter helped him put a new staircase inside the cottage where once there had only been a ladder to a hayloft. Up there, the telex machine chattered companionably, telling its tale of prices rising and falling. He read the messages once a day and never more frequently. He was on holiday. With these activities and a little trout fishing in the pools deeper into the woods, he whiled away two or three weeks of the July heat. He troubled nobody and was, in return, left in peace. There was no telephone in the cottage. The telex was enough to let him know if he should make contact with the outside world. The world should not be allowed to trouble him.

He bought his wine in the village supermarket, bread from the bakery near the *Mairie*, carrying it on his battered old bike, like a local. Sometimes he would ride the same bike into the village on a Sunday to buy the Arcachon oysters from the stall that appeared in the square, but only on Sundays. On those days he might sit down and take a glass of *vin blanc* on the *terrasse* of La Crémerie shaded by the lime trees, their perfume languorous in the warmth, which caused some jealousy as there were two other respectable *cafés* in the village. Then he would get up and go, taking his oysters with him and never a word to anyone. He was a mystery.

Jeanne, who waited on him on those rare occasions at La Crémerie, failed summer after summer to extract anything more from him than a courteous *s'il vous plaît* and a *merci beaucoup*, uttered in his outlandish accent. Each year she yearned and secretly promised herself that next year she would burst upon him like the first rose of summer and he would suddenly notice her and carry her off to the wild, sophisticated life of Paris, New York and London. He was so handsome, with his wide-open face and powerful, athletic body, not like the dark, wiry little men of the Médoc. And then his direct glance, straight into the eyes as if he really noticed her, made Jeanne's heart skip a beat every time. But Richard never saw her. His thoughts were some thirty to forty kilometres away, in Pauillac.

Now and again he would drive to Bordeaux. The expeditions were essentially aimless. Once he watched a Bastille Day parade on the Esplanade des Quinconces. He had seen her then, sitting in the stand surrounded by dignitaries. She wore a large shady hat of dark-cream straw encircled by an emerald ribbon, tied in a stiff bow at the front of the brim. Large sunglasses partially obscured her face, but it was her. The mouth, the cheek bones, he would have known them anywhere. And the way she looked intently; concentration unwavering. Nobody else could look and look so long.

In fact, it had been her. Alexa had few acquaintances among her wine-growing neighbours. For the most part, they were all much richer than she was herself and she could not return hospitality that she was obliged to sell to strangers for money. There were few invitations and even fewer that they could accept. Fabrice had made himself so universally unpopular as a young

man, that those who were his neighbours and whose fathers and
grandfathers had been the friends of his father and grandfather
were not his friends. Alexa never chafed at her social isolation
because she did not notice it. The struggle for survival had
provided sufficient companionship, and brought its own small
crop of acquaintances.

It was one of these, Monsieur Chirac, who had begged her to
accompany himself and his wife to the parade. He pitied her
isolation. Many times he remarked to his brother and to his wife
that it was a scandal that any woman with Alexa de Pies Ombre's
looks and personality should feel herself bound to that idle boor.
"There is not a man in France who would not be proud indeed
to have her at his side." "And in England?" teased Madame
Chirac. "Any man in Europe would be fortunate," Chirac af-
firmed and was rewarded with a narrow look.

On another occasion Richard had seen her talking to the manager of Château L'Agence. He had gone there idly as the place
was open to visitors, to buy a little wine and to look at the
cuverie and *chais*. She was there at the rear of the buildings,
walking with the young *régisseur* among the vines, leaning down
to examine the bunches of berries. He had left promptly. He
mustn't be seen yet. She must come to him. Again, she had
emerged from the offices of a firm of accountants on the Allées
de Tourny. She was wearing a blue shantung dress, her arms
bare and bronzed. Her head was uncovered and the light bounced
sparks off her hair, making a haze of light. Her face was sad and
serious. She looked as if her spirit had grown older. He was
near enough to touch her. Involuntarily, his hand started forward, but he let it fall back. Her name stuck in his throat and
mere fractions of seconds jerked by like the frames of old film
footage. Rooted to the spot he watched her look in the window
of an expensive flower shop. There were arum lilies such as
grew in the backyards of farms in that region, their waxy white
cornets as unreal as angels' trumpets. Her eyes examined them
minutely, with that total attention that was her chief characteristic. After a short eternity, she turned away, uttering a faint sigh
that only a worshipper could have heard.

Now she had come.

Alexa's meeting with Richard was awkward at first. It took
place in his suite of chambers in a cliff-side of a building on
Wall Street in down-town New York. There was a disconcert-
ingly rarefied air of money in the atmosphere. Money that had

not yet been made, that existed only in the minds of people like Lionel Scheitinger, who could translate a thought, an idea, into hard currency. It was not a matter of base metal coins here, or of clean or grubby banknotes, nor yet of columns of figures representing actuality. In this place, money was essentially a concept of the mind. Alexa felt it instinctively, even before she entered the building. On this street, a nod and a handshake would make all things possible without a coin changing hands or a stroke of the pen.

As the silent elevator transported Alexa to the twentieth floor, she was startled to find herself pitched immediately onto the beige carpet of the Goldstein premises. There was no interface of cold, impersonal corridor. No uninviting doors to examine, no moment in which to finally compose herself. She was there, confronting a vast smoked-glass table behind which there sat a grey-suited receptionist of steely efficiency, who presided over a small squadron of telephones. She came forward to greet Alexa and led her to a low, brown-leather chair, from which she knew there would be difficulty in rising gracefully.

"Mr. Lockwood has a call at the moment. I'm sure he'll be with you presently. Can I get you some coffee?"

Alexa shook her head, not wanting the pretended occupation of drinking coffee by herself in a strange place.

The modern sculptures, gleaming-leaved tropical plants and acres of thick carpet gave no clue to what projects might attract the smile of financial endorsement, and what would not. If anything, there was a suggestion that nothing as simple as a little vineyard in France would be understood here. The freneticism of the incomprehensible works of modern art and the astoundingly distant ground viewed from the plate-glass windows spoke of a world in which soil and season, fruit and flavour would seem primitive concerns, which should be financed, if at all, by similarly atavistic means.

The receptionist spoke quietly into a telephone, glancing covertly at Alexa as she did so.

"Mr. Lockwood will see you now," she announced, her hands folded and her eyes fixed on Alexa. She seemed to be adding the unspoken wish that Alexa should prove worthy of the honour. Her voice was as impersonal as the polished rubber plants and the bright chromium of the reproduction Mies Van der Rohe chairs.

Richard did not rise. He looked over the rims of the black-

framed spectacles. There she was at last. He detected a fierce-
ness and energy about her which brought the scent of battle to
his nostrils. She had come to fill the war chest.

She stood framed in the doorway. He regarded her steadily,
filling his eyes with her, eyes which gave no hint of their long
unsatisfied hunger. She looked older. True, she was as lithe as
ever, the smooth skin unravaged, but over the well-remembered
planes of her face the shadow of experience lay. It showed in
bones that stood in sharper relief, in the twist of knowledge in
her mobile, expressive mouth. The graceful column of her neck
rose from the severe, collarless navy coat. Her only ornaments
were small, plain pearl earrings. A neck to wreathe in diamonds, he thought. One day, my love, you shall have them.

"Come and sit down, Alexa. May I call you that?" His voice
was more transatlantic than she had remembered.

"You always used to."

"You were just a little girl then. A bright, brave little girl.
Now you are a great lady with a success story behind you."
Richard cursed himself. He had used the technique he employed
on business opponents and employees many a time. It was habitual. Knock 'em down to start with, and then build 'em up.
That way they start off owing their self-esteem to *you*. But this
was the woman he loved. The only woman he had ever really
wanted. Wanted to the point of pain.

Alexa made no immediate response. She found she did not
object to his description of her youthful self. It was true. That
was all she had been, an ignorant little girl. If she had known
more when she started, she would never have begun.

"And how is your husband?"

"Alive."

"And well?"

"Yes, I suppose so," Alexa was impatient of the preliminar-
ies. There was nothing she could say about Fabrice's health or
state of mind that would make any sense to Richard Lockwood.
She barely understood it herself.

Over the years they had lived in a state of tension. There were
long periods without overt conflict, but then there would be an
eruption of anger and resentment which would poison both their
lives for weeks. Attempts at mutual understanding and *rap-
prochement* had become less and less frequent, and those that
there were, were always instituted by Alexa. Fabrice drank each
year more heavily than the last. He drank joylessly, without

uproar but with a determined self-destructiveness. His performance as a host was correct but wooden and their guests had begun to treat him as a cipher, to Alexa's sorrow and embarrassment. It wounded her pride that people should think her husband unworthy. They knew nothing of his mordant, sophisticated wit, or the well-springs of emotion she herself had occasionally uncovered. His public indifference to her humiliated her more than his private cruelty.

Obsessed with the unconscious terror that Alexa would swallow him whole, Fabrice tried frantically to whittle away her self-esteem until she should represent no further threat. And because reason played no part in his feelings towards his wife, he was equally afraid that she would leave him. In the recesses of his mind, he believed he could make her afraid to go away from him.

Once, when he had drunk a great deal, he had held her forcibly in front of her dressing-table mirror and said, "Look at yourself, Alexa. Everyone treats you as if you were a beauty, but you can see, can't you, that you're really a very plain woman. Almost ugly. You're desirable only because you're my wife. Nobody would want you for yourself." The words had been slurred but they had hurt and bewildered her, but not nearly as deeply as the time when he had said, "I feel like a homosexual." Feeling as if the balance of her own mind was overturning, she had asked him what he could possibly mean. He had said, "It's you, it's like living with a man. You're not a woman at all." Her confusion and self-doubt had made her at times seriously question her own reason. She seemed to be living in a world of inter-reflecting mirrors where nothing was what it seemed, least of all herself. The effort of continuing to see herself as being whole had become by far the greatest trial among many.

Each time something of this sort happened, Alexa castigated herself. It's me, she told herself. It must be. If I try harder, Fabrice will love me eventually. Because, against all logic, she still wanted to love him. It was a wish separated from hope, an act of pure will, which only Héloïse could have appreciated or applauded.

Along with this determined morality there rode a fear of the future, and a longing for financial independence. If she had something substantial of her own, Fabrice could not continually accuse her of having nothing that was not his. She felt at times that this was the sole root of his enmity. But now she had reached a plateau of pain. She had begun to regard the dull ache of emotional privation as a natural condition of her existence, the only proof that she was alive. It was acceptance and peace, of a sort. Richard could not begin to understand any of this.

"I'm glad you came to see me, Alexa. We have some business to talk over. But I was coming over to Ariel's apartment anyway before you left town. I often go there since she and Lionel split up. I was going to suggest you girls go out to dinner with me, and then perhaps we could go on to a club, if you'd like it. You don't get away from the sticks very often, do you?"

"As you say, I don't get away very often and I shouldn't be here now were it not for the fact that I have some business to transact. I cannot afford to travel for pleasure, Mr. Lockwood."

"Richard, please. I thought we agreed all that years ago."

"Yes, of course, years ago."

"Well, what can I do to help?"

"First I'd like to talk about my two thousand dollars I left with you. I never heard anything about it from you and I wondered if there'd been any growth to speak of. You said you'd double it in a year, and well, frankly, I need that money now."

Richard nodded and pressed a button on his desk. A woman's voice, disembodied and distorted, replied.

"Bring me the Alexa de Pies Ombre Trust file immediately."

"Right away, sir," the voice snapped audibly to attention.

"I think you'll be pleased with my stewardship. It's amazing what you can do with two thousand dollars if you're given a free hand."

The file was brought in by a tiny, clever-looking girl in her mid-twenties. It was just an ordinary buff folder in which an untidy wad of papers was tightly fixed with a metal clip. Richard turned in his seat and took the file with both hands. "Meet my personal assistant, Carrie Morgan. I guess she'll be leaving me soon for one of the big players. She's outgrowing this outfit real fast." Alexa noticed the quick, warm glance of mutual understanding which passed between them. She felt a pinprick of jealousy. Carrie's glossy brown hair was beautifully cut and her black suit and white silk shirt were not the sort of thing, Alexa's practised eye noted, which secretaries wore. She had neat, expensively shod feet. This girl was her own age but she understood things which Alexa did not understand. She belonged in Richard Lockwood's world.

A green light flashed on the console on Richard's desk. Carrie picked up the telephone. "I'll be right there." She left the room with an easy swinging stride, coquettish and exquisite.

Reading her unspoken thought, Richard looked at Alexa. He smiled slightly and shook his head. Alexa's eyes flicked irritably away. She looked out of the plate-glass window, over his shoulder, unwilling to communicate anything but the words she chose to speak.

"I got all this stuff on computer disk now, except for yours, that is." Alexa brought her attention back to the papers on the desk. "I kept yours a low tech. account. Sort of personal hobby. Let's see now. Yes, as of yesterday at close of play, you understand that's the latest update I have on your affairs, but we'll run another check in a minute . . . you're worth, yes . . . one million, eighty dollars and sixty cents." He looked up again, above the black-rimmed spectacles. "I could have taken some risks, of course," the drawl was almost sensual, "but you don't play fast and loose with the funds of poorer clients . . ."

"I was not aware that you were a broker, Mr. Lockwood. I thought you were a banker and that my money had been invested in the Scheitinger Clinics." She spoke like an automation, barely aware of her own words or meaning. Every conscious cell of her brain was trying to absorb what she had just heard, trying to make it fit into what she already knew of herself and of the world.

"Half of it is. When I'd doubled your original stake. I started buying other stocks too. I've done rather well for you, don't you think?"

There was a pause. Alexa saw the whole of her life of the past seven years flash before her eyes. The struggles, the economies, the bitter rows, the sleepless nights, the fear of failure. It was the fear she couldn't forgive him for.

"Have you any idea how much half of that money, a quarter, even a *tenth* of it would have helped me? What it would have meant to me? Do you know that Fabrice and I have never had a holiday since the day we were married? Every penny we've made has been ploughed back into the land or the house. Did you know that my former employer, Monsieur Terry, dresses me as virtually a charity case? I wear what rich women cancel or reject. We have had no luxuries and precious little dignity. You say amassing this fortune has been your personal hobby. Well let me tell you what you've been using for your recreational equipment. My *life*. Just that, my life. Did you think of *that*?"

"Yes."

Alexa leaned her head on her hand, "How could you do it?" her voice came hard and dry as dead leaves.

"Easily. I loved you. I still do. Always will."

The shock waves vibrated around the room. There was a silence as the backwash from the unretractable statement brushed against them both, rocking them violently, silently. Eventually, Alexa said, "You hardly know me."

"I have seen you, I have heard you and I have watched you. I know all I need to know. I know I love you."

"You realise that this is impossible?"

"Oh completely, *Madame*, completely. I am unaccustomed to find myself in impossible situations, however, so you will make allowances if I appear to blunder around." He was angry with her, heartsore that years of careful work had been rejected with violent ingratitude.

"The situation and its impossibility is of your making."

"No, it is of yours. Or, if not that, of some maliciously ordained configuration of events and circumstances over which no human being has control. You could not imagine, could you, that I should wish to feel as I do? Why should I, a respectable New York banker, wish to make a fool of myself over a girl half my age, the wife of another man? No, no, *Madame*. You are not the only person with a sense of her own dignity. No, there have been times when I wished I'd never laid eyes on you, my dear. I have become unused to seeing anything that I cannot have by signing a cheque."

"Couldn't you have kept it to yourself?"

"No. Not any longer. I have kept it to myself for seven years or thereabouts. Now I consider I have a right, have *earned* the right to speak."

"Why should you draw that conclusion?" Alexa spoke with frigid calm.

For a moment, he hesitated, uncertain that what he wished to say would make any sense to her. "Because, you arrogant young fool, I have made you rich. I have made you safe and independent. I have made it possible for you to have whatever it is you came here for, even if I do not choose to advance the money to you personally. *That* is my right to speak. You spurn my gift of freedom. Perhaps you would not spurn it so disdainfully if you knew that weaving this mantle of independence for you was a labour of love, of selfless endeavour which has provided me with the best hours I have had in my entire life. I've never had a chance to do anything for someone else before. Or perhaps I've never wanted to. You made it different.''

Alexa was still for a moment. Then she said, ''It is lucky that once again you have acted in my affairs so officiously, because now, we need have nothing further to do with each other. I need not tell you why I came to see you. Just give me the money and I can go.''

''Why *did* you come to see me, Alexa?''

''I wanted to start a business. Now I can, without reference to anyone.''

''May I know what the business was, or should I say, *is*?''

''No. There is no need for that. You have manipulated me, Mr. Lockwood, but now you have me in the killing pen I need not, after all, die. Not if I refuse to co-operate. You virtually gave me the initial two thousand dollars. I did not ask for it and I always felt uneasy about taking it. Perhaps that's why I half forgot it.''

''You earned it. What do you mean, I gave it to you?'' He got up and walked to the window. Standing with his hands in his pockets, with his back to her he gazed down into the street far below. There was nobody, walking on that street now, who would not thank him for what he had done, if only he had done it for one of those unknown people. But no. Of all the people in the world, he had chosen Alexa de Pies Ombre. Stubborn, touchy, unjust, incomprehensible . . . his mind ran out of adjectives. Wealth was what he had to give, and for her, it wasn't good enough. He was sick with disappointment.

''You put it my way, let us say, then,'' her voice cut through his thoughts. ''I did not go out and get it for myself. It was an ungentlemenly thing to do, to put me under an obligation to a strange man.''

Richard laughed incredulously.

''I did not ask for the money, because I could never feel that it was honestly come by. It seemed like a gift from a man who . . . did not know the rules. And now, I find that in changing a sum that seemed to me large enough at the time, into a fortune, you have placed me in a still more questionable position. What am I to do? How am I to explain to my husband why it is that I have so large a sum at my disposal and have never seen fit to use it to relieve some of *his* problems? What *can* I do, except take the money and run, as they say? I must, before you compromise me any further.''

"You are very *delicate*, Alexa. I reckon your motives weren't so refined when you married that animal you call your husband in that sanctimonious way of yours. I bet there was some real, crude emergency *there*." Alexa's face was chalk-white. She began to rise from the chair.

"No, no. Don't go. You *are* a sanctimonious bitch, you know, but there are things you don't realise about yourself. You earned that two thousand dollars as surely as I earned every darned cent I own. The minute you walked into that ritzy dressmaker's joint in Paris and asked for a job, you began to earn it. You took what you had, assessed it, decided it was saleable and trundled it along to market. That's judgement. That's business sense. That's courage, and I applaud it. So you came to New York and someone was willing to pay for more of the same commodity. We don't chase every order in business, do we? Some just come by good luck. You got two thousand dollars and I asked you for the chance to work with it for you. You agreed. You never called it in and I just continued to deal on your behalf because I never had any instructions to the contrary. You call that manipulation? You don't owe me a thing. I've charged your account with every cent of brokerage fees I'd have charged any other client," Richard lied. "So *where, Madame*, is the condescension, the manipulation, as you call it, in *that*?"

"You're very clever, Richard, but you are not honest. You know the dangers. I *love* my husband."

"Liar! And, I'll tell you another thing, Alexa Standeven, you harp a lot on what I daresay your mother would call the *impropriety* of those two thousand dollars. But it's noticeable, you've not mentioned leaving *one million* dollars behind you out of a sense of decency. Wrap it up, darling. You may fool that decadent husband of yours and his moribund family. You may even fool yourself some of the time but remember where I come from, the same place as *you*. There are some gestures that can be afforded, and some that can't. So, you may as well tell me what you came for, at least. How's the kid?" He changed the subject abruptly, tactically.

In spite of herself, she warmed to the enquiry. Alexa could not resist answering a question about Charles. He preyed on her mind so constantly, that it was natural to speak of him to anyone who asked.

"The kid, as you call him, had a severe defect of the bone marrow at birth. It was not apparent until a year to eighteen months after his birth. I am sure Ariel has kept you abreast of these family concerns of mine."

"She has, as a matter of act. Said you were making a pretty good stab at coping. Pushing the poor kid a bit, though, aren't you?"

"How *dare* you?" Alexa flashed at him. Nobody knew the anxieties she faced on Charles' behalf. She resented this casual criticism from a childless bachelor.

"Easy, I care. How're the cats going on?"

"The cats are delightful. They seem to be the only good thing that ever proceeded from you, Mr. Lockwood."

"Except a million dollars."

Alexa was silent for a minute, her mind busy with the glorious new fact in her life. It had come too late to save her and Fabrice from the deep scarring of poverty and anxiety, but now, it *existed*.

"Touché, Monsieur." Both of the set faces which opposed each other across the desk relaxed, dissolved by the light beam of Alexa's own smile.

"Tell me now, Alexa. Why did you come here?"

"To borrow the money to start a wine business of my own. I have a little capital, you know. Just the money from my marriage settlement which has been carefully looked after. Not, with the same flair that you exhibit, I must say, just ordinary caution. And then I have some land, also from my marriage settlement. *That* has not been cared for, and it will take a good deal to put it back in good heart. I've even got a little money left from my grandfather's legacy, but I spent most of that on a nursery for Charles. The balance has been earning interest at a very pedestrian rate. Compared to what you've achieved, it's small change. Altogether, it would have been just about enough, but my grandfather told me never to use my own money for anything if I could borrow it at reasonable cost. So I came to see you. Now it doesn't seem necessary. I'm quite safe, after all."

"Safe from what?" He looked at her closely.

"You wouldn't understand. My affairs are too mixed up and complicated to explain. Anyway, I don't think it concerns you."

"No, possibly not, Alexa. But concerned is what I am, just the same. I don't like to see talent going to waste, you know. And you have talent, don't you? You really know about this wine thing. I notice *Château de Pies Ombre* got a prize last year from the *Comice Agricole du Médoc*. Yes, *Diplome de Medaille d'Or*. A gold medal, no less. What did it say? Something like, 'An excellent property, completely restored. A noble vineyard in perfect condition.' Or so I translated in my clumsy uneducated way.''

"You keep yourself very well informed. You are also very observant, or should I say curious.''

"Both no doubt. It is a banker's business to be informed and curious. If a thing is written down, I read it. If it is audible, I hear it.'' He did not tell her how close to her own territory he read and heard these things. During his annual few weeks at Villandraut, he scoured the regional newspaper, *Sud Ouest*, for the slightest mention of her area, her property, even that of her neighbours. In New York he took every magazine that ever had articles on wine. He knew almost as much as she did. About tonnages and prices, perhaps a good deal more. "So, why don't you go ahead?''

Alexa shifted uncomfortably in her chair. The conversation seemed to be going nowhere. She drummed her still-gloved fingers irritably on the steel of the chair arm. New factors in her situation required to be digested.

"Come on, let's hear about your wine business. What did you have in mind? You've nothing to lose by talking about it. By the way, why come to me? Aren't there any French banks willing to back a new venture of this sort? Rather more up their furrow than mine, I should have thought.'' His weak joke was ignored with deliberate and visible disdain.

"I went to the *Crédit des Vignerons d'Aquitaine* in Bordeaux, they were polite but unhelpful.'' For the next hour Alexa told Richard of the courteous stonewalling she had experienced in Bordeaux. The banks were unwilling to load her and her family with a further burden of debt, just when she was nearly free of it after so many years. They would, of course, help, if she insisted. But they would require a further charge on the château. And naturally, for this Fabrice's consent would be necessary. This would involve giving him some equity in the new enterprise and this was unacceptable to Alexa. It would entirely defeat her objectives. Once again, she would be dependent on Fabrice. Alexa told Richard nothing except her unwillingness to rely on her husband for support in the venture. "I wanted to do it myself, otherwise there would simply have been no point," she said in conclusion.

Richard listened with increasing admiration and hope. She could not love a man she did not trust. Not as a woman loves a man. Perhaps as a mother loves a child, but not more than that.

"Ah, the husband you love . . ."

Alexa shot him a look of pure loathing. "Sorry. I withdraw that." His remorse was genuine. "You know me, a rough diamond, at best."

"Like hell!" Her smile came again, a flash of summer lightning. She had this power to change the weather in any room, at any time. There was no warning, ever.

"So that's the banks. Now tell me what the business plan was."

"I've got five hectares of my own and the use of a further ten at a nominal rent. Our *négociant* told me years ago I could have them for next to nothing if I'd restore them. It may sound like a pathetic smallholding to you, but land capable of supporting vines in the Médoc is worth a great deal of money. In fact nobody knows just how much, because it never comes on the market."

"It certainly does sound small . . ." he could not resist teasing.

"We're not growing barley, you know," Alexa flashed defensively, "what we grow is gold, red gold."

He smiled and nodded. "I accept the high value of the crop but . . ."

"With wine, quantity is not always the first consideration. In our region it is of minor importance, what counts is quality. And quality is what the entire world now knows I can deliver.

"It is true, you know, that at one time I dreamed of producing a popular wine. Something that everyone could enjoy and that would mature fast enough to make that realistic and affordable. Something in the St. Emilion manner, based on the *Merlot* grape. But there was a problem with that. First, fifteen acres just won't feed a mass market and secondly, I found out that it's warmer down in St. Emilion. *Merlot*'s a bit of a risk with us. The vine flowers early and we suffer somewhat with late frosts." She shrugged. "That could wipe us out. I wanted to do for claret what Mateus did for rosé. But it's not practical. However, I notice that at Pétrus they are making a wine that is the reflection of my dream. It fetches the highest prices of any wine in the greater region. They only have about eleven hectares. Is it so crazy to try it with the same amount of land, a little more, in fact? I know we have the frost risk, but we can do things about that. Alarms, braziers, flame throwers . . . There are ways, I am sure.''

"Go on." Richard's concentration was intense. As before, the depth and breadth of her knowledge impressed him. Another thing struck him. She was only fully relaxed when she was addressing the subject she loved. The marks of strain dissolved and she appeared as fresh and youthful as ever, full of vigour and sap, her skin glowed and her voice was musical and strong, making point after point with total command and self-confidence. Her presence irradiated his whole being. She communicated her strength and belief as certainly as if she had injected them into his veins. It was his great luck that the Bordeaux banks would not lend. Why not, he could only imagine. Perhaps she spoke French less forcibly and gracefully than she spoke her native language. He had no means of judging.

"It would take four years before I could make any wine at all, that's if I restocked from the beginning. Or I could clear the land and do what they call *recépagement*. Cut the old vines and graft new stock onto them. They did it at Pétrus after the frost got them, more than fifteen years ago, and it's still working. It might be a way of getting a quality wine on the market faster.''

"Did you explain all this to them in Bordeaux?''

"Of course, you have to have all your facts marshalled when you go to see a bank in Bordeaux, or any bank," she amended hastily.

"I wonder why they did not advance you the money on condition you gave them a legal charge on the land? That way your husband wouldn't have been involved. If what you say is right, the land is *yours*.''

"Oh, they suggested that. But I wouldn't have it.''

"But that isn't unreasonable, Alexa. Quite usual, in fact. You surely don't expect them to lend money without some security?''

"Their security was my proven competence and experience. I've had enough of the bullying of banks. I want no more of it. They either take a chance on me or they don't. I've lived too many years with the threats of banks hanging over my head. I really couldn't stand any more of it.''

"I know how you feel." Richard's voice had a curious, bitter quality which Alexa had never heard there before. Her eyes widened enquiringly.

"But you're a banker."

"I was only a schoolboy when a bank ruined my father. The day it happened I stopped being a schoolboy. He couldn't afford to keep me there any more. I was a bank clerk when the poor old bugger died of shame and a broken heart. He never lived to see me get my own back. He was a fool, too. You're not."

Alexa, not knowing what to say, remained silent. It was an afternoon full of revelations.

"Anyway, that's what I wanted. An unsecured loan for $105,000. Crazy, wasn't it?"

"Take a banker's advice. Never admit you can see anything unreasonable about your own suggestions. Remember, to a very large extent he relies on your assessment of the business risk. Banking is the betting business. Betting on people, their knowledge and their characters. Any projections?"

"Yes, here." Alexa opened the lizard-skin document case.

"I'll take a look at these and get back to you."

"I wonder if it's all worth doing now."

"Rubbish. What are you going to do? Sit around enjoying being a dollar millionairess for the rest of your life? It's not quite as much money as you really need to be, *safe*, as you put it."

A dollar millionairess. Alexa savourved the phrase. The fact had barely sunk in. She had money, real money. "I can't *feel* that money somehow. I don't feel physically connected to it. I didn't get it by inheritance, I didn't work for it, it's difficult to realise it's mine."

"It'll feel physically connected to you all right when you've worked *with* it and made it into a one hell of a sight more than it is now. By Jove, you will. Look, let me look at your projections and think about it for twenty-four hours. I think you've got what it takes, and if these bear you out, we're in business. I don't like layabouts, not dollars, not people. You with me? Have a drink with me before you go? Just for old times' sake?"

"What old times?"

"My, a rattler ain't got nothin' on you." Richard gave a murderously accurate imitation of a Texan agricultural worker.

"All right, Richard. But for these times, not old times. Hatchet buried, but shallowly, mind."

He depressed the switch on his desk again. Her mind wandered to another office and another drink. The glass of *marc*

Monsieur Terry had persuaded her to take before he had reluctantly offered her a job as a model in his *couture* house. All of this had begun there. She hadn't really wanted that drink either. But if she hadn't had it, she wouldn't be here now, exercising the power of real choice for the first time since . . . since when? There are days in your life on which every small thing you do affects the rest of your life. That day was one of those. Today was one. An unwanted drink had been lucky before. She was too superstitious not to invoke the good luck.

In a moment, the smart receptionist, whose name was Warren, came in with two crystal goblets and a bottle swathed in a damask napkin. She was smiling as if she knew what had taken place. Alexa reflected, accurately, that she probably smiled automatically as a matter of professional habit whenever alcoholic liquor was called for. Gloom and celebration replaced themselves automatically on her hired features in rhythm with the progress of her employer's business. Alexa felt sorry for her and hoped she had things of her own to make her smile.

"I want you to try this, tell me what you think." He poured a liquid that flashed alternate lights of amethyst and garnet. He handed her a glass, avoiding touching her hand with noticeable care. "What is it?"

"Is this a test?"

"If you like."

Alexa grimaced unself-consciously as she swilled the wine around her mouth as if it were the pink antiseptic fluid provided by dentists. "It's claret, of course," she pronounced with all the gravitas of a man twice her age.

Richard smiled, "You sure?"

"I ought to know, it's certainly *Cabernet Sauvignon*, or most of it anyway. There might be some *Petit Verdot*, I can't be sure. It's a variety we don't use ourselves. Not much oak and a little hard for my taste. Still, it's good. Not a great wine, but some potential for development I guess. Whose is it?"

"Nobody you know." He removed the napkin. "Here you are."

Alexa peered at the label. She read aloud, "Julius Sparrow, Margaret River Valley Estate, Cabernet Sauvignon, Product of Australia." She looked up at him, her mouth slightly open.

"It's for sale. I think we should buy it. The estate, that is."

* * *

Reluctantly, Alexa agreed with Fabrice that the first experimental operation on Charles' legs should be allowed to go ahead. It would involve long stays in the hospital, pain and no guarantee of ultimate success. Charles himself was consulted. At nearly seven, he was too old to be left out of the discussion. The agony of his parents and the cessation of their almost constant bickering made him hopeful of their eventual reconciliation. It seemed to Charles that if attention could be concentrated on his legs rather than money, wine or even American house guests, then hospital was a small price to pay for peace.

"You'd like me to have straight legs, wouldn't you, Mummy?"

"Well, of course, darling but . . . ."

"Could I take one of the cats?"

"No, sweetheart, I'm afraid they don't allow cats in hospitals and certainly not to sleep on the beds."

"*Grand-mère* doesn't approve of it here. But we still do it, don't we?"

Alexa gave in to the temptation. "*Grand-mère* doesn't call the shots here. I do."

"What does that mean, Mummy?"

"Ask Uncle Richard when you get to New York. No, on second thought, darling, don't. It was rather rude of Mummy to say that, not at all polite. *Grand-mère* is quite right really, and Granny Standeven would agree with her." Alexa tried not to involve Charles in the family tensions, but sometimes, irritability got the better of her.

"Will I be seeing him, Uncle Richard, I mean?" Charles' face had brightened. He had never met the donor of his cats, but in his narrow world, Richard Lockwood had assumed the proportions of a legendary figure, the distant, powerful person who had given him his most cherished possessions.

"Yes, he and Auntie Ariel will be looking after you. They'll both come and see you every day. And of course, Morag will be staying in the hospital with you. She'll make sure you do your school work too. So you shouldn't be bored or lonely."

"Am I going then?"

"Yes, darling. We've got to try it."

"Will you come and see me too?"

Alexa bent down to enfold the body of her son with tears in her eyes. "Of course, baby, as often as I can."

"And Daddy?"

"We'll see darling, you know how busy Daddy is."

Charles sighed. He had a few illusions about his father. But it was tacitly agreed between himself and his mother that Fabrice's increasingly long periods of hopeless depression confused by alcoholic intoxication were to be buried under the name of *business*.

Little was understood of Charles' condition. It seemed that the inevitable post-natal fracturing of the bones followed by distorted fusing, and the treatment with huge, unwelcome doses of cod liver oil, were the sum total of medical knowledge. Doctor Kilpatrick had suggested surgically re-breaking the bones and then setting them again, in the hope that whatever malfunction had caused the distorted setting during Charles' infancy was now corrected. If this theory proved to be founded in fact, it was proposed to realign both legs during three or four such operations successively. It was a horrifying procedure and the outcome would depend entirely on the result of the first operation. If it showed a sufficient measure of success as to justify repetition, each of the subsequent operations would have to take place before puberty, in Doctor Kilpatrick's judgement. Alexa could see alternative arguments.

"It's a race against time, Mrs. Ombre." Kilpatrick had resolutely declined to attempt any approximate version of Alexa's title. "We've got to sort out those bones while they're still greenwood and pretty easy to work with."

"Mightn't we do better to wait until Charles's grown up and the legs have reached their final form, and work on them when growth can't affect every stage of the treatment?"

"Might. Might not. Look Mrs. er . . . Omber, you know my record on corrective bone surgery. You either trust me, or you don't. I don't take patients who have no confidence in me. Don't have to. Know what I mean? You want someone to straighten the kid's legs out, reckon it'll have to be me." If he were the last doctor on earth and I were dying he shouldn't touch me, Alexa thought angrily, but for Charles she would swallow any amount of pride.

Charles left with Morag after Christmas. For once both Fabrice and Alexa went to see them off from Paris. They stayed the night in the dusty old house in the Marais. Rain lashed the windows and the dismal wet of the winter streets outside seemed preferable to the catacomb gloom within.

The house was barely habitable. The party had supper together, seated at a round table before a hastily made fire in the

Grand Salon. Old Brun shuffled in and out with plates of soup and cheese and pâté, his coat as threadbare as the curtains. Morag wore an expression of disapproval the whole evening. It would have been amusing if it were not so wearisome. Alexa felt faintly irritated with her. It was all right for Morag, protected in her gilded eyrie, paid a comfortable salary and insulated from all but nursery cares. What could she know of mortgages, obligations to old servants and constant financial stringency? Care had been taken that she never should know of these things. It was part of the carefully structured cocoon of safety that had been built around Charles. But she was a good girl, loyal and dependable. Nannies must never be worried lest they communicate worry to the children. It was one of Elizabeth's wiser pronouncements.

Morag's consternation increased when she learned that she would have to bathe Charles that night in a china hip bath in her bedroom. She would have to carry copper cans of hot water up from the kitchen aided by Brun. It was the only place the ancient plumbing system could be relied upon to deliver hot water in sufficient quantities.

"You and Daddy were married here, weren't you?" Charles remarked brightly, enjoying the midnight picnic with his parents. They were so rarely together. If only Tante Héloïse were here too, it would be perfect, then he would have everyone he loved at once. Well, almost, it would be nice to have Uncle Tim Bowring too. He made everything exciting and fun when he came to visit. Piggy-back rides through the dark unused rooms of the château, games of hide and seek in the *chais*. Everyone liked Uncle Tim. Even Pierre David, and he was hard to impress. Once he'd asked him why he wasn't a daddy himself. He said he still hadn't found the kind of mummy he'd like to be a daddy with. "I want someone like your mummy," he said, "but they're very hard to find." Charles sighed.

"Yes, darling, in this room."

"It's like a horror movie."

"Film, darling, film. Where does he pick up these expressions, Morag?"

"He was watching quite a lot of American television in Mrs. Scheitinger's apartment, while you were having your meetings with Mr. Lockwood. That's the only place he can have got it, Madam."

Alexa glanced quickly at Fabrice, who hearing the other man's

name had looked up enquiringly. At that moment the telephone
rang in the little antechamber. Alexa rose to answer it and after
a few moments' muffled conversation returned. She waved away
Fabrice's half-uttered question with a warning frown.

"Come along Charles, now," Morág said, understanding the
cue, "it's long past your bedtime and heaven knows when we
shall see our beds tomorrow." Grumblingly, Charles allowed
himself to be led away on the promise of a mug of hot chocolate
in the bath.

As the double doors shut behind them, Fabrice again turned
to Alexa.

Alexa sat down again at the table, "It was your mother," she
began gently but knowing no way to soften the news. "It seems
Tante Héloïse was looking for some papers on top of the cupboard in her room this morning after we left. She fell. There
was a massive cerebral haemorrhage. I'm afraid she's dead."

CHAPTER
18

❧❧ HÉLOÏSE'S SUDDEN DEATH had hit Alexa and Fabrice hard. Each mourned separately and wordlessly. And both realised that in her they had lost the only friend who had known them both fully, and knowing all, had loved them with the same fullness. She had tried to make them love each other, and although Alexa at least, was willing to try, Héloïse could not make her patient with Fabrice. His aunt had also perceived the soreness of Fabrice's heart and the delusions of his mind, but she could not make him understand the distortions which clouded his perception of reality, or control his bouts of cruelty to Alexa, of which she knew nothing.

The preparations for Héloïse's funeral acted as a counter-irritant both to the sadness of her absence and the gnawing anxieties about Charles which Alexa and Fabrice both felt keenly, but did not mention.

The house was smothered in a pall of unrestrained gloom which assorted ill with Alexa's inbred belief that as little as possible should be made of death. The atmosphere killed whatever lingering vibrations of Héloïse's brisk, kindly personality there might have been and filled their place with a melancholy which was untrue to her own faith and optimism. Certainly the stress placed on the physical aspects of mortality was offensive to Alexa, causing her to sleep badly at night and to be oppressed during the day by feelings of irritation verging on hysteria.

Héloïse's body lay in an obscene state in her bedroom on the ground floor of the *Tour du Jardin*. Alexa was expected to view the mortal remains and she did so, reluctantly, refusing to repeat the exercise to Suzanne's triumphant disapproval. It seemed almost as if the cessation of life in Héloïse's body had resulted in a mysterious transmission of unusual vigour into Suzanne's. She walked about the château, as often as not, rosary in hand, presiding over the details of her sister-in-law's departure from life with ghoulish efficiency, glad to exhibit command over procedures which Alexa did not understand.

Alexa expressed fear and revulsion, saying she had no wish to inspect the carrion. Suzanne chose to take grave offence, and Fabrice, who made a perfunctory visit to the death chamber himself, without remark, raised his eyebrows as if to suggest his wife's behaviour was noticeable purely on account of its childishness.

"You will be so reassured, Alexa," urged Suzanne, "to see Tante Héloïse so peaceful. Death is nothing to be afraid of. She would have told you that herself."

"But *what* will be reassuring about it? I shan't feel any reassurance, I promise you, until that *thing* is out of the house. I don't want anything to do with it. It's all horrible. Why couldn't they take her to a mortuary or a hospital or something?" was Alexa's petulant response.

"Mademoiselle de Pies Ombre lies in her own home until it is time for her to make the journey to her last resting place. That is the custom and it is *our* custom. Anything else would be a breach of our duty and of our dignity. We are not paupers that we have no room to house our dead. I thought that you had a regard for Tante Héloïse."

"I *did*. But I don't like dead bodies, whoever they belong to."

But it was no use. Alexa was driven to visit Héloïse's room in order to keep the peace. She went by herself, shrinking from this encounter with a corpse. On entering the circular room, she at first saw nothing. As her eyes accustomed to the gloom, she realised with a shock that she was not alone and that two figures knelt on either side of the bed. They were in fact two nuns from the Order of the Sainte Vierge in Bordeaux, whose convent Héloïse had wished to enter so many years ago. They were keeping a vigil beside the body of their would-be sister, their orisons lit only by two large candles and a curious brass taper bracket which Alexa had never seen before affixed to the wall beside the bed.

Alexa stood shyly in the doorway, her flesh chill and the hairs standing up rigidly on her forearms. Tentatively she breathed in the air. There was a stuffy smell and the heavy perfume of some white lilies which were disposed about the room in large pretentious arrangements. From where she stood, Héloïse's body looked unnaturally small. Pale, claw-like hands clutched a rosewood and mother-of-pearl crucifix. The mother-of-pearl Christ glowed with a faint phosphorescence, echoing the tone of Héloïse's dead flesh. Alexa shuddered and turned to leave when she jumped at a light touch on her shoulder. One of the sisters led her by the hand to the bedside. Alexa wanted to snatch her hand away from the cool grasp of the other, unknown woman, but good manners prevented her.

The bedroom had been transformed by the undertakers into a funerary chapel. The walls were hung with black cloth, the bed had become a bier on which the pallid remains of Héloïse lay. The body seemed insubstantial in terms of mass and colour, but it lay there without the characteristic heaviness of death. To Alexa's shrinking eye, it looked so fragile that it might blow away in a sudden draught.

"You see, she is at peace. There is nothing to fear," the face, almost as bloodless as Héloïse's own, announced from out of the shell-like coif of white linen. Alexa nodded mutely, wondering how soon she could terminate this unwelcome conversation.

"Would you like to kiss her?" Alexa turned away, unable to respond to the revolting suggestion.

"What is this thing?" She gestured towards the brass wall-bracket which supported three small wax candles. The nun's glance followed Alexa's.

"Oh, that is always here when any member of the family dies. You see, there are places for five tapers, but when it is a woman who dies, there are only three placed in it."

"I see." Three out of five was a poor score for Héloïse. "Are there any more tapers?"

"Why, yes *Madame*, plenty," the nun answered, surprised by the question. "You see, in this box, here, I replace them whenever they burn down." The nun took a brass box from a small table, opening it to show Alexa the contents. Alexa took two of the tapers, and watched by the open-mouthed nun, she inserted them in the two vacant holders in the bracket.

"From now on *ma Soeur*, you will keep five burning while Mademoiselle de Pies Ombre remains in the house. Do you understand?"

The nun was ruffled. "But certainly, *Madame*, if you wish it, but . . ."

"Five!" Alexa forgot to lower her voice. She heard it crack the carefully nurtured silence as she ran from the room.

Since returning from Paris, Alexa felt a disturbing restlessness and was unable to sleep with her customary ease and relaxation. The loss of this ability which had stood her in good stead through the worst of her troubles exasperated and worried her. The simple self-discipline of reminding herself each night as she got into bed, which Fabrice shared very seldom, and then only when drunk, that she was powerless to affect her situation until the next day, had enabled her to refresh her mind and body in readiness for renewed struggles. Hortense prepared infusions, *tisanes* as she called them, from dried lime-tree flowers, but they did no good. Even the discreet flurry surrounding the arrangements for Héloïse's funeral and the unwelcome presence of her body in the house, together with agonising uncertainty about Charles' ordeal, did not fully account for her loss of equilibrium. She experienced a kind of hyper-perception. Colours seemed more vivid, the notes of individual voices in the household were intensified and most of all, she was aware of a heightened consciousness of her own body.

When she walked she noted the length and rhythm of her own stride, feeling the tension and individuality of each muscle. Her movements were swift, springing and deliberate. She found herself examining herself in looking-glasses for many minutes together. At odd moments of the day, she could not resist spending time with her own reflected image. It was as if it were indeed an alter ego with whom she could share a delightful and exciting secret.

But what was the secret? Restlessly, Alexa paced the turret room, unable to concentrate on the new vineyard project. Estimates for clearance work and new vine stocks lay neglected on her desk. Somehow it was difficult to focus her attention on these matters which had so completely filled her life until this moment. Eventually she identified within herself the presence of an inexplicable joy, the source of which was dangerous to contemplate.

The eye of her mind constantly retraced its steps to the hours she had spent in Richard Lockwood's office on Wall Street. She saw the contours of his face, his long upper lip pulled down in deprecation, the neat, pale ears which lay close to his skull. It was natural she should think of him. He had volunteered his services as Charles' temporary guardian in New York. She had been unable to refuse and Ariel felt better able to bear the responsibility with Richard's support. She was glad he and Ariel were friends, together they made another kind of family, a citadel of safety and protection for her child.

As she lay wakeful, turning and slapping her pillows, readjusting the sheets, her thoughts caressed and explored the crisp dry waves of his hair and the texture of his skin. There was a small scar near the corner of his eye. It made a distinct crater. The tips of her fingers knew its depth and extent. In yearning imagination, she laid the length of her own smooth and slender body next to his compact and massive one. She matched shoulder joint to shoulder joint and laid her small breasts against the rock of his chest wall. Would there be much hair? The gravelly threads in his remembered voice travelled through her veins.

These thoughts drifted unbidden across her mind. But Alexa was powerless to reject them. Her own hands conducted a tour of her body. When her finger tips sported casually with abundant pubic hair, she felt his hair. She cupped her engorged labiae in her hand and felt the firmness of an embrace she had never known and would never have permitted. The inner gates of her womanhood stood open, demanding a fulfilment, the nature of which her brain told her was impossible. The ache was a real and constant pain from which there was no escape. A strange, astringent odour of juniper haunted her intermittently, she realised that it was the smell of Richard's body. It came without warning, when she least expected it and when, for a time, she had found some respite in her work. The odd, resinous scent would assail her and destroy her concentration.

It was the day before the funeral that Maître Robinson telephoned. Alexa received the call in the turret room where she was exerting herself to study the sales literature for an automatic grape harvester. Developed from an English raspberry picker, it appeared to have some possibilities. The sound of the quiet, characteristic buzz of the internal telephone system disturbed her painstaking calculations.

Hortense's voice announced the outside call.

"*Madame?* Madame Fabrice de Pies Ombre? It is you?"

"*Oui, Monsieur. C'est moi. Qui est-ce qui parle?*"

"*Madame*, it is I. Maître Robinson, at your service."

"Good morning, Maître. What can I do for you? Are you telephoning about the arrangements between myself and Monsieur Chirac? We have decided on a peppercorn rent and percentage of the profits in recompense for the use of the land. I'm afraid poor Monsieur Chirac will be getting by far the worst of it. He won't see any return for a good many years, I fear . . ."

Alexa sat down at the desk and looked through the oriel window. Work had begun at last on the formal garden below and its old pattern had begun to emerge.

"Why don't you make a nice *English* garden, Alexa? So much kinder to the feet and livelier to the eye." Héloïse's voice echoed sadly in her head.

"No, no, *Madame*. It is not vineyards I wish to speak about. That is not the purpose of my call. Are you able to talk? Are we private? I have something to say of a confidential nature. Please, there is not much I *can* say, but I hope you will follow my drift."

At the other end of the telephone, Maître Robinson attempted to light his pipe with one hand.

Alexa was puzzled and alert. There was something almost frantic in Maître Robinson's tone. Every antenna of her brain and body bristled with attention. There was agitation in the lawyer's voice where she had never previously heard anything but calm deliberation and good-humour.

"Please go on, Maître Robinson. I am listening."

"It is Mademoiselle de Pies Ombre's will. I shall read it to-morrow, after the funeral, which of course I shall attend. It is an outdated procedure, but one still favoured by our older families, though I sometimes doubt its wisdom."

"But surely Tante Héloïse had little to leave."

"Ah, that is the problem. Mademoiselle de Pies Ombre never spent anything. And whilst she may have begun life with little enough by the standards of her class, her estate is rather more substantial than may have been anticipated by the family."

"But that is good news, surely." Alexa spoke cautiously. There was something wrong here. She must be patient, Maître Robinson was no longer a young man. Nothing would be achieved by hurrying him.

"For some, perhaps. I wonder, *Madame*, if it is really necessary for you to attend this funeral? Mademoiselle de Pies Ombre is not a blood relative of yours, and after all, your son is in New York. At a time like this, he must need his mother." There was an infinitesimal pause while Alexa swallowed her astonishment.

"But, Maître Robinson, you know surely that Tante Héloïse was more to me than an aunt by marriage, much, much more. She was a good friend. At times, I thought she was the only one I had here. I couldn't think of not attending her funeral. In a way, I'd be glad to avoid it. There's a horrible, horrible fuss here, you can probably imagine, but I wouldn't want anyone to think I didn't love Tante Héloïse because I *did*. I simply must go, unless you can give me a very good reason for being absent."

Maître Robinson said nothing. He'd got his pipe alight at last, and was drawing on it steadily.

Alexa waited impatiently. Why doesn't he hurry? What is this elaborate game about? What is he trying to say?

"*Madame*, I feel some family tension may result from the provisions of Mademoiselle de Pies Ombre's will. Perhaps it was not the most sage of testimonies, but I was powerless to dissuade her. Indeed, I did not want to, but I perceive potential dangers."

"Dangers?" Alexa wondered what possible dangers there could be in poor Tante Héloïse's will. She was going to leave everything to Charles, that had always been understood, since before he was born. It was the way things were done in the de Pies Ombre family. Maiden aunts without children of their own always, by custom, left the bulk of their estates, in equal shares, to the children of their brothers and sisters. It was perfectly fair and reasonable, but there was only Charles to consider.

"Well, perhaps *danger* is too strong a word," he amended quickly, "but, as I say, surprises are always harder to absorb at emotional times. I think, in short, that it would be a good idea, a tactful idea, if you were to be out of the way at the time the will is read. *Do* try to understand, *Madame*. I think only of *you*."

"I thank you for your concern, Maître. I am touched, as ever, by your thoughtfulness, but I think I can manage. I know this family very well, after all, I am part of it. Tante Héloïse wouldn't have done anything to harm any of us. She loved us all, in spite of our faults."

He would not say more. But her refusal to draw any conclusions from his hints left Maître Robinson in despair. What more could he say? How could he give expression to his fears? Even if he acknowledged they were fantastic, but they existed none-the-less.

Once Héloïse's coffin had been placed in the family vault which lay in a small copse of trees to the rear of the house, and Pierre David with two men from the *chais* left to manoeuvre the marble slab back into position, the family returned to the château for lunch. The sight of other, older coffins that the recent excavation had revealed took all appetite from Alexa and drowned the curiosity she might have had concerning the mysterious anxieties of Maître Robinson.

During the requiem mass at the village church, he had glanced nervously at her from time to time and she had felt his eyes upon her. Resolutely, she had refrained from returning his glance. Hints, half-stories, had always irritated her. Maître Robinson had been an invariably kind friend, not only to her, but to the family as a whole. But he had not known Tante Héloïse as she had done. However she had arranged her affairs at the last, it would only be to their benefit, and she would never, never have taken anything away from her nephew.

The *cortège* made its way back from the church to the château. Alexa went with Fabrice in the old Jaguar, Suzanne shared the limousine provided by the undertakers with Tilly. She had flown from Paris the night before. Her presence was unnecessary but she had insisted on ''supporting'' the family. ''After all,'' she had said as Alexa conducted her to one of the best guest-rooms, ''I have known that poor old woman since Suzanne's marriage and as she can have *very* few friends, I thought it my duty to swell the numbers.''

Hating to hear Tante Héloïse so brutally described, Alexa had replied smoothly ''Yes, poor old Heloise, she was just a year younger than you, wasn't she, Tilly? Sixty-three,'' at which Tilly had tapped Alexa gently on the wrist and told her she was a naughty, clever girl but she should be forgiven because everyone knew how much she missed Tante Héloïse.

Alexa had stood beneath the roof of the miniature chapel with the theatrically veiled Suzanne, Fabrice and the members of the immediate family, the only ones for whom there was room. She contributed her small handful of fading blooms to the dark pit which lay open at her feet to receive the coffin. It was so small and light that Pierre David brushed the undertaker's man on one side and lifted it reverently from the hearse in his arms and

placed it ready to be lowered into the vault. The flowers fell
with a soft, sighing sound as they hit the coffin. Flowers, not
earth, a tribute to virginity. Her stomach retched at the sound.
The priest, a young, pimply designate of the Bishop of Bordeaux, who reminded her unpleasantly of Père Lachasse, continued his prayers. Alexa's mind was deliberately elsewhere. If
she stopped to look or to listen, she would surely be sick. No
doubt he was saying ''From dust to dust, from ashes to ashes''
and all those things which insulted the memory of the dead and
increased the horror of permanent parting.

Tilly left for Mérignac airport immediately after the final cer-
emonies were completed. It was tiresome, she said, because she
would have liked to stay to luncheon, but there was no other
plane she could catch until the evening. She waited in vain for
Alexa to suggest that she remain another night at d'Ombre and
leave the following morning. Alexa was too distracted to think
of it and Suzanne had no inclination for a second evening of
Tilly's incessant chatter. And so Pierre David was deputed to
drive her to the airport in the Jaguar and she went, clearly dis-
gruntled, with a suitcase the size of which would normally have
indicated plans for a more protracted visit to Alexa's hospitable
eye.

At luncheon she was unable to eat anything. Suzanne and
Fabrice ate calmly enough with an increasing air of cheer as the
meal progressed. Maître Robinson seemed concerned to keep
the conversation to the usual items of Bordeaux gossip with
occasional courteous asides to the two sisters who had kept the
vigil beside Héloïse's bed. They remained to hear the provisions
of the will in which their convent was assumed to have an interest. They said little, murmuring politely in appreciation of the
dishes which were set before them and smiling distantly at Maître
Robinson's sallies. Nobody said more to Alexa than the minimum consistent with bare civility except Soeur Marie-Josephe,
who was seated near enough her hostess to notice her pallor and
to press a little wine and water on her.

''I am afraid you are not well, *Madame*. You must be greatly
distressed by Mademoiselle de Pies Ombre's death. When I first
entered the convent as a postulant, we were always being told
by our Novice Mistress that it was a pity none of us showed the
enthusiasm for the life that poor Héloïse de Pies Ombre did,
who hadn't been *allowed* to enter. Of course, she didn't mention
her by name, but we all knew who she meant. There is always

talk in a closely knit community like Bordeaux. I think our Superior and the Novice Mistress had not agreed about her case.''

The other nun looked up sharply from her plate and her more communicative sister flushed and fell silent. The constitutions of their order forbade idle gossip.

Maître Robinson cleared his throat and re-arranged the papers which lay before him on the writing table in the *Grand Salon*. The room, or rather the furniture at one end of it, had been arranged to resemble an office with chairs arranged in a semi-circle around the desk. They all sat there, awaiting the moment when he should begin.

The pale February sunshine fell upon the group, bleaching their sombre clothing and causing a restlessness as each twisted discreetly, trying to find some respite for the eyes. Suzanne lifted her hand to ward off the sun, the nuns looked down at their serge-clad laps and Fabrice's eyes were closed. He had drunk a good deal at luncheon but fortunately gave little sign of it. Alexa looked obliquely along the polished parquet of the floor and noted Maître Robinson's socks. They were black silk. So fine that the flesh showed through them. They had a weirdly chorus-girl look about them. He looked up and caught her smile. His expression was one of appalled anxiety. He got out his pipe, looked longingly at it and slipped it back into his pocket. He cleared his throat again.

''As you will know, the late Mademoiselle Héloïse de Pies Ombre was allocated a small capital by her father at the time when in normal circumstances, she might have been expected to marry. It was, however, Mademoiselle de Pies Ombre's desire to enter the convent of the Sainte Vierge in Bordeaux. Unhappily, owing to her state of health, the Superior at that time was obliged to refuse the application. This caused Mademoiselle de Pies Ombre much sadness although she resigned herself to the authority of the decision and acknowledged its wisdom.''

The coifs of the nuns nodded slightly in confirmation, their faces invisible. Maître Robinson continued. ''It was always Mademoiselle de Pies Ombre's wish, that the dowry that she would have brought to the convent in the event of her acceptance there should benefit the convent on her death. And in this respect, she has not deviated from her original intention.''

Suzanne shifted restlessly. Fabrice looked bored, opening his eyes only slightly. He made a gesture intended to convey to the lawyer that he should continue without excessive explanation. Maître Robinson ignored the gesture.

"It was her further intention to leave the interest accrued on that original capital to her nephew, the Marquis de Pies Ombre, in trust for his legitimate children, together with certain items of jewellery, owned personally by her own mother and left to her to dispose of as she would. It had originally been her intention to make the convent her literary executors in the hope that the community would continue to benefit from the royalties arising from her works, for some little time to come. There were, in addition, some small bequests to family servants, societies and charities in which the lady had interested herself during her lifetime. These provisions are substantially unchanged. However, some months before her death, I was instructed by Mademoiselle de Pies Ombre to re-draft the will along lines which, whilst giving ultimately a similar effect, altered the custodianship of her estate during the minority of her great-nephew."

He had prepared them as best he could. Maître Robinson could read nothing in the Marquis' expression. He seemed almost comatose, but the light of suspicion had begun to dawn on his mother's features which were darkening with displeasure. He began to read the will expressionlessly, in the tone of professional detachment that he hoped would avert any outburst. The minor legacies were dealt with first. Pierre David and Hortense were generously treated. The convent would receive the sum of Héloïse's original dowry, fifty thousand francs. It was not a great sum. Forty-one years had passed since the money had first been settled on her. The compounded interest, in all a sum of 984,844 ffs, when the principal had been subtracted, was to pass to Alexa to be held in trust for Charles. The capital and interest arising therefrom to be administered during his minority as his mother thought fit. The jewellery, of which the major items were a diamond parure and the diamond and opal magpie Héloïse had worn at Charles' christening, were to pass to Alexa for her own use absolutely, without entail or limit. "Just as the testatrix had herself owned them," Maître Robinson added on a note of redundant explanation.

A profound silence greeted the concluding clauses of the will. It was not a fortune. At the beginning, Héloïse had the price of a very good house. At the end of her life, unimaginative management had left her, in real terms, with very little more. But it was a useful sum. It was money that Fabrice had looked forward to controlling. There were debts to pay, of which Alex knew nothing. It was unforgivable. So that was what she had been doing all those hours with Héloïse. Working on the old woman.

Maître Robinson rustled his papers uneasily. A burst of indignation would have been easier to handle than this unnatural silence. He addressed Fabrice directly.

"You realise, of course, that these amendments to your aunt's will, in fact make no difference to the eventual disposal of her fortune. All will go to your son in due course and thus remain in de Pies Ombre hands . . . No doubt Mademoiselle de Pies Ombre thought that since your wife oversees your business affairs to a large extent these days, it would be helpful if you were to be relieved of the burden of administering what is, after all, a comparatively modest estate. She did not confide in me, but I imagine these were her intentions."

"Or were they my wife's intentions?"

The question was snapped out. Fabrice rose, his difficulty in doing so made him seem all the more threatening. Alexa watched him warily. He had hit her once before. The nuns remained as motionless as rabbits caught in the headlights of a car. Suzanne walked towards Alexa who remained seated, still trying to encompass the full implications of the will. She understood the compliment that Héloïse had paid her and there was a lump in her throat. But dimly, she was aware that in being given exclusive control over the small fortune left to her son, she had been led into a trespass on territory which might be disputed.

Alexa felt Suzanne's hand on her elbow. Incredibly, she seemed to be attempting to raise her from her seat, quite gently. She looked up gratefully into her mother-in-law's face. Then, very deliberately, Suzanne raised her hand and smacked her daughter-in-law's cheek. The sting brought tears to her eyes.

For once, Tilly confined herself to listening without comment. At the end of Alexa's recitation of the facts she said "I see." Alexa held the telephone patiently to her ear. She had reported the events of the previous afternoon without embellishment or omission. Now that Héloïse was gone, there was nobody but

Tilly to turn to. And, she recalled, Tilly had offered to act as confidante before her marriage took place. Now she should make good her promise. Advice might not be a realistic requirement, but an understanding capable of recognising the outrage was a necessity.

"You must realise, *ma chère*, that Suzanne would have benefited to some extent from the money had it been left in the trusteeship of Fabrice. He has always shared whatever there was with his mother. Why, I don't know. She did precious little for him as a boy. And her reaction, although it shocks you, is not entirely unexpected. Suzanne grew up in the emotionally charged society of colonial Algeria. Those families, wherever their actual roots, were more Mediterranean than the Mediterraneans. It seems that a few generations' exposure to the sun is all it takes to transform the temperaments of good northern stock. It is true that Suzanne has lived in Metropolitan France all her life since her marriage at eighteen, but when we are under acute stress, the mannerisms of our extreme youth take over. To Suzanne, a slap in the face is a trifling matter. A mere form of expression."

"It is not one I can accept."

Tilly sighed. She supposed not.

"I never told anyone, but Fabrice hit me once. When I was expecting Charles. It is the second time a member of the de Pies Ombre family has laid violent hands on me and it is the *last*, I assure you of *that*."

Alexa heard the still deeper sigh at the other end of the telephone.

Really, Tilly thought, everyone was most ungrateful. Alexa had made a far better marriage than she would have done without her interest in the matter. Suzanne hadn't been at all keen at the beginning, and now all this drama over something that was really no more than an unpleasant incident. Good Heavens, in her day, there were girls who had to put up with far worse than the occasional slap. But Alexa *had* restored the fortunes of the de Pies Ombres though not quite in the way they'd all hoped and expected. Mr. Standeven, charming though he was, was a little tight-fisted. But his daughter had rolled her sleeves up in no uncertain manner and done what neither her husband nor her mother-in-law had been able to do. And Suzanne had got a grandson and more money to waste than she'd had for years. Tilly was at a loss to see any serious occasion for complaint.

Except of course, as she reminded herself, that the pride of Alexa Standeven will not allow the dust to settle naturally. It really was too bad of them. She had arranged their lives so neatly and advantageously and now they were intent on destroying the pattern like three heedless children. It was too tiresome. Now she would be expected to arbitrate between them, Tilly considered with satisfaction.

"Does your father know anything of this?"

"No, he does not, and I don't know how I could tell him."

"Very wise. First it will be necessary to identify which elements of your life, if any, you wish to remain unchanged. Then we must see what can be done as regards the rest. If Mr. Standeven were to hear of this, I am afraid that he would give you no choice in the matter. He would take immediate steps to ensure your divorce from Fabrice. If I understand your *dear* father at all, I know he would be deeply distressed by all of this. Far better to keep him in the dark, far kinder too."

Tilly clung to an ever-strengthening fantasy that she was intimate with Alexander Standeven and could divine his thoughts and probable reactions as if she had been his closest friend.

"Fabrice wants a divorce."

"Because his aunt leaves you some money, or at any rate, the control of it?"

"Probably, but that is not what he says. He says I deny him his conjugal rights."

"And do you?"

"He is rarely in a condition to exercise them. And I'm not having another baby."

"That is naïve. You know as well as I do, *ma chère*, that there is no occasion to have babies one does not want. The matter is in your own hands and nobody, least of all your husband, need be any the wiser."

"Tilly, do you think that I should mess around with calendars and pills or horrendous contraptions on a daily basis on the off-chance that my husband may pay me one of his rare visits?"

The shrug at the other end of the telephone was almost audible.

"Alexa, it isn't like you to be so unreasonable. You cannot have it both ways. You must think, do you want your marriage to continue, or don't you? How do you wish your child to grow up? Where do you wish to live and with whom? These are the salient features of the matter. Perhaps it may be possible to find Suzanne some small and dignified house in which she could live. This may ease your domestic situation somewhat. Things might look better if that could be arranged.''

"And who is to pay for this small and dignified house. You suggest I should fund the enterprise? I am to reward the woman who slaps me in the face with a private residence?'' Tilly removed the telephone from contact with her ear as Alexa's voice rose to a crescendo of outrage.

"Alexa, pull yourself together, *ma chère*. It is you I am thinking of. Look, promise me one thing, that you will do nothing for two days at least. Try to behave normally, as though nothing has happened. Let them think that you feel it has all been a storm in a teacup. That is your admirable English expression, is it not? *Pas grand-chose*. It is impossible to think straight when one is hot with anger. You cannot act effectively in your own best interests when others are alert to your emotions . . .''

Again, Tilly held the telephone receiver at arm's length. It wasn't that Alexa was shouting but she *was* talking loudly and very, very clearly, making her feelings and sense of injustice known with a searing precision, choosing her words with a brutal exactitude that was not pleasant to listen to.

"I know, I *know*, but believe me, I have lived a long time and I know that precipitate action loses the game. Do as I say. Trust me. You will see things more clearly when another forty-eight hours have passed. Meanwhile, I will think hard and see if I can come up with a plan of action. Believe me, *ma chère*, it is best.''

Alexa almost slammed the telephone down. Tilly was right. But she had wanted suggestions for violent and immediate revenge that would have a decisive and positive effect. She had been humiliated in her own house and she was hungry for blood.

Alexa was curled up in the chintz armchair deep in thought and gazing at the dull red glow visible through the micawindows of the stove when Hortense knocked at the door.

"*Madame*, Pierre has brought the post round from the *chais*. You did not look at it yesterday, of course.''

Alexa stirred herself. "Oh, thank you, Hortense. I must go through it before lunch. Did he say if there was anything special?''

"No, *Madame*, but he hopes there may be a nursery catalogue that he has been waiting for, and there is a personal letter there."

Alexa slit the cream envelope with the London postmark open with a paper knife. Glancing at the signature, she saw it was from Tim Bowring. She laid it on one side and opened the stove to replenish it with vine cuttings. Their touch triggered the decision.

CHAPTER
19

ALEXA GAZED FOR several moments at the torpid, slack-featured child in the bed. There must have been some terrible mistake. "That's not my son," she flung the words at Doctor Kilpatrick.

The words broke the stillness of the small, antiseptic room. The white-uniformed nurse in the background was arranging hot-house roses in the sort of dull vase that hospitals provide. Morag was having the afternoon off. A well-earned rest from several weeks of almost uninterrupted vigil at her charge's bedside. The nurse ceased fussing with the flowers abruptly, stepping forward, a look of professional concern on her experience-weathered features. She laid a hand on Alexa's rigid shoulder. Post-operative shock may affect the mother as well as the child.

For a moment, Richard and Doctor Kilpatrick looked at each other. Their eyes met across the cot sides of the bed. They disliked each other, but their conspiracy was a reflex, the instinctive, primitive drawing together of men in the face of frightening feminine unreasonableness. The doctor, helpless in the face of this unexpected reaction, stared in amazement at Alexa. It was left to Richard to reach down and draw the sheet away from Charles' body. He pointed to the three, faint brown moles on the child's left forearm. They formed a perfect equilateral triangle. It was the way she had taught him to tell left from right.

"You see?" Momentarily she was relieved.

"Then why does he look so different? So . . ." she hesitated, "so *stupid*? Charles is not a stupid child." Frantically she looked from one face to the other.

"You're talking about the muscular relaxation of the features.

409

You see, Charles is heavily sedated. It's a routine procedure in the post-operative period . . ."

Alexa looked hard at the surgeon. She disliked his soothing avuncular tone. How dare he patronise me, she thought. Her son blinked up at her unrecognisingly. Kilpatrick's voice resumed its tone of kindly condescension to an intellect less able than his own.

"There is some discomfort, of course, and we dare not give him any more analgesic. He has had the maximum dose for a child of his age and weight. No more until tomorrow."

"You *promised* me no pain. And *I* promised Charles!"

"I did not say, indeed it would have been unethical to say, no discomfort . . ."

"*Discomfort!* Analgesic! Sedatives! Why don't you just say it right out, Doctor? There *is* pain. Pain you can't treat or control except by making my son into a cabbage! You lied."

Even as she spoke, Alexa knew she was being unreasonable. What Kilpatrick had promised was no *excessive* pain. But seeing Charles, his whole personality dissolved in physical hurt, bewilderment and drug-induced acceptance of both, made her feel it was all her fault. When she hated herself, she became dangerous to all around her.

"Please, Mrs. Ombre, you're overwrought. It's late and you've had a long journey. I'd like to prescribe . . ."

Doctor Kilpatrick had seen parents come close to the end of their rope many a time. They were always easier to deal with under mild sedation. Much better for them too.

Alexa read his thought instantly. "Oh no you don't, Doctor. You don't put me out of action with a pill."

Charles looked up, he could see his mother. He knew her, but he didn't know why. She seemed angry, almost threatening. He seemed to remember doing something she wanted, but she didn't seem pleased. Who was she angry with? Oh please, *please* don't let it be me. His eyes closed and he drifted away again. Even anxiety was too exhausting to sustain.

They'd broken both his legs in three places. Resetting them was difficult. The ends of each broken section didn't quite match with the corresponding ends. Not if they were to be aligned straight. The casts were hot and itchy. Correcting the curve was going to be a harder task than Doctor Kilpatrick ever imagined.

Alexa looked hard at Kilpatrick, discerning a slight atmosphere of uncertainty about him. Those wide shoulders were somehow not quite so aggressively horizontal as she had remembered them and he was having trouble finding something to do with his hands.

"I'm not sure about this," unconsciously her hand gripped Richard's wrist as it lay on the cot side. "I'm not sure about this at all. I'll let you know what I think should be done in the morning."

She reached down to stroke her son's face. She wanted to hold him. Feeling her need, Richard motioned the nurse to let down the cot side. She lay her cheek next to Charles' skin. It was smooth, suffering and innocent.

"It's all right, my darling. I'll come back tomorrow. Try and sleep now." As Alexa rose she felt a curious melting sensation in her legs. Richard caught her in time.

It seemed natural to tell him everything that had happened.

"Madame La Courbe is a wise woman. She gave you good advice.

"It's all very well to wait," Alexa sipped the brandy. "Now I have waited and still I don't know what to do. I only know I must do something. I can't forgive it. Not this time. I just can't bear it."

Alexa had tried, in spite of her unspoken vow, to forgive Fabrice for the time he had knocked her to the ground in the *chai*. She had never fully succeeded because she could not forget it. Whenever she and Fabrice found themselves arguing, that scene sprang back into her mind with the same vividness as the day on which it had taken place. But her effort had been sincere. She gave away the emerald-green dress she had worn on that day to a church jumble sale. But its colour and texture were imprinted on her memory together with every other detail.

Until she had told Tilly after the funeral, she had kept silent about that day in the *chai*. It would have been pointless to upset Héloïse with the story. And she could imagine the well-meaning lecture Héloïse would have delivered. But how could anyone forget a blow to the face? And memory made forgiveness a sterile formula, as if wishes could be transmuted into facts by the mere assertion of will.

All the suppressed anger of years had been released in the single moment of Suzanne's own violence. In Alexa's mind, there was now no difference between mother and son. They had become a single, hostile entity.

"What do you want? Revenge?" Richard sat opposite her, surveying her tense figure.

"What I want is justice. No more than that."

"Justice usually implies the punishment of someone else, you know."

"I can't help that."

Richard got up and walked about the room, his hands in the pockets of his camel-hair slacks. His opportunity had come. If he didn't take it now, there might never be another time. He could do it. He could get her justice. But it meant destroying another man. From day to day, in the business arena, it didn't matter. It was not in the private domain. This was different. Now it was *her* man. She was angry with him now. But would she always be? Fabrice was like a rotten limb, useless, a source of disease. But he was Alexa's limb. She had a right to refuse the amputation, even if it cost her her life. She had a pathological fear of anything resembling manipulation. But he would have to get her to trust him, nothing would work without that.

His glance took in the blank impersonality of the apartment. There was a weariness about it all. Here and there there was a good piece of sculpture. The Elizabeth Frink bronze, a Rodin cartoon, even one of Barbara Hepworth's rare small pieces, stood forlornly on an old pile of magazines. They were all waiting, like him, for a proper home.

He turned away from her and looked out over the winter tree-tops of Central Park. Their nudity allowed fleeting glimpses of the cars passing in the deep ravines which gave passage through the green lung of the city. Behind him, he heard Alexa pour herself another drink. Brandy. It was her third since they returned from the clinic an hour ago. It decided him. She was too good for that.

"Alexa, did you think any more about the Margaret River Estate? You know, the Australian wine we had in my office last time you were over here?"

"Yes," she answered, startled. "But with all this happening, Tante Héloïse dying, the awful, awful funeral, the will, Suzanne and Fabrice and his bloody divorce . . . and now Charles, I really . . ."

"I know, I know. I've been to look at it, though." He did not look around. The silence behind him was tangible.

At last, she replied, "But Richard, you know nothing about wine."

"No, not more than the average rich man in the street, that's true. But you see, my dear, I don't have to. The best independent advice can always be bought. In fact, I bought two opinions."

"Who did you get?" Her curiosity was only idle. None of this seemed much to do with her present situation.

"A realtor in Perth who specialises in wine properties. And then a young fellow. He wrote a pretty classy article on wine in the *New Yorker*. An Englishman. His subject was the wine properties of the Napa Valley in California. So I thought he was the right sort of chap to get."

"Sounds okay. Who was he?"

"Bowring. Tim Bowring. That's what they call 'im. Bit of a stuffed shirt, rather a lot of the old-school-tie stuff for my taste, but a nice enough guy. Seemed to know what he was talking about, anyway. I liked him."

"But I know him! We've been friends for years. He often comes to stay with us. Charles adores him! Did you say who you were looking at the estate for?"

"No, why should I? I'd no idea there was a connection. I paid him a fee. For all he knows I might have been considering it myself. Perhaps I was."

"But Richard, you would have met him at Charles' christening. I invited him, he came. I remember."

"Well, I don't. But then, I didn't see much except you, that day."

Alexa looked quietly at him as he spoke, remembering the day of Charles' christening. She remembered showing him round the *chais*, convinced he was bored, and how her parents had both liked him. He'd seemed an old man to her then.

"I had a letter from him."

"Who? Bowring?"

"Yes. Apart from being a friend. He is, or he was, the son of one of the partners of Tremayne Taylor in London. He sold some wine for us once. In fact, that's how we met. He did jolly well, too. He got some storage arranged for us, actually. There's more we haven't sold."

"And now he's branched out into wine journalism."

"So it seems. I suppose he knows an awful lot about it now. He's spent a great deal of time with us and he handles all the fine wine sales at Tremayne Taylor these days. He was really just beginning when I met him. He'll know lots about different kinds of wine, where I only know about claret."

"So why did he write to you?"

"He wants to write about us, our wine, anyway. Château de Pies Ombre."

Richard spun round and faced into the room. "You really mustn't let him do that, Alexa. At the moment that's not what we need."

Alexa looked at him in total surprise. An article in a prestigious magazine like *Decanter* could do her property nothing but good. She always thought of d'Ombre as *her* property.

"Why ever not? Look, what has all this to do with what I've been talking about? The Australian place— Tim. What's it all got to *do* with anything?"

"Everything, Alexa. Everything." He clicked his tongue with uncharacteristic peevishness. "The last thing we want is laudatory blatherings from your Little-Lord-Fauntleroy type." Seeing Alexa's gesture of protest, Richard waved it down, "He's okay. But keep him quiet. And another thing, you've got to trust me, okay?"

"I'll trust you, Richard," she looked at him. He was wearing a navy-blue cashmere sweater. She had never seen him informally dressed before. The style suited him. It made him seem less like his own Wall Street building and more like a warm and strokable human being. He was a heavyweight hunter. Massive, well cared for, expensive and strong. He shone with the gloss of health and confidence. She wanted nothing so much as to wrap her arms around him, fill her nostrils with his juniper smell and squeeze and squeeze until some of his strength flowed into her. In her abdomen there was a tension and in her thighs a tingling restlessness. She wanted him so very badly.

"But what *about*? I can't just trust you, blindly, about everything, can I? There has to be a beginning and an end to me trusting you, doesn't there? So just tell me what's going on."

Richard crossed the room and sat down close to her. He removed the brandy balloon from her hand and took both of her hands in his. For a short time he looked down at the small, delicately bones little hands with their pale nails. They seemed to nestle confidently enough in his own. He looked deeply into her blue eyes as if focusing a laser beam into those dark pools to discover what creatures inhabited their depths. Alexa returned his gaze steadily and although her heart beat a tattoo of ecstasy, she kept her guard up. He saw the veiling mist of privacy and sighed.

"That's just it. I can't. And I do want the impossible and the unreasonable. I want you to trust me about *everything* that affects you. I don't want to . . . to be any kind of burden to you, but you know I would do anything for you, don't you? And I would never do anything to harm you . . ."

He was struggling. Unaccustomed to expressing his own emotions, he found himself hampered by a lack of vocabulary. He heard with shame the wooden, avuncular phrases. It was as if he was speaking to a small, frightened child, and not a lovely, courageous woman beleaguered by a sea of troubles. He realised that unconsciously he had been gently massaging her hands. She did not seem to mind. Perhaps she understood a little of the longing and passion he was trying to express. Could a dull New York banker with an even duller background in Yorkshire ever be understood as a knight in shining armour? He doubted it. It didn't matter. The thing was to rescue the lady first and later, woo and win her at leisure. Richard felt a queer sensation of lightness; a swooping, darting, hovering bird in the heart, beating its wings for the sheer joy of living.

It was the first time he'd felt that surge of secret excitement since Michael Goldstein had died. Then it had been the scents, sounds and echoes of the stock market expeditions. The cacophony of telephones and the shouts of the dealers, the plots and the raids, the elation and the despair. And afterwards, the news of battle in the *Wall Street Journal*, telling him things he already knew because he had been there, and the warm shining pride in Michael's eyes. Now it would be a different kind of war, one of stealth and intelligence, luring his enemy into a carefully disguised snare and finishing him with a single, silent blow. It was beautiful. Alexa deserved the best he could do.

When he spoke, nothing gave away the exaltation of his emotions, "What I'm trying to say, is I can put together a plan of action which will substantially get you what you want. But an important element of the plan is that you relax, do as I say and don't ask too many questions."

"It's a lot of trust to expect." She looked up at him doubtfully.

"It is. I realise that. But it's the only way to do it."

"Do what, exactly?"

"Get rid of the things you don't want without losing the things you *do* want. I'm right in thinking, aren't I, that you don't want to lose your precious château but you could do without your husband and his delightful mother?''

She didn't answer him directly. He had voiced her thoughts, thoughts she had hoped she would never harbour. But now they had become so firmly lodged that there was no turning away from them. She had known on the day of Héloïse's funeral that she could not go on. "I've put my heart and soul into that place. Why *should* I be turned out because he wants a divorce?''

"He wouldn't necessarily get a divorce, but suppose he did, don't you think your life might be better without him?''

"Yes,'' Alexa replied heavily, "I'm afraid I do. But how? I will never willingly part with Château d'Ombre. My life's *blood* is in those vines and in that house.''

Richard smiled inwardly. He could never belittle her achievement, but she seemed strangely young to be speaking of her life's blood. She couldn't be above twenty-seven or -eight. Her earnestness and the way she took herself so seriously, without false flippancy or modesty, were the most endearing features of her character. She was like one of those grave children who inherit responsibilities too early and carry them with solemn courage. They had something in common there.

"All right, all right,'' he soothed. "Just now we're going to talk about something else. That Margaret River Estate has got to be purchased and we don't have much time. There are other parties interested. Your young friend, Bowring, said he'd snap it up.''

Alexa suddenly seemed a little more alert. The occasions on which she would not talk about wine and the things of wine were very rare indeed. Richard noticed how easily her attention was grasped with admiration. He liked a dedicated worker.

"What's it like? And where *is* it exactly?''

"It's 160 miles south of Perth in Western Australia. The climate is relatively cool by Australian standards, something like the Mediterranean with absolutely no risk of frost. Apparently that's important to you.'' He said it slyly, wanting to hear the rich, vigorous sound of her indignation.

"Obviously!'' She was scandalised by his ignorance. "If the frost gets to the vines while they're flowering, the crop is ruined. There'd be no fruit and therefore no wine. To have a property where it simply cannot happen must be like living in a *vigneron*'s paradise.''

"Well, maybe this place is just that. Let me tell you more.''

"How old are the vines?"

"Six years."

"Good God!"

"What does that mean?"

"It means they've barely begun."

"Quite. Apart from that, quite a lot of the acreage is still unplanted. More than half in fact. But it is cultivated and ready to go."

"What have they got in there now?"

"Only *Cabernet*, so far. But there's a nursery and they're bringing on some *Shiraz*, as they call it. Bowring says it's a Burgundy grape. And something else, I can't remember. But you wouldn't have to be bound by all that, there isn't a crucial amount of capital committed. Remember, the place is only half planted and there are 220 acres. Now that's big for a wine property. I've learned that much."

Alexa calculated rapidly. "Ninety hectares! Why's the chap selling?" She was taut with excitement.

"Quite honestly, I think he's bust. Under-capitalised. Sugar man really. Got a big spread in Queensland, found he can't handle them both. But, Alexa, he's anxious to sell and the price if *right*. The Perth realtor was sure it was a bargain and Tim Bowring said it was an ideal place to make a wine in the style of claret or St. Emilion. If you want it, all I have to do is lift a telephone and it's yours."

"What do I use for money?"

"Half of yours and the other half I supply. You'll need some working capital and you'll need to keep some handy for a rainy day. Let the bankers take some of the risk, that's what they're there for."

"They've never given me that impression before. Is there a house?"

"Not what you'd call a house, I reckon. Still, there's a dwelling there and it's very large."

"What's wrong with it?"

"Nothing really, it's just a big, plain bungalow built of wood. Perfectly sound and dry. But of course, it's not a Walt Disney castle like d'Ombre." Alexa mused. She could grow all the *Merlot* she wanted in a place with no frost. With ninety hectares she could make a serious impact on the world market and the bungalow was a bonus. An escape. And it would all be *hers*.

"Say yes, Richard. I've got to have it. I've just *got* to. It's fate. Life doesn't send you chances like this very often. It'll make Suzanne go berserk. Do you know? I'm almost looking forward to that part more than any other.''

"Alexa," Richard warned, "you mustn't tell her, or your husband. Do you promise? Don't tell them anything at all.''

"Well, yes,'' she replied uncertainly, "but . . .''

"You promised to trust me remember? And there's another thing. Who is your solicitor in France?''

"The family lawyer. Maître Robinson. He's very nice and very intelligent. He arranged with Daddy about my marriage settlement. I'm getting on with that, by the way. The planting, I mean.''

"Yes, well, I want you to change him, the solicitor, I mean.'' Alexa was astounded. "*Change* him?''

"There's no need to go to the trouble and embarrassment of formally sacking him. It's just best that you don't confide your affairs in his ears at the moment. I'll get my staff on to it and we'll have found you a top-flight man in Bordeaux by the end of tomorrow.''

"Okay. If that's what you want.''

"I do want it. You just said it yourself. Maître Robinson is the *family* lawyer. We want someone whose loyalties aren't pulled in more than one direction at a time. It's important. Now, is Château d'Ombre a limited company?''

"It's a *Société Anonyme*, same thing. I saw to that.''

"Are you a director?''

"Yes. But I don't hold more than a token amount of the shares. That's what's so worrying.''

"That doesn't matter. Resign.''

"What! Wouldn't that be playing into Fabrice's hands? He'd have total control then. And believe me, Richard, he isn't fit to control a cabbage patch.''

"I know. But just the same, I want you to resign. Don't ask me why, just do it, dear. You've got to trust me.''

"But wouldn't Fabrice think that very odd, when I've always seemed to fight so hard to keep as much control in my own hands as I could? He'd be sure to smell some kind of rat.''

"Not if you handle it right. You must tell him you're fully occupied over the matter of your own new enterprise with the little plots and you'd like him to take the reins back into his own hands, something like that. You'll know how to play it. And another thing. Stall him on this divorce thing. Keep him sweet, but not too sweet. Be generous with Tante Héloïse's money, but not too generous. After all, you're Charles' trustee. Act in character but loosen up the purse-strings a little. Buy him presents and give him a little cash, encourage him to spend a bit on himself. I want him brought slowly to the simmer. When I'm ready for him to come to the boil, I'll let you know. Oh, and another thing, try and discover what debts he has. There's bound to be the odd thing you don't know about. There usually is. You've kept him on a cash diet for a long time now, haven't you?''

"It's always been necessary. It's still necessary. Once he starts spending money, it gets out of control. But, Richard, I don't see how I can do this. Tante Héloïse's money is *Charles*', not mine. All I can do is look after it for him. I certainly can't go giving Fabrice expensive presents out of it.''

"There's no problem about that. You can spend the income to benefit the estate, can't you? The estate of Château d'Ombre that will eventually come to Charles, can't you?''

"Yes, but I should have to have shares in return for investment, on Charles' behalf, of course.''

"Quite. Well, the estate's a company, isn't it? And the company needs a new car. Get Fabrice a new Jag.''

Alexa's eyes were round. "Won't that be wasting Charles' money?''

"No, it'll be the best investment that young Charles ever makes. Now, don't ask any more questions. There's one other thing.''

"Yes.''

"On no account should Tim Bowring know that you know me or that I am acting for you in any matter. Do you understand? That's a potential complication I can do without.''

"I don't understand.'' Alexa's brow wrinkled charmingly. She didn't understand anything but she believed in him, he was her only chance of escape. Suzanne's slap had woken her from a long dream. She could never, ever turn to the de Pies Ombres again. Héloïse had made it possible to believe in the future but Héloïse had gone and the mysterious cohesion with which she, an unimportant maiden aunt, had held the fragmented household together had gone too. It had all come unstuck on the day of her funeral.

"That's part of my security system.'' Richard's voice interrupted her thoughts. "Believe me. I'm protecting you. This is one of the few occasions when the less you know, the better things will go and the safer you, personally, will be.''

Alexa was silent for a moment. There *had* been some good times.

"Richard, there are a lot of things I don't like about Fabrice, these days. He hasn't been a good husband to me. Hardly a husband at all, in fact, but I don't want something vile on my conscience for the rest of my days. When all's said and done, he's Charles's father.''

"Trust me, Alexa. Your marriage is between you and your husband. It is something with which I am not qualified to interfere. I am merely a man of business. Is not that the case? Concerned with purely material matters.''

By the time Charles and Morag came home, the year's work in the vineyards was well under way. The new shoots were being selected and tied in and the tender young leaves were beginning to show.

Charles' few weeks' absence in New York had taught Alexa something new about herself. She felt a longing for the presence of her child that conflicted with her gratitude that he had not been there to witness the traumatic scenes which had surrounded Tante Héloïse's death. On several nights, unable to sleep, she had walked up to the nursery to make tea, telling herself that it was nearer than the basement kitchens. She had drunk the tea standing in the doorway of Charles's vacant bedroom, looking at his empty bed, feeling a sense of privation. She wanted his familiar little body to be curled up in the miniature four-poster once again, with the scatter of soft toys lying around it on the carpet. When he comes back, she told herself, we shall do more things together. For Alexa, the château was like a body from which the spirit has departed. She understood for the first time, that Charles had inherited more than money from his great-aunt. On him had devolved the duty of infusing the walls of the château with his own sunny temperament, thus counteracting and pushing back the shadows which always threatened to engulf his family.

He was as delighted to be home as Alexa was to have him with her once again. Charles used a stick to assist his still-painful progress but grew stronger and more adventurous every day. Mother and son walked in the vine fields together discussing the work that was being done there and stopping to talk with the workers from time to time. He was only a little boy, but they all seemed to accept him as the future proprietor and answered his questions with a grave respect which was mingled with warm affection for the brave little boy afflicted with the strange inheritance of the de Pies Ombre family.

"Shall we get that automatic picker you told me about, Mummy?"

"No, darling. I've made some enquiries about it. It would knock the vines about too much. Forty-year-old vines have to be treated gently. The best properties won't have them. They'll improve, of course, and then we can look at it again. But not now, not until the scientists and engineers have made them better. I'm afraid we'll have to go on picking by hand for quite a time yet."

"Doesn't shooting rattle the vines about too?" Alexa looked at him ruefully. He was a sharp child, uncomfortably so at times.

"Yes, darling, I think it does. That wasn't the best idea I ever had. But it was necessary at the time and you know how much Pierre David enjoys it. I couldn't think of giving it up until he retires."

And then she remembered she was no longer in a position to stop or start anything at d'Ombre. She was no longer a director.

Fabrice had been astonished when she told him. But he accepted the explanation that Alexa had her own infant vines to attend to and wished to be relieved of the heavy burden of administration that running Château d'Ombre involved. "After all," she added, "Charles is growing up so quickly now, I think he should have more of my attention. I simply wouldn't have time to give it to him if I were busy all day in the *cuverie* and in the fields."

It was an act of faith. Richard seemed very far away and there were times when Alexa asked herself if the whole thing weren't a jumbled dream. Why was she giving up everything to Fabrice? It was impossible to see how any good could come of it.

"I suppose you've realised now that running a property like this isn't the mere bagatelle you thought," Fabrice remarked complacently one day at breakfast. Alexa was not tempted to react violently because of the strangeness of her husband's observation. His grasp on reality seemed ever more fragile and his ability to ignore matters of demonstrable fact increased week by week. She shook her head in a characteristic gesture of confusion, as if to clear it of misinformation, which Fabrice took to be an admission of defeat at the complexities of the wine business. His gratification was apparent and Alexa watched him with detached incredulity.

Every day she worked alongside the young man Pierre David had hired to help her in her little plots. There was much to be done and the physical work distracted her from the bemusement she felt at her own foolhardiness in confiding the management of d'Ombre into the hands of Fabrice. Pierre David was dismayed when she told him of her decision and begged her to reconsider.

"It is too late my friend. I have done it. *Monsieur* must manage for himself now, with your help. My son has reached the age when he needs more of my time and I want to concentrate on the new project. In four years we shall have a vintage. Don't pull such a long face, Pierre. Help me think of a name for the new wine. I intend it shall be famous. Good marketing never did any harm. What shall we call it?"

"I have little to offer in the way of imagination, *Madame*. But when it comes to practical experience, you know that everything I have is yours for the asking. And if you will take my advice, I shouldn't trouble with regrafting those old stocks. Start from scratch with the new stock, it will be a better investment in the end. Who knows how long the old vines will live to support the grafts? If they last fifteen years, and that is not impossible, where will you go from there?"

Summer guests proposed themselves and Alexa anticipated their coming without enthusiasm. Prudently she replied to a number who had visited in the past, proved to be good company and were inclined to spend a number of days at d'Ombre. This pattern was more profitable and less tiring than receiving new people for one night only and at short intervals. To others she wrote expressing regrets that the château was fully booked for the entire season. Far from causing a gradual decline in interest, gossip suggested that the *Marquise* and her husband were becoming selective in their choice of paying guest which stimulated a spate of importuning letters from those she had rejected begging her to reconsider.

It was no longer only the newly rich from unsophisticated parts of America who were willing to pay for the privilege of a night or two's entertainment at d'Ombre. Both the socially ambitious and the merely curious from all over Europe, America,

Canada and Australia were anxious to sample the esoteric delights of hospitality in the bosom of a *Grande Famille du Vin*.

Alexa had refined the range of programmes, from vertical tastings in the château's own cellars to Christmas shooting parties, and the whole world wanted to be among those clearly wealthy enough to buy their way into the lifestyle, as it was beginning to be called, of Monsieur and Madame de Pies Ombre. Part of the attraction was the sheer oddity of Fabrice contrasted with Alexa's natural grace and total lack of conscious grandeur. The clash of their personalities produced a weirdly unreal atmosphere which accorded well with the other-worldly quality of the house.

The house, year by year, became more and more *soignée*. Repairs and refurbishments went ahead steadily and where once there had been only neglected policies there emerged a garden of incomparable tranquillity and beauty, a fitting setting for what emerged as one of the loveliest châteaux of the region. Before it lay an extensive lawn, well-watered and tended. A true English lawn, the envy of every proprietor in Pauillac. In the centre of the lawn, a single tree had been allowed to survive, a Cedar of Lebanon. To the side, the cypresses still shaded the drive, immaculate now with white gravel and guarded by lacy wrought-iron gates purchased from a derelict estate house. The gate posts still supported the painted-stone magpies with their proudly coroneted necks. Alexa found it hard to remember what it had all looked like when she had first seen it. The changes and improvements had come little by little, transforming the old house so gradually that those who saw it every day noticed it as little as a mother notices a child growing.

None-the-less, on unpredictable occasions, Alexa would suddenly comprehend the gulf between the property she had come to as a bride and the flourishing concern over which she now presided. The signs of prosperity were not limited to the domestic aspects of d'Ombre. At the end of each vine row there nodded a red or pink rose, as on every self-respecting estate in the Médoc. Since Alexander's original gift of the first three stainless-steel vats, more had been added, the latest ones with automatic temperature-control mechanisms. Two new tractors had been purchased, the immensely tall type which could pull hoes along two rows at a time while the vines themselves passed untouched between the wheels. There was now a museum devoted to the display of all the old, traditional equipment which had been in use at the time of Alexa's marriage. Over and over again, Alexa asked herself what she had done.

Fabrice never spoke of divorce again that summer. Perhaps it had been no more than one of his periodic outbursts, a childish temper-tantrum. Alexa was torn between relief and a mounting desire to be free of him. But it was not realistic. Without him there would be no place for her at d'Ombre and without d'Ombre, she could not live. She let her imagination rove, trying to imagine the comforts and charms of a quiet and unmolested life in one of the small houses in the village of d'Ombre. There were many such and she could afford to buy one and to renovate it to her taste. She could devote all her time to the new vineyard and the future wine. To spend all day planning and dreaming in a safe place of her own ought to have been an enticing prospect but it was not. She did not know what Richard thought he could achieve and she did not believe he could achieve much. The whole thing was impossible. She was doomed to live inside an unhappy marriage in the home she had fought so hard to rescue and on the land she had laboured to make fruitful and which she loved as only a farmer can love. The alternative was to escape a sterile marriage and lose everything she cared for. At times she was swept by panic. Fabrice would lose d'Ombre. And then it would all have been for nothing.

Alexa de Pies Ombre. Richard contemplated the signature on the thick vellum sheet with interest. He had never seen it before. Its chief peculiarity lay in its legibility. There was no egotistical, self-invented cipher, nor yet any cramped secrecy. It was written in royal-blue ink with a broad-nibbed fountain pen. The ink had dried thickly and the firmly drawn characters looked both vital and resolute.

He began to read the document. It was a power of attorney. She permitted him to buy, acquire, sell or dispose of any property or stocks in her name and generally to act on her behalf and in her stead for a period of one year. That should be enough. He looked at his watch. If he sent a telex now, McAlpine would get it as soon as he came into the office. With any luck he'd respond immediately and they could fix the completion meeting. It would be autumn in Western Australia. In the future Alexa would be able to attend both her vintages. And one day, he would be with her.

Tim Bowring came to d'Ombre in spite of Alexa's prohibition

on any publicity. He came as a friend and a guest at his own suggestion and Alexa was delighted, as ever, to acquiesce. It occurred to her to inform Richard of his visit in case any gossip should reach his ears and make him doubt her promise of trust in his decision. He telephoned very early one morning a day or two before Tim's arrival. The telephone rang in Alexa's bedroom and she answered it sleepily.

"I've been thinking about Bowring. It seems to me, you could do worse than let him write something about the property, after all. But it's to be something mildly unflattering, mind."

"What?" Alexa held on to the sound of his voice. It was so conversational, so everyday, as if a mere street separated them, not endless wastes of watery miles.

"A hint of criticism, that's what's wanted."

"But how can I explain *that* to him?"

"I don't know dearest, but you'll think of something."

"You don't understand. He's a gentleman, I mean, integrity means a lot to him."

"And you're a beautiful woman asking a favour from a friend. All we want is a word in season. Say it fits in with your future marketing plans, anything."

"But it's mad! He won't belive it."

"Goddammit, Alexa! He'll believe anything those blue eyes of yours tell him to believe. Just do it, okay. Make it easy for him. Give him one of those things, what do you call them? Vertical tastings? A few duff bottles, that kind of thing. Whatever you have to do. I've got to leave this to you, Alexa. Believe me, it's important." Alexa sighed. Richard expected a lot. What went on behind that capacious brow of his?

"I'll try."

"Good lass. Tell me how it goes. Bye now." A thousand miles away, the telephone clicked. Final. The orders had been given, he assumed they would be complied with. Alexa replaced the receiver thoughtfully. It would be early evening there. She tried to picture him in his office, or perhaps his apartment. The apartment didn't seem to mean much to him. It was just a cupboard where he put himself away until the next working day. The bank was his real life. "And me, perhaps," she muttered aloud.

There was a soft tap on the door. Startled, Alexa got out of bed and slipped into her dressing gown to open the door. There on the threshold was Charles.

"Darling! Does Morag know you're awake?"

"No, she's asleep. She snores, you know."

"I think we all do occasionally. Poor Morag. I bet you snore sometimes." She realised she had no idea.

"You'd better get into bed with me for a bit, but not too long. If Morag wakes up and finds you aren't there, she'll have a heart attack."

"What's a heart attack?"

"I'm only teasing. I mean Morag will be terribly worried if she goes into your room at the normal time and finds you not there." Charles trotted into his mother's room.

"Oh, super. I go in Morag's bed sometimes but she says I wriggle. She makes me play something called spoons. It's really just a way of making me lie still. It's awfully boring."

"Whatever's spoons?"

"She lies facing one way and I lie behind her facing the same way, you know, like spoons in a drawer. It's boring."

"Well, I won't make you play spoons."

"Can I talk?"

"As much as you like, darling. But not too loud. You'll wake Daddy next door. He's not very good at waking up early."

"You don't really think he's good at anything, do you, Mummy?"

CHAPTER
20

❧ ❧ THE NEW JAGUAR gleamed under the dappled shadow of
the trees around the *chai* yard. It was British racing–green, an
"E" Type. Alexa's birthday present. Fabrice glanced back at it.
It aroused confusing emotions in him. A mixture of pride of
possession and anger. He was not able to tell whether his sensations of gratitude or outrage were uppermost. Behind the wheel
of that car he experienced such feelings of potency as he had
never thought to feel again, and yet its value and power created
equally vivid images of Alexa's own potency and his pusillanim-
ity. He hadn't thanked her for it very graciously. "How many
shares does this buy Charles, then? What are you trying to do,
Alexa? Buy back control of Château d'Ombre through the back
door?"

He loved the car, but it was hard not to have bought it himself.
In fact it was difficult at times to see the car as being more than
a symbol of his bondage. That was the sort of gesture Alexa
specialised in. With one hand she could give handsomely, but
the other would make certain that the gift was a constant reminder of their relative positions. The car was a glittering me-
mento of her domination and his humiliation. At other times it
was simply a car. A wonderful, beautiful machine that made
every eye swivel enviously. One would have to be made of stone
not to enjoy it. That sugary, dirty little blonde tart in the Rue
des Bouviers liked it too. She'd become noticeably more passionate of late.

The waterfront girls in Bordeaux were a whole new avenue
of exploration. They knew things and could do things that would
make a hardened woman of the streets of Paris blush. Things
they learned from Arab sailors, no doubt. Half of those girls

would be the by-blows of prostitute mothers and Alergian sailors. It was pleasant to think of Maddy's plump, malodorous little body on the beige calf-leather seat beside him. Her odour of sweat and a sweetish, Moroccan perfume was friendly and sexually encouraging.

She was good company, Maddy. Unambitious, undemanding, and deliciously coarse, she would do a great deal for a meal in one of the sleazy waterfront cafés. Perhaps for a real *grand repas* at the *Vieux Bordeaux* she might plumb depths of exquisite depravity which Fabrice himself could not imagine. He enjoyed the salacious hope that Maddy knew more than she had yet revealed to him. But he had no complaints, Maddy gave magnificent value for money. He would see her again, soon. Before the summer guests started coming and making it more difficult to get away.

This recent rejuvenation had done him a world of good. Alexa was not a satisfactory partner in bed. She was too intimidatingly clean, too cool and restrained. The very crispness of her sheets protested a virginal objection to all but the most unimaginative procedures. In the early days of their marriage she had occasionally shown a decent enthusiasm for straightforward marital coupling, but it was dull. She was a passionless, bossy, English schoolgirl who kept calling the game to order as though the marriage-bed of the de Pies Ombres were some windswept hockey pitch. He didn't feel in control of her and that was essential. Alexa never achieved an orgasm and hadn't the good manners to pretend. And she was quiet, unnervingly so. Apart from the occasional conventional endearment she was silent. Frigid. Not so the delightfully unwashed Maddy. She filled the air of her dark, evil-smelling *appartement* with shouts of laughter and streams of cheerful obscenity. She had blood in her veins, not lemon juice.

She was easily pleased, too. A few francs, some vulgar underclothing, the rent on the *appartement*—that was all it took to make her nestling and adoring. Fabrice smiled at the memory of her. Yes, Maddy was a find. A secret and affordable pleasure. He'd wondered about keeping a woman before, but a respectable mistress, the sort one might seriously consider being seen with, would expect an expensive *appartement* in a good area. She would expect him to visit her regularly and to bring presents of noticeable value. No. It would be like a middle-class marriage. She would try to limit his drinking, want to go abroad with him.

The expense would be followed by boredom and the trauma of kicking her out. When he tired of Maddy, he would simply not return. She would be used to such treatment and would make no embarrassing efforts to find him. She had no idea who he was. If only he could get rid of his wife so easily. Still, Alexa had resigned her directorship and he'd got the car. He could spend some of his own money now and again.

There were times when Fabrice asked himself when it was that he had begun to detest Alexa. They had got on well enough at the start. She was intelligent and capable of being companionable. There were things in her to admire. But her admirable qualities were always too much in evidence. And she was grasping. It wasn't only money, she usurped everything except what was of no value anyway. Hortense had quickly transferred her loyalty to Alexa, the same with David, the nanny barely ever spoke to him. The world of d'Ombre had *Alexa* stamped all over it, just as if each object and individual were her own personal possession. Well, he had never consented to become her property and very soon, he'd take steps to ensure that Charles didn't slide irrevocably into his mother's inventory of possessions. Morag would have to go soon. She had guarded the nursery territory fiercely for nearly eight years, now it was time for her to yield up the ground.

The 1977 bud-break had been early. Really too early. It had been the fifth of March when David had reported the first shoots on the vines. It was worrying. Too much could happen between the beginning of March and the end of April. Preoccupation with Charles had not entirely blotted out the consciousness of risk from either of his parents' minds. Now it was nearly the end of the month and the temperature suddenly became dangerously low. Fabrice shivered as he opened the door of his office. It felt uncomfortably like frost. There was that sullen dankness in the air, a lifeless, numbing cold that could so easily turn into the killing knife of frost. Perhaps Alexa's alarm system would work. Perhaps not. She had emphasised with tedious repetitions that it all depended on everyone pulling their weight.

"The minute the buzzer goes, everyone but everyone has to get themselves out of bed and downstairs and into the fields to light those braziers. It's the only hope of saving the crop. Even then we won't be able to cover the whole acreage, but we've got to try and do our best. If we can escape frost damage, the rest of the year might be good and then we'll have more to sell than other properties in a basically good year in which the crop will have been very small. We should be laughing all the way to the *Crédit des Vignerons*!''

Fabrice dug Charles in the ribs, ''You find yourself a nice quiet lady to marry when you grow up.''

''Run away to Morag, at once Charles!'' Suzanne commanded peremptorily, ''Really, Alexa, you can be impossibly vulgar at times. 'Laughing all the way to the *Crédit des Vignerons* . . .' What sort of tradesman's language is that to be teaching the future head of this family?''

''It's language which may teach him to be a businessman one day,'' she responded shortly. She bit her tongue. How much she wanted to tell Suzanne that better Charles should be vulgar than an ineffectual drunk like his father. But she had promised Richard to be careful. To do nothing to worsen the domestic situation. To be in the same room as Suzanne was unpleasant. To exchange words with her was worse. Fortunately the older woman addressed very few remarks to her daughter-in-law these days.

Everyone in the household except Charles and Morag was allotted a share of ground to cover. The problem had been how much acreage to attempt to save, how much could realistically be saved. In the end it was decided that it was better to be certain that the temperature could be sufficiently raised over a restricted area than to expend effort fruitlessly on a less than efficient job. Some of the men would sleep in makeshift accommodation in the *chais* as long as the weather remained critical. David would stay in his own little one-storey villa, isolated among the vine fields, and the family members and staff would play their part. Even Suzanne had raised no murmur of protest. Wine is wine, wherever it is grown, and Suzanne's background was enough to make her react instinctively to the demands of vines in danger.

For some days the temperature hovered above freezing and certainly during daylight hours there was nothing to concern Alexa unduly. The braziers were all in position, with their priming of newspapers, soaked in paraffin, and dry vine prunings laid on top of them. A little stack of coke stood near each one and the whole arrangement was covered with a tarpaulin of the plastic sacks in which the bentonite for fining the wine was delivered. She hoped it would all work. Pierre David was sure it would.

There was nothing she could do to save the shoots on her own infant vines if the expected emergency arose. They were too far away from the house and every pair of hands was needed on the château property to ensure the survival of the main crop. As the young vines on Alexa's own property were not to fruit during their first four seasons, she spent the daylight hours removing the shoots with secateurs, reasoning that it was better to prune them than allow them to be burnt off arbitrarily. Charles accompanied his mother on these expeditions and was entrusted with simple tasks.

"Why can't I prune?"

"Secateurs are dangerous and your hands are too small to control them properly yet."

"David lets me."

"Well he's very naughty and I shall tick him off. Where should we be if you cut one of your fingers off?"

"He says I'm *très capable* and it's important for a *vigneron* to know every job on the property as well as the work people."

"Indeed." Alexa pursed her lips. He must have thought her hopelessly ignorant for a long time. And he would have been right. She would perhaps never learn as much as Charles would absorb through the pores of his skin. In a few more years he would already possess as much knowledge as his mother now had. It was natural. He had lived among vines and their product since his birth, as she had not. It was his birthright. It felt somehow strange, looking back, to think that she had bred the future head of a *Grande Famille du Vin*.

"When am I going to go to school, Mummy?"

"We'll have to think about that hard and very soon. I think Morag has taught you all she can. I did wonder if you'd like to go to the village school for a bit. It would be company for you, wouldn't it?"

"Would I have to keep on going if I didn't like it?"

"Charles! Don't be so negative, darling. You don't know you won't like it. Why worry about that until it happens? And we don't just run away from things because we don't like them. We try very hard to see what it is about a thing that we don't like and then try to change that thing. And if it can't be changed there are other things to think about before you just walk away, like how good the reasons for staying are."

"Yes, Mummy." Charles sighed, he was not unused to these sermons on conduct from both his mother and Morag. On bal-

ance he thought his mother was very slightly worse. Her disser-
tations were longer on account of the superior reasoning.

Tim Bowring came and was flattered to be allocated a part in
the frost-prevention scheme. It would make a great first paragraph for his article, he said.

On the evening of his arrival, during dinner, he eyed Alexa
sideways from time to time. She was no less lovely, but rounded
out somewhat. Her eyes still had the inky quality, blazing to a
fire-flame blue when she was excited or angry. Her voice was
deeper. It had lost its girlish hesitancy that had been punctuated
with random bursts of gunfire imperiousness. Now it was low
and quiet. She spoke softly but her voice was distinct and carrying. The marks of authority were plainly visible in her carriage
and her gestures. And she had a weariness about her. It crept
over her like a heavy mantle. But the moment she felt herself
observed, she would shrug it off with gaiety and turn to him
with that well-remembered smile. Even that was no longer quite
the same. Alexa could call that weapon to her aid at will now.
Before it had appeared only fleetingly and of its own volition,
like some shy animal, seen only in a moment of breathless
splendour, and then vanished into the forest once more. The girl
had become a woman, wary, poised and secretive, and he was
saddened by the change.

Suzanne and Fabrice had always treated Tim with tolerant
contempt on his previous visits. He was a callow youth, harmlessly in love with Alexa. He was not a threat, her manner with
him was much what it might have been if he had been a younger
brother. And then, he was useful with Charles, giving him the
sort of boisterous masculine play that he needed and which his
father could not supply. Now they treated him with a new cir-
cumspection. After all, free publicity was as valuable as it was
nourishing to the self-esteem. Suzanne struck matriarchal atti-
tudes and took to wearing a lorgnette around her neck on a
ribbon. It had been Héloïse's but never used except on social
occasions as Héloïse had naturally preferred to wear spectacles
when working.

Now that he was in a position to be particularly useful, it was
remembered that he had known enough to sell some old wine
for a considerable sum. He was astonished at his sudden new
standing in the household. True, neither Suzanne nor Fabrice
wished to dwell on that earlier success. It was yet another un-

pleasant reminder that Alexa had, with the co-operation of this
young English stranger, brought them from the brink of bank-
ruptcy to their present state of comparative prosperity.

Alexa was amused to watch the anxiety with which efforts
were made to please and flatter Tim. His opinions on oenolog-
ical matters were sought, as they had never been before. The
chinless buffoon had been promoted to "distinguished young
guest."

"Tell me Mr. Bowring," Suzanne had enquired portentously,
"what is your opinion of the non-vintage wines produced by the
châteaux in our region?"

Tim was at a loss to know how to answer, the question was
so broadly based that it appeared to have no meaning. With an
effort he began to address the task of analysing it.

There followed a long and tedious conversation in which Tim
attempted to treat seriously questions about wine that were devoid of sense. It became clear to him that Suzanne's primary
objective was to decry Alexa's decisions and achievements in
respect of Château d'Ombre. He countered every thinly veiled
attack with tireless courtesy and growing anger.

Fabrice ate in silence, indifferent to what passed between his
mother and their guest, whilst Alexa picked at her cutlet, miserable with embarrassment. When the talk turned again to the
matter of their fears and hopes for the current year's vintage,
she was at last able to draw the conversational initiative away
from Suzanne.

"Well, I think, if we are lucky, we may have a little vintage
wine this year, but as for the rest, it would be as well to get
another label designed and printed. There may be a good deal
to dispose of the best way we can."

"I thought you had retired from running d'Ombre, Alexa,"
Suzanne said archly, animosity towards her daughter-in-law poi-
soning every syllable. "I should think you could leave this sort
of decision to Fabrice now and concentrate your efforts on the
nursery, where they should have been focused in the first place."
She turned confidingly to Tim, "Poor little Charles, he has been
so neglected. I'm sure you have felt that, Mr. Bowring, when
you have visited us."

Alexa ignored the outrageous accusation and alluded again to
the vineyards. "It is hard, *Belle Mère*, not to be interested and
anxious. Our income derives in large part from the vineyards

now, you know.'' She was unable to resist adding, ''As it always should have done, of course.''

Tim shifted nervously on his chair. He felt the undercurrents of feeling thick in the air of the *salle à manger*. The old dowager had always amazed him with her combination of fine looks, impressive voice and stupefying banality. But now, she no longer seemed the harmless figure of fun that had enlivened his previous visits to Château d'Ombre and he detected something ugly and threatening gathering behind the inanity.

Alexa noticed Tim's discomfort and embarrassment and made some excuse to take him away with her up to the turret room. As she poured two little glasses of the *marc* that was made on Monsieur Terry's brother's little Norman property, and which he sent her every Christmas in recognition of their continuing mutual regard and friendship, she tried to make some excuse for Suzanne. It was intolerable that even such an old friend as Tim should be drawn into family squabbles and she was ashamed for them all.

''You mustn't mind my mother-in-law, you've been a guest here often enough to know how strange she can be. I don't think she means any real harm. Not to you, anyway. She's showing off a little today, I think. She thinks you're very important and are going to write things about us personally. She talks rubbish a lot of the time because she doesn't know what else to say. But she's had quite a hard life, you understand,'' Alexa explained lamely.

''It seems to me that your life isn't exactly a picnic.''

''I don't suppose anyone's is perfect, and mine has had some satisfactions.''

''What's all this *had* and past tense about? You are still very young, there's a lot more you will do yet, I hope.''

Alexa knew she must not confide in him about the Margaret River estate, but she was longing to unburden herself of this new secret excitement in her life. Richard was so far away, just an infrequently heard voice on the telephone. They were trying to find a permanent manager for the place. The sugar planter who had sold it had agreed to continue to oversee the estate as caretaker until someone could be found. She really could not understand what harm there could be in telling one of her very few friends. Fortunately, Tim spoke in time to deflect the temptation.

''I had an interesting commission lately. I went to survey, or at any rate to give my opinion of a wine estate in Australia, of all places." Alexa's face remained impassive.

"Did you? Why do you say 'of all places'? I thought Australia was very much the up-and-coming country for wine and that we Europeans had better look to our laurels."

"Well, that's true of course, but I never thought to hear a *vigneron* of the Médoc admit it!"

"What was the place like?"

"Very large and there wasn't really much activity. It was summer when I was there and they were going to take their first real crop a couple of months later. The proprietor seemed to have lost interest in the enterprise and was selling up. I was there because this banker wanted an opinion on its viability."

"What did you say?"

"I said I thought it was a once-in-a-lifetime opportunity for someone. Everything you want and nothing you don't want. There's no winery of course, *cuverie* to you. The grapes get processed at a place called the Cape Mentelle winery. Apparently they're the local experts with *Cabernet*. I went there and tried some. It was pretty good. But I think what's really needed to turn it into an internationally marketable product and give you *Médocains* some competition is barrel-aging in small oak casks. Once they tumble to that, well . . . you'd better watch out. They've got a lot of space out there where this property was, and a climate you wouldn't believe."

"You seem to have been impressed."

"I was. And boy, what a place to live. This particular estate was one big clearing in a forest of tall trees, Karri and Jarrah woods, that's what they told me. Doesn't mean a thing to me, but I can tell you they were *big*. So it seemed as if you were in a private kingdom, isolated, impregnable. You should have seen the house!"

"What was it like?"

"Huge. Oh, not like this, it was completely different. It was the biggest bungalow I've ever seen. Made of wood, up on stilts with a broad verandah running all round it. Architecturally it wasn't a patch on this, but so damned *comfortable*. Cool and spacious. It would be a wonderful feeling to sit on those verandahs in the evening and look at your vine fields spreading out around you on every side, like being a king."

"Isn't there a problem with water?" She was beginning to

enjoy herself and leaned down to adjust the flue damper on the stove, concealing the dancing amusement in her eyes.

"None. It's very green and they get a good dousing of rain every winter and never, never any *frost*." Alexa's mind turned to the present.

"Yes, frost. I think it's got to come sooner or later."

"Never mind, you're dead right you know. If you can pull just some of your vines through, the price you'll get from the wine made from those will offset the loss on the others. More even. Claret's going through the roof."

"By the way, will you sell off the rest of that wine I left you with?"

"Yes, if you want. You should get good prices for it."

"I hope so. I mean to let Fabrice have it. He needs some capital of his own."

"It's his anyway, isn't it? Did that little ruse of ours work, by the way? I never did ask you." Tim put his glass down and looked at her enquiringly.

"Yes. One hundred percent. He's always had the report on that sale right there in his own filing cabinet, but so far as I know, he's never gone to the trouble of discovering what was in it. So now he's about to get a nice surprise. It's a safety net I don't need any longer."

"Fine," Tim shrugged, "it can go in next month's sale. But aren't we going to have to tell Fabrice about *that*? You can't just have money appearing from nowhere without some sort of explanation."

"I took care of that too. You would find in my unread report that I foresaw the problem. It says there, that you will sell the balance of the wine when the time is right, in a sale of your own choosing and which has been agreed between you and me. If you don't hear to the contrary, you're to take it the decision is ratified, well, after nearly eight years, I think we can regard it as duly ratified, don't you?"

"Oh, Alexa," Tim looked at her with a mixture of affectionate amusement and horror, "is this really kosher?"

"Pure as the driven snow, I assure you. You may look with your own honest grey eyes. I'll get you a copy of the paperwork tomorrow. Do you want some more of Monsieur Terry senior's firewater?"

Tim nodded, and helped himself while Alexa drew the curtains across the oriel window. The night was bitter and the moon in the cloudless black sky was a crisply outlined disc, shining coldly. "The frost alarm will sound tonight," she murmured.

She wondered how she could begin to tell him that his article on Château d'Ombre must avoid praising the property. For two days she had been steeling herself to raise the matter. As yet, she had not found the right moment. It was difficult. Honest journalists of any sort didn't submit to instructions about what to write, and of all people, Tim Bowring would be honest. She had just decided that Richard's request was impossible to fulfil, when her train of thought was broken by Tim's voice.

"Shouldn't we go down and join Fabrice in the billiard room? We can't stay up here all evening, much as I'd like to, it looks so appallingly rude. The poor fellow will think I'm busy seducing you. Come on." Reluctantly, Tim began to heave himself out of Alexa's chintz armchair.

"There's something I want to ask you, Tim, before we go, something important."

"As a matter of fact, there's something I want to ask *you*. What's all this about you withdrawing from the management of Château d'Ombre? It isn't true, is it?"

Alexa gave the explanation which she had given Fabrice. She needed to spend more time with Charles, now he was no longer a baby, and there was her own little vineyard to think of. With so little labour affordable for that project, she needed to supervise it personally.

"Fabrice is delighted, actually."

"He may be, Alexa, but I'm sure you'll be missed, by wine lovers, that is. I suppose the immediate effect will be to heighten the value of any wine that was made before this year. I'm afraid it might depress the price of subsequent vintages. Difficult to say. It isn't often a proprietor has become so firmly established in the public mind. You may not realise it, but there are an awful lot of people out there who know you, even if you don't know *them*. You *are* Château d'Ombre. Couldn't you reconsider?"

"No, Tim, my mind's made up. I've done enough. Charles has seen far too little of me since he was born. Now it's *his* turn. Château d'Ombre will have to get on without me."

Tim sighed. "Well, it's a pity. I hoped I'd be writing nothing but good news about Château d'Ombre."

As they picked their way down the ill-lit spiral staircase to the top gallery, Alexa asked herself again, what she was doing.

* * *

The alarm went off at four o'clock in the morning. It was an eerie, frightening sound. The noise-factor of David's contraption had been supplied by Alexa's father. It was an old mill siren, rescued years before by Alexander on a strangely sentimental impulse when clearing Henry's old mill before the purchaser took over, as part and parcel of winding up the old man's estate. In its time it had served as an air-raid warning siren for the district. The sound was designed to be gut-churning, strange and fearful, impossible to ignore.

Alexa shot out of bed, donning the thick corduroy trousers and sweaters she had laid ready for the expected emergency. They had been folded for days over a mahogany towel rail in her bedroom, a pair of stout, lace-up walking shoes beneath, with ribbed shooting socks tucked into them. She was almost relieved to be putting them on at last. Soon they would know the worst. This was how expectant fathers must feel, she smiled to herself. Glad to have a part to play at last. Boiling hot water or lighting braziers, it was better than doing nothing. Helpless waiting hurt more than catastrophe.

Within five minutes Hortense was rapping at the door.

"I have brought you some hot *bouillion, Madame*. Drink it, you will need it."

"Oh, Hortense, you are always thinking of our stomachs!" Seeing the older woman's crest-fallen countenance, she said, "Here, let me take a mouthful, you drink the rest. You need it more than me, you are not used to work in the fields. Better still, go and put some more on a low light on the stove to keep it hot for when we have finished. Then, we're sure to need it, all of us. Hurry!"

Obediently, Hortense trotted away. Alexa bit her lip. Hortense was too old to learn new tricks. For her, the nourishment of the body would always come before anything else. It was her life's work. For her mistress, it was the nurture of the vines. If the crop failed, she wanted to shout after the faithful cook, where would *bouillion* come from?

Out in the home fields, the dark air prickled with cold and the moon, as though drawn with a compass, shed a silver-blue light on everything. The clear sky was speckled with stars and it was tempting to waste time gazing up at them. But the nipping crispness of the atmosphere warned that there was work to be done. They would have to act fast, but there was time.

In the moonlight there was no time to look closely at who was present and who was absent. The dark scurrying figures hastened each to their own appointed territory. The *flambeaux* were ready prepared, leaning against the first brazier in each demarcated area. They were improvised from bundles of vine twigs, wrapped around with pitch-soaked strips of linen bandage. Soon pin-points of orange-coloured light flared near and distant as the workers began the task.

It took a few, achingly long moments to get the first braziers going. At first it seemed as if they would refuse to light, but they did. Alexa dashed to her next one, thirty yards away, stumbling on the pebbly ground as she ran. The next one took fire a few moments later and she ran back to the first to check its progress. It was fine, beginning to establish itself. She ran on, back past the second one which she stopped to examine for a second, then on to the third. She worked like this for an hour or more, rushing back to the previous braziers to coax and add fuel, stumbling often and falling several times.

All over the area surrounding the house, there were similar scenes. Fabrice was undertaking only half a dozen braziers to allow for his slower movements, even then he fell several times and struggled to his feet slowly, cursing loudly. David, so adept at practical things and a countryman to his finger tips, finished his own area within forty minutes and came to his master's aid.

"We have done it, *Monsieur*. This part of the crop is safe, the battle is won!" With customary tact, Pierre David did not remind his master that his wife was once again the architect of success. Fabrice's temper was uncertain, these days.

Two hours later, Alexa straightened her back and looked around her for the first time. The dawn was still not come and all over the acreage immediately surrounding the house, the fields were dotted at regular thirty-yard intervals with glowing punctuation marks, cherry-red beacons, throwing a little russet light into the surrounding vines. She felt hot. Her face was smeared with coal dust and her hands were black. A bath would seem the greatest luxury imaginable after this. She looked back at the towering pile of the chateau. Lights blazed everywhere at random. The graceful monster had some eyes open and some shut. It was home.

Back in Hortense's vaulted kitchen, in the general euphoria of a mission successfully completed, all class and age barriers were put aside. Every member of the party recounted their exploits with boisterous enthusiasm. They all laughed at Alexa's soot-smeared face and even Suzanne took the ribbing at her slow start in good part. She looked at her daughter-in-law from time to time, quickly and covertly, as if she would like to say something. Alexa did not see but passed her a bowl of Hortense's *bouillion* and a hunk of coarsely cut bread as if she had been any other estate worker. It was enough. There was a truce for the moment. The people of d'Ombre, masters and servants, had fought in a common cause and rejoiced together.

"What'll it fetch, *Madame*?" shouted young Juliot from the end of the long table.

"What? The wine?"

"Yes, what we've saved."

"Who can say that? The summer's not over yet, but at least we've beaten the spring!"

"What happens to the rest?" called another.

"I don't know yet. We'll make some sort of brew with it, the best way we can, and flog it off for something, don't you worry."

Fabrice frowned. They all looked to her for leadership. When would they realise who was the real master at d'Ombre? Alexa caught his glance. Understanding his look, she whispered to him, "I think we'd all like to hear the boss propose a toast to everyone who took part tonight, to Château d'Ombre, and the future. Go on, darling, it's your show." Alexa was sickened by her own treacly little speech but Fabrice saw nothing amiss and rose to his feet.

"*Salut*. To d'Ombre and all who serve her!"

There was a roar of answering acclaim. Alexa saw Tim Bowring raise his glass and drink from it, his eyes studying her over the rim. He was puzzled.

"Come on everybody, another glass of the best wine in the world and then bed. We've got to look at those braziers again in less than three hours' time. If we don't have clear heads, we *must* have functioning legs!"

It was after nine o'clock when Hortense gently pushed open the door of Alexa's room. She stood for a moment looking down at her sleeping mistress. The light was dim since the brocade curtains were drawn. As Hortense's eyes adjusted to the level of light, she saw that Alexa slept with one arm thrown back behind her head and the other stretched out at right angles to her body. Her hair was spread out around her on the pillow, her skin slightly flushed. With wine and success no doubt, poor lamb, thought

Hortense. Her breath came deep, slow and regular. It was going to be hard to waken her.

The little silver salver in her hand trembled. On it was balanced a small glass of cognac. An unusual breakfast. Downstairs they had chosen her, the cook, to inform the *Marquise* that her son was dead.

CHAPTER
21

ALEXA DID NOT attend the funeral. She had refused point blank to allow her son's body to be interred in the family mausoleum. The thought of that vile maw opening again to receive the pathetic remains of Charles revolted her sensibilities. It could not be contemplated. And in Alexa's precarious emotional state, Doctor Gaultier had recommended that the matter should not be pressed. Some alternative must be found.

Hurriedly, a patch of ground four metres square in extent was prepared. It lay towards the outer limits of the old, formal garden, now substantially restored, and overlooked by the *Tour du Jardin*. Railings were erected and the little grave was dug by David himself. Alexa would not go near the turret room but remained in her bedroom or downstairs in Héloïse's old study. Much as she wanted the privacy of her private boudoir, study and office, she shied away from catching even a glance of the grave whilst it still remained an open, greedy chasm.

It was Tilly, with her influential connections in the Church, who at short notice had arranged for the Bishop of Bordeaux to consecrate the ground so that it should receive the de Pies Ombre heir with a propriety at which no-one could cavil. Père Lachasse, as Charles's godfather, added his weight to the arguments in favour of consecrating a new burial ground for the de Pies Ombres who were, after all, distinguished sons and daughters of the Church and had never previously asked for any special privileges.

It was done without Alexa's participation. A cool message of acknowledgement, together with a small cheque to be applied to the charity of his choice, was the Bishop's sole reward for interrupting a busy schedule and departing from modern and more democratic procedures. He was accustomed to the peremptory manners of some of the great landed proprietors of his see, but profoundly irritated by the *hauteur* of this Protestant Englishwoman. He would see to it that Madame La Courbe heard of it. It wasn't that he exactly wanted his ring kissed, but this woman behaved as if she could command his services just as if he were a dentist or an accountant.

And of course, Tilly telephoned in a flurry of indignation.

"Alexa, *ma chère*! You might have been a little more effusive with His Grace. You know he has done a great thing for you and *very* quickly. And not a word to poor Père Lachasse! It's doubtful if the thing could have been achieved with *quite* such celerity without his interest in the matter."

"How long could we *wait* for a grave?" Alexa's intended cruelty hurt no-one so much as herself. "No doubt he has enjoyed being the godfather of a future *Marquis*. Quite an enhancement to his career prospects, I don't doubt," she continued drily. "I shouldn't wonder if he isn't hoping that I may be able to provide him with a replacement."

"Well," Tilly concluded, "I shan't intrude myself on your grief any further, *ma chère*, though I hope when you get over it you will be able to see matters with your usual clarity of vision and recover some of your accustomed graciousness. I suppose we must make allowances. Really, Alexa, I have never known you so *surly* before. Do pull yourself together, *ma chère*, life goes on you know. *I* know no-one was to blame for this *terrible* tragedy, certainly not yourself. You really mustn't be so self-indulgent. Do try to think a little more of *others*. *Think* of poor Fabrice, for instance. You have not been the only sufferer, *ma chère*. You must both think about having another child just as soon as possible. That is the best antidote to all this. Yes, I'm sure that is the only solution. Now, of course, I know . . ."

Tilly had never been a mother. She seemed to think that replacing a dead child was only a little more problematic than replacing a dead goldfish.

"Have you finished?" Alexa was icy with fury. The voice on the other end of the line was silent. "Because, if you have, I'm sure you will understand when I tell you that I never intend to entertain any de Pies Ombre spawn again. This family will get no more cripples on me! And yes, I *did* love Charles. More and more with every day that passed. I had no choice. Nature makes certain of that. But loving him hurt like knives every step of the way. It hurts now, and it will go *on* hurting. It was a wicked trick, Tilly, and very cruel.''

"Ah, nature, *ma chère* . . .''

"Nature had precious little to do with it. I was tricked into this marriage and deceived into bearing a son who everyone except me knew was likely to be damaged. Who, precisely, was responsible I have never really been able to fathom. But I've had a strong feeling for some time that you may have had something to do with it yourself. And secondly, do not presume to lecture me on my behaviour. I neither welcome your advice, nor do I need it. You have been no friend to me.''

Alexa had dropped the telephone receiver back into its cradle. She glanced out of the oriel window, her eyes drawn as if by a magnet to the raw mound on the far side of the garden. She had ordered that all the flowers be removed before she would use the turret room again. David had planted bulbs there, in the freshly turned earth that lay on top of Charles. She had not yet cried. The tears were banked up behind a rampart of defensive activity. They created a pressure that built into a dull ache and a sense of futility.

Once again, her mind travelled the familiar route. She had been responsible for Charles' death. She should have known that the Davis escape would prove too big a temptation to a red-blooded, proud little boy. Stupidly, she had never considered that Charles would attempt such a thing on his own. She had taken it for granted that he would never challenge his own physical limitations although she herself had encouraged him to do so on numerous occasions. The regular fire-practices with Morag using the equipment, abseiling down the wall of the château with Charles in his sling, had never struck her as likely to excite her son's imagination. And perhaps they would not have done so, if she hadn't spoken so carelessly about the frost-prevention scheme in front of him. It had all seemed a great adventure to his small boy's mind. He had wanted to prove something to himself and to all of them. And because of it, he was dead. His neck and back broken like dry vine twigs. He couldn't tell her all of this, but she knew as plainly as if he had spoken to her. Ariel had expressed her doubts about the attic nursery at the very beginning and she, Alexa, hadn't listened.

They didn't blame her, oddly. She would have thought they would have been glad to turn on her. But no. It was poor Morag who had found herself treated as a murderess. It was the need to defend the hapless nanny, suddenly surrounded by the baying hostility of Suzanne and the more hurtful cold glances of the estate staff, that had supported Alexa through the first dreadful hours of her knowledge of her son's death.

The night the frost alarm first went off, Morag had heard it and got up to see if Charles had been disturbed. She looked in at the door of his room. Apparently he was sleeping and Morag had no reason to doubt it. Charles had always slept soundly, as most children do, and he regularly slept through the most terrifying thunderstorms. She went back to her bed and read for a while, falling asleep herself after about an hour.

When she woke in the morning she went again to Charles' room and found that the form in the bed was nothing but a roll of blanket, artfully curved to resemble a sleeping child. She smiled. They had been reading a lot of old-fashioned English school stories lately. He had probably gone down to his mother's room. He had been doing that a lot lately. It was healthy and Morag wasn't given to jealousy.

She went to the nursery kitchen and began to make herself some tea. It was about eight o'clock. After half an hour had gone by, she began to feel some mild irritation. Time with Mother was one thing, but nursery routines were not to be disrupted lightly. It wasn't beneficial to the child and it wasn't part of her working relationship with Charles' mother. It was odd, Madame de Pies Ombre had always been so considerate where nursery matters were concerned. An ideal employer. Something was wrong.

Morag had dressed quickly with a rising sense of unease. She was still clipping the silver nursing buckle which Alexa had given her for Christmas, last year, as she hurried down the steep narrow staircase which led to the two main bedroom galleries of the château. Normally, she would never come that way. It was a rule of the house that Charles was not to use that staircase. If he wanted to reach his mother's room he had to go down in the lift to the kitchen first and approach the first and second floors by ascending the broad, shallow staircases of the main part of the house. It was safer.

As Morag emerged through the little Gothic-shaped doorway which gave onto the upper gallery, she felt an unnatural hush. Looking over the stone balustrade, she could see down into the hall with its black and white marble floor. There was no sound or movement there. She did not at first notice Hortense on the gallery below, who had paused outside Alexa's door holding a small tray in her hand. When she did, she knew with an appalling lurch of the heart that something was terribly wrong. It was not only the glass of brandy on the tray but something desperate in Hortense's attitude, a look of reluctance which informed her whole body. Morag hardly needed to be told anything. Something unthinkable had happened.

Hortense, feeling herself observed, glanced upwards. When she caught sight of Morag, she turned away immediately. Morag hurried down the next staircase calling to Hortense. The old cook said only, ''Downstairs, in the kitchen.''

Pierre David had found the body. It lay, crumpled at the foot of the château's west wall, the Davis rope dangling from the little window with its own pointed gabled roof, which jutted out of the blue slate roof. Seeing the grotesque angle at which Charles' head lay, David knew enough not to move him, but no sound of breath came from him and his flesh was cold. He wore a thick Breton sweater and corduroy trousers, like the ones his mother always wore for work in the fields or the *chais*. One of his shoes was unlaced and David saw with a rush of tears to his eyes that the little boy had put his socks on so that the heel was on the upper side of the foot. Even at seven, Charles's precocity of mind and manual dexterity did not stretch to dressing himself. Morag had unwittingly seen to that.

A local doctor was summoned who pronounced the boy dead. He was carried into the kitchen and laid on the table where his parents and all the estate workers had celebrated their first victory over the frost only a few hours ago.

The attack on Morag had been immediate and ferocious. Suzanne was beside herself. She screamed at the bewildered nanny that she was irresponsible, careless, slept like a pig and should never, ever get another appointment as long as Suzanne de Pies Ombre lived. Morag stood, rooted to the spot, unable to fully comprehend what was happening. There was a terrible noise, a lot of people were shouting and some were crying. The blanket-wrapped bundle on the table was her little Charles, they said. It was a miasma of horror and confusion, an evil dream from which she would wake.

It was into this maelstrom of sound and emotion that Alexa stepped. Hortense had told her. She had drunk the brandy and said, unbelievingly, that she had better come and see for herself.

At her entrance the level of sound dropped for an instant but then resumed.

"Be *silent*!"

All eyes turned towards the figure in the doorway, and then fell in embarrassment, except for Suzanne's. Not for the first time, Alexa saw how mother and son resembled each other. Suzanne's face was disfigured by the round crater of anger that she had seen open on Fabrice's face innumerable times.

"Go to your room, *Madame*. You are beside yourself."

Suzanne, hesitatingly, lifted her arm and pointed an accusing finger at Morag who still stood in the middle of the kitchen as if transfixed. A gobbling sound issued from her throat. She was incapable of coherent speech.

"No. We will speak later. I wish you to go to your room immediately." Suzanne left, her head held exaggeratedly high, slamming the door behind her.

Alexa surveyed the scene before her, her eyes only flicking over the shrouded form on the kitchen table. Hortense stood behind her, mopping her eyes with a large bandanna handkerchief, looking fearfully over her mistress' shoulder.

"This is a terrible thing. But it is a misfortune which *I* must bear. Please, all go back to your work. The braziers need attention. If it freezes again tonight, we will go on as before. Do you understand? Monsieur Charles would have wished it." In a moment in which nobody moved, Alexa added with a sudden flash of hindsight, "He was coming to help us."

Slowly, shufflingly, the workmen assembled in the kitchen began to leave by the yard door. Alexa shooed them mechanically, as if trying to assure them that the terrible thing on the table was an illusion, nothing more. She had not taken in the fact that all that was left of Charles was a tragic little corpse. Dimly, she realised herself that she was detached from reality. But there were more immediate things to attend to. The dislocation of Château d'Ombre must be mended. No peripheral disaster could be confronted until the vines were saved.

"Hortense, make some strong black coffee. Pierre, ring the parish priest. He must make the arrangements. I don't know how to and *Madame* is too overcome to manage. Where is my husband?"

David shrugged, looking almost shiftily at Hortense.

"I do not know, *Madame*."

"And Mr. Bowring?"

"He is already attending to his braziers. There is no need but he insisted . . ."

"Does he know of this?"

"No, *Madame*."

"Then please inform him at once, and ask him to come up to the house as quickly as possible."

"Immédiatement, Madame." As David turned to leave, Alexa went to Morag, who still stood immobile like one on trial, and put her arms around her.

"Come and sit down. You have had a great shock. You must have some coffee first, with some cognac in it and then, there are a few things we must do." Alexa led Morag to a chair near the stove. She had almost to force the girl to sit down as her own muscles and sinews had seemingly ceased to respond to messages from her brain, if indeed they were receiving any.

"No one blames you, Morag. You need take no notice of my mother-in-law, she is not in command of herself and is not responsible for what she does or says."

Morag dissolved into noisy tears and would not be embraced or comforted. Hortense and Alexa looked at each other over the nanny's bowed head. It seemed there would be few people to depend upon in this crisis.

In the end it was Tim Bowring who undertook the distasteful task of carrying Charles' little body out of the kitchen. He was laid in a cold, seldom-used bedroom on the upper gallery, there to await the attentions of the undertakers. Alexa suspected that Morag would prove of no further practical use and she herself never wished to set foot in the nursery again. She wished she could set fire to it.

She declined Tim's tentative but sincere offer to tell Fabrice what had befallen his son. She did it herself, distancing herself as best she could from his howls of animal rage and pain. She found him asleep in the dressing room next to her own room. There was a half-finished tot of whisky on the bedside table and his breath stank. He had slept in his underpants and a grubby undershirt. Tears coursed down his face, leaving streaks of vividly clean skin where the salt water cut its way through grime. With detachment Alexa noticed that he had not washed after the night's exertions.

"Please try and take hold of yourself, Fabrice. We have a business to run and other people to think of."

"You bloody, bloody heartless bitch! That's all you ever think

of, isn't it? Nothing has ever mattered to you but that. Money!
You greedy, bourgeois trollop. I wish to God I'd never set eyes
on you! Get out, Alexa, get out! And take that Scotch gorgon of
yours with you. Go where the hell you like, but get out of my
sight. You and your bloody business. Get out!''

She left him to himself. With any luck he would drink himself
to sleep again and leave her to get on with what had to be done.

It was the day after the funeral that Richard arrived.

Alexa had told him briefly over the telephone what had happened. A low moan of sorrow escaped him, issuing from the
deepest caverns of his being. The sound was repeated again
before he found speech.

"Alexa, my darling. There is nothing, nothing in the world
that I can say, except that I love you. I will do anything, I will
give anything . . .'' The futility of his words echoed back mock-
ingly in his ears. "Please, hold on, I can be with you by tomorrow morning.''

There was no effort or premeditation in what he said. The
terrible shock of her news released valves in him that undammed
a flood of feeling. It rushed out in words unhampered by reason
or reticence. He accused himself of being the author of Alexa's
agony. He felt he was to blame. In taking Alexa's life so wilfully
into his own hands, he had allowed the calamity to happen as
if it had been part of his plan. It was his stupidity, his carelessness . . . It was irrational, he knew, but nothing could wipe out
the feeling that he was intimately involved in her tragedy and he
longed to be near her to staunch the cruel gash of pain he had
so mysteriously and so inadvertently inflicted. Until he could
place his secret soul and very body next to hers, the blood of
her heart would continue to flow and stain his hands.

Eventually, he became calm and the whirling storm clouds of
words subsided. He became, to Alexa's relief, recognisably
himself, drily practical, solidifying once more into the blunt
man of affairs. But she wanted everything now to happen in
manageable episodes. Like a convalescent, she could only take
small mouthfuls of experience.

"No. Please don't come, not yet anyway. I can't bear it. I'm
not going to the funeral myself. When it's all over, I believe I
shall be able to handle things again, but at the moment, I don't
want anyone. I told my parents not to come. It would only make

things worse. I'm just not strong enough yet. If anyone comes near me now, I shall break down. I know I shall.''

''Wouldn't that be a good thing?''

''No, it's too dangerous. I have to stay in control.''

''What do you mean? Stay in control of what? You'll have to let it out some time, Alexa. You'll be ill if you don't. I mean it, dearest. There's a certain degree of self-control that isn't healthy or normal. For God's sake, Alexa, let it out.''

''I mean in control of the situation. Fabrice is trying to get rid of me. He wants me to go. He says he can't bear the sight of me. I don't know if he can do that, but I'm not moving. *This is my home*. And I have never done anything wrong.''

''I shouldn't take any of that too seriously, if I were you. He's obviously out of his mind with grief. My God, Alexa, he won't know what's hit him. I scarcely do myself. Fabrice will have no idea what he's saying or doing either, I guess. Just leave him alone, keep out of his way and let him calm down. I *am* coming, Alexa. But I'll leave it till after the funeral, if that's what you really prefer. I can't bear to think of you being there alone in that atmosphere at a time like this, but I haven't the right to intrude, if you don't want me.''

He wanted her so badly. He needed to protect, guard, cherish and possess her. It angered him that he could not compensate her for her loss. There were a few things, just a few, that even great wealth could not buy or supply. And he had hoped to give her everything. Now this irrevocable death, this chance carving of a living branch from her trunk, had cheated him. The scar would be her own, inalienable, irreparable.

''Oh, Richard! You fool! It isn't that I don't want you, I do. I'm so lonely and so frightened. But if you come here, Fabrice might start talking about adultery and divorce. I can't afford that. Don't you understand? I don't want to leave d'Ombre. I *can't*. It's more mine than his. I won't give it up. And,'' she added after a pause, with a jagged catch in her voice, ''I don't want to leave Charles. He is here, you see.''

''I understand. But Alexa, you and I have *never* committed adultery.''

''I know that. But Fabrice would grasp at any excuse, however slight, at the moment. He's just crazy. You've no idea. He ought to be locked up. But, Richard, I'm *not* running away. Do you understand? I stay *here*. It's my right.''

''Alexa, darling, just try to relax and not worry too much

about things. I told you I was working to put a few things right in your life, didn't I? Well, do you think I just talk for the sake of it?"

"No. But what *are* you doing, Richard? I don't like all this mystery. And nothing, *nothing*, will ever be right again."

"It will. It will. It'll soon be over. For the time being it's best you don't know too much, safer. Now be a good girl and look after yourself. I'll be with you soon. Oh, just one other thing, is Bowring still with you?"

"Yes, why?"

"Tell him to ring me. Make sure he does."

The line went dead. Alexa held the telephone for minutes. The silence was thousands of miles long.

She never set foot in the nursery again. Tim Bowring escorted Morag to Merignac Airport and flew with her to Paris and on to London. He would see her safely home. She took with her a hand-written reference couched in the warmest terms and a very large cheque in respect of severance pay.

Putting aside her own pain, and deciding to deal with it later, Alexa tried to heal Morag Anderson. She had kissed her affectionately at the door and made her promise to write within a week.

"We have been through so much together. I need to know that you are safe and beginning to feel better. And Morag, you must never, ever blame yourself for this. It was a terrible accident and I don't suppose you will ever forget it. But concentrate on the good times. Those are what matter. Charles's life was happy and secure, and that was your achievement. Never forget *that*. You will see what I have written about you. Yes, open it. It's for you as much as the lucky people who get you next."

"Oh, Madame de Pies Ombre, I shan't be able to face working for another family. Not after this."

"Then you will be very selfish, Morag. You *must* get over this. Somewhere, there's a little boy or girl who needs you just as much as my son did. Go on now. Oh, and by the way, you might give my mother a call and reassure her that I'm all right." Morag looked wide-eyed at Alexa.

"You're quite the best person to do it, dear. After all, she'll be confident that what you say is right. You've been keeping her in touch for so long. If it hadn't been for you, my mother and I would have ceased to know each other.''

It was Hortense who went up to the nursery to check that no signs of recent occupation were left. She stripped Charles' bed and Morag's, emptied the waste-paper bins, the refrigerator and the laundry basket.

Waterman and Quink were brought down, one cat held firmly under each of Hortense's muscular arms. They squirmed angrily but Hortense held on to them like grim death. The nursery was to be closed, virtually sealed off. No-one would live there again. The blue cats were to be rehabilitated as kitchen cats. Their yellow eyes were round and Alexa avoided looking at them. They searched for familiar things that were absent and knew that Charles was gone.

The soiled linen from the nursery was to be burnt together with the other rubbish. Alexa burnt it herself in the kitchen courtyard. The smoke stung her dry eyes but she kept poking at it with the long poker from the kitchen stove. There must be nothing left. It was absurd, she knew. She wasn't going to burn all the toys and the books. Just these things. But it was a serious and necessary ritual. A cremation of more than sheets and blankets and towels. It was a private and final goodbye.

Hortense knew she wasn't wanted. Occasionally she glanced out of the window. When would she have finished? Already the flames had died down, all that remained was a smouldering pile of rags. Alexa kept prodding them, trying to make the sulky sparks flare up again and consume the remnants of fabric. Her hair was disordered, she kept pushing it out of the way with her hand, there were flecks of ash and soot in it, her eyes were red.

When the great door-bell clanged, Hortense gave one more worried glance out of the window and, wiping her hands hurriedly on her apron, she climbed the basement stairs to see who had come at so unseasonable a time. There were no guests scheduled yet and she imagined they'd all be cancelled this year. She had no recollection of the man at the door, although he greeted her courteously and by name.

''Good morning, Hortense. I should like to see Madame de Pies Ombre, she's expecting me.'' Hortense regarded him with surprise. There was nothing about Alexa's appearance or occupation to suggest that she had any expectation of callers.

''If you will wait in here, sir, I will inform *Madame* of your arrival. What name is it sir?'' Mechanically, Hortense showed him into Mademoiselle Héloïse's office by the front door. It was clean and tidy.

"Lockwood," Richard answered, preparing to sit in the desk chair of Héloïse's study. Puzzled, Hortense descended to the basement. It was awkward. *Madame* was in a delicate emotional state. If she were allowed to get over her strangely expressed outburst of grief at leisure, all might be well with her. But she had repressed her natural feelings for what seemed to Hortense an unhealthily long time now. This interruption was inopportune. Still, the man might be important. She dared not send him away on her own authority.

"Madame!" The sight that confronted Hortense's vision bounced off her understanding like a negative magnetic field. The two refused to come together. Alexa was standing in the middle of the kitchen sobbing uncontrollably and ripping tea towels, kitchen table cloths, napkins, into minute pieces with the aid of scissors. Drawers were pulled out of the dressers and the contents spilled on the flagstone floors. Wild-eyed, Alexa was tearing and cutting, emitting sounds of frustration and rage. She did not register any consciousness of Hortense's presence.

"Oh, *Madame, Madame . . .*"

"Let me deal with this, Hortense." She felt a firm pressure on her shoulder and the calm, authoritative voice just behind her. "Go and find *Monsieur le Marquis*. Go on. I'll take care of your mistress."

"I'm taking her away, Pies Ombre."

Fabrice was slumped in a chair by the empty fireplace in the billiard room. In his hand he held a tumbler of whisky. He was unshaven. His stick had fallen to the ground, he would be unable to reach it. Richard regarded him without pity.

"Suits me. If you want the cow, take her. There's nothing I can do about it." He sniggered, "Nothing I *want* to do about it. Don't bring her back. If she goes today, that's the last I want to see of her. Understand? She's your responsibility, and you're welcome to it."

"I will show you this much friendship, Pies Ombre. I will ignore those remarks and attribute them to your own understandable grief and a pardonable lack of self-control in the surrounding circumstances. However, your wife in anxious about the vineyards and the progress of work here while she is gone. I'm sure you realise that, in view of the degree of her personal involvement, although I understand she is no longer a director of the firm, it would be a better preparation for a period of total relaxation if she could be reassured that everything will go on in her absence as she would have wished. Can you give me that assurance? If you can, then I shall be happy to convey it to her, to spare you the strain of a meeting when you are both so over-wrought.''

''You pompous bastard! Who the hell are you?''

''We met some years ago. I visited your house once and I attended your son's christening.'' Fabrice grunted.

''One of Alexa's punters. How come you take such an interest in my bloody wife's affairs?''

''I am a banker. I have been looking after her affairs for some time now. Just some little investments and trusts. The usual things. Now, what am I to say to Madame de Pies Ombre? Do you feel up to supervising things here or is there some kind of temporary estate manager we can get in? I understand your *régisseur* is a good man, but can he manage on his own?''

''You can tell that cow she's got nothing to worry about. I've had an offer for Château d'Ombre and I think I shall let the lousy place go. The whole bloody shooting match. I've had enough of it. There's nobody to keep it going for now, why should I bother?'' It was not a question but Richard could not restrain himself from replying.

''Seemingly it is your wife who has bothered.''

''Fuck off, Lockwood. Take that sodding cow with you and don't bring her back. There'll be nothing to come back to. Do you hear? I'm selling it! Tell her that. Her precious d'Ombre doesn't exist any more, not for her. And another thing, she needn't think she can come on to me for any money, if she gets any ideas like that, you can disabuse her. It's all over.''

CHAPTER
22

♋ ♋ THE HIRED MERCEDES swung onto the N10 from Bordeaux. It was a fast road. Richard glanced at the clock glowing green in the dashboard. Five minutes to midnight. They would be in Paris by first light.

He looked at Alexa sleeping beside him. Her head leaned against the door, she couldn't be very comfortable but at least she was calm now. Putting out a hand to stroke her hair, he had to swerve violently to avoid an on-coming car. Beads of sweat stood out on his forehead as he righted the vehicle. There must not be any accidents now.

He had taken her away from the château in the early afternoon and driven the forty miles or so south, to Villandraut. She had been amazed but unquestioning about the cottage.

And then it started. The nervous collapse he had witnessed earlier in the day at the château was not all. She began shivering uncontrollably. Her face was grey and her skin clammy to the touch. She could hardly speak. When he asked her what was the matter, she couldn't answer, just shook her head, helplessly. Richard searched through his memory. He had seen something like it before. Years ago. The day the bank foreclosed on his father's little business. He had reacted the same way, but not until the evening. The doctor had said it was delayed shock.

Rapidly his mind combed through the resources to hand. There was no telephone in the cottage, only the telex machine. Doctors did not have télex machines installed in their surgeries or houses. He could have contacted the bank in New York and asked them to find him a doctor in the Bordeaux area. It would all have taken a long time. And in the end, he would have found himself explaining the inexplicable to a man he didn't know,

who might want to take Alexa away and put her in a hospital.
He found he couldn't face the prospect of losing sight of her,
even for a few hours. Even so, he cursed the privacy-preserving
instinct which had led him to exclude the telephone. He had
never foreseen an emergency like this.

With clumsy hands he built a fire in the large farmhouse fireplace, laying twigs and logs across the crude, iron firedogs. He
had cut a great deal of wood on his vacations, but never yet lit
a fire. He urged it to flare quickly. Hortense had thrown an old
blond mink coat in the boot of the car. He went to get it. He
wrapped it around Alexa's shuddering frame as best he could.
It was no good, it kept slipping off.

"Stand up, darling, let me get you into this." She could not
stand but had to be supported. It made it awkward.

"Sit down again, I've got a better idea." Quickly he went
into his own bedroom and brought blankets and pillows. He laid
the fur coat on the ground with the fur facing upwards and made
her lie on it before the fire. He covered her with the blankets
and supported her head with the pillows.

"Now, you'll soon feel better." He spoke without much confidence as she continued to tremble. Desperately he readjusted
the logs and added more, willing them to become a roaring fire.

"Hot sweet tea, that's what you need." Alexa's face registered repugnance.

"You're lucky. I don't have tea in the house." His mind raced
onto coffee as an alternative and rejected it. "I'm going to make
you a drink with whisky and honey and brown sugar and lemon
juice. The lemon juice is to take some of the *glug* out of it. Do
you think you could face that?"

Her eyes never left his face. She nodded weakly.

"All right, I need to go into the kitchen. You stay here and
keep wrapped up." In the kitchen he busied himself boiling
water on the electric hob. It was slow. Alexa had had as much
as she could take. Eight years of toil and anxiety had led her to
this. Richard gritted his teeth, willing the water to boil. When
it did he poured it into a tumbler with the last of a bottle of
Cutty Sark. Fortunately there was enough, even a little left over
for him. The honey had crystallised in the jar and was slow to
melt. He cut a lemon, nicking his finger. The blood flowed and
he swore. Frantic in his haste to get back to her, he wrapped a
glass cloth round it.

"Can you sit up a little?" He crouched down beside her and

supported her with his arm. "Drink this, all of it, it will do you good." He held the glass to her lips and she sipped the toddy, slowly at first and then greedily as the hot liquid cooled. "That's a good girl." He kept his arm around her. The shivering was beginning to subside.

The fire began to take hold and he fed it with more wood. Outside a wind sprang up, sighing and moaning through the surrounding trees. A shutter began to bang in the wind and Alexa started. Her nerves are shot, thought Richard. She'll pull through. She must. Dimly he recognised she was trembling on the edge of a full-scale nervous breakdown. Nothing stood between her and an abyss of fear and confusion but his will. The whole of his being was concentrated on drawing her back from the brink.

"It's nothing, darling. Just a shutter come unhooked. I'll go and see to it. Are you warm enough now?" He laid his cheek next to hers. It was still cool but the clammy feeling was gone. He began to extract the pins from her hair. It fell in a curled mass over her shoulders, reflecting glints of red and orange from the firelight. Passionately he brought a lock to his lips, tears starting from his eyes. In a moment, he laid her gently back down on the pillows.

"Alexa, can you hear me?" She was looking fixedly at him but she seemed far-distant in her mind. She nodded slightly.

"I'm going upstairs, to send some messages. I'll only be a few moments, and then I'm going to be outside getting some more wood. Will you be all right for a few minutes?" She reached for his hand and squeezed it. It was her answer. An unaccountable surge of joy rushed through his body like a tidal wave. Its force pushing away the structures of years as effortlessly as if they had been toys. What was left was space for a new beginning. A devastated beach with clean, unmarked sands.

When he returned to her she had fallen asleep. The fire was burning fiercely now, casting moving shadows on the white-washed walls of the old house. It was growing dark and they would have to leave soon if they were to make their rendezvous with Alexander. There was no way now of getting in touch with him. He had left for London at midday, as soon as he had received Richard's call that morning. He was to get the first available flight for Paris and wait for them there.

Richard sat beside her for an hour, unwilling to wake her from the calm and healthy slumber. He watched her in the gathering darkness, occasionally adding more wood to the fire. The noise caused her to stir slightly but she did not awake.

When an hour had gone by, he rose from the chair where he had been sitting more or less motionless and lay down beside her. She woke then and entwined her arms around him. Her eyes were fully open, dark and round.

"Could you make love to me?"

The consummation was swift. They came together with the crashing impact of tide on rock. He soared above her and then dived to claim his beloved prey. When the storm subsided they were one.

There was no time for words. Alexa ate hungrily while Richard received some telex messages, the clacking and whirring of the machine in the upper room sounding as companionable as a spinning wheel. When he came down, Alexa asked him, "What have you been doing up there?"

"You ever heard of Rumpelstiltskin? You remember, that's the little bandy-legged guy who spun gold out of straw for a lady in distress."

Alexa smiled at Richard's picturesque description of his own activities, but she attached no particular significance to it.

They had drawn level with Le Mans when she woke again and began to talk.

"I am Château d'Ombre," she had said, without a trace of self-consciousness or humour. "And d'Ombre is me. Without it I am no-one again. Somebody else's creation, not a creator myself. If they take it away, I shall be invisible. I shall not exist for myself. I will see nothing in the mirror."

Richard was not saddened. For most women a man's love might be enough. But for his Alexa, it was not. She must have her work and her land or she would refuse any secondary love. Acceptance of this was the essential condition on which she could be loved or love in return.

The sudden and violent reaction of suppressed frustration and grief he had witnessed in the château kitchen had had a therapeutic effect. He reflected that many times during their years together, he had seen old Michael Goldstein formally rip the breast pocket of his jacket when told of the death of an acquaintance in the banking community. It had always made Richard wince at the expense. "How many suits are you prepared to ruin?" he asked him.

"Not so many. Look, for relatives I tear cloth, but for busi-

ness associates, I rip stitches, they would not expect more."
Rending garments. It was better than psychiatry.

He told Alexa the story. She seemed grateful to know that her
actions had not been those of a mad woman.

"Poor Hortense. I left a terrible mess for her to clear up.
She'll think you're taking me away to a clinic for rich lunatics."

"No, she won't. She knows you're going away for a short
holiday. That's all. You'll be back before long."

"Don't humour me, darling. I'm strong enough to face the
truth. I know I'm never going back. I've lost. You took the
weapons out of my hands yourself. I'll never know why. Perhaps
one day you'll tell me what it's all been about."

"Soon, my darling. Just give me another week. Everything
is going to be fine. Be good and relax."

"Why do you treat me like a child?"

"I'm treating you like a business partner. Right now it's more
important than ever that you trust me. Concentrate on getting
your strength back. You're going to need it."

"What for?"

"For one thing, you've got your Australian property to supervise. You really will have to go out there soon and give some
directions about it. What a damn good thing you decided to buy
it before all this blew up in our faces."

"The whole thing's going to seem rather tasteless without
Château d'Ombre in the background. It's not the way I pictured
things . . ." her voice trailed off uncertainly.

"Come on, this isn't like you. Things will look different in a
few days' time, I promise. Just trust me."

"I don't have a choice, do I?"

"Quite frankly, my treasure, you don't."

Tim pulled the third and final sheet out of the typewriter. He
supposed it would do. Everything he'd said was no more than
the gospel truth. All he had to do now was telex the number he'd
been given in New York. If the copy got the okay it would be
printed, subject to editorial approval. Why was it that everything
to do with Alexa de Pies Ombre was so complicated and mysterious? He'd never understand why she'd resigned, never.

Alexander arrived early. It was eight, or was it nine years since
he'd been in this office? Nothing had changed in the Rue Rod-
rigues chambers of Maître Robinson. Much as he had liked the

French lawyer, he had hoped not to be under the necessity of
meeting with him again on a professional footing. Somehow, in
spite of the increasingly hopeful state of affairs, he had always
feared that this day would come.

Alexa had not been told yet. He hoped she would take the
news bravely. This time, there was nothing he could do. She
had formed the Château d'Ombre wine business into a *Société
Anonyme* on his advice. And then, unaccountably, without consulting him, she had resigned from the Board of Directors. It
was a rash, foolhardy step. But then she was just that, rash and
foolhardy. She'd proved that eight years ago. At least she had a
little money of her own. Rather more than might have been
expected actually, or so that banker fellow indicated. Just as
well, she was going to need it. Alexander couldn't see her coming out of this affair very well. Fighting a divorce action in the
French courts at long range would be a costly exercise and was
unlikely to be a very fruitful one.

Alexander had given himself up to these gloomy reflections
when he was joined by Maître Robinson.

"My good friend. How was your journey? Did they look after
you at the Aquitania?"

Alexander rose to greet the other man, dapper in the inevitable pinstripe. "Thank you, I was quite comfortable in body, if
not in mind. What has precipitated this whole affair? My daughter will tell me nothing that sheds any real light. I gather there
has been some tension between her and her husband, and then
of course, this frightful affair of my grandson. But this hardly
seems the time to take so radical a step. I have always been led
to believe they had a successful business going there now. I
confess, I am bewildered and I feel helpless. What is it that I
am expected to achieve here today?"

Maître Robinson ushered Alexander into his well-remembered
office, speaking to a clerk in passing. "There is little you can
do, my friend. But you ought to be present to ensure that the
property conveyed is in conformity with what we know the *Marquis* has full competence to sell. We know he cannot sell the
acreage that formed your daughter's marriage settlement. You
have brought the documents?"

Alexander tapped his briefcase. "I'm bound to say, I wonder
if we should not in fact sell those plots as a separate transaction
to the purchaser of the Château d'Ombre property. Alexa is

going to find it hard to administrate them independently and I cannot believe that she would really want to.''

"She has given no instructions?''

"No, and I no longer hold her Power of Attorney, it lapsed at the beginning of this year and through some oversight, it hasn't been renewed. But we could sound the attitude of the purchaser. However, that seems to me a detail. What is of pressing concern to me is this. Monsieur de Pies Ombre, my son-in-law, appears to have constructively deserted my daughter, by making it impossible for her to continue to live at the matrimonial home. I accept that he has the power to sell Château d'Ombre without reference to her, but how are the purchase monies to be divided? Must we commence proceedings for divorce against him? Alexa is entitled to a settlement I presume?''

"Indeed, but it will be the subject of prolonged argument. The business is healthy, in that it is saleable but it is not cash-rich, and I fear that extensive litigation will use up all the money available. You will act for your daughter without charge, no doubt, but you understand, sir, I cannot act for Fabrice de Pies Ombre without a fee. The affair is likely to be protracted, and I should be seriously out of pocket.''

Alexander sighed. It confirmed his worst suspicions. His presence was little more than a formality. He thought of Alexa. She had been at Langstroth Grange for the past ten days. He and Elizabeth had left her pretty much to herself. The death of the child made them wary of taxing her nerves over-much with business affairs. But they had to be addressed and Alexander was exasperated to find himself in the gladiatorial arena with little more than his bare hands to fight with.

"I understand. There is nothing to be done from our point of view but to see to it that no attempt is made to convey my daughter's land with the main bulk of the property and to note the purchase sum agreed upon. Is it substantial?''

"We have talked in terms of fifteen million francs and I believe that is what the property is worth. We should close at that.''

"To what extent is the business indebted?'' Maître Robinson turned to the group of decanters which stood to one side of his desk. Taking the stopper from one he raised his eyebrows, his head cocked on one side. Alexander shook his head impatiently. The French lawyer replaced the stopper with a sigh and selected a pipe from the rack on the chimney piece.

"Until lately, the debts were insignificant. This happy state of affairs had been the position for a period of some three years. There was the usual working overdraft with the *Crédit des Vignerons*, but there were also some modest cash reserves sensibly invested in Government Stock. Of late months, there have been substantial drawings. The bank is becoming restive and has even threatened to call in its loan and the investments have been almost entirely liquidated."

"Where has the money gone?"

Maître Robinson shrugged eloquently. "*Monsieur*, your son-in-law has developed some expensive tastes lately, it would seem. You realise, that since your daughter resigned—such an ill-advised move, if you will excuse me from saying so—her signature on the company's cheques has not been necessary. The *Marquis* has had access to funds without control or supervision. Now in what manner he has disbursed those funds, I am not able to say. I see no trace of capital purchases connected with the vineyard. One can only assume the money has been removed under the heading of director's drawings and applied to private purposes."

Once again Maître Robinson shrugged. Alexander felt an increasing fog of despair descend on him. Alexa wasn't fit to cross the road by herself. What ever would her grandfather have said? Actually he knew. Henry would have called Alexa a bloody fool, favourite grandchild or not, and taken a horse whip to de Pies Ombre. Alexander wished he could adopt such simple and satisfying remedies to soothe his own feelings.

"We'd better begin then."

Maître Robinson pressed the buzzer on his desk. In a moment the clerk he had spoken to before looked into the room.

"Oui, Monsieur?"

"You had better tell Mr. . . . er," Maître Robinson leafed through some papers on his desk, "Mr. Jamieson, that's right, to come in, if you will." The clerk nodded and disappeared. "Mr. Jamieson is acting for the purchaser, MRE International. The company appears to be an American real estate company with diverse interests in various parts of the world. I understand from Mr. Jamieson that wine properties are a new area of investment for them. The property has not been advertised, you understand. MRE made a speculative enquiry and subsequently, an offer based on the fifteen million francs we spoke of."

To Alexander's eye, Jamieson was an insubstantial youth. He

wore a strange suit with an inverted pleat where the centre back seam should have been. It was pale grey and shiny. His shoes appeared to be made of plastic and his tie passed reasonable understanding. He wore rimless spectacles balanced on a large, formless nose which dominated his face. The two European lawyers glanced at each other with a single unspoken thought. The calibre of young men entering the profession today was lamentable, even allowing for the fact that this one was American.

Jamieson smiled revealing his only agreeable feature, teeth that were a masterpiece of the orthodontist's art.

"*Bonjour Messieurs,*" he began in passable French.

"My dear Mr. Jamieson, how kind of you to attempt to transact this morning's business in the French language, but I pray you will spare yourself the strain. Here in Bordeaux, we are practically bilingual and as ready to do business in English as in French. My friend, Mr. Standeven here, shares the natural reluctance of his admirable nation to tax French ears with any sound other than his own beautiful tongue." The savagery of the French lawyer was not lost on the American. Alexander closed his eyes, embarrassed by the incivility to his fellow English speaker, and a little amused.

"That's fine to me, gentlemen," the American snapped.

"Well now, we are here to effect the exchange of contracts and completion in the matter of the sale and purchase of the property known as Château d'Ombre, being the area of land and all buildings at present standing on the said land and delineated by the red line you will see on this map, but excluding those areas hatched in green which form the property settled on Madame de Pies Ombre at the time of her marriage and not being within the legal competence of Monsieur le Marquis de Pies Ombre to convey." Maître Robinson spoke with the breathless, drawling chant that lawyers employ when reading documents of their own composition. "That is correct, is it not?"

"Yes sir."

"And the transaction has been agreed in the sum of fifteen million French francs. That is so, is it not? You have the bankers' draft with you, I take it?"

"No sir. I have a banker's draft with me guaranteeing the sum of thirteen million French francs." The New York voice quacked sharply.

The two other men looked at each other in puzzlement and on Maître Robinson's side, some consternation. The Frenchman was silent for a moment.

"I'm afraid I do not understand, Mr. Jamieson. We agreed . . ."

Jamieson snapped open the locks on his mock crocodile briefcase. "Perhaps you gentlemen should read this. I guess it makes the point." He passed a glossy magazine over the table. Alexander at once saw a full-page colour illustration of the Château d'Ombre. Beside it was an article headed *Château d'Ombre— What price now?* The sub-heading read, *Alexa de Pies Ombre abdicates after seven years.*

"You'd better read it. It's central to the whole deal."

"You have another copy of this?" Maître Robinson enquired.

"Sure. I'll go get a call through to New York while you read it."

"*Alors*, Mr. Standeven," the Frenchman looked up after ten to fifteen minutes' solid reading. "This Mr. Bowring thinks highly of your daughter. According to him she is the sole author of success at your son-in-law's property. We know he is right, but surely it is far—how do you say it—*brought*? Far brought to say that Château d'Ombre will fall into inevitable decline without her. Let us be practical. We both know Madame de Pies Ombre's virtues. But she is not the only *vigneron* in the world. She is not the only successful proprietor in the Médoc. She is not the first person to restore a neglected property. What can this man be thinking of?"

"I can't say I care one way or the other. If my daughter's continued involvement is so crucial to the purchasers, which I doubt, then they won't buy. It makes things easier for me. I shall initiate divorce proceedings on my daughter's behalf and keep the initiative for a while longer. It would suit us better."

Jamieson returned, pushing his spectacles up his nose in the manner of one who had thoughts to conceal. He resumed his seat and crossed his legs, sitting well back from the table.

"I have read the article, Mr. Jamieson. I confess, I am at a loss to perceive its import. Is this *Decanter* regarded as an *authoritative* journal?"

"Sure is. The deal is this. Unless Alexa de Pies Ombre works for a year under contract to MRE International to manage the estate, my clients insist the purchase price be reduced to reflect

the cost and inconvenience of finding a suitable estate manager
at short notice and to take cognisance of the fact that some
disruption and loss of profit will be an inevitable consequence
of a period of uncertainty. You must understand. MRE does not
have staff qualified to undertake such management. They are a
real estate company, no more, no less. So, gentlemen, unless
Madame de Pies Ombre returns to Château d'Ombre and signs
a service contract with my clients for a minimum of one year,
the purchase price reduces to thirteen million francs, or the deal's
off."

Maître Robinson looked enquiringly at Alexander.

"Has your daughter been approached concerning this matter?"

"Not to my knowledge."

"Pardon me sir, but her Power of Attorney has been so approached and has declined the offer on her behalf." Alexander
went white.

"I was not under the impression my daughter had issued a
Power of Attorney to any individual other than myself. And that
Power lapsed at the beginning of this year and has not been
renewed."

"Well, I can assure you, sir, there is a valid Power of Attorney
in existence."

"Gentlemen, gentlemen. We can proceed no further until
I have contacted my client and taken his further instructions.
I am afraid we must adjourn this meeting for a little while. I
hope the delay will not be long. Please, since I am unable to
join you, do rely on my recommendation and lunch at *Au
Côté du Jardin*, Rue des Bahutiers. I will telephone to ensure
you have a good table and that my good friend Leclerc takes
care of you. Yes, that will be best. Wait, I shall tell them to
summon a taxi."

When the meeting resumed at two o'clock, Alexander was
somewhat resigned to his helplessness and mollified by the
splendours of the meal he had eaten at Maître Robinson's expense, for the head waiter had waved away Alexander's proffered
American Express card with a smile. He was not, however,
restored to a full approval of his daughter, who seemed to have
compounded her errors with a reprehensible secretiveness. There
would have to be some plain speaking on the subject of filial
trust when he returned to Yorkshire. This would not do. The
young American had talked incessantly. Alexander had em-

ployed his usual system of looking alert while his ears were closed and his mind was occupied with his own thoughts. Jamieson was an unpleasing boy.

"I am happy to tell you that my client has agreed to the sale of the property under the conditions you name. Since Madame de Pies Ombre will not be available, and in fact, Monsieur de Pies Ombre has made it plain, that were his wife to accept the offer of a year's employment, he would withdraw the property from the market, may we take it that the agreed purchase price is thirteen million francs?" Jamieson pursed his lips.

"Yes, but there remains the question of vacant possession. We expect your guy to leave within twenty-four hours, although we are prepared to allow a period of one calendar month during which his contractors are free to clear personal effects from the house. Okay?"

"Monsieur de Pies Ombre has indicated that this will be acceptable." Maître Robinson bowed with a freezing courtliness which was ignored by the American.

"Okay, let's get to it, shall we?" Alexander raised his eyebrows. Jamieson snapped open the locks on his briefcase once more, and a quantity of papers passed across the table. The silence was broken only by the scratching of fountain-pen nibs. Finally an abstract of the title deeds was passed to Alexander who had no other part to play, apparently, than to receive them.

"That's your daughter's title to her five acres, my friend. If there is anything I can do in the future to assist in any way, do not hesitate to contact me." It was the final dismissal. Alexander felt a surge of anger with both men.

"I am obliged to you Maître Robinson, both for your hospitality and your assistance. I am, unfortunately, certain that we shall meet again in the future. Some arrangements must be made for my daughter's maintenance. I will bid you good afternoon now. My flight leaves from Mérignac in two hours." He was damned if he'd let them get away with it. Robinson wasn't on their side. He might have warned that in view of the conflict it would have been advisable to procure the services of another *avocat* for Alexa.

"Mine too. Say, can we share a cab?" Alexander nodded reluctantly. The American had a right to expect professional detachment, even if it was not wisely exercised in the circumstances.

The journey to the airport was fraught with unspoken hostility. Alexander was furious with himself. For the first time in a distinguished career, events had overcome him. Again and again, he cudgelled his brains. What could he have *done*? There was probably something. Something that a French lawyer would have known. He should have consulted one. But he had been given no *time*. He had been as helpless as a child. They had taken away his daughter's home as easily as one takes a toy from a child's hand. He was very, very angry. He was so angry, he thought he was going to be ill. It was a bloody shambles. He could wring Alexa's neck. Poor child, she'd been done.

In the departure lounge Jamieson talked about his client. MRE International, he said, were his first important clients. He expected to make a lot of money out of them. Real estate was a profitable business worldwide. Buying real estate and selling it was just the thing to keep a law practice solvent. "The rest's just jam. Isn't that the case, Mr. Standeven? Do you have a big real estate practice in . . . where was it you said you come from?"

"I didn't," Alexander responded wearily.

"Well, look here!" The American started waving frantically. "If it isn't the man himself."

Alexander looked without interest in the direction of Jamieson's uncontrolled gesticulations. A stocky figure in a dark suit was walking towards them with a broad smile. He carried a briefcase. It was Lockwood. Beside him was a tall, elegant woman. She wore immaculately cut tweeds. There was something familiar about her. He realised with a shock that it was Alexa.

Lockwood extended his hand to the seated Alexander. Alexa bent down to kiss her father. He recognised a faint fragrance of tuberose. A switch in his brain clicked. She was happy. Women never wore perfume unless they were happy. "What the devil . . ."

"All over now. Sorry to put you through this, Mr. Standeven. I hope the explanation will make amends somewhat for the tiresome day you've had." Alexander was still speechless.

"Have you got the stuff, Jamieson?"

The young American had leapt to his feet at Lockwood's approach and stood nervously fiddling with his spectacles. He bent down to his briefcase and opened it clumsily on the floor. He handed Richard a thick packet of documents.

"That's great. Good work. You can cut along now. Guess we'll be catching a later flight." Jamieson obviously could not follow the trend events had taken. He stood for a moment looking foolishly at Richard. Richard nodded encouragingly.

"It's sure been good to work with you. I'll be in touch." Jamieson was almost stammering.

"Sure you will, feller. That was the last call for your flight. Better hurry."

They watched him scurry away in the direction of departure gate two. He kept looking back over his shoulder. All day he'd been under the impression that he was the one in the know. The two European lawyers had been putty in his hands. Jesus! You never can tell with these guys.

Alexa was smiling, the glorious search-light smile which could light up a dungeon. Lockwood took her hand and threaded it through his arm. Alexander noted the gesture with a degree of apprehension. "Come on now, we can get an aperitif here and I'll fill your father in."

"I should appreciate that, Mr. Lockwood," Alexander said, "I have not had a comfortable time and I have the distinct impression that you may be to blame."

"Let me begin my apology with a stiff whisky. You look as if you could use one." They walked towards a bar. Alexander's face was still rigid with annoyance. He did not enjoy being kept in ignorance to build climactic scenes for somebody else to enjoy. That was *his* privilege.

"Oh, by the way, Mr. Standeven, will you put these papers in your briefcase? They're the deeds to the Château d'Ombre property." There was no instantaneous dawn on Alexander's features.

"Can I put it another way, sir? MRE International is the holding company for your daughter's various interests. It stands for Margaret River Estates, which I understand from Alexa is to be changed to Magpie International. Your daughter is the Chief Executive and principal share holder."

"Daddy, it's all right. We've *bought* d'Ombre. I've got it back. There's nothing Fabrice can do about it. It's mine. I didn't know anything about it until late last night. Richard kept it quiet all this time.''

"I had a legal Power of Attorney for her. I formed the company and set about acquiring Château d'Ombre to add to other property. She knew nothing about it. Alexa could never be found guilty of fraudulently acquiring her husband's ancestral acres. It's all absolutely safe and sound.''

Alexander grunted. "One day, Alexa, you may be as devious as me.''

Epilogue

☼ ☼ THE EARLY SUMMER sunshine squeezed through the lancets of the oriel window, splitting the light into dust-flecked stripes. Alexa watched the dust in perpetual motion, whirling like a miniature snow blizzard. Nothing else moved. Beyond the formal French Garden the little green mound in its enclosure was peaceful. Alexa was glad he was safe. At least she knew where he was, the exact extent of his suffering and that it was finished. She was better off than many mothers who lived in perpetual fear of what may befall their children in the future. There would always be pain in remembering him. But it was a finite pain. Perhaps the reasoning was twisted but it had saved her sanity. Alexa never spoke of it to anyone.

Beside her on the desk a portfolio lay open. There were two or three proposed layouts for the new wine label. She would have to make her mind up sooner or later. The wine would be blended and bottled this year, and marketing plans would have to be put into effect. The advertising agency would need to know what it was they were selling.

Alexa picked up one of the sketches. It was a simple design. There was a young magpie in flight and underneath the words *Héritier d'Ombre. Mise en bouteille au Château*. "The Heir of Shadow," Alexa tried the words in English, searching for the fullness of their meaning. Their strange resonance echoed in her mind, the double-sided truth, spinning like a coin tossed in the air. That was the one. Charles' wine. His memorial.

She turned to the other papers with a sigh. There was yet another complaining letter from Tilly, enclosing a sheaf of *couturiers'* bills for Suzanne. She could never keep within her allowance, however generous it was. Alexa reached for her cheque book. Nobody's life was quite perfect. According to Tilly, old Brun had died which left the Marais house completely unstaffed. Well, it was not her affair. The Hôtel de Pies Ombre did not belong to her. It really ought to be turned into *appartements*. They would fetch a good rent. Suzanne could have one of them and that would keep her out of Tilly's hair. Perhaps she should make an offer for the house. Richard would probably like the idea. There was nothing in the articles of association of Magpie International to prevent the acquisition of residential property. A well-balanced portfolio, it was his favourite phrase. Ariel could come over and decorate the *appartements*.

She glanced up. The vines marched away into the distant blue of the Aquitaine horizon like troops in review order, spread out for their general's inspection. A tall tractor appeared, spraying was in progress. Not bad for the notary's daughter. Suzanne's old jibe was powerless to hurt her now.

A small morocco box caught her eye. The dark red leather was stamped with Cartier's distinctive cipher. It lay on top of the marquetry work table that Elizabeth had given her for her thirtieth birthday. Slowly, she reached across and opened it. The diamond and sapphire magpie flashed in the sunlight. The sapphires were different colours. They ranged from the near black of Australian gems to the soft velvet depths of Kashmiri stones. Their myriad refractions imitated the elusiveness of a magpie's inky wing. She closed the box. It would have to go back again. Richard sent it every year with his proposal of marriage. Next year, she would probably keep it.

ABOUT THE AUTHOR

Born in the West Riding of Yorkshire and educated at the same school as Charlotte Brontë, Rosemary Enright studied for a year at the Sorbonne in Paris before returning to university in Wales. She then had a brief spell as a fashion model, preceding a five-year stint in the Women's Royal Army Corps. She has also worked in a variety of industries, including the jewelry, printing, and construction trades.

She has spent much of her married life in the Middle East and North Africa but now works for an advertising agency in Leeds. She has one small daughter.